Penguin Books
The John Franklin Bardin Omnibus

John Franklin Bardin was born in Cincinnati in 1916.
After an unhappy childhood he had to leave the
University of Cincinnati in his first year to find a full-
time job. He became a ticket-taker and bouncer at a
local roller-skating rink and educated himself by
working at night, reading and clerking in a bookstore.
From 1968 until 1972 he was a senior editor at Coronet
in New York, and between 1973 and 1974 he was
Managing Editor for the American Bar Association
magazines. From 1946 to 1948, during a period of
intense creative activity, he wrote the remarkable
novels in this volume. He has also written more
conventional crime novels under the pseudonym
Gregory Tree. Other novels written under his own
name include *Purloining Tiny*, *The Burning Glass* and
Christmas Comes But Once a Year.

D1339427

John Franklin Bardin

The John Franklin Bardin Omnibus

With an Introduction by Julian Symons

Penguin Books

Penguin Books Ltd, Harmondsworth,
Middlesex, England
Penguin Books, 40 West 23rd Street,
New York, New York 10010, U.S.A.
Penguin Books Australia Ltd, Ringwood,
Victoria, Australia
Penguin Books Canada Limited, 2801 John Street,
Markham, Ontario, Canada L3R 1B4
Penguin Books (N.Z.) Ltd, 182–190 Wairau Road,
Auckland 10, New Zealand

The Deadly Percheron first published in the United States
of America by Dodd, Mead & Co. 1946
First published in Great Britain by
Victor Gollancz 1947
The Last of Philip Banter first published in the United States
of America by Dodd, Mead & Co. 1947
First published in Great Britain by
Victor Gollancz 1947
Devil Take the Blue-Tail Fly first published in
Great Britain by Victor Gollancz 1948
This collection published in Penguin Books 1976
Reprinted 1979, 1983

Printed in the United States of America by
R. R. Donnelley & Sons, Harrisonburg, Virginia
Set in Monotype Baskerville

Contents

Introduction by Julian Symons

Denis Healey was the guest of honour at a Crime Writers' Association dinner a few years ago, one of those years when he was no more than a shadow Minister, and so had time for criminal frivolity. In the course of his speech Mr Healey showed a considerable, almost a dazzling, knowledge of crime fiction. It was an impressive performance, one nearly too much for some of the audience. People who write crime stories are often not great readers of them, feeling perhaps that anything they read will be inferior to what they have written. And when, near the end of his peroration, Mr Healey picked out for special praise the crime novels of John Franklin Bardin, they looked at each other in astonishment. Who was John Franklin Bardin? One is safe in saying that no more than a dozen of the hundred and fifty people at dinner that night had ever heard of him.

Our present Chancellor of the Exchequer is not Bardin's only English admirer. Kingsley Amis, Edmund Crispin and Roy Fuller are among those who have been enthusiastic about one or all of the books republished here, but only *The Deadly Percheron* had a considerable success. And he has been much more appreciated here than in his native America, where ignorance about him is greater. I have yet to find an American writer or critic who knows his work at all.

It proved difficult, indeed, to discover whether he was still alive, for he had disappeared from literary life rather like one of the characters in his books. Neither his publishers nor his agents had heard of him for years and stories in papers about a 'Quest for Bardin' produced no response. He was eventually found through the *Third Degree*, the journal of Mystery Writers of America, alive, well, and living in Chicago, where he was editing a magazine for the American Bar Association. He was ready, and indeed eager, to see these early books republished.

They are all distinguished by an extraordinary intensity of feeling, and by an absorption in morbid psychology remarkable for the period. The crime story immediately after the Second World War was still mostly in the hands of writers who constructed ingenious puzzles, which neither they nor their readers took more seriously than one takes any other game. Bardin was ahead of his time. He belongs not to the world of Agatha Christie and John Dickson Carr, but to that of Patricia Highsmith or even that of Poe. The mental agonies of his heroes and heroines communicate a distress that makes the reader feel uncomfortable. Are they going mad, as they fear, or is there some reasonable explanation for the terrible things that are happening to them? There is a visionary lucidity about Bardin's nightmares that makes his surrealist logic both convincing and disturbing.

The opening of his first book, *The Deadly Percheron*, shows this quality. A young man wearing a scarlet hibiscus in his hair comes into a psychiatrist's office and says that Joe told him to wear the flower. Who is Joe? 'Oh, he's one of my little men. The one in the purple suit. He gives me ten dollars a day for wearing a flower in my hair.' And who are the other little men? Harry, 'who wears green suits and pays me to whistle at Carnegie Hall', and Eustace, who 'pays me to give quarters away'. We think with George Matthews, the psychiatrist, that this is a fantasy spun out of whole cloth – until Matthews meets one of the little men. *The Last of Philip Banter* begins with what seems an impossibility when Philip, an advertising man with a difficult marriage and a drink problem, finds a typed manuscript on his office desk, apparently written by himself, which confuses past and future. It describes what is going to happen as though it had happened already, and Philip, to his horror, sees the predictions coming true. The device is one that would have delighted Poe, and it is used rather as Poe might have used it, to express the course of mental breakdown, personal disintegration.

These are powerful, not perfect, novels. They suggest more than they ever say about the incestuous feelings of parents and children, and the solutions demanded by the problems of the characters seem to be rooted in psychology rather than in reason. Bardin, however, obviously felt the need to provide answers that made sense in terms of an orthodox detective story, and the details of these are not always convincing. One has to admit this, yet on reading the books again recently I found that their power to shock and terrify remained untouched by the not quite satisfactory solutions. And such a criticism does not apply at all to Bardin's masterpiece, *Devil Take the Blue-Tail Fly*, a book whose problems and solutions are conceived wholly in terms of the psychology of its heroine, Ellen. The book was written in six weeks as a first draft, taken away by Victor Gollancz from an agent's office, and never revised. Nor does it need revision, moving as it does with increasing pace and a perfect natural rhythm.

The opening is unforgettable in its blend of the commonplace and the sinister. Ellen is leaving the mental home; she is the patient whose recovery they are all proud of; her longing to see her husband Basil is natural and real. Then, as if a nail were intrusively scraped across a window pane, Ellen does something unexpected and 'wrong', in asking the nurses to turn their backs, and from that moment onwards we know that she is not well. The other moments in this opening chapter that convey the ripple of disquiet are also beautifully muted: Ellen's reluctance on leaving the home to go away from the doctor, and her desire to say good-bye to the mountainous Ella, whose Buddha-like placidity apparently 'expressing a god-like peace' contradicts her actual

9

violence. What happens afterwards, the disintegration of Ellen through a mixture of bad luck, self-deceit, and stupidity on the part of the other people (some incidents remain properly mysterious, like what actually did happen to the key), is finely judged and developed. The book is unusual also in its suggestions of the way in which creative ability can be thwarted, and even destroyed. One can believe in Ellen as a musician, and the torments she suffers are partly those of the frustrated artist, 'the agony of flame that cannot singe a sleeve'.

'My basic literary influences have been Graham Greene, Henry Green and Henry James,' Bardin says, but although traces of James and Greene can be seen, the moving power behind these stories is his own life. Without, perhaps, being exactly autobiographical, they are clearly a reworking of events in a stormy, painful childhood and adolescence. Bardin was born in 1916 in Cincinnati. His father was a well-to-do coal merchant, his mother the child of a groom, a girl who came to Cincinnati to work in an office. Misfortune pursued the family. An elder sister died of septicaemia, and a year later Bardin's father died of a coronary. He left very little money, and John had to leave the University of Cincinnati in his first year to find a full-time job. He became a ticket-taker and bouncer in a roller-skating rink. 'Mother had become a paranoid schizophrenic by then. It was on visits to her that I first had an insight into the "going home" hallucinations.' There followed that process of self-education ('I worked at night and read, clerked in a bookstore') undertaken by many American writers.

The biographical details are interesting because they fill in the background of the books and show the pressures that helped to produce them, but of course they do not explain their quality. They were published over a period of eighteen months, the result of an almost continuous surge of creative energy. Their lack of success in America must have been discouraging. *Devil Take the Blue-Tail Fly* was not published there until the late sixties, and then only in paperback. Bardin turned to writing slick, readable, unadventurous crime stories under the pseudonym of Gregory Tree. In his own name he published at least two more novels, one an interesting but unsuccessful experiment, the other disastrously sentimental. He has not published a book for more than a decade, although he has recently started writing again.

The novels sprang out of nightmare experiences, and it does not seem likely that Bardin will be impelled to write anything like them again. They are unlike anything else in modern crime literature. The first two are erratic and exotic, but they are never plodding or dull, and *Devil Take the Blue-Tail Fly* is one of the most convincing and frightening 'psychological' crime stories ever written. It is a pleasure to bring all three books to a new and wider public.

January 1978   J.S.

The Deadly Percheron

To
My Wife, Rhea

Contents

1   Easy Money

Jacob Blunt was my last patient. He came into my office wearing a scarlet hibiscus in his curly blond hair. He sat down in the easy chair across from my desk, and said, 'Doctor, I think I'm losing my mind.'

He was a handsome young man and apparently a healthy one. There were certainly no surface manifestations of neuroses. He did not seem nervous – nor did he seem to be suppressing a tendency to be nervous – his blue eyes were steady, his suit neat. The features of his face were strong, his shoulders were nicely made and except for a slight limp he carried himself well. I would not have believed he belonged in my consultation room if it hadn't been for the outrageous flower in his hair.

'Most of us have similar apprehensions at some time or other,' I said. 'During an emotional crisis, or after periods of sustained overwork, I, too, have been uncertain of my sanity.'

'Crazy people see things, don't they?' he asked. 'Things that really aren't there?' He leaned forward as if he were afraid he might miss my answer if he did not get closer to me.

'Hallucinations are a common symptom of mental disorder,' I agreed.

'And when you don't only see things – but things happen to you – crazy things, I mean – that's having hallucinations, isn't it?'

'Yes,' I said, 'a person who is mentally ill often lives in a world of his own imagining, an unreal world. He withdraws completely from reality.'

Jacob leaned back and sighed happily. 'That's me!'

he said. 'I am nuts, thank God! It isn't really happening!'

He seemed wholly at ease. His face had relaxed into a crooked grin that was rather nice. My information had obviously relieved him. This was unusual; I had never before met a neurotic who admitted wanting to lose his mind. Nor had I seen one who felt happy about it.

'That's a pretty flower you have in your hair,' I said. 'Tropical, isn't it?' I had to begin somewhere to find out what was wrong with him, and the flower was the only unnatural thing I could find.

He fingered it. 'Yeah,' he said, 'it's a hibiscus. I had a devil of a time getting it, too! Had to run all over town this morning before I found a place that had one!'

'Are you so fond of them?' I asked. 'Why not a rose or a gardenia? They're cheaper, and surely easier to buy.'

He shook his head. 'Nope. I've worn them at times, but it had to be a hibiscus today. Joe said it had to be a hibiscus today.'

It began to look as if he might be insane. His conversation seemed incoherent and he was entirely too happy about the whole affair. I began to be interested.

'Who is Joe?' I asked.

Blunt had taken a cigarette out of the box on my desk and was now fumbling with the lighter. He looked up in surprise. 'Joe? Oh, he's one of my little men. The one in the purple suit. He gives me ten dollars a day for wearing a flower in my hair. Only he picks the flowers and that's where it gets tough! He can pick the screwiest flowers!'

He gave me some more of that crooked grin. It was almost as if he were saying 'I know this sounds silly, but it's the way my mind works. I can't really help it.'

'Joe is only the one who gives you flowers, is that right?' I asked him. 'There are others?'

'Oh, sure there are others. I do things for a lot of little guys, that's what has me worried! Only you're mixed up about Joe. He doesn't give me the flowers. I have to go out and buy them myself. He only pays me for wearing them.'

'You say that there are other "little guys" – who are they and what do they do?'

'Oh, there's Harry,' he said. 'He's the one who wears green suits and pays me to whistle at Carnegie Hall. And there's Eustace – he wears tattersall waistcoats and pays me to give quarters away.'

'Your quarters?'

'No, his. He gives me twenty quarters every day. I get another ten dollars for giving them away.'

'Why not keep them?'

He frowned. 'Oh, no! I couldn't do that! I wouldn't get the ten dollars if I kept them. Eustace only pays me when I succeed in giving them all away.'

He reached into his pocket and pulled out a handful of shiny new quarters. 'That reminds me,' he said. 'I'm meeting Eustace at six, and I have all these to give away yet. Take one of them, will you please?'

And he flipped a quarter on to my desk. I picked it up and put it in my pocket. I did not want to antagonize him.

He watched me closely. 'It's real, isn't it?' he asked.

'Yes,' I said. It was real.

'Do me a favour. Bite it.'

'No,' I said. 'I don't have to bite it. I know a genuine coin when I see one.'

'Go ahead and bite it,' he said. 'So you know it isn't counterfeit.'

I took the quarter out of my pocket, placed it in my mouth and bit it. I wanted to humour him. 'It's real enough,' I said.

His grin sagged, then disappeared. 'That's what worries me,' he said.

'What?'

'If I'm crazy, doc, then you can cure me. But if I'm not crazy, and these little men are real, why then there are such things as leprechauns and they are giving away a tremendous treasure – and then we'd all have to begin to believe in fairies, and there's simply no telling where that would lead to!'

At that point I thought I was on the verge of uncovering his neuroses. He seemed very excited, almost frantic – and he had thrown a great deal of new information at me suddenly. I decided to ignore his reference to 'leprechauns' and 'fairies' for the time being, while continuing to question him about the one tangible piece of evidence: the quarter.

'What has this to do with Eustace and the quarters?' I asked him.

'Can't you see, doc? If I'm crazy – if I just imagine Eustace – what about the quarters? They're real enough, aren't they?'

'Perhaps they belong to you,' I suggested. 'Couldn't you have gone to your bank and withdrawn them, and then forgotten about it?'

He shook his head. 'Nope. It's not that easy. I haven't been to my bank in months.'

'Why not?'

'Don't have to. Why go to the bank and draw money if you're making thirty to forty dollars a day? I haven't spent any of my own money since last Christmas.'

'Since last Christmas?'

'Yeah. I met Joe on Christmas day. In an Automat. He didn't know how to get coffee out of the gadget there, and I showed him. We fell to talking and he asked me if I wanted to make some easy money. I said, "Sure, why not?" I didn't know then what a silly job it would turn out to be. But I was bored with the job I had – I was clerking in a haberdashery – and anxious to do something more interesting. I really don't have to work, you know. I have a steady income from a trust fund. But the trustee is a cranky old guy who always lectures me about the virtues of having a job. He says, "Doing a task well builds character."

'I started to work for Joe that very day and after a

couple of weeks I met Eustace and then Harry through Joe. Joe was pleased with my work. He said I was trust-worthy. He said the little men always had trouble finding guys they could trust.'

I was fascinated. This promised to be one of the more curious cases of my career. Most abnormalities adhere closely to a few, well-established patterns. It is not often that you find a man so imaginatively insane as Jacob Blunt seemed to be.

'Tell me, Mr Blunt,' I asked, 'just what exactly is your trouble? It seems to me that you lead an excellent life - you certainly make enough money. What is the matter?'

Once again I saw him discomfited. He looked away from me, and his grin came and went before he answered.

'There's nothing wrong, I guess,' he said. 'That is, if you're sure that Joe and Harry and Eustace are halluci-nations?'

'That is what I would say they probably are.'

He smiled again. 'Well, if you're right, I'm just nuts and that's fine. But what worries me is the dough! If those quarters are real, how can Eustace be imaginary?'

'Perhaps, as I suggested before, you get them from your bank, and then forget you have made a with-drawal.'

His smile broadened. He reached into his breast-pocket and pulled out his bankbook. He handed it across the desk to me. 'What about this then, doc?' he asked.

I looked at the figures in the book. There had been regular, quarterly deposits of a thousand dollars each for the past two years, but there had not been a withdrawal since 20 December 1942. I handed the bankbook back to him.

'I tell you I haven't been to the bank since before last Christmas,' he repeated.

'What about the deposits?' I asked.

'My trustee makes those,' he said. 'From my father's estate. It's in trust until I'm twenty-five.'

23

I thought for a moment. If I could only get him to give me a coherent account of what had been happening to him, I might be able to inquire a little more deeply into the nature of his trouble. 'Suppose you go back to the beginning and tell me all about it,' I proposed.

He looked steadily at me, and his look made me feel uncomfortable. I had an idea that he knew how puzzled I was, and that my confusion disturbed him.

'It's as I told you,' he said. 'I met Joe in the Automat. He said he'd give me a trial at flower-wearing and, if I was good at it, I could do it regular. He was so pleased with what he called my "earnestness" that he recommended me to Harry and Eustace. I've been whistling for Harry and giving quarters away for Eustace ever since . . .'

This was getting us no place. Absurd as his fantasies were, they were consistent. 'What do you do for Harry? Did you say whistle?' I asked wearily.

'Sure. At Carnegie Hall. At Town Hall. Sometimes in the balcony. Sometimes downstairs. I don't have to do it loud, and I may sit off by myself so I don't annoy anybody. It's a lot of fun. Last night I whistled "Pistol-Packin' Mama" all through Beethoven's "Eighth". You oughtta try it some time! It does you good!'

I smothered a smile. I had begun to like the boy, and I did not want him to think I was laughing at him.

'These "little men" – why did you say they hire you to do all these peculiar things?'

He reached for another cigarette and fumbled again with my lighter. Most of my patients smoke – I encourage them to because it makes them feel at ease – and it gives me an opportunity to watch their reactions to a petty annoyance if my cigar-lighter is balky. Often a man or woman who is superficially calm will reveal an inner nervousness by getting disproportionately aggravated at the futile spark. But not Jacob Blunt, he spun the tiny wheel patiently and phlegmatically until the unwilling flame appeared. Then he answered me.

'They're leprechauns. Came originally from Ireland, but now they're all over the world. They've had a tremendous treasure for all eternity and until recently they guarded it jealously. Now, for reasons of their own that I can't get Eustace to tell me, they've started to distribute it. Joe says they've got hundreds of men working for them all over the country. Some pretty big men, too, Joe says. People you'd never guess.'

'You mean they are fairies, like gnomes or elves?' Sometimes if you can show a patient the infantile level of his obsession, you can give him a jolt that will start him back on the road to reality. 'Don't tell me you believe in fairies!' I scoffed.

'They're not fairies,' he protested. 'They're little men in green and purple suits. You've probably passed them on the street!'

I was getting nowhere. Soon I would be arguing with my patient on his terms. I had to find a way to change the direction of the conversation. As it was, he was leading it, not I.

'Suppose you aren't mentally ill, Mr Blunt, what then?'

He grew serious. For the first time he seemed sick, anxious.

'That's what has me worried, doc! What if I'm not crazy?'

'Then the "little men" are real,' I said. 'Then there are such things as leprechauns. You don't really believe that, do you?'

He was silent, undecided. Then he shook his head violently, 'No, I won't believe it! It couldn't be! I must be crazy!'

I thought it was about time to reassure him. 'Let me decide that,' I said. 'That's my job. People who suffer from hallucinations such as yours usually defend them rigorously. They never entertain the possibility of a doubt as to the reality of their imagined experiences. But you do. That is encouraging.'

'But what about the money, doc? The quarters? They're real enough, aren't they?'

'Let's not consider that part of it now. Suppose you tell me a little about yourself. Talk to me about your childhood, your youth, your girl – you have a girl, haven't you? – whatever comes first to your mind.'

I was hopelessly confused. Usually a psychiatrist can see the flaw in the logic of a schizoid's dream world. It is patently an irrational mechanism. The difficulty normally lies in getting the patient to talk about his inner life. Here, however, this was not the case. Jacob seemed eager to confide the details of his 'little men' and their 'easy money' to me; but, besides doing that, he had presented a certain amount of evidence that at least some of his experiences were true, and if this were so he might not be insane. All I could do was to urge him to talk some more, hoping that he would say something that would help me help him.

'What will telling you the story of my life have to do with Eustace and Joe?' he asked.

'Take my word for it that it may have a great deal of bearing on your problem,' I said.

He was reluctant to begin. Nor was he as much at ease as he had been before. He had stopped smiling, and his eyes were dull.

'I'm a Dead-End Kid,' he said, 'who was raised on Park Avenue. You probably know all about my old man, John Blunt. He had more money than was good for him. Just about the time of the first World War he sold his carriage-making business to one of the big automobile companies and from then on he was rolling in dough. He bought himself a seat on the Exchange and kept right on making money until he died of apoplexy a few years back. He left all his dough to me, but he tied it up in a trust so I can't get at it until I'm twenty-five.'

'How old are you now?'

'I'm twenty-three. I've got two more years to go. But that isn't what worries me. I've got plenty of dough.'

'Yes,' I said, 'I know.'

'I really was a hell-raiser when I was a kid. I wore out two or three governesses a year. My mother died when I was a brat, that's why I had the governesses. My old man never paid much attention to me. I used to run wild. I made friends with all sorts of kids. I always had more money than any of the others, and I was so much trouble to have around that none of the servants minded much if I didn't come home for days at a time.'

'How old were you when you started running away from home?'

'Nine or ten.' He dug into his coat pocket and took out his wallet. From it he drew a well-thumbed photograph which he handed to me. 'That's a picture of me at about that time,' he said. 'The kid with me was a friend of mine – the ugliest little shrimp I ever did see. I called him Pruney.'

I looked at the photograph. It was the kind a strolling photographer makes. Jacob looked surprisingly the same – even as a child he had that lopsided grin. But it was the image of his small companion that held my eye. He was a small boy dressed in a dirty sailor suit, yet his face was uglier than I have ever seen on a child other than a cretin. It was an ugliness you would expect to find in a man of forty or more, not a young boy. And on the back of the photograph were scrawled the initials: E.A.B.

'What do these stand for?' I asked.

Jacob looked at them, shrugged. 'I don't know. I had even forgotten about Pruney and this old picture until – after my old man's death – I was going through his desk one day and found this in a cubbyhole. I guess it meant something to him.'

I stuck the photograph in my pocket. I wanted to see if my patient would resent this act of possession. But he did not seem to notice it. Baffled, I tried another tack: 'Where did you sleep when you were away from home?'

'In hotels. In the Park. I spent a lot of time around

27

Central Park. Sometimes at the houses of friends. I always had a lot of friends.'

'Hardly a normal childhood,' I said. 'Why didn't your father stop you? Didn't he know what you were doing?'

Jacob laughed. He threw back his head and laughed loudly, a harsh, cynical laugh. 'I tell you my old man didn't give a damn,' he said, 'about me, or anybody! He hired people to look after me – why should he bother?'

I said nothing. Jacob stopped laughing. He did not go on. I did not know what to think. He had obviously had an extraordinary life so far, and not a healthy one. I was not surprised that he was neurotic. He had never had a family, no one had ever loved him. Or had there been someone . . .?

'When did you first fall in love?' I asked. Perhaps, the clue lay there . . .

'When I was fourteen. With the cigarette girl at the St Moritz. She was a blonde and she had nice legs. I remember I bought her a black silk nightgown for Christmas. Did you ever buy a girl a black silk nightgown?'

His grin was contagious. 'Why, yes, I suppose so,' I said.

'Who?'

'My wife, I guess.'

'Oh.' He was disappointed. Then he said, 'Well, I suppose we all do that at one time or another.'

'But not at fourteen. That's a rather tender age, don't you think?'

He smiled deprecatingly. 'You don't understand, doc. At fourteen I'd been around. I'd been underfoot in New York hotels since I was knee-high. I knew all about cigarette girls and things at fourteen.'

'This cigarette girl was your first love, you say? How many times have you been in love since then?'

He started to count up on his fingers, then stopped and shook his head in mock dismay. 'Hundreds of times, I guess,' he said. 'Dozens of times between then and when

I went to college. At least a score of times at Dartmouth. I don't know how many times since . . . I'm in love with a redhead right now! I'd marry her if I wasn't crazy!'

'Don't you think you fall into and out of love too easily?' I asked. 'Would you agree that you were emotionally unstable?'

'No, I wouldn't!' He was emphatic. 'I'm just lucky. I've enough money and enough looks to get a woman easily, so it's only natural that I do. What's more normal than falling in love?'

'That's normal enough,' I admitted, 'but what about falling out of it? Most men eventually settle down and get married.'

'Most men don't have the money I have,' he said blithely. And then more seriously, 'And most men don't see little men in green and purple suits!'

Jacob was quiet. During his account of his early life, I was again impressed by his sanity. Except for the 'little men' – and the scarlet hibiscus in his curly blond hair – I had seldom met a more normal young man. For example, a neurotic, when invited to talk about himself and his childhood, is likely to respond in one of two ways: he may either tell a long rambling story in excessive detail that reveals a score of hidden fears and resentments, or he may shut up and refuse to talk. But Jacob had done neither. His response had been of the kind I might have made myself if I should ever have had to answer an over-inquisitive interrogator in this way. He had told a simple, brief, cogent – and, so far as I could tell, truthful – story in a casual, friendly fashion. The only induction I could make about his character that was in any way profitable from a psychiatric point of view was the fact that he hated his father. I could hardly call this abnormal. From what I knew of him, I wouldn't have liked old John Blunt either. He was the last of the Robber Barons.

On the other hand, some of Jacob's actions were quite peculiar. How had he allowed himself to be inveigled into all this ridiculous business of wearing flowers in his hair, giving quarters away, whistling at Carnegie Hall? I could think of only one probable reason why an otherwise apparently rational young man would do what Jacob had done: he did it because he liked doing it. Hadn't there been a gleam in his eye when he urged me to try whistling a popular tune the next time I attended a concert? Hadn't he said, 'You oughtta try it some time. It does you good!'? And from the way he kept patting at the hibiscus in his hair, I surmised that he enjoyed wearing it. His own account of his past history might supply the cause for the pleasure he took in such outrageous, non-conforming behaviour. He had never had a normal home life; he had no respect for authority, and he enjoyed revolt. His whole personality might be built on this latent need to protest. Being an impulsive, extraverted youth, his protest took the form of tomfoolery and thoughtless waggishness. So he fell in with the suggestions of his 'little men' and liked doing what they told him to do . . . up to a point. Yet the trouble with this seemingly reasonable explanation was that it took for granted the existence of the 'little men'. And I was not ready to take that much for granted.

So I found myself again at a loss. Each time before that I had attempted to analyse my patient's complaint, I had ended up facing a blank, but quite sane, wall of defence. Now I hesitated to try again.

It was Jacob who made the suggestion. 'Look, doc,' he said, 'we're getting no place fast!' He checked his wrist watch. 'And it's five o'clock already – I'm supposed to meet Eustace at a bar on Third Avenue at six. Why don't you come back to my place while I shave and change my clothes, and we can both go over to the bar and meet Eustace? Then you can see for yourself!'

I looked at him. His eyes were begging me to say yes. Unorthodox as it was I had the feeling that what he suggested was the correct way for me to approach his case, especially if he were neurotic. It showed him that I had confidence in his 'earnestness', and if he felt I trusted him, he might come eventually to trust me – it might be a means of accomplishing a transference. Of course, I knew that there was no Eustace, and I had an idea that all we would do at the bar would be to have a few drinks. But it was worth trying.

'I think that's an excellent idea, Mr Blunt,' I said. 'I should like to meet your friend.'

'Maybe you'd like to go to work for him, too?' he asked. I could not tell whether he was poking fun at me or not.

I laughed and said, 'I might at that. I could use a little extra cash as well as the next one!'

I told Miss Henry, my nurse, that I was leaving for the day and asked her to phone my wife at my home in New Jersey to tell her that I would be late and not to keep dinner for me. I also asked Miss Henry at what time was my first appointment the next day. And then I followed Jacob out of my office into the corridor.

He was still wearing that ridiculous flower in his hair. If I have an outstanding fault, it is that I am rather vain about my personal appearance. I have regular features and a sober expression. I am perhaps a little too fastidious, although I don't think I am conceited. Still, when I go out with others, I expect them to be similarly neat and tidy. I disliked having to walk the streets with a man who wore an absurd flower in his hair. While we were waiting for the elevator, I asked him to take it off.

'Oh, I couldn't do that,' he said. 'Eustace would notice it! He might tell Joe and then Joe wouldn't want to hire me again. I have to wear it all day to earn the ten dollars.'

'But can't you take it off now, and put it in your pocket until we're about to meet Eustace? You could put it back on then and he would never be any the wiser.'

'Oh, no! I couldn't do that. That would be dishonest! You forget that the reason the leprechauns hire me all the time to distribute their money is because I'm so trustworthy! I could never betray their trust.'

'I see,' I said. There was nothing to be gained by arguing with him.

Jacob gave me a sidewise look. 'Would you feel better if you had one, too?' he asked. 'The florist I finally found this one at this morning had another one, and his shop is quite near here. They might still have it. If you want, I think we might have time to stop by there so you could have one, too!'

'No, thanks,' I said.

'But it might be a good idea!' he insisted. 'If Eustace saw you voluntarily wearing a flower in your hair, he might tell Joe about it and it might help you to get into Joe's good graces. You might be able to work for Joe as well as Eustace!'

'No, thanks,' I said. 'I can do without a hibiscus right now.'

I was glad the elevator came just then, interrupting the conversation. Sometimes a psychiatrist's life is a hard one.

2   Gift Horse

Jacob gave away all his quarters before I managed to get him into a taxi. It was quite embarrassing. He gave one to the elevator operator, another to the starter, one to a lady in mink who was coming out of the revolving door as we were going in, one to a coloured shoeshine boy who has a stand outside my office building and the last to the doorman. I felt better when we were finally inside the taxi and Jacob had given the driver an address on West Fifty-third Street. I hadn't liked the look the lady in mink had tossed at us as she regarded first the shiny new quarter in her hand, and then the scarlet flower in my patient's hair.

He told me more about himself during the slow ride through rush-hour streets to his apartment. He had graduated from Dartmouth in 1940. The Army hadn't taken him because of an old knee injury sustained in a basketball game during his sophomore year. He was only twenty-one when he finished college because he entered at seventeen, having skipped a grade in childhood. He said he liked Bach and Mozart and Brahms, redheads and Hemingway. His present redhead was in the chorus of *Nevada!* – he had met her one night when he went backstage. She was, in his words, 'some mouse!'

The taxi stopped in the middle of the block between Fifth and Sixth Avenues on West Fifty-third, and we entered a very modern apartment building. The desk clerk nodded to Jacob, and the elevator operator smiled and called him 'Mr Blunt'. Apparently these people who saw him all the time knew and liked him. If they had thought him queer, they would have treated him

33

differently. Things were certainly not getting any simpler.

I liked his apartment. It was one extraordinarily large room, a small bedroom, a kitchen and a bath. The walls of the main room were a deep blue, one was lined with bookcases; there was a phonograph with ample record shelves and a fireplace with a good Miro hanging above it. The redhead was on the long divan in the centre of the room, half-lying, half-sitting against a striped pillow. Her hair was long, loose, in lovely disarray. Another girl sat more stiffly beside her – a small, neat, childlike creature with soft-brown curls and an open, innocent look in her blue eyes. The redhead glanced up at us as we came into the room, her eyes intense green blurs in her beautiful, blank face.

'Hello, Jakey,' she said in a low, purring voice. 'Denise and I were shopping and we dropped by a minute ago to mix ourselves a drink. Who's your friend?' Both girls were looking at me with unashamed curiosity.

Jacob had stopped smiling, and all his casual friendliness had disappeared. He seemed both startled and displeased to find that there was someone in his apartment. Not that this showed in anything he said. It was only that he was suddenly stiff and wary, even, perhaps, suspicious.

'Dr George Matthews, Nan Bulkely, Denise Hanover,' he mumbled. From the vague wave of his hand, I took it that the tall girl with the blank stare was Nan, the brunette was Denise. Jacob nodded in Nan's direction and said in a slightly louder voice, 'She'll give you a drink if you want it. I'm going to shave and dress.' And he went out of the room without saying another word.

I walked over and sat down in a chair across from the divan. Nan uncrossed her legs – they were delightful legs, long and well-proportioned, a dancer's legs without a dancer's unsightly muscles. Denise picked up her cocktail and began to sip it, and her eyes studied the glass. But Nan never took her own remarkable eyes off mine. These were as green as a cat's in the dark, but wide and open, disarmingly frank. Yet, except for her eyes, Nan's face was expressionless, empty. Even when she smiled it was like having a full-colour advertisement come to life and smile at you –something out of *Harper's Bazaar* or the *New Yorker*.

'I'm sorry,' she said, 'I didn't catch your name? Jacob mumbles so.'

'I'm George Matthews,' I said.

She opened her eyes a little wider. 'Didn't I hear Jacob say "Doctor"? Or were my ears playing tricks on me?'

'I am a doctor,' I said. 'A psychiatrist.' I did not like Nan at all. She made me feel as though I was a child being pumped by an adult. I looked at the other girl and, as I did, she stood up and walked out of the big room into the kitchen. It was as if some signal had been passed between the two women. This I resented, as well as Nan's questioning. But I was careful not to let her see my resentment – she might tell me something about my patient that would turn out to be valuable. So I answered her questions.

'Are you and Jacob old friends?' was the next one.

'No. As a matter of fact, I saw him for the first time this afternoon in my office. He is my patient.'

She was surprised. I saw her throat tighten and her shoulders grow a little more rigid, although on the whole she controlled herself well. If I hadn't been a trained observer of the subtle psychological reactions that betray a person's emotions, I would not have known how much my simple statement of fact had shocked her.

She was quiet for a moment, and then she asked, 'Did Jacob come to see you of his own free will?'

'So far as I know. Why do you ask?'

'I just never thought he would, that's all,' she said. 'I'm rather glad he has consulted you. I've been awfully worried about the way he's been acting these past few months, but I knew I could never suggest that he visit a psychiatrist. He wouldn't have listened to me.'

It was a clever act. When she asked me if Jacob visited

me on his own impulse, I felt that she actually wanted to know – in fact, there was an urgency about the way she asked the question that made me think she had to know. But the reason she gave me for asking me that question was a contrived excuse. I could not help but wonder why she was so concerned over Jacob's having come to see me.

'What has Jacob been doing lately that has you so worried?' I asked her.

'You saw the flower he was wearing, didn't you? In his hair! He says that a friend of his pays him to do that! And it has to be a different flower each day!'

'Have you ever met this friend?'

She regarded me steadily as if she meant to confide in me. 'No, that's the strange thing about it. He has described them to me – there are several of them, you know – not one – several "little men" – he's told me all about them, even told me their names, but I have never met one of them. I think they exist only in his imagination.'

'Has he ever shown signs of queerness before, Miss Bulkely?'

She shook her head, her red hair swirling about her shoulders. 'Of course, I haven't known him long – only since last year. But when I first met him he seemed altogether normal.'

I stood up and went over to the mantel to get a closer look at the Miro. I've always liked Miro. There's something marvellously fluid and liquescent about his work, something soothing like a fountain plashing in the evening's distance. But this time I paid little attention to the Miro. I went over to it for the effect, so Nan would not see how important I considered our conversation.

'Would you say he was abnormal now, Miss Bulkely?' I asked.

She stood up too, and walked over to where I was standing. She was tall, slender without being angular, high-breasted. I liked to look at her, but when I looked at her it was difficult to keep my mind on what she was saying. 'Yes, doctor, I would. I've almost decided that Jacob is losing his mind.'

'That is what he thinks himself,' I said. 'I'm not so sure.'

She was standing close to me, her eyes level with mine. 'Doctor, do you think he might get violent?'

I reached into my breast pocket for my cigarettes. That is the pocket where I keep my cards. As I pulled out my cigarette case, my card folder fell onto the floor. Nan stooped immediately to pick it up – stooped quicker than I did myself – then held it in her hand, looking at it. She tore the top card off and held it to her mouth, smiling.

'Do you mind if I take this, doctor? I see it has both your telephone numbers on it. If I have it, I can get you at any time of the day or night if anything should go wrong with Jacob . . .'

What could I say but, 'Yes, of course. Keep it if you wish'? It was as if she had picked my pocket – I had the definite impression that it was my telephone number that she had been after all along – but I would have been foolish to protest. After all, there was no good reason why she should not call me up.

I started to say, 'I have only seen Jacob for an hour or so this afternoon and I am not thoroughly acquainted with his symptoms, but I see no cause for alarm as yet –' when I became aware of the fact that someone, not Nan, had coughed. I turned around to see the other girl, Denise, standing behind us. Her face was flushed and her eyes were round and glistened. She seemed to be making an effort to communicate something to her friend, trying to speak without speaking. Then, I became aware of Jacob's presence at the same moment Nan herself did. He was standing in the doorway that led to the bath; he had changed into a dinner suit and his curly hair was carefully combed. His face was white with anger.

'What has she been telling you about me, doctor?' he demanded.

Nan rushed over to him, put her arm around him. 'I was just telling him about your friends, Jakey. I didn't say a thing you wouldn't have said yourself.'

He pushed her away from him. 'What are you doing here? Why didn't you tell me you were coming?'

She pretended to pout. That was one thing she could not do well, pout. All she accomplished was a crude parody of the childish expression. 'I wanted only to see you, Jakey. I thought you could have dinner with us before the show.'

'You could have telephoned me if you had wanted to do that. How many times have I told you not to come to my place without calling first? Do you want me to tell my man not to let you in?'

Nan was angry now. She went into the foyer and took her wrap from the closet and flung it about her shoulders. Denise, embarrassed, followed her. Nan stood staring back at Jacob and myself, her eyes bright slits of green fire. But when she spoke, she spoke to me.

'Do you see what I mean, doctor? He's mad – stark, raving mad!'

She even slammed the door on the way out – after holding it until her companion was safely outside. It was a good performance.

'Weren't you a little hard on them?' I asked Jacob as we were standing waiting for the elevator. 'I think Miss Bulkely is really concerned about you. You're concerned about yourself, you know. As for Denise, well, I think she was fairly embarrassed.'

'It wasn't that I minded so much Nan's talking about me behind my back,' he said. 'It's that she has begun to follow me around. Everywhere I go, I see her – or that friend of hers. I feel like she's trying to keep me leashed!'

I could understand his resentment and, at the same time, I could see where Nan might have good reason for acting the way she did. Although I had sensed something wrong in her attitude, I seemed compelled to defend her to Jacob – yet I dared not do so more than I had already. If I were to help him, I would have to induce the belief that I was on his side, right or wrong.

The taxi took us to a bar and grill in the Sixties on Third Avenue. This was the usual Third Avenue bar-room with Rheingold neon signs in the windows and saw-dust on the tile floor. I noticed, while I was waiting for Jacob to pay the cabby, that a large van had been parked in front of the place – a truck with deep sides and screened windows near the roof of its storage space not unlike an oversize paddy wagon. I wondered at the time what it was there for, but I forgot about it almost immediately.

We went into the bar and ordered a couple of beers. Jacob looked around the smoke-filled room and then said, 'I don't think Eustace is here yet.'

I looked about, too. I don't know what I expected to see, surely not Eustace. There were a few booths along one wall, some tables in the rear – a few of which had been pushed aside to make way for a dart game. Most of the customers were clustered around the players, one of whom seemed to be an excellent shot. As I watched I saw three clean bull's-eyes thrown into the target, a circle chalked on the wall. Then I looked back at Jacob.

'Tell me,' I asked, 'do you really expect Eustace to come?'

'Oh, he'll be here all right. He's usually a little late. He sleeps a lot and has trouble with his alarm clock.'

Was my patient pulling my leg? If he was, he was keeping a perfectly straight face and making a good show of turning around to look every time someone opened the door. I drank some beer and resumed my interest in the dart game.

It was breaking up. Men were turning away, shaking their heads and emitting low whistles. I saw that the target now contained all of the darts – the bull's-eye being particularly crowded. I peered to see who was the egregious marksman. It turned out to be Eustace.

He was a midget scarcely more than three feet high. He had on a bottle-green velvet jacket, a tattersall waistcoat and mauve broadcloth trousers. He walked jauntily from out of the crowd of normal-sized men, a broad grin on his face. Somebody yelled at him 'Where did you learn to throw darts like that?' and, without turning around, he answered, 'Once I was one end of a knife-throwing act in a carnival.' Then he saw Jacob. He came over to the bar and held out a hand to be helped up onto the barstool. When he was seated comfortably, he glowered and said to Jacob in a disproportionately bass voice: 'Who's this mug?'

Jacob waved a hand in my direction. 'This is Dr Matthews, Eustace. He'd like to go to work for you, too.'

Before I could protest, Eustace had turned his back on me. 'Can't use him,' he said to Jacob. 'He's not our type.'

This made me angry. Why couldn't I give money away as well as the next one?

'What's so difficult about giving money away?' I said. My voice was loud. 'I don't see why I couldn't do it!' I still hadn't overcome my surprise at finding Eustace was real, and I had to find some way to express my resentment.

Eustace turned around slowly on his stool and gave me a disdainful look. I began to dislike the little man intensely.

'Money?' said Eustace. 'Who's giving away money?'

'Why, Eustace,' said Jacob, 'haven't I been giving money away for you every day for the past six months?'

'Oh, that! That stopped yesterday,' said Eustace. 'Now you're giving away horses. Percherons.' He turned and whistled at the bartender. 'Hey, Herman,' he called in his deepest voice, 'how about a hooker of that lousy hog-dip you call rye?'

'Horses?' said Jacob.

'Yeah, percherons,' said Eustace. 'The kind they use on beer wagons.'

I had been examining Eustace carefully. I was sure he was only a midget. He had the typical cranium of a dwarf, the compressed features, the dominant forehead, the prematurely wrinkled skin. I pointed a finger at him.

'He's only a midget, Jacob,' I said. 'He's not what you think he is. Someone is playing a joke on you.'

Eustace got very angry. He began to jump up and down on his stool like a kid at the circus. His small face got bright red and then dark purple.

'Midget!' he croaked. 'Who the hell's a midget? I'm a leprechaun. Me father came from County Cork!'

Jacob was exasperated, too. 'Now, look what you've done!' he exclaimed. 'Now you'll never get to work for them!'

I refused to be abashed. 'He's not a leprechaun, Jacob!' I insisted. 'Leprechauns are tiny men only six inches high. He's only a midget pretending to be a leprechaun.'

'You're thinking of Irish leprechauns,' said Jacob. 'Eustace is an American leprechaun. His father came over from Ireland and Eustace was born on this side of the water. Leprechauns, like everything else in America, are bigger and better than anywhere else!'

Eustace had quieted down. He contented himself with delivering a withering glance in my direction that was intended as a *coup de grâce*. Then he ignored me.

'Isn't there some place we can go to talk business in private?' he asked Jacob.

'You can talk in front of Dr Matthews,' Jacob replied. 'I've told him about our work.'

The bartender set the hooker of rye down in front of the preposterous little fool. He grabbed it greedily and tossed it down his throat skilfully. Then he gave another scornful look.

'Well, if you've told him the harm's already done,' he said. 'But you really ought to be more careful who you talk to!'

If Jacob Blunt had not been a patient of mine, I would

have walked away and never seen him again after that. Still it was plainly my duty to stay and see what this hoaxer would put him up to next.

'You said I'm not to give quarters away any more,' Jacob was saying. 'You said I was to give away horses. But to whom?'

'That's right,' said Eustace. 'Percherons. The big ones. Tonight you're going to give Frances Raye a percheron.'

'Frances Raye!' I said. 'The Star of *Nevada!*? Why, she's the most successful actress on Broadway!'

'That's the one,' said Eustace. 'We leprechauns have decided that it's about time she had a percheron.'

'How am I going to get it to her?' asked Jacob. He was frowning – I could see he was not too pleased with this latest assignment.

'I've got it in a truck outside,' said Eustace. 'I'll drive you over with it, and then you can take it out and tether it, go ring her doorbell and present it to her. You get twenty-five dollars for that instead of ten.'

Jacob was decidedly unhappy. I had not seen his grin in some time. Eustace must have noticed it, too.

'Look,' he said, 'what's eating at you? Here I give you a promotion – take you off of quarters and put you on to percherons – and to look at you I'd think I'd fired you! I don't get it!'

Jacob tried to smile. 'You mean I'm to give away a horse every night to – to somebody like Frances Raye?' he stammered.

Eustace nodded his absurd head waggishly. 'That's right. That is, if you do a good job. It all depends on whether you're cut out for percherons. You may be just a good man on quarters.' Here he paused, significantly, and looked at me. 'Some people can't even give quarters away!' he scoffed.

I did not like Eustace at all.

Jacob regarded me over Eustace's head. 'Did you hear what he said, Dr Matthews?'

'You don't have to do it if you don't want to,' I told him. 'There's no way he can make you do it.'

'Have another beer, kid,' said Eustace. 'It'll make you feel better! Percherons are no different from quarters – only bigger. It ain't difficult once you learn the trick to it. Aaah – you'll be good at it I tell you!'

Jacob was not listening to him. He was still watching me. 'Dr Matthews,' he said, 'tell me – am I crazy?'

I was in no mood to answer that question.

Jacob and I had another beer apiece, and Eustace had another rye, before we went outside to see the percheron. It was in the van I had seen when we went into the saloon. This truck was actually a stable on wheels: the rear doors opened downwards to form a runway, the inside walls were padded, there was a stall and a bale of fodder – it was something to see. And the percheron itself was a gorgeous animal. It stood at least nineteen hands high and it had the most beautiful white mane I've ever seen. I was impressed.

'You mean I have to ring Frances Raye's doorbell and then just give this thing to her?' Jacob gasped. He was really worried. 'What if she isn't home?'

Eustace was casually lighting a cigarette. 'Then you go back tomorrow night,' he said. 'I'll give you another twenty-five dollars. If she isn't home it won't be your fault.'

'What will I do with the horse then?'

'If you can't deliver it, the driver will take it back to the stables. Then you can tell him when you want it tomorrow night and he'll bring it around to your door.'

They locked up the back of the truck and Eustace went around to the front, and stood talking to the driver. Jacob had thrust his hands deep into his topcoat pockets and was looking glum.

'I'm not crazy, doc – am I? You see him, too – don't you? He's real – isn't he?'

'You don't have to go through with this absurd joke,

you know,' I told him. 'You don't need the money. It's my opinion that one of your friends is trying to make a fool of you. I wouldn't let him get away with it if I were you.' I spoke quickly, angrily. Jacob's vacillating attitude was aggravating – particularly as I was not sure that the joke was not being played on me.

Jacob stood there, fingering the hibiscus in his hair. 'Oh, I'll have to do it tonight,' he said. 'Eustace is counting on me and I can't let him down! But I'm not so sure I'll do it after this . . . Percherons are a little too big . . .'

I was exasperated. He still might be a neurotic, and I still might be a physician bound by my Hippocratic oath – but the odds were that he was only a silly, impressionable youth that someone was playing a long-drawn-out, unfunny practical joke on. And there I was, standing on a street corner, trying to reason with him. I felt insulted!

'At least you can take that silly flower out of your hair!' I said peevishly, knowing well that it was the last thing I should have said at that time but not being able to keep myself from saying it. 'You don't have to make yourself doubly ridiculous!'

That did it. If I still stood a chance of arguing him out of his foolish risk, I threw it away by taunting him. He was immediately on his dignity – I saw his shoulders stiffen – although he was too proud to let me know I had hurt him. Instead he let me have the full benefit of that off-centre grin. 'Oh, no, I couldn't do that,' he said. 'That wouldn't be fair to Joe. Besides I'm used to having a flower in my hair. I sort of like it.'

I gave up. There is never any point in arguing with a neurotic about his obsession – not that I was convinced Jacob was a neurotic. If he ever changes, the change will come from within himself. All the doctor can do is to point it out. Jacob was either a foolish youth who was too absurdly proud to admit he was an object of ridicule, or his neurosis was so ingrown that I could not instil a desire for change. Perhaps he preferred to be neurotic. It would not be the first time I had met the symptom. If later he thought differently, he knew where he could get in touch with me. As for now, he could go ahead and give Frances Raye a percheron if that gratified any hidden urge in his psyche. I'd be damned if I'd have anything more to do with it!

I said good-bye, turned up my coat collar against the drizzle and walked down Third Avenue towards 59th Street and the crosstown car. I felt very put upon and badly used. As I ate a lonely dinner in the Columbus Circle Child's, it occurred to me that the police might be interested in Eustace's crazy scheme. Annoying an actress by tethering a percheron to her doorstep might easily be a misdemeanour, if not something worse. I thought about telephoning my old friend, Lieutenant Anderson of the Homicide Division, and reporting the whole silly routine to him. But I soon decided against that. If nothing came of it, and no one ever tried to give Frances Raye a horse, Anderson would never stop laughing at me. So, instead, I went down to Penn Station, walked to Sixth Avenue and caught the tubes to Jersey.

And as I sat in the half-light of the underground, my ears filled with the rushing roar of pent-up steel on steel, I kept turning the whole wild muddle over and over in my mind. Soon I found I had lost my carefully nurtured objectivity, and with it my scoffing attitude. I was as much a part of Jacob's mental crisis as I believed Nan to be. This is not supposed to be a healthy state of mind for a psychiatrist, but I am not too sure. How can one understand or appreciate the trauma of a neurotic if one has never experienced similar trauma oneself? I knew I would not sleep well that night – I was all but resigned to the fact that I would not sleep well any night until my patient showed definite improvement. And I was ashamed of myself for leaving him alone with his dilemma.

If I forgot for an instant the disturbing fact that at least Eustace, and that part of Jacob's story, was real, it would be a simple matter to name his complaint. He was verging on schizophrenia, if he weren't already a schizoid. But Eustace was real (and I had to admit to myself that later experience might prove Joe and Harry to be equally real); he and his peculiar proclivity for paying Jacob to give away silver quarters and blooded horses were not an irrational fancy. At this point, I could not get past that improbable fact unless I doubted my own sanity.

And a psychiatrist must never doubt his own sanity.

*

I did fall asleep that night, but only after tossing for what seemed hours. I did not get to sleep for long though. Sara's voice, sleepy and irritable, awakened me.

'The telephone is ringing, George!' she said. 'Ringing its head off! Please go answer it!'

I groped for my slippers, threw my bathrobe over my shoulders and stumbled down the stairs. The voice over the wire was Nan's. If I had been sleepy before, as soon as I understood what it was she was saying I was instantly awake.

'Jacob's been arrested, doctor!' she said. 'In connection with the murder of Frances Raye! They found her dead in her apartment, and him, outside, drunk, ringing her doorbell, trying to get in! Oh, doctor, they think he killed her!'

All I could think to ask her was: 'What did he do with the horse?'

3 A Question of Motivation

I reached Center Street about six o'clock in the morning.
Before I saw Jacob I had a talk with Lieutenant Anderson
of the Homicide Division. Anderson was a man I liked;
I had served as consultant on several cases with him and
I respected his intelligence. He was a dour, middle-aged
man with sparse grey hair. His face had a certain lean
spareness that was the only trace of the officer of the
law to be found in his manner or appearance; otherwise he resembled a dyspeptic businessman.

I was not prepared for the cold way he greeted me. He
did not look up when I came into his office. He was bent
over his desk writing; I stood for a minute or so waiting
for him to ask me to sit down, and then I sat down anyway. I had used the same technique myself on occasion
and I knew its uses and why it was sometimes necessary –
it was one of the best ways to give yourself an initial
advantage in an interview. Perhaps, this was why it
angered me. I already felt rather put upon about the
entire affair, but I had not expected Anderson – whom I
considered a personal friend – to treat me this way. I
decided I could keep silent as long as he could. I refused
to allow myself to be restless or to look at him. Yet I knew
he was watching me.

'They tell me Jacob Blunt is a patient of yours,
George.' Anderson spoke when I least expected him to
and, despite myself, I was startled.

'Since yesterday afternoon. I saw him for the first time
yesterday,' I answered.

'What was the matter with him last night? Was he
drunk or is he crazy?'

47

'I shall have to see him and examine him before I can say that,' I said.

'Cautious, aren't you?'

Anderson's way of speaking had always been terse, drily humorous on occasion, but never impolite. He was not being impolite now, for that matter. In his last curt question, I detected a hint of amused recognition of my own confusion. The difference in his manner, I decided, lay in the difference in our relationship – perhaps, even in the difference in my own point of view. Heretofore I had been a consultant working with him on equal terms, but now I was a witness. With this thought I allowed myself to relax, to drop my defences. 'It might help me if you told me what happened last night,' I reminded him.

The Lieutenant's sharp, blue eyes regarded me steadily, but I suspected that he was suppressing a smile. Why, the fellow liked having to interrogate me! 'Frances Raye was murdered last night,' he said. 'Her body was found on the living-room floor of her apartment on West Tenth Street. It was near the door, about six paces away. She had been stabbed in the back. We haven't found the knife.'

'What has my patient to do with it?'

'Blunt's queer actions led to our discovery of the body. He was standing outside the house ringing the doorbell. A big horse with a fancy mane was tethered to the nearest lamp-post. A scout car was passing by, and the boys thought the set-up looked funny. So they parked and investigated. Blunt told them a "leprechaun" had paid him twenty-five dollars to deliver the horse to Raye. The boys thought he was drunk, but one of them went inside to see if he had bothered Miss Raye. He found her door unlocked and her body on the floor.'

'What did Jacob say about that?'

'He said he didn't know anything about it. He kept repeating the same outlandish story about a "leprechaun" named "Eustace" who had given him the horse and paid him to deliver it to Raye. I questioned him myself about an hour ago and he said the same thing. Finally, I told one of the boys to lock him up until he came to his senses.'

'What's he charged with?'

'Drunk and disorderly.'

I was relieved. From what Nan had told me over the telephone, I had thought that Jacob was under suspicion of murder.

'Of course, he could have killed her,' Anderson went on. 'Or he could have seen the murderer on his way out. But when I talked to him, I got the idea he was more than drunk –' He tapped his forehead significantly.

'As I said before, I know very little about him – nothing more than I gained in a short interview yesterday afternoon – but if his mind is affected I doubt if his type of aberration would lead to homicide. Not so soon, at least,' I said.

'You mean this "leprechaun" he was talking about?'

I nodded my head. 'Something like that. He might have been suffering from hallucinations.'

Anderson leaned his head on his hand. 'The trouble is I don't have any clues. The door to her place was ajar, the building doesn't have a desk clerk or elevator operator – just one of those buzzer arrangements – and even the front door was unlocked. If your booby killed her, why did he go back outside and ring her doorbell?'

'Anyone could have done it, is that it? Were there signs of struggle? Was anything stolen?'

Anderson stood up and came round his desk. He was a short man in a neat, double-breasted suit. He fingered his tie nervously, unloosing the knot. There was a button missing on his coat sleeve. 'No, the place was in apple-pie order and nothing seemed to be missing. Raye was wearing one of those backless négligés – not the sort of thing she would wear if she were expecting company, unless it was a certain kind of company. They tell me she didn't have anything on underneath.'

'What about her friends?' I asked. 'Are you going to question them?'

He smiled for the second time. Again I had the feeling that he enjoyed the advantage of his position. The next time he consulted me, I knew how I was going to act. 'We're taking care of that,' he said, and his tone let me know that I had asked a foolish question.

'Then you don't think Jacob murdered her?'

He shook his head. 'No, I don't.' He did not sound too happy about it. 'Nobody, even a nut, who had just killed a woman would try to get by with a preposterous alibi like that.' He shook his head again as if he still could not believe that Jacob had told him what he had. 'And even nuts have reasons for doing what they do, particularly murder. Crazy reasons, but still reasons.'

'And Jacob has no motive . . .'

He nodded his head glumly. 'That's about the size of it.'

'Lieutenant,' I said, 'what would you say if I told you that I had met and talked to this leprechaun Jacob was telling you about? Eustace, I mean?'

He did not even look up at me. 'I'd say you were crazy, too.'

'But it's true. I met him only last night.' Then I went on to tell him about Eustace and the percheron. 'I heard him promise Jacob twenty-five dollars to bring the horse to Frances Raye,' I concluded.

I think that Anderson felt like quitting his job then – just throwing up his hands and walking away, never to return. His shoulders slumped and his eyes grew tired. For the first time he looked like a man who had been awakened in the middle of the night to investigate a murder. His manner seemed to say: 'There are some things no man can endure!' Well, it served him right for the way he had been acting to me. Now the shoe was on the other foot and I hoped it pinched!

'George, I must remind you that there are penalties attached to obstructing the course of justice,' he said, wearily clutching at the remains of his dignity.

'What I said was the truth. In every detail. On my professional honour. I told you because I thought the information might lead to something in connection with the case.'

Then I told him the story of Jacob's visit to my office the previous day and the events that followed. I ended by saying, 'I'm in a position similar to yours. I cannot believe these things to be true, and yet I cannot escape the evidence of my own senses. I cannot say whether we are dealing with a wily madman or the ingenuous victim of a vicious conspiracy!'

Anderson slumped down in his chair. He seemed discouraged. I felt tired and over-tense myself. The lack of sleep suddenly began to weigh on me, the four dreary walls of the small office oppressed me. I wanted to get up and walk out – to forget all about it.

'We have to find this "Eustace",' said Anderson. 'We have to make him talk – tell who hired him and all the details. Then we may get to the bottom of it.'

'Who do you think is behind it?' I asked.

He shook his head. 'I don't know. I haven't an idea.'

'We can't get at Eustace without Jacob's help,' I reminded him. And a moment later I regretted that I had spoken. The same thought entered both of our minds at once. Anderson looked at me, a smile creasing his saturnine face. Then he sat down and began to play with the pencils on his desk.

'If I release him into your custody, will you work with him and try to find out what he knows? I'll give you any police assistance you may need.'

This was what I had feared he would suggest. I did not want to do it. I wanted to be done with Jacob and his little men. And yet I was curious. 'What about my practice?' I asked. 'It would take time and I have a long list of appointments every day.'

'You'll get paid for your time. Any fee within reasonable limits.'

I wanted to do it, and I didn't want to. I felt a responsibility towards Jacob – if I did not do it he might be prosecuted for a crime he did not commit – and yet I had no desire to get entangled with Eustace and Joe and Harry. It was difficult for me to say either yes or no.

At last I made up my mind. 'I'll do it,' I said, 'if we can start now. I want to lose as little time from my practice as possible.'

Anderson pressed a button on his desk. He was smiling. 'You can find out what he knows if anyone can, George,' he said. 'I've always liked working with you.' I said nothing, but I was amused by the change in his manner. Now that I had agreed to do what he wanted me to do, there was no need for him to dissimulate and we were friends again. 'I'll give orders to release Blunt into your custody. If you could get him to open up and talk to you by – say – this afternoon, that would be fine.'

I held up my hand, 'Not so fast,' I said. 'It's going to take longer than that.' I was thinking of how unsuccessful I had been the day before when I had tried to find out what was really wrong with Jacob.

'Well, report your progress and his whereabouts every day.'

'And, in the meantime, what will you be doing?' I asked him.

'I'll be working at it from this end. I'll let you know how that goes, too.'

I found Nan waiting for me in the corridor outside Anderson's office. She was a subtly different person from the girl I had met the night before; although she was every whit as beautiful, her manner was no longer as intense – she seemed withdrawn, distracted.

'What did he say?' she asked me, and, strangely enough, she averted her eyes. I had the feeling that she did not care to know.

'Anderson is releasing Jacob to me. They should be bringing him up in a few minutes. I'll be responsible for him – he will have to stay with me, but he will be out of jail.'

'How did you manage to work that?' Her exclamation

was automatic, her voice apathetic. I looked at her curiously. She looked away again.

'I've known Anderson for several years,' I said. 'I worked with him as a psychiatric consultant on a number of cases. So I pointed out to him that parts of Jacob's story were clearly true, and to get the whole truth we would have to get Jacob to confide in us. Anderson realizes that psychiatric methods sometimes work in places where police methods fail. He's releasing Jacob – although he will still be technically under arrest – under my supervision. Jacob is not yet out of the woods, though.'

'I suppose it's like being out on bail?' Again she spoke lifelessly and gave me the impression that none of this mattered to her. I stared at her, remembering the impulsive, prying interest she had shown in my opinion of Jacob just the previous evening. She saw that I was puzzled and smiled at me. 'Don't mind my mood, doctor. I'll snap out of it. So many things have happened in so short a time that I guess it's all been a little too much for me.'

'You should go home and rest,' I said. 'I can see how this has affected you.'

'I'm all right now, or I shall be as soon as I have some breakfast. I don't want to go home now. I want to be with you when you meet Jacob.'

Oddly enough, she sounded as if she meant her last statement.

A few minutes later a man came down the corridor toward us, accompanied by a policeman. He was about thirty, of middle-size, with slick black hair and an annoyingly small moustache. As soon as Nan saw him, she rushed to meet him, throwing her arms about him and crying, 'Darling, they aren't holding you any longer. Dr Matthews is going to be responsible for you!'

But the man she was kissing, the man she had called 'darling', was not Jacob Blunt. He was not the man who had come into my office the previous afternoon and who had later introduced me to Eustace. His hair was not even the same colour.

There was something very wrong.

I waited to see what would happen. I knew I could do one of two things: either denounce him to Anderson on the spot, or let him think I did not know that a substitution had taken place and see if I could learn something important. I knew then and there that the sensible thing for me to do was to tell him that I did not know him, that he was not Jacob Blunt. But I hated to face Anderson again, to make myself doubly ridiculous. If I could find out what lay behind the muddle of Jacob, the little men and their preposterous activities, I might be able to turn the tables on Anderson. I was still brooding about being awakened in the middle of the night to rush down to Center Street only to be questioned like a common criminal by my old friend. As a result, what I did may not seem intelligent – all I can say is that it made sense to me then, it even looked like a good idea. I walked down the corridor to a desk, signed some papers and then walked out of the station with Nan and 'Jacob'. He did not say anything until we were standing outside on the street.

'It was funny my finding her body like that,' he said, self-consciously. 'I don't blame the cops for thinking I did her in.'

'You didn't, of course?'

He looked at me, feigning incredulity. He was smiling, but his face was pale and his mouth worked nervously. 'You don't think I killed her, do you? My God, I didn't! I really didn't!'

'Why shouldn't I think so? You were the one person who was found near the scene of the crime.' I thought I was testing him. I wanted to see how far his bravado would carry him before he realized that I knew he was an impostor.

We had been walking down the street. He stopped and took Nan's hand in his, pulling her around roughly so that she faced him. I saw the flesh of her wrist turn white under the pressure of his fingers, and I thought I saw her wince. 'You don't think that of me, darling – do you?' he demanded.

Nan would not look at him. 'I don't know, Jacob. I'm not sure.'

He turned to me. His eyes were cold, but his mouth was uneasy. I saw that he did not know how to take my acceptance of him as Jacob Blunt. Whatever he had expected, it was not this.

'But, doc, I didn't do it, I tell you! I did get drunk last night with Eustace. I did serenade Frances Raye and try to break down her door. But I never killed her, honest I didn't! Why, I'd never seen her before last night!'

I could not understand what he hoped to gain by pretending he was Jacob. Although he succeeded in imitating Jacob's voice and way of talking fairly well, I was certain that this man was not the man who had visited my office. And by this time I had decided that as soon as I could get to a telephone, I would call Anderson and tell him what had happened.

We continued to walk up the street to the I.R.T. station. I kept on the look-out for a drugstore or lunch wagon that had a telephone, but all I saw were office buildings. Then it struck me that if I made a call now, it would be too obvious. I had better wait until we arrived at my office and I could excuse myself for a moment. During this time neither Nan nor Jacob spoke. This in itself was strange since Nan had struck me as being rather talkative. We walked down the steps of the subway entrance and stood on the platform waiting for the Uptown Local. From far off came the beginnings of a metallic roar – the train was approaching. I remember thinking: I can watch him on the train to see if he resembles my patient in any particular. I remember sensing that someone near me had moved, that someone else had whispered words that had something to do with me. I remember beginning to turn around, the first sensation of fright . . . and at the same instant I knew that the grinding roar had increased and that the two gleaming lights of the train were almost level with me . . .

Then I felt a sharp blow in the middle of my back. I remember arching, grabbing at air – I remember twisting, falling against something that rushed past me and tore me away with it and then threw me down . . .

4   Non Compos Mentis

Two eyes were looking down at me. Two cold blue eyes in a fat womanish face. No lipstick. No rouge. A pallid, fleshy pancake of a face.

'Open your mouth.'

I opened my mouth and a cold thing went into it. I peered down my nose to see what it was and my head was one solid stabbing pain. The face swam away from me accompanied by a harsh, rustling sound, leaving me looking at a very flat pale green wall. Very flat indeed.

Was it a wall? Could it be a ceiling? But if it were a ceiling, I must be lying on my back! What would I be doing lying on my back looking at a very flat pale green ceiling?

The face was back again. It was even closer than before. The cold thing, now warm, slid mysteriously backward out of my mouth. I did not like the face. I wished it would go away.

After the face went away, I decided that the cold thing must have been a thermometer . . . and that I must be sick . . . in bed . . . in a hospital? I would ask the face.

I waited a long time for the nurse to return. And when she did, I found I could scarcely speak. The first time I tried I only made a rushing sound. My mouth was dry as felt and my tongue was twice its normal size, awkward, an impediment to speech. I tried to speak again. I managed to say, 'Nurse!'

'Yes.'

'Where am I?'

'You're sick. But never mind. You'll be all right.'

I closed my eyes. The effort had been too much. I had wanted to find out something . . . something important. But now it did not matter.

*

The next time I awoke I felt better. My head still ached, but it was easier to think and my mouth felt more natural. This time I waited eagerly for the nurse. I still could not remember what was so important, but I wanted to ask questions. I wanted to find out the name of the hospital. I wanted to know what had happened to me.

The nurse did not come.

After a while another face came. A blank, lined face such as I had seen many times before but could not remember where. Cold brown eyes like flawed marbles. A mouth that twitched.

'Aggie's got you too!' it said. 'Like me, Aggie's come and got you too. And you ain't goin' to get away! Naaah! You ain't goin' to get away. Aggie's got you!'

The face laughed. I felt sorry for it, but I did not know why. I had seen so many like it before, but where? The face kept on laughing.

'They come for me too,' it said. 'They come in a wagon. They drug me. Yaah, they drug me! Oh, I didn't wanta go, but they made me.' And then suddenly the face began to whimper – the mouth trembled and the brown marbles glistened with tears. 'Never done no harm. Never hurt nothin'. Why should they hurt me? Why should Aggie get me? Never done no harm . . .'

A flat toneless voice that went on and on. I shut my eyes. Would the nurse never come?

*

The third time I awakened I knew where I was. I must have felt stronger because I tried to sit up. I could not. I could only move my head. I was strapped to my bed. That could only mean one thing: I was in the psychopathic ward of a hospital.

That explained the second face. A paranoiac. I had seen many just like that in my days at the sanatorium – I had even encountered a few in private practice. They were unmistakable: the empty, neurotic face, the unending complaint of the toneless voice, the humourless, mechanical laugh . . .

But what was I doing in a mental ward? I was not insane. I was a psychiatrist. Who had committed me?

The fat face again. This time it was easier to talk.

'Where am I?'

'You're sick. Don't talk.'

'But what's the name of the hospital? Where am I?'

'Be quiet. Be a good boy . . .'

The last word held as if the sentence might not be finished.

'But where am I? What am I doing here?'

The fat face was gone.

*

This time I was determined to find out where I was and why. They could not keep me, a doctor – a psychiatrist – in ignorance like this. It was unethical. I would demand to see the doctor in residence.

After a long wait another face appeared. A competent face with glasses, a professional face, a man's face – the doctor?

'Where am I?'

'The City Hospital.'

'The psychopathic ward?'

'Yes.'

'But, doctor, you can't keep me here!'

'I'm afraid we have to, old man.'

'My name's Matthews, George Matthews. I'm a doctor with offices on Lexington Avenue. I'm a psychiatrist.'

He hesitated before he spoke. 'Your name is John Brown. Homeless. Picked up wandering.'

'It's not true! It's as I told you! I'm a physician, a psychiatrist. You can't treat me like this!'

'I'm afraid you're mistaken, old boy. But I'll look into it. "George Matthews," did you say?'

'Doctor, I tell you – '

But he was gone.

He came back.

'Who did you say you were?'

'Dr George Matthews of 445 Lexington Avenue and Hackensack, New Jersey.'

'There is such a doctor. How did you know his name? Has he treated you at some time?'

It did not look like a stupid face – how could it be so obtuse? I wanted to shout at it, but I knew I must keep calm, a model of sanity.

'I am that man, doctor. Look, you can call a number, can't you? You can call BUtterfield 2-6888, can't you? That won't do any harm.'

'But that's Dr Matthews' number.'

'That's what I'm telling you! I am Dr Matthews! There's been a mistake. Call that number and describe me to my nurse. If the description tallies, you will know I'm telling the truth!'

The face was gone. To telephone I hoped.

This time he was back quickly. The first I knew of his presence was when I felt the straps loosen. I sat up. A young, embarrassed intern stood at the foot of my bed. He was not smiling.

'Well,' I said, 'I was right, wasn't I?'

Only then did it occur to me that I might not be right. An irrational fear, I told myself. I knew who I was, didn't I?

'I was mistaken – ' he began.

'That's what I was trying to tell you . . .'

He spoke quickly. 'I was mistaken in saying there is a Dr George Matthews,' he said. 'There was a Dr George Matthews. But he died recently.'

He spoke clearly and distinctly. Underlining each simple sentence as if he were speaking to a child. Or a madman.

'What do you mean?'

'I looked first in an old directory. Then I found a Dr George Matthews at the address you gave me. But when I called the number, exchange cut in and said there was no such number. I checked with a later directory and I found that Dr George Matthews had died.'

'When?'

'I don't know when. Between this year and last, I suppose.'

'But I am Dr George Matthews. I'm not dead. I live in Hackensack, New Jersey. I have a wife named Sara . . .'

The intern was very embarrassed. He gripped the foot of my bed with both his hands, clenched the rail tightly as if he were fighting pain. 'I'm afraid you're mistaken. I know it seems that way to you, but that is not your name. Our records are quite accurate – I checked them again before I came back. The name on your Social Security Card, which we found in your pocket, is that of John Brown.'

Then he went away. What was the use of telling him I had never had a Social Security Card? He knew that they had never been issued to doctors just as well as I did.

*

They let me up and around but would not let me shave myself. They gave me an old pair of corduroy trousers, the ones I had been wearing – I was told – when they found me. I held them up with my hands. I could not have a belt because I might hang myself with it. There was no mirror, and I was not allowed to leave the ward. I could not see what I looked like now.

By running my hand over my head I could tell that my hair was more closely cropped than it used to be. It felt short and bristly like an undergraduate's. I began to feel like a different man, a poor man, a sick man.

I grew friendly with the young intern. His name was Harvey Peters. We talked together whenever he could spare the time. I argued with him again and again. But it never did any good.

On the second day –

'Doctor, I tell you my name is Matthews! I am married and I live in Hackensack, New Jersey. I want you to get in touch with my wife.'

'I'll try if you want me to.'

'There must have been some mistake about the other. The telephone company's error. But reach my wife, please! She'll be worrying about me.'

'I'll try – '

The third day –

'My wife's coming to see me today? You got in touch with her, didn't you? She'll be coming to take me home today?

He shook his head. 'I'm sorry, fellow. I tried. But I could not reach your wife.'

'She wasn't in? She was out shopping most likely. Sara likes to shop. But you'll try again? She'll be in the next time you call.'

'There is no Mrs George Matthews in the Hackensack telephone book.'

'But doctor, we have a phone. I know we have a phone.'

He kept shaking his head. I could see he pitied me now. 'There is no Mrs George Matthews in Hackensack, New Jersey, who is a doctor's wife. That Mrs George Matthews moved away. She left no forwarding address. I know because I've checked with the post office.'

'Doctor, there must be some mistake! She wouldn't leave like that – without a word!'

'I'm sorry, old man. You're mistaken.'

'I'm not mistaken. I am George Matthews.'

'You must not get so excited. You must rest.'

Another day –

'Doctor, how long have I been here?'

'About two weeks.'

'What is the diagnosis?'

'Amnesia, with possible paranoid tendencies.'

'But I know who I am! It's just that I can't prove it!'

'I know. I know that's the way it seems.' He was humouring me. A mild-mannered, kind, young man who was almost a doctor was humouring me. He pitied me. He had not as yet developed the necessary callousness and the aberrations of his more intelligent patients still dismayed him. He wanted to let me down gently. I knew he would comply with all my requests (or pretend to comply), because he felt that my interest in my former life – in any former life, even a mythical one – was an encouraging symptom, a sign of possible improvement.

I continued to batter my hopes against this blind construction of theory and tradition, this man for whom I was mad because my history sheet said I was – and if I were not psychotic, why then was I in the psychopathic ward of the hospital?

'But, doctor,' I said, 'I know who I am. A man suffering from amnesia does not know who he is. All, or a part, of his past life is lost – he has misplaced his identity, his personal history, even his habits. That isn't a description of me!'

He answered me patiently. He talked while his eyes looked past me, remembering the definitions and practices learned by rote, mechanically interposing the logical objections, the proper refutation to all my proposals. A neurotic catechism – a litany for the irrational!

'You do not recognize your identity. You do not recognize your name – worse! – you refuse to accept it as yours. You put forward instead another man's name, a dead man's name, and claim it as your own. You claim his wife, his profession. And, building on this delusion, you begin to think that all of us are persecuting you, holding back what is rightfully yours. That is paranoia.'

'Doctor, do me a favour?'

'What is it?'

'Call the police. Headquarters. Ask to speak to Lieutenant Anderson of the Homicide Division. Tell him I am here. Describe me to him. Tell him that there has been a mistake – that something has gone badly wrong.'

'But the police brought you here. You were charged with vagrancy. The police know all about you.'

'Just this one last favour, doctor. Please, call Lieutenant Anderson!'

He went away. This time I did not pretend to myself. This time I knew that it would do no good. Although I might still have him call my club and some of the medical societies I belonged to, I suspected that the response would always be the same. This was the last time I would try. After this I could do nothing but wait.

He returned, stood at the foot of my bed, hesitant, sorry for me. 'Lieutenant Anderson knew Doctor Matthews well,' he said. 'He committed suicide last year. His body was found in the North River. The Lieutenant said that you must be an impostor.'

After that I began to believe it myself.

*

It was terrifyingly easy for me to believe that the past that I remembered was unreal. I had been lifted out of my life as totally as a goldfish is dipped out of an aquarium; more so, for when a storekeeper scoops a fish he soon places it again in a paper bucket of water – the fish remains in its element. I was not so fortunate. I lived and breathed, but in an entirely different fashion, horribly unfamiliar.

They wake you early in a mental hospital, at about six o'clock. They feed you prunes, oatmeal, wholewheat bread, butter, coffee. Then you help clean up the ward until nine o'clock. You make your bed, you push a mop, you scrub toilets. There is enough for an hour's work, but you have until nine o'clock to do it. But that is not too long. After a while, it takes you until nine o'clock because from nine until twelve is the rest period. That means you have nothing to do between nine and twelve but rest. You sit. You listen to the radio. Sermons, recipes, the news every hour on the hour. If there is an old magazine or newspaper around, you read it even if you have read it from cover to cover ten times before. What is left of it, that is. All items that might have an exciting or depressing effect on the patients have been removed.

The big room is clean. It is warm. There are comfortable wicker chairs (made by the patients – occupational therapy), and outside the sun is shining.

This is all necessary. I knew it to be necessary, knew for a fact that I was in a model institution, but knowing it did not help me to accept. After a week, two weeks, more weeks of sitting and listening, you get so you listen, wait to hear a sound different from the rest. The sense of hearing is the last to give up hope. But you know that time will never end, and you begin to scheme against this fact, to plan lovely lies of escape and the return to a life that probably never existed. For after twelve comes lunch, a stew of meat and potatoes, wholewheat bread, butter, jello. And after lunch you clean the toilets again, push the mop (if you have mechanical aptitude you can go to the shop) until three – and after three there is a rest period until five. Then you have supper, a piece of beef or a bowl of soup, wholewheat bread, butter, rice pudding. And after supper you go to bed and tell lies to yourself until you go to sleep.

On Thursdays I saw the psychiatrist – a pleasant woman, Dr Littlefield, a behaviourist. She gave me tests. Fit the little pegs into the little holes, the big pegs into the big holes. Turn the discs over and put them back in place – one side red, one side white – see how quickly you can do it! Answer the questions, as many as you can. A king is a monarch, serf, slave, hedonist, a lucky man. Underline the one you think is more nearly right: $2 \times 2 + 48 = 54$, 62, 57, 52.

She was a small woman with a bun of neat brown hair. Her eyes were blue and she had a tidy smile. I guessed she was about my age. The first time I did the tests, she studied my paper carefully, biting her lip as she evaluated it. I waited eagerly to hear her say: Why, there must be some mistake! Why, nobody in a mental hospital should do this well!

I should have known better. She looked up at me and smiled politely. 'You show ready understanding. I think you have no trouble learning. But there is a certain instability indicated – a compulsion?'

A sane man could have taken the same tests and made the same answers. A sane man? I was a sane man. But did I think so? Could I really be deluding myself?

I wanted to tell her what I knew, prove to her that I, too, could give Stamford-Binet tests, make a prognosis, indicate treatment. I wanted to be a bright student. I wanted to outwit teacher. But I knew I did not dare.

There was only one way I could get out. I must show 'improvement'. It did not matter what the truth was. I could never prove to them that my name was George Matthews, that I was a doctor, a psychiatrist, a married man with a bank account. Or if I could it would take a very long time. I knew that what I would have to do would be to break down all the individual, carefully constructed ramparts of science and knowledge – I would have to prove to Dr Littlefield, Dr Peters, Nurse Aggie Murphy, that I was a man and not a case history, a human and not a syndrome. And I could not allow myself a short time. I had to get out tomorrow, or the day after, or the day after that!

I realized this when Peters reported my own suicide to me. He told me that Anderson had said I died last year – *last year*. I took that piece of information, so casually dropped, and with equal calm stored it in a cranny of my mind. I must have lost months! When I looked outside I saw that it was summertime. I must actually have had a loss of memory (that rushing blackness in the subway seemed yesterday or last week, not last year – but I knew it had happened on a rainy fall day, the 12 October). The problem was: had I forgotten the same period they thought I had? Amnesia cuts two ways. You can forget your remote past, your early years, childhood, youth, young manhood, or you can forget a piece of your maturity.

I knew now that I had forgotten some things – I did not realize how much.

But I could lie. I could build a past that was not true, but which fitted the role I had been given. I could report the fictional history of a destitute man, and I could do it well because I had studied and put to heart many such case histories.

They expected me gradually to recover my memory. Harvey Peters said that I showed improvement. Dr Littlefield gave me tests each Thursday and told me that I showed less fear, less anxiety. But they would never, or only after too long a time, know me for the man I was. Or had been.

Why should I be Dr George Matthews any longer? What was wrong with being John Brown? Someone wanted me to be John Brown. Why should I fight him?

Was identity worth slow decay?

No. I would lie.

I had made up my mind.

A year contains 365 days. I died last year. Dr George Matthews died this minute. John Brown is born. John Brown will escape. John Brown will find the one who wanted to obliterate Dr George Matthews – and who played with him first, twitting him with comedy! – and John Brown will destroy him.

'I was born in Erie, Pennsylvania. My father worked in the mills. I had seven brothers. My mother died. My sister ran away. I joined the Army under another name.'

'You remember now?'

'It comes back slowly. I was hurt – somewhere in France. I came home. There were no jobs. I was on relief. I went from town to town. I worked on farms up and down both coasts. Then I was away for a while.'

'Away? Just away?'

Slick, glib lies. I had to hide something. I had to make my story fit the pattern she expected, and she expected me to try to hold back some part of the whole.

'I got married. Down South. I worked for a real estate office. Then times got hard again. She was having a child. She should have had an operation. We waited too long. We didn't have the money for the operation. She died.'

'I'm sorry.'

A facile lie told slowly – a typical syndrome of self-pity. This was what was expected. This was what she was going to get.

For a few moments I said nothing. Dr Littlefield was respectfully silent. I wanted to laugh deeply. Life was bitter and good and I hated all of them. I was glad I knew how to lie.

'Then what happened?' Tentatively. Ready to take it back with silence if her timing was off. She did not want to precipitate an emotional block. This bland little trained priestess of scientific black magic thought she could steal my story from my unwilling mind. And it was I who was doing the embezzling!

'I left town. I went the rounds again. Things got worse. You know how it was during the Depression? In season I became a harvest hand. In the winter I stayed in cities – the relief is better there. I worked on the PWA, the WPA. I bummed around . . .'

Looking down as if I were ashamed. I was not ashamed. Even if this had been my life, I would not have been ashamed.

'Yes?'

'I drank.'

'Much?'

'A lot.'

She did not say anything. Had I overplayed my hand?

'It's funny but I never want a drink any more.'

That ought to do it!

'No?'

'No, not since the bust on the head . . .'

I hoped the location was right. It was usually the head.

'When did you hurt your head?' She thought she was helping me remember! It was working!

'Before I came here. I had a fight. Over a woman. He came at me with a bottle. That's all I remember.'

A classic tale. Cribbed from a million sordid lives. But it would do.

Of course they did not let me go right away. I had to run the gauntlet every day for a week. Dr Littlefield saw me again, then Dr Smithers and Dr Goldman. Harvey asked me sly questions. I fed them all the same pap. A detail here, a detail there. Careful parallels drawn from selected casework. Never too close, but always the pattern they had been taught to expect.

It worked. One day Dr Littlefield told me, 'You are much better. We think you are almost well. How would you like to leave us this week?'

A carefully nurtured smile. Must not be too much of a shock, but at the same time patient should be made to feel the doctor is pleased with his recovery.

'That would be nice. You really mean it?' Equally carefully contrived incredulity. Doctor must be made to feel patient's relief and pleased amazement, but doctor must not be allowed to perceive that the game has become very, very boring.

'Friday. You're to see Miss Willows today. I think she has a surprise for you.'

I was not surprised to find Miss Willows fat and sloppy. Social workers so frequently are. This was the woman who was to rehabilitate me! Well, I was willing.

'I've talked with Dr Littlefield about you,' she said. 'She tells me that you are thinking of leaving us?'

'Yes, ma'am.' I knew enough to be humble with her. Case-workers like humble people.

'We don't want you to go out and lead the life you've led before. Not that it's your fault. But if you will help yourself, we can help you.'

'Yes ma'am.'

'A job in a cafeteria – not a very big job – but one with a good chance for advancement.'

'You're very kind, ma'am.'

69

'And if you work hard, and be sure to remember to report back to us every month the way Dr Littlefield told you – why there's no telling where you might end up!'

'Yes ma'am. You're very kind, ma'am.'

On Friday, 12 July 1944, John Brown stepped on to a crosstown bus. In his pocket was the address of a Coney Island cafeteria where Miss Willows had told him to apply for a job as waiter and busboy. His clothes were cheap and new. His face was studiously blank. If you had looked at him closely, you would have said that he had once seen better days.

5   In Which a Man Runs Down

From then on my name was John Brown. I could not explain, even to myself, the process by which I came to refute my identity. Not so long ago I had been a specialist with a comfortable living, a wife and a certain amount of status in the community. Now the world knew me only as a counterman in an all-night Coney Island cafeteria.

I had not intended to take the job Miss Willows offered me when I left the hospital that warm July day; there had been still some fight left in me. For weeks I had been shamming, assuming a false character, because I knew this to be the quickest way to return to what most of humanity considers sanity. I had been bitter during those weeks, cynical enough to adopt a fictional character and to play a hypocritical charade; but I had not lost hope. I might well have despaired if once in that time I had been allowed to look in a mirror.

I had noticed the lack of mirrors in the ward, but I had decided that this was a precaution similar to the banning of belts and braces: a mirror can be broken into sharp shards which can be employed to slit throats. Added care must have been taken to prevent my self-inspection in the last days of my convalescence; however, if it was, I was unaware. I do not blame Dr Littlefield for not letting me have a mirror, although if I had been in her place, I might have considered a confrontation a necessary part of my patient's adjustment. But, perhaps, this judgement is unfair: Dr Littlefield probably did not realize that I had not always been that way . . .

As it was I first caught sight of myself while having a

coke in a drugstore, just after I descended from the bus
that had taken me crosstown. Behind this soda fountain
was a mirror, fancily decorated with gaudy signs urging
the purchase of egg malted-milks and black-and-white
sodas. I glanced up and looked into it without knowing
what I was doing. My mind read the signs first, felt good
at seeing a familiar sight while being as usual a little critical
of the advertising profession. Then, when the signs were
read, my consciousness became curious about the horribly
disfigured man who must be sitting next to me. He was
not old – about my age now that I studied his face –
although he had seemed older at first glance. This was
because his short-cropped hair was grey streaked with
white and his jaw, that showed the remains of strength,
trembled spasmodically. But what made him really fasci-
natingly ugly was the wide, long, angry red scar that tra-
versed his face diagonally from one ear across the nose and
down to the root of the jaw at the base of his other cheek.
It was an old scar that had knit badly and in healing had
pulled and twisted at the skin until the face it rode had the
texture of coarse parchment and the grimace of a clown.
One cheek, and the eye with it, was drawn sidewise and
upward into a knowing leer – the other drooped, and with
it a corner of the mouth, as if its owner were stricken with
grief. The skin's colour was that of cigar ash, but the scar's
colour was bright carmine. I pitied the man, then was
embarrassed to look around at him; surely he must have
seen me staring at his reflection! But as I had this thought
I noticed that his glass emptied itself of coca-cola just as I
sucked noisily at my straw, and a suspicion crept into my
mind. I fought it back, silently scoffed at it, and kept my
eyes averted while I waited for my neighbour to go. How
long I might have continued this self-deception I shall
never know since I was soon forced to admit that the
horribly mutilated face I had been staring at was my
own. A little boy came in and sat down on the empty stool
next to mine – it had been occupied only in my imagination – giggled, and said to his perspiring mother, 'Oh,

mama, look quick at the man! Mama, how did he get like that?'

I fled with the child's taunt ringing in my ears. How did I get to be like this? I asked myself. And then, before I tried to answer that: How can I return to Sara like this?

I stopped in my tracks, stood staring out into the traffic. It would be so easy to run out into the street, to feel the crushing weight of a bus or truck, a blinding instant of pain, and then oblivion! My legs twitched with this necessity, a great hand pushed relentlessly at my straining back – I took two halting steps to the kerb, hesitated at its edge as if it were a precipice. My mouth went slack and the trembling of my jaw increased. Sweat trickled down my side from under my armpits.

Then, slowly, I turned and walked down the street towards a subway kiosk. John Brown, waiter or counterman or busboy in a Coney Island eatery, belonged to that face. For the time being, I was John Brown. Dr George Matthews would remain in hiding at least a while longer. I did not know who had persuaded my wife that I had died, but she must have had good reason to think I had or else she would never have left the city. Perhaps, it was better that way. Sara had a small income of her own, enough to take care of her. In the meantime I would have a chance to think things over. I laughed. Once I had been a psychologist and had thought myself capable of adjusting to any predicament. I fingered my scar, its treacherous smoothness – well, I was capable of an adjustment. In fact, I had already adjusted so completely that I was incapable of remembering the face that had preceded that tortured grimace seen in a fly-specked mirror. I had forsworn any personality other than 'John Brown, homeless, picked up wandering.

I took the B.M.T. to Coney Island.

Mr Fuller was a small seedy-looking man with a scrubbed-pink face and bleary blue eyes. He looked like he might take one drink too many too often. The shirt he had on had probably been worn more than once, his tie was of sleazy imitation silk. His shoulders drooped, he looked harried. I know he did not mean to be unkind to me.

We sat down at one of the tables in the front of the cafeteria. It was the middle of the afternoon and the place was nearly empty. Outside the calliope of a merry-go-round wheezed and clanged and banged. A barker farther down the street exhorted a straggling, sweaty crowd of passers-by to 'Step right up and pay a dime to see "Zozo". the beautiful, delovely Latin who lives with a boa constrictor.' Mr Fuller paid no attention to these sounds. He fingered my slip of paper, studying it as if it were a text. He regarded it for such a long time that I began to debate the possibility that he would ever look up again; whereupon he coughed once, squirmed, blew his nose.

'Ever work in a cafeteria before, Mr – ' (here he glanced at the slip of paper) ' – Brown?'

'No, sir.' I had better say 'sir'. Now that I had decided to remain John Brown, I would have very little money. Dr George Matthews' resources were no longer open to me – if they ever had been – and getting this job was all important.

'How do I know you can do the work? I'm not used to inexperienced help,' he complained.

'I'm good with people. I know how to talk to them. I have patience.' As soon as I had said these words, I was sure they were the wrong ones and my heart sank.

'There's more to the job than that,' he said. He looked at me inquiringly. 'You gotta be careful, you know? I been having too much breakage lately. They don't like too much breakage.'

' "They"?' I asked.

'The company,' he explained. 'They come in a couple of times a week and look around. Once a month they take inventory. If there's been too much breakage I hear about it. I'd like to put you on, but I can't be too careful . . .'

I spoke slowly and distinctly, trying desperately to

sound sincere. 'I'd be very careful,' I said. 'I wouldn't break anything.'

He looked at me for a long time, queerly. At first I did not understand what he was looking at. Then came the shock of recognition – my hand clutched at my face.

'People hardly notice it,' I said quickly, as the tortured image rose in front of my eyes and partially obscured his face. 'I don't think your customers would mind. They haven't on other jobs,' I lied.

He thought for a moment. I could see that the effort needed to make a decision was great for him. 'I admit it's hard to get a good, steady man these days. Maybe a fellow like you has a hard time getting jobs? Maybe, if you got a good job like this, you'd be steady?'

'I'll be steady.'

He thought again. He squirmed around in his chair. He blew his nose.

'Well, I'll try you for a week. If you work hard and apply yourself, you may have a steady job. That is, if the customers don't complain.'

He stood up and walked to the rear of the cafeteria. I followed him. He gave me two clean aprons, a pair of white duck trousers and a black leather bow-tie. Then he told me to report for work at six o'clock that night. My hours would be from six until two, when I would be relieved. We shook hands and I thanked him. Then I left the place to go look for a room.

During the next month, the sultry, crowded days of August, I worked at the cafeteria six nights a week, slept or sat on the beach and read in the daytime, existed. I would be lying to say that this was an unhappy period. Indeed, I might say the opposite. I had no desire to do anything else. The books I read were adventure stories and the like. I did not dream of my former life, or of an impossibly satisfying one to come. I made no friends or enemies. Yet – if a form of contentment that was not unlike a drug-induced stupor can be called happiness – I was happy.

I had promised myself a period of time 'to think things over'. Yet I thought nothing over, made no decisions. Some day I might try again to be Dr George Matthews, the eminent young psychiatrist. Some day I would return to Sara – Sara, my heart quickened at the thought of her. Yet day after day went by, and I did nothing.

Several times in the first weeks I worked at the All-Brite I experienced recurring fits of self-consciousness. I would suddenly become acutely aware of my disfigurement (perhaps, a customer would stare at me too long), and I would leave my work, go to the lavatory and peer at my face in the looking-glass. In time, though, the first horror of my discovery passed and there came in its place a peculiar, perverted sense of pride in my distinction. No other quality of my adopted personality differed in the least from that of any man I might meet on the street or find sitting on the beach. In all other ways I was cut out of the same bolt of cloth as everyone else: I had a small job, I was lonely, I had little security. But I did have a bright scar on my face, and this disfigurement soon stood in my mind as a symbol of my new identity. I was John Brown, and as John Brown I had a scar that ran from my ear across my face diagonally. It was a strangely satisfying attribute.

There were times when a little of my old objectivity returned to me and I stood aside and looked at myself in self-appraisal; but these times were rare and soon they stopped altogether. I knew that being proud of a defect was a defence, a stepping-stone to neurosis, but I did not care. I concentrated on my tasks, saw to it that there was always one piece of each variety of pie on the counter, sufficient shaved ice on the salad trays and that the water was changed every hour in the percolators. I waited on trade and learned to be obsequious to get nickel and dime tips. And in all this time the thought of Sara, the home that had been ours, my practice and former prestige, was only a faint and annoying memory that came in the night like the ache of a hollow tooth and which I dismissed easily from my mind, ignored as I would any petty distraction. My life had become the product of my own distorted imaginings, and I did not dare let visions of a former reality disturb my precarious equilibrium, even though in my secret mind I may have longed for my former life.

Nor did I allow myself to think of Jacob Blunt. The whole warped history of Dr George Matthews' last day remained a forgotten thing. There are some memories we have, and which we are aware of, but never allow to become entirely conscious. Such memories are always lurking directly beneath the surface of our reason, and in times of crisis certain of our actions can only be explained in terms of these remembered experiences; yet they never become tangible and we never allow ourselves to speak of them in telling of our past. So it was with me regarding the details of Jacob Blunt and his 'little men' and the other vicious nonsense of that last day which may or may not have resulted in the death of Frances Raye and my accident in the subway. I knew they had happened but I chose to forget them. They were no part of my present life.

I even became proficient at my craft, if you can call being a counterman in a cafeteria a craft. There were three of us to a shift and each of us had a particular section of the counter to care for. The coffee urn, the salad table and the desserts were my province; it was my responsibility to see that the kitchen kept a sufficient quantity of these items on hand for me to replace the empty dishes as soon as the customers deplenished the stock. A simple job, but one that had its difficulties. Some of my troubles lay with the customers: patrons would insist on handling each of the sweets before choosing one or would demand special orders that took extra time to prepare and then get testy because they had to wait. Often it was the cook who was slow in preparing foods that were the most popular, while flooding me with huge quantities of the slower-moving delicacies. I worked out systems by which I could balance supply and demand, push butterscotch pie and sell less apple, get rid of the avocado salad when the avocados were not all they should be – systems that worked so well that the day came when Mr Fuller had a little talk with me and gave me a rise.

He stood behind me, watching me work and making me nervous. I heard him snuffle and blow his nose. He even cleared his throat before he said, 'They're pleased with the way you've turned out, Brown. Mighty pleased. Along with me they felt that maybe the customers would complain, but we haven't had any complaints. The breakage is down this month, too. You've turned out pretty well.'

'I try my best,' I said.

'They told me to tell you that they wanted you to stay with us, and not to get any foolish notions in your head about working some place else. We're going to raise your salary two dollars a week.'

He snuffled again and wiped his nose on an unclean handkerchief. Why should Fuller or his ever-present 'they' fear my leaving? Why should I look for another job? I was satisfied where I was.

The two dollars more a week meant nothing to me. I had been living on what I earned, spending it all on food, shelter, an occasional clean shirt, but needing nothing more. Now that I had it, I did not know what to do with it. Eventually, I put the extra money in my top bureau drawer, adding to it each week; not saving the way a cautious man saves with a goal in mind or for a prudent principle, but only putting it away because I had no desire to spend it and the bureau drawer seemed a more appropriate place than the wastebasket.

During the day and early evening the cafeteria was patronized by ordinary people out for a good time: small businessmen with their families, clerks with their girls, bands of teenage youngsters who dropped in for a hamburger and a coke and stayed long enough to be a nuisance. But after ten o'clock the character of the clientele changed radically. It was at this hour that the carnival people began to appear.

They were of all sorts and all kinds. Gaunt, under-nourished men would sidle up to the counter, order coffee and rolls, take their orders to a table and sit there the rest of the night. These were the less prosperous ones, the 'drifters'. They earned their livings by taking tickets, operating rides, selling hot-dogs and floss candy, by doing odd jobs. They sat with each other and did not mingle with the second group, the 'artists'.

Brassy blondes, flashily made-up red-heads, rarely a glossy headed brunette, showgirls, wives of entrepreneurs, lady shills – all of these were considered 'artists'; as well as their masculine counterparts in checked suits and pointed-toe shoes, barkers, grifters who operated the 'sucker' games, pitch men and the 'big boys' who owned the concessions. The 'artists' came in later than the 'drifters', spent more money and were more convivial. They were a society to themselves, but a friendly, open-handed one; I learned that the 'drifters' did not mingle with them of their own choosing, not because the 'artists' were snobbish.

There was also a third group that kept partly separate, but also sometimes mixed with the shills and showgirls. Zozo, 'the delovely Latin who lives with a boa constric-tor,' was a member of this clique, as was a man named Barney Gorham who kept a shooting gallery. Barney interested me very much. He was a great ape of a man with smoothed-back, glistening black hair and a half-grown beard. As he walked his shoulders would sway involuntarily; watching him one was always conscious of the movement of muscles beneath his rough flannel shirt. He would give the impression of having money when first met; and yet if one talked to him for any length of time he would invariably try to borrow a dollar or two. He pretended to be a painter, and it was true that he did paint in his spare time. Several times, when he brought them to the All-Brite, I saw some of his daubs; badly designed seascapes, highly romanticized pastoral scenes and gaudy portraits of those of the showgirls he had slept

79

with. For Barney was successful with the 'ponies', as the chorines were called. Usually, he had one or two girls with him, talking vivaciously, while he sat slumped in his chair glowering at the room.

I called these last the 'characters' and there were many of them, yet of the three groups they were the most difficult to define and limit. A few of them were intellectuals or pseudo-intellectuals, and what they were doing at Coney Island I could not understand. Others were freaks; dwarfs and bearded ladies, the pin-headed boy who was really a cretin yet was accepted as a member of this loosely knit society – he was always accompanied by a large, motherly-looking woman with a monstrous goitre – a man who owned a motion picture theatre and a girl who ran a photographer's studio. I decided at last that what they all had in common was a sense of dissatisfaction. Both the 'drifters' and the 'artists' were content with their life, but the 'characters' – although many of them were successful financially – were malcontents. They were not peculiar to Coney Island except in their concentration; you might find small groups such as these in the theatrical district of any middle-western city. However widely they might be separated during the winter months, as each sought a way of earning a living (some by touring the South with a carnival, some by doing odd parts on Broadway or at Radio City, others by touting the race-tracks or taking any 'rube' job they could find), they always returned to this place in the summer, met at this cafeteria, considered this the centre of their lives.

I supposed it was only natural that after a time I came to be a part of this last group. John Brown was homeless too, and like everyone else needed to feel that he belonged. It cost nothing to sit down at one of the tables that had been designed to seat four, but around which six or seven were sitting, and soon I found myself joining in the conversations. These, instead of being confined to carnival gossip as I had guessed they might be, were about almost anything. I was surprised at how learned Barney was, for example, and both amused and frightened at the thought that Zozo, who lived with a boa constrictor, had not only read Kant but also Fichte and Spinoza. One of the favourite topics of discussion was psychoanalysis (it usually came up when one of the group would remember the time when the Wild Man from Borneo with Sells-Floto – 'a quiet type who liked Guy Lombardo and Wisconsin lager' – went berserk on the midway and killed three men – 'the show did great business for the rest of the stand, we made all the dailies and that year we went 'way over our nut'), and I astonished them with my knowledge of the field. While I restrained my memory of my past life, I seemed to have no compunction about using information I had gained during that life – in fact, one of the reasons why I was soon so fascinatedly a member of this odd group was because I was pleased to find so many neurotic personalities at one time. The All-Brite was a veritable game preserve for the psychiatric sportsman. Yet by the time I had worked in the cafeteria a month, I knew several of the 'characters' well enough to consider them my friends, and also to forget that I had once considered them eccentric.

Sonia Astart was one of my friends. She entered the cafeteria at the same time each night, a few minutes after twelve. She would walk between the tables, speaking to this person or that, finally making her way to the counter where her order was always the same: a pot of black coffee. Then she would go sit with Barney or Zozo.

I joined Barney's table more often than I did the others, and Sonia was the reason for this. She seldom had much to say, but one never noticed her silence. When I was near her, I felt her presence and it was far more stimulating than words. Yet she had few of the standard hallmarks of womanly beauty. She was tall, and her features were irregular – she was not even especially fastidious. Often she was without lipstick or powder, sometimes the sloppy shirts and slacks she wore were badly in need of a pressing.

I am certain that there were times when Sonia did not know how she would manage to scrape enough money together to live the week. She was usually between jobs. And it was at these times that she would change from a listener to the most talkative of all those present. She had a marvellous fund of stories about the carnival folk, and she would talk politics or sex or a theory of art for hours on end with Zozo or myself or anyone who would argue with her, interrupting the discussion frequently to get up from the table, corner a prosperous-seeming friend who had just come in the door, speak long and earnestly with him for a few minutes, borrow money from him. It was as if she could not carry off the necessary wheedling, the tale of sudden, unexpected misfortune but certain better luck to come, without first plunging into the fever of argument. And when I considered the content of these conversations later, I realized that they were only word games, intellectual puzzles that aborted thought.

Sonia and Barney were among the more complex of the 'characters'. There were others more obviously and conventionally neurotic. One of these was the Preacher, an extremely tall man who dressed in cowboy boots, riding breeches, a flannel shirt and a Stetson hat. He would stride into the cafeteria, walk up to the first people he encountered and begin to exhort them to leave the city.

'Go find yourself a home on the plains!' he would shout. 'A free place in a wide space where you won't be bothered with no taxicabs tootling their crazy horns at you, where you can cross a street and take your time – Gawd's Country!' He would orate like this on his one and only subject, the West, oblivious to the fact that no one listened, until suddenly for no visible reason he would stop talking, stare belligerently about for a moment and then stalk angrily out. I never saw him sit down at a table or join in a conversation even with the 'drifters', nor did I ever meet anyone who knew anything about him.

I would sit with these people for hours every night, afterwards going home to my sleeping room not to leave until late in the afternoon of the next day. I cannot say I looked forward to these social hours (they were not in any way comparable to the chosen leisure of a healthy man; they were only another form of my somnambulism). When I was not actually asleep, I submerged my personality in the mechanical compulsions of my job, or in an equally mechanical participation in this society of misfits. It was a complete negation of everything that had gone before.

I suppose it was inevitable that I should sleep with Sonia, although I can say honestly that at no time did I calculate it. First we fell into the habit of sitting next to each other, an accident in the beginning and then a not unpleasant institution. Later, we would walk home together in the early hours of the morning – she lived near me. During these walks we talked little, but there existed a common feeling between us which I cannot define except to say that when I was near her in this way was the closest I ever came to awaking. Then one night by mutual consent, without a word of love being spoken, we walked by her boarding house and went to my room. From then on, although it was never a constant procedure and there were many nights when she went to her place and I went to mine, we considered this a part of our relationship and I believe we both found solace in it.

One night Sonia did not come to the All-Brite and I walked home alone. This, in itself, was not unusual. Sonia often missed a night a week at the cafeteria and I never questioned her as to her whereabouts on these nights. I cannot say that I felt lonely that night either; as a matter of fact it was a beautiful night in early September, there was a blood-red harvest moon and I took a long walk along Surf Avenue, exploring all the many side streets I had never ventured down before.

Coney Island is a terrifyingly empty neighbourhood late at night. By two o'clock in the morning most of the concessions are closed, except for a few dance halls and bars and one merry-go-round that goes all night. A few roistering sailors staggered, yipped and brawled a short way up the street that night, the three sheets and gaudy side-show signs gleamed red in the rich moonlight, the twisted skeleton of the roller-coaster stretched its conjectural latticework up towards the pitch black sky.

I felt exhilarated, almost as if I had been drinking. I remember I stood in front of a fun house, the façade of which featured roly-poly clowns with starchy faces and huge grinning lips, and bent double with laughter at my own crazy reflection in a distorting mirror. That, I know, was the first time I had looked into a mirror with equanimity. But the distortion of this flawed surface was so grotesque that it relieved the natural horror of my face, and by making it ridiculous enabled me for an instant to accept it. I was still laughing at the insanely contorted self I had seen, as I turned down my own street and started for my rooms.

Except for the main stem, Coney Island streets are dark at nights – and in 1944 they were doubly dark because of the blackout. Still the moon supplied a neon light of its own. I had walked this street many times and I had grown to like its ramshackle air; even the occasional rumble of the elevated seemed reassuring. Then, all of a sudden, I was afraid.

I do not know for how long I had been aware of footsteps sounding behind me, but at that moment I realized that they did not belong to a casual pedestrian but rather to someone who was following me. Trembling, I stood aside to let this person pass – sure that he would not.

When I turned around no one was there.

I was childishly panic-stricken. I experienced an irrational attack of terror. I remember that I put my hand up to my face to feel my scar, automatically, as if it were in some way connected with my phobia. I stood there for several minutes, holding my breath, feeling my heart hammer at my ribs and my blood freeze in my veins, ready to flee at the sight of a shadow or the sound of an echo. But no one came.

I started for home again.

And the sound of footsteps followed me! Whoever it was must have hidden in a doorway when I stopped and turned around. On the blacked-out street I did not discover his presence. I knew now that whoever it was intended to do me harm – why else hide? I walked fast.

The person behind me walked fast, too. I began to run. He ran. I ran as fast as I could, and by then I was only a block from my house. If I could reach my door, would I be safe? All I could hear was the sound of those feet. He seemed not ten paces behind me. Then I became aware of an automobile coming down the street towards me. I ran out into the street in front of it, waving my arms frantically to flag it down. I could see that its headlights were mere glowing slits, but I preferred the known danger of being run over to the unknown danger the footsteps implied . . .

The last person I thought of before the car hit me was Sonia. For some reason her hair was slicked back like a man's and she had a moustache. I hated her.

6 Between Two Worlds

There are times in anyone's life when it is possible to stand aside and see what is past, as well as what is present, with an objectivity that is unnatural if not god-like. A few minutes after I was knocked down in the street near my rooming house, I came to in what was to me then – at that moment – a strange bed in a strange room. It was a small room, clean, but cheaply furnished. The door stood partly open and through it I could see a dimly lighted hallway and a banister. Over the dresser in the place where a mirror would normally be, several cheap reproductions of famous paintings had been thumb-tacked to the plaster: a Van Gogh, a Cézanne and a Degas. I was pleased to see them since these are my favourite painters. All this I perceived in the foggy instant between full consciousness and the depths of unconscious-ness.

Then, as I struggled to awake fully, the recent past surged in on me: I felt a sharp, unyielding pain at the base of my brain, I heard again the roar of a motor racing wildly and felt the rush of wind as a bulk – huge and men-acing – hurled past me, caught at me, threw me down. At this I was greatly confused. Several conflicting images appeared to my mind's eye, many faces looked down at me: one, that of a man with a moustache, another a dwarf's face underneath a bowler hat, others I could not quite descry. The hands lifted me, and, uncannily, it seemed as if I were lifted twice at the same time – as in a double printed motion picture you see the same action duplicated, two sets of images doing the same thing – and voices said different things, different voices! One said,

'He's dead! Get the photo, quickly!' Another cried, 'Oh, I saw it happen! Is he hurt badly? Here, let me help you. He lives only down the street – we can take him there!'

Then the struggle ended, one set of memories won out. At the same time I recognized the little man who was sitting on the foot of my bed. I was wrily dismayed. He was Eustace.

While I stared at him, I remembered that I had become frightened in the street, that I had run into the path of an automobile and that Sonia had come along right afterwards and helped to carry me down the street and upstairs to my room. But what was the other memory I had awakened with, the one that had contested unequally, for a glimmering, with the more recent past? Was I remembering what had happened in the subway station? And what was Eustace doing there? Was he the one who had been following me?

As I looked at him, I realized that I wanted badly to know the answers to these questions. Perhaps, he could tell me? If I played it right, I might learn something. The thing to do was to pretend that I was confused. I thought about it and arrived at a plan that seemed brilliant. I would act as if I had suffered another attack of amnesia. I would say I had forgotten everything that had happened recently. By this tactic I would put him on the defence. And, if he had been following me with a purpose, I would find it out.

Eustace was not wearing fancy clothes this time: his suit was conservatively cut and a carefully brushed bowler hat rested on his knees. 'What are you doing here?' I asked him.

'You could have been hurt bad, chum!' he said. 'That car gave you a nasty clip. I had to come up to make sure you were all right, didn't I?'

His voice was still the same mechanical-sounding guttural, but it was not pitched sarcastically as it had been when I first heard it. In fact, he was smiling uneasily, smoothing his hat with one hand, patting his knee with the other. He was trying to be ingratiating.

'I saw you over on the Avenue,' he went on. 'I've been wanting to see you for a long time but I never expected to find a swell like you here! I've been wanting to talk to you. I followed you and you started to run. Before I could catch up with you' – he glanced down at his short legs – 'you ran out into the street in front of that jalopy.'

I rubbed my head and my hand came away bloody. I had knocked loose a hastily contrived bandage. Eustace jumped to his feet and made clucking noises with his tongue. He came over to me and helped me tie the bandage tighter.

'It's only a deep scratch,' he said, 'but you better lie still for a day or so. You can't tell, from a lick like that it might give concussion!'

I could see that my plan was working. The little man was rattled. He had not expected to find me suffering from amnesia and, now that he surmised this was the case, he did not know what to say. I was not sure that I would learn anything from questioning him, but I could at least find out what sort of a game he had been playing on Jacob. I was curious about that.

'What's he been doing? Picking at it?'

Sonia was standing in the doorway. She held a basin of water in her hands and she was smiling. Her eyes were shadowed, her hair gleamed darkly in the poor light, her slim figure was silhouetted against the brighter illumination that came from the hallway – I liked her looks. Tonight she was wearing a loose-fitting Russian blouse and flannel trousers that looked well on her long legs. I regretted that, until Eustace left, I would have to pretend that I had forgotten her.

'Why don't you introduce me to your friend, John?' she asked. 'He was very kind to wait to be sure you were all right after that awful bump you had. Particularly after the driver left you in the street like that!'

Eustace was watching me expectantly, waiting to be

introduced. Sonia was regarding me solicitously. I decided to embarrass the little man as much as I could.

'This is Eustace,' I said. 'A leprechaun.'

Sonia took it calmly, only barely raising an eyebrow. 'Irish?' she asked. I could see she thought I was joking. Maybe I was.

'No, he is an American leprechaun.'

Eustace was discomfited. He squirmed. 'I been meaning to tell you about that,' he said. 'That's one of the reasons I've been wanting to see you. I want to tell you how that was.'

'What's his last name, John?' Sonia asked.

'I don't know his last name,' I said.

'It's Mather,' said Eustace. He squirmed some more.

'Eustace Mather?' She raised her eyebrow a little higher.

'No lady,' said the little man. 'My name ain't Eustace, it's Felix. Felix Mather.' He looked at me unhappily. 'I've been meaning to tell you,' he said.

At this point Sonia put her arm around me. I liked that. 'You've never spoken of Felix before, John,' she said. 'Is he a friend of yours?'

'Business acquaintance, lady,' said Felix. 'Eustace was my trade name at one time.'

She pulled me to her and brushed her lips across my forehead. 'I like you, Felix,' she said to the little man. 'John should have let me meet you sooner.'

I looked at her and, though I tried hard, I could not keep from smiling. I was enjoying this game. How surprised she would be at what I was going to say next!

'Who are you?' I asked her. 'You tell me who you are first, and then I'll tell you about him.' I motioned to Felix.

Her wide mouth lost its smile and her eyes seemed to disappear completely into the shadows of her brows. Her arm dropped on to the bed – away from my shoulders. I missed the familiar pressure.

'I'm Sonia, darling. Your Sonia. Don't you really

remember? Oh what a bump you must have had!' She said this last as much to Felix as to me. I could not see the expression on her face, but I could tell from the sound of her voice that she was concerned about me. I found myself wanting to take her into my arms and assure her that I was all right. Instead I continued to ask questions.

'But Sonia, what am I doing here? What are you doing here?'

She gave me a frightened, non-comprehending look. But when she answered my question she spoke calmly and quietly, the way one talks to an invalid.

'You live here, John. And I live down the street. You've just had a bad fall and you're still shaken up. Now lie down and forget about everything and when you wake up it will all have come back to you.' She began to fluff the pillows behind my head and to undo my shirt for me. She was putting me to bed.

'I don't want to go to sleep,' I said. 'I don't know where I am. I don't know who you are. Nor how I got here. I'm not even sure I know who I am!' This last was the worst fabrication of all. I knew who I was all right. I was two people: John Brown and George Matthews. But I could not let Felix-Eustace know I had been leading a double life. If he knew, and he really had something to tell about Jacob, he might get suspicious and shut up. At least, that was how I reasoned then.

Sonia finished taking off my shirt and began to undo my trousers – right in front of Felix and against my protests! She undressed me, took a pair of pyjamas out of the bureau and helped me on with them, pulled the covers about me and kissed me on the lips without saying a word. After she kissed me, she said, 'I insist that you rest now, John. You may have suffered a concussion, you know. It wouldn't be good for you to over-exert yourself.'

I sat up in bed abruptly, throwing myself close against her so that she had to embrace me to keep from losing her balance. Her dark hair fell about my face and smelt strangely sweet. I kissed her again.

'You called me "John",' I said. 'That isn't my right name. My name isn't John.'

She laughed at me and laid her head on my shoulder, looking up at me, smiling. 'I won't believe that you've lost your memory to that extent! Your name is John Brown and you know it!'

Felix started uneasily in his chair. 'No it ain't, lady,' he said. 'That's Dr George Matthews you're kissing!'

Sonia pushed herself away from me. She stared curiously at the little man.

'You're kidding,' she said. 'He's John Brown and he works nights at the All-Brite cafeteria.'

'I don't know about that, lady,' said Felix. 'I only know that when I met him his name was Matthews and he was a doctor.'

I was not too pleased with this turn in the conversation. I had planned to confuse Felix in an attempt to gain information he might not otherwise let me have – but instead of learning anything myself, Sonia was learning facts about me I would rather she did not know. And there was little I could do about it.

Sonia looked at me. She was still smiling, but her smile now seemed to say, 'You're trying to fool me, but why?'

'Are you a doctor, John? You never told me that.'

'I'm a psychiatrist,' I said. I hesitated, not knowing what to say next. Then I decided that, having gone this far, I had better try to continue the deception – until Felix left. 'What I want to know,' I continued, 'is what I am doing here? The last I remember I was having a fainting spell in the Canal Street station of the I.R.T.'

Sonia stopped smiling. 'John, to the best of my knowledge you haven't been out of Coney Island in the past month. You go to work and you come home, then you go back to work again. The only relaxation you get is after work nights at the cafeteria. Why should you go to Manhattan today? And what business would you have on Canal Street?'

From now on the game got wilder and wilder. I

regretted ever having begun the gambit. But now I was in too deep. I had to continue to lie and hope I could explain away later. 'I had to see Lieutenant Anderson,' I said. 'Miss Bulkely awakened me this morning and said Jacob was being held for the murder of Frances Raye. I was home then in my own bedroom in New Jersey. What I want to know is how I got here?'

Sonia was being motherly – and the attitude did not suit her too well. She put her hand on my forehead. 'I'm going to take your temperature. You're certainly delirious and that's a sure sign of fever.'

I put my hands on her shoulders and shook her gently. 'I am not delirious!' I said. 'Please listen and try to understand what I'm saying to you!' Then I spoke slowly and emphatically, hoping that she would see that I meant more than I said, and keep quiet. 'I don't know you, Sonia. I don't remember ever having seen you before. I've never even seen this room before!'

Felix still had his hat on his head, but instead of leaving the room he came closer to my bed. He was looking at me and I saw that his forehead was even more wrinkled than was natural. His eyes betrayed his bewilderment. Sonia was regarding me too, but at last she had nothing to say. Her dark eyes had disappeared again into the hollows of her brows and her mouth quivered slightly. She reminded me of a disappointed child who does not realize why she has been disappointed.

'Frances Raye was killed the twelfth of last October,' said Felix. He put his finger to the brim of his diminutive derby as if to apologize for mentioning this fact. 'I know because they had me up as a material witness. I was in jail three weeks. I was in the Tombs.'

Sonia looked at Felix and then back at me. She moistened her lips with her tongue, but did not try to smile. I knew that she did not know what we were talking about, but the implications frightened her.

'Frances Raye was murdered no longer ago than last night!' I contradicted Felix. 'Not more than six hours after I left you with that crazy horse of yours on Third Avenue. What sort of a hoax are you trying to bring off now?'

I should not have raised my voice to the little man. He straightened up so that he seemed to have gained inches of height and his eyes became cold chips of marble. Yet, perhaps, if he got angry enough he would talk.

'You've just lost about ten months some place, chum!' he said. 'Ain't no business of mine if that's the way you want it. I came here friendly because I wanted to talk to you to explain how things were . . .' He paused and stared at me. 'Because I figured you might have been handled a little rough somewhere along the line, and maybe I knew something you oughtta know . . . and maybe you could tell me some things, too . . .' He stopped and glanced at Sonia, then shrugged his shoulders and began to move towards the door. 'But I see I'm intruding between you and the lady here . . .'

I stopped him just before he reached the door. 'Don't leave now, Eustace!' I cried, without realizing until I said it that I had called him by the name I first knew. 'I have to get straightened out somehow, don't I?'

He came back and sat down again on the chair. 'That's why I've been keeping an eye open for you all along,' he said. 'I figured there were still some things you were mixed up about.'

Sonia squeezed my arm and wrinkled her eyes at me. 'What are you two talking about? Sonia hasn't the vaguest notion!'

'I seem to have forgotten a lot of things,' I said, ignoring her question. 'Both of you will have to help me out.'

Felix and Sonia were watching me. The little man was perplexed; his mouth was straight and his forehead wrinkled. Sonia's face was expressionless. She was either dissimulating or deeply puzzled, possibly hurt. I did not know which.

'You want us to tell you? Is that it?' asked Felix.

I nodded my head.

'I'll start off,' Felix said. 'The only time I ever saw you before was on the twelfth of October last year. A fellow named Jacob Blunt had hired me to do a crazy job for him. I was to pretend I was a leprechaun, whatever that is. He had me memorize some lines I was to say to a man I would meet that night, silly lines that made no sense. I took the job because he paid me well . . .' And he went on to tell about meeting Jacob and me in the bar on Third Avenue. He left out some of the details. He did not mention the percheron. But what he did say fitted what I remembered – all except the first part. When he had finished, I had some questions to ask.

I sat on the bed across from the chair on which he was sitting. I watched him while he talked. It was a queer feeling sitting there earnestly regarding a midget, hanging on to his words, trying to discover some key to the bewildering maze of my mysterious past. I realized with a start that the more I looked at him, the less I knew about him. In fact, the more he said, the less I knew.

'You say Jacob hired you to pretend that you were a leprechaun. Why did he do that?' I asked him.

The little man shook his head. 'Don't ask me, chum. He didn't tell me. I only worked for him.'

'Where did you meet Jacob?' I asked. 'And how did he come to hire you?'

'I answered an ad in *The Times*,' said Felix. 'Then he told me his proposition. It sounded like easy money so I agreed. All I had to do was to be at a particular bar at a particular time and say a few lines to a guy he would bring with him. That was you.'

'But what about the percheron?' I asked. 'Where did it come from?'

Felix looked blankly at me. 'What percheron?' he asked innocently.

'The big horse out in the street. The horse you told Jacob he would get twenty-five dollars for delivering to Frances Raye.'

The small man clapped his derby with his hand. 'Oh,

that horse!' he said. 'Oh, I didn't have anything to do with that! Jacob supplied the horse.'

I had a feeling that Felix was pulling my leg. He was too bland about this, too eager to be helping and in helping – confuse. 'I suppose you know nothing about the flower-wearing or the whistling-at-Carnegie-Hall either,' I said sarcastically.

He shook his head from side to side. 'I don't know what you're talking about,' he said.

'And neither do I!' said Sonia. 'John, you must have a fever! You're making no sense at all. Who is this Jacob you keep referring to?' Still looking at Felix, I answered her. 'Just listen now, I'll explain later.'

'What did Jacob and you have to do with the murder of Frances Raye?' I asked the little man.

Again he shook his head. 'Nothing. Nothing at all. That was an accident.'

'You mean she wasn't murdered? That she was killed accidentally?'

'No, no.' He put his pudgy hand to his forehead. 'She was killed all right, but they've never found out who did it. The accident was that they had me in jail for three weeks as a material witness thinking I knew something about the murder.'

'What happened to Jacob? Where is he?'

'He disappeared completely. I don't know where he is.'

'Then what did you do after they released you?' I asked.

'I went back to work at Coney Island. I'm still working here. But I've been spending my spare time looking for you. I thought that maybe it was my fault you lost yourself. I thought you might be in hiding. I wanted to tell you that you were safe – that they couldn't pin it on you.'

My mind was whirling. How much of what Felix-Eustace was telling me was true I did not know. If Jacob had been deluding me, what was his motive? Could it be that Jacob had killed Frances Raye and had used me in some way to help him with his crime? I could only question.

Sonia was standing beside me, frowning. 'Darling, please tell me what this is all about?'

I looked at her, for the first time really critically. She was not a beautiful woman, but I liked the way she looked. There was an honest strength in her features and in her direct gaze. The mannish clothes she wore added to the severe simplicity of her long lines, accentuated them. I realized that few tall women could dress the way she did, successfully. Right now her hand felt soft on my arm, but I sensed that she could be hard if she wanted to . . .

'Tell me what you know about me,' I said to her. Her hand tightened on my arm. Felix stood up to go.

'Don't leave us yet, Mr Mather,' said Sonia. 'I want you to hear this, too.' She loosened her grasp on my arm, and stood up. She looked away from both of us.

'Your name is John Brown,' she said, as if speaking to the wall. Her voice was quiet, self-contained. I was afraid it was cold. 'I met you about a month ago. You worked then, as you work now, in a cafeteria.' She stopped, turned around, her dark eyes seemed to be on fire as she stared at me. 'I've been sleeping with you for some time now.'

Felix made an embarrassed movement towards the door. Sonia jerked her head in his direction. 'Don't leave,' she said, 'just as the party's getting rough.'

Felix sat down – uncomfortably.

Sonia, impulsively, put her arm around me. I could feel her warmth through the thin cloth of my pyjamas. I wanted to let go, to lean back hard against her, to hold her to me. I did not want to try to think it out.

'You haven't talked to me very much,' she was saying. 'That's partly my fault, I suppose, since I haven't asked many questions. I don't believe in asking questions.'

She hesitated, looked around the room, her gaze coming to rest on Felix. He fidgeted under her inspection. Then she went on, 'A girl gets curious sometimes . . . I got curious. I saw where you had been saving money, a lot of money on your salary. I looked through your pockets. I found a slip of paper that had "City Hospital" printed on it – a slip introducing you to the manager of the cafeteria. I knew then that you had been sick . . . possibly hurt . . .' Her voice continued, a quiet voice, a soothing voice, a voice that was nice to hear in a nightmare. I stared at the cheap colour prints above the bureau, at the well-dressed midget sitting on the rickety chair fondling his derby hat. And as I stared, I had a recurrence of the feeling – the perception of two realities – that I had experienced upon first regaining consciousness a half-hour or less before. One level of my mind seemed to be dealing with the present: I was thinking about the little man, Felix Mather he had said his name was . . . a funny name . . . I had known him earlier as Eustace, a leprechaun . . . an even funnier name. But as my eyes kept wandering around the tiny, cramped room looking at the net curtains over the unwashed window, at the reflections of a street lamp on the dark, streaked glass – another aspect of reality seemed to be lurking on the fringe of my awareness, I had the feeling that something important, something that had great bearing on the here and now which I had been forgetting, lingered on the tip of my tongue. And then my sight settled on the door, focused on the calendar hanging on it, on the large prominent figures – 1944.

'. . . I knew there were many things about you that I didn't know,' the quiet voice was saying. 'I knew that you were still sick . . . I guessed that there were some things you had forgotten . . . some things you could not remember. But that made no difference. Just as it makes no difference now that I know . . . some things. I still feel the same way about you. I still love you just the same, even if I have never told you that I love you until now. Those things that you forgot . . . those things that I guess you still don't remember . . . they don't make any difference . . .'

1944 – those numbers were all I could see. From October 1943 to August 1944 was almost a year – ten months that were dark, at least seven that were completely lost.

Time that had disappeared, that could not be retrieved and re-examined like a looking-glass from which a fragment is missing that will not reflect a full view of your face. A face? A lost mirror? My face? The memory that had been lurking just beyond the edge of recall, rushed back. A mirror? Why wasn't there a mirror in my room? Why hadn't I seen a mirror at the hospital? A child's voice taunted me with words I could not understand – I heard the voice clearly (I could see the face of the child), but I could not define their meaning. And in this confusion of previous experience, this stretto of trauma like the mingling of voices before the final cadence of a mighty fugue, I returned to the confusion that always lay awaiting me below the topmost layer of my mind.

Yet out of this welter of images, sounds, ideas, emotions, came one cogent desire that was indeed a drive, a compulsion. I wanted to look into a mirror. I had to see myself in a mirror.

'I want a mirror,' I said.

I felt Sonia drop her arm from around me. I saw Felix jump to his feet, take one step backwards. I saw Sonia watching me, looking as if she wanted to cry. 'I want a mirror,' I said again.

'You stay there,' said the girl. She went over to the bureau and opened her purse. She took a small vanity mirror from it. She looked at me for a moment, as if she had not decided what to do about my request, and then handed the small square of silvered glass to me. 'It doesn't make any difference,' she said. 'I don't want you to think that makes any difference. How many times am I going to have to tell you that I never see it any more?'

I was looking into the mirror, seeing again my face and the ripe scar, remembering my first sight of it – not too long ago – the curiosity and revulsion that had changed to apprehension and dread and then to acceptance and disgust. And now I heard again and understood the little boy's words: 'Mama, how did he get like that?'

I walked over to Felix. He stood up to meet me, but

even so I had to stoop to get at him. I grabbed his throat in my hands and began to shake him back and forth. He was choking. I was wringing his neck as I might a damp rag.

'How did you know me? If you hadn't seen me since last October, how did you know me? I didn't look like that before!'

Then I felt Sonia's hand on my shoulder, and I heard Sonia's calm voice in my ear. 'Let go of him, John. You're killing him. It is not his fault, John. He had nothing to do with it. Let go of him.'

I let go of him. He lay there gasping on the floor, trying to speak. When he managed to get the words out they came in painful phrases and his voice was a thickened whisper. I could see the imprint of my fingers on the flesh of his throat. I could still feel his skin writhing under my fingers. 'I saw your back . . . it looked . . . familiar. I tried to catch up with you. But you ran away. You ran . . . ran into . . . the car. Then I saw your face. I knew it was you . . . although you looked . . . terribly different.'

Later, I apologized. He was still afraid of me and he could not get out of my place fast enough. I made him give me his address, which he did reluctantly – writing it down on a scrap of paper Sonia found. I could not think straight. I was still unreasonably angry at him. All I could see was that bright scar dividing my face. That scar should not have been there. Felix went away rubbing his throat.

I did not lose his address.

7 The Dilemma

'What was all that about?'

Sonia was standing with her back to the door. Felix had just left. I had sat down again on the bed. My head was aching and I did not feel well.

'I pretended that I did not know who I was to confuse him,' I said. 'I thought I might learn something about . . . about my past.'

Sonia stuck her hands deep into her trousers' pockets. 'Tell me the truth, John. Have you killed someone?'

Her question surprised me. My heart jumped beneath my ribs. Then I remembered that she knew nothing about the death of Frances Raye except what she had gathered from my conversation with Felix.

'No,' I said. 'I am not a murderer. Although it looks like I was meant to be a victim.' I began at the beginning and told her the whole story of Jacob and his 'little men', the phone call in the middle of night, the impostor I found at Center Street, my accident in the subway and my awakening, late in May, in the psychopathic ward of the hospital. I described how I had lied my way out of the hospital and my shock at finding that I had a horrible disfigurement.

'But why did you continue to call yourself John Brown?' she asked. 'Why didn't you go at once to the police and try to locate your wife instead of –' She did not complete her sentence. Her face was expressionless, but from the way she blinked her eyes I could see that she was fighting back tears.

'How could I go back to Sara looking like . . . like this?' I asked. 'I did not look this way before, you know?' I stroked my face with my hand. 'I cannot bear to look at it myself. How could I go back to her?'

'I never see it any more!' Sonia said with quiet emotion. 'It makes no difference to me!'

'But, don't you see, I could not bear it to make a difference with . . . with Sara?'

Sonia did not answer. She turned her head away and would not look at me. I felt miserable.

We talked that night, Sonia and I. We had much to say to each other. I told her all I could remember about my past: my childhood in Indianapolis, my father's death, the years at medical school in Cincinnati and the postgraduate work in psychopathology in Zurich, the hard years of the early thirties, my mother's death, my marriage and my slowly rising fortunes until I could call myself a success at thirty-six. I tried to explain why I had felt apathetic when I left the hospital, why I had continued to lead the life of John Brown instead of trying to recover the career of Dr George Matthews. 'A psychiatrist should look distinguished,' I said, 'not like a clown.' I tried to make her see why I had been unwilling to attempt to recall the happenings of my black period – the seven months between 12 October 1943 and the last part of May in 1944. But as I talked I found myself losing the very apathy I was defending, and beginning to be angry instead. Who had done this to me? What had happened and why had it happened? This left me worse off than before. As long as I allowed myself to forget the blank spots, to ignore them and live only in the present, I had no immediate problems. But now I was regaining my sense of identity, and I realized what an impossible situation I was in. I had two complete personalities, John Brown's and George Matthews'. I was Dr George Matthews to myself, but I was John Brown to Sonia and all my friends in Coney Island. When I looked into a mirror, I saw a horrible face that matched the life of John Brown, not Dr George Matthews. But it had been Matthews' face before it had been Brown's.

Sonia told me all she knew about me. There was nothing new in this. After the first shock of realization that I had a wife as well as a double personality, she adopted a sympathetic attitude to my problem. I knew that she had been hurt by the way I had acted, and I guessed that she was also afraid for my sanity – especially after I attacked Felix. But she was also in love with me.

It was Sonia who suggested the theory which I later came to think of as my 'working hypothesis'. She reminded me that l had suffered at least two accidents, one in October, 1943, and another that night. Amnesia, a mental disorder that caused me to forget my past, had certainly resulted from one – if only for a short time. When I had awakened that night after being struck by the automobile, I had forgotten the scar on my face and – for an instant – I had confused the recent past with the less-recent past. If this was true, was it not likely that I had also lost my memory regarding my past life at the time of the accident in the subway? During the seven months between my fall in the I.R.T. station and my awakening in the hospital, I had called myself John Brown, had worked and received a Social Security Card.

'Or someone – the same person who had pushed me into the train in the subway, perhaps – gave me that card,' I proposed.

'Then you think someone tried to kill you, too,' Sonia said.

We were having coffee, which she prepared on the hot plate in my closet. As she said this, I suddenly realized the full extent of the injustice that had been done to me. For a long time I had been unwilling to face the fact that all these things had not just happened, but that someone had done them to me for a reason. Here I was, living in a dingy room on a counterman's wages, alienated from my wife, and I had not even made a protest!

I wanted to jump to my feet, to scream and rage. I did not do it – I have always had fairly good control over my emotions – but I could feel the anger welling up in me. Why should anyone do these things to me? 'Why should I be deprived of my profession, my home, everything of value to me including my life?' I asked Sonia.

'I don't know, John – George, I mean. I think that something like that may have happened though. Tell me, when they gave you back your clothes at the hospital, didn't they give you your wallet? And if they did, didn't it contain some identification that would have told you who you had been?'

'Only the Social Security Card with John Brown's name on it,' I said.

'But on that day last year when you had the accident in the subway, didn't you have that kind of identification on you then?'

'At that time I was carrying my membership cards in several medical and psychiatric associations, my bank-book and both my business and home addresses,' I said.

'Yet you didn't have any of these when you entered the hospital, apparently. Doesn't this point to a plot against you?'

It certainly did.

Sonia was excited. She leaned across the table and pressed my hand. 'Do you know what I think, George? I think that in that last day you must have stumbled upon some fact that was dangerous to some person or group of persons. A fact that he, or they, could not dare let you remember?'

This was what had been in the back of my mind all night, but which I had not been able to put into words.

'Why didn't they kill me then?' I asked.

Sonia shook her head. 'I think they tried – and failed. I think they might try again.'

I had nothing to say to this. It was just a supposition, of course, but an unpleasantly logical one.

'George – who is Jacob Blunt?'

'Why, I've told you,' I said. 'He was my patient. He said that "little men" hired him to do crazy things. He wanted me to help him find out if these "little men" were real.'

Sonia walked to the window. The sun was rising over the rooftops – the structure of one of the rides a few blocks away was clearly visible. We had talked all night.

'George, didn't Felix say that Jacob Blunt hired him to say certain things to you?'

'That was what he said.'

'George, don't you think you had better find Jacob Blunt?'

There was no doubt that Sonia was right. Unless I wished to give up the fight altogether, I must find Jacob Blunt. For it was inconceivable that I could return to Sara, as I was, without some explanation of how I got this way – what had happened to me and why, who had done it. But did I want to continue the fight? And, above all else, did I want to go back to Sara and resume being Dr George Matthews?

One way I looked at it, my decision had already been made. Felix had forced it by revealing to Sonia my true identity. To the one person most important to John Brown, John Brown no longer existed. It would be difficult, if not impossible, to keep up my deception from day to day when I knew Sonia also was aware of what I was doing. Despite myself, I was – again – Dr George Matthews.

But what about returning to Sara? I was thinking about the way I looked, the absurd, grotesque face I saw when I gazed into a glass. How had I managed to face people without feeling self-conscious? I realized that a major part of my composure during the short time I had worked at the All-Brite came from my rejection of the personality, and standards, of Dr George Matthews. George Matthews had looked a certain way – he had to or he was not George Matthews – but John Brown belonged to the vicious caricature of a face that he glimpsed in mirrors. If I went back to my old way of life, I had to overcome this feeling of wearing a disguise, of appearing to myself as another character. Of course I could persuade myself that my face looked much more vile to me than it possibly could to another. All my past training in mental hygiene supported this self-advice, but I could not believe in it. All I could see when I thought of going back was that lewd smear of outraged flesh . . . and it disgusted me. I wanted to cover my face with my hands.

I suppose the reason I decided, finally, to go back – to find Jacob Blunt – to discover what was behind everything that had happened to me (as well as what it was that had happened), was that I desired revenge. This emotion, which soon dominated me and drove me on like a cruel spur in my side, was in itself paradoxical. For I had always held that revenge was a motive alien to modern, civilized man, a primitive drive, a blood-lust that human nature had sloughed off. But the man who had cultivated this opinion – the George Matthews of a short year ago – was a different man from the George Matthews I had become; nor could the man who accepted the name today ever wholly return to the man of yesterday who had never known another.

Aware of this, I set out to recapture the past.

Sonia had to go to work and I was left alone. I decided not to go back to the cafeteria. There was no reason why I should work there – I had money in the bank and a home in New Jersey. Of course, I might not be able to get the money out of the bank without a bankbook, without identification, without resembling the man who had deposited it. And I did not want to return to New Jersey because Sara might not be there – and also because Sara might well be there.

Yet, despite my torturing ambivalence, I wanted badly to see Sara. What had happened to her in the past year? Had I forgotten her, too, when I fell in the subway? The only way to discover the answers to these questions was to go and find out. I put on my hat and coat and walked over to the elevated station. Since it was early in the morning, the huge, two-levelled structure was cavernously empty: it dwarfed me as the enormity of my task dwarfed my spirit. I tried to whistle, but the tones froze in my throat. I let three trains pass before I stepped on to one.

I got off at Wall Street and walked past Trinity Church and down Cortlandt Street to the Hudson Tubes. In Jersey I took a bus to my neighbourhood. When I left the bus I took all the short cuts to our street, foolishly proud that I still remembered them. But when I stood in front of my house, I did not recognize it. I knew the block and the number, yet I walked past it three times before I found it. In the beginning I could not tell what was wrong – it just did not look like my house. Then I saw that it had been painted and that some of the shrubbery had been up-rooted and that there was a child's tricycle on the front porch. Sara and I had no children.

I walked slowly up the steps and pushed the doorbell tentatively. Heavy steps resounded through the house. The door opened upon a large woman in an old silk dress. She had a stocking cap over her hair and a dark mole on one cheek. She stared at me aggressively.

'We don't need anything,' she said.

'I'm not selling anything.'

'Then what do you want?'

'I'd like to speak to Mrs George Matthews.'

'There's no one here by that name.'

'She used to live here, I know.' I wanted to say more. I wanted to say: I own this house. Mrs Matthews is my wife! I must see her! But the words clogged my throat.

'The house was empty when we came.' The woman had begun to shut the door. 'We rented it last year. We don't know anything about the people who lived here before.'

'Who do you rent it from?' I all but shouted. I had to find out more. I could not stop now!

'The realty company rents it to us. They're still trying to sell. That's their sign out there.' She pointed to a large sign stuck into the lawn. Then she shut the door in my face.

I walked down the steps to the street and turned around

to look back at the sign. A few minutes before I had stood on the same spot and looked in the same direction, but I had not seen the sign then because I did not want to see it. How many other obvious facts had I overlooked in a similar fashion? And why did I want not to see certain things?

I looked at that sign for a long time. Then I took a piece of paper and a pencil out of my pocket and wrote down the name and address of the real estate agency: Blankenship & Co., 125 West 42nd Street, New York City.

Then I walked back to the bus stop to wait for the bus back to town.

I did not learn much at Blankenship & Co. I talked to a young man with a bland manner and eyes the colour of fish scales. He said, 'We contracted to manage Mrs Matthews' property in November of last year. We are to rent to responsible people until the opportunity presents itself to sell at a reasonable figure. The present tenants have been there since June. Are you interested in purchasing the property?'

'No,' I said. 'I'm a friend of the family who has lost touch with Mrs Matthews. I thought you might help me reach her again. Perhaps, if you told me where you send the rent money . . . ?'

When I asked this question, his fish-scale eyes slid over me appraisingly. I could see he suspected my intentions. But he answered my question. 'We deposit the rent to Mrs Matthews' account in her New York bank.'

Her New York bank? Then Sara had left the city?

'Could you tell me where Mrs Matthews lives now?'

The young man stood up. 'I'm sorry, but we are instructed not to divulge Mrs Matthews' whereabouts to anyone.'

'Can't you even tell me the name of her bank?'

His mouth had compressed itself into the thinnest of lines. 'I'm sorry, but that is confidential, too.'

I took my hat and left. On the street I wondered if I would have met with more success had I told him who I was instead of saying I was a 'friend of the family'. But I could not have proven that I was Dr George Matthews. I could only prove I was John Brown.

I took a local at Times Square to Canal Street and Police Headquarters. I had decided that it was time I had a talk with Lieutenant Anderson.

The policeman at the switchboard asked me: 'Why do you want to see the Lieutenant?'

'I think I have some information about the murder of Frances Raye,' I said.

He hesitated. I could see him thinking, could tell the exact moment when he recalled the case. He did something to the switchboard, said something into the receiver strapped to his head, then looked up at me.

'Go in the second door to your right. The Lieutenant will see you shortly.'

I walked down the same corridor as I had that morning in October, 1943, but went this time to a different room. That meant the Lieutenant was not seeing me in his office. I wondered why.

I opened the frosted glass door and stepped into a brightly lighted cubicle. It contained the usual desk, three chairs, a framed map of the five boroughs of New York. I sat down on one of the stiff-backed chairs, struck a match to a cigarette and waited.

I was very nervous. Would I be able to convince the Lieutenant that I was George Matthews? We had been old friends, but would he be able to recognize me despite my disfigurement? Felix had been able to, but he had seen my back first – or so he said. It was possible that Anderson would not know me at first, and that I would have to prove my identity to him. Would he give me the information I wanted – where Sara and Jacob were – or would I have to try other means? I could advertise in newspapers. I could hire a private detective and get in touch with Sara's relatives. But I might never see my wife again. And finding Jacob promised to be even more difficult.

I do not know how long it was before Anderson came into the room. He walked over and sat down behind the desk, folded his hands on the blotter and regarded me intently. His face blenched. Then he said, 'My God! It is you, isn't it, George?'

'I'm afraid I don't look quite the same, Andy.' I did not mean to speak so familiarly – while I had been waiting I had remembered the coldness of his manner at our last meeting. But I was encouraged by his easy friendliness this time. For a few moments I relaxed into the belief that everything was going to be all right.

'What has happened to you?' he asked.

'I don't know. Or, rather, I've forgotten.' I told him about meeting the man who had called himself Jacob Blunt, walking with him and Nan to the subway, falling – or being pushed? – losing consciousness.

'But, good God, George!' he said, 'when you saw the man wasn't your patient why did you take him with you? Why didn't you come and tell me?'

I did not know how to answer him. How could I explain the impulse that had misled me without reproaching him for his strangely hostile attitude toward me? I had felt then that if I could talk to the impostor in the privacy of my office, I would have been able to get him to confess his crime or implicate the real murderer. But I had to admit that I overstepped my authority, and had subsequently paid dearly for it.

'I should have told you,' I admitted. 'But, remember, I had seen the real Jacob only once, and I could not be certain that I remembered his appearance correctly.'

Anderson shook his head. 'But where have you been all this time?' he asked.

I told him about awaking in the hospital and, briefly, about my escape from the mental ward. I told him about my job in the cafeteria at Coney Island and about Sonia. I explained the apathy that had enervated me during the past month or more and how it was related to the clown-like disfigurement that had distorted my personality. At this, he clutched at a pencil and began to roll it along the blotter on his desk. 'I can well believe that,' he said. 'As you probably know, some criminologists hold that many criminal personalities can be traced to disfigurements. Scars make crimes.'

I went on to say that I had had an accident the previous night and that when I had recovered consciousness I had experienced again a momentary loss of memory. I told him of my suspicions that Felix-Eustace had been following me and related my attempts to get him to tell me more about Jacob.

When I had finished, Anderson looked up quickly. 'You think that someone tried to kill you – once, in the subway and, twice, last night. Did you get the licence of the car that struck you?'

I shook my head. 'I am not certain that another attempt was made last night. In fact, I think not. The street was dark and I ran into the car while trying to flag it down.'

'You were frightened?'

'As I said, I heard someone following me. It turned out to be Felix, and his intentions were friendly. But I did not know this at the time.'

'Why do you think they tried to kill you in the first place?'

I paused and thought before I answered. 'I think I must have stumbled upon something, learned something, that was dangerous to whoever killed Raye,' I said. 'What this could be, I don't know – unless it was the fact that I knew the man you were holding was not Jacob Blunt.'

Anderson leaned back in his chair, a tight smile on his face. 'You're being vague, you know. You say "I may have been pushed . . . perhaps, I knew something dangerous to somebody." None of that gets us any place.'

'I know I'm being vague. I can't help it. I don't remember anything else.'

The door opened behind me and another policeman came into the room. He gave Anderson a photograph that

I recognized immediately as one of my own. It was one I had given to Sara!

'Where did you get that?' I asked as soon as the other policeman had left the room. 'That belongs to my wife.'

Anderson nodded his head. 'Mrs Matthews let me make a copy of this. She said it was the only existing photo of you.'

He held it up for me to see. I tried to look at it, but my mind played a trick on me. In its place I saw again the mocking travesty of a face that I had first seen reflected in the soda fountain mirror. I saw the twisted lips – one side of my mouth in a permanent laugh, the other in a fixed, downward sneer – and the livid slash that rode my nose like a sabre slash. And I felt a trickle of perspiration run down my back.

Anderson was studying the photograph. 'You'll pardon me,' he said, 'but this has been such a queer case all along that I did not want to take a chance on my memory – even knowing you as well as I do – when identifying you. But I see now that you are the same man as this.' He tapped the photograph, then threw it on the table. I picked it up and looked at it. This time I saw it as it was: a portrait of a self I had almost forgotten, a smiling, distinguished-looking man who knew who he was and where he was and could help other people by sharing his strength.

I tried to light a cigarette, but my hand trembled too much. Anderson had to help me. I felt weak and womanish. The sense of relief, of knowing that someone at last recognized me indisputably as me, flooded my body with warmth and made a lump rise in my throat. Now I wanted to ask Anderson where Sara was, but I hesitated. I was afraid to crowd my luck. When I had mastered my emotions and looked up to see if Anderson had noticed the effect his words had had on me, I saw that he was standing with his hands clasped behind him looking at a map of the Bronx. I still did not speak. I was terrified to ask about Sara. What if she weren't all right?

Finally, Anderson said, 'That leaves us with another problem and a very cold trail.'

'What do you mean?' I asked.

He sat down and began to scratch his cheek ruminatively. 'On the eighteenth of November, 1943, a man's body was pulled out of the North River. The head had been smashed in. The body was about your build, dressed in your clothes and had your identification in its pockets. When your wife saw that body, she said it was yours.'

'That's why when Harvey Peters called you from the hospital you said I was dead,' I said.

Anderson nodded his head. 'I remember getting a call from a Dr Peters,' he said. He smiled apologetically. 'If I had known then what you've told me just now, I could have saved you a lot of trouble, I suppose.'

I could see that he was blaming himself for not realizing that the body that had been found in the river wasn't mine. 'What could you do if Sara identified the body?' I said to reassure him. And then, 'I guess this means that whoever killed Frances Raye also killed this man and dressed him in my clothes?'

'It looks that way. Now we have two unsolved murders instead of one.'

'But why didn't he kill me?' I asked. 'What did happen to me? How did I get this?' I fingered my scar.

'That's what we're going to have to try to find out,' said Anderson. He bit the end off a cigar and stood up. 'And it isn't going to be easy.'

8   Memory of Pain

I had reached for my hat, thinking that the interview was over. I knew that Anderson would want to see me again, and before I left I wanted to ask him to try and get in touch with Sara for me. But I did not expect what happened next.

'It's strange that you should come to see me just now,' he said, his hand on the door. 'The Raye case has been shelved for months and there has been no new evidence – until this morning.'

He looked at me questioningly.

'Come with me to my office,' he said. 'I want you to meet someone.' He opened the door and waited for me. Then he led me down the corridor to his office.

Nan Bulkely was sitting there. She turned to look at us as we came in the door. When she saw me her eyes widened and her lips trembled. I could see her hand clutch her pocketbook. For a long moment we stared at each other, then she jerked her head away.

'Do you recognize this man, Miss Bulkely?' Anderson asked.

'Yes. He is Dr George Matthews.' Her voice was scarcely louder than a whisper.

Anderson went behind his desk and picked up a pad of paper on which he had scribbled some notes. 'This is the man to whom you referred when you gave me this deposition a few minutes ago?'

'Yes.' Again I could hardly hear her. I remained standing. What was all this about?

Anderson cleared his throat and began to read from the pad of paper he held in his hand. 'Miss Nan Bulkely, of her own free will, made the following statement in the office of Lieutenant William Anderson, Homicide Division, Police Department of the City of New York on the morning of 30 August 1944. "On Wednesday night of last week I visited Coney Island with a friend, stopped in a cafeteria for something to eat and recognized one of the employees as Dr George Matthews. This man did not see me at the time or recognize me. I knew that the police considered him dead, and that he had been involved in the murder of Frances Raye which was still unsolved. I had not seen him in nearly a year. When I first had known him he was a psychiatrist who had been treating a friend of mine, Jacob Blunt. I met him in connection with the death of Frances Raye, in which Jacob was at that time implicated. You (the police) released Jacob into his custody for further questioning. I went with Dr Matthews and Jacob; after we left the police station Dr Matthews had a fainting fit in the subway and nearly fell into a train. Jacob and I took him to my apartment. Dr Matthews felt better after a short while and left, making an appointment to see Jacob in his office the next day. I thought his action was peculiar then, and I do now, since he would be held responsible for any crime Jacob might commit in the interim. But I said nothing. Jacob stayed with me for a short time and then he also left my apartment. I had not seen either Jacob or Dr Matthews again until last week when I saw Dr Matthews in the cafeteria. I barely recognized him at that time because of the terrible disfigurement he has suffered since I last saw him. His face is badly scarred, but he is obviously the same man for whom the police have been searching."' Anderson stopped reading and regarded me. 'Do you remember any of this?' he asked.

'I do not remember visiting Miss Bulkely's apartment after my accident in the subway,' I said. 'As I told you the last thing I recall is the sensation of falling – or being pushed.'

'Did you see her last week at the cafeteria?'

'I did not,' I said emphatically. I looked at Nan. She was sitting rigidly in her chair, her hands clenching the arms. Her face was pale and her eyes were wide and staring. She was badly frightened. But why? Then I remembered the way I looked, the effect the sight of my own face had had on me the first time I saw it – and I understood her fright. I looked away so she would not have to look at my face.

'Do you think I killed Frances Raye, Andy?' I asked. 'Is that what this is all about?'

Anderson sat down and began to roll a pencil between his fingers. He rolled it back and forth, back and forth. It was a while before he spoke, and during this time I kept my face turned away from Nan. 'I don't think it's impossible, but I doubt it . . . at this point. I see no motive for it. But then none of us has ever uncovered a reason for her killing. You are certainly a suspect.'

I said nothing.

'Tell me again what you have been doing since you left the hospital,' he said.

'I've been working nights at the All-Brite cafeteria and living in the neighbourhood,' I said. 'I have friends that can vouch for that.'

'But you do not remember going to Miss Bulkely's apartment or anything that happened between the time you fell in the subway and the day you woke up in the hospital – is that right?'

'That's right,' I said.

'What is your impression of Dr Matthews, Miss Bulkely?' Anderson asked Nan.

She stood up, hesitantly. She had a fur over her shoulder that fell to the floor. I started to stoop to pick it up for her – then remembered how she had reacted to my face. I turned my eyes away and let her pick it up herself. When I looked back she was regarding me. Suddenly I realized that I did not like to have her look at me either. Those staring eyes, that red hair, that beautiful blank face – they mocked me. A memory of that same face seemed to bob along the surface of my mind like a brightly painted toy balloon floating on the surface of a pond.

She had not answered Anderson's question. I decided to forestall her. 'Jacob did not come with us that day when I took a man into my custody, Miss Bulkely,' I said. 'That man was not Jacob Blunt. I do not know who he was, but he was not Jacob Blunt.' And then I turned to Anderson. 'It seems to me that he would be your most likely suspect, not I.'

'He must be mistaken,' Nan said with surprising calm. (I had expected my statement to flurry her.) 'The man was Jacob Blunt. I knew him very well. I could not be wrong.'

Anderson kept playing with his pencil. I wished he would stop, the incessant movement of his fingers was making me nervous.

Nan adjusted her fur about her shoulders. 'I think Dr Matthews is ill,' she said to Anderson. 'He admits that he has forgotten a good deal. Isn't it possible that he has forgotten more than he realizes, and even that he is mistaken in some things that he remembers?' Anderson came around the desk and guided her to the door. I heard him say '. . . investigate his statement thoroughly, check it in every detail. We'll make certain there's no mistake. I have your address.' Then they were out in the corridor and he had shut the door on me. I was alone in the room.

And a frightening thing was happening to me. I was remembering . . . something. Something that had to do with a girl's face close to mine, her eyes watching me, something that was horrible to remember . . . that had to do with pain . . . my own pain or someone else's? I did not know.

I might be wrong. I might be remembering, even now, despite the assertions I had made, going to her apartment that day in October. Perhaps, I had gone there, perhaps, I had done other things I could not remember . . . both before and after that day.

I shut my eyes, but found I could not shut out the image of that beautiful face, those wide-open staring eyes. It would not go. And there was something else . . . something terrible that was coming that I could not prevent, that was coming again and again. And something else again, the sound of a violin . . . a sweet sound, yet horrible.

I heard the door click. I jumped to my feet, terrified. But it was only Anderson. He was smiling in his tight-lipped way.

'I telephoned the cafeteria,' he was saying. 'He says that you work there so you're probably all right. I want you to come along with me though and have the manager identify you as John Brown. Then we'll know that at least that part of your story is true.'

Anderson was still friendly – I thought that a good sign. I felt my muscles losing their tenseness. I tried to smile, but I could not. When I spoke, I stammered. 'You think I don't know what I'm saying, don't you, Andy?'

Anderson shrugged his shoulders. 'I don't think in black-and-white terms,' he said. 'Working with you taught me that, if nothing else. When you had a practice did you think of your patients as either sane or insane? You know that you didn't. They were all kinds and varieties of people and their mental aberrations differed in degree as well as in kind. You had to make up your mind about each one, independently. With a cop it's the same.

'All I have to do is to look at your face to see that something has happened to you – that you've been through a lot. But I know that your having an ugly scar doesn't mean that you murdered Frances Raye, or even that you are mistaken in your memory of what happened that day in the subway. But you do admit that you cannot remember anything after you fell in the subway. And Miss Bulkely says that you recovered consciousness quickly and then went to her apartment. This makes me want to check the other aspects of your story.'

'And it makes you curious to find out what happened during my blank months,' I said.

Anderson smiled. He stuck the pencil he had been worrying into his breast pocket, pulled out a cigar and began to pick at it. 'That's right,' he said. 'And that's another reason why I want to go along with you while you retrace that part of your life that you remember. I have hopes that somewhere in the process you will begin to recall what you have forgotten. I've seen it happen before.'

I followed him out of the door and down in the elevator to the street. My thoughts were in great confusion. What was I remembering about Nan Bulkely? I could still see her face in front of mine, her burnished hair, her eyes close to mine, glittering.

I shuddered.

I watched the Lieutenant as we drove across Canal Street to the bridge and over the bridge to Brooklyn. A small, spare man with closely cropped grey hair, I had thought he looked more like a worried businessman than a detective when I first met him years ago – and I still thought so. It was difficult for me to imagine him using an automatic; my mind preferred to picture him bent over a cash register or studying a chequerboard.

He talked as he drove, giving me a short history of the Frances Raye case. 'We have never been able to follow through on a single line of reasoning from the very beginning,' he said. 'That's one of the reasons I'm taking such a personal interest in you now. You might think that I would assign this sort of routine to one of my men, send a good man out to check up on you and then read his report. Well, the reason is this: the damned business is beginning to get my goat! I don't want to make any mistakes now!'

'It's kind of you,' I said. 'I appreciate your interest.'

'Look at it from the Division's point of view,' he went on. 'Over a year ago a prominent woman was found murdered in her apartment. A drunk was caught ringing her doorbell at the same time the body was found. It looked open and shut. The newspapers created their customary hullaballoo, but we thought that all we had to do was to sit tight, ask the usual questions and make a thorough check-up and the whole thing would be sewed up and ready for the D.A. in a few days.

'What happens? I ask you, what happens? You came down, visited the prisoner, I let you have him in your custody – and then both of you disappear! We pick up a little guy who says the prisoner hired him to feed you a line, and then we have to let him go. He knows nothing, or he won't talk. We still don't find you or Blunt. We question every person we can find who ever spent five minutes with Frances Raye. No results. There is no motive, no clues, no suspects. In four solid weeks of relentless investigation we were never able to follow a solitary clue to its logical conclusions. We knew less when we finished than when we started! Is it surprising that, when after all these months you show up again, I should not let you out of my sight?'

'Did you ever find Blunt?' I asked.

'He sent us a postcard last summer. I went up to see him at his place in Connecticut. It was then that I found out that the man we arrested was not Jacob Blunt. I thought we had something then and I went to work on him. He told me the same crazy story that I had heard before from you and the impostor: about being hired by this Eustace (who said his real name was Felix Mather) to deliver a horse to Raye. But he said that he decided not to go through with it and left the horse tied to the post. He went to a near-by bar and got soused – when he woke up the next morning he was in a hotel room at Atlantic City married to some blonde he had met when he was drunk. We checked his story and found it was true. By that time the newspapers were off the trail, and I saw to it that the story did not leak out. I still have a hunch that he has something to do with it, but I don't know what. Then again, if he was telling me the truth – and we could not

119

disprove his story – someone might have been plotting against him. That's why I did not want the newspapers to get on to the story of what happened to him. I can get him any time I want him, even though he lives out-of-state now. We have had the sheriff of his town watching him for months.'

I was puzzled. 'If you knew that the man in the cell was not Jacob, why didn't you question Nan Bulkely further just now when she insisted that he was?'

'I don't want her to suspect that I did not accept her story. It is possible that she's guilty of the crime, but it is more likely that she is shielding someone. She's being followed right now and I hope she will lead us to something. I have a hunch that between you and her I'll get at whoever is behind all this.'

Anderson parked his car on the Avenue across the street from the cafeteria. He made no move to get out; instead he lighted the cigar he had been chewing all this time, and went on talking. He had obviously wanted to talk this all out to someone for a long time. 'You see, if I wanted to charge Bulkely with perjury and helping a prisoner to escape, I could have done it long ago. But what good would it have done to jail her? It would not have solved the case, and we would have shut down our one possible lead to the killer – for I think Nan is in it up to her neck. We might have sweated it out of her, and then again we might not have. All in all, now that you've shown up – and Nan re-enters the case voluntarily with a cooked-up story that doesn't fool anybody – I'm beginning to feel I've played it right. One of these days this thing is going to bust wide open!'

He took a long drag on his cigar and knocked some ashes onto the seat. 'We tried to find you, too, you know. Your wife was frantic. She gave us your picture and came down to Headquarters every day for weeks. Then, in November of last year, we found that body and she identified it as yours. I can't blame her for making a mistake. After a body's been in the river for a while even its own mother couldn't tell it! Your wife finally left town – went to Chicago to her parents.'

Then I knew where Sara was! I felt better. If she was in Chicago, she was safe and I could reach her any time. But, I realized, I did not want to reach her. As long as I knew where she was that was all that mattered. I had not yet made up my mind what to do about Sara. There was the scar . . . the way Nan had reacted to it was still fresh in my mind. No, Sara could wait. There were other matters to be attended to first.

Anderson was chewing his cigar contemplatively. 'So now we got two murders,' he said, 'but this time I'm going to hold on to you. You're not going to get lost again. I'm going to have some good man on your tail night and day.'

I looked at him in surprise. This I had not expected.

'I'm taking no chances,' he explained. He opened the car door and stretched his legs. 'Come on. Let's find out what the manager of the cafeteria knows about you.'

I followed him across the street to the All-Brite. I was still thinking about Sara, and about my scar.

When I walked into the All-Brite it seemed impossible that as short a time ago as the night before I had worked there. Everything about it was strange and unfamiliar – I was seeing it with George Matthews' eyes and not John Brown's – the long steam tables at the rear, the lurid orange walls, the jumpy fluorescent lighting. Although the details of the nights that I had spent there came flooding back to me, and I could recall the feeling that went with the place – a sort of desperate loneliness, a complete and hopeless loss of personality, a fear of being jobless – I found it devilishly hard to confront Fuller, the manager, to pump his flabby hand and look down at his scrubbed-pink face and realize that he had ever represented 'authority' to me!

He sat down with us at one of the tables. He seemed surprised to see me. In fact, his first words were: 'What are you doing here at this time of day? You're not on until six o'clock.'

I did not answer him. I waited for Anderson to ask the first question. He was considering Fuller thoughtfully, chewing a little on his cigar. Then he asked, 'Does this man work for you under the name of John Brown?'

Fuller glanced at me apprehensively. He had no way of knowing who Anderson was – the Lieutenant was in plain clothes – but he seemed to sense that something unusual was happening. He answered with exaggerated caution.

'He has been,' he said. 'A good worker, too. I was worried about taking him on – thought the customers might object to – to his face. Thought they might get complaints and I would hear about it. But he's worked out pretty well . . . so far. The breakage was less this month . . .'

'How did you come to hire him?' Anderson picked a flake of tobacco from his lips and flicked it onto the floor. Fuller's eyes looked down at it in disapproval. I knew he did not like to have his floor dirtied. But he did not say anything.

'The hospital recommended him. We get a lot of our help that way now. It's the times. The war is hard on the cafeteria business.'

'What hospital? And when did he start to work for you?' Anderson was annoyed with the way he had to pull information from the seedy little manager.

'City Hospital. The social service lady there. She sends them to me with a card. It's about the best way to get help these days.'

'When did he start work for you?' Anderson was being very curt. I knew how he felt.

'I couldn't say that. I have to look up my records.'

I broke in here. 'I can tell you,' I said. 'It was on the twelfth of July.' I would never forget that date. That was the day I had first looked into a mirror and discovered a bitter, demented clown.

Fuller nodded his head briskly. 'That's right. I remember now. It was during that hot spell in the second week of July. I had had another man until the week before, but he got in a fight with one of the grifters around here and he got sixty days . . .'

'Don't you know any more about him than that?' asked Anderson. I could see he was frustrated.

'Why?' asked Fuller. 'Has he gone and got himself in trouble?' He frowned his disapproval at the thought of 'trouble'.

Anderson leaned back in his chair and flipped the lapel of his coat to show his badge. 'I'm from the Homicide Division. Are you sure you don't know anything more about this guy?' I was surprised at how tough he could be when he wanted to.

Fuller stared at us both for an instant, then jumped awkwardly to his feet, knocking his chair over in the process. It fell on the tile floor making a noisy clatter. A few people at other tables looked at us with curiosity.

'I knew I shouldn't have hired him!' Fuller was saying. 'I knew the customers would complain. I knew they'd hear about it. I kept telling myself that I should never have took him on!'

His voice rose higher and higher until it was a strangled squeak. His pale pink face had flushed a flower-pot red. Now he stopped in mid-protest and stared at me. He raised his arm slowly and pointed at me. 'You mean he's a murderer? You mean he's killed somebody?'

I wanted to laugh. It was not at all funny, but I wanted to laugh. The bug-eyed little man was so ridiculous. And I had once feared him. Now the whole thing was completely absurd.

Anderson was angry. 'I didn't say that!' he shouted. 'I just asked if you knew anything more about him that you weren't telling me. If I wanted to tell you anything else I would tell you. Now answer yes or no – do you know anything else about the identity of this man?' He glared hard at Fuller.

The manager swallowed once or twice and then backed

away. He actually cringed. He moistened his lips with his tongue, opened his mouth, croaked a few times before he said, 'I'd never seen him before that day when he came here with the card from the hospital. I never heard of him before that.'

Anderson picked up his hat. 'That's all I needed to know,' he said. He motioned to me that it was time to go. I followed him to the swinging doors. Fuller was right behind me, and I turned around to face him. He looked at me, ran his tongue around his lips, still scared. I could not understand why, unless he thought his own security was threatened in some vague way.

He wanted to ask me a question. I waited patiently for him to form the words. Finally they came. 'You are coming to work tonight?'

'No,' I said. 'I don't work here any more. I'll be in Saturday to get my pay.'

He backed away, putting out his hands helplessly. 'But what am I going to do?' he asked. 'I need a man tonight. Where am I going to get one?'

And at one time I had been afraid of that man – I could remember the feeling.

Anderson was waiting for me on the sidewalk. We walked to his car together. 'Where do we go now?' I asked him.

'We go to see Miss Willows, the head social-worker at City Hospital,' he said. 'I want to find out what those people know about you.'

'Do we have to do that?' I dreaded going back to the hospital, back to the blank part of my past. I felt I was close to remembering, and I did not want to remember. Without willing it, the image of Nan's face appeared in my mind's eye again, close to me, bending over me. It seemed to bob and beckon, urging me to delve deeper. But I did not want to delve – I did not want to remember. I was afraid and, strangely, I was listening. Listening . . . but for what?

The Lieutenant nursed the car into the traffic. He began to drive east across Brooklyn towards the river. 'We have to follow up all the leads we have,' he said. 'The hospital is one of those leads. You remember being there but, as you well know, you may be forgetting something important. Perhaps, they know what happened to you, or, perhaps, after you talk to Miss Willows you will remember it yourself.'

He talked on, reasonably. I admitted to myself that he was right and that my fear was irrational. I let him take me back to the hospital.

Miss Willows was the same middle-aged fat woman with a broad face and a placid disposition that I had known before. Her hair was still caught up in a bun at the back of her neck. Looking at her I remembered with peculiar force my desperate lies of a few months before, the cleverly halting story I had told with bated breath, the moment when I had manufactured out of a tissue of fabrication the personality of John Brown that was to fit me better than I knew then.

Miss Willows did not seem surprised to see either Anderson or me. She looked in a filing cabinet and found a manila folder with the name 'John Brown' clearly marked on it. She waddled back to her desk – one of her legs was shorter than the other – and opened the folder and began to examine the cards with their closely written records. Her lips moved silently as she read them.

'Oh, yes, Mr Brown,' she said, after she had refreshed her memory at the file. 'He was one of our more interesting cases. A complete recovery despite a rather bad prognosis. And an excellent adjustment and rehabilitation, if I do say so myself.'

'Just tell me what you know about this man,' said Anderson.

She glanced up, a little put out by the Lieutenant's crisp tone. Then she pursed her lips primly.

'He came here on the first of May this year, 1944. One

of your men picked him up on the Bowery, wandering. He seemed to have no memory of his past life. He had had a bad concussion and a deep laceration on his head. The policeman thought he had been in a fight. He was not intoxicated.'

'This was just a few months ago?'

'In May. We put him in bed and treated him for concussion and shock. When he regained consciousness he had an obsession. He believed himself to be a psychiatrist – a Dr George Matthews. He was most convincing about it. He supplied us with all kinds of details about a fictitious past life. Of course, none of them were true.'

'You checked on them, of course?'

'We found them all to be quite fictitious. There was a Dr George Matthews, but he had been dead some time.'

'You say that the prognosis was unfavourable at first?'

Miss Willows smiled quickly. 'Did I say that? Well, at first, yes. He had a persecution syndrome. He believed himself to be this Dr Matthews and he considered it unethical of us to keep him here.'

'He remembered later?'

'Oh, yes, it all came back! Occupational therapy you know. A little rest in a quiet place, an opportunity to use one's hands. Oh, yes, it all came back, didn't it, Mr Brown?' Now she had turned her smile on me, a chaste, antiseptic grimace.

'Yes,' I said. 'It all came back.'

'Mr Brown was born in Erie, Pennsylvania,' she was reading aloud from the folder. 'He came from a large family. He joined the Army and served in the first World War. He was wounded and came back home. He had a hard time. He worked as a farm labourer, here, and on the West Coast. His wife died. He was on relief during the depression. He became an alcoholic.'

She stopped reading and pursed her lips again. 'A typical case, I'm afraid. Is he in trouble again?' She spoke right over me – as if I weren't there or, worse, as if it did not matter how I felt.

Anderson shook his head. 'We just wanted to check with you. This is all the information you have?'

Miss Willows smiled again. She felt Anderson's displeasure, but she did not know why he was displeased. She wanted to make amends. I could see she was not a bad sort.

'You might try one of the doctors, though I doubt if they know as much as I. This is the complete case history, you see. Very complete, in fact. Mr Brown was an unusually interesting case.'

Anderson thanked her and stood up to go. 'Oh, that's what we're here for,' she said cheerfully. 'Any time I can help . . .'

As soon as we were outside the door, he stopped and looked at me. 'Did any of those things ever happen to you?' he asked.

'No,' I said, 'none of them.'

'Then how did you get on her record?'

'I remember that much, I assure you. I made that all up. I told it to the doctors and to her. It was the only way I could get out, you see!'

Anderson scratched his head. 'No, I don't see,' he said.

'They wouldn't believe that I was Dr George Matthews. They checked with you, and they were told I was dead. They checked with my office, and they discovered that my office was no longer in existence. They tried to find Sara and they failed. Then they decided that I had paranoid tendencies.'

'But I still don't see why you had to make all that up?'

'Because that was the only kind of history they expected me to have. They looked on me as a bum, a vagrant. I cadged that story from a hundred similar cases I have encountered in my career. I constructed it carefully so that in its every detail it would coincide with their preconceived notion of what my life history must be like, and by this

means planned to persuade them that I had indeed recovered my memory. If I had persisted in telling the truth,
they would have continued to believe that I was suffering
from an aberration. All that I might have said would only
have heaped coals upon the fire of their conviction. Every
circumstance dissuaded the possibility, to their minds, that
I might have been a psychiatrist. I was forced to create a
complex lie and offer it to them as the reality. There was
no other way out.'

'Didn't you ever doubt your own identity? By God, I
know I would have been mixed up!'

'Sometimes I was a little confused about it,' I admitted.
'But where do we go from here?'

He laid his hand on my shoulder. His eyes studied me
in kindly fashion. I realized that this man was my friend,
that he was on my side—at least, for the time being. It was
a pleasant sensation. 'I'm taking you home,' he said. 'I'll
have a man on duty all night in front of your place. When
you go out, speak to him so he can keep track of you. I
don't want to take any chances.'

I was glad to get home. In fact the car could not take me
back to Coney Island fast enough. Things were going on
in my head. I wanted to lie down and be with whatever it
was that was struggling to the surface of my memory. I was
afraid, but I knew that sooner or later I would have to
face it. Things had gone too far – someone had pushed me
too far. Now was the time to remember – and then to act.

When I reached my room, I drew the shade and
stretched out on the lumpy bed. This was all that was
necessary. Nothing clicked; there was no sudden revela-
tion. It was just that a part of me that had been sleeping
had awakened. I remembered it all, completely, in each
detail. Or, so it seemed at first.

Later I walked to the window and lifted a corner of the
shade. A man was leaning against a doorway across the
street. He was watching three small girls play hopscotch.
I smiled to myself. That was Anderson's man. I might

need him before the night was up. But right now I needed sleep. I lay down again and closed my eyes. There was no hurry now, no compulsion, I had plenty of time.

I knew who my enemies were now, even if I did not know why they were my enemies.

9 Memory of Pain II

Memories exist whole in the mind; to put them down in words demands sequence, a sense of time and space, of then and now. But when one remembers an event that belongs to the far past and relates it to another happening that belongs to yesterday, these memories exist together simultaneously – they are both, for a moment, now, not then. And so it had been with me when I stretched out on the bed in my small room, shut my eyes and with the blotting out of sight closed down upon the present, let the lost past seize me and hold me fast. I saw it whole, lived it all again – not in an hour, or even in several minutes, but in a single, incalculable instant . . .

A softly lighted room, the dusk blue against the windows, the sweet voice of a violin, a faint scent of perfume – I was alone in the room; but someone had just left it, someone a moment before had turned on the radio, someone was returning now   I could hear the steps in the hall. I fought the heavy weight of lethargy that smothered me. A pricking sensation existed on the edge of my consciousness – was it a previous feeling remembered or was I feeling it now? It did not matter and it was all-important (it seemed logical that it should be both at the same time). Everything loomed so very large: my head, the room, the beating of my heart, the intense harmonies of the violin. I could see the waves of sound, feel them breaking over me, threatening to engulf me. The wide windows darkened deeply into night; the footsteps grew nearer and nearer, their sound accumulating into a muffled loudness. It seemed as if whoever the person was who was approaching, he was taking an eternity to get to the door, to open it, to come into the room . . . an unbearable eternity. Then I heard a decisive sound, a metallic liquidness, a key turned gently in the lock. The person came in (I had been listening for so long, for forever), and I was terrified.

Now I could see who it was. It was Nan. This was her apartment. This was her living room. (I had been in this room how many days?) And I knew why she was here. It was time again for my 'treatment'.

She sat down beside me on the couch where I lay, reached out and took my hand. I turned my head away. The scent of perfume was no longer faint, it enveloped me. From the radio the thread of sweet sound was now joined by strings and woodwinds and what had been a sibilance began to swell to crescendo. It was almost dark and the outlines of the furniture blended into the long shadows thrown by the darkening window. I felt myself slipping away . . . falling.

'Won't you tell me? He can keep this up forever, you know. Neither Tony nor I want to do it, but we can't help ourselves. Why don't you tell us? Then you would never have to go again.'

I gritted my teeth and said nothing.

'I promised you that you would never have to go again. As soon as you were strong enough you could leave, go home. All you have to do is to tell us where Jacob is. Nothing more. No one would ever need know you told. You can believe me, no one would ever need know you told.'

I could feel her fingernails biting into the back of my hand. I could feel her breath warm on my cheek. She was sitting close to me, talking quietly, earnestly. I said nothing.

'Think of how I feel. Do you think I like to take you to the doctor every night? Do you think Tony likes it? We are not murderers! Do you think we like to stand by and watch you suffer? What good does it do for you to be a hero? Why can't you tell us what we need to know, say a few little words, tell us where Jacob is? Then it would all be over.'

She waited for me to speak. She waited a long time until the room grew black dark. She turned on a light, then stood in front of me. I would not look up at her, but I could not help seeing her legs, the bottom of her skirt, the belt of her dress.

Suddenly, she knelt in front of me. Her eyes were wet. She had been biting her lip and it was bleeding. Her hair was disarrayed. Her coat was flung over her shoulders, she wore a hat. She was ready to go, to take me with her . . .

'Please, Dr Matthews . . .'

I turned my face away.

She cried quietly for a few minutes, then she went to the closet for my coat, the sunglasses, the bandage. She wrapped the yards of bandage around my face, loosely so I could breathe, leaving holes so I could see. She put the smoked glasses over the bandage and handed me the cane, helped me into my coat. Tony was waiting for us in the hall, nervously smoothing his slick black hair. The three of us went down in the elevator together. As usual, the taxi was waiting outside.

I am not a brave man. At times, when I have read of the tortures men have undergone in Spain, at Dachau and Buchenwald, I have laid down the book that told of this martyrdom. What ideal could be worth that agony? Would it not be better to tell them what they wanted to know – even if you were killed for it afterwards? Then, at least, death would come quickly.

You don't feel that way when it happens to you.

There were differences in my case, of course. I was not in Germany or Spain; I was in New York. What happened to me should not have happened. But it did.

I could not have told had I wanted to. I did not know Jacob Blunt's whereabouts. I had seen him once for a few hours. All I knew about him was what he had told me himself.

But Nan, Tony and the 'doctor' thought differently. They were certain I knew where Jacob was. And 'he' thought I know where Jacob was. Many times Nan made it clear that 'he' gave the orders. They all feared 'him' and obeyed 'him'. I never saw 'him' – during all those weeks I never met my persecutor.

(I remembered it all now. It was all there. It took no effort to recall any part of it: the coming back to consciousness on the subway platform, Nan's solicitous questions, Tony's arm around my shoulders, the lift and pull of them both as they helped me to the taxi, the long drive to Nan's apartment on Central Park South, the falling asleep, the blackness returning as soon as I touched the sofa, the being awakened for the first of the daily catechisms . . .

'Dr Matthews! Dr Matthews! Wake up! It's Nan!'

'Yes.'

'You had an accident. You fell in the subway. But you're going to be all right.'

'Where am I?'

'In my apartment. You said you did not want to go to the hospital. I brought you here.'

I wondered at the time why I should have requested not to be taken to a hospital. But my head hurt. I could think about that later.

'Do you feel well enough to talk?'

'Yes.'

'I want you to tell me where Jacob is.'

'Jacob? Why isn't he with you?'

'Not that Jacob. The real Jacob!'

'The last time I saw him was last night . . . with Eustace.' I did not want to talk. I was not thinking about what I was saying. I was answering her questions guilelessly.

'You haven't seen him since last night?'

'Seen whom?'

'Jacob. The real Jacob.'

'Who was that in the cell? The man who came with us? Didn't you call him Jacob, too?' I was beginning to remember, and I was becoming conscious – but too late.

'That wasn't Jacob.'

'Where is he now?'

'He's here with us. You'll see him. His name is Tony. But answer my question. Where is Jacob?'

'I don't know.'

'Are you certain?'

'Yes. I really don't know.'

Then she was silent for a long time. Then she went away.)

The doctor's office was near the Third Avenue 'El', not more than a five-minute drive from Central Park. Although I was taken there every night for I do not know how many nights, the bandages on my face and the dark glasses over my eyes prevented me from discovering the exact location. I know I had to walk up three steep flights of rickety stairs and I reasoned from this that the building was probably a tenement – once I brushed against a child's tricycle, always there were smells of cooking in the corridors. But while all these details were vague, there were others that were etched into my recently rediscovered memory with disconcerting clarity.

The room in which I found myself when they removed the bandages was of average size, but without windows. I suspected that the 'doctor's' office was part of a railroad flat. There were no chairs, no pictures – not even a framed diploma – on the dirty brown walls. Both doors were kept locked and bolted from the inside. The single piece of furniture was a chipped white enamel operating table, complete with straps. This was in the centre of the room and over it a glaring naked electric bulb hung by its cord from the ceiling. An autoclave hissed in one corner of the room beside the wash-basin. The 'doctor' was always washing the stiff lather off his hands when I entered the room.

He was a thin man with small, brown, bloodshot eyes. His apron was usually slightly soiled. What was left of his hair was ginger-coloured, but there was a large, circular bald spot on the top of his head – with kalsomine on his face he would have resembled a circus clown. I never heard him speak. He would look around at me, then point at the table. That meant that the 'treatment' was about to begin. He never hurried his wash: he took his time about smoothing and rinsing the suds from his arms, working with an automatic coordination, methodically. When he had dried himself, he would walk briskly to the table where I was lying to inspect the straps. Sometimes he would tighten one, or loosen another . . .

The first night I lay down on the table of my own free will. The next few times I fought bitterly with Tony (of the slick black hair, the bristly moustache), but each time I lost. Finally, after several nights of futile struggle, I submitted to the 'treatment' as inevitable – Tony was amazingly agile and strong and he overcame me easily. I feared and hated what happened next. I knew it for what it was and was aware that there were limits to the number of times they could do it to me without impairing my faculties, but it was useless to struggle. Even if I could break loose, where could I go? The doors were locked and there were no windows. Soon it would be over until the next time . . . the spasm only lasted a fraction of a second.

I'll say this for the devil: he knew how to make an injection. I never felt the needle – it was on me with the quickness of lightning. I would be flat on my back, the brilliant light from the bulb overhead glowing dully in my brain despite my shut eyelids. There would be a wait while he went back to the sterilizer for the hypodermic. Then I would feel his hand steadying, probing my arm . . . The dull red of the light would spin and swell with maniacal celerity to a blinding, vivid, all-encompassing sheath of white heat. My spine would writhe, my neck arch . . . (I have seen patient after patient in 'shock' . . . I have seen remarkable recoveries, too . . . but I shall never prescribe it again.) Then cool blackness would swim in.

I do not know whether I was given insulin or metrazol or one of the new compounds. I do know that I was taken to the 'doctor' every night for what seemed forever. I know that I always awakened back in Nan's apartment, awakened only to fall asleep again. I know that during the last few nights and days I was under morphine a good part of the time, otherwise I might not have stood the strain. They questioned me each day, of course, but I told them nothing. There was nothing I could tell them.

They had devised a perfect form of torture. Shock treatments left no trace, if the patient were strapped properly and the dosage regulated with care. They knew I had been a psychiatrist and they knew that they could count on my experience of the special effects of metrazol or insulin on others to add to the normal dread of the 'treatment'. They knew that I knew that if the 'treatments' were continued long enough, something would break.

It was a precisely calculated means of extracting the information 'he' thought I had. But the joke was on 'him'. I did not know where Jacob was. I could not supply the desired information even if they killed me in the attempt to get it.

It was a grim joke.

Sometimes I questioned Nan about 'him' and his motives. She would sit beside me in the afternoon, her head burnished by the slanting sun – the sun yellow in the large living room, her hair copper-gold, glinting.

'Why is Jacob so important to "him"?' I would ask.

She would look away. 'I can't answer that question, Dr Matthews.'

'Who is "he"?' I would ask.

She would walk over and turn on the radio, fiddle with the dials until she got music, soft music, she did not seem to like the more martial *allegros*.

'Why are you helping him? If it is true that you would prefer to have nothing to do with this, why do you keep it up?'

Her face would go pasty, her lips would tremble. 'I work for him.' She would come back and sit beside me. We would listen to Delius or Mozart or Schumann. Sometimes she would read. The sun would go down behind the high apartment buildings facing the Park. The sky would begin to darken. All this time I would be thinking of what was coming, planning ways of escaping, wild schemes, foolish daydreams. But they were better than the reality of the night.

One of them I tried. One night, when we reached the street, I broke and ran for it. I could see dimly and then only directly in front of me because of the bandages and the dark glasses ('he' was very clever – 'he' had thought of everything). I ran desperately towards Fifth Avenue and heavy traffic. I could hear Tony running behind me, gaining on me. I saw a broad fellow in a Homburg hat in my path. He had some sort of a terrier on a leash; he must have been out walking the dog after dinner. I swerved to miss him, seeing for an instant his over-fed countenance, his porcine eyes. Then I heard Tony yell behind me 'Stop that man!' No reason given, only a peremptory command, yet the fat fool stretched out his arms. I tried to elude him, but there was too much of him to elude. I heard him gasp 'Oof!' as I hit him, yet, surprisingly, he held his ground. I suppose he thought he was being very brave – he probably related the incident to his bored wife later, exaggerating it proudly. The damn dog began to race around us excitedly, tangling my legs in his leash. Then Tony came up, thanked the man profusely, gripped my arm firmly and led me back to Nan and the waiting taxi.

That was on one of the first days. Later I did not have the energy or the hope.

I was never able to think effectively about my predicament. The 'treatments' every night prevented that. My waking hours were dominated by the memory of past nights and the dread of those to come. After I had undergone many 'treatments' – by that time the 'doctor' listened carefully to my heart each night before he administered the drug – the lethargy that fell on me precluded anything but fugitive imaginings, vague dreams of surcease.

One thing I did do. I memorized the furnishings and descriptive details of Nan's apartment. This was mainly an intellectual exercise, an automatic attempt to keep a disused member functioning, for I had little hope. I felt sure that eventually the 'treatments' would be carried too far – one spasm would prove too rigorous – and I would die or suffer severe brain damage. But it is difficult to kill hope. While I despaired, I looked about me, memorizing.

It was a large room with a fireplace; wide French windows opened on a terrace that overlooked the Park. Above the fireplace was a circular mirror of blued glass, on either side of it stood two figurines – a man with his hands outstretched, reaching, a woman kneeling in the attitude of propitiation. The carpet was a neutral grey; the bookcases along two of the walls held brightly-jacketed novels. The large radio-phonograph was of blond wood . . .

I had no need to study the faces of my captors, Tony and Nan. I was confident that I would never be able to forget either of them (how misplaced my confidence was, since I was only now remembering). Tony's clothes were of good cloth, but too severely cut, the patterns too distinct, the shoulders padded. For hours on end I watched his reflection in the fireplace mirror as he stood guard by the front door or lounged in one of the chairs in the entry hall. Regularly every few minutes he would smooth his slicked hair with the back of his hand, then run his fingers over his moustache. He seldom smoked; only infrequently did he exchange more than a few monosyllabic words with Nan. They seemed unwilling companions.

Nan was unhappy. She managed to keep busy, spending her time reading, listening to the radio, preparing our food. But there were periods in each day when she would stand by the windows and look out over the Park. She never ventured out on the terrace, nor did she ever comment on the weather. She would stand quite straight, her hands at her side, barely breathing. It occurred to me that she might well be as much a prisoner as I, and that Tony might guard her as well as myself. But when I tried to get her to confide in me, she repelled me with silence. Or 'I work for him,' she would say. 'He pays me well.'

And I would curse myself for being a sentimental fool.

My escape came entirely by accident. One night the taxi we were riding in – we were bound for the 'doctor's' office – collided with a truck. The door beside me was thrown open by the force of the collision. Tony, who had been sitting beside me on the collapsible seat, and I were thrown to the sidewalk violently. I fell on top of him; his body cushioned my fall. I was not hurt; but he was badly injured, I think. His head was twisted strangely around and his eyes were staring and glassy, although he was still breathing. I did not linger to examine him closely – the circumstances were such as to make me forget the Hippocratic oath; instead I staggered as fast as I could down the crowded street towards the river. I looked back only once. A crowd had gathered around the upset vehicles and a police car had already reached the scene. I thought I saw Nan waving at me, motioning to me to go on.

But I am not sure.

The sound of the door opening brought me back to the present. Sonia came into the room. She reached up for the cord that dangled from the ceiling and pulled on the light; it had grown dark without my knowing it. Now I felt Sonia's body next to mine on the bed – her lips soothing my forehead – before my light-dazzled eyes could construe the outlines of her face, her soft, dark hair. I held her close to me.

'My poor darling,' she said. The soft stuff of her blouse whispered against my shirt. I half rose, then fell – convulsively – upon her, bore her to me. We were together many minutes under the bald brilliance of the unshaded electric bulb. Her body had the warmth of fever, while I rid myself of a cold, mechanical urge. Later, the shame-lessness of the dangling light bulb seemed to mock me and I walked across the room to turn it off. Sonia lay watching me, a smile on her lips.

'Why did you do that?' she asked.

'It hurt my eyes,' I said. I sat down on the chair. The slats were cold to my flesh.

'Aren't you coming back?'

'I have come back. That's the trouble.'

'I don't understand you, John.'

It was queer sitting there on the cold chair in the black-ness of the small room. I felt then that Sonia was hardly real, and that I was even less so. Although I heard her voice, I would have been only too glad if I could have per-suaded myself that she did not exist . . . that my being in this room, at this time, close to her was but another part of a continuing nightmare. But I could not deny her reality. The last quarter-hour had been only too real.

'You're acting so peculiarly.' Her voice sounded hurt.

'My name isn't John,' I said. 'I told you before that my name is George Matthews.'

'I've always called you John.' Her tone was flat, subdued, a dissonance.

'I explained how that came to be,' I said. 'Perhaps, I should have told you that I still love my wife . . . that someday I hope to go back to her . . .'

Sonia did not speak. I felt I knew what she was thinking. 'Yes, I will,' I said, as if my affirmation could, once and for all, refute her unspoken denial. 'I know the way I look. I know that many things could have happened to come between us in this past year. But I'll take the chance. I tell you that she loves me. I know that she will understand . . .'

I could hear Sonia moving about on the bed. She was dressing. I went over to the bureau, knocked against the wall and scraped my shin in the dark, and found my shirt. While I was groping for my trousers (I had thrown them on the floor a short time before), Sonia spoke again.

'I'll need the light. You might as well pull it on.'

I did. She was standing beside the bed trying to button her blouse. I saw that I had torn it badly. The fabric was hanging loose from one shoulder.

'I'm sorry,' I said. 'I'll get you another.'

'It doesn't matter. I have others.' She walked to the closet and began to take her clothes off the hangers. When she had all her slacks and sweaters she laid them on the bed. She went over to the bureau and began to empty another drawer that contained her other things. I watched.

'Where will you go?' I asked stupidly. I had become used to her – more than that – and now I realized that I did not want her to leave.

'I have a place of my own.' She said this sharply. Then she glanced up at me. 'Surely you remember that?'

'Yes. I haven't forgotten.'

She sat down on the bed. The vari-coloured garments

in her lap began to slip and fall on the floor. She made no move to pick them up. 'What's wrong with you?' she asked.

'I think I am suffering from the after-effects of prolonged insulin shock and repeated concussion,' I told her. 'That kind of shock frequently results in extended amnesiac periods. At least, I think that is what is wrong with me. I have all the characteristic symptoms.'

She put her hand to her forehead and looked away from me. 'I don't understand.'

I told her what I had remembered about Nan and the 'doctor' and his 'treatments'. I tried to tell my story quickly and not to emphasize its more terrible aspects, but even so she reacted emotionally. It was the first time I had seen her cry. 'Oh, how terrible!' she said. 'Why did they do all that to you? What was behind it all?'

'That's what I want to know,' I said. 'And that's what I intend to find out – not only "what", but also "who".'

She sat quietly. Her eyes never left mine. 'Why won't you let me help you?' she asked.

'I told you. I am married. I have a wife. This business between us can't go on.'

She hesitated before she spoke. Her eyes were still wet and some of her hair had fallen over her brow. 'That doesn't matter – you must understand what I say. Your wife, what you intend to do later – none of that matters. Only let me help you now. I don't want to leave you . . . alone.'

After Sonia had hung her clothes back in the closet and put her other things back in the bureau drawer, we sat across from each other while I told her again (she insisted on knowing every detail) the entire story of my strange experience. I began at the beginning with Jacob's appearance in my office and worked slowly forward to the accident in the taxi and my escape. There, as before, I stopped.

Sonia leaned towards me, her dark hair eclipsing her eyes. 'Can't you remember anything more? That's a lot of it, of course, but not enough to take up the time from the middle of October until the first of May.'

'There is more,' I admitted. 'Not much . . . I don't think it tells us anything.'

'Let me judge that,' she said.

I stood up and walked to the window. The street lights were out and only an occasional glimmer from a house or restaurant enabled me to descry the man who was still leaning in the doorway across the street. Anderson's man. A chill ran down my back as I remembered that he was placed there for my protection. I turned back to Sonia.

'After the accident I ran for blocks until I could run no more. By then I was in the neighbourhood of the East River. I entered the courtyard of an apartment house and sat on a bench opposite a fountain. I don't know how long I sat there. It must have been for hours. I know it was late at night when I finally got to my feet and began to walk to the other side of town. I had only one idea: to get home to Sara. It was like an obsession.'

'Sara is your wife?'

'Yes. Haven't I told you her name before?'

'If you have, I don't remember.'

'I had a very hard time getting home. I had no money. They had been thorough – they had thought of everything, even of taking my billfold away from me. I had to walk. By the time I reached the George Washington Bridge, far up on Riverside Drive, and clear across town, I was literally dead on my feet.'

'How did you get into Jersey?' Sonia asked.

'There is a bar near the approaches to the Bridge. I went in and begged. I had little success at first. I guess I was dishevelled and weary enough to look drunk. Then a man gave me a quarter and another man gave me a dime. That was enough to get home on.'

'Poor George!' I looked at Sonia, aroused by the feeling in her voice. There was no doubting the depth of her emotion. She was sincerely moved by my story – I only hoped she did not pity me.

I hurried on, embarrassed. 'I took a bus to my town,' I said. 'And then I was on my own street, walking towards my own house. Only then did I begin to wonder about the reception I would get; until then I had not realized that, since I had no way of knowing how long I had been missing, I had no way of knowing whether Sara was still my wife!'

'Did you have doubts?' Sonia was surprised.

'Only for a moment. Put yourself in my place. How would you have felt if you had gone through what I had? My experiences had been so terrible that I found it difficult to believe that they were over and done with and that I would be allowed to resume a normal life. It was too much to expect that in a few minutes I would be home, kissing my wife, safe at last.'

'Then what happened?'

'I'm getting to that. I remember going up on the porch and ringing the doorbell. I remember noticing that there were lights on downstairs, although it must have been after midnight. I don't remember anyone answering the doorbell though . . .'

'Don't you know?'

'No. I can't be sure. The rest is very confused. The next thing I remember and, I believe, the last thing I remember until I recall coming to in the psychopathic ward of the hospital is a terrific, blinding pain in my head – not that I feel again the pain, but that I know that I felt such a pain. After that . . . nothing. I must have lost consciousness at that point.'

'But what happened?' Sonia had jumped to her feet. Her eyes seemed to be starting out of her head. I went to the window and lifted the blind to look for Anderson's man. The sight of him lounging in the dark doorway across the street was reassuring to me.

'I don't know what happened,' I said. 'Somebody must have hit me on the head with a blackjack or a gun butt or something equally murderous. I suppose that blow, coupled with the incessant strain and stress of the shock treatments, did me in for sure. I must have suffered a concussion in the subway, you see; amnesia often follows concussion. Amnesia also often follows metrazol or insulin injections. And severe amnesia almost invariably follows frequent head injuries. Concussion plus the repeated shock of the "treatments" plus another concussion . . . I marvel that I am alive!'

'But why would anyone try to kill you on your own door-step? And who would do such a thing? It couldn't have been Tony – you said he was injured badly in the auto crash.' Sonia thought for a moment, her hand at her fore-head. 'Could Nan have followed you?' she asked.

I shook my head. 'Sonia, I tell you I don't know! It's only one more thing I must find out.'

We talked it all over a thousand times that night, in fact, we talked until the light began to seep under the drawn blind. I crossed to the window and saw that another detective stood in the doorway across the street, a heavier, older man than the one who had been there before. The night had fled; it seemed as if the hours had never been, yet neither of us felt tired or needed sleep. Indeed, we were both ravenous and Sonia set about at once to prepare breakfast.

With the smell of fresh coffee and bacon in my nostrils, I thought back over the tentative conclusions we had arrived at during our night-long discussion. 'Sonia,' I said, 'I am going to call out the major steps in our plan for action while you're busy there. I want you to stop me and correct me if you think of anything I've missed.'

'All right, George,' she said, 'I'm listening.'

'First of all,' I said, 'there is what I shall call the "time-table" of my amnesia. It begins when I fell or was pushed in the subway on the morning of 12 October 1943. I then lost consciousness for a short period of time, no more than a few hours, regaining it when I awoke in Nan's apartment. From then until I escaped from the taxi and made my way home a month to six weeks later, the period of the "treatments", I must have been conscious a good part of the time. When I was struck a second time on the porch of my house, I lost consciousness for a longer period – or if I did not lose consciousness for the entire period, I did lose my ability to remember what happened then. As it is I have no memory of what happened from that instant until I awoke in the hospital – an interval of probably seven months.'

Sonia gestured with the cooking spoon she held in her hand. 'What do you suppose did happen during that time, George? Are you sure you can't remember anything?'

I shook my head. 'Not a thing. I believe that the key to the puzzle lies hidden in those lost months. Or I may have just wandered aimlessly. Remember the police report they had at the hospital said, "John Brown, homeless, picked up wandering".'

'But you must be able to remember something that happened during all that time!'

'Not necessarily. Amnesia plays queer tricks, especially amnesia that is at least partially conditioned by the use of shock therapy. When they were first learning to administer shock treatments to patients, before the improved electrical methods were perfected, I have seen schizoids return to consciousness after the spasm to find that they could not remember their names or their previous illnesses! Those patients often effected a complete recovery, except that it would be days or even months before they regained their memories. Now, however, with the refinement in technique such amnesia is only an occasional concomitant of the treatment and short-lived. But I have no assurance that the "doctor" who administered the drug in my case knew or even cared about modern methods. It was his job to make each injection as traumatic as possible to make me tell Jacob's whereabouts. He may not have known that amnesia would be the result, or he might not have cared.'

Sonia laughed abruptly. 'But you're not suffering from schizophrenia!'

'That makes little difference. It is the extreme effect the sudden shock has on the brain and nervous system that induces amnesia. Although I have never seen it used on a sane patient, I think such a patient would be just as likely to forget after extended treatment as a schizoid.'

Sonia went back to her cooking. 'I hate to think what you must have been like during those months without a home or money, not being able to remember who you were or what.'

I did not like to think of it either. It is difficult to think of oneself as being destitute, vagrant, a bum. No wonder the staff at the hospital scoffed when I claimed to be a psychiatrist: they had seen me when I was admitted and thought I was just another wandering lunatic with delusions of grandeur.

'Let's get back to the "time-table",' I suggested. 'I can't remember what happened from the moment I lost consciousness in Jersey until the day I awoke in the mental ward. We do know, roughly, how long that was. Frances Raye was murdered on the twelfth of October 1943. Since it must have been at least a month or six weeks after that when I escaped from the taxi and went home that would make that day sometime in the last part of November or the first of December 1943. Then from December 1943 until the first of May – the day I entered the hospital – is still a blank.'

'How long did you stay in the hospital?' asked Sonia.

'Until the twelfth of July 1944. That's a little over two months. I shall never forget the day "John Brown" walked out of that place a free man.'

Sonia smiled slowly. She finished putting the plates of bacon and eggs on the card table. 'And now it's the end of August and if you don't come eat your eggs they'll get cold.'

I joined her at the table. 'The other night when I was struck by the car, the knock on my head did something again, relieved a pressure, perhaps. I believe that eventually I'll remember everything, even that long blank

147

period. Yesterday, when I came to after my accident in the street, I was confused for an instant. It seemed as if something I had forgotten, something I have not remembered yet, was struggling to come to the surface of my mind.'

'You can't tell me what it was?' Sonia was watching me intently. A frown wrinkled her forehead.

'No. As I said it is all coming back, but in its own way, capriciously, in patches. I am still confused but ultimately everything will fit into place.'

'Then when you awakened night before last in this room, the first person you saw was that funny little man, Mr Mather, and you thought you were awakening from your fall in the subway!'

'Only for a moment, for one perplexing instant, did I think that. But I pretended that I did not remember anything more at that time in an attempt to learn something from Felix.'

'Are you glad I was here?' she asked, not looking at me.

'Very glad,' I said.

We ate our breakfast and afterwards I helped her wash the dishes. When the room was straight again, the dishes back in place in the closet next to the hot-plate (we used the washstand for a sink), we lighted cigarettes. Sonia sat on the bed, while I sat on the one chair.

'Now what are we going to do?' she asked.

'I've decided to wait until Anderson comes,' I said. 'He promised to be around this morning. Then we'll get the facts on Frances Raye's death from him, how she was killed and under what circumstances – if possible, we'll get him to take us to the scene of the crime. Until you spoke of it last night I had never realized how incongruous it was for me to know practically nothing about the murder that seems to have gotten me into all this trouble.'

Sonia sat swinging her legs over the side of the bed. 'Yes,' she said, 'there must be some connection.'

'Then I think we should call on Eustace – I mean Felix

Mather – and take Anderson along to see if we can't get him to tell more of what he knows,' I said.

'Do you think he knows more than he is saying?'

'I still don't understand how he knew me now that I have this.' I fingered my scar. 'When he first saw me I looked entirely different.'

'Perhaps not as different as you think. Anyway, that was no reason for trying to strangle the poor little fellow!' Sonia came over and put her arms around me to show that she did not mean to sound too severe. I looked up at her long, intent face. 'George,' she said, 'don't be hard on Felix. I think he was telling you the truth the other night.'

Sonia was too near me – suddenly I did not like the feeling I had when she was close to me like this, as if Sonia, not Sara, were my wife. As if Sara was over and dead like the past. 'But you should love Sara,' I told myself. 'It is not her fault that all this has happened. She will want you to be with her again. You cannot go on like this.'

I pushed Sonia away and stood up. She went over to the bed and began to smooth the covers; she was trying not to show me that I had hurt her. I walked to the window and looked out. Anderson's man was still there. 'I think we must see Felix again,' I said.

'You're probably right,' sighed Sonia. 'Only the one I'd see first would be Nan. You know what she did to you!' Her voice had risen until she was almost shouting. I realized that we were on the verge of a quarrel and I did not want to quarrel with Sonia. She was right about Nan, too. I should see her first.

I stood staring out of the window, biting my lip to keep from saying the hot words I felt compelled to say. I knew that I was being unfair to Sonia and that my desire to talk again to Felix was nothing but a hunch. I also knew that the real cause of my irritation had nothing to do with the investigation I proposed to make. If I had a friend it was Sonia, yet somehow she stood between me and Sara. Sara who was . . . well, for all I knew . . . little more than a comfortable memory.

149

I had been looking at nothing in particular, but all at once I realized that the man who had been on vigil across the street was no longer there. I half-turned to comment on this to Sonia when the doorbell rang. Sonia answered it.

Anderson stood outside, his mild face dour. The heavy-set man who had been on watch was directly behind him. I asked them in.

The Lieutenant walked into the room, then stopped in his tracks. He looked at Sonia and again at me. 'Bill, here, tells me that neither one of you left the building all night. Is that right?' he demanded.

Sonia answered, 'We haven't left this room.'

Anderson's shoulders drooped. He clenched his fist, then relaxed it. 'I told you yesterday that we had a mighty cold trail to work on, Doctor. Well, it's warmed up a little overnight. Nan Bulkely was found shot to death this morning.'

His usually pleasant blue eyes were boring into mine. I returned his stare. 'Where? In her apartment?' I asked, more to make a response than because I was curious; more to hide my own amazement than because I expected the place of Nan's murder to be significant.

'Her body was found on the doorstep of an apartment building on West Tenth Street five minutes after seven o'clock this morning by a milkman who was making a delivery. She had been shot through the temple with a .45 automatic equipped with a silencer that was found lying in the street a few yards away. The medical examiner has set the time of her death as occurring at any time during the previous six hours.' Anderson recited these facts rapidly and mechanically, and with a trace of disgust. He continued to stare at me so steadily that I was discomfited.

'I'm sorry to hear that,' I said. 'But we didn't have anything to do with it. Your own man will tell you . . .'

He cut me short with a wave of his hand. 'I'm not saying you had anything to do with it. I just want to know where the goddam horse came from!'

'What "goddam" horse?' I asked.

Anderson's face was a mask of exaggerated disapproval. 'A percheron, one of those big truck horses, was found tethered to the lamp post next to where the body was found. He had a feedbag tied on and a red ribbon in his mane.'

I regarded Anderson and Anderson regarded me. It was one of those looks that convey absolutely no meaning, but establish a community of disbelief. I kept thinking 'This is where I came in.'

But there was no convenient exit that led out of the movie and into the sane and sunny street.

11   The Beginning of the End

Anderson wanted us to go with him to the scene of the crime. On the way over in his car, I realized that for some reason West Tenth Street was significant to me. I turned around and asked Sonia, who was sitting in the back seat, 'Do we know anyone who lives on West Tenth Street in Manhattan?'

Before Sonia could answer, Anderson cut in, 'If the street sounds familiar to you, the address would sound even more so. It's the same address as Frances Raye's.'

My voice showed my surprise. 'Do you mean that Nan Bulkely was killed in front of Frances Raye's house? Why that means both killings have occurred at the same address! Why?'

Anderson shook his head. 'Don't ask me why. The more I get to know of this case, the more "whys" I can think of myself.'

'But doesn't that mean that the same person must have murdered both Raye and Bulkely?' Sonia asked excitedly.

'It may indicate that,' Anderson conceded. 'Or it may mean that whoever killed Bulkely wanted us to think that she was killed by Raye's murderer.'

Bill Sommers, a fat detective, sat forward in his seat. 'You know, lady, murderers do funny things sometimes. Take this horse that keeps popping up, for instance. Now I gotta theory about that horse.'

'Yes?'

Sommers laid his large hand on Sonia's trousered knee. 'I think that horse is the most important clue we got to who done these murders,' he said. 'Only a guy with a sense of humour would think up a gag like that. The horses don't serve any useful purpose that I can see. He just thought it would be cute to tie a big horse to a lamp post every time he killed somebody.'

'Well,' said Anderson, over his shoulder, keeping his eyes on the road ahead. 'Let's hear your theory, Sommers.'

'That's it,' said the detective. 'We gotta look for a guy with a sense of humour. A funny guy. A card. That's all.'

'Huumph!' was Anderson's only comment. He kept his eyes on the street. Sommers kept his hand on Sonia's knee. She looked down at it, regarded it as she might some peculiar creature that she had just laid eyes on for the first time in her life, then gently removed it.

But Sommers had given me an idea. There was something in what he said, although that something was probably not what he had intended. In the last analysis the psychology of the murderer and of the practical joker did differ only in degree. Both were sadists, both enjoyed the pleasures of the grotesque and of inflicting pain on others. Murder might be termed the ultimate practical joke; similarly, a practical joke might be called the social form of murder.

There was little to see at the scene of the crime. Both the horse and the body had been removed. Two policemen stood talking to the superintendent of the building; Anderson approached them and joined in the talk. Sonia and I looked around at the sidewalk, the lamp post. What we expected to see, I do not know – blood, perhaps? We saw nothing. Sommers stood leaning against the fender of the police car, his hat tipped over his face to keep the morning sunshine out of his eyes. He seemed about to fall asleep.

After a few minutes, Anderson came back to us. 'I talked to the super,' he said, 'and he's going to let us into the apartment that used to be Frances Raye's. The lady who lives there now is out for a few hours.'

As we followed him into the foyer of the small apartment building, I said, 'You don't expect to discover any significant fact about Raye's murder here now, more than nine months after it happened, do you?'

Anderson jabbed the elevator button. 'You never can tell in this business. Finding that body outside this morning makes me wonder.'

'Won't you need a warrant?' Sonia asked.

'The super is taking the responsibility and I'll back him up if necessary. We won't touch anything and they'll never know the difference. A warrant would take too long.'

The elevator came and we went upstairs. Anderson opened the apartment door with the superintendent's key. It was a medium-sized flat, impeccably clean, furnished with severely modern furniture. Anderson stood in the middle of the living room and pointed at the floor. 'This is where we found Raye's body,' he said. 'She lay flat on her face. She had been stabbed in the back, but the knife was not to be found. There were no signs of struggle. The doors and windows were all unlocked, but the apartment was in order. We took fingerprints all over the place, but the only recognizable impressions we found were those of Raye herself and her maid's. Since the maid could prove that it was her day off, that got us nowhere. The only conclusion we could reach was that the murderer was a friend who had just walked in. and since she knew him she did not raise a fuss.'

I kept looking about the apartment – it fascinated me. I wandered into the bedroom and Anderson followed me. This room was finished in powder blue and one whole wall was a mirror. There was a low vanity and a chaise-longue beside the bed. Nothing else was remarkable.

We walked into the kitchen. Anderson opened the dumb-waiter and peered down the shaft. 'This is big enough for a man to get into,' he said, his voice reverberating in the empty shaft, 'but the super says he keeps it locked at both the bottom and the top. He insists that it was locked on the night of the murder, too. So whoever did it couldn't have escaped that way, not that there weren't other ways, plenty of them, that he could have used.'

I cleared my throat. 'Andy,' I said, 'I know something more about the man who pretended to be Jacob Blunt. The man you released into my custody.'

He looked at me suspiciously. 'You do?'

'Yes. He held me prisoner for many weeks. He and Nan Bulkely. His name is Tony. I began to remember it all last night . . .' And I told him about my ordeal in Nan's Central Park apartment, about the 'doctor' and his 'treatments', Tony's probable death and my escape.

When I had finished Anderson said, 'Why didn't you tell me this before?'

'I only remembered it last night.'

'Do you know when this took place?'

'Not exactly. It must have started the same day Tony was released, the day after Raye's murder. But when it ended I can't tell for sure, perhaps a month or six weeks later.' I told him about my 'time-table' then.

'When you went back to Jersey after your escape, did you see anyone you knew? Somebody who could remember seeing you and help us arrive at a probable date?'

'No, I didn't.'

'Are you sure you didn't see your assailant before you were struck that night on your front porch? Haven't you any idea who it might have been who attacked you?'

'No. I'm sorry, but I did not see who it was.'

'There was someone in the house though?'

'There was a light on in the house.'

'Are you sure you didn't see your wife?'

'I tell you I saw nobody, Andy.'

Anderson sat down on the kitchen stool, pulled a cigar out of his pocket and bit off the end. Sonia, who had been in the living room, came into the kitchen. She saw the frown on Anderson's face and looked questioningly at me. 'I have just told him what I remembered last night,' I said in answer to her unspoken question.

Anderson kept silent for a long time. Finally, he looked

up at me. 'You are certain you don't remember anything after you lost consciousness on the porch of your house? From then on remains a blank? You're not holding back anything?'

'That's all I remember. You see,' I said, 'I think being hit on the head served to bring on my amnesia. It might have overcome me anyway, or it might not – but with the effect of the concussion to add extra pressure, my loss of memory was certainly aggravated. I may have recovered from the actual blow in a few minutes, returning to a state of consciousness that resembled the normal, but at that time I probably could not remember my name.'

Anderson looked at his watch and stood up. 'We're not doing anything sitting here,' he said. 'Let's go back to Headquarters and see what the boys have dug up on the Bulkely murder. I had a man following her last night, you know. He says she left her building about ten minutes to one this morning. She met a man outside and then they took a taxi. My man was too busy hailing a cab himself to see what the man looked like. He followed their cab to Sheridan Square where he was stopped by a traffic light. He would have had the driver crash the light, but he saw them draw up to the kerb across the street and leave the taxi. He jumped out of the cab and followed them into a night club – there are several there, you know. But when he got inside he could not find them. Like a fool he looked all around the club before he asked the doorman where they had gone. The doorman had seen them. He said they came in, looked around at the crowd, then left. Somehow my man had missed seeing them. When he reached the street, they were nowhere in sight. And that's the kind of rotten break we've been getting all along!

'I've a hunch that whoever it was that Nan met is the one we're looking for, the one behind it all. Now, at least, we know that Bulkely had a part in your kidnapping. She may have been killed because she knew too much.'

'Don't forget that only yesterday she was in your office making a big point of having seen me in the cafeteria.

There must be a reason for that stratagem,' I reminded Anderson.

Anderson nodded his head. 'That might have been an attempt to discredit anything you told me in advance.'

'If so, a pretty clumsy one. Because it tied right in with my story.'

He shook his head. 'Don't be too sure about that,' he said. 'It might have been just clumsy enough to look like the truth. I remember thinking yesterday that perhaps I was wrong in believing your story without more investigation. You had been released from a mental hospital recently – then this girl comes down with a report that she had seen you. She reminds me that you might be the one uninvestigated suspect in the Raye case, and that it might be profitable for me to look you up. When you walk in and ask to see me – Nan could not have expected that you would come so quickly – it would have been better for her if you had come the next day – it looks like you know you've been recognized and had decided you had better give yourself up before we came and got you.

'As I say, I wasn't at all sure I believed your story yesterday, and if I hadn't known you before I would not have been inclined to give you the benefit of the doubt. That's one of the reasons why I left a man outside your door last night – not only to protect you, but to watch you. Now, of course, I know you didn't kill Bulkely, but only because I know you didn't leave your house last night.'

'You think it's likely that the same person killed both Bulkely and Raye, don't you, Lieutenant?' Sonia asked.

Anderson smiled briefly. 'I'm not answering that question yet.'

We went outside to the waiting car. Sommers was still leaning against the fender, apparently more asleep than awake, but he stiffened to attention when he saw Anderson. I looked back at the apartment building as we began to move away. A woman was climbing the steps to the front door, a small, well-dressed woman. I saw only her back, but my pulse began to pound in my throat. The woman was Sara, my wife, who was supposed to be in Chicago. I would know her anywhere. I craned my neck to stare back at her. She was fitting a key into the lock as we turned the corner and lost sight of her. Only then did I realize that Anderson had been watching me out of the tail of his eye.

'See somebody you know?' he asked casually.

'I'm not certain,' I said. I saw he was not going to let me off with that. I could lie, or I could be honest. I surprised myself by being honest. 'I guess my eyes were playing tricks on me,' I said. 'I thought I saw Sara.'

Anderson swerved the car abruptly down the next street, ignoring completely the one-way signs. 'We'll go back and see,' he said. We sped dizzily around the next corner and screamed to a stop on West Tenth Street. No one was to be seen. Anderson and I jumped out of the car and ran up the steps. Anderson rang the superintendent's bell.

'Did anyone come into the building just now?' he asked the man when he appeared.

The fellow shook his head. 'I didn't see anybody.'

Anderson glanced at the long row of doorbells. 'We could search each apartment,' he said to me, 'but we would have to get warrants for that many.'

'I wouldn't do that,' I said, having noted the hesitation in his voice. 'My eyes were playing tricks on me, I'm sure.'

He turned and started back to the car. 'Yes,' he said. 'that must be it. The last I heard of your wife she was still in Chicago staying with her parents. She said that if she ever came back to New York she would notify me.'

'I was imagining things,' I said. But as I said this, I made up my mind to come back and see for myself as soon as I could. I was certain that I had not been imagining things, but I was not sure that it would be a good idea to let Anderson know that.

We climbed back into the car and this time we went to Police Headquarters.

12 Percherons Don't Come Cheap

Anderson's desk was piled high with reports from the various men he had working on the Bulkely slaying. Sonia and I sat down while he read his way through the pile of official-looking papers. When he finished, he spoke into the inter-com on his desk: 'Tell Arnheim to report to me.'

Minutes later, a swarthy, dark-haired detective opened the door to the Lieutenant's office. He had narrow shoulders and a broad, jovial face.

Anderson spoke to him without looking up from the reports. 'You checked on that horse and its owner?'

'Yes, sir. Bide-Away Farms at Algonport, Long Island. A Mr Frank Gillespie. He rented the horse to a Miss Bulkely yesterday and delivered it to a stable on Seventh Avenue. I checked the stable, too. The horse was there from three o'clock yesterday afternoon until five o'clock this morning. It was delivered in a closed van and called for by the same van. The van belonged to Mr Gillespie. It has not returned yet although Miss Bulkely promised to have it returned last night. I reported it stolen this morning.'

Anderson snapped, 'I know all that. It's down here on your report. What I want to know is did any of your men see that van last night? Somebody must have seen it between upper Seventh Avenue and West Tenth Street!'

'I checked with all precincts, sir. No one reported it. A general alarm is out now and it may be picked up any minute. Or one of the men who is off-duty may have seen it and will report it later. Then again, it may have been noticed, but not reported because there is nothing unusual about seeing a moving van on the street, sir.'

Arnheim spoke quietly and rapidly. He had his facts well in hand. Anderson remained surly, but I could see this was his way of showing one of his men that he was pleased.

'You say here that this is the same man who sold another percheron to Miss Bulkely at the time of the Raye case,' Anderson tapped the report he held in his hand with his fingernail. 'Why didn't that come out then? Didn't we contact every horsedealer in this vicinity in an attempt to find the owner of that horse – and didn't we draw a blank on every one of them?'

Arnheim bobbed his head in agreement. 'That's right, chief – but this guy, Gillespie, admits he lied now. He says this dame, Bulkely, paid him ten grand for the previous horse. The price was so high because the horse was bought only on the condition that Gillespie asked and answered no questions. So when we came around he claimed to know from nothing.'

'How did you get him to talk this time?'

'I recognized him. He used to be in numbers before he went straight and I've seen him in the line-up again and again. He called himself by another name in those days – we got his record – and he's been up the river twice. He knew it would go hard for him if we cracked down, so he sang.'

'Promised him protection, hunh?'

Arnheim opened his eyes wide. Surprisingly, they were baby blue. 'Yeah, chief, I did. That was right, wasn't it?'

Anderson waved his hand in weak protest. 'I suppose so. You should have checked with me first, though.'

Arnheim's eyes gleamed. 'I didn't get a chance, chief. I could see this guy knew something. So I pushed him around a little.'

'How did you find him so quickly?'

'That was easy. Bide-Away Farms was printed on the nag's blanket. That was because this horse was rented, I figure. When Bulkely bought the other horse, she used her own blanket. Then we didn't have the clue.'

Anderson nodded his head. 'OK, Arnie,' he said 'that's nice work. Now I want you to trace that van. If necessary send a special squad out after it. If we find it quick enough, we may get another lead.'

When the detective had left the office, Anderson turned to me and asked, 'What do you make of that?'

'It looks like whoever is behind these killings has plenty of money,' I said. 'Ten thousand dollars for a horse! And, as far as I can see, it plays no essential part in the murder!'

'It certainly lends a grotesque touch,' Sonia commented.

That reminded me of what Bill Sommers had said about the murderer being a man with a sense of humour. I could not get that idea out of my mind. 'Just what part do you think horses play in this murder?' I asked Anderson.

He swivelled around in his chair. 'Criminals, especially murderers, are fond of the sensational. They frequently trip themselves up by adding a useless, but melodramatic, touch to their crimes. I hope it works out that way this time.'

'Doesn't Mr Arnheim's evidence prove that both these murders are the work of the same person?' asked Sonia. Womanlike, she insisted on coming back to the same point. I smiled.

Anderson was also smiling at her. 'It proves that Nan Bulkely played a part in both of them. But we knew that much already.'

I had a thought. 'There is something else, too,' I said. 'Supposing that Sonia is right and that the same person did kill both Frances and Nan – then we know that he had less money to spend this time than before.'

'How do you figure that?'

'The first time the horse was bought, wasn't it? This time it was only rented. Doesn't that indicate something?' I asked.

Anderson smiled and shook his head. '"He" didn't buy or rent either horse. Nan Bulkely bought one, rented the other. She may have been acting as agent for someone else, possibly she was. But we still have no proof of that.'

He picked up another of the reports and, after regarding it intently for a moment, flicked the switch of the intercommunications system. 'Send Miss Hanover in,' he said into the microphone. Then he looked up at me. 'Denise Hanover was Bulkely's room-mate. When my men examined Bulkely's apartment this morning they found her there. Here, I'll read from the report: "When told of Miss Bulkely's death, Miss Hanover was hysterical. Later she said, 'I know who killed her!' She was placed in protective custody."'

I felt suddenly cold. I was remembering the previous afternoon and Nan's attitude towards me. She had acted as if I were the guilty one. Could this Hanover girl know something about me that I did not know myself – that I had forgotten? I knew that my fears were neurotic and that they were conditioned by the extreme hardship and insecurity of the past months of my life, but they remained real enough. I put my handkerchief to my forehead to wipe the perspiration away. I saw that Sonia was concerned – she must have noticed my sudden pallor. Luckily, Anderson stood facing the door with his back to me so for once he did not see my reaction. Denise, seeming younger and prettier than ever before, walked into the room. Her eyes were red with tears.

I stood up and gave her my chair. She stared at me for a long moment before she sat down, her eyes glimmering with curiosity, her lips curling with revulsion. I knew that look well by now – it was the price I paid for showing strangers my face – and I had learned to take it.

Anderson introduced us and explained our presence as persons interested in the case. I said, 'Miss Hanover and I have met before in Jacob's apartment.' I saw that her eyes still stared at me and that they were large with hate. Her shoulders kept quivering. It was some time before she could speak.

'Nan's dead,' she said to me, 'and you killed her!'

Sonia jumped up and seized my arm. 'Are you sure of what you're saying, Miss Hanover?' Anderson asked.

'I know he killed her,' she said softly – so softly that her words were almost inaudible.

'How do you know?'

'He phoned her last night. She went right out to meet him. And I never saw her again.'

'You say Miss Bulkely received a telephone call that caused her to go out on the night of her death. But how do you know that the call was from Dr Matthews?'

She pointed her finger at me. 'He has been calling her up and threatening her life since last January. Sometimes, always against my advice, she would go out to meet him after one of those calls. That's what she did last night.'

'But how do you know these telephone calls, including the one you say she received last night, were from Dr Matthews?' Anderson asked again.

'She told me,' said Denise. 'But I knew it without her telling me. She used to get calls from him at the theatre – that was when she was still going with him. Then she caught him out with one of the girls from the chorus, and they had a fight and she broke off. It was then he began to threaten her. Finally she was so scared of him she asked me to come to live with her. That was this spring.'

Denise was very young, even younger than I had thought the day I first met her with Nan in Jacob's apartment. She wore too much make-up. Her face was garish now, a tear-streaked mask. Her lips were trembling so that she could hardly form her words. Strangely enough I was not surprised at what she said, perhaps, because I was past being surprised.

Anderson, though, was taken aback. He shot me a quick glance, then looked down at the papers on his desk. I could see Sonia's back stiffen and her eyes harden. All the sympathy that she had been prepared to give this girl was now gone in the face of what was, to her, an outrageous lie. But she said nothing.

'Are you certain of what you're saying, Miss Hanover? To accuse a man of murder is to make a mighty serious charge, you know? You must have the evidence to back it up.' Anderson's voice was level and steady.

Instead of answering the girl began to cry again. Her head sank until it was buried in her gloved hands and her whole body shook with genuine grief. Anderson came around from behind his desk and stood helplessly beside her, patting her back clumsily. He looked to Sonia for assistance, but Sonia's eyes were cold and indifferent. Denise quieted soon though, and took the paper cup of water that the Lieutenant had fetched from the water cooler.

She dabbed at her eyes with her handkerchief, sitting up straight in her chair, her high heels caught under the bottom rung as a child might sit.

'Let's go back to the beginning, Miss Hanover,' Anderson suggested. 'You've known Miss Bulkely how long?'

'I met her in 1941 when *Nevada!* began its run. We were both in the chorus at that time. I've lived with her since March, though.'

Anderson glanced at me. 'I didn't know that Miss Bulkely was in *Nevada!*' he said. 'What part did she play?'

The girl continued as if she had not heard his question. 'I was only in the chorus. But Nan understudied the lead. I was lonely – I had just come to New York – and she was kind to me. She never changed after she became a star.'

'When did she become a star, Miss Hanover?'

'After Frances Raye died, of course – everyone knows that!'

Sonia broke in. 'But the girl who replaced Raye was Mildred Mayfair! I ought to know, I've seen *Nevada!* three times!'

Denise nodded her head. 'Mildred Mayfair was Nan's stage name. She thought it sounded more romantic.'

'Was Miss Bulkely still playing the leading rôle at the

time of her death?' I asked. I did not notice how maladroit my question was until Denise began to cry again. 'No, Nan left the cast in June. She was tired and needed a vacation. Now she'll never be able to play it again!' Her face was taut with grief.

'What happened after she became a star, Miss Hanover?' Anderson's question was put gently, but I could see that he did not intend to be halted by her continual tears.

Denise sniffed and patted her eyes with her handkerchief. 'We didn't see so much of each other for a while. Don't misunderstand me, please. It wasn't that she went upstage. Nan was always sweet to me. It was just that she didn't have so much time to herself being a star and all . . . and having so many boy-friends.'

'You say she had many men as friends. Who were they?'

Denise sniffed again. 'I'm sure I don't know. I never pried into her personal affairs.'

'But surely you must have heard her mention some of them by name?'

'Well, yes.' Denise paused. 'Right after – no, just before she became leading lady – there was Edgar. I never saw him but he was real nice to her. He gave her a mink coat and . . . and other things. She didn't like him much though.'

'Do you know his last name?'

The girl hesitated, her face blank with concentration. 'No, I don't think I ever heard his other name. But there were others I do remember. There was Jacob Blunt. She liked him. I think he was younger than Edgar. But she stopped seeing him right after she became a star. She said he might get her into trouble about Frances Raye's death.' Denise stopped, shut her mouth tightly as if she had just realized that she might have said too much – then rushed on. 'And then there was the Doctor. He started to call her up a couple of months after she became a star, about January I think. And when she wouldn't

see him, he began to threaten her. He said she knew
something about Frances Raye she wasn't telling. And
she didn't know a thing! – not a thing, I know that! But
from then on until just last night he kept after her. Sometimes she would go out to see him, although I always
begged her not to, and when she came back she would be
limp and bedraggled looking. She'd be so frightened. And
she had reason to be frightened! Didn't he kill her?'

Denise was pointing her finger at me again.

Anderson ignored her accusation. 'When did you come
to live with Miss Bulkely? Did you say this spring?'

'It was in March. That was the funniest thing!' she
said. She hesitated, pulled at her gloved finger with her
teeth. 'She called me up one day – right out of the blue
sky! She said she was lonely and wouldn't I share her
apartment with her? Would I? Well, I should say! Her
with an apartment on Central Park South!' She stopped
and looked at me. 'But it wasn't because she was lonely,'
she said tragically. 'It was because she was scared of him!'

'Did you ever see Nan with Dr Matthews, Miss Hanover?' asked Anderson.

The girl started to speak, then stopped. She looked
down at her gloved hand and picked at a loose thread.
Looking up again, she flared: 'No, I didn't! But that was
only because he was so cagey! Always meeting her some
place late at night – never coming to see her backstage or
at home the way a decent person would!'

'How do you know then that the person who was
threatening your friend was Dr Matthews?' Anderson
was quiet and reasonable.

'Because Nan told me, that's why! Because I had no
wish to doubt her word!'

Anderson smiled, but shook his head. 'I admire your
loyalty, Miss Hanover, but such blind, unsupported belief
isn't very reliable as evidence. We know for a fact that Dr
Matthews could neither have telephoned nor murdered
Miss Bulkely last night. One of our men was watching him
all last night. He made no telephone calls since there is no

phone in his room, and he did not leave his room all night. Someone else may have been threatening your friend – someone else may have telephoned her last night – someone else certainly killed her. But it wasn't Dr Matthews.'

Denise was on the verge of tears again. 'But I tell you she was afraid. Afraid of him! I lived with her and I know!'

'Miss Hanover, would you go out to meet a man in the middle of the night if that man had been threatening your life for months?'

She shook her head.

'But that's what you say Nan did. Can't you see that she must have gone out to meet somebody else, somebody she said was Dr Matthews to keep you from knowing who she really had an appointment with?'

'But why should she lie to me?'

Her lips trembled and I thought she was about to cry again. But I was mistaken. Instead, she unhooked her heels from the rung of the chair and stood up unsteadily. The mascara about her eyes had run over her cheeks and her lipstick was badly smeared.

'Before you go, Miss Hanover, I'd like you to identify these,' Anderson said. He was holding a sheaf of letters and postcards out to her. 'One of my men found these in Miss Bulkely's desk when he searched the apartment this morning.'

Denise took them hesitantly, glanced at all of them, and handed them back quickly. 'Those are Nan's own! Why are you meddling in them?'

Anderson ignored her question. 'Are these part of the correspondence Miss Bulkely carried on with Jacob Blunt?' he asked.

Denise stood very erect and tried to look cold and dignified. 'I really wouldn't know. I never read Nan's mail.'

'But you know his name. Didn't you just say that Nan used to see him, but had stopped because she was afraid he would get her mixed up in Frances Raye's murder?'

'Yes, but – '

'But what, Miss Hanover?' There was a sharp edge to Anderson's politeness.

'But I thought she hadn't seen him since last October. She never told me that she wrote to him. I didn't know.'

'Isn't it possible that there are many things you don't know about your friend's affairs, Miss Hanover?'

'Yes, but – '

'Isn't it possible that, if Nan could carry on so lengthy a correspondence with Jacob Blunt without your knowledge, she was also deceiving you as to the identity of the person who made those threatening telephone calls?'

'I suppose so. But – '

'Then you aren't really sure just who she went out to meet, are you, Miss Hanover? You really don't know who murdered her, do you?'

'No. But that doesn't mean – '

Anderson was peremptory. He picked up one of the letters and waved it. 'You don't know anything more about this correspondence?'

Denise shook her head. 'I thought she had broken off with him.'

Anderson opened the door for her. 'I want you to remember, Miss Hanover, that Dr Matthews could not possibly have had anything to do with your friend's death. I want you to remember that he was under surveillance all last night, including the time when she was killed. I don't want you to say anything to anybody about what you've told me here. I don't want you to let anyone know you've been to see me or anyone at Police Headquarters. Keep it all to yourself. You will remember that, won't you?'

She looked up at him and fluttered her eyes. 'If you say so, Lieutenant.'

Anderson was holding the door for her. She gave him one more lingering glance that was intended to be dramatic, then swept her fur about her throat – an absurd gesture – and bounced into the hall. Anderson shut the door violently, then leaned against it. He was obviously relieved.

'What do you make of that?' he asked us.

'I'm interested to find that Nan Bulkely was Frances Raye's understudy and thus profited directly by her death. How is it that you didn't know that before?'

Anderson's face was grim. 'I should have known!' he said. 'Somebody slipped up on that one. At the time of Raye's death my men interviewed the entire cast of the show. But no report I ever saw indicated that Mildred Mayfair was Nan Bulkely.'

'That was probably because Nan did not want you to know that if she could help it.'

'Still we should have discovered it,' said Anderson.

'We all make mistakes,' said Sonia.

'Yes, but none of my men should make an error as bad as that.' He returned to his desk and jotted down a memorandum. I could see heads rolling on the Homicide Squad.

'I don't see why Nan lied to Denise about the name of the man who was threatening her,' I said. 'Why should she say it was me? Could it be that whoever was threatening said he was me as long as he confined his actions to telephone conversations? Then, when he finally made himself known to her, she was afraid to reveal his true identity and continued to pretend to Denise that it was me?' I put this explanation forward self-consciously. I was still very much aware that I had just been accused of murder.

Anderson was chewing contemplatively on his cigar. 'Then you would interpret her visit with me yesterday as an attempt to get the police to investigate the case again and in so doing uncover her real enemy?'

'Something like that,' I agreed. 'Isn't that the way a girl, afraid for her life, might act if she wanted police protection yet was unwilling to accuse the man who was threatening her? She used me as a pretext for coming to see you, for getting you to re-open the case.'

'But how did she know where you were?'

He had me stumped. I felt that if I could know the answer to that question, I would be able to lay my hands on the murderer. I said as much to Anderson, and added, 'I feel that Nan is the link to the murderer, in fact, we already have a certain amount of evidence to prove it. But I still don't see how.'

'What about those letters?' Sonia asked. 'May we see them, too?'

Anderson picked the sheaf of correspondence off his desk and handed it to Sonia. His eyes twinkled. 'Feminine curiosity or pure intellectual interest?' he asked.

I read them over her shoulder. They were all signed either 'Affectionately' or 'With Love'. They seemed to be in order of receipt: the earliest dated back more than six months, but the latest was no more recent than six weeks back. If she had received any letters from Jacob since then, they were not included. I pointed this fact out to Anderson.

He nodded his head. 'I noticed that. But I don't know if it's too significant at this stage of the game. There is nothing remarkable in her corresponding with Blunt. They had been close friends before. What we must find out is whether Jacob is in any way, other than that we know already, connected with Frances Raye's death, your kidnapping or Nan's murder.'

'I should think you had better get in touch with Jacob and ask him some pointed questions. Even if he is innocent of all connections with Nan's plotting, he may be able to throw additional light on the whole affair.'

Anderson agreed. 'I telephoned the New Britain police this morning and asked them to bring him to New York. I'm expecting to hear from them any moment. He has been under surveillance ever since the Raye case was tabled, however, and I doubt if he is involved in this latest development.'

'It seems to me that you ought to have investigated Jacob Blunt much more thoroughly than you have up to now,' Sonia commented drily.

Anderson stood up, pushing his swivel chair back

against the wall with a resounding bang. 'Why?' he demanded of the room. 'How can I question or hold a man when I haven't a particle of direct evidence against him? What did he do? He got drunk and assisted in tying a horse to a lamp-post. I have no definite proof that he even did that, although he admitted it. He left the scene of the crime before it occurred – again on his own word, but we have no direct evidence that he even visited the address. Before that he went to a psychiatrist who was later kidnapped – again Jacob had nothing to do with the crime. A man who is suspected of murder registers in jail under his name. That's peculiar, but not criminal as far as Jacob is concerned. The only charge I could have held him on, to the best of my knowledge, is that of disorderly conduct. And with a good lawyer he could beat that!'

'But,' protested Sonia, 'looking at the whole case from the day Jacob stepped into Dr Matthews' office until today, you must admit that Jacob Blunt has a great deal to do with it. And from what Dr Matthews tells me, whoever the person was who had him held prisoner and tortured was seeking information about Jacob's whereabouts. I just can't see how you can ignore the question of Jacob Blunt!'

Sonia was walking back and forth across the room, her dark hair swinging loosely about her shoulders. She was wearing slacks and a light polo coat, and her stride, as usual, was uninhibited by skirts. Her excitement had grown while she talked to Anderson – I had never seen her as close to anger. Anderson's ire was aroused, too. He stood behind his chair, his knuckles drumming the wood, his teeth clenched. It might have been the beginning of a real row . . . if the intercom had not buzzed just then. Anderson had to lean down to the microphone to answer it.

The voice of the receptionist sounded in the small office, 'A Mr Jacob Blunt to see you, Lieutenant. He says he wants to report a murder.'

Anderson collapsed in his chair. He was so astonished that he failed to respond to the loudspeaker's question. He sat still as a stone, staring at me blankly, while the mechanical voice kept repeating: 'What shall I tell him, Lieutenant? A Mr Jacob Blunt, Lieutenant, wants to report a murder. Shall I send him in?'

At last, Anderson leaned forward and flipped the switch. 'Yes, you might as well tell him to come in,' he sighed.

I think things were just a little too much for Anderson just then.

13 A Knife Stained Darkly

Jacob was surprised to see me. He stood in the doorway of Anderson's office looking just about the same as he had on the day he visited me. He stared at me with astonishment. This time there was no flower in his hair and he was not grinning. His brown suit seemed in want of a pressing and he needed a shave. But he was enough the same that I had the feeling that I had suddenly been carried back ten months into the past – that instead of this being the last day of August, 1944, it was 11 October 1943 – and I found myself at the beginning of it all again. I guessed from Jacob's manner that he was experiencing a similar sensation.

'Come on in,' Anderson grumbled. 'Don't just stand there. It's only Dr Matthews and he is alive and well.'

Jacob shut the door behind him. 'I thought you said he was dead.'

'It turned out I was mistaken. The body we found in the river, the one his wife identified, wasn't his – obviously. But that's a long story that will keep. Tell me what you want to see me about.'

Jacob approached Anderson's desk, but he kept looking sideways at me. I knew that he was discomfited by my appearance and that he could not take his eyes off my scar. By now I should be used to this initial revulsion people felt when they looked at me, but instead I had begun to doubt if I ever would get used to it – although I had learned to stare it down. Finally, he said, 'I'm glad to see you, Doctor. You seem to always turn up when I'm in trouble.' He swallowed and then faced Anderson. 'I – I want to report the murder of Nan Bulkely,' he stammered.

Anderson's hands had been playing with a pencil on his desk. Now they went limp and the pencil rolled off onto the floor. 'How do you know about that?' he demanded. 'Who told you?'

'I – I was with her when it happened,' Jacob said. 'I ran away afterwards. I didn't kill her, but I knew you would think I had. I went and ate breakfast and I thought it all over. Then I took a walk in the park and thought about it some more. I decided to give myself up. I – I want to face – the music.'

Anderson slammed his hand down on the desk and jumped to his feet. 'I might have known when I saw that horse,' he exclaimed, 'that this guy would be mixed up in it somehow!' He turned and glowered at Jacob. 'What do you mean you didn't kill her?'

Jacob put his hand to his head. 'We were walking along West Tenth Street,' he said, 'early this morning – we had been to a night club in the Village and we wanted a little air – when I heard a silly pop. Nan grabbed at me, started to say something, then fell in a heap as if someone had tripped her. I looked around, but I didn't see anybody. I'm sure there was no one around. But I didn't do it.' He looked appealingly at Anderson.

Anderson stared at him belligerently, his mild face twisted into a frightening scowl. 'Do you expect me to believe that story?' he asked sarcastically.

Jacob smiled submissively. 'It's the truth.'

'Haven't you forgotten something?'

Jacob shook his head. 'No, that's all that happened. We were walking along, and there was this pop, and –'

Anderson walked around his desk and laid one hand on Jacob's shoulder, an almost fatherly gesture. 'Tell me, son, didn't you forget that goddam horse? Didn't you forget all about that stinking percheron?' Anderson was being nasty, but I could not blame him for his bad temper. Too many things had gone wrong in the last few hours.

But Jacob did not understand the reason for Anderson's irony. He was only puzzled. 'What percheron?' he asked.

'I didn't see a horse this time. We were walking along and I heard –'

'Yes, yes, I know!' cut in the Lieutenant. 'You heard a bang and you looked and there was Nan, dead. It's a sad story – a very sad story.'

Jacob was shaking his head in obstinate disagreement. 'It wasn't a bang, it was a pop. A sound like – like a paper bag makes when you bust it, only hollower. It was so quiet I couldn't tell where it came from.'

Anderson glared at Jacob. I knew that he was venting all the irritation and bad temper that had accumulated during the past day on this boy. Jacob had the misfortune of being the straw that broke the back of Anderson's camel. 'Why don't you let him tell his story in his own way?' I suggested.

Anderson glanced at me, then returned his glare to Jacob. 'All right,' he said. 'Begin at the beginning. Tell me what you were doing in New York, and tell me' – he reached into the pile of papers on his desk and grabbed one of Nan's letters – 'what is the meaning of this?' He shoved the letter at Jacob.

Jacob looked at the letter and handed it back. 'That's only a letter I wrote to Nan,' he said.

'But why did you write to her? I thought you told me you were married?'

Jacob ran his hand through his curly hair and looked steadily at the ceiling. 'I am,' he said. 'I'm married all right.'

'But these are love letters,' said Anderson. 'You say all kinds of silly things in them. They're enough to turn a man's stomach!'

Jacob stood stiffly, but not without dignity. His face was flushed and he was perspiring heavily. 'What difference does it make to you what kind of letters I write?' he demanded weakly. 'I'm not living with my wife any more. In fact, she's getting a divorce. But what do you care about that?'

'I care this much,' Anderson snapped. 'The woman

who received these letters was murdered this morning. She had been receiving threatening telephone calls for some time. She received the last of these calls last night, about twelve-thirty. She went out to meet the person who called. You tell me that you were with her last night and that you were with her when she was shot. It looks to me like you – who wrote her ardent love letters, who were the last one to see her alive – were also the same person who made the telephone calls and finally carried out your repeated threats by killing her. And to think that now you have the brass to come into my office and try to lie your way out of your crime with the most absurd, damn-fool story I've ever heard!' Anderson slammed his fist down on his desk, knocking papers in all directions. 'Well,' he snorted, 'you may fool the Doctor, but you aren't fooling me!'

Jacob looked dazed. He hesitated, then he said in that worried tone I knew so well, 'I didn't call Nan up last night. I met her outside the apartment building.'

Anderson continued to stare belligerently at him. 'Go on, Jacob,' I said. 'Tell us what happened.'

Jacob's eyes rolled nervously, his face twitched. Anderson had frightened him badly and it was a moment before he could speak. 'I decided yesterday to come to town for a few days. My wife had just left me for good – we never did get along, and now I know I never should have married her – and I felt like being alone and getting good and drunk. So I gave the sheriff's man you had watching me the slip and came on into town.

'I had been writing Nan off and on for the past year. Recently she had stopped answering my letters, why I don't know. I thought I might drop around to her place and see if she wanted to go night-clubbing with me. As my taxi stopped in front of her building, I saw her coming out of the apartment door. She saw me about the same time and she rushed up to me and threw her arms around me. She was very excited about something, in fact, as I held her I could feel her tremble. She said, "Oh, Jakey, I'm so glad to see you! Take me some place quick!"'

'Did she say why she was glad to see you?' I asked. Anderson was leaning back against his desk pretending not to listen to what Jacob was saying. He had a you-can-go-on-with-this-if-you-want-to-but-I've-made-up-my-mind expression on his face. 'Or did she say why she wanted you to take her some place quickly?'

Jacob nodded his head. 'As soon as we were in the taxi I asked her what was wrong. She said she had just had a fight with Denise and that she was so disgusted she did not want to think about anything. I didn't think she was telling me the truth, but I couldn't say so. "Take me some place where there is music and dancing, Jakey," she said. I felt sure she wasn't telling me all that was wrong. But I didn't feel like quibbling just then. I let her lean back against my shoulder and I told the driver to take us to this place I knew in the Village. I had troubles of my own I wanted to forget, too.'

'Then what happened?' I asked.

'There isn't much else to tell,' Jacob showed me that bashful grin of his for the first time since he had come into Anderson's office. 'We did what you would expect us to – we got drunk. Nan was sick and I took her outside for some fresh air. We sat in the park for a while, and then I suggested we take a walk. We were walking along West Tenth Street when it happened. I just heard this pop and I felt Nan grab at me and then she fell over in a scrambled heap. At first I thought somebody had pushed her . . .'

'What time was it when you left the night club?'

'It was closing time, around four o'clock.'

'And how long did you sit in the park?'

'I don't know for sure. I was pretty drunk, you see. It was still dark when we left.'

'Make a guess.'

'I don't know. Maybe an hour, maybe longer.'

'Then it was probably between five and six o'clock when you were walking along West Tenth Street?'

Jacob nodded his head, but he looked dubious.

'And you didn't see anyone on the street when the shot

was fired? Did you notice which direction the sound seemed to come from?'

'No. All I heard was a pop, and then I was too busy trying to help Nan to look around. When I did look around, I saw no one. The pop didn't sound too close, though. It wasn't loud enough to startle me.'

I could not think of any more questions to ask. I believed Jacob's story just as I had believed his story when he had come into my office that day so long ago. But I could see where Anderson would never believe it.

'Are you through?' Anderson asked me.

I nodded my head.

Anderson pushed the buzzer on his desk. We waited until Sommers, the fat detective, came into the office. Then Anderson pointed at Jacob, 'Take this man downstairs and see if you can get him to talk. Book him on suspicion of murder, but see that he gives you a statement first. I'll be down to talk to him later.'

Jacob started to protest, then thought better of it. But he looked at Anderson for a long time before he turned and followed Sommers to the door. As he was going out the door he turned around again, and this time he decided to speak.

'I didn't see a horse,' he said falteringly. 'I didn't see a horse all night.' Then he went out the door.

Sonia and I left Center Street a few minutes later. I promised to report to Anderson the next morning – by then he would be through with his questioning of Jacob. We went up to the Village and had lunch at a sidewalk café. While we ate I told her about seeing Sara enter the building on West Tenth Street and about my intention of returning there to see if I couldn't find her. I explained that I wanted to do this alone, but asked Sonia to meet me at West Tenth Street in a couple of hours. Sonia said she would pass the time at a movie.

We parted and I walked through Washington Square to Fifth Avenue. It was one of those wonderful, clear sunny summer days when everyone seems glad to be alive. Washington Square was crowded with students, families and Fifth Avenue buses. The dogs were out in full force: pomeranians, schnauzers, greyhounds, cockers, collies, terriers of every sort and a few more weird breeds I could not name. Even the stately façades of the Fifth Avenue apartment building seemed warm and friendly, instead of cold and majestic.

But when I came to the building on West Tenth Street that we had visited that morning all my good feeling vanished. As I gazed at the long rows of mailboxes, each equipped with its own doorbell, I felt faint and weary. None of the names on the boxes was Matthews. How would I know which apartment Sara lived in? I could ring them all, but that would create a disturbance. I could ask the superintendent, describe Sara to him; but he would certainly recognize me and report the conversation to Anderson. I stood undecided, not knowing what to do.

And I began to think of my face. I saw again the first glimpse I had had of my disfigurement in the drugstore mirror; my flesh began to creep as I visualized that livid slash that divided my features, made my mouth twist into a permanent sneer. I put my hand to my cheek, feeling the smoothness of it, and imagined the look of revulsion that would come over Sara's face when she saw me. My stomach felt empty and a great weight pressed upon my chest. I was about to turn away . . .

Then I heard the door click behind me. I looked around and found myself face to face with Sara. She was smiling at me . . . she knew me . . . she seemed to accept me as I was. She was the same, unless she was a little more wonderful than I remembered. I looked at her for a long moment, afraid to speak as if in speaking I might break the magic – and then she gave a little gasp and fell into my arms. We held each other close like two kids in love. 'George,' she whispered in my ear. 'I'm so glad I've found you!'

I held her tighter, but I did not speak. I knew I did not need to tell Sara how miserable I had been. There was so

179

much to tell, enough for days, and these first few moments of reunion were precious. But if I did not speak, I nevertheless communicated my emotions to her: I could feel her trembling in my arms. 'Oh, George,' she sighed, 'I was afraid I might never see you again . . .'

We went up in the elevator to her apartment and into a small living room. This room seemed strangely familiar to me. While she took off her hat and coat, I wandered around wondering at this sense of familiarity, so similar to the feeling I had had that morning in the apartment on the floor above. When Sara came back into the room I asked her, 'Why did you take a flat in the same building as Frances Raye's?'

She seemed puzzled by my question. 'Why, that was your idea, George – don't you remember? You wanted an apartment in the building because you wanted to be on the scene of the crime. You felt it was a safe place to carry on your investigation – a place where they would never look for you.'

I sat down beside her. 'Sara, I've forgotten so many things.' For the next ten minutes I told her briefly all that I remembered in just the way I had remembered it. I told her I could remember nothing from the time I was attacked in New Jersey until I came back to my senses in the hospital. 'And now you say I was carrying on an investigation,' I concluded. 'If I was I know nothing about it now.'

When I had finished Sara put her arms around me and held me close to her. I kissed her brown hair, her up-tilted nose, marvelled at the way she wrinkled her eyes when she smiled. 'George,' she said, 'you were right here in this apartment with me all that time you can't remember. We came here after you had me rent the house in Jersey. You were terribly sick from the wound in your cheek, and you wanted no one to know where you were. You would sit in the dark and tremble at the slightest noise.'

In my joy at finding her again, I had forgotten my fear that Sara would recoil from the scar on my face. Now I was amazed to discover that she knew about it already. I asked her to tell me what had happened.

She went over to a secretary and took a long box and a small notebook from the bottom drawer. She handed them both to me, then sat down on the floor at my feet, her legs crossed under her skirt the way she always used to sit, and told me the story of my blank months. 'I was frightened the first week of your disappearance last October,' she said. 'I visited Lieutenant Anderson every day to see if he had news of you. All he could tell me was that you had left his office with Jacob and that girl – later you were to tell me that the man was not Jacob but an impostor – and that Nan had told the Lieutenant that you had left her apartment after falling in the subway and refusing medical assistance.

'All through October I heard nothing of you. I was worried sick, I didn't know if you'd been killed, or if you had suffered amnesia. Then, about the tenth of November, one night as I was packing to leave on a visit to my parents in Chicago, the front doorbell rang.'

'You say this was on the tenth of November?' I asked.

'Yes. I threw the porch light on and answered the door. At first all I saw was what looked like a bundle of old clothes slumped on the porch. I also heard a rustling noise in the yard, as if a small boy were running away. But I did not see who it was. By that time, I had recognized the bundle as you and I had seen that you were unconscious and bleeding profusely from an ugly wound in your face.'

Then my 'time-table' was off! The time I had spent at Nan's apartment was less than a month, instead of a month to six weeks.

Sara was pointing to the long box she had given me a few minutes before. 'Open it,' she said, 'and look at what is in it.' I opened the box cautiously. Inside was a thick layer of cotton-wool which I unwrapped. I saw a long, horn-handled hunting knife. The part of the cotton that had rested next to the blade of the knife was stained darkly with dried blood. As I looked at the wicked implement I felt the scar on my face begin to burn and all the hate that had been pent-up during the many months of my half-life repossessed my brain. I threw the box that contained the dagger aside.

'George,' Sara was saying, 'someone had thrown that knife at you! I found it buried in the lintel. Whoever threw it meant to kill you, George. Instead the knife struck you an awful, glancing blow and ripped half your face open!

'When you came to you told me about Nan and the "doctor" and the "treatments". You told me that you wanted to find the person responsible for Frances Raye's death, your kidnapping and the repeated attempts on your life, yourself -- that you felt that you should be the one to bring the murderer to justice.'

I realized suddenly that I had not suffered a loss of memory at the time I was struck on the porch. This meant that another, later blow caused the amnesia, and by chance I forgot what had happened when I came to on the porch! But when had I suffered the second, later blow? I felt as if this knowledge were on the tip of my tongue, that in a few minutes I would be able to say it.

'I tried to dissuade you,' Sara went on. 'It seemed to me that you had suffered enough and that it was dangerous for you to try to hunt down the killer. But you wouldn't listen to me. You had me rent the house in New Jersey and assign an agent to manage it. You even had the agent deposit the rent monthly in our bank, and to send his reports to my parents' address in Chicago where they were forwarded to us in New York! I rented this apartment, in this building, on your theory that it was the safest place to carry on the investigation unobserved because it was the last place the murderer would expect to find you. But, beyond that, when Anderson asked me to look at a body that had been found in the North River wearing your clothes – you had been dressed in an old pair of pants and a torn shirt that were not yours when I found you on the porch – you had me identify the body as you to throw even Anderson off your track!'

'But whose body was that which Anderson found in the river?' I asked.

'From the description I gave you at the time you decided it was Tony's – the man who had guarded you, who had posed as Jacob and who must have died of injuries received in the taxi accident.'

I nodded my head. It all began to fit together, although there were still many questions to be answered. And, as Sara recounted these buried details of my past, I remembered things, too. There had been a notebook that I had kept . . . a notebook in which I had put down all my findings during my investigation. I asked Sara about it.

'You're holding it in your lap, George,' she said. 'I gave it to you a little while ago when I gave you the knife. Remember, you hired the Ace Detective Agency to do most of your work for you. They interviewed Nan Bulkely and later her room-mate, Denise Hanover. From them you found out that Nan had been receiving threatening telephone calls which she said you made. You knew that you did not make those calls. I think you decided that if you could discover the identity of the person who was threatening Nan, you would have a clue to the murderer.'

I looked at the fat notebook in my hands. Here was documentary evidence about the blank months of my life. At last the past was on the verge of being recaptured! 'How long did I carry on this investigation?' I asked Sara.

Sara paled. She knelt and pressed my hands next to her breast so that the notebook fell on the floor. 'Oh, George, promise me you won't take up the investigation again. Please, promise me that!'

'It's out of my hands now,' I told her. 'Anderson has re-opened the investigation.' And I told her about the events of the last few days and of Nan Bulkely's death that morning. 'But answer my question. How long did I carry on the investigation?'

Sara stood up. She walked away from me. 'Until the last of April of this year, George. One day you went out on one of your rare trips – you know you very seldom left the house but let the detective agency do most of the actual spadework for you – and I never saw you again until this afternoon.'

'But where did I go that day?' I asked. 'And what happened to me?'

Her answer was amazing. 'I don't know what happened to you – apparently whatever it was caused you to lose your memory – but I know where you said you were going. It was an address in Coney Island. You'll find it in the notebook.'

For the next half-hour I read hurriedly through the notebook, my 'dossier' as Sara called it. The whole first section was devoted to newspaper clippings and these provided a history of the police investigation of Frances Raye's murder, most of which I already knew. I noticed that one of the tabloids had used the murder as a point of departure for a seething editorial on the inefficiency of the Police Department – small wonder Anderson was so concerned over the case!

After the many news stories came reports of what I had done from day to day. These began in late January. From them I saw that the investigation had proved slow and arduous and I had progressed little at first. As I read, I began to remember this period of my life – sometimes fragments of days would return to me before I read my curt précis of them, sometimes afterwards. I remembered the decision I made to confide in a private detective agency, and the fears that I had then that my activities would be reported to the police. But after the reports from the Ace Detective Agency began to come in, the investigation began to go forward again.

The agency had concentrated on Nan Bulkely. I had had them interview her after I had attended a performance of the long-time hit show *Nevada!* and discovered that its star, Mildred Mayfair, was Nan. One report told of a 'mysterious admirer' who had been sending anonymous gifts and making queer telephone calls. Another told of the gift of a fur coat accompanied by a card. I had pasted the card to a leaf of the notebook – how the detectives I hired managed to secure it I never knew, probably by bribery or theft. It contained only the scrawled initials: E.A.B.

On 15 March, the Ace Detective Agency had reported: 'Mayfair went out with E.A.B. after last night's performance. At the matinée today she was visibly nervous and frightened.' Later, 'Mayfair has asked Hanover to share her Central Park apartment.' This was the last of the detective agency's reports.

The next entry, and the next to last, was a long account written in my own hand of a visit I paid to a famous law firm on Broad Street. As I looked at this I remembered that interview. I had spoken to a Mr James G. McGillicuddy, an ancient barrister of Scotch descent, who had served as attorney for John Blunt's estate. His answers to my questions, all concerning the estate, had been especially guarded but he had admitted that there had been 'another bequest made by Mr Blunt that was not part of his will'. I had not been able to garner much more information on this point. Some person, or persons – Mr McGillicuddy's wording was too cautious to reveal which – had been fortunate enough to be the beneficiary of a sizeable living trust fund which had been established during old Blunt's life. I could not get the name of his beneficiary and by the terms of the trust agreement it was not a matter of court record. I stressed the fact that I was Jacob Blunt's psychiatrist and needed this information for my patient's peace of mind. 'I have heard rumours about the younger Mr Blunt which, if true, do his father's memory a disservice,' the old lawyer had said with an air of chill dignity. Then he had stood up behind his fine old colonial desk and had dismissed me with a wave of the hand and an exaggerated nod of the head that might, under more favourable circumstances, have developed into a courtly bow.

But it was the last entry in the notebook that brought memories rushing back into my mind helter-skelter, head over heels. This was nothing new. It was the photograph of Jacob's childhood friend, 'Pruney', which he had handed me that first day in my office and that I had never returned to him. As I looked at it I remembered that black moment in the subway as the train rushed past me hurling me down, and I heard Nan's voice say: 'Get the photograph!' And I remembered stepping out of the elevated station at Coney Island and looking around me. Then there were many snatches of memory, images and sounds, that were not orderly or related to one another. One was a feeling of walking down a long, twisting passage and listening to a high tittering voice mock me. Another was of just one word, the word 'ocean'; I saw it in blinding letters before my mind's eye. And then, for some queer reason, I remembered the night I had stood outside the Fun House at Coney Island and stared laughing at my crazily distorted image in the flawed mirror . . .

I felt that it was all there, that in just a moment I would understand . . . I looked down at the picture in the notebook, examined the desperate face of the small boy standing beside Jacob. I saw that the picture was pasted down only at one end and that it could be lifted up. I lifted it and saw the same initials again, this time in old Blunt's handwriting as Jacob had told me when he gave me the picture – E.A.B. But there was something else, too. I had written under those initials the name, Edgar Augustus Blunt, and the address, 5755 Ocean Avenue.

It all came back to me. I remembered every detail of my expedition that day I disappeared: the second visit to the lawyer's office when I had told him honestly what I wanted and why and he had surprised me by giving me the name and address of John Blunt's mysterious beneficiary. And I remembered going to 5755 Ocean Avenue.

And I knew who killed Frances Raye and Nan Bulkely.

*

I laid down the notebook and looked up expecting to see Sara. At first I didn't see her, although I noticed that the door to the hall was open. I smiled to myself – had I been so intent on reading the notebook that I had made Sara restless? I called, 'Sara, Sara! Where are you?' She did not answer.

I stood up to walk to the door to see if she was out in the hall. As I crossed the room I found her body stretched out where she had fallen against the sofa. She had been stabbed to death with a knife just like the one that had been thrown at me.

I picked her body up and laid it on the sofa. I bent down and kissed her gently on the forehead. I stayed there, my lips brushing the still-warm cheek. My grief was dry-eyed, perceptionless, embittered. I felt as if my life-blood had run out with hers.

Then something snapped inside me.

Epilogue

My hands will-lessly wrenched the blade from Sara's body, held it high for an instant, then threw it to the farthest corner of the room. My voice cursed. My glands poured sweat from my pores; I felt it cold and trickling. Tears purged my cheeks. Yet inside I was numb, more asleep than awake – somnambulistic.

Finally I straightened up and retreated to the chair that faced the sofa. I sat on it heavily, my gaze still riveted to Sara's body, my breathing slow and stentorian. How long it was before I lifted my eyes and looked around the room again I do not know. All I remember is that when I looked at the open door to the hall, Lieutenant Anderson was standing there.

I did not recognize him. I saw only a middle-aged man with greying hair and a sober expression. My first reaction was to be angry at this intrusion and to order the man out of my apartment. But I did not act on this impulse. A lethargy weighed on me and I sat staring at the man in the door. Then I saw that he was not alone, but that there were others behind him. I saw Jacob and Sonia. At this moment, Anderson stepped into the room, and walked over to the sofa to bend over my wife's body. I had the uncanny sensation that I was watching myself, seeing my own recent actions relived. I wanted it to stop as I felt I could not bear to watch this parody. 'Sara is dead,' I said.

Anderson turned and regarded me. His eyes were cold. 'I know,' he said. 'Why did you do it?'

Sonia and Jacob had come into the room. Sonia started towards me as Anderson spoke, but an abrupt gesture of his hand stopped her. 'Why did you kill her?' he repeated.

His question had no effect on my emotions. The split continued: one part of me heard his query, considered it, responded ('I did not kill her,' I heard myself saying); while a second part of me ignored the words, did not even hear the sound of his voice, saw no intruders, remained intact and lonely.

'Then why did you call the police a few minutes ago and say, "I want to report that I have murdered my wife, Sara Matthews"?'

'But I didn't,' I said. My answer was matter of fact, a direct response to a direct stimulus. Reason did not enter into it. My mind was numb.

'Someone did. Someone made that statement, then gave this address.'

'I made no call,' I said. 'I did not kill her.'

Anderson went over and picked up the blood-stained knife. He held it carefully in a handkerchief and held it out to me. 'You killed her with this,' he said. 'Then you threw it in a corner. I think we'll find that the fingerprints on it belong to you.

'I was reading,' I said. 'I must have been concentrating since I heard nothing. I don't know how it happened, but it did. The door to the hall must have been ajar. Someone must have thrown a knife through it and killed her. There was no sound. I think it was meant for me.'

'You say "someone". Who?'

'I don't know. The same person who killed Frances Raye and Nan Bulkely.'

Anderson shook his head. 'I think that person is you. Oh, you've been very clever, Dr Matthews, both bold and clever. If I had been you I would never have had the courage to come to the police and enlist their aid before I committed two more murders. And it almost worked. You recognized the fact that the best sort of alibi for a murderer is a psychological set of the detective's which causes him to ignore the possibility of the murderer's guilt and to seek the culprit elsewhere. I've thought it over since last night and I can see that the story you told me about your amnesia, your persecution, your experiences in the hospital, all these things were carefully calculated to render me incapable of conceiving you as the killer.

'I followed this line of reasoning and investigated further. I found that Detective Sommers was guilty of gross carelessness. He was not on duty all the time outside your house last night. When he started his shift he had not eaten breakfast and he sneaked off to an all-night restaurant. He now admits to having been off duty between five and six this morning, the very time Jacob Blunt gives as the approximate hour of Bulkely's death. Since it was early in the morning when traffic is at low ebb, you could easily have left your place, taken a taxi to West Tenth Street, shot Bulkely and returned before Sommers got back.'

Sonia protested. 'But I was with him all that time. He never left the room!'

Anderson turned to her. 'I have only your word for that. You are his friend, and probably his accomplice.'

I listened to what Anderson had to say with unnatural calm. This could not be happening to me, and even if it was – what did it matter? Sara was dead, murdered. That was all that mattered.

But Sonia was not willing to give up so easily. 'You're bluffing, Anderson!' She was standing very straight, her shoulders thrown back, her dark eyes glowering. 'You can't prove this and you know it! If George is the murderer, where is his motive?'

Anderson smiled confidently. 'I was coming to that,' he said to her. Then he looked back at me. 'You didn't succeed in "disappearing" last year as well as you thought. I knew your every move from the time you rented this apartment until I finally lost track of you last April. You did some peculiar things during those months. You hired a detective agency, interviewed a lot of people. You may have had an accident of some kind as you say, but it made you forget your whole past life, not just the immediate past. I had a man watching you day and night and I know. I had a man on duty here when you had your wife rent the apartment under an assumed name. That's how I knew where you were. I knew you visited Mr McGillicuddy, an old gentleman who was trustee of John Blunt's estate – I visited him, too. What I did not know from having you watched all the time, I learned from this – '

Anderson picked the notebook up from where I had thrown it on the floor. 'This apartment was searched thoroughly one week-end recently when your wife was away. I had photostats made of the leaves of this notebook.' He picked up the knife. 'There was another knife just like this one in the apartment then and it had your fingerprints on it.' He looked at it, then back at the body, saw that there were two identical knives in the room. 'Why, this is it!' he exclaimed. 'And I think we'll find it is the knife you used to kill Raye just as that one was used to kill your wife.'

He laid down the notebook and pointed to it dramatically. 'This alone contains all the circumstantial evidence we need to convict you. It's a very complete record of a man in search of his past. Oh, you were cagey about it – the separate entries are cryptic, but with a reasonable amount of study they lead to only one logical conclusion: your real name is not George Matthews as you would like us to believe, but Edgar Augustus Blunt!'

Jacob interrupted, 'But, Lieutenant, I don't know an Edgar Augustus Blunt. If he exists, shouldn't I know him?'

Anderson shook his head. 'No, it isn't likely you would. His existence was a well-kept secret. Your father never let you know you had a half-brother. But this man is legally your half-brother and I think blood tests will prove it. His mother was a chorus girl in a Broadway musical at the turn of the century. His father was your father. They were never married. Later his mother married a ne'er-do-well actor and threatened to reveal the existence of a son by old Blunt if he did not pay for his support. John Blunt established a living trust which was to continue only as long as the child made no claim to the name of Blunt. In the event of your death, Jacob, this man would inherit your entire estate!'

Anderson turned back to me. 'In a way I'm sorry for you,' he said. 'You must have led a hell of a life as a child. McGillicuddy told me that your mother died soon after giving birth to Frances, her second, and only legitimate, child. You were both raised by her husband and successive nursemaids, your income was stretched to support this man – a broken-down actor – and your half-sister. At one time you even met your half-brother, Jacob. McGillicuddy told me some story about you being fast friends before old Blunt found out about it and separated you. Then your step-father got a contract with a carnival and started touring the country. That is how you and Frances lived for the next five or six years until your step-father died in a drunken brawl.'

Jacob came over to me and stood looking at me. 'Then you must be Pruney,' he said wonderingly. He examined me closely, then turned back to Anderson. 'But he couldn't be, Lieutenant. He doesn't look like him! And Pruney was only a little older than me!'

Anderson riffled the pages of my notebook until he found the photograph of Jacob and his childhood playmate that I had pasted in it. When he found it, he handed the notebook to Sonia, asking, 'How old would you say this person was?'

Sonia looked at the photo for a short while, then handed the book back to Anderson. 'In his teens,' she admitted, 'although he might be almost any age. I never saw such an old face on such a stunted body. But he certainly doesn't look like Dr Matthews!'

'This snapshot was taken fifteen or more years ago,' said Anderson. 'A person can change a great deal in that length of time.'

'Dr Matthews is not Pruney,' Jacob insisted stolidly.

I felt it was about time I came to my own defence. I resented Anderson's absurd claims, particularly since I had reasoned from the same evidence to entirely different conclusions. 'I was born in Indianapolis, Indiana,' I said. 'My father's name was Ernest Matthews and my mother's name was Martha. My name has never been any other. I am in no way related to Jacob, and if you will check the records at the courthouse in Indianapolis they will prove it.'

'You will be given the opportunity to prove it,' said Anderson, 'but I doubt your ability.' He looked searchingly at me. 'I think your name is Blunt, and I know your half-sister's name is Frances Raye. I think you hated this half-sister, just as you hated your mother before her. I think you hated Jacob, too, and felt that all of them stood between you and your rightful inheritance. I think that you had planned for a long time – '

I broke in. 'Do you really want to know who killed Frances Raye, Nan Bulkely and – ' my voice broke – 'and now Sara?' I had grown tired of his wrong-headed charges.

'I think you did,' said Anderson.

'Give me a chance to prove you wrong,' I pleaded. 'Give me until tomorrow morning. If I don't have final, irrefutable proof of my own innocence and the murderer's guilt by then, you can do what you think best.'

Anderson studied me for a long moment. I thought he was going to grant my request, but then he shook his head. 'No,' he said, 'once before I took a chance with you, George – and I regretted it. Now I'm placing you under arrest – '

He reached out to take my arm and handcuff me. I hated to do it, but there was no other way out – I stepped forward and hit him hard on the side of the jaw. He fell sprawling on the floor. I ran out the door, vaulted down the stairs to the street. A policeman and a detective – Sommers, dozing as usual – stood on either side of the entrance to the house. I went past them so fast that I was in Anderson's car and had released the clutch – the motor was running – before they knew what I was doing. The car roared down the street in second. I shifted into high as I turned the corner. In rapid succession I heard shouts, the shrilling of police whistles and the windshield shattered as a bullet struck it. But by then I was in the clear – I had turned on to Eighth Street from Fifth Avenue and was racing for Third Avenue. Canal Street and the Bridge . . .

2

I had never driven that recklessly before and I hope I never have to again. I drove through traffic lights, busy intersections – once I narrowly missed colliding with a brewery truck. I ignored the brakes, using them only when the police car began to sway dangerously going around a corner or when a street car blocked my path. I turned on the radio and heard news of my escape being broadcast to all other scout cars. But by the time I reached 5755 Ocean Avenue none of them had found me yet.

I went there because this was the address I had scribbled under the name 'Edgar Augustus Blunt' on the back of the photograph months ago, and also because I had now remembered what I had done that last day of April: I had gone to 5755 Ocean Avenue to confront the murderer. One other time I had visited this address, if by accident, and that was a few nights ago when I had taken a walk in the Coney Island neighbourhood and had stood and laughed at my reflection in the crazy mirror.

Yes, 5755 Ocean Avenue was the address of the Fun House! As I drew up along the kerb in front of it, I noticed that there was a sign pasted over the box-office window that read 'Closed for Repairs'. I paid no attention to this sign but pushed up the latch that barred the flimsy, gaudily streak-painted door and walked inside.

It was pitch dark. I stood still until my eyes became

accustomed to the blackness. My heart pounded against my ribs as I saw that the only way to go was along a steep, narrow, twisting passageway. I told myself that this place was just like many amusement concessions I had visited in my childhood at Indianapolis; but my head told me that it differed in one essential: somewhere inside lurked a murderer. I began to climb the tortuous passage.

Soon I could see nothing even when I looked around for the slit of light that marked the door by which I had entered. I felt along the wall as I climbed to find that it was of the roughest plaster and an old nail that obtruded tore at my hands. I kept climbing, higher and higher. Sometimes the floor seemed to drop away from under me – these were the hinged boards meant to give pleasurable scares to amusement-seekers. Then, after I had climbed for about five minutes, the passageway began to steepen. Jets of air blew up my trousers, a thin stream of water spurted into my face. Another time I would have laughed, but instead I climbed grimly upward.

What I expected to find at the top of the passage was a way down into the interior of the Fun House. I remembered only vaguely the time I had been here before; that is, I could remember entering and climbing the same steep ascent. I remembered that other things had happened too, horrible things, but what had gone wrong? I stopped and decided to try to collect my thoughts, sort out my memories, so I would be prepared for what would happen next.

From the moment I had struck Anderson and dashed pell-mell for the car until then I had not paused for deliberation. I knew roughly what my plan was, but it had been formed under great pressure of time. Now I could afford a breathing spell. I fumbled in my pocket for a cigarette and a match and in so doing I must have shifted my weight heavily from one foot to another and pressed a movable board for the floor fell out from under me.

I was slipping, sliding, madly scrambling down, down,

down. And, at the same time, I heard a shrill laugh that went on and on in a spasm of hysterical merriment!

I slid faster and faster until my body began to scorch through my clothes because of the awkward position I had fallen into and the needless friction it caused. I knew from the way I was falling that I was going down a slide, but it was many seconds before I was thrown forward at last on my hands and knees at its bottom. As I stood up on what was apparently a gently sloping, polished surface, the lights went on dimly. These were only a few dusty bulbs strung haphazardly in odd corners of the cavern-ous, vaulted structure with its mazes of passages and sur-prising devices. The slide had deposited me in the centre of a turntable – one of those rides that begins to revolve slowly as you cling to the high centre and spins faster and faster until centrifugal force tears you away and flings you off tangentially. High above me were tier after tier of balconies, partly covered, that ringed the barnlike build-ing. When the Fun House was open, customers entered from the street as I had done, walked along these ascend-ing balconies until they reached the drop-off unexpec-tedly and fell headfirst down the slide . . . Just as I came to this conclusion, I heard again that laugh.

I looked upwards towards the ceiling and saw a catwalk high in the rafters – there, partly in shadow, his back turned to a giant switchboard, I saw my adversary – Eustace.

He was dressed in the same absurd velvet jacket, tattersall waistcoat and ridiculous mauve broadcloth trousers as he had been the first day I saw him. He looked down at me and laughed again.

I had been a fool. Now I remembered fully my previous experience in this same Fun House not more than three months before. Then, too, I had tracked him here, caught him, only to find myself caught, a helpless prisoner. And I remembered how he had freely admitted his crimes at that time, bragging about them to me. He had tried to kill me then and he had failed. Now it was my turn.

'Well, Doctor, shall we try it again?' As Eustace leaned down from his platform high above me, he flicked a switch and the turntable I was on began to revolve very slowly. 'You have regained your memory, haven't you? You have rediscovered your theory that I am the murderer!'

'Yes,' I said. 'Aren't you?'

Eustace leaned far over the guard rail of the high platform. 'Why ask me, Doctor? Why don't you tell me as you did once before? You had it all figured out. My name was not Felix Mather, not even Eustace, but Edgar Augustus Blunt, old John Blunt's unacknowledged son. You even told me why I killed Frances. You said I hated her because she was my mother's daughter and that I hated my mother because she bore me. You said that who I really hated, and could do nothing about my hate because he was dead, was my father. John Blunt. You even had a name for my motivation – you called it "illicit transference". You said my natural love for my mother had been thwarted when I was a child by my father and had turned into an unnatural obsession against Frances and Jacob, my half-sister and half-brother.'

'And I was right!' I exclaimed. Eustace leaned over the rail until he seemed to be dangling by his hand, which clung to a lever on the wall behind – actually a slim guard rail protected him.

'Yes,' he cried, 'you were right. Of course, I hated them. I hate every one of you long-legged, straight-bodied, huge, overbearing people. But Jacob and Frances I hated particularly. One of them had my father, the other shared my mother. Yet neither of them was like me. Why? I've asked myself that question a hundred thousand times. My father did not reject me because my mother was not married to him. No, he rejected me because my face and body revolted him, because he could not stand the sight of me!

'Why should Jacob be straight, handsome, tall, while I

was a dwarf? Why should Frances be beautiful, while I was loathsome and frightening? Why should I be content with a trust fund and the name Mather when a great fortune was Jacob's? Mather! I hate that name! It was my mother's name before she married Raye. When I lived with him and Frances after my mother's death – when we travelled back and forth across the country with a carnival – even then I was different. Raye lived off my money and called himself my guardian. That brat of his, that pig-tailed Frances, wouldn't even play with me! She called me Pruney. It was then, years and years ago, that I made up my mind to kill her eventually. Then one year we came to New York . . .'

'Where you used to play in Central Park. Where you met Jacob and the two of you became good friends. Why should you hate him now?'

'Jacob!' the dwarf screamed wrathfully. 'All he has is mine rightfully!' He was nearly hysterical, maniacally angry. He yelled some incoherent sentences I could not understand. Then he paused and went on more quietly. 'Jacob was my brother at one time. Really my brother. Those were the days when we played together in Central Park. I knew who he was because my mother had showed me a picture of him she had clipped from the papers before she died. He did not know who I was, yet he accepted me, liked me, was my friend. But that did not last. One day my father came and found him with me in the Park, took him away. He was never allowed to play with me again after that. And I grew to hate him, too!' His voice had risen shrilly again.

'You travelled with the carnival some more after that,' I said. 'When you came of age, what did you do with your income?'

'I bought this place for my amusement,' he shouted down at me. 'I run the controls, see?' He pressed a lever and the turntable I was on began to revolve faster. 'Every summer I sit up here, high above everyone else, looking down at all the fools who come in here, playing tricks on them. I throw the switches, press the buttons. I blow up the girls' skirts, tilt the floors, cause farting noises to sound, scare them, bedevil them, make them even more ridiculous than they seem to think I am . . .'

'When I came here in April, you admitted that you killed Raye,' I shouted up at him. 'You killed her in such a way that the police were bound to think Jacob did it – or that was the way your plan should have worked. You hired midgets from a side-show to help you persuade Jacob to do insane things, dressed them up in queer suits and provided them with money. Jacob fell in with your plan, but he acted intelligently twice. He came to see me and he refused to deliver the percheron. So when you murdered Raye, there was no one to blunder into her apartment afterwards.'

'That's right as far as it goes,' said Eustace. 'I hired Tony to drive the truck that carried Jacob and the percheron to Raye's apartment. But I did not know that Jacob would get wary and refuse to ring her doorbell. I planned to have him discover her body, phone for the police and tell them his crazy story. If he didn't get convicted of first degree murder for that they would certainly declare him criminally insane and either way I would get his fortune.

'But he told you too much for my good. And, while I was inside Raye's apartment, he decided not to go through with the delivery of the horse. I had knifed Raye and made my escape through the dumbwaiter – I got out at an empty apartment and waited in the hall until the coast was clear – when a scout car frightened Tony, the driver of the truck, just as he was delivering the horse. Caught in the act he, stupidly, told the story Jacob was supposed to tell.'

The turntable was spinning faster and faster and I was growing dizzy. But I knew I must keep Eustace talking. I remembered what had happened before, how I had tried to escape by one of the exits and he had pushed a lever that brought a crushing weight down on me . . .

'So then you sent Nan down to Police Headquarters to

bail Tony out and to try to get hold of me. You wanted to get me to tell you Jacob's whereabouts. After I was foolish enough to allow Tony to be released into my custody, Nan pushed me into the train and searched my pockets for the photograph of you that Jacob must have told you he had given to me. She didn't find it because it was in my other suit hanging in my closet in my house. So Nan and Tony took me to Nan's apartment and you conceived of the brilliant idea of having a quack doctor administer shock treatments to me to make me tell you something I didn't know: where Jacob was.'

'I'll never believe that you didn't know,' Eustace said. 'I still think you know where he is.'

'You mean you haven't found him yet. But why are you still looking for him?'

'And you,' said Eustace. 'Both of you know too much about what I've done. That's why I killed Nan this morning. And that's why I killed your wife this afternoon. I came into the hallway of your apartment house and saw the door open. I crept inside and threw a knife into her back from a distance of six feet. It was a perfect shot – she didn't make a sound.'

I hated him. His small figure made a great swinging shadow that whirled and danced in ellipses and circles as I revolved around it. I had to crane my head to see him, high on his tiny catwalk, and this accentuated my dizziness and made the pit of my stomach reel.

'Why didn't you kill me then?' I asked.

'I wanted to talk to you. I knew you would find me again, and I wanted you, of all people, to know my plan. And then you could tell me where Jacob is.'

'Yes,' I said. 'I can tell you that. But first you must answer some questions for me. Do you agree?'

He bobbed his head in assent. I had an idea. It was dangerous, but that did not matter. If it did not work, I would die anyway – only, perhaps, a little sooner. 'One thing I want to know,' I asked, 'is how you managed to get Nan Bulkely to help you with your plan?'

'I gave her presents at first. Then I promised her the lead in *Nevada!* – although she did not know I planned to grant that promise by killing Raye – and a Central Park apartment. Until Raye was murdered she thought the things I was doing were all parts of a complicated practical joke I wanted to play on a friend. After that she was afraid to do other than what I told her for she knew I would kill her.'

I was right when I guessed that Nan had been as much a prisoner as myself, and that she had been acting against her own will. 'Another thing I want to know,' I said, 'is why you had Nan get you percherons to tie to the lamppost when you committed a crime?'

Eustace threw back his head and cackled. This time his laughter was higher and shriller than before, an especially grisly sound to hear. 'I like percherons,' he said. 'They're my trademark. My way of setting a seal on my work–they're so big and powerful, just the opposite of me.'

'Were you the one who called Nan last night?' I asked.

'Yes,' he said. 'That was after I had Nan rent another percheron. I told her I wanted it for you and that I would telephone her and tell her where to have it delivered. But when I phoned she told me she was through. Then I knew I had to kill her. I trailed Jacob and her to the Village, waited until they left the night club and the park and were walking a deserted street. Then I shot her and went to get the percheron which I had had delivered in a truck a block or so away.'

'Why didn't you kill Jacob then?' I asked.

'I planned to, but just as I was taking aim I heard somebody open a window in the house behind me. I might have had a witness if I had shot again. So I beat it and threw away the gun. If I had used knives it might have been different. I'm good with knives, and knives are even quieter than a silenced gun. I learned to throw them at the carnival. See?' And as he spoke, his figure lunged and a long hunting knife buried itself in the wood of the turn-table inches from my head. I knew then that I had only seconds to wait. I clambered to my knees, clutching desperately for handholds on the smooth wood as the machine whirled faster and faster.

'One more question, Eustace,' I cried up at him. 'What did you do with me after you tried to kill me here in this place last spring and what did you do with Tony's body after the taxi accident?'

'I put a fake Social Security Card in your pocket after frisking your identification,' he said, 'and hired a couple of friends of mine – good boys who work around here – to dump you along the Bowery. I thought you were dead at the time or I wouldn't have let you go. As for Tony, he died in Nan's apartment after the taxi accident. We put your clothes on him and threw him in the river. It was the safest place for him.'

He was silent. I could see that he was leaning far over the guard railing, peering down at me, his hand on the lever. The turntable was going so rapidly now that I knew I could not hold on much longer. I saw him raise his small hand, saw the gleam of a disproportionately large knife in it . . .

'You told me that you would tell me where Jacob is now. I've got to find him. As long as he lives I shall not be free. This morning, if I had had this, I would have killed him. Now, quickly, tell me where he is!'

I stood up dizzily, balancing precariously on the very centre of the turntable. I knew I made a better target like that and also that I would soon be thrown off. But if this came off I would have to be as dramatic as I could . . .

'Right behind you, Pruney!' I cried. 'Look, Jacob is right there behind you!'

It worked. I don't know whether it was the old taunt, the sound of the ancient ridicule that startled him, or whether he so ardently desired to see Jacob that he did not think. But he tried to face about instantly and, delicately balanced on the guard rail as he was, he wrenched his hand free from the controls, swayed sickeningly and fell off the catwalk. He gave one whistling cry before he struck the floor thirty feet below. He must have died instantly. Unhappily, in death his stunted body and absurdly wrinkled face looked as much a caricature of human features as they had in life.

But I was not pitying Eustace then. I maintained my balance for one moment more, time enough to see Lieutenant Anderson and one of his men detach themselves from the darkness of a balcony and come clattering down a stairway to the ground floor – and to realize that they had been part of the greater shadow long enough to have heard every word of Eustace's confession.

Then I just let go and swung off into space.

The Last of Philip Banter

To
Estella M. Martin

Terror can strike by day as well as by night.
Although the frightful is, perhaps rightly, conjoined
in our minds with the darkly coloured, the harshly
dissonant – with bludgeon blows and the odours of
decay – the most terrible experiences are often bereft
of these properties of melodrama. The words 'I love
you', spoken on a sun-streaked terrace during a
joyous day, can cement a betrayal. The unchecked
gratification of an impulse, conceived in sensation,
can bear the bitter fruit of misery. And a prophecy
can – by auto-suggestion or soothsaying? – deliver a
man to evil.

The First Instalment

'Philip Banter,' he said to himself, 'you are in a bad way.'

He stood on the corner of Madison Avenue and Fiftieth Street blinking his aching eyes against the mild winter sunshine. He was trying to decide whether to cross the street or not. If he crossed the street, he would be confronted by the entrance to his office building and he would have to go through the revolving door and into the elevator and up to his office. But if he did not cross the street . . . if he turned right instead . . . and walked down the side street a few doors . . . he would find a bar and have himself a drink. Just one little drink, no more. That was what he needed. Just one little drink.

He did not cross the street. He turned right and walked to the bar and went inside and sat in the rear booth and ordered a double shot of rye whisky when the waiter came. That was what he needed. That would get it over quickly. That would clear his head.

In a few minutes the ache that had gripped his eyeballs had relaxed until it was only an occasional flickering, the slightest hint of pressure. He found he could think again – he could look straight at things – the bar mirror was what he was looking at right then – without flinching. Now everything would be fine if he could just remember what had happened last night.

He was convinced that something terrible had happened last night. If he could remember one detail, one tiny circumstance which could give him a clue to the calamity that had befallen him, he would feel reassured. But he had no memory of the night before. He knew that he had been drunk, very drunk. And he did not know this because he recalled being drunk – no, he deduced his previous state from the way he had awakened, sprawled across the bed in his rumpled dinner suit, and from his monstrous head and brassy tongue. He also knew that he had hurt himself, or had been hurt, last night. There was the ravelling bandage on his wrist, the steady throb of pain in his arm, the ugly, deep cut he had found beneath the bandage. Putting fresh gauze and antiseptic on the wound, he had tried desperately to remember how he had suffered it. Had he been in a fight and, if he had, with whom and about what? Or was the slash self-inflicted? Had he tried to kill himself? There were no answers.

When he had showered and dressed and come to breakfast, Dorothy, his wife, had not been at the table. The maid had served him sullenly, only bringing him his paper after he had called her twice. There was no doubt about it, he had done it again. But with whom had he gone off this time? If he could only remember how the evening had begun, whether Dorothy had been with him – she must have been or she would have been at the breakfast table – when he had started drinking . . .

He hailed the waiter and ordered another double rye and sat there shaking his head until it came. His wrist still throbbed steadily and he had to resist continually the desire to lift the bandage and inspect the wound. Luckily, he had been able to find a shirt with full, soft cuffs this morning; he could pull his cuff over the bandage to hide it from the curious. Otherwise he would have to answer question after question as best he could. If he could only remember what had happened!

After about five more minutes of introspection, he threw a couple of dollars on the table and walked out of the bar. This time the sun did not hurt his eyes nearly as much as before. He did not hesitate when he reached Madison Avenue but, since the light was green, walked directly across the street. As he went through the revolving door that had seemed such a hazard so recently, the sudden darkness of the building's lobby was marvellously refreshing. And as he entered the elevator, the quick smile of Sadie, the operator, was a welcome challenge. 'Philip Banter,' he said to himself, 'you've still got what it takes.'

Sadie, he saw, was eyeing him. 'How was the love-life last night, Sadie? Satisfactory?' They were alone in the car. By ten o'clock even the late rush was over.

'Mr Banter! What makes you go on like that?' Sadie brushed at her rusty hair provokingly. She was obviously pleased at his sally, indeed she had invited it, yet she felt she should pretend to be shocked and her pretence came off badly – awkwardly and self-consciously. Philip smiled to himself. She acted this way every morning, accepting and responding to his easy familiarity. Their exchange of knowing witticisms had become a ritual.

'Why, I'd think a healthy girl like you would need a little relaxation now and then. Nothing wrong in that.'

Sadie turned away from him to watch the tiny ruby lights wink on and off on the indicator as the elevator sucked itself upward. She played at being embarrassed.

'I'm not going to talk to you any more, Mr Banter, if you must go on like that. It's not nice for a nice girl to hear such talk!' The car subsided at Philip's floor; the automatic doors whispered open. '

'You're not a "nice girl", Sadie.' Philip flipped her backside lightly and left the elevator. This was something new in the ritual.

He heard her voice. 'Misss-ter Banter!' She sounded rather pleased at this added attention. He would have to remember that. Not that Sadie was the type to be considered seriously . . . but you never could tell. There might come a time when she would fit in nicely.

He walked down the hall, his lips pursed, whistling sourly. It was exactly five minutes after ten when he pushed open the door of Brown and Foster, Inc., Advertising.

The house goddess of the agency, Miss Campbell,

turned swiftly in her chair to grant him a tight-lipped smile of good morning. Philip smiled back at the receptionist, feeling – if anything – a little more undone than usual as long as he remained within the orbit of her formal cordiality; he pushed open the swinging gate and ushered himself through it as quickly as possible. He had never considered Miss Campbell either, nor would he ... she was indubitably frigid. He walked down the inner corridor to his office, no longer whistling, fighting a sudden desire to turn around and leave the office, to go back to that friendly bar on the side street and have another little drink.

As he entered his secretary's office – through which he must trespass to reach his own – Miss Grey, his secretary, looked up at him from a copy of *Tide,* said, 'Good morning, Mr Banter', and watched him cross to his own door. Although he did not see her do it (he shut his door on the sight), Philip knew that as soon as his back was turned she had gone back to *Tide*. This annoyed him. Not that he would say anything – she was so damnably efficient – but did she always have to make such a point of doing nothing when she had nothing to do? The other men's secretaries usually managed to seem busy, why couldn't his Miss Grey? And that awful complexion! Why, in God's name, didn't she do something about that?

As he hung up his hat and coat, Philip was still grumbling to himself and feeling put upon. This being so, it is not surprising that his subconscious aided him in prolonging his martyrdom: he grasped the hanger clumsily and it slipped out of his hands and clattered to the floor; he stooped for it awkwardly and caused a momentary twinge in his side – the protest of a muscle that had grown too used to lax habits – and when he finally managed to hang his topcoat, he discovered a spot on the lapel. Even after he turned around and faced the desk, he did not at first notice that his typewriter was lying open upon it; his mind was too occupied with vague resentments and too inclined to gloat over personal suffering to be quickly observant.

When he did discover the typewriter on his desk, it caused no break in the flow of his inner discourse. Had he left it like that again? If he kept that up, it would need another cleaning, since dust got in it overnight. Here was something else Miss Grey could attend to if she really cared about her job! She could come in after he left each night to see if he had put the machine away. He would want to make a note of that so he would be sure to speak to her about it. She would soon learn to do more to earn her money than burying her nose in the latest issue of *Tide* or the *New Yorker*! Philip did not see the manuscript until he sat down at his desk, then he could not avoid seeing it. There, placed next to the offending typewriter, was a neat pile of pages, double-spaced, well-typed. Why, there was a sheet in his machine that had typing on it, too! Who had been using his typewriter?

He reached for the button that would summon Miss Grey to ask her whom she had let use his machine, when he noticed that it was his own name and address that were typed in the upper, left-hand corner of the first page of the sheaf. He did not press the button. A new idea occurred to him: it might be better to read the pages first before he mentioned their existence to anyone. Someone might be playing a joke on him, trying to make a fool of him . . .

So Philip leaned back, lighted a cigarette and began to read. He was a large man in his middle thirties with a long, good-looking face. His mouth was disproportionately broad, enough so as to be almost disfiguring when he grinned. Yet this horizontal slash added a kind of distinction to his otherwise even features – it unbalanced the narrowing lines of his nose and jaw, suggesting a latent violence, a brooding force. Philip's fond opinion was that women found his face both likeable and disquieting. One of them had been foolish enough to confide this ambivalence. 'Philip,' she had said, 'your face is so innocent and your mouth is so evil.'

But, although Philip frequently remembered this remark and had, on occasion, used it himself at the proper point in a flirtation, he was not thinking of his good looks now. Instead, his attention was focused on the typed page he was reading; and after he had laid it aside and gone on to the second, and then the third, sheets of the pile, he underwent a subtle change. Where before he had been sitting erect in his swivel chair, now he began to slump. Where before he had let the manuscript lie on his desk while he read it from a distance, he now held the pages progressively closer to his eyes. He forgot about the lighted cigarette clenched in his dry lips and let it burn until it scorched him. Then he dropped the smouldering butt onto the floor, impatiently grinding it out with his heel.

There were only fifteen pages of the manuscript, but Philip read them slowly – and then he read them over again.

Philip Banter
21 East 68th St.
New York

Confession

I

I thought I was done with that sort of thing. I thought I had settled down, that I would spend the rest of my days being a model husband.

It isn't that I don't love Dorothy. I even respect her. Although I can imagine life without her (I am not a romantic), if I had to choose I would prefer life with her. I cannot explain my need to be unfaithful to her.

I know the risk I run. Last night, as on all the similar

nights before, I gauged the full extent of my jeopardy by the look of sheer hate she threw at me as I left our apartment with my 'latest'. I know how jealous Dorothy can be. I know, too, that some day I shall try her jealousy beyond the self-erected barriers of her admirable restraint. Then it will be too late.

Knowing this, why do I continue the way I do?

*

Sometimes, most times, I must admit, I have brought it on myself; but not last night. When I left the agency at five, I intended a slippered evening: a good dinner with Dorothy, some brandy and a little talk afterwards, then the radio or a book until time for bed. A new flirtation? Impossible! I loved my wife last night when I left work. I loved her all the way home on the subway, and on the short walk to the East River. I was never a more normal American husband than when I fitted my key into the lock of our door, threw my hat and coat on the table in the foyer, went into our room where she was dressing and after kissing her, asked:

'What's for dinner?'

She wrinkled her eyes at me in the mirror, but kept on working the rouge into her cheeks, patting at them with an absurdly large puff, a pink plush blob.

'Something you like.'

'What?'

'Guess!'

'Must I? A roast of some sort?'

'Darling, we had a roast just the other day...'

'A rarebit?'

'No. Try again.'

'No, you tell me. I'll never guess.' I do not like guessing games and though I realized that Dorothy, like all other women, must be coy at times, I was not inclined to encourage her on these occasions. It was tiresome.

'We're having chicken and rice, the Spanish way. You've always liked it so much. But there's something else, too.'

'For dinner?'

She turned halfway around on her vanity stool, throwing her dark hair back, smiling at me. She had just been putting her lipstick on; one lip was smudged vividly like a child playing at being grown-up.

(I tell you I loved her then. I meant no infidelity. I contemplated no sin . . . not that I believe in sin.)

'Yes, in a way, for dinner,' she said.

'Oh, come out with it, Dottie,' I said. 'Stop teasing me!'

She tossed her shoulders and affected to ignore me. But she returned my stare by way of the mirror – her eyes never left mine.

'Jeremy called. He's coming around to dinner and bringing a friend.'

'Jeremy? Jeremy Foulkes?'

'The very same. I thought you'd be pleased. Why, Philip, whatever is the matter? You look positively sick!'

I passed my hand over my damp forehead. I was breathing wildly, my thinking was blurred. What could I say?

'Pleased? Of course I'm pleased. I'm always glad to see Jeremy. You know that. And any friend of his is always welcome.'

'I didn't mean to startle you, darling,' Dorothy said. 'I just thought I'd make it a pleasant surprise.'

*

That was last night, Tuesday, 1 December 1945. A few short hours ago. So much has happened since then.

*

I am confused. I simply cannot understand my own motives. Motives? Drives? Insane urges? Was I wholly sane last night?

*

It may help to clear my mind if I put down a few facts about myself, Dorothy, my friends.

I am in the advertising business, an account executive. Occasionally, I write a little copy.

Before I drifted into advertising, I was a newspaperman: first in Indianapolis, my home town, and then in New York.

*

Philip's hand shook as he laid down the manuscript. The pain in his bandaged wrist had been increasing as he read the typed pages. He pressed his wrist against his mouth. What was the meaning of this 'Confession'? Why did it refer to Tuesday, 1 December – today – as 'last night'. Was he supposed to have written it, or was someone kidding him? He would have to read further to find out.

He picked up the manuscript, slouched down in his chair and propped it against his knee so he would not have to use his injured wrist. He began to read again. His forgotten cigarette smouldered in the ashtray.

*

I met Dorothy during my newspaper days in this city. Jeremy introduced her to me at a party. It was one of those intellectual gatherings Jeremy was always sponsoring in those days; perhaps he still does, I don't know.

I had never thought I'd marry. There was always another woman. Any one woman's individual attractions dulled for me and became enervatingly habitual after a few weeks' intimacy. Matrimony was a fisherman's hook with a fancy lure, and I was a wise old fish who admired the bright, twirling feathers but refused to rise and be impaled . . .

Unless, of course, the woman had money, besides intelligence and beauty. A starved fish will on occasion chance snatching the bait from a hook, if the bait is exceptionally tempting. For that matter, fish have been caught with three or four rusty hooks imbedded in their mouths.

I had never met an intelligent, beautiful girl with money until I met Dorothy. I married her.

It wasn't quite as cold-blooded as all that. I fell in love with her, as might be expected. I still love her. But I am honest with myself: if her father hadn't been a partner in one of the larger, more affluent advertising agencies, if Dorothy hadn't had considerable money in her own name, I can scarcely believe our relationship would have lasted.

I don't mean to imply that our marriage hasn't been a happy one; I think it is as happy as most. We are kind to each other. I believe I have worn worse with Dorothy than she has with me (isn't this the way it should be?). I left the newspaper business at her father's suggestion and became a copywriter in his agency; it wasn't long before he gave me several accounts to handle and I found my salary in five figures. We would be completely happy if I could only be a little more circumspect about my personal affairs. The trouble is I don't try. Dorothy might never know of my flirtations, if I didn't insist on flaunting them in her face.

Or if she learned, I know she would be proud enough to pretend ignorance – if I allowed her the pretence.

But she can't overlook an event that happens before her eyes: the way I made up to Jeremy's 'friend' last night, for example.

Why couldn't I have waited?

*

Our guests arrived while I was still dressing. Dorothy had left the room earlier to see how things were in the kitchen; I heard her go to the door when the bell rang and then I heard muffled conversation. I knew Jeremy and his 'friend' had arrived.

It has been a long time since I last spent an evening with Jeremy. Until about a year ago he was my closest friend; then we had a falling out. Nothing dramatic occurred, no quarrel, not even a disagreement. We just stopped seeing each other. Several months passed before I realized what had happened, and then when I thought about it I knew that our estrangement had been progressing gradually for years. Our community of friends was dispersed by the war, for one thing; I believe that Jeremy and I were the only 4-F's in the group. We might have had the newspaper business in common if I hadn't left it, and Jeremy, too – he went into radio shortly after I married Dorothy. I know nothing about radio, and I must confess I dislike most radio people. They're queer. I've noticed Jeremy growing queer since he has become an announcer. He wears hand-painted ties now, and Irish linen shirts – that sort of thing. I suppose it is another reason why we have drifted apart.

Dorothy might have kept us together. She was our last link. Jeremy had known Dorothy before I knew her, and he had liked her a lot at one time. They were great friends and it was good to see them together. Jeremy was the only one of Dorothy's friends that I did like, for that matter. But then that might have been because he was my friend, too; I don't know.

Thinking back over it I can't understand why I was surprised to learn that he was coming to dinner. As Dorothy said, I should have been pleased. And I was, after a while, yet at first it was a shock and almost disagreeable.

It was as if I had a premonition.

*

She was the first person I saw when I entered the living-room. To that moment I hadn't thought about the 'friend' Jeremy was bringing around. If I had been asked, I should have guessed that Jeremy's companion would be a man. I seldom think of Jeremy with women, principally because he doesn't often have a feminine friend. Jeremy is some-thing of a lone wolf, or he used to be. He had a girl with him last night, though.

I could not take my eyes off her. She was small and slim, and she stood very straight. Her eyes were brown, flecked with a lighter shade that changed from hazel to green and back again within the duration of a glance. She wore a severely simple suit of black broadcloth set off by a tailored shirtwaist. Her hair was darker than her enigmatic eyes and it fell to her shoulders in soft abundance. There was something taut and alive about the way she held her head, something imperious and demanding about the quick, restless gestures of her hands . . .

Jeremy came over and introduced us. He looked well, if a little fat; he had been one of those small, compact men who seem to take the highest gloss, but now his clothes bulged slightly and there was a fold of flesh at his collar.

'This is – –, Philip. She's going to be a writer, too.' (I do not want to write her name. It's not that I have forgotten it – how could I? – indeed, I have been saying it over and over to myself all the while I wrote this, as if it were an incantation. But I refuse to set it down in black and white. A silly quirk, perhaps . . . or a sensible caution?)

I looked away from her to see if he had said this last with malice. But Jeremy was smiling in the best of nature. I tend to remember insults and to cherish resentments, to be sensitive about wrongs long after others have forgotten them. Once Jeremy had lashed out at me unmercifully for taking a job in advertising. He had called me a parasite. But, of course, he no longer remembered that, even if I did.

'What sort of thing are you going to write?' I asked her, sitting down beside her on the sofa. Dorothy had moved over to make room: 'Stories, or something serious?'

Her eyes glinted and changed colour. 'Can't stories be serious?' she asked.

I felt foolish. I had made a snide remark that had turned out to be anything but clever. I had asked a meaningless question, been guilty of an inanity, and her manner let me know she knew it.

'Of course,' I said. 'Of course, they can. I didn't mean that.'

'What did you mean?'

'I meant are you going to write fiction, or – or something more serious?' As soon as I said this, I marvelled

224

at my own stupidity in repeating the very remark I had wanted to efface. Now I wanted to add something else, quickly, that would bury it. But she did not give me the chance.

'I can't understand the typical American business man's attitude that art, writing in particular, is an intricate game, a child's play. I think I detect that in you. And I want you to know that I resent it!' She licked at her lip with her tongue as if a drop of the acid that formed her words had fallen upon the sensitive membrane and must be expunged.

'I didn't mean that,' I protested. 'I wish I could write fiction, good fiction. I admire an honest writer.'

She stared at me incredulously. And then she smiled and looked away. I knew that it had begun all over again.

*

We went in to dinner soon after that, but before we did Jeremy came over to talk to me. He didn't have much to say, just asked the usual questions about business and my health; but he gave me the opportunity to ask him about her.

'Where did you meet her?'

'At a party in the Village a while back,' he said. 'We're pretty good friends. What do you think of her?'

I looked at her again. She was sitting back on the sofa talking to Dorothy (I had walked over to the fireplace with Jeremy). She held her drink in one hand and was gesturing with it, the other hand was poking indefatigably at her long bob. I thought to myself, I've never seen a person who was so alive . . .

'She's attractive,' I answered Jeremy, 'and she's got spirit. I like the way she stands up and fights when she talks.'

Jeremy nodded soberly, but I could see he was pleased. His next words proved it.

'I'm in love with her, Philip. I'm going to marry her.'

'Are you? Congratulations!'

'Oh, I haven't asked her yet,' he said, and his face flushed. 'She may not want me . . .'

'I wouldn't say that,' I said.

He was asking for it, but then Jeremy always asks for it and thanks you afterwards.

*

I said earlier that this time it wasn't my fault. That isn't true. I don't know whose fault it could be except mine. If I had said I couldn't help myself, that would have approached the truth.

All through dinner I could not keep my eyes off her. She noticed my continued attention, and Dorothy noticed it; only Jeremy seemed to be unaware of what I was doing. I don't think I was conscious of the food I was putting into my mouth; I know I paid only enough heed to the conversation to keep up my end. She had pre-empted my mind.

And I could tell that she favoured my attention. Sometimes when you look at a woman she pretends to ignore you – that can be either good or bad; but if she shows you by returning your look that she knows you are watching her – that can be only good. During dinner I think that she returned my gaze as often as I regarded her – that's what I mean when I say I couldn't help myself. I'll admit that I didn't have to look at her . . . that was where I was to blame. But once I had begun our wordless exchange, the only thing either of us could have done to have stopped would have been to leave. And I don't believe that she ever thought of that – I know I didn't.

*

There was a telephone call for Jeremy about nine o'clock. We had been talking about the modern novel: I remember having said something rash about Henry Miller, only to feel her eyes on me again, to hear her soft, harsh voice challenge me.

'At least, he's honest!'

'I didn't say he wasn't. I said only that his books were

226

execrable, his hatred of America and things American old-fashioned and absurd.'

She was half-smiling. There was a pleasurable antagonism between us. 'I don't believe you've read him!' she exclaimed.

She was right, I hadn't. Although I believe I did read a review of his latest book.

That was where we were when the 'phone rang. Dorothy answered and said it was for Jeremy. We could hear him out in the hall, arguing. 'But I can't. I'm at a party,' I heard him say. And then later, 'Well, all right. If it can't be helped, it can't be helped. But I do think that you could plan these things better. Yes. Yes, I understand. I'll be over right away. Yes, I'm leaving this minute.'

And while this was going on, I was acutely conscious of her and she was comparably aware of me. Each time we spoke we were at each other's throats, but it was a different kind of aggression we intended. This verbal sparring was a substitute; even when we were silent we were at war, the oldest, most fought and best war of them all.

Jeremy returned to find three people with that look on their faces that says, 'We didn't mean to, but we couldn't keep from listening.' He stood in the doorway and made his excuses.

'That was the station. One of the men is ill and I have to fill in unexpectedly. I tried to beg off, but I couldn't.'

'You don't have to go right away?' asked Dorothy.

'I'm afraid so.'

Jeremy walked away from Dorothy and over to her. She stood up – it seemed reluctantly. She looked at me, then shook her head and looked away.

'You don't have to leave, darling,' said Jeremy. 'I'd only have to take you home anyway. And I don't want to spoil your evening.'

She hesitated. She looked from Jeremy to me, ignoring Dorothy. I wondered if she realized how obvious this all was. There was no reason why she could not accomplish the same end more subtly.

Jeremy, the fool, was throwing her at me. There is an example of why he never has a woman of his own. He knows nothing about them. He should not be trusted with them.

'Why don't you stay, darling?' he was saying. 'Phil will take you home, won't you, Phil?'

She was watching me again, this time eagerly. 'If you're sure it's no trouble,' she said.

'Of course it's no trouble.'

Jeremy seemed relieved. 'Then I'll be going. I've really got to dash! Thank you, Dorothy, for a magnificent dinner.' He waved his hand at us and was gone – an absurd little man in a shirt too big for him.

As soon as he left, she sat down beside me. I was uncomfortably aware of Dorothy, standing by the fireplace, too pointedly paying us no attention.

'Dorothy,' I asked, 'what do you think of Henry Miller?'

'I haven't read him either,' she said. 'I'll reserve my opinion.' I could feel —'s leg against mine.

*

There are times in my life that I remember well and of which I can recall every detail, yet I have to force myself to think of them at all. The rest of last night is such a time. Until about eleven o'clock we sat and listened to the radio and talked. I think I can remember every word that was said, but I cannot make myself put that conversation down. What we said had no relation to what was happening. Last night was an emotional crisis, a conflict between three people that existed by itself without the aid of words or overt action.

I believe we talked about the plight of the American writer, of his peculiar homelessness and the strange feeling of futile striving you get from our fiction – as if the author were inarticulate. Actually, it was ourselves who were inarticulate. We felt a need to talk, as if our talk clothed and made decent our naked emotions, but what we said was frustrate. There seemed no end to it.

At times I felt myself to be a bystander; these were the times when Dorothy and – were concerned only with each other in their contention over me. And there were other times when Dorothy must have felt herself excluded – when – and I were alone despite her presence. (I still cannot bring myself to confide her name to paper.) Yet no anger was expressed. No words of love were spoken. We talked about Cain and Dos Passos and Wolfe; it was all very intellectual and civilized like a scene from a bad play.

About eleven o'clock, she stood up abruptly. 'I'm going home.'

'It's early yet,' I said. At that moment I wanted to delay the inevitable. I believe I would have backed out if I could.

Dorothy yawned. 'You might as well take her home, Philip.' Dorothy wasn't being impolite; she was acknowledging defeat, and letting me know that it would be an armed truce. 'I'd like to get to bed, too,' she added.

I went out to get our coats. She was standing in front of the mirror over the fireplace fussing with her hair, and I saw that Dorothy was watching her. Dorothy was looking at her the way she would inspect an obstacle in her path, coldly, dispassionately – but the emotion she was hiding was hatred instead of annoyance.

I brought her coat back into the room and helped her into it. In the mutual struggle with the fur she brushed against me more than was necessary. Dorothy saw this as well. I felt I had to say something to take the curse off the silence.

'I'll be back within the hour,' I said. Dorothy smiled at me, and then looked at her. 'You know you won't,' she said.

I turned around to look back at Dorothy as we left. She had craned her neck to watch us leave. She was still smiling, but that was because she had forgotten to stop.

I looked down at the woman beside me. I resolved that I would take her to her house and leave her. I told myself that I would really come back to Dorothy within the hour. I was married. I loved my wife. I was getting too old for this sort of thing. And I believed myself for the moment it took to shut the door on Dorothy.

She stood still beside me, her eyes answering my look, her lower lip trembling. After acting like that all night, now she was shy . . .

But I tasted blood when she kissed me in the taxi.

*

Later, while I was dressing, she asked, 'Why did your wife say that?'

'Say what?'

'What she did just before we left. When you said you would be back, and she said you wouldn't.'

'I don't know.'

'Oh yes you do, Philip.'

'But I don't.'

'It's because this happened before, isn't it? Many times before?'

'I don't know what you're talking about.'

'Oh yes you do!'

'What are you getting at?'

'I mean – this isn't the first time you've been unfaithful to Dorothy, is it?'

There was no use lying. 'No, it isn't.'

'You do it all the time, don't you?'

'Not quite "all the time".'

She threw me a strange look and ran into the bathroom. 'Why does she put up with it, Philip?' she called to me over the sound of running water.

'I suppose she loves me.'

'If I loved you . . . and you did that to me . . . you know what I'd do?'

'No. What?'

'I'd kill you, Philip.'

I didn't say anything. I finished brushing my hair. I was ready to leave.

'Philip.'

'Yes.'

'I wouldn't try her too far, Philip. She might kill you, too . . . sometime.'

'I know. I'm leaving now.'

She came to the bathroom door. She had thrown a rough, terry-cloth robe over herself.

'You have my number, haven't you?'

'Yes, I have. Good night.'

She was smiling at me, imitating the way Dorothy had smiled. She mimicked Dorothy's voice. 'Go straight home, Philip. Don't stop at any bars.'

'Good night,' I said, and slammed the door.

*

The manuscript ended there without reaching a conclusion. As if there would be more – later.

Philip threw it down on the desk and reached for the calendar pad. He sat staring at it, fingering its leaves. The 'Confession' purported to be written by himself about events that had occurred the night before. But the date given in the manuscript was Tuesday, December 1 – today. Did that make the 'Confession' actually a prediction?

He had thought while he was reading it that he might possibly have written it himself, and the thought still plagued him. He had also thought that the 'Confession' might be a distorted account of what had happened last night, what he could not remember. Of course, if he had written it himself, he might have mistaken the date – that would account for the discrepancy. But if he had written it himself, when had he had the opportunity? Had he returned to the office to record the details of his latest conquest before he went home to bed? Hardly. He had been drunk the night before, but not that drunk. Nor had he ever been inclined to keep a diary. No, this must have been written by someone else and was intended as a prophecy.

But by whom? Dorothy? Dorothy would not stoop to so

cunning a device; besides, hadn't he always been most cautious to be at all times discreet? He was sure Dorothy suspected nothing, but even if she did she would have too much good sense to jeopardize her own happiness by threatening him. For that was what the 'Confession' did – there was no escaping this conclusion – it constituted a threat.

Jeremy might have written it. Jeremy had always been a little jealous of him, especially since he had married Dorothy. But why should Jeremy come forward with such a preposterous device as this now? He had not seen Jeremy in a year or more. And was Jeremy that subtle? No, Jeremy could bluster – he had once in the past – he could try to bully, but he would never think of planting a 'Confession' on a man's desk. A 'Confession'! Why, the very idea!

What the hell was it all about?

Philip stood up. His face was very red and he had run his hand through his hair again and again. Now he seized the sheaf of manuscript and, turning the pages quickly, re-read a line here, a paragraph there. It was a strange sensation, that of reading an account of actions that were supposed to be his – a sensation that left him with an emptiness in the viscera and a heady feeling of pleasure, much as he supposed he might experience if, upon the completion of a dangerous exploit, he had heard himself praised for his daring. Even while he was first reading it, he had been particularly pleased by certain passages and significantly disturbed by others, although why he should feel either pleased or frightened he could not say. The whole thing was ingenious, and surprisingly accurate, in places. Of course, most of it was nonsensical. He knew no one who fitted the description of the mysterious woman and it was fantastic to predict that he would meet such a person. For the 'Confession' did predict . . . the day it concerned itself with was today . . . the events it described had not happened yet. And wouldn't, if he had anything to say in the matter!

But who had placed it on his desk? Suddenly, he thought of Miss Grey, and, as he did, his face grew livid. He tossed the 'Confession' violently aside and jabbed the button that would call her. While he waited for her to appear at the door, he cursed her under his breath.

When she came into the room, her pencil and notebook in her hand, he asked, 'Did you put anything on my desk this morning, Miss Grey?'

'Just the mail, Mr Banter.'

'Nothing else? No papers, or anything like that?'

'No, Mr Banter, just the mail.'

Philip hesitated. He felt he could not refer openly to the 'Confession'. He did not want anyone else to know about it. But he did want to discover who had put it on his desk.

'Did anyone else come into my office this morning before I arrived?' he asked.

'No, Mr Banter, not while I was here.'

'Or last night – after I had left?'

'Nobody's been near your office, Mr Banter. Is there something wrong?'

Philip thought quickly. 'It's just that someone else has been using my typewriter, that's all!'

The girl look puzzled. 'Nobody has used your typewriter, Mr Banter. I know.'

'I found it open this morning, Miss Grey!' He felt himself growing angrier. She was playing innocent. He knew she was. She had to be!

'Why, Mr Banter, is that what's the matter? That doesn't mean someone else has been using it. That just means that you left it open last night yourself. I remember noticing it.'

Although the girl's blotchy face was wholly earnest, Philip felt she was laughing at him. She wanted to make a fool of him, did she? He would show her a thing or two!

'You're sure of that, Miss Grey?'

'Yes, Mr Banter, I remember you left it open.'

'Why didn't you cover it up then? Isn't that one of the

duties of a good secretary? To see that my desk is in order before you leave?'

'But, Mr Banter –'

'Don't "but" me, I mean it! And another thing, from now on you can spend your spare time cleaning out the correspondence files or helping Miss Campbell. You're not to sit around all day long with your nose in a magazine as if I didn't give you enough to do!'

The girl looked as if she might cry. Philip felt foolish now that his anger was spent. What had been the good of that? Not that he had not been justified, but had he learned anything?

'I'll ring when I need you, Miss Grey.' He watched her leave the room. He was right about it; she had been growing awfully slack of late. Still, he could have gone about it more successfully. He was convinced that she knew more than she said. But what could he do about it?

Someone had to write that story, someone had to put it on his desk. The only possible times this could have happened were after he left the previous afternoon, and that morning before he came in. Miss Grey had said she had been in the office both times. She had to be lying . . . unless he had written it himself. And then forgotten about it . . . impossible!

Philip thought he heard the door to his office click. He did not look up. He waited for the door to open . . . for the person who was there to step into the room. But the door never opened . . . instead, his vision grew dull, the light grew grey and scummy, there was a faint . . . but persistent . . . ringing in his ear. And he felt as though he were breathing cobwebs . . .

He tried to get up, and he could not. He tried to cry out, and he could not. And then he heard the voice . . . a familiar voice . . . one he had heard many times before . . . although he never recognized it as his own until it had stopped . . . his voice when he had been a child . . . a petulant, whining, coaxing voice . . .

'Philip,' the voice said, 'why can't you remember last

234

night? I want you to remember, Philip. We had so much fun.'

Philip buried his head in his hands to shut out that foggy light. He knew that if he opened them before the tinkling in his brain went away, he would still see the light that soiled every object in the room. For a month or more he had been having these spells – that was why he got drunk so often. He never saw the light when he had been drinking, never heard that voice . . .

There it was again. 'Philip, why can't you remember? It was just last night, Philip.'

He clenched his teeth and forced himself to stand erect. Despite the vague fuzziness of his vision, he found the calendar pad and began to check off the day's appointments. Lunch with Peabody at one. Copy conference at two-thirty. Mr Foster's office about the new campaign at four. He looked at his watch – it was a few minutes to twelve. Time enough to have a quick drink and then catch a taxi for the ride downtown.

He stumbled across the room, grabbed his hat and coat and plunged blindly out of his office. 'Philip, why can't you remember?' the voice was saying. As he waited for the elevator in the corridor, he shut his eyes and listened for the voice again. It did not come. By the time he had reached the street his vision had begun to clear and the tinkling sound was fading. The sun was still bright and he had to blink his eyes to see anything. Then he saw a taxi pull up across the street, an empty taxi.

As he stepped forward, the dull, black truck turned out of the next side street – moving with clumsy rapidity. It bore down on him. Philip did not see it. His eyes were intent on the taxi. The taxi driver saw it and shouted at Philip. At the same moment, a woman screamed. The great, dully painted truck swerved – in an attempt to miss Philip, or to make sure of hitting him? Philip looked up and saw the looming headlights, the tarnished radiator grill, the kewpie doll on the front of the hood.

He jumped, sprawled, stretched himself forward and down. A great blast of wind tore at him as he hit the hard pavement. The woman screamed again – and again.

Then the cab-driver was standing over him, helping him up. Automobile horns were honking and a policeman's whistle shrilled. 'Cripes, that was a close one, buddy!' the cabby was saying. 'He looked like he was out to get you – like he swerved right at you! And he kept on goin', didn't even stop for the cop! Are you all right?'

Philip smiled weakly and thanked the driver. He climbed into the cab and told him to get away as fast as he could. 'I'm already late to my appointment,' he explained.

In reality, he wanted some time to think about what had just happened. Was the cabby's hunch correct? Had someone aimed that truck deliberately at him? Was this near-accident and the 'Confession' all part of a scheme – a scheme either to kill him or to drive him out of his mind?

Philip just did not know.

Dr George Matthews was looking at his appointment book. '11 a.m., Mr Steven Foster and Mrs Philip Banter,' he read. Mrs Philip Banter? – that would be Phil's wife, Dorothy, wouldn't it? And Steven Foster – wasn't he Dorothy's father? Dr Matthews was surprised to find their names in his book, but then his appointments were usually made six or more weeks in advance and during the interval he often forgot them. He lighted a cigarette and tried to remember when and why he had made this one. Phil and he had had lunch together a few weeks before – they had kept up their college friendship and they liked to talk over old times. Had Philip asked him to see his wife and her father then? George Matthews doubted it. He made a policy of not accepting his friends as patients and if he had broken this rule, he would remember why he had broken it. No, he had not made this appointment. He picked up his telephone and buzzed Miss Henry, his nurse. She might remember . . .

Miss Henry did remember. 'I made it for you only yesterday, doctor,' she said. 'Mrs Campbell called to say she could not keep her eleven o'clock today. Then Mr Foster called right afterwards and said he wanted to see you as soon as possible. So I squeezed him in today.'

'Thank you, Miss Henry. Will you ask them to come in now?'

Matthews hung up, and ground his cigarette out in the ashtray. Miss Henry had no way of knowing that Mrs Philip Banter was an old friend, but he wished she had checked with him before making the appointment. Dr Matthews did not like analysing his friends or his friends'

friends. Psychoanalysis and friendship belonged in different worlds. But there was little he could do about this now.

The door opened and Miss Henry ushered a beautiful, dark-haired woman and a tall old man into the office. Matthews stood up and shook hands with Steven Foster, while smiling warmly at Dorothy Banter. She acknowledged his greeting. He saw at once that Dorothy was tense and unnaturally excited. She kept glancing back to her father (they had come into the room separately, Dorothy with Miss Henry, her father a discreet distance behind). Now Dorothy sat down and as she did, jerked open her purse, spilling its contents. Matthews came around his desk and stooped to help her pick up the money, powder and cigarettes that had scattered over the carpet. He saw that she was embarrassed, her face flushed as she stammered her thanks, and he wondered at this because Dorothy had always before had remarkable poise.

But if Dorothy's behaviour was puzzling, Steven Foster's attitude was even more interesting. Dorothy's father had not spoken a word. He had nodded his head and smiled grimly when Matthews had shaken hands with him, but he had said nothing. Rather than sit in a comfortable chair, he had walked to the other end of the large, book-lined office and sat on the couch – he was sitting on the edge of it, his cane imprisoned between his knees, his gloves entangled in his fist. It was as if he wanted himself considered a spectator, not a participant.

And yet Dorothy looked at her father and waited until he nodded his head again before she began to explain their presence. 'We have come to see you about Philip,' she said, smiling apologetically. 'You have known Philip as long as I have, and you are a psychiatrist. We thought you might be able to help us.'

Steven Foster thwacked his fist against his thigh. Dorothy, nettled by the unexpected sound, glanced at him. But still he said nothing.

'You see, my husband has been behaving strangely lately,' she added a moment afterwards.

'I saw Philip last month,' Matthews said. 'We had lunch together. He struck me about the same as usual. Although, as I remember, he didn't have much to say. But then I don't think about my friends the same way I do about my patients.'

Dorothy smiled at that, and for an instant regained some of her normal composure. She leaned forward and spoke eagerly. 'You don't expect to find psychoses in your friends, you mean?'

'I don't seek them in my friends.'

'Then, perhaps, you can understand how unnerved I am. I didn't expect to find my husband psychotic. But little by little that is the conclusion that is being forced on me . . .'

Dr Matthews made a tent of his hands and peered through it. He was a well-proportioned man in his middle thirties with a face that had once been handsome but had suffered a scar that made it saturnine. Yet there was a kindness in his eyes, a gentleness about his mouth, that told you that here was a man to whom you could talk and he would listen.

'What does your husband do that seems psychotic to you?'

Dorothy fretted with her necklace. 'There are so many things I've noticed, it's hard to decide which to tell you about at first. I suppose I should tell you that he drinks. He drinks a terrible lot. The way an alcoholic drinks.'

'Have you any idea *why* he drinks?' Matthews asked.

Dorothy shook her head. Her dark eyes were half-closed and her full lips were tightly compressed. She seemed to have to fight down a desire to withdraw before she could speak. 'He is unhappy. I can tell that, although he never says so.'

'Do you know why he is unhappy?'

'I thought he might be worried about business. But Dad tells me that he seldom comes into the office any more – and that he's losing all his accounts.'

239

Dr Matthews turned to Steven Foster. 'Has he talked to you about this?'

The old man pulled at his stick. '*I* have talked to him. I told him he was a loafer. I warned him that if he lost another account, he was out of a job.'

'And what was Philip's reaction to your warning?'

Foster tossed his head in disdain. 'He begged me to give him another chance. He said that he had not been himself.'

'Did he say he was ill?'

The old man snorted. 'Ill? Do you call hitting the bottle being ill? If so, Banter's dying!'

Matthews smiled to himself and turned back to Dorothy. He could see that Steven Foster had no wish to cooperate, and he surmised that his antagonism for Philip had deeper roots than he would admit.

'So far, you have told me nothing about your husband's behaviour that would support your fear of insanity, Dorothy. Hasn't he other symptoms that have alarmed you?' Matthews asked. Or else, why are you here? he added to himself.

'The scoundrel has been seen with other women,' growled old Foster.

'That, even when coupled with chronic alcoholism, is not necessarily psychotic,' Matthews said drily. 'Although such men are often neurotic enough.'

Dorothy smoothed her dress, looked at her father and then at Matthews. 'It's been going on a long time. A long, long time. Since before we married, perhaps. And I have never known until recently . . .'

This was growing more and more embarrassing, Matthews thought. If only Philip were here to defend himself! 'Are you sure of what you're saying?' he asked.

Dorothy nodded her head.

'I would think you needed a lawyer instead of a psychiatrist.'

'You don't understand.' Dorothy stood up and walked around her chair, stood holding on to it. 'There is no "other woman". There have been scores – hundreds for all I know. I found his address book. It was full of . . . of their names.'

'The scoundrel!' fumed Steven Foster.

George Matthews was shocked. Philip had been a gay enough blade in college; in fact, he had a reputation then for this sort of thing. But he had seemed to settle down, to be in love with Dorothy. It was difficult to be professional about his wife's confidences: as a friend, he felt he should spring to Philip's defence; as a doctor, he felt his interest should be strictly clinical, probing. He solved this dilemma by straddling.

'Promiscuity is relative,' he said. 'It can be a sign of arrested adolescence, of perpetual self-love, narcissism. Or it can be the end result of a driving fear of impotency. However, by itself, it can hardly be regarded as a sign of insanity – unless it attains the proportions of satyriasis.'

'Of what?' asked Dorothy.

'Satyriasis. Abnormal, excessive sexuality. Fortunately very rare.'

Dorothy thought for a moment. 'There are other signs, too.'

'Yes?'

'Philip disappears.'

'Disappears. What do you mean?'

'He did it only last night. We had dinner together. Afterwards, we sat together for a while, then Philip discovered that he hadn't any cigarettes. He said he was going down to the corner to get some. I waited a half hour for him to come back – and then an hour. He did not return. I went down to the drugstore. He had not been there. I went to the bar across the street. The bartender knows us. Philip had been in, he said. He had had several drinks and then had left with a woman he met there. The bartender was reluctant to tell me this, but I wheedled it out of him. He said he thought Philip had picked her up . . .'

'I see,' said Dr Matthews. He did not know what else to

say. He knew that he did not want to have anything to do with this. Philip had been his friend for a long time. If his actions were peculiar, who was he to say they were amoral – let alone that they were evidence of insanity? And Matthews did not like the way old Steven Foster sat on the couch and glared at him without saying a word.

'This isn't the first time this has happened,' Dorothy was saying. 'Philip disappears like that often – increasingly often. Once he left me at the theatre. Just said he was going out for a smoke. I didn't see him until the next morning. He was drunk and he smelt of cheap perfume. I asked him where he had been and he said he didn't remember. I pressed him, and he began to tell me a wild story. He said he kept seeing a "dingy light" and hearing a "persistent ringing as if a tiny bell was tinkling somewhere far off". He also said that he heard a voice – he asked me if I heard it! – that repeatedly chided him for not remembering what he had done the night before. And that was all I could get out of him.

'Another time he was to meet me on a street corner. I saw him across the street. I saw him look at me and then go into a bar. I waited a few minutes and then crossed the street. But when I went into the bar he wasn't there. He must have gone out a back entrance. He didn't come home for days that time. And, as usual, he said he could not remember what he had done or where he had gone.'

Dorothy had been speaking furiously. Now she stopped, to catch her breath, and glanced at her father. The old man's posture and mien had not changed. His hand still clutched his gloves. His cane still shot upright from between his knees. His unyielding gaze seemed to Matthews outrageously malevolent. But Dorothy was relieved – she sighed and some of the stiffness left her face – when Steven Foster nodded his head curtly.

'What do you think, doctor?' Dorothy asked.

Matthews spoke slowly, emphatically. 'I've known Philip for a long time. He was always sensitive. When I first met him his adjustment was dependent and precarious –

he leaned heavily on his friend, Jeremy Foulkes, used him as a model and mentor. But then Jeremy did the same with him. It is not unusual in college to see two friends who mutually idolize and patronize each other in this way.

'But after Phil met you, it seemed to me that he matured quickly. If he was something of a Lothario in college, I thought he was now a devoted husband. I am surprised, and a little shocked, to hear your testimony to the contrary. And I am put in an uncomfortable position. Your husband is still my friend, Dorothy – even as you are my friend. A doctor, especially a doctor of the mind, must put aside all emotional allegiance when he accepts a patient. If Philip had come to me, and told me that he was ill, I might be able to work with him. But when you and your father come to me, and tell me these things without Philip's knowledge, there is little I can do. It is not that I doubt your word, but just that I do not see how I can act honourably, as a friend, or effectively, as a physician.'

'You could talk to the man!' exploded Steven Foster, projecting his resonant voice across the room. 'You could call him down, tell him he is ruining his life!' The old man's rugged face was infused with colour.

'A psychiatrist never calls anyone down, Mr Foster,' Matthews said abruptly. 'Nor would I, as an individual, think of dealing that way with Philip. Neither is it sound medicine, nor sound friendship.' He looked at Dorothy, who had also arisen. 'I would like to talk with Philip though, Dorothy. Perhaps, the next time we have lunch together, he will ask my advice. You must understand that it is psychologically necessary for the patient to come to the doctor. All you can do is inform me that Philip is ill. Of all that you have told me, only the "voice" that he hears seems symptomatic to me. That doesn't mean that you aren't right in your suspicions that Philip is facing a break. But you should realize that while drinking – even heavy drinking – and promiscuity are often neurotic, they are not by themselves signs of a psychosis.'

George Matthews had walked to where Dorothy was

standing: now he took her hand. Her dark eyes were quiet and brooding. Her mouth trembled. 'I'm afraid he doesn't love me,' she said simply. 'He has changed so. I don't know what I've done.'

Matthews did not know what to say. He was concerned, too, but he was not sure whether it was Philip who was ill. He tried to be matter-of-fact. 'Talk to him. Encourage him to talk to you. Try to get him to tell you why he leaves you. Don't be jealous. Don't attempt to watch him every moment. Give him his freedom. Suggest that he come and speak to me.'

They were at the door. Matthews glanced at his watch and saw that it was time for his next appointment. Then Steven Foster, who had at last gotten to his feet and walked over to them, broke in irately.

'You doctors are all alike!' he cried. 'You never have any time for common-sense, direct methods. I thought you might be different from what I read in the newspapers, and what my daughter told me, of how you solved the Raye case.* But no, all you can do is to mumble scientific terms and beat about the bush. Why don't you come right out and tell the girl that the only thing she can do with a man like Philip Banter is to divorce him or have him horsewhipped?'

Dr George Matthews, for the first time in his life, held the door of his office open for a patient. He was exceedingly angry, although he did not show it, and he wanted Steven Foster to leave immediately. But he answered his outburst with courtesy. 'I never prescribe horsewhipping as therapy. Corporal punishment is at once mediaeval, cruel and ineffective. As to divorce, that is not for me to decide – certainly not on such skimpy evidence. Since you have been rude enough to allude to my experiences with the police, and my abilities as an amateur detective, all I can

* Steven Foster referred to the mysterious death of Frances Raye, in which Dr Matthews was innocently involved. The psychiatrist solved this mystery with the aid of the police and gained some fame. cf. *The Deadly Percheron*.

say is that both have been exaggerated – and that I hope I shall never have the opportunity to add to them.'

Dr Matthews smiled again at Dorothy, turned and went to his desk. His mind was already on his next patient. Dorothy took her father's arm – the obstinate old man was still enraged – and led him from the room.

When they had reached the street, Steven Foster hailed a taxi and told the driver to take them to the Algonquin. He sat in a corner of the cab, his lean fingers caressing the polished knob of his stick, his eyes intent upon the taxi-meter. Dorothy smoked a cigarette nervously and tried not to keep glancing at her father. She knew now that she should never have come to him that morning and told him about Philip. She had found him at breakfast, alone at the long table in the formal dining-room of the town house in which she had spent her girlhood – and the sight of her father at the head of the table had, as always, vanquished her. He had looked at her and asked, 'What have you done?' The question had stripped her maturity from her, made her a guilty daughter again, forced the conversation into a well-known pattern that allowed the full expression of parental authority.

Within a few minutes she had told her father all the most secret of her fears and suspicions about Philip – the accusing words had come tumbling out in response to his probing, skilful questions. And, as she confessed, she felt the full shame of her self-betrayal. She realized that she was damning both Philip and herself by giving in to her father, yet this knowledge did not deter her. She had only wanted to come to her father's house for a few days, to stay away long enough for her absence to worry Philip. Her father would not have known, indeed, she had not wanted him to know, what was wrong. If she had not forgotten that she had never been able to withhold the truth about any of her misdeeds from her father, she also had not recognized that she felt guilty about her relationship with Philip. And yet she must have felt guilty, why else had she confessed? It was this unpremeditated action of hers that bewildered her.

Once she had told Steven Foster about her husband's loose habits and queer ways, the old man had become coldly angry. He had wanted her to see his lawyer at once. This she had refused to do since she felt a need to defend Philip against her father's authority. Not that she had not thought of divorce before; she had on many occasions when Philip had deserted her or by some chance she had uncovered fresh evidence of his chronic infidelity. But to have her father suggest that she see a lawyer was, in some way she did not understand, treachery. Instead, she had said that she wanted to consult George Matthews – whom she knew to be Philip's friend – and her father had gone to arrange the appointment, grumbling about 'that modern fad, psychoanalysis'.

Dorothy had never expected to get an appointment that day, in fact, she had hoped that the time set would be weeks in advance and that by then she would have solved her difficulties with Philip. When her father had come back from the telephone and announced grimly that 'Dr Matthews will see us at eleven o'clock,' she had been horrified. Her mouth had gone dry and her pulse had pounded. She had wanted at that moment to call Philip, to ask his help. But this she could not do, nor was there any way she could escape the appointment.

The taxi jolted to a stop at a traffic light and the sudden jar interrupted her thoughts. She looked out the window and saw that they were nearing the hotel. Her father still sat rigidly in his corner, and the sight of him made her want to shudder. In the past such fits of taciturnity meant that he was arriving at a decision which he would ultimately force upon her. Now he was probably planning how to deal with Philip. Dorothy leaned forward and deposited her cigarette in the bent and battered ashtray that clung to the side of the door. This time, no matter what Steven Foster decides, I will not do it, she said to herself. And the part of her that always quarrelled with her highest ideals and most fervent resolutions, her materialistic conscience, reminded her – 'If you don't, it will be the first time since you married Philip that you have gone against your father's wishes.'

The light changed to green, the taxi lurched forward and turned down the side street to the hotel. Steven Foster did not change his position until the cab had come to a full stop in front of the Algonquin, then he flicked a bill at the driver, clambered out and stood stiffly while his daughter stepped down. Taking her arm he said, 'We shall have luncheon here and while we eat we can decide what to do about Philip.'

Dorothy shook her arm free of his firm grasp and walked ahead of him into the lobby. She walked rapidly, as if she wanted to escape him. He stepped forward slowly and resolutely, as if he knew that for her escape was impossible.

While Dorothy and her father lunched at the Algonquin, Philip and Mr Peabody had luncheon at Angelo's in the financial district. The Peabody account had not been a fortunate one for Brown and Foster. Sales had fallen off during the first year's campaign, despite an enlarged budget and additional space in the latter half of the year. A few weeks before Philip had submitted the suggested programme for the next twelve months, a campaign which Philip had worked out himself, supervising it down to the last detail with the copywriter and the art director. But Philip had not given it much thought since it had been submitted. The fact was that recently he had found it impossible to think about advertising matters at all. He sat at his desk, when he was at the office, and tried to remember the intervals that he had forgotten. Sometimes, his vision would fog, the dingy, dirty light would soil everything he looked at, and the voice would begin to pester him about yesterday or the day before.

'Philip, why can't you remember. Think hard, Philip . . .'

So Philip was not prepared to defend the merits of the

campaign, and this was exactly what he was called upon to do. He had left the taxi at One Wall Street, still shaken by his narrow escape from death a few minutes before, and had taken an express elevator to one of the topmost floors of the tall building. As he stepped out of the car at his floor, a large man pushed past him hurriedly, knocking him off his balance. He fell backwards into the elevator just as the automatic doors were closing. He knew that these doors did not bounce back from an obstruction like subway doors, but kept closing inexorably. He struggled desperately, off-balance, to lunge forward – spurred on by the helpless cry of the elevator operator who was reaching to reverse the controls. Suddenly, he was struck in the back, slammed forward onto his knees. And at almost the same moment, the heavy doors whispered together and he heard the car drop down the well. He knelt on the floor, breathing heavily, cold sweat on his forehead. Had there been two attempts on his life inside of a half-hour? Or had the burly man, who had entered the elevator successfully and without Philip's seeing him full on, only accidentally knocked him off-balance? Both his near collision with the truck and his almost being crushed to death *might* have been accidents – but they also *might* have been attempts on his life. He was going to have to be very careful.

Philip stood up, brushed at his knees and walked down the corridor to Peabody and Company. He gave his name to the receptionist and she showed him into the board room where Evergood Peabody, the president of the company, was surrounded by his vassals. The campaign was spread out on the long table and the men were hunched over it, exhaling cigar smoke at it, peering at it malevolently. As he entered the room. Philip heard one of them saying, ‘I agree with you, Mr Peabody. Even the theme, the basic gimmick, hasn't the “Peabody push”.’

Philip saw at a glance that the campaign was being torn apart. All the men, every one of whom depended on Evergood Peabody for his opinion but – once the line of argument to follow was established – were quite capable of destroying good copy and art in any number of ingenious ways, jumped on Philip at once. 'The headlines have no zing,' said one, another said, 'The copy's too long, it takes too much time getting in the sales punch.' 'I miss the "Peabody push",' said a third voice. 'This thing hasn't enough class, no real distinction,' complained another.

Fighting off these generalities as effectively as he could, Philip tried to concentrate his sales talk on the essential – tried at all times, even when he was addressing a subordinate, to aim his argument at Evergood Peabody. For, as everyone knew, the president made all decisions at Peabody and Company.

At one o'clock, Evergood called off the discussion. 'I just wanted you to get my department heads' reactions,' he told Philip, chummily putting his arm around him. 'Let's you and me go to Angelo's for lunch where we can talk this over quietly. Then we can decide what to do.'

Philip followed the client out of the board room and down the hall. He knew that the dogfight he had just been in might mean nothing at all, or it might be highly significant. The real decision would come from Evergood Peabody himself in the next half-hour or so. Even now he was making up his mind.

And Philip did not really care. He was preoccupied with his own problems: the two 'accidents', the voice he heard, the 'Confession'. He was especially concerned with the voice, because – as they walked down Wall to Pearl Street and Angelo's – the voice kept sounding in his ear. 'You have to be more careful, Philip,' it was saying. 'You're so forgetful – you even forget to look when you cross a street. Please remember what I say, Philip.' He was glad when they reached the restaurant and found a table quickly. Now, for a few minutes, Peabody would be busy eating and drinking and telling his interminable stories, now he could relax and perhaps the voice would go away. But he did not relax and the voice did not go away.

While Peabody talked at length about a hunting trip

he had taken in Canada, Philip listened to the voice. There had been moments when he had not been able to hear it since he left the office. But the sound of bells had persisted, as had the queer, dirty light. He picked up a knife from the table and held it in front of his eyes. If he could only see the silver gleam, he would feel better. But, no, the same greasy film seemed to cling to it, too, just as it covered his hand, the tablecloth, yes, even Peabody's face!

Only then, as he looked hard at his face for quite another reason, did Philip realize that Peabody had asked him an important question, a very important question.

'I beg your pardon,' Philip said, 'I didn't understand.'

Peabody coughed pompously and patted his chin with his napkin. 'I would have thought you'd hear that! I asked you if you can think of any good reason why my company should retain your agency's services.'

The ringing ceased. The fogginess faded and in its place were the hard outlines of Peabody's heavy-jowled face, brightly, sharply defined. Philip's mind baulked at the meaning of the words it heard. Why, the man was firing the agency, they were losing the account! And only a moment before he had been talking about the seven point buck he had shot!

By now Peabody was glowering at him. 'Maybe you don't hear so well today, Mr Banter,' he said. 'If so, I'll repeat my charges. Our sales are off twenty per cent – thirteen per cent in the last five months with December yet to come in. They're falling in the face of the biggest Christmas season this country's ever known. All the time our advertising costs are going up. Every time you have recommended more papers, a bigger budget, fancier art-work. The copy remains the same. Oh, you change a few words here and there and tack on a new headline – but that's all. Now, you submit a new campaign. And what do I see?' He stopped and flopped his fat hand down on the presentation. The diamond on his middle finger glared at Philip. 'I see the same old crap!' he snarled. 'The very same pretty girls, the same old reason why copy, the same boilerplate layout. There's not a new idea in that whole campaign. Peabody and Company couldn't use an inch of it – let alone hike the budget by five hundred grand the way you have the gall to suggest!'

He peeled the band from a panatella and stuck it in his mouth. He did not offer Philip a cigar, although there were two in his pocket. 'In view of that,' he went on, 'I ask you if you can tell me any reason why we should continue your contract?'

Philip said nothing. All he could think was: if Peabody walks out on us that will be the third client in two months. What will the old man say?

The silence grew. Peabody puffed away at his cigar until the booth they were sitting in was clothed with smoke. Philip tried several times to speak, to say something like 'If you could be a little less destructive in your comment, Mr Peabody' or 'Now, suppose we look at just one ad. and you tell me what is wrong,' but each time he failed to get the words out of his mouth. Finally, Peabody reached for his hat.

'If you haven't got anything to say for yourself, young man, we're just wasting our time.' He pushed the cloth-bound presentation across the table. 'Here, maybe you can use this some place else. It isn't a bad programme. It's just not the thing we need right now with sales falling off.' The heavy jowls relaxed into a grin. He was being proud of himself for being sympathetic.

'We can have another programme on your desk next week, Mr Peabody,' Philip managed to say. 'If you will just show me what's wrong, where we took the wrong turning –'

But Peabody was shaking his head. 'You heard what the department heads had to say, son. They're the ones that know – they're the ones that have their hands on the public's pulse. I'm not saying it's your fault, son. I know you try your best to sell our stuff, but you just don't seem to have what it takes.' His eyes glinted. 'Get your hat and I'll walk you to the Battery. The sea air will do you good.

Looks to me like you haven't been getting enough exercise, son.'

Philip reached for his hat and the check. Three accounts gone in two months. What would old Foster say? And, as he walked glumly out the door behind Peabody, he heard the voice again. 'Philip,' it coaxed, 'we had so much fun last night. Why can't you remember?'

Steven Foster returned to his office in the middle of the afternoon. He walked through all the departments of the agency, looked into all the offices, stopped and talked to a man here, a girl there. Foster had been in advertising for over thirty-five years. He had started his own agency with Brown, long since dead, twenty years before. There had been times when he had written most of the copy – he had even helped with layout – when the agency was hard-hit by the depression and they were losing most of their clients. He was of the old school of advertising men, a man who could write a book or a rateholder, sell banks or soap.

He took a paternal pride in his force and showed an interest in their welfare that was frequently unwelcome. It was not uncommon for him to stop a secretary whose eyes seemed tired and whose face was pale and command her 'to get more sleep at nights'. And he had been known to sniff a copywriter's breath. He walked into the art department without knocking and loved to make detailed comments on finished artwork that drove the art directors out of their minds. Each ad. had to be personally approved by him – he was reputed to know every schedule in the agency. On occasion he had kept the production men working day and night to get an intaglio layout proofing up right – he had once even invaded the precinct of a syndicate's rotogravure shop to demand a sharper definition in the printing of a client's trademark. But he made up for this driving mania for perfection, or so he reasoned himself, by his generosity. His wages were among the highest in the business, his employees shared equally in the agency's profits, his Christmas bonuses were enormous. But as one paste-up boy put it, 'I'd rather do without an extra finn at Christmas so's I didn't have to worry every day in the week that the next minute I'd find old S.F. breathing down my neck telling me to move the logo a sixteenth of an inch and watch that I set that cut down at exactly a 40 degree angle.'

The aloof severity that marked Steven Foster's manner was actually a kind of restraint. He was naturally a man who itched to get his hands into everything, who was supremely confident that he could do any man's job better than that man. Often he could, but he had learned that he could not always prove his abilities. And he was the same way about his loves and hates. He liked few people. He loved many and hated many. A man could become his deep friend, without the man's knowing it, within the duration of a handshake – and a man could become a bosom enemy in as short a space. But Foster kept his feelings hidden, revealing them, if at all, only in crisis. As a result, everyone feared him, even his daughter – for whom he held the deepest love.

When he had finished his stroll through the agency, Foster returned to his own office and seated himself behind the broad desk. He kicked open the bottom drawer on which he rested his foot, picked up his telephone and asked the switchboard girl to tell Miss Grey to come in to see him. While he waited for Philip's secretary to arrive, he bit the end off a fresh cigar, lighted it and exhaled clouds of smoke at the ceiling.

Like many wealthy men, he was unused to having people say no to him and when it happened he was hurt; although he usually hid his feelings behind a gruff taciturnity. His temper was particularly short at this moment because Dorothy had refused to agree to divorce Philip. Foster had argued with her for an hour at lunch, yet she had remained steadfast. 'You know that I have usually followed your advice, father, but you must realize that this is one problem that I have to solve for myself. You can grumble and berate me as much as you like, but I shall make up my own mind.'

Her adamancy especially rankled Steven, since he had never liked Philip and was pleased that Dorothy's marriage was not working out. His reasons for not liking Philip were, for him, the best ones. He knew no Banters, had never heard of the family, and none of his friends had either. But Dorothy had insisted on marrying him, and he had been unable to prevent her since she had been of age. He had toyed with the idea of disinheriting her, but had dismissed that as being petty. Actually, he had been more than generous. He had given the puppy more than enough rope: a good job, a handsome apartment, a responsibility in the agency. He chuckled. It was working out just as he thought it would . . . although no one could say he had not been willing to give Philip a chance . . .

'Yes, Mr Foster?' Miss Grey had come into the room without him hearing her. She was standing in front of his desk, a slight smile on her face. Good girl!

Steven Foster glanced at her, and then nodded his head. He did not speak.

'Mr Banter came into the office about four o'clock yesterday afternoon. He had not been in all day. He seemed as if he had been drinking. I am not sure as I did not get close enough to him to catch his breath.' The girl spoke mechanically as if she were reciting. 'I waited around until five-thirty, at which time he came out and told me to go home. Remembering your instructions not to do anything suspicious, I left. However, I gave the charwoman a dollar and asked her to tell me if Mr Banter was still there when she cleaned his office. She told me this morning that he was still in his office at six o'clock, and that he was very drunk. She said he had his typewriter out on his desk, but he was just staring at it. He had not written a thing.'

The girl paused and looked at Foster. He nodded his head again, and she went on. 'This morning Mr Banter arrived about ten o'clock. He had been drinking. He went into his office and, a moment later, called me in. He asked me why I had let somebody use his typewriter. I told him that nobody had used his typewriter but himself. Then why was it open on his desk? he asked. I told him that he had left it open the night before. He got very angry and told me that I was to make sure that his typewriter was shut up before I left. Apparently he had forgotten that I left ahead of him last night.'

Miss Grey stopped, and stood waiting for her employer to speak.

'Where is Mr Banter now?'

'He went to lunch with Mr Peabody shortly before noon. His appointment was for one o'clock. He has not returned.'

The old man smiled. 'Thank you, Miss Grey. That will be all for now.' He held up his hand as she started to leave. 'Except that you might tell Mr Banter to see me as soon as he comes in.'

Miss Grey opened the door. 'Yes, Mr Foster,' she said.

She shut the door and Steven Foster sat staring at it, chewing vigorously at the end of his cigar. 'I'll teach the puppy!' he said.

Philip had a drink, and then another before he returned to the office. He would not have come back that day, if he had not had an appointment with old Foster at four. As it was, he needed the false courage of the whisky.

He joked half-heartedly with Sadie on his way up in the elevator, and was careful not to look at the starched elegance of the receptionist as he entered the offices. He did not go back to his own cubicle, so Miss Grey did not have a chance to deliver her message. Philip knew that there was no use putting off the inevitable. He strode right into Steven Foster's private office.

The old man was still sitting, chewing on the end of a now dead cigar, his feet propped up on an open drawer. He did not look around when Philip came into the room, but he did glance up when Philip laid the presentation down on the polished surface of the desk.

'How many O.K.s did you get?' Foster asked.

Philip shook his head.

'Not a one?'

Philip did not answer.

'What does he want us to do?'

Philip cleared his throat. Everything was bright and clear now. He heard no ringing, no voice. But still it was all he could do to hold on to himself. He stared at the hard lines of Steven Foster's face, the etched wrinkles and the wide, compressed angle of the mouth, the obscenity of the limp cigar. He felt himself sinking into that face, being devoured by it . . .

'There will be no new campaign,' he said. 'We have lost the account.'

The old man took his cigar out of his mouth and laid it gently in the gold-plated ashtray. He stood up slowly. He walked slowly around the large desk until he was standing directly opposite Philip.

'I am going to give you a month's notice, Philip,' he said pleasantly. 'Through the end of December. Call it a Christmas present if you want.' He held out his hand.

Philip took it and shook it grimly. There was nothing else to do.

Miss Grey saw Philip go into Steven Foster's office. She went to the water-cooler, which was near the president's office, and stood by it. She had finished two Dixie Cups of water and was about to start on a third, when she saw Philip come out of the door. His face was flushed, his lips compressed, his eyes defiant. Miss Grey turned slightly so that as he went past the water cooler, he would not see her. As soon as he had gone down the hall to his own office, she followed him. But she did not go back to her desk. Instead she knocked on the door of the office next to Philip's. And when a masculine voice cried, 'Come in!' she went inside.

This office was as large as Philip's and hers put together, but four desks occupied it. Two of these were empty, at a third a young woman was diligently typing – she did not look up when Miss Grey entered – and at a fourth a young man was sitting staring out of the window with his hands behind his head. Miss Grey went to this last desk. The young man looked up at her.

'What is it, Alice?' he asked.

'I'd like to see you tonight, Tom. For just a few minutes.'

The man smiled, he had a nice smile, and looked at his watch. 'The usual place? After work?'

Alice Grey nodded her head.

'Good,' said the young man.

The girl at the other desk went on typing.

'The usual place' was a restaurant on the lower level of the R.C.A. building. Alice Grey was there at ten minutes after five, and she waited another ten minutes before Tom Jamison arrived. They found a booth and ordered beers.

'What do you have to tell me that couldn't wait until I came for you at eight? Or did you forget we have a date tonight?'

Miss Grey reached over and squeezed his hand. 'I didn't forget, of course. But I just learned something that was too good to keep.'

'What?'

'I think that Philip Banter is going to be fired!'

Tom looked at her, barely suppressing a smile. 'Are you sure?'

'No, I'm not sure. But he's been getting worse and worse. And, you know, I've had to report everything he did to Mr Foster each day. Well, when I told him he was drunk again last night, you should have seen his face! He thanked me, but he was very angry. Then I saw Philip go into his office and come out within two or three minutes. Something had happened, Tom – I'm sure! I could tell by the way Philip acted. I'm thinking that he fired Philip this afternoon!'

Tom sipped his beer. 'What has this to do with me?' he asked coldly.

Miss Grey bit her lip. 'But, Tom, this is just what we've been working towards.'

'Just because Philip loses his job – that doesn't mean I get it again.'

'Who will S.F. put in his place but you? Someone will have to take care of those accounts. You always did it well, before Philip came. Oh, Tom, this is what we've been working towards for months!'

Tom Jamison allowed himself a smile. Actually, he agreed with Alice that if Philip had lost his job, old Foster would give it back to him. And why not? Had Foster ever had any reason for taking him off those accounts in the first place, except that of making room for Philip? Now, Tom would get a little of his own back.

But all he said was, 'Drink up, Alice, and let's get out of here. Someone might hear us talking.'

3

'Oh, Philip, how beautiful! How sweet of you!'

Dorothy could not keep from beaming. Philip was pleased by her pleasure. It was ever-surprising to him to see how ingenuously happy a woman could be over a simple gift of flowers. Childish, yes, but wonderful – a constant in an inconsistent world.

'Whatever made you think of them, darling?'

She was fussing with the stems, filling a vase with water, arranging them on the mantelpiece. While he watched, he noticed for the first time that she was wearing a dinner dress. Were they going out? He would have to remember to ask her.

'I saw them in the window,' he said, 'and I thought of you.'

Dorothy had finished arranging the blood-red flowers, but she seemed loath to leave them; she stood looking at them, her head tilted upwards. Philip could discern the whiteness of the part in her glossy hair. He walked over to her, placed his hands gently on her bare shoulders, turned her about and kissed her. She was warm and sweetly scented.

'It was nice of you to think of them tonight, Philip – when we are having company that we can show them off to.'

There was a circular mirror above the fireplace; Philip looked into it, over her shoulder, and saw his own long face grow grim. 'Company? Tonight? Whom?'

'Jeremy and a friend. He called up this afternoon and asked if we'd be in. I tried to get you at the office, but the switchboard girl said you and father were in conference. Why, Philip, what's wrong? Are you ill?'

Dorothy put her arm around him and helped him to the sofa. Her dark eyes were suddenly anxious, her hands quick to feel his brow, to unbutton his shirt – her voice was sincerely worried.

'Your face changed so abruptly, Philip. You're still pale – tell me what's wrong.'

'I'm all right. I was . . . startled.' It had been a shock. He had quite forgotten about the 'Confession'. He must hold on to his wits. He dare not let her know.

'Well, if you're sure you're all right . . .?'

He patted her hand. He was very fond of her: the gentleness of her ways, the ease with which she moved, her sincerity. 'I'm all right, Dorothy. I don't know what came over me, but it's passed.'

'I was telling you about Jeremy, when all at once I thought you were having some sort of an attack.'

'You said Jeremy called and told you he was bringing a friend. Are they coming to dinner? Did he mention his friend's name?'

'Some girl. He said we hadn't met. He said he wanted me to see her. Philip, do you know what?'

'No.'

'Philip, I do believe Jeremy's in love! It certainly sounded like it over the 'phone. Oh, I hope he is! It would do him so much good. You know I've always said . . .'

Philip stood up. He staggered. Dorothy jumped up, caught at him – but by then he had found his balance.

'Philip, are you sure you're all right? You almost fell.'

'I'm perfectly all right. I'll go in and change my clothes now. Nothing is the matter with me. It was just that something you said startled me.'

'But, Philip, I was only telling you about Jeremy. Why should that have startled you?'

'I must have been thinking about something else at the time. I'll go in and change now.'

'I'll be in the kitchen with cook if you need me, Philip.'

He looked back at her as he left the room, and he saw

that she was watching him. She looked like a little girl in a sophisticated dress. A worried little girl.

Philip felt sorry for his wife. He almost felt like crying.

He sat on the bed, his fingers fumbling with the buttons of his shirt, thinking. Was the impossible about to happen? Was all that the 'Confession' predicted about to come true? No, he couldn't believe that. This was a coincidence. To think otherwise was superstition. And it was to deny his own will. The rest of the prophecy would not happen because he would keep it from happening. If he knew the danger he had to face, as he did, he could avoid it. He would not allow himself to look at this girl Jeremy was bringing, not even one glance.

But it had been a shock. Wasn't it strange how he had managed to forget that damnable story? Not so strange, after all. You don't get fired every afternoon, and when such a calamity does befall you tend to think of nothing else. If the 'Confession' was so good, why didn't it predict that? No, of course, the manuscript had said nothing about what would happen that afternoon. It concerned itself only with what was to happen that evening.

Why couldn't he have continued to forget about it? If it was going to happen anyway . . . He had been completely happy in Dorothy's happiness, her unalloyed joy over his gift. He had even managed to stop thinking about the things Foster had said, the curt way he had discharged him. And then she had said that – practically the way she had said it in the manuscript. Or had she used the same words? Was this only a trick of his imagination? He could not tell without re-reading those pages still safely locked in his desk drawer at the office.

Why not plead illness? Why not go to bed? Dorothy would believe him since she already feared that he was ill. If he said he was sick, then he would not have to meet Jeremy or his friend.

Or his friend. Was he admitting the possibility that Jeremy's friend would be the woman in the manuscript?

261

Did that mean that, so soon, he was ready to give up? Was superstitious panic this close to the surface? A few mysterious occurrences, none of them definite proof of the manuscript's predictions, and he was ready to abandon all logic, all reason, to a savage irresolution!

It did not have to happen. It could not be ordained. There was no such thing as fate (and even if there were, the author of the 'Confession' was not privy to it). He could not be made to do something he did not want to do.

But what if he wanted to do it? Suppose he was attracted to this girl, would he then have the will to ignore her? Suppose she was attracted to him (as the manuscript said she would be), would he then be able to ward her off?

He had to. There was no escaping that conclusion. If it all came to pass (it was impossible – it could not – these events could not possibly occur!), would he be able to withstand the temptation?

When Philip finished dressing, he lay down on his bed and tried to smoke a cigarette. He found that he was breathing too rapidly and too irregularly to accommodate the habit of smoking: he gasped and choked until his eyes watered. He threw the cigarette away and stared at the ceiling, his hands clasped behind his head. He waited. He could hear his wife moving about in the living-room, and he could catch occasional fragments of her conversation with the cook, who must be setting the table. He felt detached and lonely. As a boy he had often had the same feeling when visitors came to call on his mother and he hid himself in his room because of his reluctance to meet strangers. He had been modest and reticent in those days, and he suffered from feelings of inadequacy. Now, emotionally, he was the groping adolescent again. His mother's face (she was long dead) hovered in his mental eye, a vague, disembodied face that seemed to be trying to tell him something, to communicate with him . . . He shut his eyes to concentrate on the evasive image; it enlarged in size and foreboding, but it became no more distinct. Warmth, an uncomfortable warmth, pressed down on him and, at the same time, he knew that he was sinking into timelessness, an unnatural kind of sleep. Then, all upon an instant, he was awake again, wholly alert, sitting forward, strained and tense with shock. He had heard the ghost of a tinkle, the last faint vibration of the doorbell – and now, voices – not a voice, not *the* voice he had come to expect to hear, a man's voice and a woman's voice . . . in the hall.

Not until Dorothy called to him, concerned about him, 'Philip, are you all right? – Jeremy and Brent are here, Philip! are you about ready?' did he go out to meet his guests.

As he entered his own living-room he was still existing partly in the emotional context of his youth; it was as if he had walked into his mother's parlour: the warm, un-aired, shut-in odour oppressed him (the sliding doors had been kept closed, the windows shut and locked against the dust so that everything would look nice when company came). He found himself comparing Dorothy to his mother – the likeness about the eyes was particularly remarkable. He promised himself again that he would not look at Jeremy's friend, even while being introduced to her. He glanced at Jeremy once; as soon as he saw how fat his friend's formerly open, boyish face had become, and had seen the fold of flesh that bulged slightly above the purposely loose collar of his shirt, he turned back to Dorothy (remembering how as a child he had kept his gaze steadfastly on his mother while forcing himself to mumble the polite words, to say 'I'm glad to know you').

No one noticed his shyness. Jeremy was being boister-ous, as usual. He had walked over and clapped Philip on the back, and had pumped his hand. 'Where you been keeping yourself, Phil? Long time no see! Auld acquaint-ance shouldn't be given the brush-off, you know!'

'Philip has been kept very busy at the agency, Jerry,' Dorothy was saying. 'Neither of us meant to neglect you. It's just that we hardly ever have a day to ourselves.'

Philip saw that Dorothy was frowning at him. Then she had noticed that something was wrong. He would have to do better than this. He would have to look at the woman, at least.

Jeremy again. 'Phil, I want you to meet Brent Holliday, a little something special I've picked up since last we met. Smile your prettiest for the nice gentleman, Brent dear!'

Had Jeremy always been like this? Philip did not remember him as being quite so blatant, so downright vulgar. Had a year really made that much difference?

And then, thinking about Jeremy, trying to compare the man before him with the memory of a friendship that was over, Philip forgot and looked at Brent. His mind neglected its principal concern for the duration of an instant and, in so doing, dropped its defences of shyness and withdrawal. He turned and looked directly into her eyes, and he did it as much to get away from Jeremy as for any other reason. He did not look away.

Brent was not beautiful. He saw at once that she was even careless of her personal appearance: her mouth needed fresh lipstick, her long bob fell naturally, loosely, to her shoulders – it had not been trained to fall that way by a hairdresser – the gold pin above her breasts was fastened crookedly to the high-necked tunic of her dress. But her eyes were alive, brown flecked unevenly with a glinting, changing colour, commanding. She was half-leaning against the back of the sofa, regarding him mockingly. He realized that she had noticed his awkward reticence, too, and had been amused by it. Where, at first, he had thought no one was aware of his shyness, and he had been able to hope that it was but an inward state of himself, now he knew that both Brent and Dorothy had sensed his fear at once, and that only Jeremy was unconscious of it.

'I'm glad to know you, Philip,' Brent was saying, looking past him at his wife. 'Tell me, Dorothy, is he always this shy? Why, he's just like a little boy. A frightened, little boy!'

But as she said these cruelly jocular words, Philip saw her face change; or was it that he was seeing her as she was instead of the façade she wished him to see? The badly rouged lips were actually quite controlled; the slurred words were slurred consciously. Her eyes held his like a man's; it was almost as if she had put out her hand, grabbed the stuff of his stiff shirt, held him at arm's length and cried, 'Here you are – I have you!'

'Philip – shy?' Jeremy exploded into laughter. 'Oh, he's shy all right. Tell her how shy he is, Dottie. Go on, tell her!'

'It isn't that he's shy, Brent. It's just that he had a dizzy spell before you came and he still feels a little shaky. Are you all right now, Philip?'

At this cue, Brent's expression changed again, became demure, penitent.

'Oh, I'm sorry, Mr Banter, I didn't know you felt badly. I wouldn't have said what I did.'

Philip thought he detected a sense of disappointment in what she said, as if he weren't all that she had expected. Or was he reading too much into a few casual words? He looked away from her and went over to sit down next to Dorothy. Jeremy was still laughing. 'Phil, tell her about how you met Dottie. Go on and tell her, Phil. Oh, he's shy all right!'

Brent's face stiffened. She seemed annoyed by Jeremy, sympathetic to Philip. 'Do you have to go on so, Jeremy?' she asked.

'It is rather amusing, Brent,' said Dorothy. 'What Jerry's referring to. You see I met Jerry before I met Philip. In fact I met Philip through Jerry. Jerry was always telling me about Philip. It was always "Philip did this" or "Philip said that" – so I got curious about this man I was always hearing about, but never seemed to meet –'

'Do we have to rehash all that, Dorothy?' Philip asked. He felt enough of a fool already.

'He's just shy, Dottie!' Jeremy insisted. 'Don't let him stop you now.'

265

Dorothy looked at her husband. She smiled at him. 'I suppose it's really only amusing to us. It would only bore you, Brent.'

'No, really, Mrs Banter.'

'Call me Dorothy as you did before.'

'I really feel like I've known you quite a while, Dorothy. Go on. Tell us about how you met Philip.'

'I finally persuaded Jerry to take me to a party that Philip was giving. It was in one tremendous room that hadn't been cleaned in weeks. There were scads of queer people milling around or being very quiet in corners. And Philip! The first time I laid eyes on Philip he was standing in the centre of this crowd, with his shirt torn and his trousers sagging, ashes and cinders sprinkled in his hair and all over his clothes, reciting T. S. Eliot's *The Waste Land* in sepulchral tones!'

'Good old Phil! The life of the party!' laughed Jeremy.

'I tell you, Brent, I never saw a drunker man in all my life. I was mortified when Jerry insisted on taking me over to him right away and introducing us.'

Brent had nothing to say. She was watching Philip and smiling. He turned away from her deliberately.

'But that was only one side of you, wasn't it?' Dorothy was smiling at him, too. Only her smile marked the indulgence of a wife, not the mocking acknowledgement of Brent's manner.

'I wasn't always drunk,' said Philip. He wished he could have kept Dorothy from dragging in that extraneous bit of his past. She meant nothing by it – her reasons were probably sentimental – but it annoyed him.

'No, darling,' she said. 'And you made love beautifully.' She turned to Jeremy and asked him coquettishly, 'He took me away from you, didn't he, Jerry?'

Jeremy seemed about to bulge out of his dinner jacket as he made a comic bow to them. A lick of his sandy hair fell onto his brow, and Philip could see beads of sweat on his forehead.

'To the brave, the fair,' he said.

Philip felt Brent's eyes upon him, but this time he did not turn away from Jeremy. He did not dare look her way. He wanted to too badly.

They talked more naturally during dinner and Philip found himself taking part in the conversation. Jeremy seemed to forget his delight in retelling sensational details of Philip's past. Dorothy was the inquiring, solicitous hostess. Even Brent ventured to talk about herself and her work. She was a writer who had been published in several of the 'little' magazines and was now working on a novel.

Philip drew her out about the novel, but cautiously. He could not forget certain lines in the prophetic manuscript. He felt that if he heard her say anything that was even an approximation of the predicted dialogue, then all of it would also come to pass, inevitably.

'I feel vaguely uncomfortable when I hear someone say "I'm working on a novel",' he said, taking care to address the remark to them all, not to Brent alone.

'Why say that, Philip?' Dorothy asked. He could see that she feared he was going out of his way to be rude.

'I think I know what he means,' Brent interrupted. 'I feel the same way at times. You're wondering what the person has found to say.'

This was not what Philip had meant. Philip had not intended anything so definite. His question had been an attempt to draw Brent out about her writing, and it was succeeding.

'There are so many kinds of novels,' he said.

'It is difficult, I admit,' said Brent, 'and if you asked me what it is I want to say in my novel, I don't believe I could answer you. Not in so many words. I could give you the plot, of course. I could describe the characters for you . . .'

Brent lifted a spoonful of pudding as she said this, but it never reached her lips. She made a small gesture with the spoon and the chocolate stuff fell off onto the front of her dress. She stopped speaking and stared at the mess she had made, frowning. At the same time a lock of her dark bob slipped forward, obscuring one of her eyes and making her seem more than ever like a wilful child. Suddenly Philip wanted to kiss her, to hold her in his arms . . .

'I'll get some hot water,' said Dorothy, getting to her feet. 'If you apply it immediately it will come off.'

'Never mind,' said Brent. 'I'll just scrape it off. It doesn't matter.' And she did as she said, not too carefully, leaving a brown smear on the light cloth of her bodice. 'I'm going to have to send this to the cleaner's anyway.'

'It would only take a minute.' Dorothy continued to protest.

'No really, Dorothy. It does not matter.' She had become aware of Philip's steady gaze and her own expression now changed, became serious, intent. It was as if she had only then made an interesting discovery. When she spoke, her words were made indistinct by the smile on her lips. 'What was I saying, Philip? Not that I suppose it matters . . .'

'You were telling us what your book was about.'

Brent laughed a little too loudly. 'Or rather I was telling you what it wasn't about. I was being awfully vague.'

'You said you could tell us about the characters,' Philip said hopefully. As long as she was talking to him, he could maintain the fiction that she was talking to the group. And he could look at her without rousing Dorothy's suspicions.

'They are very stuffy characters. I'd only bore you.' She was teasing him. She wanted him to coax her openly, before his wife.

'Let me decide that,' he said.

Brent glanced at Dorothy – to see if she gathered what was going on? And if she did – to see how she was taking it?

Jeremy yawned. 'Brent's always going on about that damned book, but she's never let me see it. I'm beginning

268

to doubt its existence.' He began to eat his pudding again. After making this one morose comment, he was definitely uninterested in the conversation.

'It's about a man and two women,' Brent said. 'The man is in his thirties and attractive. One of the women he has known for a long time; the other he meets in the subway quite by chance. He loves both of them and cannot choose between them.' She paused.

'There's more to it than that?' Philip asked.

Brent twisted the pin on her dress. 'Much more. You see, he only meets the second girl in the subway. At first, he meets her accidentally, and then, later, he plans to. She talks to him, lets him kiss her, but she will never leave the train with him. He trails her, follows her, tries to see where she gets off. But she never gets off.'

'She would have to leave the train sometimes, wouldn't she?' asked Dorothy.

'No,' said Brent, 'she never does. She stays on the train. One night the man stays up the whole night with her on the train waiting for her to get off. But she never does.'

'She's a symbol?' asked Philip.

Brent looked down at her empty plate. 'Yes, you might call her that. You see, he talks to her on the train about everything, simply everything. The world, politics, art, the education of the young – just everything. She's well-informed, intelligent, nicely dressed, beautiful . . . his ideal woman.'

'But she never gets off the train . . .'

'That's right. She never gets off the train.'

'What happens in the end?' Philip asked.

Brent smiled secretively, and traced a pattern on the damask with her fork. Then she looked directly into Philip's eyes. 'He dies. He commits suicide by jumping under the train. He has realized his love is hopeless.'

'And what about the other woman, the one he has known a long time?' Dorothy asked. 'Does she just stand by while all this is happening and . . . and let it happen?'

Brent turned to Dorothy. 'She never knows what is

wrong. She thinks she is at fault. At the end, she blames herself for his suicide. And, in a way, she is right . . .'

Jeremy jumped to his feet and threw his napkin down on the table. 'Rot! Unpleasant, pretentious rot!' He glared at Brent. 'And what's more. I think you were making it up as you went along!'

Brent made no response, nor did she seem discouraged by Jeremy's comment. He excused himself, and they watched him leave the room. And then, since dinner was over, they followed him.

Coffee was served in the living-room. Philip and Jeremy could find little to say to each other, but this was not the case with Brent and Dorothy. They sat together on the sofa and talked about those subjects women always talk about and men never listen to, while Jeremy and Philip sat on either side of the fireplace, in the two large chairs, facing each other glumly. Jeremy, who had been boisterous before dinner, had grown surprisingly taciturn. Philip concentrated on beginning a conversation with him. He was glad that Dorothy and Brent were taken up with each other – if he could get Jeremy to talk, perhaps he would be able to forget his obsession: Brent.

'I have some brandy that should go well with this,' he said to Jeremy, setting his coffee cup on a low table and getting to his feet. 'Would you like some?'

Jeremy gazed vaguely at his own cup and slowly shook his head. 'Never touch the stuff any more. My doctor advises against it.'

'Ulcers?' Philip tried to make his inquiry sound sympathetic.

'No, palpitations. And high blood pressure. I work too hard.'

'Still doing the same thing?'

'I'm on sustaining. And then I get calls for extra shows at odd hours. I did ten extras last week. They pay well, but I'm on the go all the time.'

'Do you still live down in the Village?' Philip asked.

'No. I found a place uptown last fall. It's closer to the studio, in the Fifties near Madison Square Garden. It's a loft that I fixed up. Roomy, and you can play the radio loud or have company to all hours. The only thing is you have to pay off the inspector.'

'The inspector?'

Jeremy lighted a cigarette and drained the rest of his coffee. 'The building inspector. You're not supposed to live in lofts. I keep my bed covered with a studio couch cover and pretend to be an artist. When he comes around I say the bed is a couch for my models to rest on. I keep an easel under the skylight to further the impression that I'm an artist and I only work there.'

'Where does the pay-off come in?'

'The last guy who came around was nosy. He prowled into the kitchen and saw the stove and refrigerator and the dishes in the sink. He asked some questions so I made him a present.'

'What's the advantage of living in such a place?'

'It's roomy. The rent's cheap. Nobody bothers you and I can walk to work.'

'Sounds interesting.'

Jeremy nodded his head. 'It is. You and Dorothy should come up some time.' He was not enthusiastic.

'We'd like to,' Philip said. 'I've been busy myself or we would have looked you up long ago.' He hesitated, not knowing what else to say.

Jeremy threw his cigarette into the fireplace. 'I know you've been busy. I can understand that. I've been busy myself. If Dorothy hadn't –'

'Philip! Jeremy!' cried Dorothy. 'What on earth are you talking about over there by yourselves? Brent and I feel we've been deserted!' Dorothy's manner was very bright and gay, but her eyes glittered at Philip. Why is she so intent on having me make up with Jeremy? he wondered. Why did she interrupt us like this? Did she think we were having a row?

Jeremy crossed over to where Brent and Dorothy sat;

Dorothy moved to make room for him on the sofa. 'Why don't you get us some of that precious brandy of yours, Phil?' she asked.

'I offered some to Jerry, but he tells me he has stopped drinking,' Philip replied. He walked over to the credenza and began to fumble with the bottles. He had almost forgotten about the 'Confession' again, and he was certainly not thinking of Brent at that moment. But before he found the bottle of cognac he had been saving since before the war, the telephone began to ring.

He ran into the foyer and answered it himself. At least that much of the prophecy would not come true, he told himself as he picked up the receiver; Dorothy would not answer the 'phone. And if it were for Jeremy, he would make sure the call was genuine and not tricked-up. 'Hello?' he said.

'I'm trying to reach Mr Jeremy Foulkes,' said a woman's voice. 'Is he available?'

'Who is this calling?'

'This is Mr Foulkes' studio calling. Can you ask him to come to the 'phone, please. It is urgent.'

Philip started to ask what was so important, but then he realized that Jeremy was standing beside him. 'Is that for me, Phil?' he asked.

Philip handed him the telephone. 'It's your studio,' he said. He walked back into the other room.

Dorothy and Brent looked up at him expectantly. 'Philip,' Dorothy asked, 'what was the name of the awful book you were telling me about the other day? The one you said I should read? Was it by Henry Miller? I can't remember.'

Philip sat down on the edge of the sofa. He tried to make his face blank. He did not want to show the sudden panic that had again seized him. 'What book?' he asked. 'I don't know what one you mean.'

'You know the one I mean, Philip – I'm sure you do. It had something to do with an American living in Paris – it was Bohemian, I think.'

Brent smiled archly at Philip. He had not noticed that he had sat down beside her, that she was close to him – that if he leaned forward he could touch her shoulder. 'Dorothy was telling me that she found the modern novel difficult, Mr Banter, and often revolting.' Brent's tone indicated that she wanted Philip to help her deride his wife's opinion. What bothered Philip most was that what Brent had said did not sound like Dorothy's opinion of contemporary writing. Dorothy liked most modern novels.

Philip's mind was whirling. He was afraid to speak or to try to answer Brent's question. The 'Confession' had predicted that Jeremy would be called to the telephone after dinner, and the prediction had come true. It had also predicted that the conversation would turn to Henry Miller, and that Philip would venture an opinion which Brent would attack – but what the devil was the opinion he was supposed to come out with? He could not remember. Did that mean that anything he said *might* be what the 'Confession' had predicted he would say? How could he keep this part of the prediction from coming true, if he could not remember what he must not say? He took his handkerchief out of his pocket and patted at his damp forehead.

Brent was puzzled by his silence. Dorothy was smiling at him vacantly. Philip tried again to speak, but all he managed was a mumble. He saw Dorothy frown. Then, before anything else could happen, Jeremy came back into the room.

'Sorry folks, I've got to go to work. One of the boys has reported sick and they've got no one to do his trick for him.'

Brent was dismayed. 'Oh, Jerry, again? Why don't they leave you alone one evening in the week, at least? We haven't had an entire evening together for a month!' She stood up to go.

'You don't have to leave, do you, Brent?' asked Dorothy. 'Why don't you stay and talk for a while?'

Jeremy patted Brent on the shoulder. 'That's right, honey. I don't want to break up the party. Why don't you stay with the folks?'

273

Brent was watching Philip. She was smiling the way she had at dinner, baring her teeth at him. He heard himself saying, 'Yes, Brent, why go now? I'll be glad to see you home, if that's what's bothering you.' It was the polite thing to say.

Still Brent was undecided. She looked at Jeremy again. 'I don't see why you should leave if you want to stay,' he said. 'I could only take you home, you know.' He glanced at his watch. 'No, I don't even have time for that. I'd have to leave you in the taxi – you might as well stay and get to know these good people.' He started for the door; obviously he did not have much time.

Dorothy went after him. Philip heard her saying, 'You will come again, won't you, Jerry?' Brent sat down on the sofa beside Philip. Whether by chance, or because she wanted it that way, she sat uncomfortably close to him – he could sense her body next to his. 'I don't think your wife likes me,' she said.

Philip was startled. The 'Confession' had not predicted this remark. 'What makes you say that?' he asked. 'I don't think it's true, you know.'

'May I have a cigarette, please?' Philip handed her his case and held a light for her. She inhaled, then blew out the lighter's bluish flame with a harsh exhalation. Her eyelids lowered as she looked at him through a brief cloud of smoke. 'Oh, I can tell. She's jealous of you. I don't think it's just me she's jealous of. I think she doesn't like any woman near you.' Perversely, she leaned against him. He could hear the cloth of her tunic rustle as she breathed.

'I think you're imagining things,' he said. He stood up to get away from her, although escape was not what he most wanted. 'Dorothy isn't like that at all. She hasn't a jealous bone in her body.'

He went over to the credenza, found the brandy and poured three glasses. As he was carrying a glass to Brent, he happened to glance at the mirror above the fireplace. He saw Jeremy and Dorothy standing by the door in the mirror. He saw Jeremy take Dorothy in his arms and begin to kiss her. Then Philip was past the mirror. He gave the brandy to Brent, and went back for his own – passing the mirror twice and twice glancing at it. The first time Jeremy was still kissing his wife. The second time he had released her and was opening the door to go.

Brent raised her glass for a toast. 'To us,' she said softly. Philip did not understand what she had said.

'I beg your pardon.'

'To us,' said Brent, her glass still raised, a tempting smile on her lips. 'To you and me.'

'I'll drink to that,' said Philip.

4

It had been inconceivable to Philip that Dorothy might ever be unfaithful to him; it had not occurred to him that other events, aside from those specified in the 'Confession', might take place on the same night that the 'Confession's' predictions came true. Seeing Dorothy kiss Jeremy came as a double shock to him. Not only was this an event that had not been foretold, but it was also one he had not thought possible. Of course, if he wished, he could excuse Dorothy's conduct on the grounds that she had known Jeremy for many years and could kiss a good friend if she so wanted. But he did not find himself wanting to excuse Dorothy. Instead he found himself wanting to kiss Brent.

He did not kiss her then. Dorothy came back into the room before they had finished their brandy, a moment after Brent had repeated and clarified her toast, in fact. Philip discovered that it was difficult for him to look at his wife. He gave her a glass of brandy, and then sat down in one of the chairs by the fireplace.

'What sort of a job has Jerry got that he has to run off to it at all hours?' Dorothy asked Brent.

Brent was sipping the last of her brandy. 'He's the head announcer at one of those small stations that play records all night,' she explained. 'They've had a run of illness lately, and he has been having to substitute for somebody almost every night. Then, sometimes, he has a half-hour show at one of the big stations.'

'He must work awfully hard.'

'That's not like Jerry,' said Philip.

Dorothy glared at her husband. 'Philip, what's come over you? Whatever made you say a thing like that?'

'It's true, isn't it? Did he work in college? You ought to know about that, you wrote as many of his papers for him as I did. Did he work when he was a reporter? How many times times did I file his stories for him when Jerry had a little too much party? It just seems damn queer to me that all of a sudden he should develop into such a hard worker!' Philip gulped the rest of his brandy and banged the empty glass down on the table.

'Philip, I don't understand you. I watched you all evening, and I saw you were as unpleasant as you could be with Jerry. It seemed to me that you were deliberately trying to pick a fight with him.' Dorothy was angry. Brent was amused. She kept sniffing her empty glass of brandy and glancing from one to the other of them.

Philip did not know what to say. He could not remember having tried to pick a fight with Jeremy, although – since what he had said to Jeremy had not been uppermost in his mind – he realized that his actions might have been taken that way and even, possibly, his words. But why did Dorothy come out with all this in front of Brent?

'I wasn't impolite to Jeremy,' he said. 'If anyone was impolite it was he. I tried my best to get him to talk after dinner. I was as pleasant to him as I could be.'

Dorothy was quietly indignant. 'Philip, that's not true and you know it. I watched you all evening and I know.'

Brent stood up to find an ashtray. Philip and Dorothy were oblivious of her in their concern for each other. After she had extinguished her cigarette, Brent walked over to Philip and rested her hand lightly on his shoulder. 'What do you think of Henry Miller?' she asked. 'Don't you find his work exciting?'

Philip was hurt and angry at Dorothy's unfounded accusation; he answered Brent's attempt to change the subject without thinking about what he said. 'Miller's just a little old-fashioned, isn't he? Rather an overdue romantic, I think.' Not until he had spoken, did he begin to wonder if what he had said had comprised what the

277

'Confession' had predicted he would say. He kept his eyes on Dorothy. She had withdrawn, as she usually did after losing her temper, and was affecting to ignore him.

'At least, he's honest,' Brent pressed him. 'He says what he thinks.'

Philip gave his attention to her. He had to keep his wits about him, he reminded himself. Or else he might say something that would lead to disaster. 'He makes a cult of it, doesn't he?' he asked. That had not been in the 'Confession' he was sure.

'A cult of what?'

'Of saying what he thinks. Of calling a spade a spade. I'll admit that he's thought out his position, and I'll admit that his position may be a sound one for him, personally. But I rather resent having him shout his invective at me at the top of his lungs. I'm an American. I live in America. I like it. If he doesn't, that's all right with me. I don't go shouting at him!'

Brent was leaning against the fireplace, her head tossed back, her dark hair falling crookedly against the mantel. 'Why do you American business men insist that the artist sing your praises? America is business. That's all we have. Is it surprising that Miller doesn't like it – that he refuses to pay lip service to your phony values?' Philip could see that she was not angry; instead she was enjoying the argument. He felt as if she were slicing away at him, peeling him to ribbons with the cutting edge of her tongue. Queerly enough, he enjoyed being attacked.

'It's been a long time since I read Miller,' he said. 'I still can't remember the title of the book Dorothy asked me about. You may be right. I'd have to read more of him to tell.'

Brent smiled, allowing him to elude her. But he knew she was aware of the full measure of her victory. She advanced to the sofa triumphantly. 'May I have another cigarette, please?'

Philip offered the case to both Dorothy and Brent, and then he got some more brandy for the three of them. 'Why

278

don't you see what's on the radio, Phil?' Dorothy suggested. 'You might be able to get some music.'

Philip turned on the set and they listened to the last movement of Brahms' Fourth. This monumental music seemed absurdly incongruous to Philip amid the confusion of his thoughts, which called for cacophony and a mixing of tongues. As the mighty chords of the *passacaglia* died away, Brent stood up. 'I think I had better go,' she said. 'I want to get some work done tomorrow.'

Dorothy did not rise. 'You will persuade Jerry to bring you again, won't you?' she asked. 'And I hope your novel turns out well.'

Philip escaped to the foyer to get Brent's coat. After he had found it he stood watching the duel of platitudes between his wife and Brent: the spectacle of two women who dislike each other yet are intent on maintaining the pretence of sociability. The sight disgusted him.

Brent finally completed her good-byes and came into the foyer. He helped her on with her coat. They went out the door. He tried to kiss her in the hallway, but she evaded him. He succeeded in the taxi.

Dorothy waited ten minutes after Philip and Brent left before she put on her old tweed coat and a mannish hat that made her look drab and different and went out herself. While she waited, she drank two brandies and paced the room. When she reached the street, she set off westward, walking swiftly. She walked with her head down, her hands thrust into her pockets, blindly. She ignored traffic lights and several times bumped into other pedestrians. By the time she had gone four or five blocks, her pace had quickened to a rapid trot. When she reached the stone steps of her father's house, she fled up them as if she were pursued.

The butler let her in and told her that her father was still in the library. Dorothy did not wait to let him take her coat and hat, but pushed past him and walked down the high-ceilinged hall, her heels clattering on the tile floor.

She threw open the heavy oak doors of the library and strode into the large, comfortable room. A fire blazed in the fireplace, and Steven Foster sat beside it in a high-backed chair. His hand clasped a book, by his side was his glass of port. His posture was as rigid, as uncompromising, as ever. He did not lift his eyes from the page he was reading until Dorothy stood before him, her breasts rising and falling from the exertion of her pell-mell haste, her breathing sibilant.

'What have you done to Philip, father?' she demanded.

The old man returned his attention to the book. The gilt letters on its spine glinted in the firelight. She could read the first words of its title, *Statistical Report on* –

'I've discharged him. Gave him a month's notice this afternoon.'

Dorothy paled. 'Oh, father, why?'

'He lost the Peabody account today. His work has been going steadily downhill. There was nothing else I could do.'

'I asked you not to . . . I knew at lunch that you were going to do this . . . I begged you not to . . .'

Foster glanced up again. His mouth curved slightly. 'Why are you so concerned? You know I'll take care of you. Philip can very well get himself another job.'

'But to do a thing like this . . . now.' Dorothy's voice trailed off. She put her hand to her mouth, pressed it hard against her colourless lips. Her body wilted. She crumpled and fell at his feet.

Foster looked down at his daughter. He laid aside his book and mumbled, 'Damn!' Then, he knelt stiffly beside her, put his arms carefully under her, picked her up and, carrying her high against his breast, walked over to the leather couch. He laid her down gently, bending his body until his face was close to hers; his lips lingered over hers. He stayed this way for a long moment, before he crushed her mouth with his own. 'He never deserved you!' he muttered savagely.

*

Later, after the butler had brought smelling salts and

brandy, Dorothy was able to sit up. Her father sat beside her for a long time, holding her hand, imploring her to stay with him and not to go back to Philip.

'I can't do that,' she said.

'Where is he now? Is he waiting for you?'

'I don't know.'

'Has he gone off again?'

'I don't know.'

'What do you mean "you don't know"? Either you know where your husband is or you don't.'

'We had people in tonight. Jerry and a friend. Jerry was called away unexpectedly and Philip promised to take his friend home. Her name is Brent. They left just before I did.'

'He's coming back?'

'He said he would.'

'But you don't believe him?'

Dorothy stared at her father, then, putting her hands to her eyes, she stood up. 'I don't know, I tell you. I don't know!'

Steven Foster clenched his fists. 'If you tell me where he went, I'll go fetch him myself!' he cried.

Dorothy backed away from him. Now her face was determined, her mouth set, her body as straight and as unyielding as her father's. 'No, I know what to do. And I have to do it myself. There is no other way out.' She walked resolutely to the door.

'What are you going to do?' Foster asked, running after her.

'Oh, father, I'm going home, of course. I'm going to wait for him like a good wife. What else can I do?'

And she slammed the heavy door in her father's face. Foster gazed at it and smiled. Things were working out uncommonly well.

Brent's apartment was on Jones Street in the Village, a street that exists for one short block between Bleecker and West Fourth and is lined its entire length by six-storey tenements only occasionally interspersed with newer, efficiency apartment buildings. Philip was panting before he had finished climbing the five flights that led to three small rooms on the top floor of the newer buildings; he was glad for the pause outside the door of her apartment while Brent fumbled with the lock; he sank down on the studio couch by the window as soon as they were inside. Brent went into the kitchen and came back a few minutes later with two highballs.

She looked much younger in the tidy, cramped flat. Her body was thin and angular in places. She moved awkwardly, in sudden spurts and sidesteps, as if she were confined by the box-like room. He drank half his highball while watching her pick up and arrange some books and papers that had been lying on the seat of the maple armchair. When she sat down beside him, he put his arm around her and pulled her to him. She allowed him the intimacy, but she did not respond. She squirmed away from him when he tried to kiss her again.

'Why are you doing that?' she asked.

'Because I want to.'

'Must you always do what you want to do?'

'It's generally more satisfactory that way.' Her attitude puzzled him. Why had she acted the way she had, if she had not wanted him to make love to her? Even in the taxi she had been inexplicably cold and, while she had not repulsed his advances, she had given him no encouragement.

'Suppose I don't want you to?' she asked.

'Don't you?'

'I don't know. I know I don't love you. I'm not sure I even like you. And I'm surprised you're not content with Dorothy. She is nice.'

'She wasn't nice tonight.'

'I wouldn't have been either the way you were making up to me.' She jumped to her feet and sat in the other chair.

'I thought you wanted me to make up to you,' he said. 'You certainly acted that way.'

'You're attractive. I like to play with the idea of you making love to me . . .' She watched him, a smile on her lips, her eyes half-closed.

Philip went over to her, seized her hands and pulled her roughly to her feet. He held her tightly against himself. He could feel her trembling. He grasped the collar of her tunic and tried to rip it from her throat. 'It won't do you any good to tear my clothes, you know,' she said matter-of-factly – although her body was wire-taut and throbbing. 'I'll sleep with you if I want to – you can't make me.'

He continued to hold her. He relaxed his grip on her dress, but his hands refused to release her body. She stood stiffly against him; her eyes stared openly at his flushed face; her mouth was a line of anger. 'And now I know that I do not want to,' she whispered.

Philip felt exhausted. Although he knew that he could overpower her physically, he also knew that he could never possess her. The advantage had exchanged hands – had it ever been his? – and he could only withdraw. As if to jeer at him, the memory of the manuscript and its misleading prediction returned to his mind. He smiled and let his arms drop to his sides. Brent walked nobly away from him. She went over to the closet and picked up his hat and coat. 'In a way I have scored a victory,' he mumbled to himself.

Brent was holding his coat for him. He could see that he had not even succeeded in tearing her dress, although he had wrenched the collar loose from the rest of the material and it was hanging awry. 'I wouldn't call it a victory,' she said. 'Or did I hear you right?'

He turned his back on her and shrugged himself into the coat she held. 'I was thinking about your novel,' he lied. 'About the poor devil who keeps chasing the girl until he falls off the train. In one respect, at least, I'm better off than him. I haven't fallen off the train.'

'Haven't you?' asked Brent. She was holding the door open for him.

5

After Philip left, Brent went into the bathroom and brushed her teeth, making wry faces in the mirror as she manipulated the brush. When her mouth felt clean again, she undressed and put on a pullover sweater and a pair of corduroy slacks. Her hips were small and the slacks outlined them pertly. She went into the kitchen, mixed and drank another highball. Then she turned out the lights and left the apartment.

She took a taxi to Jeremy's place in the Fifties. This was a loft located in the tenement district near Madison Square Garden. She unlocked the battered door and climbed a steep flight of broad stairs. Inside the loft she went to the rear of the barn-like room and switched on a lamp that made a small circle of warm light in the greater darkness. A half-partition hid a kitchen, a tub and shower, as well as an improvised closet. Brent filled the tub with warm water, took a pair of pyjamas out of the closet and laid them on a chair, then soaked herself in the tub until the water grew lukewarm. She jumped out and rubbed herself down with a rough towel that dry-scrubbed her flesh until it was brick-red. She put on her pyjamas and combed her hair, then went into the other part of the room where she turned down the cover on the studio couch and made it up for the night. Her movements were quick and showed her actions to be habitual; she was obviously accustomed to the place as she knew where everything was and lost no time in deciding what to do next. After she had made the bed, plumping up the pillows that served by day as the back of the couch and sheathing them in slips, she took a book off the shelf and twisted the lamp so that its pool of light fell on the head of the bed and climbed under the covers.

Brent read for ten or fifteen minutes before she fell asleep. Jeremy awakened her when he came in about four o'clock. He turned off the light that had burned all night, bent over and kissed her brow. 'Jerry,' she said sleepily, 'you took so long.'

Later, she wanted to know about Philip and Dorothy. 'I've seldom felt so uncomfortable, Jerry – what's going on between those two? And why did you let him take me home? Didn't you know he would make a pass at me?'

Jeremy's face paled at her last remark. 'Did he do that, the bastard! What did you do?'

Brent laughed softly. 'I didn't let him, silly! I think I gave him a shock. He looked very strange when he left.' She told him about Philip's unsuccessful attempt to make love to her. 'But that doesn't help me find out what interests me,' she said later. 'Tell me more about his wife, Jerry. She hates me and I want to know why.'

Jeremy hesitated before he answered her. His hair was tousled and his eyes were tired. He was still a young man, but he was the kind of young man who already shows some of the signs of middle age. 'First, let me ask you a question,' he said. 'What do you think of Philip?'

'I think he's fascinating in some ways. He's so sullen and dissolute-looking. But I don't like him.'

'Because of last night?'

'Partly.' She sucked in her lip, thinking. 'But I felt I disliked him before he tried to make love to me. I think perhaps, because of his attitude towards you.'

'I didn't think that showed.'

Brent nodded her head. 'Yes, it did. After you left, Dorothy bawled him out for it. She said he had been trying to pick a fight with you all evening.'

Jeremy smiled. 'I wouldn't have believed she would take my part,' he said.

Brent bit her lip and began to pound him playfully with her fists. 'Stop being so mysterious!' she cried. 'Tell me what's behind all this. What kind of people are they? And how long have you known them? Does Dorothy look that way at every woman who comes into her house? Each time she looked at me, I felt like she was thinking up ways of murdering me!'

Jeremy laughed. 'She probably was.' Then he grew more serious. 'Dorothy's one of the nicest people I know. We've been friends ever since we were in college together. She was my best girl then. Does that make you jealous?'

Brent leaned up against him. 'A little,' she admitted. 'But not seriously, as long as it's in the past tense.'

'It's in the past tense all right. She didn't stay my girl, you see. I introduced her to Philip, my closest friend, once when we were in New York for the holidays. The next year they were married.'

'I know most of that from what Dorothy told me last night,' said Brent. 'But why is she so jealous of him?'

Jeremy was silent for a few minutes. Brent waited patiently, sensing that what he was about to tell her was painful to him and that he would prefer not to speak about it. It had begun to grow light outside; the skylight in the front part of the loft had become an ill-defined grey patch latticed with darker shadows, as had the great, wide front windows, the sills of which rested on the floor. Slowly the cavernous darkness of the loft began to recede, to grow dim and vague; objects began to take their day-time forms beyond the previous frontiers of sight: an easel, a door, the slanting roof of a tenement across the street seen foggily through the rain-streaked windows. 'I believe Philip loves her.' Jeremy spoke at last, quietly and contemplatively, spacing his phrases with intervals of silence. 'And I believe he loved her when he married her. I have never blamed him . . . for taking her from me . . . she was there to take . . . and I have never blamed her for preferring him to me . . . Philip had so much more to offer her . . .

'We had the same ambitions, Philip and I – I suppose that is why we were friends. Both of us wanted to write . . .

Philip even started a novel. It was a good novel; at times I thought it came close to being profound . . . but who am I to judge profundity?'

'I would never believe that!' Brent exclaimed. 'Philip's a fool! Why, I asked him his opinion of Henry Miller last night, and the comments he made were the standard clever remarks with which they always try to write off Miller. I don't think he has ever read a book by him. I know that when Dorothy asked him the title of one of Miller's books, he did not know it and pretended not to have heard of it!'

'Philip is not a fool. That is part of his act, which you mistake for the whole man. He likes to make one think that he knows the least, to make a pretence of ignorance, in the hopes that he will be able to lay a trap for you and catch you in it. But that's beside the point. The point is that Philip could have written a good book had he wanted to.'

Brent rested her head on Jeremy's shoulder. 'But, of course, he didn't,' she said.

Jeremy stared at the growing patch of daylight on the floor. 'And I have never understood why not. It sometimes seems to me that all Philip cares about is to prove to himself that he can possess something that he desires and which seems unattainable. But once he knows he can have it, then he is no longer interested in it and is more than likely to throw it away. Most of us have some touch of this folly in our natures, but the objects of our desires are inanimate: books, pictures, automobiles or, at the most, a way of life – a complex of people and things. Most of us learn to accept a modicum of dissatisfaction and we manage to adjust ourselves to imperfectly attained goals. Not Philip. I wonder if I am right when I say he loved Dorothy? What I mean, I think, is that he desired the things Dorothy stood for and, if he was in love, he was in love with the process of achievement. Once the exploit was over, the goal attained, Dorothy lost all value to him. He is throwing her away . . .'

Brent sat up, surprised. 'What are you talking about, Jerry? How is he throwing Dorothy away? I don't understand.'

'You saw the way they were last night. You saw how jealous Dorothy was of him. Fear lies beneath her jealousy, fear of losing him. Once Philip made sure of her, you see, once he had married her and held a secure position in her father's agency, he began to be consistently unfaithful to her. And Dorothy knows this. That is why every woman she sees him with she looks upon as a threat to her own security.'

Brent considered what he said. Her fingers busied themselves with pulling a ravelled thread from the blanket, but she was deeply concerned. Did what Jeremy was telling her mean that he still loved Dorothy? If it did – and how else was she to interpret it? – what would happen to her?

Jeremy responded to her silence, came close to her, held her to him so that her dark hair smothered his face and her warm breath moistened his cheek. 'Don't worry, Brent, dear,' he said. 'That is all past. It's you I love, not Dorothy.'

'But you were just saying . . .' she began.

'You asked me to tell you. I loved Dorothy once, and so did Philip. He married her, not I. I feel badly that he gets into bed with every piece of fluff that comes his way – I feel even worse that Dorothy knows this and still wants him enough to be savagely jealous. But I can assure you that I no longer desire Dorothy, now that I know you.'

'You mean you did . . . before?'

Jeremy nodded his head. 'Sometimes when I went to their house for dinner, it was all I could do to keep from kissing her every time Philip's back was turned. And Philip was supposed to be my best friend! That's why I stopped seeing him.'

'You know what I think, Jerry,' said Brent. She was smiling and baring her teeth the way a kitten does. 'I think Philip is your personal devil. I don't believe in his talent the way you do. I think he has been lucky. He didn't finish that novel because he couldn't – not because "he was no longer interested in it". I talked to him last night and I think he is a fool!'

Jeremy stared at her and slowly shook his head. 'You've seen him only once. You don't know what he's really like.'

'I saw all of him I intend to see, I can tell you that. As for Dorothy – well, I think she's a nice person.' Brent spoke cautiously. She did not want to say anything that would alienate Jeremy. She was afraid of Philip's wife, and the hold she had over her lover. But she did not want to let Jeremy see her fear. 'She's a nice person, and I like her. Perhaps you're right, and the only reason she doesn't like me is because she thinks of me as a threat to her. But I do believe that what goes on between Philip and her is their business, and you had better not concern yourself with it. If Philip wants to be unfaithful to his wife, let him! Why should you bother about that?'

Jeremy rumpled her hair and kissed her. Then she pretended to resist him and he pretended to overcome her resistance. Then they both laughed for a long time.

'All right,' he cried finally. 'You win! Philip, I hereby give you the right to sleep with anyone you desire!' Jeremy was kneeling on the couch, the blanket draped over his shoulder toga-wise, his face severely pontifical. He made an imperious gesture, then pulled Brent to him and kissed her. 'As long as it isn't you!' he added.

6

As Philip came out of Brent's apartment building and turned down Jones Street, there was a sudden sound of glass splintering above him and a small hard object struck him a glancing blow on the temple. He crouched instinctively, over-balanced and fell to his knees. The street was now totally dark. Glass continued to fall near him. Then he heard a shrill whistle, which was followed by spasms of childish laughter. As his eyes grew accustomed to the dark, he saw that a street lamp overhead had been smashed – out of the corner of his field of vision two small boys disappeared from view, running wildly towards Bleecker Street. He stood up, touched his stinging forehead tentatively with his handkerchief. He was not bleeding. He laughed self-consciously. Only kids shying rocks at the street lamp . . . he had thought they were stoning him!

He walked down the deserted, darkened street, his mind intent on the strange scene he had just had with Brent. The 'Confession' had been wrong. Although many of its predictions had come true, its major prophecy had not: he had not been unfaithful to Dorothy with Brent. But he could take no credit for this. He had made all the necessary advances, as the manuscript had foretold: if he had not done his wife an injustice, it was because Brent would have none of him, and this the manuscript had not foretold.

What was the purpose of the 'Confession'? Had someone deliberately egged him onto Brent, knowing that she would not find him acceptable, as a crude joke? Would this fit Jeremy's sense of humour? He wondered.

At Sixth Avenue, a flashing neon sign that advertised a

bar met his eye and beckoned him inside. The bar was crowded, but a booth was empty at the rear of the room. He sat down and when the waiter came, he ordered a double scotch.

His mind had grown numb and the whisky tasted like tap water. He gulped it down and ordered another . . . and then another. He knew very well that he was going to get drunk again, that he would forget again. But somehow it did not matter. He had a problem to which he had to find a solution, a problem that would require reasoning. Now, of all times, he should stay sober. That was all very true, and yet it was all very false. He had another whisky. Now he would stop drinking and try to think it through. First of all, there was Jeremy. But who was Jeremy? Just what did he know about Jeremy . . . ?

He had another whisky. This one burned a little and did not taste like it had come out of a faucet. As he sat and stared at the seat on the other side of the booth it seemed to him that he began to see Jeremy vaguely. This is an hallucination, he told himself. Jeremy is not really sitting there. I am alone. But the vision became clearer and clearer. Jeremy was still wearing the same suit he had been wearing earlier in the evening. The same fold of fat bulged around his collar. And, while Philip was trying to assure himself that he was not real, it seemed to him that Jeremy spoke.

'Remember me, Philip?' he asked. 'Do you remember how I was when we first met? I was the fat boy who was your room-mate all through college – the kid you were jealous of all through the first term because I had so many friends and I played on the Freshman team.

'And do you remember the night that you came home to find the fat boy – that was me, of course – crying over his books? It was just before exams and I was failing. I told you that I would be eternally grateful if you helped me. And you helped me, with bad grace even then, but you helped me, Philip. And I am still grateful.'

'I remember,' said Philip, hoarsely.

'I was your best friend for years to come, wasn't I, Philip?' The vision smiled mockingly. 'You imitated me, dressed as I did, made my friends your friends. I encouraged you to go out for sports. You pledged my fraternity. You wouldn't have received that bid, Philip, if I hadn't sponsored you. Oh, I know what you're going to say. You helped me, too. Of course, you did. You had to keep up the pretence of the friendship. You tutored me. You had me major in English Lit. and taunted me into becoming a journalist. Oh, I'm very grateful to you, Philip – don't think that I'm not. But it was you who became president of the senior class. And would that have happened if you hadn't been my friend? Or would I have had the honours you received, if I hadn't boosted you?'

Philip stared at his empty glass and slowly shook his head. He knew that Jeremy was not there and that the apparition was due to his nervous tension. He had been thinking about Jeremy, arguing with himself about Jeremy – and suddenly his imagination let him see Jeremy, argue with Jeremy. It was all in his own mind.

But what about the argument? All the things 'Jeremy' said were true, and yet they weren't motivation enough for him to have written the 'Confession'. Philip raised his finger and summoned the waiter and ordered another double scotch. And then 'Jeremy' seemed to speak again.

'What about the women, Phil boy? What about the women? I not only refused to compete with you when it came to campus politics, but I let you take my women, too. I guess I just liked being a sucker – but does anyone really like being made a fool of, Phil? I knew you excelled me at all my own specialities. I even tried my hand at one of yours. Do you remember the chapter of a novel of mine – that's about as far as it got, one chapter – I read to you, Philip? Do you remember what you said, Philip? Now was that kind? After I had listened so patiently to the sections you read me of your novel, too. Oh, I could have written the "Confession", if that's what you're wondering.'

Philip smiled to himself and averted his eyes to avoid looking at the apparition. He felt a little good now that the scotch was taking hold. He had been a different man in those days; his face had been as long then as it was now, but the line had been firmer, his jaw had been less heavy, his hair had been . . . thicker. And then he thought he heard Jeremy's voice again.

'You were quite a boy with the girls, weren't you, Phil? You had had several affairs by the time you were a senior. You seemed to like taking your friends' best sweethearts away from them. Why were you so successful with the women, Philip? Was it your eyes, that way you had of looking that left no one up in the air as to what you wanted? And what you wanted was usually someone else's woman, wasn't it? Sometimes it seemed to me that you made a point of ignoring the beauty of a woman until some other fellow, whose taste you respected – myself, for example – had selected her for his own!'

Philip let the glass slip out of his hand as he laughed loudly. Now he knew what he had been evading. Now he knew why it must be Jeremy who was writing the 'Confession'. Dorothy had been Jeremy's girl. He had not fallen in love with her when he first met. He might never have fallen in love with her if Jeremy had not mentioned that her father was the head of one of New York's largest advertising agencies.

Philip rolled his glass back and forth under his hand as he looked up for the waiter. Oh, he was a realist about his own motives. He knew how large an element of profit there had been in his choice of Dorothy for a wife. But she had been attractive to him, too. He had loved her . . .

He pointed his finger at the apparition. 'You never did like the idea of Dorothy loving me more than she did you, did you?' he demanded. 'I saw you change, Jeremy. At first you were pleased that Dorothy and I liked each other. Then you were miffed when Dorothy and I had dates on nights when you wanted to be alone with Dorothy. Finally you were angry when you realized that you no longer rated with Dorothy. There was the night I proposed to her. I took her for a long drive in the country and asked her to marry me – we stayed out quite late. When I came home, I found you, Jeremy, waiting up for me. "By God, Phil!" you said. "I've had enough of this! If you want to marry her, marry her. But if you won't, then leave her alone. If you make a slut of her, I'll kill you!" Do you remember what you did next, Jerry? You started swinging wildly and I had to hit you – to knock you out. I didn't get the chance to tell you that Dorothy was going to marry me until morning. Then you insisted on being a gentleman and buying me a drink. Do you remember all that, too, Jeremy?'

But, as Philip watched, Jeremy disappeared. He faded away all at once, blending into the dark wood of the booth. Philip had known all along that he was not actually there. But now that he could no longer see him, he felt relieved.

It was late and the room was growing hazy – with smoke? Philip sat staring at his empty glass. Only a few stragglers were left at the bar in the front of the room; a fat blonde leaned on the juke box next to the booth where Philip sat and crooned the words of the tune the machine was playing. Her voice was raw and beery. After a time, she came over and sat down next to Philip without asking for an invitation. She put her arm around him automatically and hugged him to her. Philip's thoughts had been in the past and he was only partly conscious of her presence until she ventured intimacy, then he was too startled to take any action for a moment. 'Would'ja like to meet a nice girl, dearie?' the blonde whispered in his ear. He pushed her away from him, stood up and went to the bar and paid the bartender. He did not look back although he could hear her cursing him drunkenly. Outside it was drizzling and a low-hanging fog partially obscured the street lights. He began to walk uptown, looking for a taxi.

'. . . if you make a slut of her, I'll kill you!' Those words of Jeremy's, spoken many years ago, still rang in his ears.

Jeremy had meant them at that time, but did he still mean them? After all those years did Jeremy still love Dorothy enough to conspire against her husband? If he did, then it was probably he who was writing the 'Confession'.

Philip shivered, only partly because of the cold, clinging fog. His eyes searched the misted streets for a taxi. He wished the mist would blow away. It made everything loom dim and vague, made him fear that he was about to hear the voice again. Very few automobiles were about, mostly early trucks. He kept walking uptown.

What he could not understand was what Jeremy, if he were writing the 'Confession', hoped to gain by it. Did he think that a reading of it would reform Philip and make him faithful to Dorothy? That was laughable. Did he hope to drive Philip into some action that would make him a fool in Dorothy's eyes? If that was his objective, Philip had to admit that he had already come close to succeeding. But there was another possibility that Philip considered even more disturbing: suppose Jeremy *was not* writing the manuscript, suppose he was writing it himself – and then forgetting he had written it! This was what he might have been doing the night before, what he had been trying to remember all day.

And it was not impossible. He had thought so at first, but now he was not sure. Who else, besides himself, could have written it? No one else knew his mind that well, but even if someone did, how could this person have forced him to make love to Brent? No, he had made love to Brent because he desired to, not because the 'Confession' had predicted that he would – to think differently was madness.

He had a theory – it might not seem sensible in the light of day when he was cold sober, but he could see no holes in it now. He was afraid that he had written the 'Confession' out of some latent, autobiographical urge, and then suffered a kind of amnesia about it. Later, he discovered it again, but then it seemed new to him and the work of someone else. He had some reason for thinking this since once before he had had a similar experience. This had happened back in his college days when he was still rooming with Jeremy and while he was working on the novel he never finished. One day, he had gone to his desk to resume writing only to discover a newly-completed chapter that he must have written himself – but which he could not remember writing. His first impulse had been that Jeremy had written it as an ill-humoured joke. He had sat and stared at the totally unfamiliar pages until Jeremy had come into the room; but when he had told Jeremy about them, Jeremy had been able to solve the mystery. 'You wrote them last night,' he had said. 'I remember waking in the middle of the night. I heard the sound of your typewriter. I got up and slammed the door of my room in hopes that you would take the hint and stop disturbing my sleep. But you went on typing until dawn.'

Last night, drunk as he must have been, he might have decided to go to his office and write. Then he might have gone back home after he finished, gone to bed and, when he awakened the next morning, have forgotten about it. The flaw in this reasoning – if there was a flaw – lay in the time sequence. How could he predict that he would meet and make love to a woman he did not know? And yet, who was better equipped to make such a prediction?

But then there was the disturbing fact that not all the events foretold in the 'Confession' had come true. He had not slept with Brent. This he still found hard to believe. He had never before been rejected so ignominiously – why, the woman had lured him on, teased him, led him to expect an easy conquest by her every action, only to refuse him coldly. If he had written the 'Confession' he would have been certain that he would be successful with Brent. Did this mean that he had written the 'Confession'?

A taxi came into view. Philip hailed it and ran into the street to meet it in his eagerness to climb inside. He gave the driver the address of his office building. He intended to find out if his mind was playing tricks on him again. By going to his office now, and staying there all night – he planned to sit at his desk and await the culprit if the second manuscript were not already there – he would either catch the author or frustrate him. He expected that there would be another instalment as the first manuscript had been titled 'Confession I'. Of course, if he were the author . . .

The building lobby was deserted. One elevator was open and the light was on inside, but the operator was not to be seen. Philip rang the night bell several times, listening to its metallic clangour resound in the vaulted lobby. After about five minutes, the night operator appeared – an old man who limped as he walked. Philip strode impatiently into the elevator.

'Aren't you supposed to be on duty at all times?' he demanded. It was insufferable to have to wait so long for an elevator in a building that advertised twenty-four-hour service!

The car started its flight upwards with an unseemly jerk. 'I ain't got no relief from twelve to six. It ain't human to ask a man to stay in one spot all that time,' the operator complained.

'It's your job, isn't it?' Philip demanded.

'Mister,' said the old elevator operator, turning around as the doors opened at Philip's floor, 'there's always the stairs.'

Philip walked down the hall towards the frosted doors of Brown and Foster. He was angry at the old man's impertinence as he fitted the key in the lock. Philip had never seen the office after hours and its dark emptiness dismayed him. He could not find the switch to the bank of lights that illuminated the corridor leading to his office. Never before had he had an occasion to turn on those lights since it was always done for him. He gave up trying to locate the switch and groped his way down the hall, striking matches until he found his own name on one of the doors. He stood looking at it long enough for the flickering flame to burn down to his fingers, remembering the brief, calamitous interview with Steven Foster. Then he pushed the door open and went in, turning the light on in Miss Grey's office and looking around carefully before he went into his own.

It seemed as though the light dimmed as he went through the door to the inner office. A bell started ringing somewhere, a faint tinkling. He felt as if he were falling forward as he groped across the room to his desk. A scream began in his mind, but stifled in his throat. And then he was swimming in furious circles in a pool of blackness that lapped over him and swallowed him until all was deafeningly quiet.

Out of that quiet came a voice – the simpering voice – speaking clearly and distinctly. 'Oh, Philip,' it wailed, 'you aren't going to forget again, are you? Please, Philip, try hard not to forget . . .'

The Second Instalment

I

Brent, Jeremy and Dorothy stood in a circle about him, pointing their fingers at him, chanting words he could not distinguish, although he sensed their meaning was shameful. An overpoweringly bright light, originating he knew not where, shone in his eyes and dimmed his vision so that when he shut his eyelids he could not escape the haunting, blue after-images of his friends ringed about him, pointing accusing fingers. Then Brent stepped forward, seized his shoulders and began to shake him, shouting more words at him that he could not understand. His head swelled with a pain that throbbed like the motor of a relentless engine, coming and going with piston-like regularity. Once again he dared to open his eyes and this time they were dazzled by bright sunlight. He felt hands – Brent's hands? – release his shoulders. He twisted his neck to see who it was who had been shaking him, and again his head was possessed by spinning pain. Brent, Jeremy and Dorothy had disappeared. He realized that he was alone in his own office. But, if he were alone, who had been shaking him? Again he tried to turn around, this time more slowly, and this time he succeeded despite the persistent pain in his head. Miss Grey was standing beside him, her blotchy face sympathetic and solicitous. 'Are you all right, Mr Banter? You gave me such a turn when I came in and found you slumped over your desk!'

Philip stood up. His whole body felt cramped and his muscles ached. How had he gotten here? He searched his memory in an attempt to recall the events of the night before. A number of scenes and jumbled incidents jostled for precedence: he had been in a bar, he had looked for a taxi, Jeremy's words – had they been spoken last night? – 'If you make a slut of her, I'll kill you!', Brent's face at dinner, slowly smiling so that her teeth were bared, the elevator man telling him, 'There's always the stairs.'

Philip tried to pretend to Miss Grey that his conduct was in no way unusual. But, even as he straightened up and smiled, he knew from the wondering expression on her face that she was aware that something had happened and that he did not know what it was. Still he had to make the best of it he could. He said, 'I came back to the office after you left last night. I had some work to do and I kept at it until late. I must have fallen asleep.'

Miss Grey began to walk towards the door. 'I didn't know what to think when I saw you there-like that. I guess you scared me. Did I hurt you shaking you? It seemed the thing to do at the time.'

Philip managed another smile, another attempt to put the girl at ease. She was not a bad sort, if she would only do something about that complexion. 'Thank you for waking me,' he said. 'I'll just wash up and then go out for some breakfast.'

Miss Grey answered his smile with an embarrassed grimace of her own and then left the room, closing the door behind herself. Philip sat down again and ran his hands through his hair. What had happened to him? He still could not think very clearly. He could remember coming to the office building, waiting an unbearable length of time for the elevator, unlocking the door to the office and searching for the light switch – but after that his mind was a blank. Why had he come to the office at such an odd hour? He thought for a moment about this and then remembered that it had had something to do with the 'Confession'. That was it! He had come back to the office to see if another instalment of the manuscript would be awaiting him, possibly to have the good luck of catching the author in the act of writing it. But what had he found? He could not remember.

He looked down at his desk. Only then did he realize that his typewriter was open as it had been the day before – when he awakened he must have been lying on it, but only now did he see it – and there was a sheet of paper in the machine also as before. Beside the typewriter was a second neat pile of manuscript that bore his name on the upper left-hand corner of the first page!

This must mean that he was writing the damned thing himself! How could he reason otherwise? He remembered coming into the office after midnight, turning on the light . . . no, he did not remember turning it on, he just remembered reaching for it . . . and nothing else. His amnesia must have set in as he began to write. But why should he want to torture himself in this devious fashion? That was yet another question to which he had no answer. He sighed and picked up the first page of the new manuscript. He might as well read it to see what he had dreamed up for himself this time . . .

Philip Banter
21 East 68th St
New York, N.Y.

CONFESSION

2

My head aches today; I feel ten years older overnight. I cannot blame it all on the liquor. I was drunk enough last night, but not too drunk to know what I was doing. Have I lost all control over my impulses? I know I cannot experience many nights like last night and survive.

But didn't I make much the same sort of vow yesterday? I seem to have a store of good resolutions . . .

I must be losing my mind. Certainly there is something

badly wrong with me if I don't learn a lesson from last night.

Philip laid the first page aside. He stood up and walked to the window and looked down on Madison Avenue. The street below him swarmed with people, all types of human beings, leading all kinds of lives. Why had this happened to him? Why not to one of them? He inserted his finger between his collar and his neck and ran it nervously along the starched edge. The 'Confession' was positively uncanny! Reading it this morning was almost like hearing his own unspoken thoughts declaimed in an echoing, resounding room. Certain sentences, phrases, were still reverberating in his ears: 'my head aches today' – his head did ache; 'have I lost all control over my impulses?' – well, had he? – his actions left the matter open to serious question; 'I must be losing my mind . . .' Philip pulled the cord that controlled the Venetian blind, jerked at it, shuttered the view of hurrying pedestrians from his sight. Was he losing his mind? His fists clenched his temples – he could feel the blood pounding in his ears. He stood like that for several minutes, cataleptically rigid, a panic-stricken statue. Then his fists relaxed, his arms drooped and his hands, now open, dangled at his sides. He turned slowly around and stared at the pile of manuscript beside the typewriter. For a moment longer he resisted it, a tense moment during which he felt as if he were about to collapse; but instead of collapsing he sat down again at the desk and seized the second page . . .

When I reached the office yesterday morning, I was ashamed of myself. I had not seen Dorothy since the night before, when I had left our apartment to take – home, and I didn't know as yet how she was going to react to my behaviour. It did not seem possible that she could overlook my misconduct this time. As long as I kept my affairs to myself, as long as I did not force her to acknowledge my infidelity, I was confident of Dorothy's reasonableness. I did not bother her and she would not bother me. But now I had broken our tacit agreement: I had made love to – before her eyes. I did not know how she would take it.

I did not work all morning. A few minutes after eleven o'clock my telephone rang. It was Dorothy on the other end of the wire. Her voice seemed pleasant and cheerful. She was going to do some shopping and would need extra money, would I stop at the bank and make a withdrawal and then meet her at the Three Griffins for lunch? I asked her how much money she needed. She mentioned a staggering sum which would all but take our balance. I started to protest, then hesitated and finally said nothing. She said she would have to hurry if she were to be on time and hung up. I sat looking at the receiver until the switchboard operator asked me if I wanted another line, then I hung up, too. I could not believe my ears. Dorothy had seemed natural, as if nothing had happened. Yet why did she need so much money?

I reached for my hat and went out the door, telling Miss Grey I would not be back until after lunch and to get the name of anyone who called. I would go to the bank and from there to the Three Griffins – I would see Dorothy and judge for myself.

The Three Griffins is a small restaurant on East Fifty-Third Street run by a hunchback. The *décor* is pseudo-Gothic: the booths along each wall fit into *papier-mâché* groined arches, the lighting fixtures are hidden in candle wind screens of pierced metal, the atmosphere is murky, romantically dismal. Dorothy had discovered it during our first year of married life and the place had some obscure, sentimental significance for her that I quite forget. Yesterday, she was as late as I had feared she might be, and I sat there under one of the mouldy-looking arches chain-smoking cigarettes and staring at the repulsive proprietor perched on his high stool behind a very modern cash-register. I was on my second martini when Dorothy arrived.

'Darling! I'm so sorry to have kept you waiting! But

Mimi dropped by to show off a hat she had just bought, and to tell me about a hairdresser she has discovered who has simply done miracles for her – you know how ratty her hair always looks? – well, you should have seen it today! it was miraculous! – and I could not get rid of her for the longest time . . .' Dorothy was being bright and gay and artificial as hell. I knew there was a reason for this pose; Dorothy is not usually like that. She went on, 'Order me a martini, darling, won't you? That one looks so good!'

I ordered her a drink, and then later the hunchback brought us a cutlet and vegetables, a salad, coffee and brandy. It was a good lunch, but I did not enjoy it. Dorothy kept on talking frippery in that phony, very-very manner with a 'darling' tacked onto the end of every other sentence, while all the time I was uncomfortably aware of what thin ice her chatter skated on so glibly. Sooner or later we would get down to cases; I could have done nothing to hurry her, just as I could do nothing to defend myself when the time came.

This was when I lighted a cigarette and Dorothy was finishing her brandy. She had just asked for the money I had drawn out of the bank and I had given it to her; she had thrust the thick wad of bills into her purse without counting them. But she spent an inordinate amount of time fussing with the catch on her purse, and said without looking up. 'And how is – ?'

'Well enough, I suppose.'

'She got home safely, I trust?'

'I took her to her door.'

'Just to the door, Philip?' Dorothy had taken a cigarette from her bag and was bending forward for me to light it. I struck a match – the spurting, spluttering crack it made sounded deafening. I did not answer her.

'You admit it then?' Dorothy had turned her eyes away from mine. It was queer. A stranger might have judged us conspirators from the way she was acting.

'I don't know what you are talking about!' I said loudly and distinctly. Too loud, in fact – I saw the hunchback swerve around to look at me. I smiled back at him to assure him that he had not been addressed.

'Oh yes you do, Philip,' Dorothy was saying softly, insinuatingly. 'Don't you think I know what goes on?'

'Nothing is going on,' I insisted.

She was silent. She held her anger for a moment or two longer as if she savoured it and was loath to part with it. This interval could not have endured more than a span of seconds, a minute at the most; but to me it seemed ten, twenty times that long. I could hear my pulse in my throat, feel the hot throb of blood in my temples . . . but I could also hear two shopgirls eating their lunch in the next booth talkatively comparing the salient points of their 'gentlemen friends'.

'You slept with her last night, Philip. You needn't deny it, I know you did. And it isn't the first time, Philip. This sort of thing has been going on for years. You've been quite . . . brazen . . . Philip.' Her manner was deliberate, like a judge on the bench; only this judge had a swarm of dark hair in place of a powdered wig, dark eyes that in the past had been merry more often than judicial, dark lips . . .

I said nothing.

'I'm leaving town tomorrow, Philip. Don't try to stop me. You'll hear from my lawyer. This time you'll have to talk to Dad yourself.' She had swept up her gloves and her bag and was gone, leaving me staring at a piece of green paper that I had folded and refolded so many times in the previous few minutes that the scribbled figures on it were nearly worn away – the check.

I went over to the hunchback and paid it; I walked outside and stood looking up at the tall, blue sky; I was not surprised or angry. Now that it had happened, it seemed inevitable.

*

I didn't go back to the office; instead I walked over to Third Avenue, entered the first saloon that I saw and started in to drink. I drank very methodically. I drank rye and water, and I would take two drinks in one place and then go to the next one. By four o'clock in the afternoon I had worked my way down to the Twenties and I had run out of money. The bartender in the place I was in then would not cash my cheque, so I went outside and into a pawnshop next door and hocked my watch; the heavy-jowled, bent-over pawnbroker gave me ten dollars after much hesitation although I had paid fifty for it. I kept on drinking. I reached Astor Place by nightfall – the clock on Wanamaker's told me it was after six. I searched my pockets but could find only a dollar and some change. There was a cigarstore on the corner of Ninth Street and Third Avenue where I went to telephone Jeremy. He told me yes, he could lend me ten until the end of the week if I would meet him at a bar on Sixth Avenue in the Radio City neighbourhood within half an hour. I promised to do that. He sounded surprised. I took a taxi uptown – the fare and the tip took my last cent. If Jeremy didn't meet me, I told myself, I would have to stop drinking, and the thought of stopping drinking made me tremble.

But Jeremy was waiting for me at the bar. He glanced at me and handed me a crumpled bill. 'What in God's name have you been doing to yourself?' he asked.

I stared at his fat face. One crease of flesh which rolled over his collar revolted me particularly. I could not understand how this man could ever have been a friend of mine.

'You look like you've slept in those clothes,' he went on when I didn't answer his first question. 'My God, Phil, what's come over you?'

I had intended to have a drink with him – I needed one badly – but I could not stand there and let him question me in his sneering way. I pushed past him towards the street.

'Hey, Phil! Wait a minute!' I walked faster. It became a matter of paramount importance to put as much space as possible between myself and him; when I was through the door and on the sidewalk, I began to run; there were many pedestrians – it was the tag-end of the rush hour – and I had to weave through the crowd like a broken-field runner. I heard him shout, 'Hey, Phil!' one more time, that is I heard a faint shout – it might have been somebody else; but I didn't stop running until I neared Central Park. Then I went into a package store and bought a bottle and took it with me into the park where it would be quiet and I would be left alone to drink in peace.

*

I am not too clear about all that happened in the park. I remember that I found a secluded bench behind a rocky upcropping that was not close to a street light; sitting on the bench I drank about half the bottle before I began to feel alive again (the ride uptown in the taxi and the energy I had spent in escaping from Jeremy had sobered me; I felt dead). I looked around me and saw that the trees, the distant lights of the theatre district, had all receded into a soft and comfortable haziness. There was a small, but intense, fire in the pit of my stomach that warmed me and encouraged me to feel that everything fitted into place and that I belonged to the world again. I remember stretching out on the bench, my head on my rolled-up coat, lying there gazing entranced at the starry, clear, cold sky. It was December, yet I had drunk enough to make it seem like June.

I must have fallen asleep for the next that I remember is the impression of being on a subway train: the roar of steel wheels on steel rails bottled up and rushing past me in the tunnel, the pale light of the cars. — was sitting across from me, but I was aware of Dorothy's presence also; although I could not see her anywhere, I sensed that she was there watching me. Then, as I sat trying to decide whether to speak to — or get up and look for Dorothy, the car began to cave in. First, the vestibule careened wildly inwards, then the walls began to collapse and the floor rose to meet them; there was a shrill, screaming rending and I found myself thrown against — on the lurching floor, a warm wetness spreading over me, flooding me, fogging my sight. I tried to get up, to stand on my feet, to force my way out – but I was pinned down, helpless. I opened my mouth to cry out my anguish, but no sound came . . .

Still trying to scream, I swam upward through the blackness, a blackness that was now relieved by the pinpoints of bright stars. I kept struggling to rise, but something held me down. I fought to free myself, as yet only half-consciously, and then suddenly awake and aware that this was no dream. I heard someone curse and I felt a staggering blow that knocked me from the bench onto the sloping ground; I rolled with the momentum of the blow down a small grade behind the bench, clutching at the slippery earth, trying to stop my fall. I continued to roll all the way down the hill and fell, at last, face down in a pool of icy, revivifying water. Someone was scrambling away up above me; I could hear running footfalls dying away in the distance.

I sat up, cold sober. My clothes were torn and muddy and drenched with rye whisky where the bottle I had been drinking from had spilled over them. My hands were bleeding for they had been scratched in my long, tumbling fall down the grade. I stood up and made my way painfully to the top of the hill. Only when I reached the bench where I had been lying, did I realize that my wallet was gone and with it my money. I had been robbed by a thug.

I set off towards the entrance of the park in search of a policeman. I did not find one; one found me. He walked up behind me, seized me by the collar and pushed me in the direction of the nearest drive out of the park. 'Get along with you,' he growled, 'before I have to run you in!' There was no use arguing with him. He took me for a bum. At that, I must have been a pretty sight: my clothes were muddied, one trouser leg was torn, I reeked of whisky and my face was scratched and dirty. I left the park and started walking downtown again.

*

I did not know where to go. If I went back to the apartment, Dorothy might be there and I didn't want to face her after what she had said at lunch. On the other hand, if she weren't there, I didn't want to be there either – I had too many associations connected with that apartment, too many mementoes of our life together. I couldn't go back to the office in my present condition. Jeremy might have let me sleep at his place, but I didn't want him to see me looking the way I did. Sooner or later he would have told Dorothy about it, and I never wanted her to have the satisfaction of knowing how her decision had affected me. There was no place I could go.

*

Philip let the pages fall onto the desk. He pressed his hand against his forehead and eyes to shut out all light. As he had read, he had been overcome with a feeling of unreality – as if he did not exist in this room, but only in the pages he was reading. Even now, with his eyes shut and the friendly, self-consoling pressure of his hand to remind him of his own, incontestable existence, he was not certain. The 'Confession' goaded him, tormented him. After another moment, his hand dropped, he picked up the manuscript and began to read again.

But I kept walking downtown along Sixth Avenue. Distances which I had covered many times by bus or taxi, I now had to cover on foot. I was near exhaustion from exposure and the after-effects of the quantities of liquor I had swilled, yet I forced myself to keep moving as if there were a great spring inside me that once it started to unwind was to continue inexorably until the last erg of tension was released. When I reached Forty-second Street, I considered going into Bryant Park; but I was afraid that if I did the police would only chase me out again. I kept on walking, stopping for street lights and when the press of traffic required. I was hungry and I had begun to feel sick when I was in the garment district around Herald Square; I went down into the subway to go to the comfort station before I realized that I would have had to pay a fare to get in there, and I had no money to pay a fare; instead, I stood looking at the exit gate with its 'No Admittance' signs, watching it swing open widely and invitingly whenever anyone pushed out. I didn't have the courage to try to sneak through when the man behind the change-window wasn't looking. I went back upstairs to the street and started walking downtown again.

When I reached the Village, I went straight to Jones Street. It might have been that my subconscious had been directing my steps that way all the while, although if this were true I had not consciously planned it or semi-consciously abetted it. Nevertheless, it made no difference to me then whether I saw – or not; either way I had lost Dorothy, hadn't I? And, queerly enough, I felt that – was the one person I could trust. I waited in front of her building until there was no one near to see me go in, and then I rang her doorbell. As soon as the buzzer sounded I pushed the door open and started to climb the stairs to her apartment; on the second landing an Italian woman with her arms full of groceries stopped to stare at me – but I didn't give a damn what anybody thought by then.

I remember – letting me in, her mouth agape when she saw how bedraggled I was. 'What happened to you?' she asked. I mumbled something that satisfied her for the moment. She helped me into the other room and let the water run in the tub while I took off my clothes. She was wearing a housecoat that featured a slit from her ankles to above her knees and showed the outside of her thigh when she walked, but I was too tired to do anything about that. She made me some coffee and some hot soup while I was in the tub; later, I sat in the kitchen drinking it and matching her questions with what I thought were convincing lies. Afterwards she took me into the next room and made me get into bed.

The next thing I remember it was morning and I was

awake and staring at —'s dark head beside me on the pillow. One of my other suits was lying on a chair across the room, neatly laid out for me. I jumped out of bed and began to shake – to waken her. She looked up at me drowsily. 'Whassa matter?'

'Where did you get that suit?'

'I went to your place last night. Dorothy gave it to me. You couldn't go out looking the way you did when you came in.'

'But how did you know to go to my place? I mean didn't I tell you not to go there?' If she had been given that suit by Dorothy, that meant that Dorothy knew how cut up I had been over her decision to divorce me. I had not wanted her to know that.

— was smiling at me, that cocky smile of hers that is half a sneer. 'You talked in your sleep last night, darling,' she said. 'You told me all about Dorothy's leaving you. There's just you and me now, Philip. Isn't that nice?'

I hit her when she said that. I knocked her down on the bed and beat the bejesus out of her. It made me feel like a man again.

Philip's hand shook as he laid down the last page of the manuscript. If Dorothy were to leave him . . . he did not know what he would do. He might take it like that. It would mean that he was not only out of a job, but that he had lost his home as well. It would mean the end of his comfortable life and the start of a whole new chapter.

But what concerned him most was the apparent fact that he must have written what he had just read. What kind of mental disorder did he have that would prompt him to try himself in this fashion? It was a kind of slow suicide. And there was a sly masochism about it – a delight in tormenting himself with personal revelations – that was dismaying. If anyone else should see it! And if any of the events predicted in it should actually occur! Yet wasn't this exactly what he must want to happen – if not, why else would he have written it?

313

His one consoling thought was the fact that of what had happened the night before in *reality*, as far as he could remember, there had been a serious discrepancy: he had not slept with Brent. As far as he could remember – ah, that was the catch. He could recall having gone to Brent's apartment, drinking a whisky and soda with her, holding her to him and having her refuse him. He could remember getting drunk and returning to the office . . . but he could remember nothing else. What had happened during the rest of the night? Had he written the 'Confession', or returned to Brent's apartment – or both? It could be that his memory was playing him false again, that he did not remember what he thought he remembered. It could be . . . as the idea occurred to him, he snatched at his desk calendar to check the date. If he had gotten mixed up on his dates and everything that had been 'foretold' in the manuscript had already happened it might not have been last night that he had met Brent at a party at his house – but the night before. His heart stopped beating as he looked at the calendar, and then it started beating again. The day was only the second of December – not the third – the events prophesied in the 'Confession' had yet to happen. If he wished, he might still prevent them. Some-how he must prevent them!

Then Philip thought of Dr George Matthews. He had known George when he was finishing up his pre-med course and they had kept in touch ever since, even writing back and forth to each other while Matthews was doing post-graduate work in psychopathology in Zurich. Once or twice Philip had nearly dropped his end of the corre-spondence; but Matthews had always persisted, writing letter after letter until Philip was shamed into answering: Matthews had said that Philip interested him since he was 'perhaps, the archetype of the narcissistic personality'. Philip had intended to look that up and find out what it meant, but he never had. Now that George Matthews had offices in New York and a booming practice, they met about once a month for lunch. George was a full-fledged psychiatrist, certainly the one best person to consult about this. He might be able to tell Philip what to do.

Philip reached for the telephone and had the girl get him Dr Matthews' number. He was lucky and George, although he said his appointment book was filled for six weeks in advance, was free for lunch. Philip said he would meet him at their club at twelve and hung up. He checked his watch and saw that it was already after eleven and he had not washed or shaved since the evening before. Well, he could have a wash, at least, before he met George. He put on his hat and went out the door, telling Miss Grey that he was going to lunch and then to the barber, but he would be back afterwards.

As Philip passed the switchboard girl, she signalled to him. 'Pardon me, Mr Banter, but I have a call for you.'

Philip remembered the 'Confession's' first prediction. 'Ask who it is,' he said.

The girl spoke into her mouthpiece, listened for a moment and then looked up at Philip. 'It's your wife, Mr Banter. She wants to meet you for lunch.'

A chill warped at Philip's neck. 'Tell her I've just left,' he said quickly. 'Tell her I didn't say when I'd be back.'

Philip slipped through the door hurriedly and walked rapidly down the hall towards the elevator. He was still seeing the look of startled, slightly pleased – here was something to gossip about! – surprise on the frigid face of the receptionist; he could still hear her haughty voice exclaiming, 'But, Mr Banter!'

He jabbed the down button. That had been a close call.

As soon as Philip left the office, Miss Grey reached for the telephone and asked the operator to connect her with Tom Jamison. When he answered, she said, 'I have some more news.' She listened for a moment. 'I'm going out at twelve; I know that's early for you, but can you make it then? All right. Twelve-fifteen at the usual place.'

She hung up the receiver, stood and went to the door. She looked up and down the hall before she closed the door quietly and walked into Philip's office. Sitting down at his desk, she began to go through the drawers methodically – shaking her head in displeasure from time to time. The large bottom drawer was locked. She pulled at it several times, banged it hard with the heel of her palm. She took a hairpin from her hair and inserted it in the lock, but then she thought better of it. She shook her head again and withdrew the hairpin. Standing, she walked to the window – 'Damn!' she said.

After looking out of the window for a few minutes, she went back into her own cubicle, opened the door to the hall and seated herself at her desk. A copy of the *New Yorker* caught her eye and she picked it up. This would help pass the time until twelve o'clock.

Tom Jamison was a young man whose face wore a perpetually worried expression. If the corners of his mouth had not turned down, and his forehead had not been scored with wrinkles, he might have been considered handsome. As it was, his habitual frown belied his even features and good bone structure. Now, his frown deepened. He regarded Alice Grey, who was sitting across from him at the table, and tried to speak above the din of the crowded restaurant. 'Why didn't you pick the lock?' he asked.

The girl did not understand him. She asked him to repeat his question.

'I don't want to speak too loud,' he said. 'You never can tell who might hear.'

'Silly!' Miss Grey smiled at him. 'No one's listening to us. They're all too busy making themselves heard.'

'Why didn't you pick the lock?' he asked again. This time the girl heard his words.

'I was afraid that I'd scratch the finish of the desk and he would notice it. Then I had no way of knowing that he had put it there.'

'It was the only locked drawer, wasn't it?'

'Yes.'

'Well, wouldn't that be the logical place for him to put it?'

'I suppose so. But he could have taken it with him.'

'Did he have anything under his arm when he left?'

The girl thought about this for a moment. 'I don't think so. If he did, I didn't see it. But I wouldn't be sure.'

Jamison was angry. 'Why not? Weren't you making it your business to keep your eye on him? Now we may never get it back! And, if we don't, sooner or later he's going to put two and two together . . .'

'Oh, Tom, I'm sorry. I do the best I can.'

'I wish we had never gotten into this,' he said.

'But when I told you about it, you had no objections.'

'If you got each one of them back. Anyway, you had already gone ahead with the first one before you told me.'

'But, Tom, a hundred dollars – now it's two hundred dollars. You know how long it takes us to earn that!'

Jamison cut a piece of meat with his knife and started to put it into his mouth. Then he thought of something and his fork stopped halfway between the plate and his lips. 'You never did tell me what you did the other night,' he complained.

'What other night?'

'Day before yesterday. The night I couldn't get away.'

The girl looked down at her plate. She spoke without looking at him. 'I waited around for your call – you could have 'phoned, you know, even if you couldn't make it. After more than an hour I gave you up and went out. I took a bus up to Central Park and walked around. Later – I don't know when – I left the Park and went to a bar. I – I had a few drinks and – and then I went home.'

He looked at her questioningly. 'Is that all you did?'

'Don't you believe me?'

'I suppose I do.'

She looked up at him. Her eyes were wet and her cheeks glistened. 'Tom, you must believe me. I work so hard. I look forward to the time when we can be married. Now

317

that it is almost within our grasp – and I'm sure it will be, Tom, if you get Banter's job – please trust me.'

Tom laughed. 'You're so certain Foster will give me that job – that Philip will leave. How can you be so sure?' he spoke bitterly.

'I've told you as much as I can. You know that by rights it's your job – it always was your job.'

'Not when the white-haired boy's around. And he's still around as far as I can see.'

Miss Grey shook her head. 'But not for long, Tom. I can assure you of that, I think. Philip Banter is on his way out.'

They finished their meal in silence.

Dr George Matthews finished tamping tobacco into his meerschaum, struck a match and puffed strenuously until his head was wreathed with a laurel of heavy smoke. The delicately tinted bowl of his pipe glinted merrily in a ray of sunshine that slanted from one of the club's vaulted windows. Matthews held it out at arm's length and admired it: this was a fine pipe, an excellent example of a kind of workmanship found only in Switzerland before the war and now, doubtless, irreplaceable. Still paying homage to his pipe, Matthews addressed Philip. 'Your secretary does seem a bit of a nuisance, Phil,' he said. 'and I can't say I blame you for being irked with her. Yet there is a tenseness about you, a drawn and hectored air, that leads me to wonder if there isn't some other flaw in your – at least up to now – enviably prosperous existence.' The corners of Matthews' wide, heavy-lipped mouth (he always reminded Philip of a Saint Bernard about the mouth) curled with sly humour. 'Then again I noticed a quality of *angst* in the hasty telephone call with which you summoned me to lunch this morning, and – if I may say so – almost traumatic apprehension. "Banter," I told myself, "has got the wind up over something."' He drew his pipe slowly back towards his mouth, inserting the stem carefully between his thick, sensual lips as if it were a piece of laboratory apparatus. 'Tell me, am I not right?'

Matthews had been pleased when Philip called him. He had not expected to have the patient come to him so quickly. Yet all through lunch Philip had talked around the subject that Matthews knew, from his interview with Dorothy and her father the day before, must be uppermost in his mind. So, although he firmly believed that the patient must bring his troubles to the psychiatrist, Matthews decided to make a leading comment that might make it easier for his friend to speak of his disorder.

Philip's reaction was complex. He laughed, and lifted his coffee cup to keep Matthews from seeing his confusion. 'No,' he said, 'you're not right. Or, rather, yes, you are – but not in the way you think.'

'"Yes and no" is a good enough answer to a general question. In fact, I can think of few questions of the kind I just posed that deserve any other answer. There are times when "yes" can be an evasion and "yes and no" quite forthright.'

As usual, Philip realized, George had managed to relieve his embarrassment. He set down his coffee cup and lighted a cigarette. For once he decided he would be frank. Sometimes it was wisest to lay all one's cards on the table. But, although candour was his earnest desire, when Philip spoke he found his words taking a devious path.

'I am disturbed,' he began, 'greatly disturbed. But not about myself or anything that has happened to me.' He paused after saying that and wondered at how he could resolve one moment to be frank and yet be so incapable of simple honesty the next. 'I've come to you about someone I know who . . . who is suffering from a delusion.' Philip's face went damp and his breath caught in his throat as he lied. However, now that he had framed it, the subterfuge seemed necessary. I shall tell the rest of it straight enough, he promised himself. And Matthews, at the same time, recognized the most familiar device of the inexperienced confessor and redoubled his interest in his friend's conversation.

'What kind of delusion does this person experience?' he asked.

Philip hesitated. 'I may be wrong in calling it a delusion,' he began again. 'It is a very real experience to my friend.'

'Would it be a delusion if it weren't?' Matthews asked soberly.

'Of course. But what I mean is – suppose a man came into his office one morning and found a manuscript there, piled beside his typewriter, one sheet still on the machine. His first impulse is to ask his secretary who has been using his typewriter, then, on second thoughts, he decides to read some of it first to see what it is about.'

'Natural enough. Might be blackmail,' George commented.

Philip nodded his head vigorously. 'Exactly. So he reads it. He finds it is a self-termed "Confession", supposedly written by himself, of events that the manuscript says have happened to him – only they haven't.'

Matthews laid down his pipe and studied Philip closely. 'What kind of events?'

'My friend says the manuscript predicted that he was to meet a girl at a dinner given by his wife. He was to make love to her, to have an affair with her. And his wife was to be aware of what was happening.'

Matthews spoke deliberately, soothingly. 'You say "predict". And yet you say the manuscript purports to be a "Confession" written by your friend. Isn't this a contradiction in terms?'

'You would think so, wouldn't you? That's one of the reasons why I called what has happened to my friend a delusion.' Philip pushed his chair away from the table and restlessly crossed his knees. 'But he says no. He says that although the manuscript was entitled "Confession" and although it was supposed to be about events that happened the night before, the events told about in the manuscript did not actually happen until after he had read about them, that evening in fact. So the "Confession" was really a prophecy.'

Matthews picked up his pipe, stuffed more tobacco into it, tamped and re-tamped it. He genuinely enjoyed the strongly aromatic smoke and he fancied himself as a pipe-collector; but his habit had a practical, as well as an aesthetic, advantage. A man who plays with a pipe is able to keep silent for long intervals and is free to observe his companion's actions – a necessary trait for a psychiatrist. Thus Matthews' pipes were wont to go out more often than those of most smokers so that when he fiddled with matches and cleaners his patients would be unaware that their doctor's eyes were upon them. Now, as he used this device to regard Philip obliquely, he grew more certain of his friend's anxiety. Where he had been sceptical about Dorothy's fears, and inclined to reassure her, he was now sure that Philip was badly neurotic. This onslaught of neurosis was not entirely unexpected; on the contrary, George had never understood why his friend had not had a break sooner. He had first known him as a shy, withdrawn lad who was sensitive about his unusual good looks; he had watched at the sidelines, figuratively speaking, while Philip drew on an inexhaustible supply of compensatory energy to spurt with unnatural rapidity into a position of leadership and to acquire a Byronic reputation; later, at a veritable distance, he had kept in touch with the mature life of this compulsive Casanova whose narcissism combined a perpetual, wily aggression against the distaff side with an uncanny acumen in the masculine, competitive world. Philip reminded him of his first acquaintance with him today: he had a diffidence that was disarming, and his attempt at dissimulation in telling the story of his hallucination was completely ingenuous. Matthews was frankly fascinated.

'You think he has been writing it himself, don't you, Phil?' Matthews puffed the words out with the first fog of rank smoke from his re-lighted meerschaum. He wanted the blunt question to have full shock value.

Again Philip hesitated. Now that he was talking about what was happening to him, it all seemed silly. But he had begun, he had said enough to pique George's curiosity so that he would have to continue. 'No, it's not like that, or rather maybe it is. He could be writing it himself. He won't ever admit that he ever suspected himself of it, but I am sure he has thought of it. Yet I am inclined to think that someone else is writing it, you see.'

Matthews shook his head. 'I wonder if you really think so. I know you say you think this is being done to your friend, but then you come to me to ask my advice. Am I right in supposing that the contents of the "Confession" are slanderous? Well, then, if you really believe that your friend is not be-devilling himself – but is being be-devilled – why don't you go to the police?'

Philip's hand was trembling. He thrust it into his pocket so that the doctor would not see. 'I wanted to rule out the possibility that he might be writing it himself before I advised him to do that. If it's a matter for the police – well, then he will have to talk to them himself. But I promised him that I would speak to you about it first.'

'Oh, he knows that you are consulting me? Doesn't that mean that he does suspect himself to be the author of this mysterious manuscript?' Matthews made a sound that resembled a deep chuckle, but his expression remained grave and the chuckle might have been an indication of digestion.

Philip knew that he had been caught up and that this was his friend's way of telling him to come clean. Instead, his explanation became more involved – partly out of the perversity that makes us defend a lost argument for just a little longer after we know it is lost. 'I've tried to make him see the bad logic of his position. But he insists every time that although I suspect him, he does not suspect himself. When I mentioned you, he even urged me to talk to you about it – but he professed to want me to see you only because I needed to be reassured that "it was impossible that I should be writing it". Those are his very words.'

This time George Matthews laughed openly and resonantly. 'He's an obstinate cuss, isn't he?'

Philip smiled and nodded his head. 'Tell me the truth, George. Could my friend be writing this story about himself – could he be telling himself what he planned to do and at the same time pretend that what he planned had already taken place – without his ever knowing it?'

Matthews rested his pipe against his cup and saucer; although he no longer held it in his hand, one of his fingers lingered beside the bowl and caressed it, taking pleasure in its warmth. 'You will have to tell me more about your friend before I can answer that. What does he do for a living?'

'He's a writer.'

'What does he write? Advertising?'

'Yes.'

'Is he married?'

'Yes, he is.'

'Is he happy with his wife – and is she happy with him?'

Philip paused. How could he answer that? Until yesterday there would have been no doubt in his mind that Dorothy and he were happy. But now? 'Yes . . . I think so,' he said slowly.

'Why aren't you sure?'

Again Philip thought before he spoke. He did not want to come too close to his own personality in describing this mythical friend, or Matthews would realize that he was talking about himself – if Matthews hadn't realized that already. Yet he did want to strike a fair parallel to keep from misrepresenting his problem. At last he decided to risk it. George had given signs of seeing through his pretence anyway. 'He, my friend, that is, has played around a little lately. He hasn't been doing all his sleeping at home. He is afraid his wife might know.'

'How do you know this?'

'I've heard gossip.'

'Do you hear voices, Philip?' Matthews asked casually.

'I beg your pardon.'

'Do you hear voices? Do you hear someone speaking to you when you are alone?'

'Why should I hear voices?'

Matthews smoked his pipe in silence. He did not speak,

but his eyes were kind. Why must I continue to pretend when I know there is no reason for pretending? Philip asked himself.

'Sometimes.'

'Do you want to tell me about them?'

Philip coughed. A great hand seemed to seize his stomach and twist it. He coughed again. 'I hear a voice. A child's voice. But first I hear a bell ringing in the distance. The sound keeps coming closer and closer. The lights dim and everything I see looks as if it were covered with scum. It's then I hear the voice.'

Dr Matthews carefully kept his own tone casual. 'What does it say, Phil?'

'It says, "Oh, Philip, why can't you remember? We had so much fun! Why did you have to forget?"'

'And what have you forgotten?'

Philip fumbled for a cigarette. His hands shook as he struck a match, the flame wavered and danced as he held it up. He dropped the match in the ashtray and stared defiantly at Matthews.

'You drink a lot, don't you, Phil?'

'Why do you ask?' Philip's voice had an edge to it. Inwardly, he was frightened.

Matthews nodded at his hand, which was still trembling as it held the cigarette. 'Your hands,' he said. 'They shake so.'

'Yes, I drink a lot.'

'Too much, do you think, Phil?'

'No. No more than many people I know.'

Matthews smiled. 'Why do you drink, Phil?'

Philip felt bright shafts of anger spear their way into his brain. He wanted to pound his fist on the table and shout George Matthews down. But he spoke quietly because he was afraid to shout or show his rage. 'I do it to get away from the voice. I never hear it when I'm drunk.'

Matthews nodded his head. He was silent, gazing at the design he had traced on the tablecloth with his fork.

'I know whose voice it is,' Philip said.

Matthews still did not speak.

'It's my voice. My voice before it changed. My voice as a child, saying "Philip, why don't you remember?"' Banter said.

'And you drink to escape the voice, drink until you forget what you do – and then the next day you hear the voice again. Is that it?'

Philip nodded his head. 'And now I'm writing this "Confession", threatening myself. It looks as if I want to drive *me* mad!'

Matthews picked up his pipe and stroked it against his cheek. He looked away from Philip at the deeply recessed windows of the club's dining-room. 'Tell me more about this "Confession" – what did it predict? And what happened?'

Philip told him the circumstances surrounding his discovery of the manuscript and related briefly the predictions it had made about his meeting Brent and his attempt to make love to her.

'And did these events take place exactly as predicted? Or were there disparities?'

'There were disparities,' Philip said. 'But I met the girl as the manuscript predicted, and I made love to her.'

'You had not known her before?'

'I am sure I never met her.'

'You could have met her and then forgotten about it, couldn't you?'

Philip had not considered this. Yes, he might have met Brent during one of his 'forgotten' periods.

'But if I had done that, why wouldn't she have said something when we were introduced?'

'There might have been a reason, mightn't there? Your wife was present . . .'

Then Philip had to tell him what had happened after he took Brent home the previous night. He ended by saying, 'She finally ordered me out of the apartment.'

'And this the "Confession" did not predict?'

'That's right. The "Confession" had stated definitely that I would sleep with her.'

Matthews sucked noisily at his pipe and again studied the high sunny windows. But he said nothing, nor did he seem to expect that Philip would have anything more to say. His reaction was disquieting – it made Philip feel uncomfortable.

'After I left her place I had a few drinks and then I went back to the office,' Philip went on. He felt a need to continue talking in the face of his friend's, the psychiatrist's, taciturnity. 'I do not remember what happened at the office clearly. I must have been pretty drunk. And I must have fallen asleep eventually. I know I do not remember having written anything. But I found a second instalment of the "Confession" on my desk this morning when I awakened.'

'And what did it predict this time?'

'That Dorothy would meet me for lunch today and ask for a divorce. That I would get drunk in Central Park and be rolled by thugs. That I would wind up at Brent's apartment as before.'

'And what do you intend to do about it?'

'I am going to do my level best to keep any part of it from coming true. I avoided having lunch with my wife. I won't go back to the office today or home tonight.' He hesitated and stared grimly at Dr Matthews. 'I won't let it happen again!' he cried.

Matthews laid down his pipe. 'I've heard of cases similar to yours, but not in all particulars. Of course, every love-sick swain since time began has kept a diary of his peccadilloes. I have encountered adolescents who laid down time-tables for themselves to follow in these matters. "Watch the girl who works in the candy store and find out where she lives. Manage to meet her alone. Ask her to the church supper." That sort of thing.' Matthews sensed the extreme anxiety of his patient (for he now regarded Philip as his patient), and he was trying to allay

327

it in part by relating the strange facts of the 'Confession' to other more natural diaries.

But Philip stiffened. 'I see no similarity,' he said with dignity. He mistook Matthews' easy casualness for joking familiarity.

Matthews grew more serious. 'It really isn't as different as you would think. The basic mechanism is the same. Narcissus looking into the pool. Your predicament is only more complex. For example, you have always been quite a lad with the ladies, haven't you?'

Philip's hand, hidden in his trousers' pocket, began to tremble again. 'Yes. Why?'

'And you're in your middle thirties, I take it?'

'Yes.'

'And once or twice lately, you have experienced unexpected failures?'

'Yes, I – I have,' Philip stammered. And then wondered why he had not lied.

'That might have a bearing on your case,' Matthews said. 'If you have a growing fear of impotency – as well as earlier feelings of guilt . . .'

'But if I did – and if I have, I don't know it – why would I write a "Confession" about an affair I was afraid I could not have? Wouldn't that be ridiculous?'

'Not as ridiculous as it seems. I'll admit that the part about actually writing down your wishes and then forgetting that you have written them is unusual – although I dare say I could find a similar case if I looked it up. But the mechanism is classic! The young boy who has never experienced sex and the old man who doubts that he will ever experience it again share common feelings of guilt and inadequacy. They both spend an inordinate amount of time daydreaming about exploits they don't have the courage or opportunity to make real. Sometimes this happens to a man in his maturity, and then his fears are often false. They are only symptomatic of a deeper wound, a hidden conflict. Some men never get over adolescent feelings of inadequacy and guilt, and with such men, every time they have a new relation it is a fresh trial of their ever-doubted prowess – you might call them sexual athletes since they are always trying to break their own records. These men often become psychically impotent prematurely. They day-dream compulsively – you do it on paper! – about imagined triumphs and then force themselves to make them real. Often they come a cropper . . .'

'Then do you think I'm writing the "Confession" myself?' Philip clenched a table knife spasmodically as he asked this question. His heart was jumping in his throat.

Matthews was lighting his pipe again. 'You do, don't you?'

'Yes, I suppose I do.'

'Philip, I don't think that "Confession" is so terribly important – if you are writing it. If you are not writing it, and that is possible – who could it be?'

'I don't know. I have no evidence against anyone. Anyone who knew me that well. Jeremy. Dorothy. Miss Grey hears a lot of my 'phone calls, I'm sure – she might be doing it, but that seems a stretch of the imagination. Steven Foster. Even Brent, if your guess is right and I knew her before during one of my blank periods.'

'Why would any of these do such a thing?'

Philip dropped the knife on the floor. He bent to pick it up. His head was reeling and he was breathing rapidly – his heart hammered at his ribs. He could see that George thought he was insane. What would he do next? The important thing was to act natural, rational.

'Dorothy might be jealous of me. She might want to get even, to scare me.'

'So she plants a "Confession" on your desk every morning?'

'It sounds weak, doesn't it?'

'A jealous woman has done queerer things before. What about the others?'

'Jeremy has always resented my success – I suppose you know that. And Dorothy was his girl before she was mine.'

'And now you are making love to Brent?'

'Yes, that would give him a motive. But, if he's writing the "Confession", why should he *suggest* her to me?'

Matthews nodded his head. 'Steven Foster?' he asked.

'The old man has never welcomed me as a son-in-law. But his methods are more direct.'

'Your secretary?'

'She resents me, too. But I don't think she has the wits to arrive at such a scheme, let alone the drive and stick-to-it-iveness to carry it out.'

'In other words, you don't think that anyone but yourself could be doing it.'

Philip tried to smile. 'I'm afraid that about sizes it up.'

Matthews knocked out his pipe. 'If you are writing the "Confession", we can regard it as a symptom. If you aren't of course, it might be a matter for the police. But since you and I both come to the same conclusion about it, I think we can look upon it as part of your syndrome.'

Philip had taken his hand from his pocket. His shirt sleeve was pushed back by the movement, revealing the soiled bandage about his wrist. Dr Matthews now saw his friend's bandaged wrist for the first time. 'Have you hurt yourself, Philip?' he asked casually.

Matthews had not considered this an important question. His only reason for asking it, beyond that of natural curiosity, was to break the tension his last remarks had created in Philip. He knew that an irrelevant question which shows human interest can often put a patient at ease during a difficult interview. But Philip responded quite differently from what Matthews had expected. He became highly excited, all but hysterical.

He jumped to his feet, clutching his injured wrist. 'I don't know, George, I don't know!' He held his wrist up to his mouth, sucking at it as a small child might do. 'I must have hurt myself the other night. But I can't remember. When I woke up yesterday morning, it was bandaged. I don't know how I did it.' His voice had become petulant, a child's voice. He whined rather than spoke and tears appeared in his eyes. Matthews saw that his pupils had dilated with anxiety. 'I can't remember a thing,' he said piteously.

'You found your wrist hurt the same morning that you found the first part of the "Confession" – is that right?' Matthews asked.

Philip gulped and nodded his head. 'And when I left the office to go downtown, I was nearly run over. A truck came out of a side street – I didn't see it coming. I think the driver swerved to hit me, although I could be mistaken. It might have been an accident. But then later, in the elevator, I was nearly crushed between the doors.' And he told Matthews about the large man, whose face he had not glimpsed, who knocked him off balance as the elevator's safety doors were closing.

Dr Matthews listened, but he made no comment. Philip gradually calmed. He realized that he had become abnormally excited – the blood was still pounding in his temples. Suddenly, it had seemed to him that everyone, everyone in the world, was against him and persecuting him. When Matthews opened a package of cigarettes and offered him one, he took it gratefully.

'Do you think that these "accidents" – both the ones you remember and the one you don't – could be part of a plot against you, Philip? Is that the way you feel?' Matthews asked.

Philip hesitated. 'Sometimes, I think so. Other times, I think that something's wrong with me – that I am trying to kill myself.'

'You mean that you are afraid that you might have slashed your own wrist while drunk? That you might have stepped into the path of the onrushing truck? That you bumped into the man in the elevator and threw yourself off balance?'

Philip nodded his head.

'You're highly disturbed emotionally, Philip. I prescribe a good, long rest in some quiet place where you can get the proper medical attention. Once you have tapered off on your drinking, your other symptoms may disappear. Why don't you come around to my office now and let me make the necessary arrangements?'

Philip had again become more and more uneasy as the conversation grew more clinical. Now he jumped to his feet. 'I'm sorry, George, but I've just remembered an appointment I must keep! I will come to see you though. I'll call you up and make an appointment.' And he began to walk away.

Matthews walked after him. There was little he could do, if Philip did not want to come with him. And he was uncertain as to his diagnosis. From Dorothy's evidence, and Philip's own admission, he did know that Philip had become an alcoholic. The first thing to do would be to treat his alcoholism; then – when he was less disturbed – would be time enough to attempt analysis. So when he caught up to Philip, who had been walking very fast, he had this to say: 'I don't want to alarm you, Phil, but you need a psychiatrist's care. If you don't want to come to me, I can give you the name of a good man . . .'

But Philip, smilingly, shook him off. 'I'm not as batty as you think, George. Just been working too hard, that's all. But I'll remember what you've said, and I'll come to see you some day.'

Then they shook hands and Philip hurried away. Matthews puffed at his pipe and looked at the check in his hand. He shrugged his shoulders, went over to the cashier and paid it.

As he walked back to his office, taking pleasure in the cool, clear light of the December sun and the cloudless blue of the winter sky, Matthews thought over Philip's peculiar story. And he grew more and more concerned about Philip. If his friend's neurosis were sufficiently advanced, he might worsen seriously before Matthews could persuade him to submit to treatment.

So when he reached his office, he gave his nurse Dorothy's name and the name of Steven Foster. 'Keep ringing both of them until you get them, and then tell whoever answers that I want to see them both tomorrow morning at Steven Foster's office.'

Later in the day, Miss Henry left a note on Dr Matthews' desk. It read: 'Unable to contact Dorothy Banter. You have an appointment with Mr Steven Foster at ten o'clock tomorrow morning.'

3

Jeremy and Brent had just finished breakfast and Brent was washing the dishes, when the telephone rang. Jeremy walked to the far end of the great loft room to reach the instrument. He spoke into the receiver in a soft, controlled voice, not because he felt the need to be surreptitious, but because an announcer habitually modulates the tone of his speech. When he realized that it was Dorothy at the other end of the connection, he did not speak more loudly. There was no need to, of course, and the rush of water from the faucet would probably have prevented Brent from hearing the conversation had there been a need; but the fact was that Jeremy, if he changed his manner of speech in the least, lowered his voice as the dialogue progressed.

Dorothy wanted Jeremy to meet her for lunch. She wanted to ask his advice on a matter of importance. When he began an embarrassed apology for his impulsive act of the previous evening, she cut him short with a pleasantry. She told him that she had not been aware until that night of how much Philip and she had missed him. She emphasized Philip's name when she said this, as if she feared that Jeremy might otherwise infer that she, alone, had appreciated his company. 'You must come to see us more often, Jerry dear,' she went on. 'And you must bring Brent along.' This time she emphasized Brent's name, as if it were her particular caution not too imply too much. 'She is such an interesting girl, so intelligent – with such *verve*!'

As Jeremy said less and less, Dorothy's voice rushed forward. 'But about today, Jerry. You would be doing me such a favour if you could have lunch with me. I know it's an imposition – please don't say it isn't, I know it is. But I really feel I must see you. Yes, it is important. No, it would be difficult over the 'phone. Yes, it's confidential, but that's not the only reason. Well, darling, you see it's so involved. I wouldn't know where to begin, but at lunch I can just talk at you and let it all come out. You can sort out and pick up the pieces, and then, perhaps, you'll tell me what you would do. Oh, Jerry, you are a dear!'

Jeremy hung up the telephone and walked to the long windows that overlooked the street. He did not stand too close to their sills, even though they were shut tight, because these sills were flush with the floor and this always made him dizzy and filled him with the crazy urge to jump. At the moment he was especially upset. Why had he found Dorothy's request so disquieting? And why did he feel he was being dishonest by accepting her invitation and not letting Brent know about it? Of course, he could tell Brent. No harm would be done, but it would do no good either. Not that he thought Brent was jealous of Dorothy – she had said she was not – but only curious about her. Nor was there any cause for jealousy on Brent's part, he was sure. If once he had been deeply in love with Dorothy, and had continued to love her even after she had married Philip, he no longer cared for her. A year's absence had effected that. Last night, a fugitive impulse had forced him to embrace her; it had been a childish passion and a wholly irresponsible one. He knew – he was certain he knew – that it had been only an incident, an inconsequential by-product of a dull evening. Nothing would come of it, because he did not want anything to come of it.

Or did he? As he stood at the window looking down on, but not seeing, the busy street – in his own apartment with the woman he told himself he loved, and with whom he had spent the night, only a few paces away – suddenly, he was a part of another reality, intensely aware of another presence. Now Dorothy stood between him and the window; Dorothy's aura, a combination of fond memories and the actual, physical pressure and warmth of her body as he had held her to himself the night before, surrounded him and overwhelmed him. Her scent was in his nostrils; her dark hair brushed lightly against his brow, cobwebby, enticing . . .

He stiffened and forced himself to withdraw from the dream that had seized him. Had Dorothy had a similar experience that morning? Was this why she had telephoned him and insisted that he spend an hour or two with her? Jeremy was afraid this was so. Faced with the possibility that Dorothy might desire to renew their love, he was not nearly as sure that he would be able to will it otherwise as he had been an instant before. Then he had thought of his action the previous night only in terms of his own wayward, selfish impulse. Would he be able to stand up against her longing as well as his own?

A sound made him turn quickly about to stare at the other end of the room. Brent had just come from the sink and was wiping her hands on her apron; her face was flushed with the heat of the water she had been using, and this unnatural colouring heightened the sensuality of her wide mouth and her brooding, changeable eyes. As he regarded her, he knew that for him Brent, too, was very desirable.

He continued to stare at her while she walked to the sofa, which the sheets and blankets still disguised, took a cigarette from the pack lying open on the end-table, lighted it and with a sigh of satisfaction bent over to unmake the bed. He watched her work, rapidly and efficiently peeling the sheets off, folding them, unmasking the pillows and fluffing out the dents made by their heads in the night. He felt a lump rise in his throat, and thought himself a sentimental fool.

'That was the studio,' he said.

'Again?'

'Joe's still sick. He has four shows this afternoon.'

'And they want you to work them? Jeremy, when are

336

we going to have some time to ourselves?' She straightened up and let a pillow drop to the floor. He could see that she took his words at their face value, and did not suspect that the call might not have been from the studio. But then, why should she? He had never lied to her before.

He looked at his wrist-watch. 'I'll have to be there inside a few minutes. The first show's at noon and I'll have to work it up.'

Brent had returned to her work. 'When will you be back?'

'This evening. They'll have to get someone else for tonight. I'm as tired of this as you.'

She did not answer him. He went to the closet for his hat and coat. As he was leaving, he asked, 'Will you stay here this afternoon?'

Brent looked up again, and smiled. Jeremy wondered if the guilt he felt had expressed itself in his voice. But if it had, Brent said nothing to indicate it. 'I may try to write this afternoon,' she said. 'If I do, I'll go home since I can never get into the mood here. If I'm not here when you get back, you can give me a ring.'

Jeremy shut the door and went down the stairs. Now that he had actually left the apartment, he felt he was making a mistake. He stood outside the building, hesitating. He could telephone Dorothy from the drugstore on the corner and make some excuse for not keeping his appointment, and then return to the apartment and Brent. But if he did that, he would have difficulty explaining why he had decided not to go to the studio. Or he could go back and tell Brent that he had lied, and that instead of going to the studio he was meeting Dorothy for lunch. Brent would be jealous of Dorothy if he did that, though, and angry at him for lying to her. The simplest thing to do was to keep his appointment. So, having reached this decision, he set off down the street, walking a little faster and with a little more determination than usual.

*

337

As soon as Jeremy had left the apartment, Brent had gone to the windows. By opening one of them, steadying herself on the ledge and leaning out a bit, she saw Jeremy leave the house and then pause momentarily as if he had not made up his mind which way to go. Brent watched him intently, her face strained with quick anger. Only when he began to walk up the street did she turn and go back into the room. She went over to the couch and lay on it and tried to cry.

Many times in past months Dorothy had thought of Jeremy, and had remembered his boyish, open face, his quick enthusiasms, with an uncomfortable nostalgia. Finally, she had called him and asked him to dinner. He had tried to refuse her invitation – she knew this was because he had been hurt by Philip's neglectfulness – by saying he had a date that evening and would be busy every other night that week. He had described Brent to her over the telephone, and Dorothy had insisted that he bring Brent along. Once done, she had delayed telling Philip that she had invited Jeremy and Brent, had delayed so long that she realized she did not want to tell him . . . that she feared his meeting Brent. She had not told him until the evening before, and she had been frightened by the effect her news had had on him. But she soon forgot this in her joy of meeting Jeremy again. All evening she had been afraid Philip would notice that she could not keep her eyes off her old friend. But what difference would it have made if Philip had noticed?

Dorothy knew that she had made a mistake by marrying Philip instead of Jeremy. Not that she had been unhappy with Philip during the first years of their married life. No, then, she had been almost unreasonably happy. But later, especially in the last year, she had felt Philip eluding her – slipping from her grasp. Philip was so relentless. He always had objectives he was working towards, but he seldom made them known to her. Frequently, she guessed them. Many times she had been angry, but it was a kind

338

of ingrown anger that she could not express. 'I am as much to blame for my husband's immorality as he is,' she told herself. 'Yet this self-shame makes me hate him. But would life with Jeremy, if I had married him instead of Philip, have been so different?'

Dorothy was enough of a realist to sense that it might have been much the same. Any good-looking man flirts. Yet she felt Jeremy had a straightness in his character that was alien to Philip, a kind of self-restraint that recognized a law that had been freely accepted and cleaved to it. Besides, Jeremy was friendly; he liked people for what they were, not for what they were worth. Jeremy had loved her, while Philip had only recognized her value to him . . . and had set about to obtain it and her.

When she thought of Philip and Jeremy, Dorothy also thought of her father. He, too, was a handsome man, erect and tawny even in his old age. As a child, her father had been a god, a bronzed, golden-haired image of majesty. She had seen him usually at a distance: at the foot of the table when she was allowed to dine with him, on the polo field at the championship matches which she had observed from the grandstand, standing by the fireplace, tall and unbending, when nurse brought her in to say good-night. To this day she perceived her father through the wrong end of an imaginary telescope; there was a barrier to scale or a distance to span between them at all times. Of course, she knew, it had not always been so. There had been times when her father had taken her in his arms and held her, one of them as recent as her wedding. But this was a memory that her consciousness usually denied, a holy thing to be kept in a safe place and reverenced, not a well-worn pocket-piece to be fondled at odd moments and perhaps mislaid. Only in the stillness of calm and peace or at the height of euphoria, did she ever think of that wedding-day embrace. Her father, rigid in his dignity, had closed her into his arms with inexorable strength and had kissed her acceptant mouth with lips and tongue; there had been greed in his

339

ardour and immeasurable satisfaction. Philip's husband kiss, a breathless moment later, had been father-like.

This was the way Dorothy thought – compulsively, circularly – about her life and Philip. And each time her thoughts reached the same, questioning *impasse*: would Jeremy have been different? Then, the night before, she had seen him, talked to him, and had grown jealous of Brent. Jeremy was just the same as he had always been, a little effusive, perhaps, and getting slightly stout – but good-hearted and still youthful. When Philip had passed the time by being impolite to Jeremy and paying court to Brent, Dorothy had at last decided that she had had enough. As Jeremy was leaving, she followed him into the hall, interposed herself between him and the door, and smiled and waited. He had kissed her and held her in his arms while she whispered in his ear. Later, she had to leave the house, to get out on the streets and feel the cold wind on her face. She had not returned until late in the night, and she had not been surprised to find that Philip's bed was unoccupied. She had waited until the middle of the morning, suffering a kind of dry-mouthed terror, before she had picked up the telephone and dialled the number of Philip's office. She intended to speak to him of her feelings, tell him that she doubted her love for him and that she wanted to leave him. It had come to that; which is not to say it was easy for her to do. Her pulse pounded in her ear while she waited for the connection to be completed, and she gasped with great relief when the switchboard girl told her that Philip had left and had not said when he would be back. But, as soon as she had hung up, she was alone again and miserable. She went over to the piano and played a little Mozart, but this did no good either. She lighted a cigarette, and then let it go out. Finally, she went back to the telephone and called Jeremy. When he answered, she spoke brightly, affectedly, begging him to have lunch with her. She would tell him about Philip and ask his advice – it would be the sensible way to let him know that she now considered herself free and unencumbered. Philip would not mind if she had an affair with Jeremy. The thought of Philip's minding made her smile bitterly to herself. The chances were he might even be pleased.

Dorothy had told Jeremy to meet her at the Three Griffins. This was a small café that Philip and she had visited often during the first months of their marriage, and she felt it somehow fitting that she should go there on the day she had decided that she must end their relationship. She put on her silliest hat, a tiny perky affair with a wild-eyed peacock's feather stuck in it, and daubed her fingernails with a gaudy polish that she had bought once when she was feeling gay and had never dared to use. She spent an inordinate amount of time dressing: taking a long, long bath, brushing her hair for many minutes before her mirror, carefully painting her mouth with lipstick that matched her nails; so, of course, she was late to her appointment.

Jeremy was sitting in a booth at the rear of the long, narrow, dimly lighted café glumly considering a martini. He did not see Dorothy until she was standing beside him, then he jumped to his feet and smiled quickly. Dorothy was suddenly nervous. She dropped her purse as she sat down; Jeremy stooped for it at the same time she did, and their heads bumped resoundingly. The mutual, ridiculous pain established a bond; by the time Jeremy had ordered a martini for Dorothy, and the waiter had brought it, a warm feeling existed between them and Jeremy's hand was groping for hers beneath the table. They talked about small, topical things at first: the weather, Dorothy's hat, the fact that the martinis were rather good – at this point they ordered two more – gossip about a mutual friend, the latest shows they had seen. Then Jeremy remembered a Gershwin show and Dorothy hummed its tunes, her head tilted back, her dark eyes glinting; and Jeremy's hand became bolder.

341

They had seen that show together on a weekend in New York when they had happened to meet; it had been a rainy, miserable day and they both had been unhappy about a party that had been a frost the night before. Now, that day came to life again and with it the Thirties. Jeremy remembered the words of a Cole Porter song, and Dorothy reminded him of a dance they had gone to together at which another mutual friend had gotten very drunk and made a scene. It was all of a piece, a mood that owed much to the martinis – they were now drinking the third round – and to that queer feeling of opportunities missed and illusions mislaid that comes upon us all when we try to remember. It was very inappropriate, too, they both realized, for what they were doing in actuality was endeavouring to escape the cage of the present by admiring and reconstructing the bars that had made the cages of the past. Neither of them mentioned Philip or Brent; Dorothy delayed because she was not at all sure that now was just the time, and Jeremy forgot on impulse because it was pleasant for the moment and he was confident that this hour would never influence the future. At last, they ordered lunch, although they were not hungry; Jeremy came around to Dorothy's side of the table and they ate off each other's plates – soon she was in his arms and he was kissing her, and getting the tulle from her hat in his mouth and her mouth, and feeling her warm form go soft and supple in his grasp.

He stiffened. 'Dorothy, I don't think we should.'

She did not answer, but only looked at him and then dropped her head. He glanced down at her bowed head and was taken by surprise by the whiteness of her part. It was difficult to speak. 'I'm not a prude, Dorothy. But I don't think we really should.' (All the while staring at her dark and complaisant head, feeling the vague outline of her soft warmth.) 'We are older now, mature, with responsibilities to think of. Don't you see, Dorothy, it's really not the same?'

Dorothy did not understand herself what had come

over her, except that she felt that Jeremy welcomed her and wanted her, in a way that Philip never did. She inched closer to him and laid her head on his shoulder. Her voice crooned softly to him in a broken, murmuring sing-song. 'It is the same . . . that's why I had to see you. You see, he's been so strange . . . so distant . . . he never looks at me any more . . . he never comes to me. I'm used up . . . no good . . . a formality. I tried to tell him . . . today . . . before I called you. He wasn't in. I thought that it mattered that I tell him first . . . but it doesn't . . . no, it doesn't. It's you I must tell. You're the one who has to know . . . before it's too late . . .'

She pressed her mouth against his, her tears dampening his cheeks. He saw the shielded lamp on the wall through the diffusion of her dark hair. He felt the points of her breasts against his chest and the oblique pressure of her thigh across his hip. Brent, he thought, Brent. He tried to remember her face, the soft slur of her voice. But Dorothy was whispering again. 'Hurry, darling . . . let's go some place . . . away from here . . . oh, dear!'

4

Philip was afraid. He tried not to think about what George Matthews had said, tried to distract himself by carrying on the small matters of life just as if nothing had happened. Since he had slept in his clothes, and badly, he stopped by a barber shop for a shave and a facial. The barber talked monotonously while he kneaded his face and applied hot towels; Philip tried to concentrate on the barber's patter, but it was no use. His mind kept reverting to its central problem: who was writing the 'Confession'? He remembered the dream with which he had awakened and saw again the faces of Dorothy, Brent and Jeremy ringed around him pointing accusing fingers. He began to tremble. Soon he was shaking uncontrollably. The barber put his hand on his forehead, but said nothing – Philip was grateful for the firm, cool fingers, yet he could not help but wonder what the fellow was thinking. He might have decided that this particular customer was recovering from a binge – what would he say if he knew what was really wrong? Had he looked out of his mind when he entered the shop? Was his confusion so readily perceptible?

What was it that distinguished the aspect of the sane from that of the insane? Surely there was a difference. He knew that many times in his life he had encountered psychotics, casually, in buses or on the subway, on the street, almost any place. They were not all locked up by any means. Some he had known by their peculiar attire, such as the man who was in the habit of making incoherent speeches at Columbus Circle wrapped in the flags of the United Nations; others had a compulsive gesture or an eccentric characteristic: they jerked or swayed, they shouted strange sounds, they talked continuously to themselves. He doubted if he had acquired suddenly any of these symptoms. But hadn't he occasionally identified madness in others by some other, subtler sign? Yes, he remembered a reporter who used to work next to him in the city room of the *Herald-Post,* a quiet, sensible chap who had a pretty wife and a bright little boy. He had gone queer overnight. They had all noticed it, and had talked it over amongst themselves – Philip and the other reporters and the men at the desk – so it had not been his imagination. Yet there had been nothing obviously wrong with this fellow, except that those characteristics that had always been his had asserted themselves to a greater and greater degree: he had been quiet to begin with – he grew quieter; he had been affable and polite – he grew extraordinarily apologetic; he had frequently paused in his work to gaze out the window – he got so that he did little else. Then, one night after work was over, he went down to the Lexington Avenue Subway and stepped off the platform in front of an express.

Philip had known that something had gone badly wrong with him, and so had everyone. There had been a blank look about the fellow's face. His eyes had seemed dead and lack-lustre. His movements had been slow and listless. Now Philip wondered if the barber who kept talking such drivel had seen the same things in himself. Was he actually frightened of him? Was this why he kept talking so much, and why he had made no remark when Philip began to shake?

He waited anxiously for the massage to be over. As soon as he was out of the chair, he darted a quick glance at himself in the mirror. He seemed the same; if anything he looked healthier than usual as his skin was fresh and pink from the hot towels and the massage. But then he would not recognize any change in himself if there were one, would he? Wouldn't it be a part of the disorder to seem unchanged even as one changed, particularly to oneself?

345

He paid the barber, tipped the man a dollar and walked rapidly from the shop. As he went down the street he felt as if everyone were looking at him. Several times he was on the verge of stopping to turn around and see if he were being followed, but each time he assured himself that he was only nervous and upset from his strange experiences and the disquieting talk with Dr Matthews. Yet he walked from 50th Street and Madison Avenue to Times Square without knowing where he was going or why, and he might have kept walking indefinitely in this aimless fashion if he had not glimpsed out of the tail of his eye a gigantic purplish hand. It had a cluster of huge, misshapen fingers and the thickest, longest finger was pointing directly at him. He stopped dead in his tracks, rigid with terror, unaware of the other pedestrians who kept pushing and shoving their way past him, too panic-stricken to face the tremendous symbol of guilt that had sought him out.

Philip first thought that he did not know where he was. He had been walking, thinking about and reconsidering everything that had happened to him in the past two days, wholly unconscious of his surroundings except that he had known that he was out on the streets of midtown Manhattan. Now he was isolated in his terror and acutely conscious of the fact that just behind him – without moving he could see it darkly – a hellish finger designated him, silently accused him – of what? A terrible idea arose in his mind, an idea that was in itself the configuration of evil: had he crossed the threshold that divided the appearances of sanity from the misapprehensions of insanity – had he literally *walked* into a madman's world? Was this thing that lurked behind him the first, weird landmark of the distorted landscape which would be his natural environment henceforward? Great waves of fear battered him, his tongue grew dry and felt like cloth in his mouth, his legs threatened to collapse. He seemed to be shrinking, gradually losing weight and stature, dissolving into a mammoth lake of terror. Yet a shred of reason, a grain of scepticism, remained in the welter of his emotions like

346

flotsam adrift in the surf. Before he gave up, before he surrendered entirely, wasn't he capable of turning around to stand full face with this apparition that had descended upon him? He fought to turn, finding that to perform this simple manoeuvre he had to assert all his strength as if he were defying gravity or forcing his way through an almost impenetrable obstruction; he moved slowly, somnambulistically, until he stared directly at the giant, pointing finger that soundlessly menaced him.

As he stared, he became aware again of light . . . of people . . . of shining chromium . . . and glittering glass. He saw that the great hand and menacing finger were not flesh and blood, but were *papier-mâché* and part of a motion picture theatre's lobby exhibit. A large sign hung above the monster that read: 'See *Man Alone* – A Tale of A Man Fighting Against Desperate Odds – And As You See it, Remember, It Could Have Happened To *You*!'

Philip walked around the dummy hand, examining it carefully and shaking his head, still doubting his eyes. He must have walked past the theatre front without knowing and have seen this advertising come-on with only the lesser part of his senses: what his eyes had seen communicated itself to his mind, which had been busily debating the question of his sanity – thus the theatre eye-catcher had been neurotically garbled and magnified into evidence of lunacy by his overwrought intelligence. He felt like laughing, like crying aloud his joy at discovering the mistake he had made. He did chuckle, and then grinned, and finally went up to the box-office and bought a ticket to *Man Alone*. Although he had not planned on seeing a show it was as good a way as any of wasting time and it was also a form of activity that had not been predicted by the 'Confession'. He was still smiling to himself as he selected a seat in the welcome darkness of the balcony and fastened his eyes on the screen.

Philip, willingly surrendering his objectivity as he centred his attention on the motion picture, saw first the

347

back of a tall man walking away from him. He was immediately struck by the fact that something about the scene was extremely familiar to him, but he was not allowed time to follow this thought to its conclusion since his mind was registering the images seen and the sounds heard, to extract their meaning. He had entered the theatre after the feature picture had begun, which meant that he did not know what action had transpired before. He saw a man walking down a busy street, a New York street, in fact (he realized this with a shock that was strangely unpleasant), a street he had walked himself only a few minutes ago! Before he could consider the full meaning of this coincidence, something else happened on the screen: a girl, a beautiful, dark-haired girl, stepped out of a doorway and smiled at the man – who still presented only his back to Philip – welcomed him without words. The man stopped walking and his back grew larger until it forced itself, obtruded itself, to the very edges of the screen. All Philip could see were the man's back and, over his shoulder, the smiling eyes of the girl which, as he watched, ceased smiling and became dull with fright. A scream shrilled in Philip's ears and the monster's back and shoulders began to rock to and fro, the eyes dangled and jumped and shook – again the scream shrilled, then formed itself into terror-stricken words: 'Oh, don't, Phil, don't! I never told on you. I swear it. He lied! He lied!'

Philip was charged with anger. He leaned forward until his chin rested on the seat in front of him – he did not feel the prickle of the upholstery since it was a part of the reality he rejected when he looked at the screen. His fingers clenched and closed spasmodically as the scene changed: now he, Philip (or was it the shadow-Philip?), found himself in a night club. The place was dark except for a single spotlight that picked out the figure of a girl, a beautiful blonde, who was singing a blues song into a chromium-plated microphone. As she sang, she bobbed and minced in time to the thud-ting, thud-ting of the hidden orchestra.

Philip picked his way to a table. When her number was finished and the lights went up to show a large, circular room with a dance floor of black plastic that shone like a mirror, she saw his inquiring eyes and came to his table and sat opposite him. Philip questioned her in low, threatening tones spoken out of the corner of his mouth, and when she refused to answer he clamped his fingers on her wrist and began to turn it slowly, torturously until she cried in pain. Then he slapped her face and walked out of the night club . . .

It was a grade-B movie he had stumbled on, and one that was in no way distinguished except that its principal character happened to be named Philip. Philip had often seen plays or movies where he shared his name with one of the characters involved in the drama. But this time, coming in when he did as the murderer was strangling his first victim, the familiar magic worked too well. The narrative continued on the screen – as the man who had escaped from prison killed his first victim and went on to kill another and another, all the time searching for the man who 'sent him up' – and each time Philip performed, partly in his mind and partly in elaborate, unconscious pantomime, each of the killer's actions. In the climactic moments of the movie, the detective, who had been following the murderer from city to city and murder to murder, at last caught up with him and killed him just as he had found and was about to kill the man for whom he had been searching.

Philip had long since lost all track of reality. The action on the screen was his action, he was the murderer – and each time the girl who was murdered was Brent. He killed her again and again, every time a different way: by slow strangulation, by poison, by shooting and once by pushing her from a high window. He was a hunted man, even though his actions were not his actions but the fictional acts of the shadow he watched – still they were real to him to a greater extent than the giant finger had been real to him, and they carried with them a sense of guilt that

349

was overwhelming. The sounds and shadows which he watched, the shape and darkness of the theatre, the actual sensations of breathing and contact with the material world, all became merged into an amorphous, phantasmagoric delusion. Philip killed, felt remorse, anger, jealousy, lust; he drank, ran, strangled, sweated, feared; he heard jazz bands, saw the other shadows as he had seen Brent and confused them with her, enacted crimes with the ease of any of a hundred odd actions in his normal life. The climax of the picture left him hysterical. He sat and sobbed through the news-reel, the Mickey Mouse and the Coming Attractions. These short subjects, instead of breaking the continuity of his delusion, served to confuse him more than ever so that the second time he saw *Man Alone* his experience was even more terrible.

About six o'clock the balcony began to fill up. A woman sat next to Philip for a little while and then went to an usher and complained. 'There's a man up there who keeps grunting and tearing at his seat like an animal. I won't sit beside him!' The usher investigated. He had to shake Philip to bring him to his senses, and he insisted that Philip must leave.

Not until he reached the street – as he groped his way down the stairs and walked through the ornate lobby, he still felt he had done some heinous wrong for which he was being pursued – did Philip begin to understand how extraordinarily he had acted in the theatre.

Then he went across the street to a bar and had a drink.

The bar was small and unpretentious, and it was not crowded. This was the kind of bar Philip liked. He usually drank at a table – he would find the table or booth farthest from the door, the one least exposed to view, and then sit at it in the most inconspicuous position. There was no conscious reason behind this habit; in fact he was not aware of his preference for privacy when drinking. Today, however, he sat at the bar. He wanted to be near people and he was eager to start a conversation. If he could talk to someone, he thought he might get his mind off his fear.

He drank three double bourbons in rapid succession and felt much better immediately. He had been acting the fool's part all along – he saw that now. Yesterday, when he had read the first instalment of the 'Confession', he should have made no secret of it. He should have questioned Miss Grey thoroughly, as well as every other person in the office who might have had the least thing to do with it. He should have told his wife about the 'Confession', too, if for no other reason than to judge her reaction. During the evening with Jeremy and Brent, he might have joked about it. Certainly one of these persons, Miss Grey or Dorothy or Brent, had written it. Or himself.

He had made another mistake at the same time. He had allowed himself to forget about the manuscript from the time he had first read it until Dorothy told him that they were having friends for dinner. As a result he was unprepared for the shock of having the 'Confession's' predictions come true. He had grown nervous and withdrawn, and he had either thought too much or not at all about every word he said, everything he did. If someone had written the strange prophecy with an aim to get him to follow a particular course of action, he could not have done more to help this person's plans or to hurt himself. He had walked into every trap that had been set for him – if, indeed, traps had been set for him at all. Now, what he should have done . . .

'Have a drink on me?'

A deeply tanned face was looking into his, a young man's face. But this face, though still recognizably young, was fleshed so tightly that the cheekbones seemed drumheads and the thin, smiling lips were as worn and polished as an old coin. He was a soldier and the service ribbons of three theatres of war were displayed on his breast. Apparently, Philip did not answer him as quickly as he expected, for the smile left his lips and the eyelids closed down on his dun-coloured eyes. He no longer seemed friendly, only lonely, and disheartened and grim. 'Yes,

351

thank you,' said Philip, and he added quickly, 'if you'll have one on me.'

The boy – for Philip saw he was very young despite his grizzled look – whistled at the bartender and ordered drinks. He ducked his head in Philip's direction. 'I'm celebrating my release.'

'Have you been in the Army a long time?'

'Four years.'

'That is a long time.'

'It's all my life.'

Philip did not understand. The drinks came and he reached for and fingered his glass. He wanted to ask the youth what he meant by his remark, but he desisted.

'Do you like it here?' the soldier asked.

Philip glanced around him. 'It's all right as these places go. I've been in worse.'

The soldier shook his head. 'Not *here*,' he said. He made a wide, sweeping motion with his hand, an all-embracing gesture. 'I mean all around.'

Philip felt put off by his terse way of talking. 'Do you mean New York?' he asked.

The boy grimaced. 'New York, Chicago, 'Frisco, all the places I've been State-side.'

'I like New York,' Philip said.

The soldier looked him unblinkingly in the face. He might stare at me like this if he wanted to start a fight, Philip thought. But he is not belligerent. What is wrong?

'Does it seem real to you?' the soldier asked.

'New York?'

'Yeah. New York, Chicago, any place here.'

'Of course it seems real to me. It is real.' Then he remembered his bewildering afternoon. 'Although, at times, it can seem very unreal.'

The soldier's eyelids unshuttered his eyes and a thin smile lurked on his die-cast lips. His next question was put forward eagerly. 'Does it sometimes seem to you like this' – he waved his hand again – 'is not here, that you are not here, that you are only dreaming it?'

Philip did not answer. Yet, because he did not want to seem unfriendly, he smiled.

The boy had not noticed that Philip had failed to understand him. 'It's like that all the time with me. I look at a building, I crane my neck up at it and I laugh. It ain't real, and I know it ain't real. It stretches way up to there' – and he pointed upwards with his hand, causing Philip to look up with him – 'and down to here' – and he pointed downwards, Philip's eyes following – 'and yet it isn't. If I weren't looking at it, it wouldn't be.'

Philip nodded his head. Now he thought he understood what the boy was driving at and he became interested. Had he read Plato or had he thought this all out for himself?

'You mean,' Philip said, 'that you doubt the verifiability of the existence of things. You can only be sure of their appearance, the way they seem to you. Is that what you are saying?'

'Here,' said the soldier.

'Here? What do you mean by "here"?'

'Things ain't real here. Chicago, New York, all the places I've been here, ain't real.'

'Are they any more real anywhere else?'

This question had an effect on the young soldier. He began to glower, his face was torturously twisted and a tic developed in his cheek. 'All I have to do is shut my eyes and' – he waved his hand – 'all this crumbles.'

Philip threw his drink down his throat. His entire system had by now been invaded by the fire set by the liquor and he felt well and strong. But he did not like what his companion was saying. It horrified him.

The soldier had shut his eyes to test and prove his statement. 'The sun is everywhere. It glimmers and shakes in front of me. The canvas of my tent stinks. The water I am drinking stinks. The coke and beer I get at the P.X. stinks. I call it the sun stink. Can't you smell it?'

'No,' said Philip.

'I can. That's real. That won't crumble. It'll always be

here.' He opened his eyes and tapped his forehead. Philip saw that two of the fingers of his right hand were gone, and in their place was a badly healed scar. The soldier saw him looking at it. 'That's real, too,' he said. 'Jungle rot got in it. That won't crumble.'

'I don't understand you,' Philip said slowly. 'I thought I did at first, but now I'm not sure I do. Do you mean that you think you're not in New York?'

'It don't matter what you call it,' the boy said roughly. 'It ain't real. It will crumble.'

Philip was fascinated. He decided to tell his companion about what had happened to him that afternoon. He wanted to see what would happen when he told it. Before he told anyone else, he wanted to try it out on someone he did not know. He began at the barber-shop and told him about the giant finger that he had thought had been following him and pointing at him. He told him about his fear of losing his mind and of the queer, dream-like incoherence of his experience at the movie. When he had finished he was at once afraid that he had gone too far. He ordered another round of drinks for himself and the soldier.

'Does it come back to you when you shut your eyes?' the soldier asked. 'Can you shut your eyes and step right into it? Then it's real. Then you see the same thing I do. The stink – ain't it hell ? – the stinking sun !'

Philip shut his eyes. He did see the monstrous finger. It was pointing directly at him. But, he told himself, this is only because you are thinking about it, remembering it. Then he saw Brent's face the way it had looked when she had asked him to leave her apartment. And he heard Dorothy's voice saying, 'I'm going to leave you, Philip.' And Jeremy was saying, 'Good old Phil, always the life of the party!' He opened his eyes. The bar room did look unreal, his face in the mirror looked unreal, the soldier's voice droning on about 'the stink' was unreal. Nothing existed.

He ordered another drink for himself and the soldier.

'I was in Greenland,' the soldier said, 'and then North Africa and Normandy. I was wounded at Caen and invalided home, and then, after a delay in route, they shipped me to the Pacific. We were stationed on an atoll that didn't have a name, only a number. The war had passed it by; we were guarding ammunition and an airstrip that was never used. A dozen bull-dozers and a couple of excavators were rotting in the sun – we were supposed to keep them in working order. They were covered by canvas and we oiled them regularly, painted their metal, polished, scraped. Every week we'd hack the jungle back, burn the vines, make a little clearing around them.

'The rest of the time we sat around, or, when the C.O. got worried about us, we drilled in the sun. The sun was everywhere. It got inside your skull and beat at your brains. It was like prying fingers inside your skin, always moving, always hot, always tormenting you. We got so we hated each other. One of my buddies would say something to me – something like "Have you got a match?" – or "Hell, ain't it hot?" – and I'd want to kill him. We all got so we never said an unnecessary word. We just sat around and thought and sweated.

'It was then I thought of home' – he waved his hand – 'of here. I'd shut my eyes and try to see it the way I remembered it, and sometimes I would see it. But most of the time all I could ever see was a dull, red glare – the stinking sun. It got so that even at night, when I shut my eyes, I'd see that red glare – sometimes I'd even see it in my sleep.

'I kept telling myself that the day would come when I'd go home, leave the island for good, and then finally, the day would come when I wouldn't even remember what it was like. I kept telling myself that the day would come when I'd shut my eyes and try to see the tent and the goddam, stinking sun – and I wouldn't be able to! If I hadn't kept telling myself that I'da gone nuts!'

The soldier talked on and on. Philip bought round after round of drinks and sat with his eyes shut while the soldier talked. He said the same things over and over again. When he had been in the Pacific, he had tried to dream of home and only rarely had he succeeded – home had been distant, unreal, the blinding sun had stood between him and his dream. He had consoled himself with the thought that the time would come when he would not be able to recall the atoll, and the sun would be eternally vanquished. But this had not happened. Now that he was in the United States, he could not believe that the world he saw and the experiences he had were real. All he had to do at any time was to close his eyes, and he was back on the atoll facing the shimmering, relentless sun. He had convinced himself that his reality lay in his mind's picture of this past experience, that he was dreaming when he saw New York but not dreaming when he saw the high Pacific sun, that the drinks he was having in this bar – even his conversation with Philip – did not exist.

Philip did not try to shake his conviction. On the contrary, every word the obsessed soldier spoke strengthened a conviction of his own that he was no longer able to discriminate between real and mental images. By now, when he shut his eyes, Philip saw many different scenes. He lived over again all the events of the past day and a half, and he was freshly horrified by their import. He remembered, or thought he did, each word and phrase of the two instalments of the 'Confession', and he saw in his mind's eye each of the scenes depicted in it – including some that had not happened, some that had partly happened and some that had not happened yet. His memory confused these scenes with the actualities of the previous night and that afternoon, just as on the street and in the theatre he had misinterpreted and jumbled together real perceptions and imagined ones. As the soldier's voice buzzed on, compulsively reiterating his distorted version of reality, Philip grew more and more frenzied. His pulse pounded. His fingers were numb and it became increasingly difficult for him to pick up the jiggers of whisky that followed each other incessantly across the bar. Finally, it seemed to him that he was not sitting at a bar, but rather that he was placed beside an endless conveyor belt that kept moving past him. On the belt were glass after glass of whisky. It was his task to pick up each glass and drain it, and throw a half a dollar after it, before the next one came along. He had been doing this for years, it seemed, and so far he had been able to keep up – but now they were speeding up the belt. He could not continue . . . he could not . . .

He turned around to ask the soldier to help him, but the boy was no longer there. He looked around him. There was no one in the place (as he stared groggily, the room gradually assumed normal proportions, although it kept wavering and fading before his eyes), except for a man in a long, white apron who was doing something to the door. Now, the man was beckoning to him, saying something to him in a loud, harsh voice that was wholly incoherent. He stood unsteadily and walked towards the man and the door. As he reached them, he put his hand out to support himself (he felt as if the room were listing badly, as if the floor were slipping out from under his feet). But his hand met with no substance; the lights about him dulled and went out. His hand groped forward, still expecting to find a door, and he followed it, uncertainly, slowly, with exaggerated care. And then he saw a street lamp shining on a green and yellow taxi – was it real? – and he guessed that the scene had changed again.

The cab-driver saw a well-dressed drunk stagger out of the bar. He opened the door to his cab and the drunk stumbled into it – 'as if there'd been a magnet in there that drew him to it,' as the cabby explained to a friend later. He knocked down the flag on his meter, eyed his customer for a moment – he wasn't a bad-looking fellow – and asked him where he wanted to go.

'Home to Dorothy,' said Philip. 'Home to my lovin' lil' wife.' And he gave an address on Jones Street.

5

Tom Jamison and Alice Grey had been to a movie and now they were sitting in the Times Square Child's. Jamison's face was especially glum and Alice, while she ate her sandwich, kept glancing at him. He paid no attention.

'You haven't said a word in ten minutes, Tom,' she said.

He looked at her and smiled slightly.

'What's wrong?'

'You lied to me this afternoon.'

Her face flushed. 'But, Tom, I didn't.'

'Do you have to lie again?'

She laid her sandwich down. 'Tom, what did I say that you thought was untrue? Tell me, Tom! I want to know.'

'You said you didn't meet anyone the other night when I was late in calling you.'

She looked at him defiantly. 'Well, what if I did? What's wrong in meeting someone else?'

He stared at her, then dropped his eyes. 'It was a man, wasn't it?' His voice was cold.

'What if it was?'

'Who was he?' Anger made his voice squeak.

'Why should I tell you that? I don't have to.'

Tom was silent. He took a cigarette from his pocket and lighted it without offering her one. 'No, you don't have to tell,' he said.

'It was an accident.'

He did not speak.

'I just happened to meet him. He came into the bar

while I was having a drink. He spoke to me and I had to speak to him. I couldn't ignore him. He asked me to have a drink with him. I was angry with you and I did. It was awful. He told me the story of his life. He's so queer, Tom.'

Jamison was now paying close attention. 'Who are you talking about?' he asked quietly.

'Philip Banter,' she said. 'I met him in the bar. He sat and talked to me for an hour or more. He told me about his wife and how he was unfaithful to her. He told me about his mother and how he had never obeyed her – though what that had to do with his wife, I don't know. He kept telling me there was evil in him and he knew it. I tried to kid him out of it, but he got awfully excited. Then he did the strangest thing!'

'Why didn't you tell me this before?'

'I was afraid to tell you. But let me tell you what he did –'

Jamison shrugged his shoulders. 'Go ahead.'

'Philip kept saying there was a devil in him – that he was possessed with evil. I told him that I did not believe in devils, that it was childish for a grown man like him to talk like that. Then he got awfully excited. He said there were things he did that were so terrible that he could not even remember doing them. His eyes grew wild and crazy-looking. He said that he could tell when he was going to do evil. He said the lights grew dim; he said that he heard a tiny bell tinkling in his ear and a voice – his own voice, he said – would speak to him. That was when he was going to do something bad.' Miss Grey had been speaking rapidly and quietly. Now her voice was suddenly louder. 'Then he did the craziest thing, Tom! He stood up and reached across the table at me – we had left the bar and were sitting at a table in the rear – he started to claw at me. I don't know if he meant any harm, but he scared me. I picked up a seltzer bottle and hit at him. The bottle broke on his wrist – it cut him badly. When I saw the blood, I ran. I ran right out of the bar and I didn't stop until I climbed on a bus!'

Jamison shook his head. 'Do you mean that after all this had happened the night before, you were foolish enough to take that money the next morning – and put that thing on his desk?'

'Yes. I was mad at him.'

'But hasn't he ever referred to what happened?' Tom asked.

'Not a word. He had a bandage on his wrist though. I saw him looking at it.'

Jamison leaned forward and spoke earnestly. 'Look, Alice, you're getting deeper and deeper in this. If you don't watch out, something will happen and you'll be blamed for it. The best thing for you to do is to tell him you're quitting. If he ever remembers what he told you that night, he'll fire you anyway.'

'I had thought of that. But, Tom, I don't want to give up my job. We need the money.'

He held her hand in his. 'You can get another job – maybe a better one. You know as well as I do that something very queer is going on in that office. And you've had a hand in it. If you get out now, you won't be impli- cated. But if you hang around, you'll only be courting trouble.'

'When do you think I should give notice?'

'Tomorrow morning. The first thing. Don't lose any time doing it.'

'All right, Tom, if you say so. But I don't see why you're so alarmed.' Alice Grey smiled. She would like telling Philip Banter that she would not work for him any longer. It would be satisfying.

At about the same time, in her apartment on Jones Street, Brent had nearly finished the writing she had been doing all afternoon. After Jeremy had left her to keep his appointment with Dorothy, she had returned to her apartment. She had written the rest of the afternoon and evening and now it was close to midnight. Her eyes were tired from the continued effort and her back ached in that inconvenient place under the shoulders which she could never reach to rub or soothe. As she completed the last page of what she was typing, she ripped the sheet of paper from the platen of her typewriter and let the lid fall on the portable with a triumphant bang. She pushed her chair back, stood up – her hand pressed to her forehead, her manner dejected. Wearily, she crossed the small room to the telephone and slumped down beside it on the sofa. She stared at the instrument several minutes before she began to dial.

She was calling Jeremy's place again. Since six o'clock she had been trying to get him, but the only response had been the familiar sound of persistent ringing. He had said that he was not working that night, still she had called the studio once just to see if he might have changed his mind. But he was not there and the night operator could not tell her whether he had been there at all that day. Brent had doubted him when he had told her that morning that he was going to work; there had been something about the way he said this, a hesitancy, perhaps, that had informed her that he lied. She suspected that the telephone call he had received had been from Dorothy, and that he had left to meet her. He was probably with Dorothy now.

But each time Brent came to this conclusion, she rejected it. She did not want to believe that Jeremy had lied to her about Dorothy, especially since she had no evidence to support her suspicion. You resent Dorothy only because she knew him first and because he loved her before he loved you, she told herself. You are insecure in your relationship with him as you have been insecure in your relationship with all men since your childhood. You never let yourself forget your father, his glib tongue and his dark negligence – do you? You can always remember, without half an effort, that first night alone after your mother's death, when your father had gone out saying he would return, and he did not – can't you? That loneliness, that horror of moving shadows and unexplained sounds, that shriek that has been caught and held and never

361

uttered in all these years – they are always there waiting for the unguarded moment, the flickering instant when restraint is loosened and the walls of reason crumble – aren't they? This implacable, childish terror (it has grown strong despite its fetters) was swallowed when your father at last returned, after a day and night of your vigil, somehow shrunken and dishevelled by his absence, swaying on his feet, clutching at you avidly while you eluded his drunken advances and shut your ears to his mutterings – it was swallowed then, but never digested – wasn't it? 'Yes,' she said aloud, as if hearing her own voice speak the words would render their truth harmless, 'it has remained a part of me, yet apart from me. It arises again and again and I re-swallow it as I might my heart's bile. I must continue to try to reclaim that which I can never assimilate.' (Except by wild rationalizations, by catch-as-catch-can plausibilities, by the butterfly nets of reason, her conscience added.)

Each time she had beaten back her suspicion in this way, had paced the floor and wrung her hands, had argued back and forth with herself, and each time she had returned to the typewriter to lose herself and her fear of losing Jeremy in her work. But now work was done for the night. The stream of words was stopped, the complex of thoughts and fingers, of words and ribboned ink and metal keys, was inaccessible to her. She was written out, and she would have to sleep another night and live another day before that escape would be possible again. Yet she knew that she could not sleep, that there was no use in lying down or trying to invite it in any of the usual ways for it would not come to her until she had heard Jeremy's voice and listened to him excuse his absence. If this did not happen, dawn would find her still alone with the ghost of her childhood . . .

The doorbell jangle broke in upon her self-torment. She stood stock still and listened to its dying vibrations. Was it Jeremy? She made no move to answer. It rang again, this time a prolonged signal that forced her to press the buzzer button in response. Then, her weight thrown against the door as if to ward off the visitor, she listened for the footfalls on the stairs. When they came they were heavy . . . hesitant . . . not Jeremy's.

Suddenly, she was a child again, the same child that had listened and waited for her father. The room became the hall-bedroom of a St Louis boarding-house – she could feel the brush of pig-tails on her back and her hand felt spontaneously for the golden locket, that had clasped a strand of her mother's hair, which she had always used to wear about her neck. The empty yearning that belongs to children was hers again, and with it the fear of the un-known – the yet to be – which as an adult she had learned to forget. She fought against the foolish dread that accompanied this throwback to the past, chided herself for harbouring such a silly fear. Yet the hammering on her heart prevailed against all reassurances, insisting that her senses were right: that the lumbering footsteps she heard were her father's . . . even though she knew him long since dead!

The sound of a large man walking uncertainly con-tinued up to her door. There was a silence, and then a fumbling and scratching – as if whoever it was was trying to fit a key into the keyhole – and a belched curse.

Brent pushed as hard as she could against the door. Her body was shaking with fright and her mouth was open and moaning. She wanted to cry out, to scream and end this nightmare (for one distraught moment she managed to convince herself that it was not happening, that she was only dreaming and, if she fought a little more desperately, she would succeed in awakening) – but the same thing in her that had held back any cry of protest as a girl, forced her to bite her lip and quiet her whimpering now. The scratching continued and with it the sound of harsh, whistling breaths.

Then she heard a tinkle, followed by another curse. He's dropped his key just as he used to do! she thought. But then something even more terrible happened. There was a heavy, slumping thud – a scrambling sound of cloth and leather on polished wood. And then a gurgling retching . . .

When Brent finally dared to open the door, she did not find her father there. Philip's limp body sprawled in upon her feet. He was not dead, only very drunk. And he had been sick in the hallway.

The Third Instalment

I

It had come to pass. Philip awakened with this conviction – he knew *where* he was, in the moment before he
opened his eyes, even if he did not know *how* he happened
to be there. He was in Brent's apartment and in Brent's
bed. Somehow, in some way, he had betrayed himself.
The 'Confession' had triumphed again.

When he opened his eyes, he saw the same small room
that he had visited once before, the same cheap maple
furniture. He was lying on the studio couch and across the
room on a chair lay his brown tweed suit, his brown snap-
brim felt hat and his brown brogues. But the suit he had
been wearing the night before was his grey urquhart plaid,
his hat had been grey and his shoes black! If this were
Brent's apartment – and he was sure it was – how did a
change of clothes happen to be ready for him? He sat up,
clutching the blanket about himself. A sound of dishes
being rattled in the next room prompted him to call
Brent's name.

'So you're up?' she answered matter-of-factly. 'The
bathroom is across the hall. I put a towel out for
you.'

Philip pulled on his trousers. 'How did I get here?' he
asked.

'That was one of the things I was going to ask you.'

Philip tried to remember the events of the previous
night. What had happened during the afternoon, especially
his nightmarish experience in the theatre, came back to
him with great clarity and a sense of immediacy – as if it
had just occurred. He could also remember leaving the
theatre and going into a bar to have a few drinks. He had

met a soldier who had talked very queerly . . . but what had happened after that?

'I don't remember,' he admitted. 'Was I drunk?'

Brent came out of the kitchen alcove. She was wearing a house dress and her dark hair was done up on top of her head like a little girl's. But her eyes were not those of a child's; they flashed with suppressed rage. 'You were drunk,' she said flatly. 'You rang my doorbell and you managed to get up the stairs. I found you in the hall. You were being very sick all over yourself.'

Philip blushed. He looked away from Brent and, as he did, he felt a wave of nausea rise inside him. He fought to keep it down, swallowing desperately. Then he rushed out of the door and across the hall to the bathroom. He thought he could hear Brent laughing.

Later, after he had finished dressing, he went into the small kitchen. Brent was having breakfast; she poured him some black coffee and offered him some toast. Philip drank a little of the coffee. 'I'm afraid you've been terribly inconvenienced,' he said.

'That is an understatement,' she said coldly.

'I don't know what made me do it.'

'The only reason I did not call the police when I found you in the hall is because I did not want the neighbours to know what had happened. I took you in, put you on the couch and took your keys from your pocket. You had ruined your clothes, so I went to your apartment – letting myself in with your key – and got you a change. When I came back here, you had managed to undress yourself and get into bed. I had to sleep on the floor.'

'What can I do by way of apology?'

'Nothing.'

Philip had never before experienced so thoroughgoing a rebuff. Brent's contempt was coldly magnificent. She regarded him steadily with concentrated animosity that was almost warlike.

'I want you to understand something, Philip,' she said.

'I never want to see you again. What I did last night, I did in my own interests. I should have called the police, but had I done that I would have awakened the house. Everyone would have known that a man had tried to force his way into my apartment, a besotted fool who could not even hold his liquor. So I took you in, and what I did you might mistake for kindness, Philip. It was not kindness. If I got you fresh clothes, it was only to keep some of my friends from seeing you leave my apartment the way you would have looked in those rags.' She pointed to a bundle that lay next to the refrigerator. Philip recognized the suit he had been wearing the day before. It was badly stained and still odorous.

Brent had not finished. 'When you are through with your coffee, I want you to leave. I want you to take that with you. I do not know where you got the idea that you could act this way with me. I do not care to listen to any excuse you might make or any apology you might offer. I only want you to get out of my house. And, please, stay away from me hereafter!'

Philip stood up. His action was automatic, a will-less response. He felt inert and nerveless, as if he were a thing, not a person. Brent's anger had turned to quiet tears. Her face was pale with emotion and her lips trembled.

Philip picked up the bundle of clothes and left the apartment. When he reached the street, he threw it in the nearest trash can. He began to walk uptown. After he had gone a few blocks, he realized that, although Brent had said that she had visited his apartment in the middle of the night, she had not mentioned seeing Dorothy. Did that mean that Dorothy had not been at home? Philip searched his pockets for a nickel to make a telephone call. In the last pocket he found a nickel and a dime. He would make a telephone call with the nickel and use the dime to pay his bus fare uptown.

He went into the first drugstore he encountered to telephone Dorothy. There was no response. He hung up and dialled the same number again, thinking that in his haste he might have made a mistake. But there was still no answer. He looked at his watch. It was not yet nine o'clock. Knowing Dorothy's liking for sleeping late, he found it probable that she had been out all night and had not yet returned.

He left the drugstore and walked along twisting Village streets to Fifth Avenue. He hailed an open-deck bus and climbed the stairs to the top deck. It was a beautiful morning. The sky was wholly clear of clouds and of the deepest blue. The sun was strong for December, and it was even unseasonably warm. Yet Philip noticed none of these things. His mind was on the many-faceted problem he faced and which he seemed impotent to solve. If Dorothy had not spent the night at home, where had she been? Had she already left him? Wouldn't he be given a chance to explain his actions?

But one question, of far greater significance than any of the others, was present continually, was, in fact, so well known to him that he scarcely needed to formulate it. When he reached the office, would he find another instalment of the 'Confession'? And if he did, what would it predict this time?

Philip descended from the bus at Fiftieth Street and went to his bank in Radio City to a cash a cheque. Then he had another cup of coffee at a Whelan's. He smoked several cigarettes and contemplated not going to the office, so intense was his desire to avoid finding a third section of the 'Confession' on his desk. But, in the end, some part of his will remained to make him face up to what he had come to consider his fate. He left the drugstore and, walking slowly and with great hesitance, headed for Madison Avenue.

The desperate confusion that had marked all of his actions of the day before had passed away; in its place was a superficial calm. The despair he felt no longer showed itself in his actions, except, perhaps, in the subdued unsteadiness of his gait. To the casual eye, if it had paused to inspect him, he might have seemed to have been suffering from a bad hangover – which, of course, he was. A more critical appraisal, such as George Matthews might have made had he met him at this time, would have considered his state an exaggeratedly neurotic and depressed condition. Philip, when he entered the lobby of his building, was walking with the measured, yet sometimes faltering, strides of a condemned man marching to the place of his execution.

Sadie, the elevator operator, did not say good morning to him, although they were alone in the car. She kept her eyes fixed on the ruby lights of the indicator so that all Philip saw of her was her back. He took this as an omen, deriding himself for being superstitious even as the thought occurred to him. Something was badly wrong about him – this he was sure of by now – if a girl who had always been flirtatious and friendly in the past should now make a point of snubbing him. As the elevator doors opened at his floor, he tried to catch her eye. If she would only smile at me, he thought, it would be encouraging! But, whether her indifference was due to a change in himself or not, he did not succeed. Sadie paid no attention to his wink.

It was the same with the receptionist. Her smile, and her way of saying good morning, had always affected Philip adversely; but this time her mien was so bleak as to be frightening. He felt that she must have discovered some part of what was going on and had grown thoroughly contemptuous of him because of it. As he walked down the corridor to his own office and Miss Grey, it seemed to him that all the girls in the office were watching him, pointing at him behind his back and saying things to each other about him. With his hand on the knob of his door, he stopped and tried to make himself turn around to face their derision; but he did not have the courage. He opened the door and went through it hurriedly.

'Good morning, Miss Grey,' he said as soon as he was

371

inside the door and before he had looked at her. She was seated at her desk, her pocketbook lying open on her typewriter, busily filing her nails. She barely nodded to him.

'Good morning, Miss Grey,' he snapped again. He was not going to allow such impertinence.

She glanced up at him. 'Good morning,' she said, and she smiled briefly. But she went on filing her nails.

Philip hesitated. His anger had flared momentarily, but now he was unsure of himself. Miss Grey was the one person in the office who was closest to him – the person who might logically know most about the 'Confession'. She could have seen it on his desk on the other two mornings. She undoubtedly knew what was on his desk now. Was it because she had read the latest chapter of the 'Confession', that she acted so casually indifferent to him as he stood before her? Was she secretly smiling and waiting to see what he would do when he went into his office and read it himself? Philip turned his back on her and opened the other door. His heart was pounding violently . . .

At first he thought there was nothing on his desk. His typewriter was not open on it. There was no neat pile of manuscript. He sighed and hung up his hat. Then he walked around and sat down. He checked all the articles that belonged on his desk top: the blotter, the fountain-pen set, the calendar, the file boxes, the clock, the buzzer buttons. He saw that he had been wrong, that there was one new thing lying on his desk – a blank piece of paper.

He picked it up in his hands and stared at it. Good bond paper, he noted, watermarked. He turned it over, held it up to the light. No, there was no marking on it whatsoever. He might have left it here himself the day before. Or it might have been here a long time and he had not noticed it. He laid it down again. A blank piece of paper signified nothing. The main thing to remember was that there was no manuscript on his desk. Which meant, of course – he was absolutely sure of it! that what had been happening to him had come to an end. He leaned far back in his swivel chair and laughed loudly, so great was his relief.

'Mr Banter?'

Philip had swerved around in his chair so that he faced the window. Now Miss Grey's voice cut his laugh short. He turned around and saw that she was standing in the doorway that connected their offices. She had her hat and coat on.

'What is it?'

'I wanted to tell you, Mr Banter, that I'm leaving. I've got another job. I've already told Miss Rossiter.' (Miss Rossiter was the assistant cashier who also acted as supervisor over the secretaries and stenographers in the office.)

Philip gaped. The girl was smiling at him, openly showing her pleasure at being able to speak these words. All Philip could say was, 'B-but I-I thought you were ha-happy here?' And he cursed himself silently for stammering.

Miss Grey looked down. She fiddled with her gloves for a moment before she answered. When she did, she looked up, her eyes wide, her mouth trembling. 'I didn't want to tell you my real reason, Mr Banter. I thought I might hurt your feelings, and I know how sensitive you are – I didn't want to make you feel bad.'

She paused, Philip waited quietly. She is going to tell me that she has read the 'Confession', he thought.

'You've been so queer lately, Mr Banter. You look at me in such a funny way, when you look at me at all. It's as if you weren't seeing me, as if you were looking through me at something behind me. Then you get angry at the least thing – like the other day when you implied that I had been using your typewriter. You make me feel uncomfortable all the time.'

Philip did not know what to say. She was embarrassed, too, and stood twisting a glove that was half-off one of her hands. Then Philip remembered that he had promised himself to ask her some questions the next time he saw her.

'I'm sorry you feel that way, Miss Grey,' he began. 'But if you're not happy here, you had better leave. Before you go – since you have referred to the episode of the typewriter – I would like to ask you a few questions.'

Miss Grey stripped her gloves from her hands. 'I'll answer what I can,' she said.

'Both yesterday and the day before, when I came into my office I found my typewriter open on my desk. But that's not all.' He stooped and fitted the key to the bottom drawer of his desk into the lock, opened the drawer and withdrew the two sections of the 'Confession'. 'I also found these manuscripts on my desk, Miss Grey. Have you any idea who put them there?'

The girl did not step forward to inspect the thick sheaf of manuscripts Philip held. Instead, she put her hand to her mouth and began to whimper. 'I don't know anything about it. You keep accusing me of things I didn't do. I don't know.'

Philip shook his head. 'I'm not accusing you of anything. I'm simply asking you for information. Do you know how these manuscripts could have gotten on my desk? Could they have been put there at night – or early in the morning before anyone's at work? Is the main door to the office kept closed and locked, and, if so, who has a key?'

Miss Grey leaned against the jamb of the door. Philip could see she was frightened. Good God, did he have this effect on everybody? What was the matter with him?

'I don't know who put those papers on your desk, Mr Banter,' the girl said weakly. 'I'm sure I didn't. And I don't think anyone in the office did. Are you sure you didn't put them there yourself, and then forget about it?'

'I am certain I did nothing of the sort,' Philip said.

'Well, the door to the office is left open for the cleaning women. They're supposed to lock it, and they usually do. Although some of the girls who get here earliest say that on some mornings the door is unlocked. We all have keys, of course.'

'What would I do if I wanted to get into the building late at night, and I had forgotten my key?'

'You could ask the watchman for one. You'd have to sign the register, but he'd lend you one.'

'So anyone could procure a key to our offices and walk right in and steal anything, I suppose?' Philip asked sarcastically.

Miss Grey shook her head. 'The watchman wouldn't give just anyone a key. He would have to know you.'

'I suppose the watchman knows all the tenants of this building?' Again Philip's voice was heavy with sarcasm. Miss Grey began to cry. 'Oh, I don't know, Mr Banter – I just don't know. I don't see why you keep after me like this. I didn't put those old papers on your desk!'

Philip realized that he was not succeeding. He sat down and regarded the pile of manuscript bitterly. Miss Grey started to speak, then thought better of it. Still sniffling, she left the room.

Philip continued to stare at the sheaf of papers. Until now he had been looking at it, not reading it. But, without being fully aware of what he was doing, he began to read it. He started reading about the middle of the first page.

Dermo not only cleanses clothes faster – people tell us a day's laundry takes only half a day when they use Dermo – but it actually makes clothes brighter, cleaner, than old-fashioned bar soaps. Dermo – spelled D-E-R-M-O – is the modern way of washing clothes, the economical way. Ask your grocer for the big, family-size today. Don't forget, get Dermo – spelled D-E-R-M-O – today!

Philip looked at the next page. What he read was also part of a radio script for one of his clients – a script for which he had written the commercials weeks ago. Quickly he thumbed through the entire pile of paper. They were all the same! He threw them on the floor in disgust.

He jerked the bottom drawer of his desk out and shuffled through its contents. He did not find the 'Confession'.

375

He pulled out all the other drawers of his desk and searched them all. Still he did not find it. He went to the file cabinet and spent a good fifteen minutes disrupting its orderly rows of folders – without success. Finally, he had to admit the fact that the 'Confession' was gone.

Had it ever existed? Philip sat and stared at the blank piece of paper that he had found on the top of his desk that morning. There was no doubting the reality of this – he was touching it, he could feel it – although he could doubt its significance. Well, there was one good use for it. He took a pen from the stand and began to scribble on it. He put down all of the events of the past two days from the moment he walked into his office and found (or thought he found) the 'Confession' on his desk until a short time before when he had discovered its theft and the substitution of several old scripts in its place. Or had he discovered only that he had been deluding himself?

By the time he had finished writing, he had covered both sides of the sheet of paper with fine writing. He had it all down on paper, concisely – and yet the puzzle remained. Who was writing the 'Confession'? Who had placed that sheet of blank paper on his desk?

He opened his drawer and withdrew another sheet of paper. He held it up to the light and matched its watermark with that of one he had found. The marks were the same. He took his pen again and wrote down these names:

Steven Foster
Miss Grey
Dorothy Banter
Jeremy Foulkes

He studied them for many minutes, then read both sides of the other sheet of paper again. Then he underlined the last name on the list like this:

<u>Jeremy Foulkes</u>

2

Dorothy and Jeremy had attempted to recapture their past, and had failed. The irresponsible holiday, that had begun the day before at lunch in the Three Griffins and had continued with a drive up the Hudson, dinner at a roadside inn and a night together in one of the inn's upstairs rooms, was ending gloomily with each feeling dislike for the other. Yesterday, their high spirits had scarcely outlasted the effects of the martinis they had drunk at lunch. The stiff river breeze – the only car Jeremy had been able to rent was a shabby, well-ventilated convertible coupé – had been sobering. They had first quarrelled about where to stop, Jeremy being all for pushing on to the next place, and the next, while Dorothy felt headachy and hungry and favoured each roadhouse they encountered. When they did drive up to an inn, it was late and the dinner they were served was bad. They ate cold ham, canned peas and soggy boiled potatoes and drank lukewarm coffee. After dinner they managed to patch up their injured feelings briefly, taking a walk along the wooded cliffs that overlooked the river until the gale forced them back inside. They went up to their room as a last resort and played at being lovers like actors reading their parts for the first time, each aware of the other's fumblings as well as his own inadequacy.

The inconvenience of the room contributed to their disillusionment. The brass bed was lumpy, the bath was at the wrong end of the dark corridor, the light bulbs were bald and over-brilliant, the linen had been used before. Jeremy, in pyjamas, could not hide the soft roll of fat that had enveloped his stomach; their intimacy was curt and conventional. Afterwards, neither had been able to sleep for the unfamiliar creakings of the old house and the sighing wind in the pines. But they had both feigned sleep to avoid the pitfalls of nocturnal conversation, and had lain stiff and tense listening to the other's breathing and uncomfortably aware of the absurdity of their situation.

The truth was that Jeremy had found himself thinking more and more of Brent as the day had darkened into night, and increasingly conscious of his disloyalty to her. There had been no reason for it. He had drunk too much at lunch and felt an appetite for a woman he had once loved; but she was no longer the person he remembered fondly; she was, in fact, a stranger. He had told Brent that he would return to her that night, yet when he had visited his loft apartment to pack a bag, he had not left her a note or telephoned her. He could only guess what she would make of his behaviour. By the time he was having dinner with Dorothy, he wanted more than anything else to drive back to town, to return to Brent. But there was Dorothy to consider. He had accepted her advances and had responded to them, had acted as a lover. Now they were alone together and the scene demanded to be played out. To have declared his feelings, would have been to scorn her. So Jeremy continued to pretend ardour, although he lacked desire.

Dorothy's attitude was more complex. She had reached out for Jeremy because she felt she had lost Philip. Jeremy was to be a test, a way of proving to herself that Philip had lost interest in his marriage for some cause other than her own inadequacy. Jeremy had wanted to marry her once, and she had chosen Philip instead; now she tried to use Jeremy to substitute for Philip, in the absence of his love, as she might have worn a charm about her wrist to substitute for him, in his physical absence. Either way Jeremy's value to her derived from Philip: she felt that if she could win Jeremy's affection away from Brent, then Philip's dereliction would not be due to any fault or lack of her own; and she felt that, having lost Philip, if she could gain Jeremy, she would be choosing again as she had chosen before.

This expedition along the Hudson had been to Dorothy an unusual experience which she understood, if at all, only on the level of her emotions. She partly knew that when she looked at Jeremy she was seeing Philip, and also her father before Philip. Unconsciously, and this she did not realize, she was re-staging the rejection scene that had shaped her personality and made her life. If Jeremy, as they drove farther and farther along the Hudson at first disagreeing and then openly quarrelling as to where to stop, thought more about Brent and less about Dorothy, it was not accidental. Dorothy was that unfortunate type that must always cast experience in the same rigid mould: she forced Jeremy to think of Brent, even when she tried to attract him. There was that in her that made her circumvent her ends.

So when the night ended and there was an excuse for breakfast, Jeremy's infatuation with Dorothy, that had lasted a number of years, was finished. They spoke to one another in monosyllables at breakfast, and on the trip back into town did not break the silence for miles at a time. They had not spoken for many minutes when Jeremy turned off Riverside Drive and headed for the midtown area, and he was the one to speak then.

'Do you mind if I stop off at your place for a moment?' he asked. 'I want to make a 'phone call before I go home.'

'Why shouldn't you?' Dorothy asked, shielding her eyes against the morning sun that suddenly confronted them as they drove East.

'I thought Philip might be there.'

Dorothy considered this. She dropped her hand and stared at the sun until the glare caused her eyes to glisten. 'Philip won't be there,' she said.

She spoke quietly, with resignation and sadness. Her manner disturbed Jeremy and made him turn to look at her. He saw that the lines of her beautiful face were set and her eyes stared forward blindly. He sensed that something was about to happen . . . that Dorothy was allowing herself to be drawn to crisis as iron is drawn to a lodestone.

After Philip left, Brent finished her breakfast unhurriedly and then passed the next hour tidying the apartment. She went to the phone and began to dial Jeremy's number several times during this hour, but each time she broke off before the connection could be completed. When there was no more to do about the house, she curled up on the couch and tried to read. After a few minutes of this, however, she tossed the book aside and returned to the telephone. This time she waited until the sound of persistent ringing had lasted for several minutes, long enough to prove without doubt that there was either no one at home or whoever was there was not answering. Slamming the receiver down in exasperation, she took a hat and coat from the closet and left the apartment. When she reached the street, she walked to the corner, hailed a taxi and gave the driver Jeremy's address.

She did not expect to find him home, yet after she had paid the driver off and was climbing the steep stairs to the loft she could not escape the fear that she might. If he were in, Dorothy would be with him; if he weren't in, he might possibly have spent the night with other friends – or so Brent reasoned. She knew that this line of thought was little better than an incantation with which she attempted to ward off the catastrophe she was certain had befallen her. Nevertheless, she was relieved when she found the wide door of the loft ajar, and walked into the barn-like room to see that, in actuality, Jeremy was not there.

She took off her hat and coat and, womanlike, began to do the same things in this place that she had been doing in her own. She swept the floors, dusted the furniture, mopped the kitchen floor, rearranged the dishes in the cupboard. Even so, she soon had exhausted the housewifely tasks the loft had to offer since most of its cavernous depth had never been properly domesticated – Jeremy lived in the corners of the great room – and there was no point in trying to straighten and clean the piles of ruck he had let accumulate in the disused portions. At last, she was reduced again to the couch and a book, albeit a different couch and –

While stretching for a novel that rested on top of the end table, Brent noticed a pile of paper that lay beside it. How did I overlook that when I was dusting? she wondered. She picked it up, instead of the novel, and began to read it. Her interest quickened when she saw that on the first page of what appeared to be a typewritten manuscript was the name and address of Philip Banter and the one word, 'Confession'. She continued to read; by the time she had finished the first few pages her interest was consuming.

A half-hour later, a moment after she had read the last page, the doorbell rang. Laying the manuscript down on the couch, she walked to the door and pressed the buzzer button – most of her thoughts were occupied with what she had just been reading. If she thought at all about who was ringing the bell, she decided that it was Jeremy and he had lost his key again.

It was quite a shock to her when she opened the door and Philip walked into the room.

3

Miss Grey had come back into Philip's office shortly
after he had decided who was the most likely author of the
'Confession'. She was still wearing her hat and coat and
her eyes were red-rimmed. Philip had thought she had
left, and he showed his surprise at seeing her.

'I have something to tell you,' she said. She put out her
hand to steady herself – she was swaying noticeably – and
it came to rest on the edge of Philip's desk. He got her a
chair.

'I lied to you this morning,' she continued. She spoke
hesitantly and in broken phrases. Her hands constantly
fretted with her gloves. 'I do know something about the
manuscript you found yesterday morning . . . and the
morning before that . . . I put it there.'

'What!' Philip exploded.

'When I came into the office day before yesterday . . .
there was a messenger waiting for me. He had a package
. . . and a note. The note was addressed to me. It was
typewritten . . . but it wasn't signed. With it was a
hundred dollar bill.' The girl paused. Her face was grey
and contorted. She forced the next words out. 'The note
asked me to put the manuscript . . . that was in the package . . . on your desk. It said you would be expecting it
. . . but that the contents were confidential . . . that I
must never speak to anyone about it . . . not even you.
Even if you asked me directly . . . I was to say nothing.'

Now that it was coming out, Philip was surprised at his
own calm. He stared at the girl, who had caused him so
much annoyance in the past, as he might have regarded a
convicted murderer. 'And you believed that?' he asked.

The girl nodded her head. She sobbed histrionically. 'I know I should have told you. I know it was wrong. But I'd never had a hundred dollars before in my life . . . and you had been bawling me out all the time. I had come to hate you!' She said these last words not defensively, in justification of her offence, but defiantly, accusingly. Philip felt himself shrink inside.

'So when you asked me who had been using your type-writer . . . I told you the truth . . . that you had used it yourself the night before . . . and hadn't put it away. I knew what you were hinting at . . . but I couldn't let you know I knew . . . I didn't want to . . . and I had been told not to . . .'

'What about yesterday morning?' Philip asked. 'What happened then?'

'When I came in the messenger was waiting for me again . . . this time I asked who sent him . . . he had a uniform on and I thought he might tell me . . . but he had been instructed not to tell. He left another package . . . and another envelope with a note . . . and a hundred dollars. The note read, "Do as you did before." I did. But when I saw you asleep slumped over on your desk, I was scared. At first I thought . . . you were dead . . . but then when I came closer . . . I saw you were all right. I put the manuscript down beside you . . . and then I awakened you.'

'Do you know the name of the company for which the messenger worked? You said he wore a uniform.'

'I noticed that particularly. It was the Zephyr Fast Delivery Service.'

Philip picked up the telephone and asked the switch-board operator to get him the messenger service Miss Grey had named. After a few minutes' wait the connection was completed and Philip explained to the voice on the other end of the wire that he had received two packages on each of the last two days and wanted very much to know who had sent them. The voice listened as he gave his name and address, and then asked him politely to wait a few minutes longer. Philip cradled the receiver between his head and his shoulder and returned his attention to Miss Grey.

'How did my typewriter come to be open on my desk yesterday morning, too?' he asked. 'I know I did not leave it open a second time.'

'I put it there,' the girl said. 'While I was deciding whether or not to wake you up.' She looked away from Philip's steady gaze.

'Did the note tell you to do that?'

Miss Grey shook her head.

'Then why did you do it?'

'I was angry at you . . . you had scolded me for not putting it away. I had made up my mind to quit . . . and I felt like being nasty. I know I shouldn't have done it . . . but I don't care. I can get another job.'

Philip nodded his head and listened for a moment to the crackling sounds that came out of the telephone. 'Then what happened this morning? Did you find a messenger waiting for you when you came to work?'

The girl shook her head again.

Philip leaned forward. 'I put the manuscripts contained in those packages in the bottom drawer of my desk, Miss Grey. And I locked that drawer. When I opened it this morning, they were gone. Do you know anything about that?'

Miss Grey reached into her purse for her handkerchief and began to dab at her eyes. At the same time she nodded her head violently. 'When I came in this morning, your chair was pushed way over to the window. The drawers of your desk were pulled out. The papers in the bottom drawer were in a mess. I was afraid . . . I thought you'd accuse me of being careless. I rearranged the papers in the bottom drawer to make them look as if nothing had been disturbed. When I did this I saw that the lock had been forced. It still works . . . but it will unlock if you pull hard on the drawer. There are scratches on the varnish . . . as if somebody had used a knife on it.'

Philip glanced down at the bottom drawer. There were scratches around the lock all right. Why hadn't he noticed them before? He was reaching for his key to try it in the lock, when the phone that he had been cradling next to his ear came to life. 'Mr Banter?' the voice said. 'So sorry to keep you waiting, Mr Banter. I have the information you requested on those two deliveries. You sent us a letter earlier this week enclosing two one hundred dollar bills and accompanying a package containing a manuscript. Your letter instructed us to deliver the manuscript and the note with one of the bills to your secretary, a Miss Grey, at your office on the morning of the first of December. Your letter also stated that another manuscript, together with another note, would be sent to us the next day. You asked us to follow the same procedure then, enclosing the second bill with the note and delivering the manuscript to Miss Grey. Both deliveries were completed as requested and I have a record of Miss Grey's signature on the receipts. Is there anything wrong, Mr Banter?'

'No,' said Philip, 'everything is quite satisfactory. I just wanted a check-up. Thank you.' He hung up. He looked at Miss Grey and wondered if she could possibly have heard. If she had, she was not letting him know. She had her purse open and was fumbling in it. As he watched, she withdrew two crumpled one hundred dollar bills. She laid them on his desk.

'I know I shouldn't have taken them, Mr Banter.' She gulped and looked away. Her voice had fallen to a whisper. 'But I had never seen that much money before . . .'

Philip stared at her pimply face, her straggly, mouse-coloured hair that was always either all over her face or tightly curled in disgusting little spiral knots. 'You can keep it,' he said. 'And you can forget about everything that has happened this week. It was all a mistake.'

Miss Grey stood up. She picked the bills from the desk hesitantly, and looked at Philip and tried to smile. Slowly, she put the bills into her purse and snapped it shut. She waited a moment longer – plainly expecting Philip to change his mind – then began to inch towards the door.

Philip turned his back on her and went to the window. He stood looking out at the buildings across the street, his mind blank and purposeless. When he heard the door shut behind him and knew that the girl had left the room, he went back and sat in his chair. For a long time he did nothing at all.

And then, he decided to visit Jeremy.

4

Dr Matthews arrived promptly at ten o'clock at the
offices of Brown and Foster, and he was shown in at
once to Steven Foster's office. 'Mr Foster will be with you
in a few minutes, doctor,' the receptionist said, and went
out closing the door softly behind her. Matthews was
annoyed at this. He had cancelled several appointments
to make this call because he had felt it important to talk
to a member of Philip's family about his illness. But he
had not expected to be kept waiting.

Steven Foster's office was large and luxuriously
appointed. A broad mahogany desk commanded the
room, but there were also several comfortable leather
chairs, an imitation fireplace, books and paintings along
the walls. Most of the books dealt with advertising and
business, but one brightly-jacketed volume caught his eye:
William Seabrook's *Witchcraft*. Matthews pulled it off
the shelf, riffled its pages and then put it back – shrugging
his shoulders. He had just finished lighting his pipe when
Steven Foster belatedly entered the room.

He came forward and shook hands cordially with
Matthews, but his eyes reflected no warmth and the lines
of his face were as tense as before. 'I had not expected to
see you so soon,' he said. 'Is it about Philip?' He waited
until Matthews had sat down in one of the leather arm-
chairs before he took his place behind his desk.

'Philip had lunch with me yesterday,' Matthews said.
'He is concerned about himself. He has some unusual
symptoms.' And he went on to tell Foster everything
Philip had told him about the 'Confession', the voice he
heard and his other delusions.

Foster listened expressionlessly. He sat rigidly in his chair, his gaze fixed coldly on the doctor. When Matthews had finished, he said, 'What is your diagnosis?'

Matthews waved his hand. 'Philip is an alcoholic. Like any alcoholic his chronic drinking is a symptom of his disorder and not the disorder itself. However, it should be treated first. If Philip could visit a sanatorium I know in the Catskills, where he would be able to rest and get the best of care, we might be able to prevent a subsequent breakdown.'

Foster's eyes glinted and the corners of his mouth curled tightly. 'Then in your opinion he has not had a breakdown yet?'

'The line of demarcation between neuroses and psychoses is so slight as to be often imperceptible. In very few cases is there a definite point at which you can say, "This patient is now insane." Insanity encroaches. It bores from within gradually, seizing possession of the intellect. I could make tests, subject Philip to a complete mental and physical examination – this I would do anyway – but I doubt if my diagnosis would change until the alcoholism is cleared up. Then we may be able to say definitely whether Philip has had a break.'

Foster raised his eyebrows. 'I had not been prepared for so encouraging a statement from you, doctor. Frankly, I've been worried about Philip. I have watched my daughter lose her spirits and grow pale in the past few months. I have heard what she has had to say about the way her husband has treated her – we are very close, you know – and I had come to the conclusion that the man was both a rotter and crazy. He would have to be crazy to do some of the things he has done.

'Now you tell me about a "Confession". This is something I know nothing about, and I think I can say Dorothy also has not heard of it. Philip must be writing it himself, or else it is an elaborate excuse to explain away his other actions. I want to see him and talk to him about this!' And he reached for the telephone.

Matthews held up his hand. 'Before you call Philip in, I want you to know that the purpose of my visit today is to get help in persuading Philip to go to a sanatorium. You know, of course, that we must have Philip's consent or that of some member of his family. Dorothy could commit him, if that becomes necessary. But it is much better for him if he goes of his own free will. I spoke to him about it yesterday afternoon, and he suddenly invented an appointment that he must keep to get away from me. I thought if we both talked to him, he might see things differently.'

Foster nodded his head and reached for the telephone. He called Miss Grey and asked her to have Philip come into his office. When he replaced the instrument, he sighed and said, 'You know, just this morning I had one of the girls come in to tell me that she was leaving us. She has been with us several years and most of that time she has worked as my son-in-law's secretary. Recently, when his condition became obvious to me, I called Miss Grey aside and asked her to report to me anything that Philip did that seemed to her peculiar. She has done this faithfully and I have relied upon her. Yet she told me today that she is quitting, that she can't stand to work for Philip any longer. She says he is too strange, that he frightens her. I tried to persuade her not to leave us and told her that she did not have to work for Philip. As a matter of fact, I gave Philip notice yesterday afternoon, but I didn't want to tell her that. She said that she would think it over.' He spread his hands dramatically to indicate his confusion. 'So you see how Philip has affected Brown and Foster,' he said.

Matthews started to speak, but he heard the door open and turned around to see Philip enter the room. Philip's eyes were bloodshot and heavy lidded, his skin was pale and he held himself badly. When Matthews had seen him yesterday, he had been unshaven and his clothes had been slightly crumpled. Today his clothes were neat enough, but he looked ill.

'You wanted to see me?' Philip asked. He stood just inside the door which was still ajar, his hand on the knob.

'Come in, Philip,' Foster snapped. 'Dr Matthews is here to see you.'

Philip glanced at his friend. 'I told you that I'd call you and make an appointment,' he said sullenly.

'Sit down, Philip,' Foster commanded. 'What's this Dr Matthews tells me about a "Confession"?'

Philip had not expected this. Matthews could see him grow tense. He looked at him and said, 'I didn't think you'd tell everybody about that, George.' He spoke quietly but each word expressed his anger and disappointment.

'I have only told your father-in-law. I wanted to talk to Dorothy, but my nurse could not reach her yesterday afternoon. I thought that someone close to you should know how ill you are, Philip.' Matthews spoke quietly and kindly.

Philip looked at him coldly. 'You want to put me in a sanatorium, don't you? You think that I am losing my mind. And if I refuse to commit myself, you intend to persuade Steven or Dorothy to commit me.'

Old Foster pounded his fist on his desk. 'Dr Matthews has just been telling me why he did not think you were insane,' he snorted. 'If he wants you to go to a sanatorium, it's because he thinks it will cure your drinking. Not that I think that's all that is wrong with you!'

Philip smiled at his father-in-law's outburst. 'Suppose I told you that I now have evidence that I am not writing that "Confession", George?' He turned and looked at Matthews. 'And suppose I said that if you would give me the rest of the day to prove to you that someone else has been writing it, someone else who wants to drive me out of my senses – what would you say to that?'

Matthews regarded his pipe which had gone out. He did not look at Philip. 'I would still say that you need a good long rest. And a doctor's care.'

Foster sat rigidly, his eyes unswervingly on Philip, who went on speaking, hurriedly, anxiously.

'Well, this morning I came down to the office expecting to find another instalment of this "Confession". Although the last section had been wrong about many things, it had predicted that I would do a terrible thing last night – and I did. I was unnerved this morning. But when I got to my desk I found only a blank piece of paper waiting for me. I could have left it there myself for all I know, although I doubt it. I had told Miss Grey to clean up my desk every night before she left, and she said that she had not noticed this piece of paper.

'Then I looked in the drawer of my desk for the two previous instalments of the "Confession". They were gone. My desk drawer had been forced and its contents stolen. Now, I ask you, if I had been writing the "Confession", and then forgetting I had written it, why should I steal it from myself?' He looked at both Foster and Matthews and waited for them to answer.

Neither man spoke. Philip continued, 'Doesn't it seem likely that whoever was writing that manuscript, for whatever reason, wanted it back? Wasn't he afraid that I might do what I should have done in the first place, go to the police with it? So he came to the office last night or early this morning. He broke into my drawer and stole the manuscript. And by now he has destroyed it.

'But it won't do him any good. I know who he is, and why he has been doing this to me. He is a man who has hated me ever since I married Dorothy. He has resented my success, coveted my wife. He did not have the courage to attack me to my face. But, since he is a thwarted novelist, he conceived of the "Confession" as a subtle way of getting rid of me. He used Brent and me as pawns in a game – his only goal was to get Dorothy to divorce me. He did not care if I landed in an asylum or not. All he wanted was my wife.'

Philip stood up. He swayed on his feet, his eyes blazing. 'I am going to see Jeremy Foulkes, gentlemen,' he said.

'I am going to wring the truth out of him – and neither of you can stop me!'

Both Matthews and Foster were on their feet and approaching Philip. He backed towards the door. And as he did, he picked up a heavy leather chair and brandished it at them. They kept coming on – he kept backing. When he reached the door, he threw the chair. They both fell flat to avoid its crashing bulk. When they stood up, he was gone.

Foster was white with rage. 'I'm going after him!' he cried. 'Why, he'll kill somebody!'

Matthews was cooler. 'First, we have to find out where Jeremy Foulkes lives. I knew him in college, but I've lost track of him since. And then I want to call a friend of mine in the Police Department and ask him to stand by.'

But Foster already had his hat and coat on. 'Forget the police. We can handle this ourselves. And don't worry about finding Jeremy's address. I know where he is.' And he plunged out the door.

Matthews followed him, reluctantly. He was afraid this would develop into a wild-goose chase.

5

Philip was as shocked to see Brent, as Brent was to see Philip. They stood for a moment, each on his side of the threshold, frozen with consternation. Brent was the first to move; her hand crept to her mouth to cover her trembling lips. Then, without willing it, she stepped back a pace . . . and another . . . and another. Philip followed her, waiting for her to cry out, to scream – knowing that he should turn about and go away – but following her anyway. He was compelled to enter the room.

Brent never screamed. Instead, she managed to recover her poise and even smile. 'I wasn't expecting you,' she said.

Philip felt like laughing, but some inner decency prevented it. 'I'm afraid that's an understatement. I didn't expect to find you here, you know. I wouldn't have come if I had.'

Brent sank down on the couch, Philip remained standing. He had not even taken off his hat. 'You came to see Jeremy?' she asked.

Philip nodded his head. 'I wanted to talk to him.'

There was an unusually long silence. He kept waiting for her to speak to him the way she had earlier in the day, to order him out of the loft. She was trying to remember all she had just read in the 'Confession', to piece it together and to make sense out of it. And she was afraid . . .

'You aren't feeling well, are you, Philip?' Brent smiled and her changing eyes were unexpectedly soft and kind. 'You're confused, aren't you?'

Philip did not know what to make of her questions – he had expected an entirely different reaction. He had not as yet seen the manuscript that was lying on the sofa. All he could say was a wondering, 'You aren't angry with me?'

Brent tossed her head. 'I was this morning, Philip. Can you blame me? But I'm not now.'

Philip smiled. He took off his hat and coat and put them over the chair hesitantly. Despite her reassurance, he still expected her to revert to her previous attitude. He certainly did not expect what came next.

'Sit down, Philip. Make yourself comfortable,' she was saying. 'I want to talk to you about this. As a matter of fact, I'm glad you came.' And Brent picked up the 'Confession' and placed it on her lap, thumbing a page. Instantly, Philip's eyes were riveted on the manuscript.

'Where did you get that?' he demanded.

Brent shrugged her shoulders. 'I had been trying to get in touch with Jerry,' she said. 'We had a date last night which he broke. When I 'phoned him here this morning after you left my place, I found he still wasn't home. I decided to come here and wait for him.' She smiled disarmingly. 'I wanted to give him a chance to present his excuses.

'When I got here, I found the door ajar. That's not too unusual. Although I keep telling him that he should be more careful, Jerry's the type that likes to leave everything unlocked. Well, I walked in and made myself at home. I took care of a few things, and then I sat down to read and wait for him, I was reaching for a book when I found this' – she tapped the manuscript with a finger – 'lying on the couch. I started to read it. I had just read the last page of it when you rang the bell.'

She paused and looked at Philip. Her eyes were kind, but inquiring. Philip thought about the contents of the 'Confession'. A deep flush burned its way up his throat to his face.

'I found it very interesting, Philip – extremely interesting.' She hesitated, looked down at the manuscript. 'I don't know quite what to make of it, Philip.'

He tried to speak and could not. He felt completely helpless, as if her words robbed him of everything but his consciousness and this they intensified, focused, so that all of him – his present, past and future – was concentrated in this moment that had stopped, stood still and confronted him.

'Philip, do you really believe all this happened? Is this your version of last night – and the night before?'

'No,' he said, 'that was the way it was to happen. The "Confession" said it would happen that way. But, luckily, it didn't.'

'I don't understand.'

Philip wet his lips. He was breathing more easily now, and his heart had stopped hammering erratically. 'That manuscript,' he began, 'the one you're holding in your lap, came in two parts. I found the first part on my desk Tuesday morning when I came to work. I read it, pondered over it and forgot about it. I thought perhaps that someone was playing a poor joke on me. But when I got home, it began to come true!

'I didn't know that you and Jeremy were coming to dinner at our house that night – I had not met you yet, of course, and I did not know your name. But as soon as I got home Dorothy told me that you were coming, just as the manuscript predicted. And, throughout dinner and afterwards, other little things happened just as they had in the prophecy!

'Some of the events predicted did not occur. But those that did occur were often uncanny. The conversation even turned to Henry Miller, for example. And I did make love to you – although I tried very hard not to!'

'Auto-suggestion,' said Brent, blushing.

'You mean I wrote it myself?' Philip asked. 'I had thought of that. And a psychiatrist I talked to about it said the same thing. But I can't bring myself to accept it.'

'You said the "Confession" was in two parts. What happened the next day?' asked Brent.

'I was coming to that,' said Philip. 'After I left you

that first night, I went down to the office. I intended to sit and wait for whoever was writing the manuscript, if anyone was. I wanted to catch him – or her – red-handed. But when I reached the office, something happened. The next thing I remember it was morning and my secretary was shaking me. I had fallen asleep apparently. My typewriter was open on my desk again, and there was another section of the "Confession" lying beside it. You know what it predicted. You read it.'

Brent nodded her head. Her expression was intense and troubled. Philip looked at her, realizing again how desirable she was to him. 'I tried my best that day – yesterday – to avoid doing what the manuscript predicted. I had lunch with an old friend of mine, a psychiatrist. I went to a movie, usually the safest of activities. I spent the evening drinking. And you know what happened.'

'What did you do this morning after you left me?'

'I went to the office again. This time there was only a blank piece of paper on my desk. I felt relieved . . .'

Brent's hand flew to her mouth. 'A blank piece of paper!' she sighed.

'Why, yes.'

'Oh. Oh, I suppose it's silly of me, but – '

'But what?'

'If this "Confession" were your fate . . . if it really were a record of what is about to happen to you . . . A blank piece of paper might signify . . .'

'My death?' Philip concluded drily.

Brent bit her tongue. 'Something like that,' she admitted.

Philip shuddered. This was one possibility he did not want to consider. He tried to be nonchalant. 'That's a little silly, isn't it?'

'I suppose so.' Brent was not convinced.

'Mere superstition.'

Brent nodded her head. Philip laughed. 'Well, if it is that, there's nothing I can do. I have an appointment with death – and I'll have to keep it.'

They looked at each other, and their looks said: 'We're sensible people living in an era of scientific knowledge. If we acknowledge fate, we call it environment or conditioning or determinism – or by some other rational tag. What we are thinking now is fatalistic nonsense. It can't be true!'

The telephone jangled.

Brent reached for it, picked it up, listened a moment and then covered the mouthpiece with her hand. 'It's Jeremy,' she told Philip. 'He says Dorothy is with him. Do you want me to tell them you're here?'

Philip considered this. If he could get Brent, Jeremy and Dorothy together in the same place, he felt sure he could talk the whole tangled affair out – and discover who had been writing the 'Confession' and why.

'Ask them both to come here,' he said. 'I want to get to the bottom of this.'

Brent spoke into the receiver again. After listening a little longer, she said. 'All right, I'll be seeing you,' and hung up. She smiled at Philip. 'They're coming,' she said.

'To get on with my story,' said Philip, 'soon after I reached the office this morning, Miss Grey came in to tell me that she was quitting. She said I had been acting "queer" lately. Then she left. I thought she had gotten her pay and gone for good. But she came back. She confessed that she had been paid to put the manuscripts on my desk!' And then Philip told Brent all about the messengers and the hundred dollar bills.

'Did you check with the messenger service?' Brent asked. 'I should think they would be able to tell you who ordered the messenger.'

'I did that. And I found out who ordered the messenger. A fellow by the name of Philip Banter.'

Brent was thunderstruck. She stood up and walked over to where Philip was sitting. 'But, don't you see, this proves that you must have written the "Confession"?'

Philip held up his hand. 'That's not all the story,' he said. 'When I looked into the drawer of my desk for the manuscripts this morning, I found the drawer had been forced and the manuscripts were missing. This theft must have occurred between the time I left the office yesterday morning and my arrival there today – nearly a twenty-four hour period.'

'Can you account for every minute of that period, every one of your movements?'

'Perhaps not all. But I think I can account for most of them. I had lunch from noon until one-thirty with Dr George Matthews. I was in a barber shop until two-thirty. I walked from the barber shop to the theatre district from two-thirty to three. From three until six I was seeing a movie through twice. After I left the theatre, I went directly across the street to a bar where I drank and talked to a soldier until far after midnight. When the bar closed I took a taxi to your building where I passed out in your presence.'

'And, after I got you inside,' Brent reminded him, 'I left you alone for an hour or more while I went to your apartment to get you a change of clothes – remember? When I came back, you were not where I left you – but asleep in my bed *which you must have made.*'

'You mean I could have gone to my office, stolen the manuscript from myself and taken it here to Jeremy's place, and then returned to your apartment while you were uptown? It's possible. But wasn't I out cold?'

'You were when I dragged you into the apartment. But drunks can do amazing things and not remember a bit of it afterwards. And you could have sobered up. I rather think you had lost most of your liquor.'

Philip nodded his head. It was possible. But – 'If I stole the manuscript myself, why did I have to force the lock on the drawer of my desk?'

Brent smiled. 'I've thought of that, too. Don't forget, I had your keys!'

Steven Foster and Dr Matthews had to wait several minutes before they managed to hail a taxi outside the office building. Then, while Matthews filled the inside of the cab with a thick cloud of rank smoke, the driver proceeded to get into one traffic jam after another. When he finally drew up at the address Foster had given him, it turned out to be a commercial building and obviously not the loft where Jeremy lived. Another five minutes were wasted in finding a drugstore, a telephone book and Jeremy Foulkes' correct address. By the time they reached their destination, a good forty-five minutes had elapsed and their cab parked at the kerb behind another car from which Dorothy and Jeremy had just alighted.

Matthews spoke to them and explained that Foster and he had followed Philip after he had broken away from them in Foster's office. He also told Jeremy that Philip suspected him of having written the 'Confession'. Dorothy wanted to know what Matthews was talking about and, to add to the confusion, Foster came up and solemnly warned both Jeremy and Dorothy that 'Philip is a danger-ous madman'.

'But he's alone upstairs with Brent!' cried Jeremy. He brushed past Matthews and began to run up the wide steps two and three at a time. Matthews hesitated an instant, and then ran after him. He caught up with him just as he reached the top of the two long flights. 'Don't break in on him like that,' he said. 'Let us all go in together and give him a chance to explain.'

They did not have to open the door themselves. Philip had heard the commotion on the stairs and he opened the door and asked them in. Brent was standing beside him, obviously unharmed, and much of Jeremy's agitation disappeared. But Steven Foster, still panting from the exertion of climbing the stairs, roared at Philip. 'What have you done!'

Philip was calm now. 'Nothing, I assure you,' he replied and, glancing over his father-in-law's shoulder, said to Matthews, 'If you will ask them all to come into the apartment and let me talk to them for a few minutes, I think I can get to the bottom of all this.'

399

They all came in and seated themselves in corners of the great loft room. Philip talked for a few minutes and told them briefly about the 'Confession' and the events of the past two days. He handed the manuscript around so each could see it for himself, and while they looked at it he told them of Brent's theory. He said that he found that he could accept every part of it as a theory except the basic premise that he had been writing the 'Confession' himself. To accept this was to admit that he was mad. And, although yesterday he had almost convinced himself of his own insanity, by now he had sufficiently recovered from his nightmarish experience to fight the idea. 'For one thing,' he said, and he looked directly at Dr Matthews, 'too many people seem to want me to think that I am insane.'

Dorothy's reaction to what he had to say was to sit quietly, to withdraw, and – as the story Philip told grew more involved and terrible in its implications – to come over to where he was standing and to take his hand. Jeremy was amazed. 'Why, Philip, that's damnable! Who would play such a rotten trick on you!' he cried.

'One of us here,' Philip replied, looking at each person in turn, Brent, Foster, Jeremy, Dorothy, and, walking to the mirror, at himself. 'Brent may be right and I am just bedevilling myself. If that is so' – and his voice grew lower – 'you may have to follow Dr Matthews' wishes and have me placed in a sanatorium, Dorothy.'

His wife gripped his hand tightly. 'I'll never do that, Philip,' she said.

'However,' he continued, loosening her grip on his hand, 'I am not convinced that I am even neurotic, let alone insane. I think each one of you had a motive, as well as an opportunity, to write the "Confession", steal it and all the rest.'

He glanced at Steven Foster first. 'My father-in-law and I work at the same office – or I should say worked, he discharged me yesterday. As you know, he was my employer. I think I can say that he never approved of me as a son-in-law. I also have my doubts as to whether he

400

would approve of any man as a son-in-law. From what I have observed of his reliationship with my wife he has always loved her deeply.' Philip paused and searched Foster's eyes. The old man did not flinch under the inspection. 'You had the opportunity, Steven,' Philip went on, 'and we need not fool ourselves that you wouldn't rather be rid of me. You certainly knew as much about me as anyone. I know that Dorothy has long made a practice of coming and talking to you about her troubles with me. Yes, I think you would even have known whom we were having to dinner and whether I had read Henry Miller. But, I think, if you had chosen to get rid of me, you would have taken a gun and shot me. You would never have considered as subtle a weapon as the "Confession".'

Philip turned away from Steven Foster, and Dorothy squeezed his hand. Matthews noticed this by-play. Several times so far he had wanted to interrupt but had not because he felt that Philip, of all people, deserved a chance to clear up the muddle. He saw now that Philip had turned his attention to Brent. And Jeremy had noticed that she was the next to be suspected.

Jeremy's florid face grew grim. 'Look here, Philip, you're going too far. If you keep this up, *I'll* say you're insane!'

Philip remained cool. 'Is that a threat, Jerry?'

'Take it any way you damn please. All I'm saying is that Brent has no motive – and that you owe her an apology.'

Philip bowed to Brent. 'I have already made my apologies to Miss Holliday. But I must say that she has a motive for this crime –'

'Crime?' cried Jeremy. 'What crime? Since when is writing a manuscript a crime?'

'Writing a manuscript is not a crime. But when you sign another person's name to it and present it to that person in such a way that it seems the handiwork of his own mind – with the intention of frightening him out of his wits – I call that a crime. Certainly, some of the statements made in the "Confession" are slander as well!'

Jeremy sniffed and walked over to Brent. Now they faced each other across the big room – Jeremy and Brent, Philip and Dorothy.

'Brent loves you, Jeremy. You have talked to her about me. She knows what our relationship is like and what it has been in the past. I rather imagine you have expressed many of the resentments you have felt against me to her. She is a sensitive, artistic person. She is equipped to write a long narrative. She might have conceived of this fiction with harmless intent as a means of shaming me into behaving better towards you.

'But, when she met me, she took a dislike to me. She sensed a conflict, not only between you and me, but also between Dorothy and myself, and impulsively decided that I should be taught a lesson. Knowing enough of psychology to employ it to a bad end, but not enough to realize that the end was bad – she might have written the second chapter of the "Confession" to frighten me even more. After all, she might have reasoned, I am committing no crime – you reasoned that way yourself just now, didn't you, Jerry? – doing no serious harm.'

'You said that the person who wrote this strange manuscript had to have the opportunity, too, didn't you?' Dorothy asked. 'When could Brent have stolen it from your desk? And how would she have known the essential facts about you?'

'She could have stolen it last night. She had my keys, and I know from experience that she could have gotten past the night watchman. Jeremy could, inadvertently, have supplied her with all the information she needed. There is surprisingly little background material in the "Confession" and the most startling aspects of it, the predictions, Brent could have forced to happen.'

Jeremy exploded. He rushed at Philip and shook his fist under his nose. 'I did no damn such thing and she did no damn such thing!' he cried. 'The whole idea is preposterous!'

Philip backed away from his old friend's wrath. It was

becoming more and more difficult for him to hold his temper, Matthews saw. But at the same time, by the very fact that Philip was remaining calm in crisis, he was proving his own contention that he was not unbalanced. 'I didn't say that Brent had done it,' he said. 'I brought up the possibilities so that I could consider them all and then eliminate her. I don't think she did it, although I can't be sure. I think her motivation is weak in comparison to other suspects, and I believe her story. Beyond that, outside of myself, she is the one person who has suffered unpleasant experiences because of this.' Philip stepped forward and gazed directly at Brent. 'Did you write the "Confession", Brent?' he asked.

Her answer came loud and clear, and with a smile. 'I did not.'

Philip motioned to Jeremy. 'You're the next suspect, Jerry. And until I talked to Brent, my most likely. Now I'm not so sure. You had motivation. You've hated me ever since I took Dorothy away from you, to put it bluntly. As to opportunity – well, where were you during the last twenty-four hours?'

Jeremy reddened. He started to stammer when he tried to speak. 'H-h-hate's a h-hard word, Ph-Phil. I was j-jealous of you, I admit. B-but I never hated you.'

Philip's voice was low. 'Where were you yesterday afternoon, last night and this morning, Jerry?'

'I won't say.'

Philip realized that Brent was no longer standing beside Jeremy, that she had slipped away and now was standing closer to himself. Jeremy had gotten up from his chair and was walking towards Philip, his jaw tense, his body in a crouch. Philip heard his wife sigh. He glanced at her and saw that she was excited.

'I wouldn't try anything if I were –' Jeremy was on him, his fist crashing into the pit of his stomach – before Philip could finish his sentence or Matthews could spring between them. Philip spun, crouched, weaved, lashed out with a left, blocked a wild right that Jerry threw with all his might. Then, as Jeremy charged past, Philip hit him on the back of his neck with the side of his hand. Jeremy sprawled on the floor.

Dorothy and Matthews rushed over to him. Philip could see that he was breathing hard, but was completely unconscious. Matthews was taking his pulse. 'I'm sorry I had to do that,' Philip said.

Dorothy stood looking down at Jeremy. Then, savagely, she turned and faced Philip. Her hand stroked at her dark hair, clawed at its abundance, came away leaving it in wild disarray. Her eyes glistened, her lips writhed in anger. 'I'd like to do some accusing now, Philip. I'm not afraid to look you in the face and say you're mad. I've lived with you, shared the experience of marriage with you, and I know your twisted ego!

'You're vain, Philip, vain and ageing. You're slipping, Philip. And you know it. You've built your life on the satisfaction of your senses, taken as much as you've wanted and paid as little as you could for it. But now the pace has begun to tell. Oh, I know – I can see it in your eyes. They look tired, you know. You see it, too. I've watched you look in mirrors. You did it only a little while ago. You've no need to worry, Philip, not for another year or so at least. Some of it's still left, darling. You have a bit more to spend!'

She paused and threw back her dark, disordered mane. 'But not with me, Philip. I shall divorce you. Poor Jeremy wouldn't tell you where he was yesterday, but I shall. He was with me, Philip. We spent the night together. We went down to your office, Philip, yesterday after lunch to tell you – but you weren't there. Then we went to Jeremy's place while he packed a bag. He was with me, Philip, all last night. Now do you understand? Isn't it plain why your weak mind has to invent stories to tell itself to hide the unpleasant facts of your decline? Face up to it, Philip. You've suffered a defeat – I'll never come again to your beck and call!'

Brent had withered in a moment. Her hand was to her

mouth again, but her eyes – those eyes that could be so brave – were piteous. Dorothy did not see what her words had done to Brent. She was watching Philip, and she was dismayed by his passivity. He was actually smiling.

'If I wrote the "Confession", Dorothy – and, mind you, I'm not saying I didn't – how did I know that Brent and Jeremy were coming to our house for dinner when you didn't tell me until I reached home that evening?'

Dorothy was confused. 'But didn't I tell you before that?' she asked. She turned to Brent. 'When did you and Jeremy decide to come to dinner?'

Brent thought for a moment. 'You asked us earlier in the week. You gave us several days' notice.'

'Dorothy,' said Philip. 'You never told me until that night. And you said Jeremy had called up and told you that he was bringing someone to dinner – that you didn't know her name.'

'Really, Philip, you can hardly hold me responsible for so small a thing. How can I vouch for what I said about a detail two days ago? What difference can it make?'

Philip spoke quietly, but his words carried weight. 'It means this much, Dorothy, that if you wrote the "Confession" you made one small mistake. You neglected to tell me about Jeremy and Brent before I read the manuscript.

'You could have done the rest with ease. Like anyone else in this room you could have ordered the messenger service to deliver the manuscripts to Miss Grey by simply writing a letter and forging my name. You just admitted that you visited my office yesterday afternoon. You knew Miss Grey, and she would have let you in to my desk. You forced the lock on my drawer and stole the manuscripts. Then you and Jeremy came back here to his apartment. While he packed, you dropped the manuscript on the couch. I think you wanted someone to discover it so you could use it against me. It was written in the first person singular, wasn't it? To the uninformed reader such a "Confession" would look damning. You planned to hold it over me – perhaps, you wanted to try to win me back by such a threat.

'Behind all this was your own inadequacy – mostly imagined – which forces you to blame me for your coldness, your faults as a wife. Whenever I looked at another woman, instead of trying to attract me, you shrank from the conflict and commiserated with yourself. Your self-inflicted martyrdom grew until it became necessary for you to strike out at me – to have an affair with Jeremy – now to divorce me!'

Dorothy stared at him, and then she laughed. 'Can't you see that what you have just said is only your own neurosis turned inside out? The reflected image of your own narcissism which can never admit its own blemishes but must blame them on the mirror – in this case me? Philip, you wrote that "Confession". You must face that fact if you are not to lose everything!'

At this point, Jeremy groaned and sat up. Dorothy did not notice. Dr Matthews and Brent helped him to his feet and into the kitchen where they began to apply cold cloths to his head. Philip walked to the front of the great room and stood looking down out of the deep windows. He noticed that the frames reached to the floor and that there were no sills. It would be easy to open the latch and just step out . . . he put his hand on the latch . . . and then he withdrew it as he became aware that Steven Foster was watching him.

Philip turned around. Dorothy had lighted a cigarette and was watching him, too. Philip felt trapped, hemmed in by animosities. 'I'll admit there's truth in what you say. And I suppose that I'll never know which one of us was right.' He walked to the chair where he had laid his hat and coat, put them on and walked out the door. Then, as they stood looking at the door, he reappeared in it.

'I'll say this much, Dorothy. If I have hurt you, I'm sorry.'

He closed the door behind him. Dorothy stood staring

at it, unable to move, yet feeling cheated. Dr Matthews came into the room.

'Where is Philip?' he asked.

Dorothy stood clenching and unclenching her hands, her mouth working but no words coming out. Her face was blenched and her eyes were stark, whether from grief or frustration Matthews could not tell.

She put her hand up to her face, cried out inarticulately and ran out of the room and down the stairs. 'She's gone after Philip!' Foster shouted. He grabbed his coat and strode across the room to the door. 'And I've got to stop her!' Matthews heard the door slam, and then heard him pounding down the stairs.

Matthews had gone to the telephone and was calling Lieutenant Anderson. This was a matter for the police.

When he had finished his call, he, too, ran out of the house and up the street.

As he went down the steps of the subway station, Philip had the feeling he was being followed. 'You can't begin that again, old man,' he told himself, 'or the first thing you know you'll be hearing things.' But even as he got change and put his nickel in the turnstile, he could feel the hairs on the back of his neck bristle with the knowledge that someone was behind. Someone was coming down the stairs, pushing his way through the turnstile . . . after him?

He stepped onto the platform. A local was rounding the slight curve and came roaring into the station. 'People are always behind you in the subway,' he reassured himself. But as the noise increased, became a din, he heard a voice. 'Philip, you're cra-zee!' The voice seemed to sound in his ear – he though he could feel the moist, warm breath against the sensitive membrane. 'Oh, Philip!' the voice said.

Although he knew he should not do it, Philip swerved quickly around – threw up his hands to protect himself – screamed.

But his scream blended in with the roar of the train.

Epilogue

By the time Dr Matthews reached the subway station, a large crowd had gathered about the entrances, the police emergency squad had arrived and two scout cars were parked across the street. Next to the scout cars Matthews recognized the car of his friend, Lieutenant Anderson, and surmised that the Lieutenant, on the way to the address Matthews had given him on the telephone, had stopped to see what was wrong at the subway station.

The policeman guarding the entrance Matthews entered was one of Anderson's men – he recognized Dr Matthews and let him by, touching his fingers to his visored cap as he did. Inside the station a large crowd had gathered on the edge of the platform where members of the disaster squad were working at uncoupling the cars. Matthews had guessed what had happened when he had seen the curious mob in the street, now he was even more sure. But he looked around for Anderson. He found him at the far end of the platform talking to a pale, shaken Steven Foster. Dorothy was seated beside them on a bench, her face in her hands, sobbing hysterically.

Anderson was a middle-aged man with thin grey hair. His manner was dour, his habit of speaking terse. As he saw Matthews approach, he asked, 'Did you know this was going to happen, George?' He had worked with Matthews many times in the past and they knew and respected each other.

'I can tell you better when you tell me what happened,' Matthews answered.

'But didn't you say that I was to come to a particular address to prevent an accident? Before I got there, I saw this commotion and investigated. From what he says' – and he jerked his hand at Steven Foster – 'the fellow under the train is a friend of yours, Philip Banter.'

Matthews swallowed hard. 'He jumped in front of the train?' he asked.

Anderson shrugged his shoulders. 'That depends upon which one of the three witnesses is talking to you. According to Foster there, who I understand is Banter's father-in-law –' He turned to Steven and said, 'Will you please repeat your account of what happened, Mr Foster?'

Steven Foster nodded his head and passed his handkerchief over his mouth. His cold eyes twitched and his forehead was beaded with sweat. 'My son-in-law has been mentally ill for some time. This morning, in my office, Dr Matthews and I tried to persuade him to enter a sanatorium. He ran away from us then and we followed him to Mr Foulkes' apartment which is down the street a way.

'He ran away from us a second time, after Mr Foulkes, my daughter and another friend, Brent Holliday, had taken turns talking to him. This time my daughter followed him, and then I ran out after her. They both had a good start on me, so I took a taxi I found in front of Mr Foulkes' apartment and told the driver to catch up with them. Before he could, they had both entered the subway station.

'I paid the driver and entered the station myself. Just as I reached the foot of the stairs, where I could get a clear view of the platform –' He paused and mopped at his brow. Matthews saw that his hand was shaking. 'A train was coming into the station. Philip must have been standing on the very edge of the platform, his back to me. But as I watched, he turned. Dorothy was standing behind him. She must have spoken to him. Anyway, he turned quickly around – lost his balance – fell in front of the train. He screamed as he fell. I ran forward, but there was nothing – absolutely nothing – I could do.'

Anderson broke in. 'Thank you, Mr Foster,' he said.

'I won't make you tell about it again for a while. Why don't you sit down beside your daughter?'

'What is Dorothy's version of what happened?' Matthews asked Anderson.

Anderson looked at him, his eyes quizzical. Matthews knew that the Lieutenant was trying to think out a problem. He wondered how much Anderson knew. But all Anderson said was, 'Mrs Banter corroborates her father's story in every detail, except that she says she did not speak to Philip. Is that right, Mrs Banter?'

Dorothy raised her eyes. Her face was puffed and tear-streaked, and her shoulders drooped. 'I had just reached the platform when Philip turned around. I did not have time to speak to him. I don't think he saw me. He just let himself fall backwards . . .' And she began to sob again.

Anderson walked away from both Dorothy and her father. Matthews walked with him. 'There is one other witness,' Anderson said. 'A blind man who must have been standing near Philip. There were other people on the platform at the time, and plenty more who came downstairs before I put men at the entrances to keep them out – but nobody else saw or heard anything. It's just our luck this man is blind!'

He pointed to a slim negro man who stood talking to another policeman. The man was neatly dressed and his hand held the harness of a sleek, well-fed German Shepherd dog. When Anderson asked him to repeat his story, he said, 'I started to listen when I heard Bozo here growl. Bozo never growls unless there's a reason. Bozo is a good friendly dog. But then I heard a scuffling, and someone panting for breath. All the time the train was coming in and making an awful racket. Bozo backed up and I backed up with him – away from the edge of the platform that is. I knew there was danger or Bozo wouldn't have done that. He's used to trains. Then I heard the voice. It was the nastiest voice I ever did hear. It said, "Philip, you're cra-zee!" – and then it said, "Oh, Philip!" The next thing I heard, a man screamed a terrible sound. And I said to myself, somebody's gone and pushed that poor guy under the train.'

Anderson shrugged his shoulders again. 'Could you tell whether this voice you heard was a man's or a woman's?' Matthews asked.

The fellow thought for a moment. 'That I couldn't do,' he said, smiling blankly. 'All I can tell you is that it was the nastiest – the meanest, cruellest – voice I ever did hear. I hated that voice.'

Anderson thanked the man and told him to give his address to the patrolman and he could go. Then he looked at Matthews.

'This is my mistake, Andy,' Matthews said. 'I had a chance to prevent it, and if I had put things together right I would have prevented it, too. But I put things together wrong – and Philip Banter was murdered.'

Anderson pushed his hat back on his head. 'Murdered, you say? How do you know the blind man's right? He is only telling us what he heard, you know – he couldn't see. I admit there are disparities between his story and that of Dorothy and her father. But if the guy was murdered, who murdered him?'

Matthews smiled tightly. 'If you will get these people together in your office this afternoon, I'll name the murderer.' He gave Anderson a slip of paper on which he had written the names of Jeremy, Brent, Dorothy and Miss Grey. 'Miss Grey works at Brown and Foster. If she isn't there the switchboard girl will tell you how to reach her,' Matthews added.

He took Anderson's arm. 'Why don't you let one of your men round up these people? You and I can have lunch together and I'll bring you up to date on what has happened before this.' Matthews was smiling, but he did not feel the happiness he simulated. He knew that if he had acted more quickly, Philip would not have died. Now all he could do was to make certain that his murderer was brought to justice.

Even psychiatrists sometimes make mistakes.

Anderson's office was sparsely furnished. It usually contained a desk, three chairs and a framed map of the five boroughs of New York City; however, for this occasion several extra stiff-backed chairs had been added. When Matthews and Anderson came into the room, the others were already there. Brent and Jeremy sat together, holding hands. Jeremy's neck was bruised from where Philip had struck him and he kept rubbing this sore spot. Miss Grey sat by herself near the door. She carried a large black purse and her fingers played restlessly with its catch – her nose and eyes were red as if she had been crying. Dorothy and Steven sat near Anderson's desk, but not together. Dorothy had changed into black and by some effort of will she had recovered her poise. Her glossy head was carried high and her gloved hands rested calmly in her lap. Steven Foster was the same as he had been when Matthews first met him: he sat rigidly erect on the edge of his chair, his eyes staring forward, his cane upright between his knees.

Anderson seated himself behind his desk, but George Matthews remained standing. He knew that all of them were looking at him, waiting to hear what he would say. Taking advantage of this interest he turned slowly around and regarded each one of them before he spoke.

'Most of you, I believe, know why you are here. Philip Banter died this morning. He was crushed to death beneath the wheels of a subway train at the 50th Street station of the 8th Avenue Independent Subway. All but one of you were present at the scene in Jeremy's apartment a few minutes before Philip's death, and you know that Philip tried at that time to discover who was writing a "Confession" – a series of threatening, prophetic manuscripts – that had been appearing on his desk.

'I thought, and I know that some of you agreed with me, that Philip was writing these manuscripts himself. I knew him to be neurotic, and alcoholic, and from his wife's testimony as well as his own I knew that he had been experiencing certain schizophrenic symptoms.

Schizophrenics often bedevil themselves by writing diaries or journals with one half of their personality which they do not recognize as their own handiwork during saner intervals. And Philip was a recognizable schizoid type. I went so far as to recommend that he commit himself to an asylum – although only as a cure for his alcoholism.'

Matthews paused and looked around the room again. Lieutenant Anderson had lighted his cigar. Brent was watching him intently. 'Philip uncovered proof this morning that he was not writing the "Confession". Miss Grey admitted that she had received payment on two occasions from a messenger for placing the manuscript on his desk. At the same time that she told him this, however, she resigned her job, saying that she could not stand to work for him any longer. And when Philip called the messenger service, he discovered that so far as that company knew he himself had arranged to have the messenger pay Miss Grey to put the manuscript on his desk.

'I say that Miss Grey's admission that she attended to the delivery of the "Confession", was positive proof that Philip was not writing it. I think it was. For if Philip had been writing the "Confession", why would it have been necessary to go through the complicated business of hiring a messenger service to pay Miss Grey? He would have been writing it at the office, and he would have left it on his desk. But, what had been happening was that someone had been preparing the manuscript and having it placed on his desk so that it looked like he had left it there. And it was the mechanism for simulating this – the business of hiring the messenger service in Philip's name to pay Miss Grey one hundred dollars for placing the manuscript on Banter's desk – that Philip discovered.'

'Yet when he told me about it,' Brent interrupted, 'he made it sound like further evidence that he was writing it himself.'

'And so it was to him, although he denied it in part. It was a shock to him to have the messenger service tell him that he had ordered the deliveries – and he never had the time to reason it through. Shortly afterwards Steven Foster summoned him into his office to talk to me and the whole affair worsened.

'Philip was ambivalent about the "Confession". He knew himself well enough to know that he was a rake, an alcoholic. He knew that he was losing his job at Brown and Foster and that his marriage was breaking up. He knew that he had spells during which he heard voices. But he did not think he was sufficiently insane to write a long narrative that predicted his own future actions, and then forget about it.'

Matthews paused and lighted his pipe. This operation took several minutes of tamping and fussing with the shining meerschaum; during this time he studied his audience. Everyone was listening intently. Miss Grey was the most visibly nervous, Brent and Dorothy were equally calm, old Steven Foster showed his usual hostility.

'It never occurred to Philip that the "Confession" might be a prelude to his murder. Nor, do I think, did it occur to the murderer until a few minutes before his crime. No, Philip thought of the "Confession" as a subtle means of frightening him, perhaps, an attempt to drive him out of his mind. First he suspected Jeremy Foulkes of this. You heard what he had to say in Jeremy's apartment. Jeremy's motive, he thought, was jealousy. Philip had married the girl he loved. Jeremy was throwing Brent at Philip to make Dorothy divorce him, and if in the process Philip had a breakdown – well, that would have complicated matters a little, but the end result might have been the same.

'As you know, Philip rejected this theory. He realized that Jeremy loved Brent, that while he was infatuated with Dorothy he would not go to the extreme of writing the "Confession" to win her away from Philip. Besides, in these times among people in this income category, divorces can be arranged easier than that.

'So Philip turned to Dorothy,' and as he said this Dr Matthews regarded her, too. 'Much of what Philip had to say this afternoon was painful for you to hear, Dorothy. But you know that much of it is true. You *might* have written the "Confession" out of your own feelings of inadequacy, as a neurotic device that you hoped one day would drive Philip from you, and the next day you hoped would bring him back to you. Philip believed you were doing it. And, I think, you were a little afraid – like Philip – that you might be doing it, too, and then forgetting about it.

'You need not have feared that. Philip said that the person who was bedevilling him both hated him and wanted him out of the way, and had the continuing opportunity to place all three instalments of the "Confession" on his desk.' Matthews looked around the room. 'Yes,' he said, 'I said *three*. Each of you could have written the first two instalments, each of you could have hired the messenger service to do its tricks – but only one of you could possibly have placed that blank piece of paper on Philip's desk!' Matthews' eyes swept the room.

'Miss Grey,' he barked, and the girl, startled, jumped to her feet. 'Did you clean and tidy Mr Banter's desk last night before you left?'

The girl stammered, 'Y-yes, s-sir.'

'Did you see a blank piece of paper on his desk then?'

'No, sir.'

'Did you clean his desk this morning before he arrived?'

'Y-yes, sir.'

'Was there a blank piece of paper on it then?'

'N-no sir.'

'Did you sit in your office until Mr Banter arrived?'

'Yes, I did. I wanted to see him early. I wanted to tell him I was quitting.'

'Did you see anyone go into his office from the time you cleaned his desk until he arrived?'

'N-no, sir.'

'No one at all?' Matthews raised his voice an octave on that last syllable.

The girl thought for a moment. 'Only Mr Foster,' she

said. 'He had been paying me extra to tell him all the queer things Mr Banter did. He came in and asked me if I had seen Mr Banter this morning. I told him no. He said I must have seen him since he had come in a good five minutes ago. He said he would just look inside and see . . . he was only inside a minute.'

Steven Foster jumped to his feet and threw his cane at Dr Matthews – all in one movement. Before Anderson could stop him, he had reached the door and jerked it open. But a uniformed policeman stood outside. Foster halted abruptly, gazed at the man for an instant and then slowly turned to face Matthews. His face was a study in disdain. 'I did it,' he said deliberately. 'I killed Philip Banter. He was a rotter and a waster and he did not deserve my daughter!' His face had grown taut and ashen, his eyes protruded.

'Philip came very close, didn't he, Steven?' Matthews asked. 'He said you had the opportunity, and he was right. You were the only one who could have written both sections of the "Confession" and placed the blank piece of paper on his desk. He gave your motive when he said that you had never liked the idea of having a son-in-law and that you had always loved your daughter *deeply*. And who but Philip knew that Dorothy talked to you so frequently and freely? You knew that Brent and Jeremy were coming to visit Philip and Dorothy before Philip did. In fact, you took it for granted that Philip knew, and in so doing made one of your few mistakes.'

Steven Foster, although he stood very straight, seemed to be experiencing difficulty in speaking. 'I saw that he did not honour my daughter. I set about to ruin him. I could only attack him through his vanity, his self-love. Dorothy had told me of Jeremy and Brent, of how Jeremy felt towards Philip. I saw in their visit an opportunity to suggest Brent to Philip. I started to write the "Confession" . . .'

'And, after Philip had read the two instalments, you stole the manuscript from his desk and left it in Jeremy's apartment. Since Jeremy habitually left his door unlocked, you had no trouble getting in. You wanted him to read it, to grow jealous of Philip – to take its slander for truth – you wanted Jeremy to kill Philip. You even misdirected our taxi this morning to delay us and give Philip time to reach Jeremy's apartment in the hope that Jeremy would attack him.

'But several things went wrong. You had not thought it possible that Jeremy was still attracted to Dorothy – that Dorothy would go away with him. So Brent read the "Confession", not Jeremy. And without Dorothy to inform you, you did not know whether Philip had conformed to the "Confession's" predictions last night or not. All you dared place on his desk this morning was a blank piece of paper.'

Matthews was silent, looking at the old man who now swayed as he stood before Anderson's desk. 'Your scheme was ingenious. In many ways it corresponds to the witchcraft of primitive man. Did you get the idea out of Seabrook? I saw his book on your shelf. You should not have relied on a secondary source. Yet it almost worked.

'But Philip, though frightened, was not demoralized. He would not agree to enter the asylum – and leave Dorothy to you! – even with my pressure. He ran away to Jeremy's and questioned each of you in turn – if you could have known the conflict in his mind then, you would realize what an heroic act that was. Dorothy saw, and Dorothy respected him for it. When he left the apartment, she went after him . . .'

'They were coming together again,' sighed Steven Foster. 'I had failed and . . . instead of driving them apart . . . I had driven them together. I hailed a taxi and reached the station before Dorothy did – she lied to the Lieutenant to protect me. I went down the stairs just behind Philip. There was no one on the platform except Philip and a blind man.'

Matthews took it up. 'Philip's back was turned to you. You came close to him and said, "Philip, you're cra-zee!

417

Oh, Philip!" He must have thought he was hearing the voice again. He turned about, saw you –'

'And I pushed him into the path of the train,' said Steven Foster. His face had grown very pale and his nose had begun to bleed. Matthews stared, fascinated, at his face for an instant; then he sprang to help him. He had recognized the signs of cerebral accident.

Old Foster held up his hand and shook his head. His knees sagged – his mouth gasped. Rigid, even in death, he fell forward on his face.

Dr Matthews knelt beside the body and noted the absence of a pulse. Dorothy, behind him, began to weep. But there was nothing he could do about that . . .

Devil Take The Blue-Tail Fly

To
John C. Madden
WITH RESPECT AND
ADMIRATION

When I was young I used to wait,
On massa and give him his plate,
And pass the bottle when he got dry
And brush away the blue-tail fly.

Chorus:

Jimmy crack corn and I don't care,
Jimmy crack corn and I don't care,
Jimmy crack corn and I don't care.
My massa's gone away.

And when he'd ride in the afternoon,
I'd follow after with a hickory broom,
The pony being rather shy,
When bitten by a blue-tail fly.

Chorus

One day he ride round the farm,
The flies so numerous they did swarm,
One chanced to bite him on the thigh –
The devil take the blue-tail fly!

Chorus

The pony run, he jump, he pitch
He threw my massa in the ditch;
He died and the jury wondered why –
The verdict was the blue-tail fly!

Chorus

They lay him under a 'simmon tree
His epitaph is there to see –
'Beneath this stone I'm forced to lie –
Victim of the blue-tail fly!'

Chorus

AN AUTHENTIC NEGRO MINSTREL SONG OF *circa* 1840

I

Today is the day, was her first waking thought—and she repeated it, charmed by the echoing syllables, the rise and fall of the cadence, saying the words aloud this time, playfully accenting one of them: 'Today is *the* day.' Ellen breathed deeply and stretched her arms upward towards the pale-green ceiling until her joints cracked and her tendons strained. The clear morning light washed the immaculate box of a room, splashed it with sun as a dasher splashes cream in a churn. Ellen laughed at the image, pleased with the ingenuity of her mind. Why, she hadn't ever really forgotten anything, had she? Only once in her life had she seen a churn, only once – during that month, the first month of their marriage, when Basil and she had stayed at that farm in Vermont – had she seen the thick yellow cream, the queer whitish butter that had tasted so marvellously rich, the frothy paddle. Oh, she was well again, there was no doubt about it, or she would not have thought of that. And it was so apt – the sun on the bland green walls did look like cream turning to butter, and she did feel happy. In fact, she felt as happy now as she had felt that month, that incredibly idyllic month, when Basil and she had first been married. Her mood and the sun and the butter, they were all the same; it was all of a piece. Ellen let her hands fall abruptly and, with a tremendously contented sigh, let her lungs empty out the huge breath she had been holding in, guarding jealously, as if in this way she could clasp the perfection of the moment to her. And, bounding and bouncing despite the stiffness of the springs and mattress, she threw back the covers and jumped out of bed. 'Today I am going home!'

Basil was coming for her. She would take his arm, a little gravely, a little self-consciously, and walk down the corridor with him. She would stand beside him while Martha – or would it be Mary? – unlocked the door, only this time she would not clutch his arm any tighter, her fingers would not tense against the rough tweed of his sleeve. For this time she would not have to stop at the door, she would not have to stand there, helpless, while Basil kissed her cheek, her brow, and then, with a caution he had not once known, her mouth. She would not have to smile and say something casual, something meaningless but cheery, to Martha – sometimes it had been Mary – while he walked rapidly past the door, down the hall, clattered on the iron, the fireproof, stairs. She would not have to turn around and walk back up the corridor to her room, just like the others, even with the monks' cloth hangings, the bound scores of Bach and Handel, Rameau and Couperin, Haydn and Mozart, in the bookcase that she had requested and Basil had brought her from town. Not today! No, never again would she sit by the window, her back turned so she would not see him walk down the flagstone path with Dr Danzer, the limp volume of her favourite Bach spread open to the first page of the text, the black notes swarming before her eyes, her fingers arching in elaborate dumb-show as they practised the first trill, her mind on the beats, the leaning upon the upper note, the precise apperception of the stopping point – not a moment too soon, not a moment too late – and in her ears once more the sound, the slow dignity, of Anna Magdalena's sarabande, a delicate ornament for her melancholy.

'I am going home today!' She said it again, laughing under her breath, brushing her brisk blonde hair until it was vibrant and sparkled when touched. She dressed quickly, surely, not hesitating over what she was to wear, but choosing irrevocably the forest-green suit, the brown oxfords with sensible heels, the hat with the feather which she did not particularly like but which Basil had selected himself and brought to her so proudly. There had been no choice, of course, or rather she had done the choosing months ago, when she had first dared to look forward to this day. All except the hat, that is; she had decided on another hat – a mannish affair that suited her and the occasion better. But then Basil had brought this hat and she could not but wear it, since she would not hurt him for all the world. No, from now on Basil's happiness came first, was her *sine qua non*, for he deserved it. Where would she be without Basil? Who had looked after her, talked and reasoned with her when she was sickest, stood by without faltering? Basil. Who had come to see her every visiting day, even when he knew there was no use, that they would not let him see her, coming from the city by train to the town, from the town by crowded bus to the hospital? Basil. And then, the last time he had come – after they had told him – he had brought her the hat. A silly hat, a frippery thing with a nonsensical feather, the kind women buy when they're in love and men buy when they go into a store and are embarrassed and say, finally, stammering, 'I want a hat.' And both times the betrayal is accompanied by the same sales-girl words, 'Madame will find it so chic!' – the same slurred speech, the same shamed groping for purse or billfold, the same flush when one thinks of the incident later and knows, whether one admits it or not, that one's been had. But, after all, what did it matter? What if the day did seem to require a more serious head-dress, a more sober hat? Hadn't Basil bought this silly thing, and wasn't that one fact worth more than any female prejudice? Oh, there was no question about that hat – she would wear it and love wearing it, for she loved Basil, and today she was going home with him. That was all that mattered, that was the wonderful fact.

After she had finished dressing, after she had made the stiff, high hospital bed for the last time, she looked at her watch, and saw that it was yet only a few minutes past six. Breakfast would not be until seven, the doctor would not see her before eight; even if Basil had taken the afternoon train yesterday, as he had promised he would, and stayed overnight at the town's one hotel, he could hardly be at the hospital before nine. She had three hours or more to pack her clothes, her books and scores, to say good-bye to Mary and Martha, to thank Dr Danzer for all he had done for her – three more hours, at least, of leave-taking. It would be a long time, now it seemed that it would never be over; but, then, would it be long enough? What are three hours in two years, especially when those hours are heavy with the burden of those years, when all the past time endured weighs on the present interval, makes each moment massive with meaning? From six to nine she would be aware of each instant in its passing, as it seemed to her she had known intimately every hour of the night and day of the two years that were ending. But – and she looked at the window, saw through it the green lawn and the curving flagstone walk, the elms that lined the high stone wall, the wrought-iron gate and the brick cube that was the gatekeeper's lodge – nine o'clock would come; although the intervening time would pass slowly, Basil would come, and she would take his arm, smile up at him, and then, finally and irrefutably, the years and the hours would be over.

She went to the bookcase and ran her hands over the narrow-backed, gilt-stamped volumes of her scores, her fingers arching and pointing, forming arpeggios, appogiaturas and glissandos, feeling the firmness of the buckram, the softness of the vellum, aching for the last time for the hard, polished veracity of keys, imagining the bright, satisfying, metallic sound of a plucked string, hearing in her mind's ear the heart of the note, the vibration of a chord, the tinkling precision of a sweeping run, a trill. A few hilly miles on a lurching bus, Basil beside her holding her hand, the rush of a train drawn as by a magnet to the city, the frustration of a taxi's stops and starts, Basil close to her, enclosed in the small space with her, his ears annoyed like hers by the metronomic tick of the meter, and she would be going up the stone steps of their house, exchanging bows with Suky, the butler – his a lithe swoop, hers a dipping of her head, a shrugging of her shoulders – then she would be past Suky, running up the stairs to her study, pausing at the door to seek the rose walls, the soft overhead lighting, the long couch where she could stretch out when her back was tired, the bow window, but pausing only an instant before stepping confidently forward to her instrument, sitting on the bench and running her hands softly over the old wood of the lid, then lifting it back on itself to reveal the manuals, the rows of keys, bringing her hand down abruptly; but, as she felt the ivory surfaces give, drawing back, holding back, slightly, hearing the chord and its overtones as her foot pressed the pedal, the sharp cleanness of sound's heart surrounded by a cloud of overlapping tones, the essence of music that only with a harpsichord can one distil. That would be noon – noon at the latest; but it might be before, when she could play again. Her fingers would not obey her; she was reconciled to this – although she had tried to keep them supple throughout the years of her alienation by exercise and silent practice. She would know the scores – she knew them backwards and forwards, she had scanned them so many times – but she was sure that at first her fingers would stumble, her coordination would be poor, her attitude tense, her rhythm inconsistent. But she would be at the keyboard again, she could strike the plangent notes whenever she desired, pick out a melody, devise an ornamentation, and with the days that lay in the future would come long mornings and afternoons at her instrument, her fingers working at the keys bit by bit reassembling the knacks, learning again to translate the ideal sound she heard in her head into actual music. It would come, it would come – it would all be hers again. And, thinking this, she began to pick the volumes from the shelves, one and two at a time, and carried them to the suitcase that lay open on the bed, fitting them carefully inside, walking back and forth, quickly, quietly, happily.

When she had packed all her books and scores and had closed the large suitcase, had tugged its heavy bulk off the bed and set it on the floor, she placed the two smaller travelling-cases on the room's two chairs and went to the closet to gather her few clothes. Two old dressing-gowns, a few dresses, several more pairs of oxfords and one pair of pumps that she had worn but once, on a day soon after she had first come to the hospital; had slipped and fallen in them, had had them taken away from her – they had not been returned for many months – along with her manicure scissors, her watch, her fountain-pen, her nail-file: all the little objects she had become used to, depended on, but which they had taken from her, saying, 'You won't need these now, will you?' and, of course, she had needed them – more than that, she had wanted them; but she had known that to protest would have been useless, that they had their routine, their methods, and that even Basil said that they knew best. Besides these shoes and dresses, the closet held her coat which she had used this winter for the first time to take long walks with Martha and Mary, her other hats, and that was all. She made three or four armfuls of them and dumped them into the two cases, straightening them with hurried pokes and deft pattings, taking much less care with them than she had with the volumes of scores, knowing that she would not wear them again, except, perhaps, around the house – the styles would be so different; she would need so many new things.

She emptied the drawer of the shiny, white metal cabinet where she had kept her stockings, her underclothing and other oddments, and put them all together in one bag, without looking at them, closed and latched it swiftly and decisively. Standing in the centre of the room, she looked around to see what she had forgotten, what remained that belonged to her and she wanted to keep – not that there had ever been much. The radio she had given to Mary months ago, since the only stations she had been able to get on it had played insufferable programmes, dramatic serials, jazz, commercials, the news; although once it had served her well – during the days when she had first begun to grow better, when she had been allowed to see Basil again and he had bought her the little set with its gaudy dial and varnished cabinet: days when it had been reassuring just to hear a voice in the room, a voice that belonged to a stranger, with a stranger's false warmth and affability, a voice that was without a doubt human, yet belonged to someone who did not know her, was not concerned with her, could not possibly have any designs on her. The pictures that she had asked Martha to clip from magazines and which she had taped to the wall, a line-drawing by Picasso, a four-colour version of one of Renoir's auburn-haired girls, a severe Mondrian diagram and one of Leonardo's drawings for a flying-machine, she had pulled off and torn up and thrown away the night before, knowing that no patient or nurse would want them – that they had had their purpose of reminding her of the order that still existed in the world and which she must emulate, but that now their function was no longer needed, she would soon be back in her own house, surrounded by the paintings Basil and she had bought together, and that these substitutes were better destroyed. There was nothing left but the monks'-cloth drapes at the windows, and she hesitated to pull them down; they would leave the room naked, make obvious its sterility, emphasize its restrictions. Although she knew she should not, that what came after was no concern of hers, she could not help thinking of its next occupant, could not help projecting upon this person the despair, the aloneness, the fear she had herself felt when she had come into this room for the first time, saw its green walls, its high bed, its lattice-guarded windows, knew that it was a locked box, a cell, a grave for the living. She remembered the nights she had lain awake, fighting off the sedative they had given her, watching the moonlight, shattered into glowing fragments by the criss-cross of the lattice, creep along the floor, the walls, the bed, menacing her. And she recalled the sharp shards of splintered sun that stabbed

431

like daggers at her eyes on brilliant days. And she walked to the other chair, bent over the second travelling-case and slammed it shut, clicked its latches and turned the key in the lock, deciding that she would leave the drapes at the windows where they belonged.

Mary brought her breakfast a few minutes later, a familiar breakfast that she had eaten many times before: orange-juice, cold but tasting of the can from which it had been poured; oatmeal, thick and warm and gelatinous; two slices of whole wheat bread and a pat of bright yellow butter; coffee with a little bottle of cream and one packaged lump of sugar which she never used but which she still found on the saucer every time. Mary's face was as scrubbed and shining as ever – Ellen had a fancy that after she washed it she must rub it with a cloth until it shone like ten-cent store silverware–her iron-grey hair, neat as coils of wire, bulged at her cap, obtruding here and there, as it always had before. But this morning Ellen felt that the smile on the attendant's face was less automatic than usual, that the quick gestures of her hands showed a certain nervousness that might be attributed to enthusiasm, that Mary, like herself, was glad that Basil was coming, that she was going home.

'Dr Danzer will be a little late this morning, Mrs Purcell,' Mary said, and then, without pausing, 'where shall I put the tray – here, on the table?'

Ellen came across the room, nodding her head, plucking the glass of orange-juice from the tray before the attendant could set it down, gulping the cold stuff to escape the tang she did not like.

'I'm going home today, Mary,' she said, knowing it was superfluous, but wanting to say the words aloud again just to hear their wonderful sound, as she might hum a tune of Mozart over and over to herself because to hear it made her happy.

The nurse nodded briskly, but the lines about her eyes crinkled, and Ellen could see that she was relaxed, that for once, at least, Mary stood before her, if not as a friend, as a neutral person. 'We are going to miss you, Mrs Purcell,' she said, and as she said this she really smiled. 'You are our favourite patient, you know.'

Ellen tried the oatmeal with her spoon, looked down at the tray to keep the attendant from seeing how pleased she was to hear her say that. 'Am I?' she said, not that she doubted it, but, childishly, to coax more praise. 'I did not know.'

'That's what Dr Danzer says.'

Ellen let the spoon drop on the plate with a clatter and turned around to see who had spoken. It was Martha, who stood in the doorway – she was smiling, too; but, then, Martha always smiled.

The two attendants were very different types: Martha, tall, young and blonde, with a lovely face which she made-up carefully and the kind of long-limbed grace to her movements that is more common to a model or an actress than an attendant; Mary, short and heavy-set, but firmly-fleshed, older than Martha but not yet old, quick and machine-like in her habits, grave and ever-watchful. Still, in them, it was not their differences that were remarkable, but their similarities. They seemed always to be present, always alert, always wary – even when Ellen had not seen them, she had known that they were lurking some-where. They were always looking at you when they were with you, their eyes were upon you no matter what they were doing, they kept you under surveillance. Ellen had at one time resented their vigilance and had complained bitterly to herself about it. She had felt isolated by it as a prisoner under armed guard must feel isolated from the rest of humanity. Even this morning, when she knew that there was no reason for them to regard her in any way other than a friendly one, she looked for indications of their wariness, was relieved to find it absent, but kept seeking it again, as if expecting it to return.

Martha had come into the room and had walked over to the table. If she would only turn her back to me! Ellen thought, then I would be sure that she means what she

433

says. She looked down at her plate again and picked up her spoon, this time actually scooping some of the oatmeal into her mouth, swallowing the warm, gluey mess. Martha was still talking, her voice casual and pleasant, confiding, 'Yes, Dr Danzer was telling us just the other day that you are his *triumph*. That he had never had a patient who responded to treatment as well as you – who effected such a complete *adjustment*.' The second attendant had an emphatic manner of speaking that Ellen had often found annoying. She accented words not because of their position in the phrase, the clause, the sentence, as Ellen liked to do herself, but to underscore their meaning. Martha talked to one as she might to a child. Even when she did not repeat what she said, the effect of her words was that of repetition, of deliberation, of instruction. And beneath this emphasis Ellen detected the ring of authority, the hint of command.

She looked up from her food at both of them, tall and short, standing beside her. 'It's kind of you to say that,' she said. 'But how could anyone keep from getting well with such good care?' She had thought this out and sensed that this was what she should say: it was a statement that showed poise and equanimity and assurance – all the qualities that once she had not had. But, in some subtle fashion, it was also a lie, an untruth that she found troublesome. Mary and Martha, she liked them well enough, and they had never been unkind to her – but it was also true that she was glad that she was never going to see them again; that their personalities, their watchfulness, formed as much a part of the life she was escaping as the lattice-work on the window.

'Some don't – ' said Mary, and then shut her mouth on the rest that she had been about to say. And, as a member of a team helps a mate to recover a fumble, Martha stepped into the gap of silence that followed, saying:

'Dr Danzer tells us that you are going to take up your music again – that you are going to play in concert. Will you send us tickets to your first recital?'

434

'I shall – I promise,' Ellen said, eating several spoonsful of the oatmeal; 'the very first concert I give. But I warn you that you may not like it – my fingers are so stiff. I'm afraid I may have lost the knack.' And while she talked she was thinking. What had Mary meant by 'some don't – '? Had she meant that some don't recover completely ever? Of course, this was true, and she knew it. Or had the older nurse started to say, and then stopped because of tact, that some seemed to recover, but relapsed, that some did not stay adjusted, that the old fears returned and with them the old malady?

On impulse, with false bravery, more to test herself and the strength of her will than out of any inner necessity, Ellen said, 'Martha, now, before I leave' – she stopped and laughed to make it like a joke – 'I want you to do me a favour. I want you to turn your back on me, I want both of you to turn your backs on me – both you, Martha, and you, Mary – and keep them turned for more than a minute!'

Martha smiled and said nothing. Mary did not smile. They both looked at her in silence, not for long, although it seemed long to her, while she took another spoonful of the oatmeal. She lowered her eyes, thinking that they might want to look at each other, to gauge the other's thoughts to see if they both thought it wise. But as soon as she looked down, she forced herself to look up again – if they had regarded each other, it had been only a flick of a glance, yet she felt that somehow they had managed it, for Martha was smiling again. But then, Martha always smiled.

'Why, of course, if you want,' said Mary. 'But I don't see why?' And then, after having said she would, she did not, and neither did Martha. But they both stood there looking at her, awaiting an explanation, smiling. And Ellen knew that once more she would have to explain.

'It's silly of me, I know,' she said, 'but all the time I've been here I've been aware that whenever either of you come into my room you never turn your back on me. I know why it is, too, and don't think I blame you for it. But now – well, you see,' and she spread her hands, arched her fingers, splayed them to reach an octave, knowing that the gestures showed her nervousness but helpless to prevent it – 'what I mean is that I'd just feel better now that I'm going home if you both did that.'

She glanced up as she finished speaking, and this time she did see them exchange a look. Then Martha laughed and smiled. 'Well, I do think it's a little silly, but if you insist.' And she started to turn, then hesitated. And Mary said, 'Why, of course, we can if you want – ' She started to turn, too, and stopped. Ellen saw that, for some reason, her request was too queer, that the very fact she had made it had broken their friendliness, that now, even though they knew they did not have to, they were thinking of her again the way they thought of the other patients, that the watchfulness was returning, not all at once, but by degrees, to their manner.

So she laughed again, more nervously than before, and said, 'No, don't. I don't want you to. It was silly of me – just a notion of mine. You don't have to really.'

And Martha said, 'But we can, if you *want* us to.' And Mary looked at her watch and said, 'It's getting late and I have all those other diets. Martha, you must help me!' And Ellen laughed again and watched them leave the room, but she did not eat any more oatmeal.

After she had drunk her coffee, she wanted a cigarette, and went to her purse for the pack, took one out of it and put it in her mouth before she realized that she still had no matches. None of the patients was allowed matches, even on the day they went home. She could ring for the nurse, who would bring her a match, and who would stay close by until the cigarette was smoked and safely extinguished, but this she did not want to do. Instead, she walked to the window, stood in front of it and a few paces away from it, so she could see through the lattice-work, looked down on the rolling lawn, the curving path to the gate, the elms.

The sky she could see was the deep, clear blue of mid-summer, the leafage of the elms had darkened in the sun's heat, the clipped grass was spoiled with bare brown patches; although it was only late July, the season already had sown the seeds of its own destruction. The warmth of the day had begun to seep into the room; she felt flushed, and when she passed her hand over her forehead it came away damp. She went to the washstand and held a washcloth under the tap, then pressed its cold wetness to her face. She put on fresh powder and a little rouge, new lipstick, bending over the basin and putting her head close to the mirror as she made a new mouth. Her hair, she saw, still passed muster; her eyes were still the same transparent blue; there were very few wrinkles. Her lips were quiet, her chin forthright, her neck was not too long, her skin smooth. But what can I tell of the way I look? she asked herself – if there is change it goes on from day to day, I grow used to it, and although in months and years my face matures, coarsens, mocks its youth, the tiny advance age makes each day I never see, I never know. Thinking this, she picked up her toilet articles, which she had forgotten before, and carried them to one of the travelling-cases, unlocked it, put them inside and slammed it shut again. But when she had done this she was more than ever aware that it was just seven-thirty, that the nurse had said the doctor would be late, that even if Basil arrived early he would not be allowed to come up for her until she had seen the doctor and he had signed her discharge, that it would be more than an hour before she could go home.

Her books were packed, and so was her music – there was not even a newspaper she could read. If she sat and did nothing she would begin to remember all the incidents of her illness, she would become morose. As it was, her happiness had not left her, she was only sensing its peril. Of course, she could open the suitcase, unpack a book – in fact, that was the sensible thing to do. But the packing of those cases had marked a significant moment, had stood for the end of her life in this room; she had not even liked opening one long enough to put her cosmetics into it. No, she would not read; but she knew what she would do; she would pay Ella a visit; she would say good-bye.

She went to the door and put her hand on the knob, turned it – half-expecting that it would not turn although she knew that they had not locked her in for months – heard the quiet click and swung open the heavy door. After she walked into the corridor she pushed it wide and pressed down the plunger that would hold it open, for this was a rule. Then she went down the long, green-walled, tiled-floor hall to Ella's room. Its door was open, too, and she walked in without knocking.

Ella was sitting up in her chair by the window, her face turned toward the sun, her great body limp and sagging, while an orderly fed her breakfast. Ellen stopped just across the threshold, waited for the orderly to nod his head before she walked to the window and the huge, ageing woman. Ella held a fascination for her, an attraction that could not be explained wholly in terms of the similarity of their names, as Dr Danzer had once tried to explain it, although she admitted that a part of the compulsion had originated in that. Last winter, when the other patient had been admitted to the hospital, she had heard the nurses and the orderlies talking about 'Ella', about her violent intervals, her generally disturbed condition. And when she had first heard the name she had thought it her own, 'Ellen', and had been frightened. For days she had hidden her fear from Dr Danzer, although he could detect its effects in her personality and kept giving her word-associations and took a renewed interest in her dreams – she could smile at her panic now, but then she had thought that Ella's symptoms, which she overheard them talking about, were her own; she had thought that she was having violent episodes and then forgetting them. She had finally confided her fears to Dr Danzer and, to quiet them, he had taken her to see Ella, as he said, 'to show you that when we say "Ella" we do not mean "Ellen".'

As she walked across the room she remembered that first time she had seen Ella: the large form collapsed on the bed under an upheaval of covers, the twisting and turning of that mountainous body, the heaving breaths and the remarkably placid face that surmounted this disorder, the grey lumps of cheeks, the broad, fat lips, the open, staring, watery grey eyes. Her first reaction had been revulsion, and then relief, and then pity. Dr Danzer had told her something about Ella's history – how she had been a successful business-woman with many friends, convivial, a sport; how liquor had first been a pleasure for her, and then a passion, and now a mania. She had taken 'the cure' several times at less reputable institutions, but the last time she had gone on a binge it had been far worse than before – there had been some other complication; degeneration had occurred. 'She had never had a Wassermann,' the doctor had said, 'until a friend brought her here. She is under treatment now; but, of course, although we can arrest the disease we cannot hope to restore what has been destroyed.'

She had fallen into the habit of visiting Ella's room a few times each week, of sitting beside her bed or her chair by the window, of watching her placid face. Now she was rarely violent and she spent most of her day by the window – why she enjoyed this Ellen did not know, although she had noticed that the older woman's eyes sought and found the sun, followed it, and only on days when it was sunny did her expression change and something that seemed more like a smile than not inhabited her features. The great woman rarely made a sound, and on those occasions when she did it was a whimpering, and not an attempt at speech. But her face, for Ellen, held as many mysteries as the sea; its mask-like placidity, she was sure, was but the uppermost surface of a deep, many-levelled world of turmoil. To sit and watch those immobile planes and curves, those empty eyes, that gaping mouth, and then to return and search her mirror, inspect her own sentience as revealed by her own solid flesh, her changing mien, was to restore her faith in her own intelligence. So she always went to Ella's room when she doubted herself, when she was afraid.

Today Ella was eating, was being fed, and she knew that her presence was a bother to the orderly. But he had nodded his head, so she crossed to the window and stood looking down at the seated giantess, watching the thin youth in the white coat spoon up the oatmeal and lift it into the open mouth, watching the broad, fleshy hands grip the arm of the chair and then relax, grip and then relax, as a baby clenches and unclenches his fist as he sucks at his mother's breast. Yet in no other way was Ella childlike; rather her placidity seemed like the visible sign of superhuman maturity, expressing a god-like peace. In fact, her physical lineaments were not unlike Buddha's; although she did not sit cross-legged, she was huge enough, mysterious enough. When she was calm it was as if she were petrified, her only movement the swivelling of her head as her vacant eyes followed the sun; but this motion was an encroachment, like the lengthening of a sundial's shadow, like the slow progression of the smaller hand of a clock from one numeral to the next. They say Ella has no perception of reality any more, she thought, but if this is so why do her eyes follow the sun? Doesn't this compulsion indicate a sensing of the passage of time, a knowledge of the continual, gradual destruction of life? Couldn't it be that she does know, that she is still intelligent, but has just lost the power of speech together with all controls over most of her muscles except those of the head and eyes? If this is right, then to hold her head steady and to seek out the sun is her way of letting us know her great determination to live. And, it could be, her violence is but a great spasm of exasperation, of despair, a catastrophic assertion of her plight. And, if this is so, her imbecility is a tragedy to her, as well as to us.

When the orderly finished giving the meal to his patient he wiped her face with brusque, masculine tenderness, picked up the tray and offered his chair to Ellen. She sat down in it, her back to the window, and stared at the woman's blank face, trying to envisage it as it had been when she had been a success in business and had had many friends. Her face had always been large – that was certain from the outset: you could tell by the shape of the skull and the structure of the bones. And she was inclined to believe that it had always possessed some of the mask-like qualities it had today. Not in the same degree, and with greater variety: there had been a jolly mask, a serious mask, and, perhaps, a pouting mask. But Ellen felt quite sure that her near namesake had never shown her true emotions; she had been too much of an actress for that, too much of a saleswoman – and had she not been convivial and had many friends? So what she saw when she looked at her today was not disintegration, but an accretion, an intensification. The conflict that had been there all along, which Dr Danzer was certain had been the initial cause of her break, and not alcohol, was as much hidden today as it had been then, and this conflict, Ellen felt intuitively, was the core of her personality. How could one plumb these placid depths and find it? Where was the clue, the key, the entering wedge? Ellen felt she knew that, too – it was there for everyone to see – the one eccentricity, the one vestige of character: the woman's eyes and their habit of looking at the sun. Here is a person, she thought, who has found time out, for whom it holds no terrors, who is one with its destructive genius.

Thinking this, she looked at her watch and saw it was after eight. She stood up to go, not wanting to be out of her room when the doctor came, looking once more at Ella, her taciturnity, her mystery. In some way knowing that Ella had given her strength, had built up her hope – she would remember this calm one, who could be so violent, fondly – she walked past the door and down the hall to her room. Dr Danzer was there, waiting for her.

He stood by the window, his hand against one of the

441

drapes, his body half-turned towards her, his eyes thoughtfully upon her. He was a small man, a slow man, a kind
man. As she came into the room and walked up to him,
she felt the same surprise that she had felt many times
before on seeing him: she was taken aback once more by
the slightness of his build, the smallness of his hands and
head, the seeming immaturity of his features. His dark
eyes behind shell-rimmed glasses had the intensity, the
capacity for feeling pain, that one expects in adolescence;
his mouth was impressionable, the way he held his lips
conjectural, as if anything he might say was tentative and
he was no more certain of his own mind than he was of
others. But when he spoke, as he did now, this vagueness,
this indecision, ceased. His words existed in their own
right, were spoken deliberately and exactly, though
quietly, implying the logic that had chosen them, the
knowledge behind the logic, the intuition behind that
knowledge. Ellen had always felt safe with this man, had
liked him for himself as well as for the security he gave.
And she liked him even more at this moment, all but cried
aloud with joy when he said the words, *her* words, that
meant so much to her. How he had known to say them she
did not know, but that was not important; what was
important was that he did say them, slowly and precisely,
giving them to her as a symbol of her freedom.

'Well, Ellen,' he said, 'today is *the* day!'

She sat beside him and looked at him, not trusting herself to speak. She felt close to him – close to him as a friend.
There were many things she had wanted to say, had
planned on saying, at this time – she had wanted him to
know how she had resented him at first, hated him,
fought him with all her being; how she had come gradually to look forward to his visits, had learned from him to
be wryly amused at the deceits a part of her practised on
the rest of her and on him, had grown accustomed to testing all her motives, all her reasons for action, to questioning her least impulse, to looking upon herself as she
might look upon a character in a play, critically, analyti-

cally. But now the time had come and he had spoken first, had miraculously used her own words and expressed her own feeling, and she had nothing to say.

He was not at a loss, however. He put his hand in his pocket and turned his back on the window, so that now he faced her and regarded her directly. 'Did you sleep well last night?' he asked.

Now that he had asked the question, commenced again the familiar ritual, she could answer him directly. 'I slept very well,' she said, 'though it was a long time before I fell asleep. I was too excited, too anxious for the morning – but when I did, I slept like a log.'

'Any dreams?' He had his notebook out, and the little pencil on which the gold-plating was worn in places so that the base metal showed through.

'I didn't have a dream all night.'

'One always dreams. Think. I'm sure you can remember.'

And she thought. And she did remember something. It came to her as it usually came, visually at first, a scurrying, a slipping away, a something that was perceived, yet not known, not recognized, disturbing in its evasiveness. But she did not let it go, she refused to let it slide away, she held on to it by asking herself questions: Was it dark? – was it big? – was it someone? – a man or a woman? – what was it doing? – was something happening? – to her or to someone else? And as she questioned, the image did not disappear, although she did not know it for what it was yet, but at the same time it expressed itself in words, sometimes in syllables, sometimes in whole clauses, the way a melody would form in her head, sounding itself little by little, and she would try to identify it, break it up into intervals, phrases . . .

'What did you dream?' he asked.

'I dreamed – I dreamed' – she was sure of herself now, it was coming, she could say it in a moment – 'I dreamed I was playing. What it was I was playing I don't know – some large, cumbersome instrument. It kept crawling away from me. I'd arch my fingers at it, I'd claw at it and catch hold of it to keep it from getting away. I'd try to play it – but the melody wouldn't come. I could hear the melody in my head – strangely, I could see it dance in front of my eyes. I don't know how I can explain that. It wasn't notes I saw, not really, but a sort of flowing, a kind of sunny, twisting river of sound. I know what I'm saying is peculiar, but it seemed natural in my dream. I kept playing, or trying to play this tune, you see. And the instrument – it was a large instrument, but not as large as a piano – kept trying to run away. And I couldn't play the tune, no matter how hard I tried – I couldn't!'

'What was the name of the instrument?' he asked.

'A harpsichord,' she answered, not surprised that she had known it all the time, for this had happened often before. 'And, now I remember, it was most peculiar, although I liked it for the peculiarity – and that, I suppose, is the reason it was so hard to play the tune! – the harpsichord, you see, has only one . . . only one . . .' She stopped and looked at him, and laughed.

'Blocked?' he asked.

'I am. I don't know why. It was just on the tip of my tongue.'

'Let's try a word test. You know, say what first comes into your mind. Green?'

'Lawn.'

'Gate?'

'Home.'

'Basil?'

. . .

'Basil?'

. . .

'Blocked?' he asked.

'Yes, I am. I don't know why.'

'Keyboard?'

'Piano.'

'Clavier?'

'Only one Basil.'

He looked at her, and smiled and looked away. He was smiling still – she could see that. But why had he looked away? 'Why did you say "Only one Basil"?' he asked.

'Because a clavier has only one – oh, I meant "manual". That was what was strange about the harpsichord in my dream – that was what I kept blocking on. *Man*-ual. Only one man. Basil. I was dreaming of Basil. And of music, and how hard I would have to practise. That was all there was to it, wasn't it? But why did I block?'

'Because you did not want me to know,' he said. 'Because Basil is your husband.'

She looked at him, startled, then laughed. He laughed, too. 'I think it's about time you went home, Mrs Purcell,' he said.

The doctor walked away from the window, leaving her, going towards the door. As he did this, something went wrong in her throat; she felt empty inside, forlorn. This must be how a child feels, she thought, when her father walks away from her for the first time, leaves her standing alone, and she knows that she must either walk or fall. And then she set her lips, made a face at the thought – she was independent of Dr Danzer; she knew it and he knew it; there was no doubt that she no longer needed him. But she did take a step forward, was drawn towards him against her will, stopping only when she saw the way he stood, the way he watched her, the remnants of his smile still about his lips, his dark eyes testing her.

'Your husband should be downstairs by now,' he said, 'attending to the formalities. I'll go and see if I can speed things up a little.'

'There are forms to be filled, I suppose,' she said, not because she wanted to know, but because she wanted to talk, to say a little more, to hold to him and his waning interest in her for a few more minutes.

'The administration office must have its red tape,' he admitted. And then he snapped his fingers, 'Oh, say, I forgot! You are coming to see me next week, aren't you?

At my New York office? I'm there Wednesday mornings and all day Fridays.'

'I can see you any time you wish.'

He took out his pencil again, and his pad. 'Wednesday, at eleven?' He looked up, smiling. 'It's just for a check-up, you know. We can have a talk. I think we should see each other for a little while more . . .'

'Eleven will be fine.'

So she would see him again. Now that she knew, she was disappointed. She was on a long rope that let her roam, but she could be pulled back at any time. Yet, as always, he was right. She would want to see him again.

He had finished scribbling in his notebook, had tucked the worn pencil away. His hand was back in his pocket, and he took a few more steps toward the door. But then he stopped again. 'May I ask you a question?' he said.

'Of course.' She wondered why he asked her per-mission. For the last two years he had asked and she had answered many questions – why should she resent another now?

'This morning, when you talked to the two atten-dants, you asked them to turn their backs on you – didn't you?'

'Yes, I did.'

'Why did you ask that?'

She was afraid. She could feel the rope tighten, could feel herself being pulled back. She moistened her lips and spoke carefully, remembering that her words must be assured, indicate poise, self-confidence.

'It was just a whim. I awoke feeling very elated – I would say happy, but you would say elated. I felt very good towards everybody – I still do. But when Mary came into the room, and then Martha, I could not help remem-bering other times. I remembered how they used to look at me, to watch me – how careful they always were not to turn their backs on me . . .'

'So you asked them to turn round,' he said. He looked

directly at her, and his eyes were serious. 'You know they couldn't, don't you? It's a hospital rule that is never broken. It had nothing to do with you.'

'It was silly of me,' she said, 'and I admit it.'

'We are all of us a little silly at times.' His eyes broke away from her glance, looked down at his pocketed hand. 'Well,' he said, 'good luck to you. I'll go down and see what's keeping that husband of yours.' He walked side-wise through the door, backed into the hall, smiling at her, pulling his hand from his pocket and raising it, then dropping it, as if he wanted to wave but decided he had better not.

She watched him go, thinking to herself, what a nice guy he is, what an awfully nice guy! But when she stood aside, as he had taught her to do, and thought of him objectively, she realized that his niceness was all probably just a part of his professional manner, a bag of tricks to effect a transference, that she did not know his real personality because he had never shown it to her. If I had met him at a party, if I had been introduced to him by a friend, what would I have thought of him? she wondered.

She turned her back on the door he had forgotten to close, deciding to let it stand open, and went back to the window. He is meeting Basil now, she thought; he is talking to him, first about the weather, then about me. How do they get along together? she asked herself. Do they like each other? She would have to ask Basil some-time what he thought of Dr Danzer – sometime in the future, when this moment lay in the remote past, when the answer Basil gave to her question would be unim-portant, when she could ask it casually, idly. She tried to visualize them together, Basil and the doctor, one large and blond and forceful, the other small and dark and dif-fident. She shut her eyes so that she might concentrate, but she did not succeed in seeing them both at once. First, she would see Basil, and then she would see Dr Danzer. It was as if she saw them with separate senses and had to

447

switch back and forth from one to the other, could never use both senses together. But it was not important, it was only a game she was playing to pass the time. She would see Basil soon. He would be coming down the hall, coming through the door . . .

Suddenly she was afraid. Something had entered the room as she thought of Basil coming through the door, something old and well known, something archaic and dreadful. She had met this thing before – although not for many months, she had thought she had quite got over it, that she need not fear its return. It had come each time in the same way, unexpectedly, when she was thinking of something else. It had fallen upon her, embraced her, shut out the light.

She struggled against it, wanting to cry out, but knowing she dare not. If she screamed, one of the attendants would come running, would ask her what was wrong, would tell the doctor. And a part of her knew that nothing menaced her, that the black thing she feared came out of her past, that she had once even seen it in a dream, clearly and distinctly, and had known it for what it was. Remembering this, she also remembered her own formula for vanquishing this terror: all she had to do was to think of that dream, spend all her efforts in recapturing that experience, seeing it fully and precisely so that she could identify it – and laugh at it. For it was not very awful really – only her father's body with the light behind it, swaying drunkenly over her crib, magnified and distorted by the shadows cast in the lamp's light; and her mother's voice, hoarse and shrill, crying, 'Don't you do it! – if you touch a hair of her head, I'll murder you!'

But even knowing what it was that terrified her, seeing it again in her mind's eye as she had seen it first in reality, as a child of three, she still had to fight its present form – the pervasive blackness that assailed her, the great, smothering blanket of panic that hung over her and threatened to descend upon her. She forced herself to go to the mirror, to look into it at her face, her bulging eyes, her straining, tensing mouth; at her hand that pressed against her cheek, pushed the flesh aside, stopped the flow of blood. And as she examined herself, held her eyes on the mirror and suppressed the desire to turn round, to look over her shoulder, she felt as if she were climbing up from the depths, struggling higher and higher, out of the dark and into the light. Her hand fell away from her face – although it left white fingers on the reddened flesh as a reminder – her lips relaxed and she managed to smile at herself. Her breathing became regular and her body seemed her own again; once more she was compact and whole, her natural self.

She stayed in front of the mirror, applying fresh rouge and lipstick, combing her hair. She reminded herself that Basil would be coming in shortly – this time as she thought these words the black fear did not strike, she was not even nervous – and she must look her best for him. This would be a difficult day for Basil – the first day in two years that he had spent more than a few hours with her. Two years was a long time; lovers had become strangers in less. She must do everything she could to make it easy for him, she must meet him more than half-way, she must stand aside and judge herself and him, as Dr Danzer had taught her to, try all along to be objective about their relationship. He will have changed, she told herself, Basil will have changed.

She had changed, too, although she could not tell how much or in what ways. Would he find her too different from the woman he had married? Would he like her now that she had learned to hide her conflicts, to face up to the darkness when it threatened her, to stand on her feet and fight back? Would he love her as he had once? Or would there still be the restraint that she had felt was due to the surroundings, her long absence from him, the difficulty of attempting to put back together the pieces of their former life for an hour or two once or twice a month? Perhaps they would never get the pieces back together again, no matter how much they had in the future. And,

449

thinking of time, she looked at her watch, and saw that it was after nine o'clock.

Minute by minute the hours had fled until now the time of her life in this room was all but used up, would soon be forever past. She found herself listening for a sound in the corridor – Basil's heavy, rhythmic stride, like drumbeats in the symphonies he conducted. And, at the same time, she thought about the world she was entering again, her unguarded future, the causes and effects that would shape her life but over which she would have only partial control, the conditionings. She looked around the room again, the familiar, enclosing scene, the four protective walls, the door which she could open or close – letting in or shutting out the sounds of other lives – the checkered pattern of light and dark on the floor cast by the sun as it invaded the latticed window. I shall leave all this order behind me, she thought, and enter into chaos. I shall never know from one moment to the next, although I shall pretend that I know, as I always used to pretend before, what will happen, how I shall behave, what awaits me. Life lies before me, and, ultimately, death – I can escape neither. I shall have to choose what I do, make decisions; only in the largest, most indirect sense will they be made for me. Once I hear Basil's step, see his face, take his arm and go through that door, I shall have to keep on moving, acting, believing . . . believing in myself and in others.

Do I want to go through that door and leave this room and this reliable order forever? Wouldn't it be safest to stay here, to accept this known, unchanging world rather than to leave it and submit to the unknown flux? She stood rigidly, her eyes shut, her hands flattened stiffly, pressing painfully, against her thighs. For an instant her mind was blank with indecision, she thought nothing, existed on the edge of her consciousness, balancing on the tight-rope that lies between sensation and numbness, thought and nullity, affirmation and negation. And then

450

a scene flooded her vision, brightly and gloriously as foot-lights reveal a furnished stage – her room at home, her study, the rose walls, the long, low couch, the forthright elegance of the harpsichord. Quietly, precisely, the notes of Bach's aria sounded in her mind, and she saw herself seated at the instrument, breathing with the gentle movements of the melody, safe within another, kinder discipline. And she opened her eyes, once more unafraid, to see Basil standing silently in the door.

2

Basil had been a fanfare, a bright cry of trumpets, a skirling of woodwinds. He stood easily, negligently, his face relaxed as if awaiting a smile, his fine blue eyes regarding her lovingly. She had seen him all at once, as she saw herself in the mirror: the high relief of his cheekbones beneath the tense, tanned face flesh; the wide, fond slant of his mouth; the dramatic arcs of his eyebrows and the deep sculptured sockets that held his eyes: the stone of his forehead and the blond verdure of his bristling hair. She had stepped forward towards him, then ran, was in his arms, her head against his shoulder, her cheek and mouth against the rough wool of his coat. He had held her close to him, his arm long and tight about her waist, had kissed her head, saying her name to her as he might to himself, 'Ellen, Ellen.' When she looked up at him he had kissed her on the mouth – there had been no hesitancy, no caution – frankly and firmly, ardently. She found it hard to breathe, and broke away, but had stood beside him a little longer, her hand lightly on his shoulder, looking at him and smiling when he smiled. 'There are three bags,' she had said – knowing she did not have to say anything of greater import – 'a big one and two small ones. Will you help me?'

Could she have put it in this drawer? What a key would be doing in her vanity drawer she did not know, but she had to be systematic about her search, she had to look every place, in every cranny – even the most unlikely places – if she hoped to find it. How barren a long-unused drawer looked, the stockings stiff in their dusty tissue paper, the powder that had been spilled smelling

stale with the years. What a blatant, pinkish shade of powder!
When had she used it? No, there was no key there. But, while she
was at it, she might as well look in the other drawers.

The flagstones had been uneven beneath her feet, the
handle of the suitcase had begun to cut into the palm of
her hand (she had insisted on carrying the heavy bag;
the two travelling-cases were enough for Basil). The
direct heat of the sun had made her dizzy, its steady
brilliance had made the grass seem greener than ever
before, the sky bluer. At the lodge they had stopped while
Basil picked through his pockets for the slip of paper he
must show the gatekeeper; she had been able to put down
the suitcase, to rest her hand, to stand in the shade of the
elms until the man had telephoned to the main office and
verified her credentials. Actually, she had stepped through
the gate because the shade was deeper on the other side,
had not been aware that by taking this action she had
crossed the line, had passed into the world and out of the
cloister; later, she regretted not having done it consciously,
had even forgotten when she had gone through the gate
until Basil reminded her, 'You went past it when you
wanted to stand in the shade while I talked to the man,
remember' – this was when they were on the bus going
down the mountainous road to the town and the railroad
station – was sorry that so soon she was blinded to the
greater reality by the immediate demands of cause and
effect.

The bus had been hot and stuffy, crowded with tired-
looking people of all ages, solitary men and women,
taciturn families, one young girl with staring eyes and an
impassive face. She had felt self-conscious holding Basil's
hand, and childishly exuberant in the face of this mass
restraint. They had been the first ones on the bus, and
had taken a seat in the rear – they had watched the others
file crookedly down the hill and past the gatekeeper's
lodge and out the gate.

'Are they all patients?' she had asked Basil, breaking a

silence that had become uncomfortable, 'and if they aren't, why are they leaving so early?'

'Visiting hours start at six on Sundays,' he had told her. 'If they didn't, they would never be able to accommodate all the visitors. Each bus brings its load, and takes another away – they run every fifteen minutes all day. Sunday is the only day most people can come, you see.' He had looked out of the window at the crowd that seemed to grow thicker as the bus filled. 'Some of them are patients, of course,' he had gone on. He pointed his finger at the girl with immobile features. 'She is. I talked to her once on the train. She lives a few stations away in a town on the river. They let her go home every Sunday, but she must be back by nightfall.'

She had held his hand tighter, smiled at him, fighting down the fear that had risen in her throat while he talked. She could feel the tether about her waist, feel it tighten, feel it begin to draw her back irresistibly. And then she realized that the bus had begun to move, that the driver had released the brake and slipped into gear, that they were rolling downhill, away from the crowd that was being left (people were standing in the aisles, the driver could not have taken any more), away from the man who had thought himself next to get on, a tall man with a florid face, who shook a great fist at them and mouthed inaudible curses.

She had looked in her study, in the music cabinet, in the bedroom, in all the drawers of her vanity. Now she went downstairs again and into the library; she began to look through the desk; she would look in each cubbyhole, underneath the blotter, the secret compartment . . . 'What are you doing?' Basil's voice behind her, questioning, a little curt. 'I'm still looking for the key,' she said, turning to face him, surprised to see his face flushed beneath his tan. 'I can't seem to find it anywhere, and I'm sure I left it in the keyhole. Where did you see it last?' He shook his head and came to stand beside her, his hand resting on the desk, casually barring her from it. 'I'll look here,' he said. 'I have

*some manuscripts I don't want disturbed. Why don't you go to the
kitchen and ask Suky if he's seen it? I'll bet you he has it safely
put away.'*

The train had been dirty and just as crowded as the
bus. Some of the same people were in their coach, along
with others: farmers and their wives visiting the city to
see a movie or go to the beach, several railroadmen riding
as far as the next stop, a junction, and a few she could not
identify. She had wondered how Basil and she looked to
these people, if any of them were doing what she was
doing – trying to deduce who they were, where they were
coming from and where they were going. Basil, she knew,
stood out in any group. What distinguished him was the
way he held himself. He always seemed, to her, at least,
to be standing on the podium. His hands gripped an
imaginary baton. His head and neck were stiffly erect,
his eyes shifted position quickly, found what they sought,
turned from it as swiftly to something else, keeping the
entire car under surveillance as they were accustomed to
survey an orchestra – first the strings, then the woodwinds,
the 'cellos, the brasses, the percussions, the 'basses.

'Any new scores this year?' she asked him, abruptly
deciding to abandon her game of trying to discover what
the other travellers thought of her, because it was difficult
and unprofitable.

Basil had at that moment, when she asked her question,
looked out of the window at the mountainous terrain, the
dark-veined rocky cliff-face that overhung the right-of-
way. He had turned about at her words, but not to look
at her, his eyes elevated and musing. 'There is a new
symphony by D—,' he had said, naming a contemporary
Russian composer whose works, although they had been
highly acclaimed and had won great popularity, she had
always thought vulgar, stilted and derivative. 'I have been
lucky enough to obtain the exclusive rights to the first
American performance. I intend to open the season with it.'

She had quite forgotten how different his taste in music

455

was from hers. Not that they did not often like the same things – Beethoven, Mozart, Stravinsky – but that there was so much which he either liked, or espoused because the public liked it, which she thought insipid or meretricious. D— was a case in point. Like most concertgoers, she had been forced to listen to a number of his works, since his music had been widely performed from the very start of his career. Except for some early chamber music that had been timidly experimental, she had found it all dull. And she had often suspected that Basil, even though she had never put him in a position where he would be forced to admit it, was of the same opinion. Yet he had championed D—'s works from the beginning, not the least of his fame as a conductor had been gained from his interpretations of them (he generally favoured a faster tempo than anyone else, and he took care to extract the last decibel of thunder from a climactic crescendo), so that now he had been honoured by being granted the right to introduce the composer's latest production to the American audience.

'Is it very long?' she asked.

'Surprisingly short,' he replied. 'There are six brief movements – two slow and four fast. One, believe it or not, is a charming minuet. A little ironic, perhaps – a few barbs of wit here and there. But, on the whole, melodic and beautiful.'

'I should like to see the score,' she said, knowing this was the thing to say, wanting, at any cost of pride, to avoid the old, useless antagonism. In a way, it was good that they inhabited separate worlds of music – there was no competition. He played Bach only in orchestral transcriptions, programmed Mozart and Haydn to pad out an evening of more bombastic works, to act as foils that in their drabness display the talents of a trickster.

'I am having the parts copied now,' he said. 'I understand it won't be published until spring. As it is, I have only the microfilm copy of the original.'

'I'll wait until you have other copies.' She was relieved

that it would not be necessary to scan the symphony and comment upon it. If he had asked her opinion, she would have told him the truth – which, she feared, he would not have liked. Yet, by showing she was interested, she had pleased him, and she was reassured to find that he still looked to her for approval. He had taken her hand again, and was holding it more firmly than before.

Basil she thought, I love you; but, dearest, I have never thought of you as a musician. Oh, you can *conduct* – you can force a hundred men to play the way you want them to – but with you it is a business, a means of winning fame and fortune, a chance to lead and make others follow, not really an art. I think you look at D—'s symphony for the first time, eagerly thumbing through its pages, humming its themes to yourself, not to find out what it is, to appraise it and learn from it, but to discover, if you can, how effective it can be, how you can twist and turn it to display your personality as a politician looks for catch-phrases in a speech: I think, Basil, that what you want – and must have – out of music, is a sense of personal power. You pit yourself against the orchestra and the audience, and the composer, as well. You stand on the podium at their mercy and drive them all into bondage by a toss of your golden head, a restless shirk of your well-placed shoulders, your angry glance, your stamping foot. And what about me? Why, I like to watch you, darling; I admire your trickery and allow you to beguile me. But, then, our relationship, Basil, is not a musical one . . .

A sandwich-hawker had come into the coach, his hoarse cry breaking into her thoughts and stimulating Basil to action. He had begun to gesture imperiously at the man – as if cueing in the brasses, quieting the strings – but when the man ignored him, he had to whistle peremptorily. This the hawker had heard, and he had offered them his basket, from which they chose cheese sandwiches on white bread and waxed cups filled with brackish-tasting coffee. For only then had they realized that it was after ten o'clock and they were inordinately hungry.

Suky was polite, bowing and mumbling neat excuses, but he was also adamant. He did not have the key, it had not been given to him, he had not seen it. He stood aside, muttering, angry at her invasion of the kitchen, while she searched the drawers of the tables, the kitchen cabinet. She left the kitchen quickly, relieved to be out of range of his subservient animosity.

She walked into the hall and went through the small drawer in the console table. It was packed with an accumulation of cards, and one lavender envelope, addressed to Basil in a small, cramped, feminine hand – whoever had written it liked to make a tiny circle in place of a dot over the letter 'i' – that gave off a faint scent of pungent perfume. She picked this up, saw that it had been opened, and even considered reading it. But she knew what it was – a mash note from some young admirer who had attended one of his concerts and had fallen in love with his noble back. Basil was always getting fan mail; he had probably found this with his letters, had read it on the spot before going out, had dropped it on the table, and Suky – who never threw anything away unless told to – had put it in the drawer. She pushed the drawer shut. The key was not there, and now she did not know where to look.

She stood in the hall, gazing through the front door at the busy street, people walking up and down in Sunday clothes, vari-coloured taxis streaming past in the still-brilliant sunshine, think-ing of where she could possibly have put that key. She had looked in her study, in the library, in the bedroom, in the kitchen. No, she had not looked in the library. Basil had been fussy about his desk, and had insisted on looking there for her. He might have found it by now.

Turning her back on the door and the street, she went into the library again. Basil was at his desk, a score – D——'s symphony? – spread out before him. She hated to interrupt him at his work. but until she found that key she could do no work either. 'Basil,' she asked, 'did you find it?'

He looked up at her, his eyes questioning, his hand holding his pencil, tapping with it. 'I beg your pardon?'

'I asked you if you had found my key. You were going to look for it in the desk.'

His eyes lost some of their distraction as he understood what

*she asked. 'No, I didn't find it,' he said. And he bent over the
score again.*

She was not sure he had even looked for it.

They had stood far to the front of the Weehawken ferry,
the late morning sun hot on their heads, their arms about
each other, watching the spectacular skyline of midtown
Manhattan loom closer and closer. There had been nights,
when she had lain in bed unable to sleep, that she had
doubted the existence of the city, of any reality greater
than the four green walls of her room, the door opening
on to the corridor, the latticed window with its view of the
lawn and the elms. Now, already, as the ferry surged
forward through the turgid waters of the Hudson and the
bone-white buildings seemed to momentarily creep higher
and higher into the dazzling blue of the sky, she could
doubt the reality of that room, wonder if it had only been
the worst of her dreams. She began to tremble with
excitement as she sensed the nearness of the life this vista
stood for; the bustle of 57th Street, the façades of Town
Hall, of Carnegie Hall, the silence of broadcasting studios,
the rose walls of her study at home, the clamour of voices
at a cocktail party, the sound of a harpsichord.

Basil felt her trembling and held her more tightly. 'It's
a wonderful town, isn't it?' he said. And, for the first time,
he referred directly to the circumstances of the day: 'It
must feel fine to be back after so long.'

'I don't ever want to leave it again,' she said quietly,
aware of the petulance in her voice, but not ashamed of
it, because that was the way she felt.

'Not even for a trip?' asked Basil.

'Not even for a trip.'

The ferry shuddered as it struck the slip, rebounded
sluggishly, nosed forward into the wharf. A clanking noise
startled them into picking up their bags and pushing
forward with the crowd – the ferry had docked and the
gangway was being let down. In a few more minutes they
were on a New York street looking for a taxi.

As the cab turned into Forty-second Street she asked him the question she had wanted to ask all morning. 'Are you glad to have me back, Basil?'

He turned to her, his features not composed, his mouth slightly open, his eyes glinting. 'You know I am glad,' he said. 'I didn't think I'd have to tell you that. You ought to know that for the last year I've lived in antici-pation of today.'

How nice to hear him say this! she thought – if only he had said it without my asking. But, since I asked, how can I believe him? Oh, I do not doubt he thinks so; but why did he need prompting? Why couldn't he have come out with it naturally as another man might? And then she caught herself, stood aside and inspected herself, knowing that once more she was looking for trouble, seeking umbrage. Basil had not said he was glad to have her home until she asked, because Basil habitually with-drew, was normally aloof. They would never be married in the sense that they would share a community of thoughts, nor would she have wanted their marriage to be like that. Basil lived in his own world, and she lived in hers; their worlds were contiguous, sometimes they over-lapped, but they would never coincide.

'Suky and I have been lonely,' he said, interrupting her internal discourse. He smiled ruefully. 'I'm afraid our house doesn't look the same. It lacks your touch.'

She leaned her head on his shoulder, shut her eyes. 'A few weeks will fix that. Although it may take longer,' she said. 'I shall have to practise at least six hours a day. You know, I haven't touched a keyboard in two years – I'm afraid I'll have forgotten how.'

His shoulder stiffened, his body grew rigid. She lifted her head and opened her eyes to look at him, to see what was wrong. His hands were clenched in his lap, his lips were compressed. 'Do you think you had better?' he asked. 'Isn't it too soon? Shouldn't you take it easy and rest up? You don't have to give a concert this year, you know. The public will remember you – there will be no question of a "comeback". Your records are all best-sellers still –'

She interrupted him. 'I am giving a concert in November, Basil. I've talked to Dr Danzer about it, and he agrees that I should concertize whenever I want. It's my way of life, just as it is yours. It's my function.'

'There are other ways to fulfil yourself – ways that are less exacting. I know how you drive yourself when you shut yourself up in the little room. I think it is still too early for you to do that again.'

They sat silent while the taxi sped down Park Avenue, coming nearer and nearer to their street and their house. Then Basil unclenched his hands and allowed his body to relax, turned to her and took her hand again.

'I won't stand in your way, Ellen,' he said. 'What you want is what I want. I don't want you to think anything else.'

She lifted her face, and he kissed her. She shut her eyes to keep him from seeing the tears of anger that had involuntarily arisen. As soon as he was not looking – when he paid the cab-driver – perhaps, she would take out her handkerchief. For a moment she had thought that he did not want her to play again.

Ellen remembered thinking that now, as she stood outside the library door, after having asked Basil if he had found the key to her harpsichord. She did not believe he had looked for the key in his desk – did this mean that he knew the key was there but did not want her to find it? She walked slowly, deliberately, down the hall. Suppose, for some strange reason of his own, that her suspicion was right and he would prefer that she did not play again. Would hiding the key to her instrument keep her from playing? Of course not! Tomorrow morning, if she had not found the key by then, she would call in the locksmith and have a new key made. And had he not said in the taxi that if she wanted to practise, to give a concert in November, he did not wish to stand in her way? In the future she must be careful about her resentments, her suspicions. She must remember to stand aside and appraise herself at every juncture so that she might understand her fears and, in knowing them, dispel them.

Basil had intended to look for her key in his desk – of this she was now certain. But, on sitting down at it, his eyes had fallen on the manuscript, and the particular problem it presented; he had begun to work at it, and soon he had forgotten why he had gone to the desk in the first place. Later, when he was finished, she could ask him again, and he might admit that he had forgotten, go back and look. But if he did not, it really would not matter – although it was frustrating not to be able to open her instrument.

She began to climb the stairs, remembering one place she had not looked – her old purses. When she had gone through the drawers she had seen two of them; there might be others in the closets. Purses and keys went together, the key she was looking for might well be in one of those purses. Reaching the head of the stairs, and catching a glimpse of the study through the door that she had left open, she had to go into the small, functional room. Functional, but not in the modern sense – congenial might be the better word. There was nothing out of place here, nothing unnecessary or merely ornamental. The harpsi-chord stood in the centre of the floor, where the light from the bow-window fell full upon it. By its side stood a great-bulbed lamp to illuminate her page at night. The walls were covered with a deep rose-coloured paper above the low bookcases that held the bound volumes of her scores, the set of Grove's, St Lambert's *Principes du Clavecin*, Couperin's *L'Art de toucher le clavecin*, Dolmetsch and Einstein, Tovey and Kirkpatrick. A small rosewood table held a tabouret, a box of cigarettes and an ashtray, the long, low couch stretched itself in a corner; but other-wise the room was without furnishings. Standing on the threshold of this sanctuary from which she had been alien-ated for so long, she felt calmer, more at ease; the tight coil of her compulsion, that had been driving her from room to room and drawer to drawer ever since she had discovered the key's absence, slackened and ran down. But she remembered her disappointment a few hours earlier, when she had flung open the downstairs door and run up the stairs, when she had stood on this threshold for the very first time in two long years, her eyes absorbed with the unquestioned reality of a scene that had existed for so long only in her memory – and then she had stepped to the harpsichord, run her hand over its old, smooth surface, had attempted to lift the lid, only to find it locked – she could not budge it – and the key was missing!

Suky had rung the gong that announced luncheon before she could begin her search for the key; throughout the meal she had had only one thought – where might it be? Basil had been talkative and had told her all about his plans for the orchestra during the new season. He had gossiped about his fellow conductors, told choice anecdotes about famous soloists and their quirks, once more shown his enthusiasm for D—'s new symphony. She had forced herself to respond to his talk, to smile and laugh in the proper places, to exclaim and ask questions; but all the time she had kept thinking of where she might have put the key, trying to trace her mind back to the last day she had played the instrument – a hopeless task, for it had been a muddled day, a time she would rather not remember.

And after lunch she had smoked a cigarette with Basil – her mind upstairs in her rooms, going through drawers, ransacking closets. He had come and sat beside her, had showed her the microfilm score of the new symphony. It had seemed only a jumble of notes to her, a blurred, black page. But he had not known her confusion, had mistaken her vague effusiveness for ardour, had taken her in his arms and kissed her passionately. And she had given herself almost completely to his caresses, rejoicing in the thrusting strength of his embrace, postponing for a little while her search. It had been two o'clock before she had begun to look for the key, telling Basil that she must unpack, not yet wanting to admit her carelessness, her frustration. Yet now that she had admitted it, he was peculiarly unimpressed.

Sighing, she turned her back on the study and went down the hall to her bedroom. If she remembered correctly, she had kept her purses in the top drawer of the dresser. She opened the drawer, and was pleased to find them there: a moiré bag, a pigskin satchel, a small billfold and coin-purse that she used to slip into the pocket of her covert cloth coat, and a gold-mesh evening bag. Oh, here was another, a patent leather cube; it opened sideways, on the bias – she had forgotten this one. When had she bought it? She usually favoured more conservative styles than this. But, then, how could she expect to account for all her actions of two or more years ago, especially those of the last six months before she went to the hospital? She sighed again, and began to go through the purses.

She found coins, a lipstick and a compact, a rhinestone-studded comb – this in the patent-leather bag – two tickets to Carnegie Hall for 23 January 1944, several handkerchiefs and a number of hairpins. But she had not found the key, although when her fingers, groping in one of the pocket-books, had first touched a hairpin, she had thought that at last she had it. Joy had leaped in her throat, she had held her breath; but a moment later she had realized that she was mistaken, that the key was still lost. By now she saw the small object in her imagination; it shone and glittered before her eyes; she could count the irregular indentations in its upper edge that fitted the tumblers of the lock, the tiny notches: there were five of them, and one was cut more deeply, more jaggedly than the others – seeing it so clearly was especially frustrating, it was as if she had had it in her hand only yesterday, had laid it aside in some safe place, and if she only thought about it, concentrated on what she had been doing and why she had laid it down, she would remember where it was. Actually, this was impractical, since it had not been yesterday or even the day before that she had last held the key, but years; and she knew that when she found it – oh, was she ever going to find it? – it would not look the way she saw it now, that she would not have remembered it accurately, but altogether different. It was like searching for a passage in a book when your memory tells you that it existed at the bottom of a right-hand page and somewhere towards the end of the last chapter, so you think, all I have to do is to leaf through all the right-hand pages of the last chapter and I shall find what I am looking for. But you look through all these pages, and all the left-hand ones, too, and then you repeat the process for each chapter of the book – working from back to front, from right-hand pages to left-hand pages – until at last you find the passage. And you are disappointed when you find it, since it really does not say what you had thought it did, it is not nearly as moving as you had remembered it – in fact, now that you think about it, isn't it quite commonplace? – but what is most disturbing of all because it reveals what a gross betrayer your memory is, what makes the print blur before your eyes and a dry knot of futile anger clot your mouth, is the fact that this line is the first line of a chapter, the second chapter of the book, high up on one of the book's earliest pages!

There was no need for further search. It was late afternoon; dinner would be ready soon, perhaps; she should not work on the first day she was home. She would look for the key again in the morning, and if she wanted to play something in the meantime there was always Basil's piano. If she did not find the key, she would call the locksmith and he could make her another one. It was really as simple as that.

She stepped into the hall just as a loud, reverberating, crashing chord resounded through the house. The membranes in her ears, long-accustomed to the disciplined quiet of the hospital, twanged in outrage; a shudder seized her frame, shook her as a great fist might brandish a sceptre. Almost before the sound of punished strings had ceased echoing, a raucous, percussive melody rushed pell-mell forth, each note jostling its neighbour, cramped by a strong, crude rhythm. Basil was playing the piano.

Resolutely, her back rigid and her facial muscles tensed, Ellen went down the stairs and toward the source of the sound. As a means of controlling the angry cry of protest that threatened to burst out of her throat, as a means of overcoming the desire to turn about, to flee back up the stairs and into her study, to throw shut the door and fling herself on the couch, clamp her palms to her ears, she tried to decide what it was he was playing, who had written it, what tendencies the work represented and whether she had ever heard it before.

The piece was not by D—: of this much she was certain. It showed none of his characteristic mannerisms: his love of the long line, his extreme modulations, his intervallic melodies. Nor was the harmony spare – lean and pared – enough for Hindemith. The intent of the piece was satirical – just listen to that banal reprise! – and, occasionally, there was a lilt to it. It seemed to combine the worst features of both jazz and European folk material. But its composer's identity escaped her.

She walked into the library, still straining with the effort to hold herself in, and saw her husband struggling with the piano. His body pranced and danced – it looked as if it might be being jerked this way and that by a puppeteer's invisible strings – fought the keyboard with huge, hammering motions. And when he came to a gentle passage – this was a slow dirge that remembered the blues – instead of relaxing, he only returned to a state of readiness, as a wire, that has been vibrating but is now still, even in its stability cannot be said to be at rest, since its very shape and aspect belie the phrase. His hands now picked out the mournful notes as the claws of a crab grasp and roil the sand of a beach; suddenly his fingers poised for the attack – his shoulders hunched, she thought she could see his muscles heave under his coat – and as they dived into the ranks of the keys, like fleshly bombers strafing a column of ivory soldiers, the crude, bumptious rhythm rocked again, the melody of the dance returned, and he ended with a catastrophic cadence that hung about and pestered her even as he turned around, tossed his head and smiled at her, acknowledged her presence.

'What is it, Basil?' she asked. 'I know it – I'm sure I've heard it many times before – the name seems to be on the tip of my tongue, but I just cannot say it.'

He came to her and clamped his hand over hers, his touch gentle but his gesture authoritative. 'It's by Shostakovich,' he said.

'Of course – how could I forget! An early work, isn't it? A rustic dance, a polka. From "The Age of Gold"?'

He nodded his head and smiled more widely. How he adores my interest! she thought. He must have it, mustn't he? What would he do if he were ignored, unable to attract anyone's attention? Or, worse than that, what would he do if he had to live alone?

'Have you been lonely, Basil?' she asked, shyly.

He had taken his pipe from his pocket and was cramming it into his pouch. Her question arrested the movement of his hands. 'Why do you ask that?'

'Oh, I don't know. It occurred to me, I suppose. I wondered.' She looked at him straightly, her eyes on his, to hide the confusion his response had forced upon her. His question had been the kind Dr Danzer asked: direct, unexpected, at first, seemingly incongruous, but later, obviously insight's entering wedge.

And he kept after her. 'But you were just talking about music,' he said, 'trying to identify that piece I played. And then, suddenly, you asked me if I have been lonely. Why?'

She laughed. 'The next I know you'll be giving me word associations and asking me what I dreamed last night. Honestly, it just occurred to me and I asked. Perhaps it was the way you played that quiet part. You made it sound like a dirge when it's supposed to be comic . . .'

His fingers returned to their task and finished packing his pipe. Slowly he put the stem into his mouth, struck a kitchen match against the rough cloth of his trouser. She felt that he did not believe her, and she hardly blamed him. Too many times in the past when she had wanted to lie, when her whole self had insisted that she protect it with a falsehood, she had not been able to bring it off. She could tell him the truth even yet – it would do her no harm. But it would hurt him, and uselessly; he was intelligent, sensitive, he would recognize the perspicuity of her observation, would be forced to admit to himself – although he might shrug it off in front of her – his own weakness.

'You still haven't answered my question,' she remarked lightly. 'Perhaps there's a reason why you don't want to answer it?' She walked to the table and took a cigarette from the silver box, looking back at him, her lashes lowered, over her shoulder.

'Of course,' he said. 'Of course, I've missed you. I've missed you very much.'

She averted her eyes, walked to his desk and picked up the massive silver cigarette lighter that lay upon it, busied herself with the ritual of igniting her cigarette. Now that he had said what she had wanted him to say, she was embarrassed. She felt foolish and slightly wary. Not that she did not believe him – he had been lonely, he must have been lonely. But he had not said it until she forced him to, and there was something in this fact that made her wish that he would leave the room, go away from her for a short while.

Instead, Basil came over to her and stood beside her. He looked down at the desk and rested his hand upon it. 'Did you find your key?'

'No, I haven't. And I've looked every place I can think of!'

'You may look in my desk if you wish. I'm afraid I was rude before.'

'No, thank you. I'm sure you would have found it if it were there.'

He shook his head and looked away from her. From the way he held his shoulders, the unexpected slump of his bent head, she knew that he was about to apologize. Her embarrassment left her, giving place to a feeling of warmth, of sympathy. He has lied to me, she thought, and now he is sorry.

'If you didn't want to look for the key, you didn't have to tell me that you had – that it wasn't there,' she said.

He jerked around. 'How do you know I didn't look?'

She put her hand on his shoulder. 'By the way you stood. By the way you held your head.'

'I sat down at the desk to look,' he admitted. 'But then I saw what seemed to be an error in the part for the bassoon. I started to study it, and I forgot. When you came in and asked me, I didn't want to tell you that I had forgotten. I get stubborn streaks, you know.'

'I know.'

'We could look now. Together.'

'In a moment,' she said. She laid her face against the roughness of his coat, the hardness of his shoulder. Her hand clenched his lapel, his breath was warm and tickling on her neck. 'In a moment will be soon enough.'

*

But when they looked through his desk, they did not find the key. She was not surprised – in fact, she had expected it. After all, what did it matter? Tomorrow she would have a new key made. But Basil, his interest aroused, insisted that Suky must have it.

'It must be in the house,' he said. 'Suky has been most careful of that instrument of yours. He's polished it lovingly every single day.'

They went to the kitchen, arm in arm, and confronted the man-servant again. Suky bowed, and backed away; he was more polite than ever, but he did not have the key. Basil questioned him closely, and Suky answered in detail; his precise, aspirate speech seemed eager to her, solicitous.

469

Yet when I asked him, he seemed hostile, she reminded herself – or did I just imagine that?

Before she could think this through, Basil had turned and pushed his way past the swinging doors that led to the dining-room and the hall. The dining-room, the buffet, the curious little drawer in the buffet where she had always stuck those things you kept because they did not seem to be quite the sort of things you threw away – why hadn't she thought of looking there before? Good for Basil! Now, she was sure, he would find the key!

But he did not. He found an old penknife which he said he thought he had lost months ago, some spare parts for his oboe, a tube for the radio. Somehow these unrelated objects made them feel sad, made them remember that they had once been younger – although they were not yet old – symbolized the difference between then and now. Or so *I* think, she said to herself. How can I know what Basil thinks, what makes him look sad (if he is looking sad – he may not be; it may only be that his mouth, with his head half-turned aside as it is now, is shadowed), unless I ask? And if I ask, how will I know that he is telling me the truth? Not that he would lie deliberately, out of malice or for selfish reasons, but just that he might prefer not to confess an emotion he would rather keep to himself. But, then, how does one ever know, since it is impossible to live inside any other skull but one's own, how can one ever tell?

Again she had to drop the discourse, abandon the question, leave her own inquisition in the lurch. Basil had walked abruptly out of the dining-room, down the hall, was standing by the stairs and was gazing at the console table.

'You looked in there, didn't you?' he asked her, without turning around.

'Yes,' she said, and he began to climb the stairs – 'I'm sure it isn't there' – and went up the stairs behind him.

They looked in her room, in the closets, the drawers, in

a trunk and some old suitcases. They went through his room and even the guest-room, but they found nothing. When they had finished, their hands were dusty and her body ached, her eyes were tired from bending over, pulling out, looking, always looking, peering, expecting to see, to touch, to discover, something that was never there.

At last even Basil gave up. They were in the hall, outside her study. He laughed and drew her to him and said, 'Well, Ellen, I suppose you were right. You'll have to wait until tomorrow and have a new one made. Unless –' He stopped and looked past her, stared at the door of her study. 'You know,' he said, 'that's one place we haven't searched.'

She smiled at his egotism. 'But I did, silly. At the very start. I looked there several times in every nook and cranny. That's the one place I'm absolutely certain it couldn't be!'

He patted her head. 'Just the same, I'm going to see.' And he pushed past her, walked in front of her into the rose-walled room. She saw him go to the harpsichord – he did not gaze around, but went straight to it – she saw him pause in front of it, standing between her and it. He did not bend down, he did not touch the instrument. But he did emit a low, unmusical whistle. Then she was at his side.

The key, looking just as she had visualized it, was in the lock. She reached out and touched it; it was real. She turned it, felt the tumblers click, softly, easily, lifted the lid, doubling it back on itself slowly so as not to scratch its polished surface. The two manuals, two banks of black and white steps to Parnassus, lay before her eyes. She reached forward, fingered a note, and heard an A twang its call to order. Her fingers stretched, she sighed, she played a major triad, a scale, a bar or two of Anna Magdalena's sarabande.

Basil spoke, as if from a distance, although he was right beside her: 'You know, darling, it must have been there all the time . . .' His blue eyes were intently upon her, his forehead was wrinkled, his wide mouth was partly open, expectant. In a moment he will laugh at me, she thought. She hated him, and she slapped his face hard.

3

She had felt it before seeing it, felt the yielding warmth of flesh beneath her outstretched, clawing fingers, felt the sting of pain that set fire to her taut skin, felt her nails scrape his cheek. But when she opened her eyes – she was dreaming, yet in the dream she opened her eyes – she saw her hand outspread before her, saw, to her horror, that the blow she had struck had opened a great hole in his face, revealed a view, a distant, beguiling perspective, that peeped between the lattices of her fingers. Suddenly it was as if his face had ceased to exist, as if the slap of her hand had swept away a barrier that had stood between her and another scene, and she walked between her fingers, seeking what lay beyond, Basil, behind her, following her . . .

'That night I dreamed of striking Basil,' she said, her eyes on the slatted light and dark of the venetian blind, her ears fretted by the sibilant sound the doctor's pencil made as it glided over the pages of his notebook. 'It was most realistic. I actually felt the blow. My hand stung, my nails dug into his cheek. and then I looked at my hand and – how shall I describe this? – it was so very strange – it seemed as if my slap had split his face apart, although there was no blood, no flesh or tissue to be seen. What I saw instead was a vista, a long, narrowing perspective, and something – I could not be sure of what it was, it was too far away, too vague – something that I wanted to see more closely, that aroused my curiosity, existed there in the distance. But my hand was still between me and this – this vista – I saw it only between my fingers, the way a child peeps at a strange and fascinating sight. I remember worrying about this, thinking, "If I take my hand away

473

the vista will be gone, but if I don't my hand will always stay between me and it." Then, before I had stopped worrying, I decided to walk through my hand – I remember smiling to myself and saying, "Now, you know, this is impossible; it can happen only in a dream" – but, despite my scepticism, I did walk through my own hand, and Basil did, too. He was right behind me.'

She paused and looked around the doctor's consulting-room. They sat in chairs that were placed at a comfortable distance from each other. They might have been friends, talking. There were some books in the room, not many. The lighting was soft and came from bulbs hidden in the moulding. Dr Danzer slouched in his chair, his knees crossed, his notebook balanced on his knee-cap; most of the time he did not look at her, but kept his eyes on the page, on his writing. She snapped open her purse and took a battered pack of cigarettes from it, shook it until one fell out, then probed with her finger to see how many she had left. There were one or two more, but she would have to get another pack soon. She had bought a carton Sunday night, and it was already half-gone. And this was only Wednesday –

'Can you remember more of your dream?' The doctor's question was put quietly, with total lack of emphasis; but it carried full weight just the same. She knew he was reminding her that she must continue, that she must leave nothing out – that there could be no evasion.

'I remember walking faster,' she said. 'I remember wanting to get away from Basil, but when I walked faster, he did, too. Soon we were both running. And yet it wasn't like any running I had ever done before. My feet seemed hardly to touch the earth, each of my strides covered many yards, but there was no sensation of great effort, I did not breathe heavily, I felt no wind on my face.

'We ran for a long time. Although I had gone through the hole because I had wanted to reach the vague object I had seen in the distance, when Basil followed me I forgot my original intention. All I could think of was trying to

474

escape him. I kept on running and running, and it seemed that the longer my strides were, the closer came the sounds of his footfalls. Then, all at once, they stopped; I heard nothing. I ran a few more paces before I stopped, too. I turned around slowly, half-afraid to face Basil. But he wasn't there. He had disappeared!

'And, while I was still recovering from the shock of his disappearance, I began to be aware that the scene around me was changing. The distance was closing in on me. The sky, the ground, everything was shrinking, rapidly growing smaller everywhere I looked. I put my hand to my mouth to keep from screaming. I shut my eyes, thinking, "If I am going to be squeezed to death I would rather not see it happen." But I did not die. I waited a long time, expecting from moment to moment to feel a great weight begin to press in on me from all sides, to feel myself crushed in an inexorably contracting vice. But nothing happened and, after another long wait during which I gathered up my courage, I opened my eyes.

'I found myself back in my own room, standing in front of my chest of drawers. I had one of the drawers open and was staring into it, looking for something. Basil was still behind me. I remember thinking, "So I didn't escape him, after all. He didn't disappear. He came here before me, that's all." And then, as I thought this, Basil spoke to me. He said, "Ellen, why do you keep looking for it, expecting to find it? You know that you're looking for something that isn't there, that hasn't been there for a long time, if it was ever there at all." And I looked, and he was right – it wasn't there.'

She stopped speaking. Her lips were dry and her throat ached. She closed her eyes and let her head sag into her hands. Thinking about the dream again depressed her, made her want to get out of the doctor's room, out into the street, into the open air. As she recalled, the sun had been shining and there had been a breeze.

'That's all?'

'Yes. Then I woke up.'

475

'You are sure you can remember nothing else? There isn't some little detail that you didn't tell me because you thought it really didn't matter? These little details can be very important, you know.'

'No. That is all I remember.'

'Hmm.' Dr Danzer sat forward in his chair, shutting his notebook and laying it aside on the table. 'Let us see. One thing is certain. The beginning of the dream – the slapping of your husband – was merely a re-enactment of something that had happened that day. Isn't that true?'

She nodded her head. The doctor was smiling inquiringly, as if he almost expected her to say to him, 'No, that isn't the way it was! How can you be so stupid?' What would he say if she did say that? But she said nothing, just kept nodding her head.

'And what do you think is the significance of the opening up of the wound, the running through the aperture, the pursuit?' he asked kindly.

'I suppose you would say that was a womb symbol. That I was expressing a desire to escape from reality.'

He stood up and walked over to her. 'A natural desire at this time. You must remember, Ellen, that you have been ill. You have lived in a small world, a world that was fitted to your needs. Now you are back in New York, and it is very different. A little frightening, perhaps. Oh, you won't admit it to yourself. When you talk to yourself you are brave. But when you dream at night, then it is different.' He turned and looked at the darkened window. 'Tell me, Ellen, what was the object that you saw in the distance? The thing you saw and wanted to reach. What did it look like?'

'It was a harpsichord,' she said, hating him for the way he managed to pull secrets from her, hating him for the time it took to say the words. But afterwards she was ashamed of herself and she smiled guiltily.

'So, after slapping your husband's face, you tried to run away from him to your harpsichord. But he ran after you and wouldn't let you escape.'

'And I never reached the harpsichord,' she said. 'Even after he disappeared I could not find it. And then things began to close in on me, and I shut my eyes. When I opened them I was in my room, looking in my drawer, searching for something. Basil was beside me, saying it was not there – whatever it was I was looking for.'

'What do you think it was?' Dr Danzer asked.

She thought about his question before answering. She had not told him yet about the search for the key on Sunday. It had been such a silly thing to do – to think she had lost that key when it had been there right before her eyes all the time. Why should she tell him? She didn't have to tell him everything, did she?

'Haven't you any idea of what you were looking for?' the doctor asked again.

'I might have been looking for the key to my harpsichord,' she said with impulsive honesty. He knows that if he only asks me enough questions I'll tell him everything, she said to herself. Why can't I keep a secret?

'What makes you think that?' he asked.

'I lost the key to my harpsichord Sunday. I looked all afternoon for it. I looked in every drawer and cubby-hole in the house ten times. Then Basil found it – right where it had been all the time – in the keyhole of the harpsichord. I was awfully embarrassed. That's why I slapped Basil's face. He was going to laugh at me!'

'Why do you think you lost that key?'

'I don't know.'

The doctor looked down at her, his finger pointed, touching the arm of her chair. He turned around and walked to the window, stood with his back to it, facing her. He did not speak.

'You think I lost it for a reason? That, perhaps, I didn't want to play my harpsichord? But that's absurd! Why shouldn't I want to play my instrument? For months I've thought of nothing else!'

'You've been practising hard since you came home?'

She felt herself shrink inside, draw up and contract.

Somewhere the cruel teeth of a trap had snapped shut, biting into the gentle flesh of a small, warm, helpless creature. She tensed her jaws to keep her lips from trembling, spoke slowly and carefully, confessed. 'No, I haven't had the chance to practise yet. I've been too busy.'

'I imagine there are a great many things to do, especially since you've been away so long. But I am a little surprised to hear that you haven't played your instrument. You used to talk to me about how you were going to practise six hours each day. Aren't you going to give a concert this fall?'

'Oh, I shall. Every day I've intended to, but there have been so many things to do. I can't begin to tell you. The house! Everything's out of place – everything's upside down –'

She had meant to say more, to tell him about how yesterday had been such a lovely day and she had gone for a walk in the Park in the morning, with no idea in her head that she would be out more than an hour, and had not come back until dusk. Or how Monday she had gone shopping, had gone from store to store, had bought dress after dress; of how today, after she left his office, she had to go to Julio's to meet Nancy for lunch. Nancy had telephoned yesterday and asked her. She could not have refused her husband's own sister, particularly when she knew that Basil must have suggested that she call. It would have been rude.

'Everything is so strange,' she said instead, 'so different from what I had expected it to be,' she said, not knowing why she told him this, not having realized before she spoke that it was true.

'What do you mean?' he asked. 'In what way are things strange?'

'The house,' she said, whispering; 'it's changed. Oh, the furniture is all there, the pictures are in place. But when I look for something, it is never where I expect it to be. And I keep finding . . . finding things.'

'What is it that you find?'

'Little things. Nothing important. Some powder spilled in a drawer. Of a shade I dislike, that I do not remember having used. In the drawer to my vanity. A pocket-book of black leather, a queer, square purse, that I do not remember owning. Little things like that.'

'Have you spoken to your husband about this?'

'No.'

'Why haven't you?'

'He would think it peculiar of me, wouldn't he? He would think that I had forgotten that these things were mine. He might think I was accusing him, mightn't he?'

'Aren't you accusing him? Didn't you accuse him in your dream?'

'Accuse him? Accuse him of what?' She was indignant. Why couldn't Dr Danzer ever come out and say what he was thinking? Why did he always have to imply his meanings, make her say them to him?

'Isn't that for you to say, Ellen?' he asked.

'I don't know what you're talking about.'

The doctor placed his hand over his eyes, pressed it against his brow. He hesitated before he spoke, as if he wanted to make sure of what he would say next, think it over in his mind and phrase his thought exactly, make his precise intention clear.

'Ellen,' he said, 'at the end of your dream, when you were back in your own room and Basil was standing beside you, when you had failed in your attempt to escape him and reach your harpsichord, what did he say to you? I could go to my notes, you know, and read your own words of a few minutes ago back to you. But I think it would mean more to you – in this particular context – if you would speak them again. What did your husband say to you in your dream?'

She shut here eyes and saw again her bedroom, the chest of drawers. She was looking down into a disordered drawer, a drawer in which powder – pink powder of a disgraceful shade – had been spilled. And she could feel

Basil's presence beside her – if she looked up she would see his face in the mirror. And he was saying . . .

'He said, "You know that you are looking for something that isn't there, that hasn't been there for a long time, if it was ever there at all." ' The words came out of her mouth haltingly, seemed unnatural to her lips. A part of her cried, you have never said anything like that – you have never dreamed anything like that – it isn't true! But another part of her, the cold, reasoning faculty, knew that what her mouth reported was unequivocally true.

The doctor nodded his head, 'And what do you think this means?'

'I was afraid I had lost something. The whole dream was about losing, wasn't it? I had lost something – something that was connected with Basil, something I may never have had. Although I kept looking for it as if I had it.'

She was silent, waiting for him to speak. But he did not speak, just as he never spoke at any of the difficult times. 'It has all to come from you,' he had often said. 'You know what it is, only a part of you keeps it well hidden. But you only have to think and it will come to you.'

'In my dream I ran away from Basil – ran to my harpsichord. But Basil kept running after me and, even after he disappeared, I never found my harpsichord. Could it have been my harpsichord I was looking for?'

'In a drawer?'

'Perhaps it was the key to my harpsichord that, in reality, I looked for in the drawer. In my dream the harpsichord might have stood for the key, just as in life the key stands for the harpsichord.'

'And where does this lead us?'

Basil. Basil had kept running after her, had kept her from reaching her instrument. 'Could it be that in my dream Basil stood between me and my harpsichord, that Basil kept me from playing my instrument?'

'Has Basil ever tried to keep you from playing?' Dr Danzer asked.

'Sometimes I think he resents my taste in music. He likes other things. Great, cacophonous, modern symphonies. He likes D—'s work.'

'But has he ever kept you from your instrument?'

'When I was ill. Before I went to the hospital.'

The doctor smiled and looked away. He said nothing for a few minutes, seemed to wait for her to speak, to add to what she had said. But she refused to speak. Why did he place so much importance on this dream? She had dreamed many more bizarre happenings on other occasions, and he had brushed them aside briskly with a few curt words of explanation. Was he trying to find something wrong? Did he expect her to relapse? She was going to have to be very careful, to choose each word, to deliberate before she spoke.

'Ellen,' he said, looking at her again, smiling, 'you know as well as I why your husband forbade you to play your instrument when you were ill. You know that playing excited you – made you worse. But you haven't answered my question, Ellen. I didn't ask you about before – I know about that, and you know I do. I want to know if Basil tries to keep you from the harpsichord now.'

'No,' she said, speaking slowly. 'He did say that he thought I shouldn't practise too much, that it was too soon for me to give a concert. But he hasn't kept me from it. He even helped me find the key.'

The doctor was lighting his pipe. She watched the ruddy flame come and go as he sucked on the stem, whetting the embers. Then he exhaled a thick, dark cloud that swam lazily towards her and made her want to cough. 'And what about the dream, Ellen? What were you looking for in the drawer?'

'Something I had lost.'

'But what had you lost? Say whatever comes into your mind. Quickly now!' His voice was all at once surprisingly sharp and peremptory.

And she responded. 'Basil,' she said, without thinking –

481

just when she had promised herself to be most careful, to examine every word she was about to say, to weigh its consequences. 'Basil,' she repeated, dismayed at how easily her mind could become a traitor, how like an old circus dog it was, a shaggy old dog who jumped and did his trick whenever the ringmaster snapped his whip. How well you have me trained, Dr Danzer! she thought, scornfully.

'You were afraid you had lost Basil? His love, you mean?'

'Yes, I suppose.' Unfortunately, he was right. He was always right. That was what her dream had been about. She had been afraid that Basil no longer loved her, that two years had been too long . . .

'Have you any reason to suspect that your husband doesn't love you?'

The doctor spoke quietly now, as if he, too, were ashamed of the trick he had forced her to perform. Now, if I were an old dog, he'd give me a lump of sugar and scratch me behind the ears, she thought, smiling wryly to herself.

'No,' she said; 'he has been very attentive, very loving. But –' And she could not continue.

'But there is something wrong, something has changed – is that it?' Dr Danzer asked. 'He is nice to you, he obviously loves you – or he says he does – but he isn't the way you remember him. Am I right?'

'Yes,' she said. 'That is the way it has been.'

The doctor stood up, surveyed the room, moved his hand back and forth in the half-light. When he was sure her eyes were upon him, he strode to the window, tugged at the controlling cords, threw open the shutters. Bright, blinding, yellow-white, noonday sun scourged the darkness from the room. The doctor turned his eyes away from the dazzling window, blinked at her. 'It is not the same, is it?' he inquired.

'No,' she said, 'it is not the same.' And she stood up to go because when he opened the windows in his hospital office it had always been a sign that the interview was ended.

But he waved his hand at her, indicating that she should sit down again. 'Isn't it a beautiful day!' he said.

She nodded her head. Actually, the sun was so bright it made her head ache. 'I hadn't realized how intense the sunlight was,' she said. 'I think it was a little cloudy when I came in. Or I was thinking about seeing you and I did not notice the weather.'

'But now you notice it,' he said. 'First, you know it has changed. Then, you begin to wonder how it has changed. "Was it cloud before? It hasn't been raining, I'm sure. Was the sun this bright or has it grown brighter? Perhaps, I didn't notice how it was when I came – I was too preoccupied." That's the way you talk to yourself. And all the time it is a beautiful day, but you are too worried about how it has changed to enjoy it.'

Now she did stand up. Now she would go. 'You mean that you think I worry too much about things – that I'm too introspective?'

He came forward and took her hand in his. It was the first time he had done this. He looked at her, hesitantly, as if he might look down at any moment. 'I think you are a little anxious, wary – that you have stage-fright. Don't you?'

'Yes,' she said, 'I suppose I am.'

He withdrew his hands, stuffed them into his pockets so that his jacket bulged comically. But the expression on his face was serious. 'Ellen,' he asked, 'what if your husband had fallen in love with someone else? Would that be so terrible?'

'Oh,' she said, 'I've given you the wrong impression. I don't think he has. It was just a silly dream.'

'There is no such thing as a silly dream, Ellen.'

'I mean I was just being neurotic. It isn't true. Basil loves me very much.' What he had said had embarrassed her, and she had begun to back towards the door. If she could only think of something casual to say, something

483

about the weather. 'You know,' she said, 'I lied to you a moment ago. I did notice that the sun was shining brightly before I came here. I don't know what made me say that I thought it was cloudy.'

'Ellen,' the doctor said, 'you are evading me again. Would it matter too much if Basil didn't love you?'

'I don't know,' she said. 'I honestly don't know.'

And, having said this, she was no longer frightened. She turned again and regarded the doctor, saw that his manner was as shy as before. 'You know, Ellen,' he was saying, 'your husband might have met someone during those two years. You may be right – he may have changed. You will have to face that fact.'

'I know.'

'But that isn't what matters, Ellen,' he said. 'Basil is not you. You are you. You cannot run away from yourself. You must live with yourself, take your life as it comes.'

'Yes, I know. But I really don't think – I don't know, of course – but I don't think that Basil –'

'I'm not saying he has, Ellen. I'm not saying he will. I'm just saying that you must not be afraid of change.'

'I understand, doctor. Thank you. Good-bye.'

'Good-bye, Ellen. Speak to Miss Nichols about your next appointment as you leave, will you, please? I think next month will be soon enough – you know you may always telephone me if you need me.'

She closed the door on his voice, without turning back, and walked up to Miss Nichols' desk. As she waited for the nurse to stop writing and look up, she realized for the first time that she was crying.

Julio's was not yet crowded – she had arrived a little before the popular time – and she found a table on the terrace. From where she sat she could see the zoo in Central Park, the masses of children in their brightly coloured clothes weaving back and forth, the shaggy ponies pulling gaudy carts, the red and blue balloons tugging at their cords high above a vendor's stand. It was so beautiful, so lively and appealing, that she found herself willing to sit still and do nothing but search for details in the shining scene, details that she was sure were there if she only had the perseverance to find them: the lost child – there was always a lost child at a zoo, wasn't there? – the barking seals, the monkey house.

Nancy was late; but, then, Nancy was usually late. She had never really learned to like her husband's sister, although at one time they had been friendly enough; but she did not dislike her either. To her Nancy was one of those people who make up the preponderant part of anyone's acquaintanceship, that she thought of as being neither pleasant nor unpleasant, attractive nor unattractive, whom she could ignore or accept as she wished. Basil was fond of Nancy, and for this reason she had used to see her frequently, and now probably would again. Nancy was brusque and unfeminine, careless and off-hand, chattering. Sometimes her aimless talk was like a knife drawn across a china plate: it set her teeth on edge. She hoped that today would not be one of those times, today, when the sight of the zoo made her feel rested and acquiescent, when she would be so glad to leave off thinking, to detach herself from the bustle of the city and the problems of her return to life.

The waiter came, and she ordered a drink, something cooling and frothy which she had often seen others have but until that moment had not had the gumption to ask for herself. And as she turned her gaze back to the park, settled her vision once more on the kaleidoscope of children and animals, balloons and buildings, a small wisp of pink caught her eye and a thready shriek, interrupted by the gusty breeze, pricked her ear. She saw the blue coat, the foreshortened, stooping back of a policeman bending down to comfort a small girl, a child with gold curls and a tam, stalk-like legs and a starchy dress. The little girl was lost – who could doubt it? – the policeman had found her; perhaps her cries had led him to her. Now he was patting her head, consoling her, telling her not to worry, that everything would be all right, that mama would come for her soon.

The waiter set her drink down on the table, and she turned her eyes away from the scene to take a sip, to taste it and see if she was going to like it, to be disappointed because it was so sweet. When she looked back, the wisp of pink and the patch of blue were gone, the kaleidoscope had whirled again and a different pattern met her eye. She felt sad and, almost, bereft. The lost child, for the briefest of instants, had been a part of her; they had shared an alienation, been united in distress. But now the spell was broken and the park became just another park with a small, cluttered zoo, and she was a silly woman, wasting time while waiting for a friend, drinking a sweet concoction that she did not like and should have known better than to order.

'Darling! You look so sad, and on such a sunny day, too. Whatever is the matter?' Nancy had arrived, her hands flying in wild gestures as she spoke, her eyes inquiring and aggressive, her teeth clenching an over-long jade holder from which a half-burnt cigarette drooped. 'Whatever are you drinking? Pop?'

Nancy flopped down on the chair on the opposite side of the small, green, metal table, crouched and began to fumble with something. She kept making cooing noises, saying, 'Now, now, sweetums – hold still! – now, ooh, isn't he the sweetest thing! – hold still, damn you – there, there!' Ellen looked over the table to see what was happening, and only then did she realize that Nancy had brought her dog along, a small animal of some obscure breed with outlandish ears and a frisky disposition. Nancy was busily tying a leash to one of the table-legs while her pet fretted at it, chewed her hand, growled playfully. 'That's Dangerous,' said Nancy. 'Isn't he sweet?'

'Why do you call him Dangerous?' she asked. 'He looks like he is only a puppy to me.'

Nancy had at last fastened the leash to the table, and

now she assumed a proper posture. 'He is only a puppy,' she said. 'He is only six months old. But he is Dangerous all the same. He likes to chew my canvas and paint-brushes. He has a frightful temper.'

This was going to be worse than she had supposed. Had Nancy been this exuberant before? Or was she putting on a show for her, hiding her embarrassment at meeting her again after – after what had happened? She remembered that during all the time she had been at the hospital Nancy had not been to see her once. Not that she had minded. There had been days when she could not have coped with Nancy. But she could not keep from wondering why.

'How have you been, darling? It's so good to see you – it's been such an age! And what is that you're having? You didn't tell me, you know – although I asked. If it's really good I think I'll have one, too. It's such a pretty colour.'

She told her the name of the drink and that she did not recommend it. Nancy beckoned a waiter to her and ordered a martini, 'But dry – very dry. It must be all gin with just a dash – a dash, only a dash, mind you! – of your best vermouth. And a walnut half – just half of a walnut, you know – in place of the olive.'

Nancy seemed older, and slightly grim about the mouth. Her broad, large-featured, peasant's face, which she tried to make look feminine by copious use of rouge and lip-stick, pancake make-up and mascara – but which she only succeeded in making look garish – seemed more than ever to have been crudely hacked from recalcitrant granite. Her hands, that she never quite managed to scrub free of pigment stains, now seized the menu and twisted it side-ways, to catch the light, for her inspection. Her eyes swept over the printed page as they might appraise a model, noting the appetizers, the entrées, the desserts, the anat-omy of luncheon. But her mind returned to her original quest, and she asked, 'Ellen, you look so sad. Is anything wrong?'

'I am a lost child,' she said. 'I am wandering through

the park. I don't know where I am – how I am going to get home.' As she spoke, she smiled, taking a perverse pleasure in confusing practical, down-to-earth Nancy.

'Whatever are you talking about?' Nancy cried. She laid down the menu and regarded Ellen with frank curiosity.

She expects me to be strange, but not this strange, she thought. But she said, 'I was looking at the zoo across the way, and I saw a little girl who was lost – she was crying her heart out. A policeman found her and took her away. But, for a moment, just before you came, I thought I was that child – I felt a little lost, a little sad, myself.'

'Well! I'm glad it isn't anything more than a fancy. I was worried about you when I saw you looking so melancholy. Let me have a taste of that stuff will you? I can't resist its colour. Faugh! It's positively insipid. I'm glad you're drinking it, not me!'

The dog jumped up and created a diversion. First, he had to have his head petted – then, when he began to lick her hands, she had to discipline him, to slap his muzzle and push him down.

'If he doesn't learn when he's young, he'll never obey,' Nancy said.

'And how is the painting, Nancy?' she asked, aware that she must keep the conversation going, keep Nancy well supplied with topics, prevent her from asking questions about herself. For Nancy was a painter, and not a bad one – she had had several shows – although her paintings did not sell and she was forced to live off her brother's generosity. But Ellen knew that Nancy liked to talk about her work, her great, forceful canvases that seemed to stand back and fling the fieriest hues of the spectrum at your eye.

'Oh, well enough,' the woman replied glumly. 'Although I've not sold anything yet this year. Basil says it's because I'm experimenting with Duco. The stuff they use on autos, you know. You spread it thickly on to masonite – it gives you a glistening opacity, a strength and vigour you can't get with anything else.'

'I would think it would be rather gaudy.'

Nancy stretched her hand out across the diminutive table and clasped Ellen's wrist. Her eyes sparkled. 'But, darling, it is! That's the whole point, you see. With it you can paint violently. It forces you to be vigorous, darling. You should see some of the wonderful things the Mexicans have done with Duco.'

'The Mexicans? You mean Riviera?' She tried to concentrate on what Nancy was talking about, as one listens to a parrot's garbled speech intent on discovering what catch-phrase is being cawed so raucously; but her mind kept going back to the doctor's consulting-room. Until now she had forced herself not to think of what the doctor had said, had kept herself from trying to unravel the hidden meaning in his allegory of the sunshine and the changing weather. But it was becoming more difficult, even in the face of her companion's vivacity.

'Not Riviera!' cried Nancy. 'The *real* Mexicans, Orozco. Sequieros. They have done remarkable things. Genuine people's art.'

'Isn't Riviera a real Mexican?' she asked. She remembered when Nancy had been furious about the destruction of the Rockefeller mural, when Riviera had been, for her, the greatest painter alive. Had she changed her mind? It was not really surprising if she had. Wasn't that what Dr Danzer had said? Everything changed. Even Basil. Perhaps, even herself, Ellen.

'But, darling,' Nancy was saying, 'surely you know about that? The great Diego has gone completely commercial – really, the whole hog! Of course, he was always unreliable – politically, I mean. But now he does murals for night clubs in Mexico City to titivate the tourist trade. Great, obscene, maundering things. And when one looks at his other work – what he did before – well, really, you know, one wonders. Yes, one wonders if one hadn't been taken in!'

She had forgotten how readily Nancy's opinions were likely to be influenced by current events – by politics, in fact. Both of them, Basil and Nancy, liked to think themselves liberals, although she sometimes doubted if they understood the meaning of the word. With them it was what everyone was doing that counted; they were adept at scenting out the popular attitude, the trend, and did not scruple to follow it even if it meant the destruction of old gods. They were not afraid of change; but then, they had no roots. They were adrift on the sea of the present, driven on to this or that shoal of opinion by the winds of the moment, by cant and prejudice.

'I thought you liked Riviera?' she asked, to see how her friend would wriggle free from the past, how she would disclaim an old loyalty. 'Didn't you use to paint in his manner? And weren't you one of the group who formed a meeting of protest when Rockefeller refused to let his mural stand in Radio City?'

Nancy laughed and tugged at her dog's leash. 'But, darling, that was ages ago. So much has happened since.' Her eyes widened as she tried to express incredulity. 'One makes mistakes. I'm the first one to admit I do. One's taste changes. I know mine has. One grows, one progresses.'

A car backfired, punctuating her phrase and disturbing her pet, who began to scurry frantically around the table-leg – entangling his mistress and himself in the leash – barking furiously. It all made a very pretty symbol of confusion.

Not until they were having their coffee did Nancy refer to Ellen's illness. Throughout lunch she had continued to talk about her painting, telling anecdotes and gossiping about her friends, many of whom were even more eccentric than herself. Dangerous had kept barking and begging for food. Nancy had at first refused to feed him, slapping at his muzzle and shouting at him to 'Sit down, sir – down, damn you! – will you look at that! – what a pest he is!' But later the dog's constant racket had worn down her desire to train him properly and she had tossed him those morsels which she did not want to eat herself: bits of salad, a chop bone and a corn stick. After pushing them around in a greasy circle with his nose, the puppy had disdained them, too, until the waiter had stooped to retrieve them – then he had growled and snapped and created an even greater disturbance.

He was yapping again now, as they sipped the coffee. Nancy ignored him and smiled at Ellen. 'It must be good to be back in New York after so long a time,' she said. 'But tell me, don't you find everything just a little strange?'

She had been looking out at the Park, watching the trees and bushes sway in the breeze; Nancy's question startled her. For an instant she thought she was back in the doctor's office, facing the glaring sun that streamed through the window, trying to distinguish his face against the bright background. But when she turned around, she realized it was Nancy who had spoken.

'What do you mean?' she asked.

'Oh, I don't know. When I've been away and then come back, I'm always slightly dismayed to find that nothing is ever quite as it was before. The impression isn't the same; but, then, it's never different enough for me to know what has changed – if anything has changed. Doesn't it seem that way to you?'

She nodded her head. 'Nothing seems to fit,' she admitted. For it was an admission; when she thought about it she felt guilty and wanted to keep it to herself. Then, remembering that Nancy was Basil's sister, she added hastily, 'Basil hasn't changed, though. He is just the same.'

Nancy's mouth opened in surprise, and at the same time her eyelids dropped until they all but covered her eyes, She put down her coffee-cup with a small clatter and shifted uneasily in her chair. 'Is he, really?' she asked.

She pretended not to notice Nancy's surprise. She picked up her own cup deliberately and held it to her lips, but it was only with difficulty that she opened her mouth and swallowed the hot coffee. 'But that may be because I haven't stopped seeing Basil,' she said, watching her companion closely. 'He came to the hospital every visiting day, you know. He was very good about it.'

Nancy started to smile, and then stopped. 'Of course, you are the best judge of that, darling,' she said, speaking slowly and not unkindly. 'If I were you, though, I'd expect some change. Men are queer animals.'

She laughed and the sound of her laughter annoyed her because it was forced and discordant. 'You forget that Basil is so wrapped up in his music that he isn't likely to know what goes on around him for months at a time. Unless, that is, you know something I don't know . . .' She paused, trying to decide whether to ask the question she wanted to ask and, if she did decide to ask it, whether to pose it bluntly or casually as if it did not matter. Then, before she had decided, she laughed again, this time even more loudly and harshly than before. And the question asked itself – she certainly had not willed it, the words, as they came out one by one, seemed strange to her, and the voice that spoke them did not seem her own. 'He hasn't fallen in love with someone else, has he, Nancy? That isn't what you're trying to tell me, is it?' And her fingers stretched themselves compulsively, her nails scored the table-cloth, her body trembled.

Nancy's face turned serious, but only for a moment. Then she was smiling again, while she looked in her purse for a comb and a mirror with one hand and patted her hennaed bob with the other. 'Darling, how should I know that?' she asked. 'I'm only his sister. I'd be the last to know.'

Nancy lived in a tall apartment building that overlooked Washington Square. Basil paid the rent for the roomy studio, which had great, wide windows and a skylight, just as he paid most of her other bills. The furnishings, however, were old and well-worn; they had come from their mother's home in Connecticut and were sufficiently out of date to be fashionable. Nancy had arranged them with an artist's talent for dramatic effect – everything faced the huge windows, viewed the Square; only her easel turned its back on the sky. So, when one sat on the ponderous horsehair sofa, as Ellen was doing now, one felt as if one had been launched into space, catapulted from the earth to the clouds, delicately suspended in the empyrean.

She did not know why she had come home with Nancy. It had not been her intent to stay with her any longer than was necessary; when they had finished their coffees at Julio's and were squabbling over who should take the check, she had been on the point of remembering another appointment, of making her excuses and abandoning Nancy. There had not been another appointment, of course; what she had wanted to do was to walk in the Park, visit the zoo, wander freely for a couple of hours. Yet when her companion had suggested that they find a taxi and come down to the Village – 'I want you to see my new canvases, Ellen – I want your opinion on one of them' – she had nodded her head and agreed. It was not that she had wanted to be with Nancy – if anything she had wanted to escape her – but Nancy's mysterious manner, her off-hand warning, when coupled with the doctor's parable, had whetted her curiosity and encouraged her insecurity. If I stay with her, she had reasoned – sensing as she thought this that her reasoning was merely after-the-fact rationalization and that it was fear that was her true motivation – she will keep on chattering and may say something else that is even more meaningful, that will let me know where I stand with Basil.

But Nancy had been more taciturn during the drive down-town. After having given the address to the cab-driver, she had settled back on the seat with her pet in her lap and had passed the time stroking his back and patting his head. When they reached the tall building and had gone up in the elevator to one of the topmost floors, Nancy had unlocked the door to the apartment, ushered her into the studio, taken her hat and wrap and disappeared.

Ellen was still waiting for her to return, facing the great blue deeps of sky, clotted with massive cloud-formations, that disrupted her equilibrium and all but convinced her that she hung perilously above the pit of the world, staring down into it with sickening dismay, beckoned by its immensity, taunted and harried into flinging herself down, down, down, to destruction. But I am only sitting on a comfortable sofa looking out of a high window, she cajoled herself, stretching her legs forward, making them long and tenuous, ambiguous appendages. I could not throw myself out and down from here. I would first have to stand and walk to the sill, to loosen the catch, lift and climb and heave. All I need do is to remain calm and quiet on the sofa, to shut my eyes and pretend I have not seen the sky; after all, this feeling is nothing new, I have fought it off many times before.

But when she shut her eyes, she saw the lattice-work, the diamonds of sun and stripes of darkness, the cool green facets of lawn and elms; and she remembered the helplessness of that other vista, the caged loneliness, the night panic. The blackness crept upon her, shutting out even the image of the bars, smothering her, forcing her breath to rush past her teeth, her mouth to part and moan. She opened her eyes again, quickly turning her head about, by this legerdemain avoiding the window and the immeasurable view. She found herself looking backward towards the hall that led to the other rooms, listening to a queer scribbling sound, a rapid scuffle, as if death had resorted to little feet, to rat's claws and a tinkly bell. Her mouth still open, her eyes fixed in terror, she tried to rise, to jump up, to scream. But her position was an awkward one, her body was twisted and her legs, still outstretched, acted as props rather than levers. She was caught and held, pinioned by her own limbs, a cold, anonymous hand caressed her spine, her throat was contracted and numb, incapable of speech. If I weren't so frightened, I would be amused, a part of her thought – the cynic inside her who could only scoff – for I have tricked myself into being my own jailer. But the scrabbling sound came nearer, mixed now with an aspirate murmur, a hideous snuffling, seemed behind her, every moment nearer, at her feet. I cannot bear it any longer, she told herself, her fingers prodding into the hard weave of the upholstery, her back arched and cataleptic in its effort to shrink away from the source of the sound – and she made one last effort to swerve around, remembering this time to attempt to bend her legs, striving to recall the mechanics of sitting up, of changing one's position, but frustrated again by the stiff hasps of her knees. And then the horror touched her, a cold, tiny wetness at the ankles – the black mists swam before her eyes. A coarse, grating noise, sharp like a gun's cough, broke the silence. And reason returned, mingling for a moment with confusion's retreat – as sun and rain exist together on a summer's day; she went limp and at the same moment blindly reached out a hand, felt backward and downward, still too panicky to turn – not yet remembering how to face about, reached short, bristly fur and a cold nose just at the time Nancy bustled into the room, a tray with a decanter and glasses on it in her hands, crying, 'Dangerous! Where did you go? Where did you scamper to, you nasty thing? Oh, there you are, you brute! Why, you've frightened Ellen!'

She began to giggle, her hand at her mouth to hide her grimacing lips and stifle the witless sound; her body, released from the tension of terror, went limp; she felt herself to be a grinning rag doll out of which the stuffing had leaked. Nancy turned from berating the dog, from setting the tray on a low table, to a proper, social concern over her fright, sat beside her on the high, old sofa, chafed her hands and smoothed her brow. 'He really is a nasty thing,' she said. 'What did he do? Jump at you and make an awful fuss? There's nothing to his tantrums, you know. All bluff and bluster. All you need do is scowl at him and he sulks. Just look at him now!'

And it was true. The absurd puppy, abashed by his mistress's voice, was crawling towards them on his belly, his tongue lolling, his eyes idiotic with craven humility. The sight was sobering, and she managed to stop laughing, although the obvious harmlessness of the animal that had frightened her so badly made her wonder again. Was there something, still undiscovered, that lay beneath the surface of her mind, hidden except on occasion when some accidental association – what had it been this time? the blue depths of the sky? the memory of the barred window? the blackness of the past? – allowed it to bob up into consciousness, a submerged monument resting on an unknown foundation, a landmark of her disorder? And if there were something there, something not so remote that it could, in an instant, come near and overwhelm her, how might she get to know it and, by knowing it, vanquish it? Would the old trick suffice, the pretended separation of judgement from emotion? Could she stand aside, even now, and inspect herslf, lying flaccid on the sofa, listening to Nancy's cooing noises, discover the flaw and eradicate it? No, she could not; for once she was certain that it was impossible – and, what was more to the point, she did not want to.

The dog, laboriously creeping, had reached their feet, and Nancy stooped to pet him. Her touch was magic, galvanic, transforming his propitiation into ecstasy; with demonic verve he began to yelp and cavort, to chase his tail. A shower of chromatic notes sounded in her head as she watched the puppy rejoice; Chopin and his little waltz descended upon her, illogically – or was it logically? he had written it after watching just such a frolic, hadn't he? – and she was able to laugh sensibly at her fright. 'I have been silly, Nancy,' she confessed. 'Please forgive me.'

'But, of course, darling,' Nancy replied, pushing past the dog, who was barking explosively, to grasp the decanter and pour wine into one of the glasses. 'Have a little of this. It will clear your head.'

She had more than a little; she had many glasses. She sat and drank the slightly bitter wine while Nancy displayed her canvases, great red and yellow blots they all seemed – although here and there she descried something, a worker, a building, a conjectural tree–one like another. But she nodded her head and hemmed and hawed over each; several she professed to like particularly; she even made a play of choosing one that she preferred above all the rest. Actually, she did not mind being with Nancy as much as she had supposed; perhaps it was because she had drunk enough wine to be comfortably hazy, or it might simply be that one could grow used to Nancy. And then she was glad for someone's presence; she did not wish to be alone after her fright.

A set of Westminster chimes echoed portentously, and Nancy, who was putting her canvases back in the closet, bending over, pushing, pulling, straightened up and exclaimed, 'That must be Jimmy!'

'Who is Jimmy?' Ellen asked.

But her friend had already run into the hall, leaving behind her the open closet, from which a pile of paintings protruded. Nancy's face had seemed suddenly flushed, from bending over or from embarrassment?

She turned her head towards the door, which Nancy, having opened, was now standing in, effectively hiding whoever had pressed the doorbell from view. They were holding a muttered conversation, or, at least, Nancy was. She was talking rapidly, but not loudly enough to be heard from where Ellen sat. Then, as she watched and strained her ears, the door opened more widely, Nancy backed a few steps, and a man came into the studio. She turned her head quickly – she did not want them to know she had been watching – too quickly to see anything more of him than a shock of uncombed hair. She busied herself with the decanter, pouring herself another glass of the tangy wine, and affected indifference as she heard them walk into the large room.

'Ellen,' said Nancy, 'this is Jimmy. Jimmy is one of my closest friends.'

Stubbornly, only partly out of the shyness that usually

overcame her at the moment of meeting, she at first refused to raise her eyes. She saw only his shoes – shabby, brown oxfords, run down at the heels like *her* Jimmy's. Why did I think that? she asked herself. I haven't thought of him for months. Not that I can't think of him. I can review the whole past, recall every separate incident, with equanimity, even that part. Thinking this, she raised her eyes, looked upward far enough to see a pair of baggy grey flannels, the same kind of unpressed slacks that the Jimmy she had known had always worn. She shut her eyes, then opened them quickly, glanced higher yet, to see a scuffed leather jacket with a zipper down the front, a pair of tanned, short, muscular arms and large thick-fingered hands that lay placidly along the flannels, seeming to contain the thighs, as the jacket wrinkled neatly at the middle, and she was aware, pleasantly and confusedly, that *this Jimmy* had bowed. She blinked again, saying to herself: what an odd way to look at a man! – and then she gazed all the way up at him, expecting to see a new face. *But the face she saw was dead, lying on its cheek, its dark hair tangled on the pillow, its lips drawn back torturously, its eyelids half-opened, as if the dying man had found he could bear only a glimmering of sight. She gasped again and saw the black blood, the battered head . . . she turned again and tried to run but, as once before, she felt the invisible wires that held her up sag and collapse . . . it was not that she was falling, just as it could not possibly be Jimmy who was dead, who had been dead, who is dead, who must be dead, it was not, it could not . . .*

'Damn!' said Nancy. 'She's fainted.' (Her voice came from far away and wavered, rose and fell, repeated itself.)

'Devil take it!' drawled Jimmy. 'Have ah done anything?' (His voice, *his* soft tenor, mingled with the wang of a carelessly picked guitar – contrasted sharply, in jarring counterpoint, with the steely perfection of the harpsichord's falling cadence, so distinct, so distant – his voice hummed, then sang to her against the casual chords that were not chosen, that seemed to be born):

Jimmy crack corn, and ah don't care!
Jimmy crack corn, and ah don't care!
Jimmy crack corn, and ah don't care!
My massa's gone a-waa-ay . . .

*

The strong, assaulting, pungent stench in her nostrils
made her jerk her head back, made her eyes stream with
tears, made her say loudly, 'Now, now, I'm all right!'
But Nancy was pressing the little bottle on her, forcing her
to whiff the ammoniac, saying, 'The poor thing! she's so
on edge – why, just a while ago the puppy barked at her
and nearly frightened her to death!' And the soft, slurred
voice – *his* voice – was saying, 'Ah've had gals makeover
me afore, ma'am – but ah'll swan if that ain't the fust time
one's fainted dead away at the sight of me!' And she sat
up straight – as much to get away from the flask of
smelling-salts as for any other reason – and stared into his
lean, weathered face, the face that had always reminded
her of homespun and worn saddles and, paradoxically, of
cramped rooms, bad air and a blue spotlight, the face she
had thought no longer existed. Now, not knowing what
to do, seeing that Nancy, her ministrations spurned, had
gone away – probably to put the bottle back in the medicine cabinet – she winked at the face. And it winked back,
slowly masking its eye, boldly, dramatically, announcing a
conspiracy.

'You're feeling better, ma'am, ah trust!' he said, even
before finishing the wink.

Ellen withdrew farther along the sofa and Jimmy advanced. She saw that he had brought his guitar – how like
him that was! – and had laid it on the table next to the
decanter. 'Yes, I'm much better now,' she said. 'It was
nothing, really. I've been sick a long time you know, and
I still get a little hazy, sometimes.'

'You must mean dazey, ma'am. You said "hazy".'

'I meant hazy. You see, I've been in a mental hospital.'

'Have you now, ma'am?' He did not pause, but went on with the silly act, pushed her along, maliciously. 'My grandmammy's gone to the State Hospital; but she's old and a little teched. You're not old.'

'Do we have to go on like this, Jimmy? It isn't funny.'

'Ma'am?' His eyes widened, but his mouth was tight to hold back the grin that longed to be there. 'Did ah understand you rightly, ma'am?'

Before she could answer, Nancy was back – Dangerous prancing around her, nipping her skirts – and Jimmy was on his feet again.

'Do sit down,' Nancy said. 'What a fuss you make – you Southerners are all alike! I see you're getting acquainted?' This last to Ellen.

'Yes,' she said, knowing she should say more, that it was imperative that she should say more so that Nancy, of all people, would not suspect. But she could not say anything, only, 'Yes.'

'Jimmy is quite the rage in the Village – all over town, for that matter. He sings folk-songs – the way they really should be sung, not jazzed up. You would like them, Ellen.'

'Yes.' (It was as if she had learned to speak that one word, as if she knew no other – yet it had no meaning, no phrasing, no sound; it was nothing but a mechanical action, a formation of lips, a button pressed, a light lighted.)

'Won't you sing something for us now, Jimmy?' Nancy was trying to be pleasant, but she could see that her curiosity was aroused. *She knows that something has happened, something that I hadn't foreseen – she is wondering what it is.* If he only doesn't sing . . .

He lighted a cigarette and held the match, curling with flame, uncomfortably in his hand as he looked for an ashtray. Nancy, obsequious, ran across the room – the dog barking after her – found one, ran back. Miraculously, he was saying – 'If you'll let me off today, ma'am – ma throat is sore and ah have to do two shows tonight.' He flicked the match into the ashtray, and Nancy, apologetically, snatched the cigarette from his mouth.

'Of course you can't sing! I won't let you!' she cried. 'And I won't let you ruin your throat with those things either. You're just like any other artist – never thinking of the consequences!' She paused and eyed him to see if her tirade had any effect.

He stood up, drawled, 'Ah can still plunk a *gui*tar, ma'am.' And, before Ellen realized what was happening, he had swung his yellowed instrument over his shoulder, let his large hand pass over its strings, while another depressed them at the fret. The melody began, gravely – a little self-consciously – but right, beautifully right, sounding just as it should, spacious, balanced, a form within a form, a line of thought . . .

'Why!' exclaimed Nancy, 'that's lovely! But it isn't a folk-song, is it? I mean, really?'

'No, ma'am,' he said, ducking his head – sometimes he carries the act a shade too far, she thought, but oh, does it get results! 'That ain't a folk-song. A feller told me Bach wrote that.'

She stood up. Now was as good a time to make a break as any. 'I'm sorry, Nancy, but I really have to go. My head, you know.' And she regarded him, standing, slouching, looking at her coolly. 'I'm glad to have met you, Mr – Mr?'

'Shad, ma'am. Jim Shad. Just call me Jimmy.'

She had to keep up the pretence. 'You play beautifully, Mr Shad. Do you know all the Goldberg Variations?'

'All thirty-two, ma'am.'

'Well, really, I must be going. Perhaps I can come again.'

Then Nancy: 'I don't know what I'm thinking about. Ellen, you can't go alone! Why, you've already fainted twice this afternoon. Jimmy, you go along with her – take her to her door. I insist!'

And Shad, grinning, his guitar hitched over his shoulder, said, 'I been intendin' to, ma'am.'

She did not trust herself to speak to Jim going down in the elevator or standing on the sidewalk in front of the building, the sun glinting on the varnished yellow wood of the guitar which he had leaned against one of the canopy's supports while he hailed a taxi. He said nothing, either, contenting himself with several ear-splitting whistles which brought a green-and-white cab from the rank on the other side of the Square. As soon as the taxi slowed to the kerb, she ran forward and jerked open the door, jumped in and tried to close it behind her before he could stop her.

'Drive away as fast as you can!' she cried to the driver.

But Shad was too quick for her. Although surprised by her swift tactic, he managed to grab his guitar and clutch the door just as it was about to slam shut. He opened it wide and climbed in, holding his instrument in front of him carefully, fell back into the seat as the automobile began to move.

The driver, grinding gears as he shifted, looked over his shoulder at her. 'Is everything all right, lady?' he asked.

She hesitated, glancing at Shad, saw his large hand grip the fret of the guitar compulsively, saw that his long lips were tense, his dark eyes bright with temper. Did she dare tell the driver to stop? Could she chance leaving the cab? Wasn't the sensible thing to do to talk to Shad first and find out what he wanted – how much he knew?

'Go ahead, driver. Everything's all right.'

'But, lady, you have to tell me where you're going.'

I must not let him know my address, she thought, I can't tell the driver to take me home – I must tell him to go some place else. But where? Where?

'Hotel Plaza, please.' Her voice sounded calm to her, but small and distant.

'O.K., lady.' The driver shrugged his shoulders and slumped down in his seat: he shifted gears again, and the taxi swerved around one of the curves of the Square.

'Is that where you live?' Shad asked. He did not drawl. His words were clipped, precisely spoken, lacked accent and twang. 'You've come up in the world.'

She did not answer him, did not look at him. She was afraid to look at him. But she heard him begin to whistle softly, brokenly, a few phrases at a time, the song she knew so well – that at one time she had wanted to forget but had not been able to – 'The Blue-Tail Fly'. Then he stopped whistling and cleared his throat. 'You thought I was dead,' he said. It was not a question, but a simple statement of fact.

She did not answer. Someone kept tightening and then loosening, tightening and then loosening, a velvet band around her head. All the many street noises, that were there all the time but which she had never listened to before, kept increasing in intensity – a policeman's whistle, a truck's backfire, the sound of a siren in the distance – rose to a tumultuous crescendo that threatened to deafen her. If I could only focus my eyes on some one thing, she thought, some fixed object – if I could only concentrate on that, ignore *him*, until this taxi-ride is over – everything will be really all right. But she could not look in Jim's direction; even when she glanced out of the window she saw a faint, ghostly reflection of his saturnine face, his mocking eyes, in the glass. And if she looked straight ahead, all she could see was the back of the driver's neck, his framed licence with its hoodlumish photograph, the ticking taximeter which already registered oo DOLLARS and 40 CENTS.

'You thought you had killed me,' he said.

There was a fly on the back of the cabby's neck. It was crawling all over, now on his collar, now on the wrinkled flesh just below the hairline. Why didn't he brush it off? Surely he must feel it! She could almost feel it herself, crawling on her neck, sending cold chills creeping down her back. No, now she saw, it was not on the cabby – but on the glass partition between him and her. That was it! – the fly was on the transparent partition and at first it had seemed to be actually on the driver's neck. Just another example of how one's eyes could mislead one . . .

'Aren't you interested in finding out what really happened?' Jim Shad asked the question quietly, maliciously.

She knew that if she looked at him now she would detect the traces of a smile at the edges of his mouth, would see a deceptive friendly twinkle in his eyes. He had always enjoyed prodding people; antagonism was for him the juice of life. But this time she could not allow herself to become angry – too much depended upon her retaining control of herself. She looked for the fly again, searched for the brief area of the glass partition that she could observe without turning her head, and was just in time to see it stop flexing its legs and fly away.

'I have a big file of clippings at home,' Jim was saying. 'They're some mighty interesting stories among 'em' – he was lapsing back into the drawl and, as he did, his words seemed to grow more sinister – 'some mighty big, black, scarey headlines: headlines about *you*, ma'am, that 'ud make somebody some mighty interesting reading –'

The taxi had stopped for the light at Forty-second Street. A double-decker bus was on one side of the cab, a truck on the other – she could not tell for certain how thick the traffic was. If it were thick enough, but not too thick, she could risk throwing open the door, darting between the jammed cars, running down the street and away from Jim – losing him in the crowd. But she could not gauge the density of the traffic without looking around, without looking at him. And if she looked him in the face, she was afraid that it would be as it had been so many times in the past – that she would give in to him. She would let him do what he wanted. It would begin all over again. No, she dare not take that chance.

He was going on in that half-joking, consciously-slurred, conversational tone, his warm, musical voice having, even when he talked like this, some of that bewitching quality that made his singing simple, good and true – only what he was saying was not simple, was not good, *was* frighteningly true.

'Ah can't understand why you ain't interested in what ah'm telling you. I know you would be if you could take a peek at some of the pictures the papers ran when they was lookin' all over the country for you. I let them have some of your professional pictures – the ones you had took of you in that purty – a little scanty, but still mighty purty – blue costume you always wore . . .'

The taxi started up, bolting across the street, the driver spinning his wheel to ease it through holes in the traffic, past Forty-third, Forty-fourth, Forty-fifth Streets. Keeping her eyes fixed on the taximeter, which now read 01 DOLLARS and 05 CENTS, she decided to call his bluff.

'Are you trying to blackmail me?' she asked him.

He did not speak for a moment, a moment during which they passed two more streets and stopped for another light just short of Radio City. The Plaza is at the Park – that's Fifty-ninth Street; ten more blocks, two more traffic lights away, she thought. If I can only put him off until then – he thinks I live there, and he won't be expecting anything – I might be able to escape . . .

'You surprise me, Ellen,' he said, dropping the drawl again. She had never realized before how effective it was to have two voices, two different voices which could be used both to threaten and cajole. 'I thought you would treat your old friends better than this, Ellen. I wanted to see you again, nothing more – I wanted to talk over old times. Blackmail is a harsh word – a terrible word, Ellen. You should think carefully before you use it.'

The taxi was waiting an interminable length of time for the light to change. The velvet band was growing tighter around her skull, the taximeter ticked louder and louder, the little black-and-white wheel that turned around to show that the mechanism was operating spun crazily, seeming to go backwards and forwards at the same time. She decided, thinking slowly, cautiously, that now was

505

not the time to speak, that she would gain time, make him repeat himself, if she kept silent.

'I can see where you might be worried about blackmail,' he said, raising his voice slightly on the last word, lingering over it as if he enjoyed saying it. 'Your husband is a very important man, the conductor of one of the oldest symphony orchestras in the world – a man with a reputation. Come to think of it, you have a reputation, too, Ellen, a good name you have to keep before your public. It's been a long time since you gave a concert – a long time since the newspapers have mentioned your name. Yes, now that I think of it, I can see where you might be worried about blackmail.' Again he seemed to pause, to weigh the word. 'It wouldn't be very nice, would it? – not nice at all – if the newspapers started printing those old stories again, I mean. I think they'd have a Roman holiday, Ellen. And there wouldn't be a thing you could do – not a thing.'

The motor of the taxi roared as the driver raced it impatiently. Then there was a harsh, rasping sound as he shifted gears ruthlessly. The cab jerked forward, subsided, the driver cursed. The automobile behind them sounded its horn, and a green-and-yellow monster of a bus nudged past them like the tortoise passing up the hare. She held her breath, the ticking of the meter clattering loudly in her ear, dug her fingers into the leather of the seat, hoping desperately that nothing had gone irrevocably wrong with the machine, that the cab would start up again. And it did, eventually, but only after another bus and several automobiles had honked their way derisively past. Unfortunately, now that they were moving again, they moved slowly, gradually rolling past Forty-sixth Street, hesitating, slipping forward, hesitating, stopping once more for a light at Forty-seventh Street.

'Yes,' Jimmy said, 'I can certainly see why you might be worried. But what I don't understand, ma'am, is why you think I would stoop to blackmail . . .' He paused at the word, let it hang in the air.

She did not speak. The taxi was in motion again, this time silently. An opening in the traffic loomed before them, and the driver, twisting his wheel compulsively, darted into it. The blocks sped past: Forty-eighth Street, Forty-ninth Street, Fiftieth, Fifty-first – they were going even farther this time! – they might even reach the Plaza! But no, they had to beat the light to cross Fifty-second Street, traffic thickened, and they halted in the middle of the block.

'Aren't you going to answer me, Ellen?'

How could she answer him? All she could think of was getting away, escaping from the cab, from the contrasting shades of his insolent voice, from the familiar Southern drawl and the clipped, brutal precision of his other way of speaking. Seven more blocks and they would be at the hotel, seven more blocks, one – or, if luck was against her, two – more traffic lights. That was all she could think of, and she dare not talk to him about that. As it was he probably knew just what she was planning to do and had already devised a way of preventing it.

He commenced to whistle again, softly, but connectedly – he whistled 'The Blue-Tail Fly' through, and then he said, musically slurring his words so that they seemed to grow out of the old tune, 'Ah allus liked you in that costume, Ellen. It was mighty purty.'

A flush spread down her face, warming the surface of her skin even under her clothes. He was looking at her speculatively, sizing her up again, measuring the Ellen he saw now with the Ellen he had known years before, seeing her again in the brief, diaphanous costume. She wanted to look away, but for some reason she could not. Her eyes met his gaze, sparred with his, their tempers met and clashed. Then he moved closer and, before she sensed what he was about to do, caught and held her in his arms.

It was a familiar place to be. His arms were as strong as she remembered them, his mouth as frank and probing. She uncurled inside – a cat, warm and fat, walked across a room, stretching itself proudly, lazily – and met his kiss.

And, at the same moment, the blackness swam in, swooping and billowing, clinging to her, claiming her, friendly, not hostile. She gave herself to it. This return to darkness was a homecoming, a yielding to placid oblivion. There was no threat here; she felt none of the dire excitement of the other times that she had fallen back into this pit, let herself go upon the surface of this sea, clothed herself in the mists of this engulfing night. Before it had seemed incalculable, formless, unknowable – a catastrophe, and she had fought against it, struggled to drive it back where it impinged, endeavoured to stand aside from it, to remain separate and by this means prevail over it; but now the sable ocean seemed bounded, had shape and substance, was meaningful – a beatitude, and she submitted herself to it, as unequivocally as she gave her consciousness to sleep, became one with it as willingly as, when a child, she had crept into her father's lap, rejoicing in her loss of identity.

Her father had been a strong man, not kind, but passionate. He had enclosed his family, locked them within the bounds of his own personality, fed them the world as he had seen it. His world had not been wide: it had centred about his store with its shelves of books and piles of stationery, its meek, maidenly clerks, its scholarly façade with leaded-glass windows and a hanging sign that creaked when the day blew gusty; but his world had been experienced intensely, for his daughter and his patient wife, as much as for himself. They both had served his clients, his wife had kept the books and paid the bills in her painfully tidy script, Ellen had dusted and polished, creamed the leather bindings, taken down the orders and done up the packages, run the errands. The bookseller had seen the great events of his day through the burning glass of his trade, the War then just a few years past had been referred to as 'the years when we stored the German stock in the cellar'. The decade of prosperity had been concentrated in his annual summer trips to Europe, which had meant long, confining hot days in the store for Ellen while she helped her mother wait on trade in her father's absence, and had resulted in crates of musty volumes, French portfolios of plates, fine bindings to be cared for during the long winter evenings. Even the happenings of the city they lived in came to them filtered through their protector's contacts with his customers: the warehouse fire, in which four workers lost their lives and which all the other inhabitants had gathered to see incarnadine the night, had been casually mentioned in conversation by Reverend Sawyer on the day he bought a set of Jonathan Edwards, and had been referred to with equal casualness by her father, that night at dinner, when he had told them how he had sold the set to the minister, how shamed he had been to find one of the deckled edges slightly dusty and how much he had got for it. All they heard of politics, of foreign doings, of local matters, one way or another seeped out of this steady flow of information on the selling of books – all they read, when they read at all, were the volumes that had been damaged that could not be sold, or those that for some reason or other incurred their master's displeasure and were cast aside as unfit merchandise. For her father had been proud of his ability to deduce when a book had been read, and the act of perusing served to lower its value in his eyes. 'Books are as perishable as butter or eggs,' he had used to say, 'and must be handled with consummate care.'

The blackness, the swirling, once frightening – but now calming – mists were intimately engaged in all this, as well as other memories: the days at school when the children had laughed at her for her affected manner of speaking and excluded her from their games because of the queer way she dressed, the upright piano her mother had inherited from an uncle, and the marvellous spectrum of sound, the ever-varying colours of notes and chords, the hushed dim silences and the clamouring, bright splendour of mounting sonorities that it had allowed her to evoke. The piano had helped her gain her freedom from the store, too, although it had not let her fly from her father, since he, for reasons as inscrutable as those that underlay his other passions – the store, his family, his upright, manly person – shared her hunger for music, standing over her while she practised, hands clenched behind his back, ready to show her a scathing grimace of disgust for a wrong note, a torturous yank at her pigtails for any indication of sloth.

He was standing over her now, as she dreamed this – hard upon her, he bore her to his will. Her fingers arched, attacked, clashed at the enigma of the keys, the old, taut strings echoed their long-spent vibrations, sustained jarring harmonies and excruciating rhythms. His shadow encloaked her; he was the sea, the night, the menacing yet benevolent image which she must fight off even as she submitted to it. And, in the background, clear and far away from the night, another music sounded, a series of graceful phrases, a pattern of notes etched in metallic tones that were above all this, complete in themselves, in touch with an ease and perfection, an essence, which was not hers then nor now, but for which she was meant, to which she was dedicated. Yet the aria she heard was in conflict with the black, engorging shadow, did not arise out of it, seemed to exist apart from it in a different time. These sweet sounds had nothing to do with the comforting pressure she felt, the warm, close darkness, the cold, blank countenance of her dead father, resting on a pillow of peach plush in a fetid atmosphere of roses, the mourning draperies that hid a relative's kneeling form. They persisted in the face of the jolting, alarming, hammering intrusion of an even stranger dissonance, a noisy, chaotic uproar that dissipated the blackness in ever-widening eddies of bright sunlight, that shaped itself ultimately in images rather than music, in a black leather world starred with a brown leather face, a wildly ticking wheel that spun black-and-white like an insane roulette table, a croaking, guttural voice that commanded her (she was aware that it was now for the second or third time), 'This is the Plaza, lady! That's where you said to go . . . you sure she's all right, buddy?'

And another voice – a soft, drawling voice she knew well enough to fear – was saying, 'Reckon she'll do. Just had a little faintin' spell, but she's comin' round. Purty soon she'll be chipper as a tom-tit. Thank you kindly for your trouble.'

She opened her eyes. Jimmy was smiling at her blandly. He had just handed the driver some money, and the man had turned his head. She started to get up, but Jimmy's arm held her own, held it down. This restraint reminded her of her predicament, added to her resolve, caused her to fight his grasp. He laid his guitar aside and helped her out of the taxi with both hands. They walked side by side, her arm locked in his, to the doorman.

'The lady had a faintin' fit,' Jim drawled to the uniformed man. 'Will you see to her while I get my instrument?'

The doorman helped her up the steps as Shad went back to the cab.

As she reached the top step, she shook off the doorman's assisting hand and turned about. Her movements seemed slow and ponderous, and Jimmy, too, seemed to be walking down to the cab with great deliberateness. The scene, glaringly illuminated by the blazing sun, was unreal, theatrical. This is not a familiar hotel, where I have danced and dined, that I am standing before, but a backdrop – the man beside me in his elegant uniform is not actually a doorman, he is only an old character actor, and that man I am watching, who is opening the door of the cab now, is reaching in for his guitar, he is not Jim Shad, but just my leading man! But as she thought this, as she tried to convince herself that the conversation in the taxi had not taken place, had been but a larger part of the dream she had had when she fainted, her cold, sceptical self withdrew and acted. She turned to the doorman – he was an old man, with a puffy red face and china-blue eyes – and said, 'That man has been annoying me! Will you please prevent him from following me?' And before he could answer her – she waited only long enough to see his tired eyes begin to kindle with indignation – she ran into the dark, cool lobby of the hotel, down a corridor she knew well and out a side entrance. Another taxi was waiting at the kerb.

She gave the driver her address, and sat back in a corner so she might not be seen from outside. Her fright was by no means spent, but she knew that she was now relatively safe from Jim. Oh, he would get around the doorman without difficulty by telling him some sort of lie and perhaps pressing a bill into his hand. But by then she would be blocks away – it was the delay she had effected that had assured her escape for the time being, at least.

For the time being! She sighed and pressed her cold hand to her brow. What would he do next? Would he go to Basil and tell him the truth? Hardly yet. He would first try to see her again – if it was money he wanted. And it probably was, although he had denied it. But then he would deny it, of course. Hadn't it always been a part of his character to do things obliquely, to force another to infer what he wanted from his actions?

But what if he did go to Basil? She reached into her bag and lighted a cigarette with trembling fingers. If he did that, if he told Basil all he knew . . . She would not let herself consider what might happen. Basil had been patient and – what was the phrase people used when they thought a man's wife took advantage of him? – long-suffering, that was it. He had been inordinately kind to her throughout her long illness. Now, just as they were ready to begin all over again, Jim Shad had to appear!

She looked out of the window and saw that she was within a block of her house. A sudden caution made her rap on the glass partition and stop the cab. She would pay him now and walk the remaining distance. By doing this she could make sure she was not being followed.

Crossing the avenue, she saw that another taxi was parked directly in front of the house. That might mean nothing, or it could be dangerous. She slowed her pace, hesitated every few feet, waited to see who was going in or coming out. At this moment the sun, which had been hidden by the western skyline, streaked red-golden fingers of fire along the street, lighting it eerily. And someone opened the door of the house and ran down the steps to the taxi.

She saw her only for an instant and in unusual light, but her profile was clear; it had the stamp of youth; the grace of her movements was unforgettable. When she looked up at the door out of which the girl had come it had closed. And when she looked back at the taxi, it was pulling away.

As she walked more rapidly to the house, Ellen could not help remembering what the doctor had said to her: 'Your husband might have met someone during those two years. You may be right – he may have changed.' When she had opened the door with her key, she went at once to the console table in the hall, jerking open its drawer and searching anxiously through the letters and cards inside it.

It was not there, although it had been there only a few days before, the lavender envelope addressed to Basil in an interestingly feminine hand. That it had been there, that she had not been mistaken, there was no doubt – the pungent perfume which had scented it still lingered provocatively in the drawer. But the letter itself was gone.

4

The lid of the mailbox felt cold and wet to her fingers as she held it down, gazing for the last time at the square envelope, her own handwriting on it, watching the raindrops fall upon it, the wet circles of damp form and spread. Reluctantly, she released the lid, heard the noise it made as it shut. The letter was gone now – she could never get it back. Tomorrow he would be reading it! This thought pleased her, and made her glance around to see if anyone had seen what she had done.

The curving village street was deserted. The low-sweeping branches of the oaks that marched along its either side were heavy-laden with the rain, their leaves rustled with its weight, and rivulets of black water ran down their trunks. She would have to be getting back to the dormitory or she would catch her death! Pulling her slicker tighter about her, she started to trudge down the street. It was silly of her to pay so much attention to one poor little letter! She laughed at herself, and a big drop of rain ran down her nose and wet her lips, making her laugh harder. A famous man like Jim Shad would never pay any mind to a note from a schoolgirl. Still, he might – you never could tell – and if he did, if he granted her the interview for the *Conservatory News*, wouldn't that smart Molly Winters be jealous!

This hope warmed her even though the spring rain was cold, and she began to hum the aria by Bach that was her very own. She usually felt better when she hummed it, and when she felt fine she would hum it, too, because it was so appropriate. She liked the way it rose and fell, its quiet dignity, the ease with which it moved, the perfect little trills and decorations. But, and she sighed, she could never play it – let alone hum it! – the way she heard it in her head. Mr Smythe said that one day she would, that all she had to do was practise and practise and *practise*; that he had never had a pupil with such fine natural gifts. But, then, funny Mr Smythe, with his curly hair that never quite hid his bald spot, was an old dear. He just liked her, that was all.

She had first had the idea of writing to Jim Shad two weeks before, when Molly and Ann and herself had slipped out, after the house superintendent had gone to bed, and had taken a taxi to Middleboro. They had heard him on the radio before that, and had been planning to go to the Black Cat to see him for many months. The trouble was that the Black Cat, a popular roadhouse outside of Middleboro, was ten miles away from the conservatory, and the girls were not allowed out later than eleven o'clock, even on a Saturday night. It was expensive, too – it had cost them nearly five dollars the last time they had gone, what with taxi-fare both ways and cokes at fifty cents apiece. They wouldn't have been able to go even at that if Molly had not just received her next month's allowance and if Ellen had not found out when the house superintendent went to bed and how they could sneak out through the cellar door without awaking her.

But Jim Shad was worth it. He was simply gorgeous! He was tall and thin and his face was sunburned and he had a dark curl of hair that fell down over his eye. He sang in a lilting tenor voice, real slow and easy like, just drawling out the words in a way that made you know he was singing for you. Ellen was especially fond of the songs he sang: some of them came from England and were centuries old, others came from the mountains of Kentucky and Tennessee or from far out West. She remembered one of them more than any of the others – it was the one about 'The Blue-Tail Fly'. She liked that song almost as much as she liked Bach's aria.

Today was Monday; that would mean he would get her

letter Tuesday and, if he sat right down and wrote a reply, she would get it Wednesday – or Thursday at the latest. Oh, what she would give to see the look in Molly Winters' eyes right now! She would be so jealous when she saw that Jim Shad had written to Ellen! Then, when they went to the Black Cat on Saturday, Jimmy – she liked to call him Jimmy to herself, but of course she would have to call him Mr Shad to be polite – would come to their table and talk to her. And all he said, except the most special parts, she would have printed in the interview for the *Conservatory News*. Oh, it was just too good to be true!

The rain began to fall torrentially, great, curtsying, misty sheets of it danced down the dark street to meet her, the street lamps became submerged globes of cold fire. Running, her rubber-soled sneakers made queer, rhythmical squishing sounds on the flowing pavement, and the gutters, flooded by the downpour, raced and gurgled. If the rain soaked through her hat, as it had done several times before, the curl would be gone from her hair and she would have to have a new wave set in it on Saturday. She just did not have enough money for the hairdresser and the Black Cat, so she began to run faster and faster, her heart pounding, the rain smarting as it struck her face. The last block of her way back to the dormitory was uphill, and by the time she reached the low, white-columned veranda her every breath was a painful gasp. She stood for a moment on the rain-swept porch, gazing at the glistening rockers and the swing that creaked in the wind, before she scraped her feet on the coco-mat and pushed open the door.

Her father, tall and spectre-like, barred her way. Behind him she could see the narrow hallway of her home and she smelled the hot, cloying scent of flowers that pervaded the atmosphere. Why, this could not be! Hadn't she only a few minutes before mailed a letter and walked back to the dormitory in the conservatory town? Why was it that when she opened the front door of the dormitory she saw, not the wide corridor and red-carpeted stairs she was used to, not the broad, complacent face of the house-mother, but the stern, angry visage of her father? Puzzled, not understanding what was happening, she inched forward, tried to sidle past her father, her eyes on the streaks of dampness that mottled the rug as water ran from her hat and slicker.

Her shoulder was seized, clutched compulsively, and she felt herself drawn towards her father, felt the harsh, unyielding outline of his body. The hot smell of the flowers, an insinuation of decay, pierced her nostrils and filled her mouth and throat with nausea. Embarrassment and resentment made her stiff and bold – adamantly she refused to raise her eyes and look at him. Somewhere, above her, perhaps, someone was playing scales, going over them again and again, each time missing the same note. Then, as she listened, she heard her father's voice, dry and rattling, catarrhal, saying, 'Shameless! You are shameless! Going out, with your poor, your sainted, mother dead in the house. Running the streets like a loose woman. Speak to me! Say something! Tell me where you've been!'

But she did not speak. Instead, the angry words with which she wanted to answer him clogged in her throat, battered against her tight lips; she pushed past his arm, ran down the hall and up the steep stairs. And he ran after her, his breath whistling between his teeth, caught her and pulled her down to him, his hand under her chin pinching the flesh, forcing her head up. But she would not open her eyes – she would not look at him – even when he began softly to curse her, to call her names she did not know the meaning of, to push her head back and back until her senses reeled and the black depths, like a furry animal, like a soft drape, like the night of sleep, drowned her . . .

She was next aware that she was kneeling in a flower-banked room, her hands pressed to her side, the thick, hot, sweetish scent of flowers all about her, walling her in, enclosing her with the thing in the casket. They had forced her to gaze at the thing, the cold, inanimate flesh that had been her mother, the pale, waxy eyelids, the powdered cheeks, the insipidly smiling lips that had never curved in just that way in life. They, her father and the minister, with soft, coaxing words had commanded her to kiss those lips, insisted that she know that chill. Then, with the murmuring of friends and relations at her back, the murmuring of a Roman crowd in an amphitheatre awaiting the spectacle, she had sunk trembling to her knees, had closed her eyes but refused to clasp her hands to simulate prayer, had held them rigid to her sides while the resonance of the minister's voice above her intoned the eulogy.

'. . . a good woman who has walked with us, a woman we have all known and cherished, a woman who has cared for her child, nurturing her, protecting her and now, having reached her allotted span, has surrendered the bowl of life to this child, bade her drink from it, bade her live the good life she has lived, do as she has done, be her mother's daughter and to live in God's presence all her days . . .'

The words horrified her, swam in her head like great, ugly, murdering monsters. Her eyes still closed, her hands weighted and inert, she rose, swaying, and turned about. The minister's voice droned on, a buzzing machine that manufactured a tone, a mechanical exhalation: the mass of friends and relatives sighed, a great, mingled breath of disapprobation. She opened her eyes and confronted them, the blobs of cloth, the bulges of legs and arms, the bobbing pink balloons that were their faces. She confronted them for an instant as the starch of terror ran through her veins, immobilizing her, making her a fitting companion to the thing in the casket. Then she fled down the aisle, past the neighbour's child dawdling on the piano stool, out into the hall, up the narrow stairs. As she reached the landing, she heard her father call, heard his anger echo and rebound in time, begin its existence in limbo. And she knew that it was already too late to return, that, having fled, she must continue to flee; that, once having left that scene, she would not go back and be a part of it again. But she ran on, down the second-floor corridor, which she did not even pause to inspect, throwing it open with a wild gesture, propelled through it by her fear. And she found herself, not in her room at home, but in her room in the dormitory – safe in the dim darkness of a familiar place that had yet to know her father's wrath, apart in distance as well as time from the house where she had passed her childhood, the place of rage and death, the sweet miasma of funeral flowers.

Molly Winters, her room-mate, was sitting at the desk, her head pillowed in her hand, asleep over the text-book on orchestration that she had been studying. On impulse, she slammed the door, causing Molly to jump into frightened wakefulness, to demand reproachfully, 'Where have you been?'

'I went out to mail a letter. It's raining very hard.'

She went to the closet and hung her streaming coat and hat, fluffed her wet hair with her hands and walked to the mirror to see if the wave was gone. No, it was still there – although she did look bedraggled! She began to brush her hair vigorously to dry it, ignoring Molly, who continued to stare at her as if she had never seen her before and never would again. The silly girl, she thought; wouldn't she be jealous if she knew I'd written Jimmy Shad!

'Ellen, I won't be able to go to the Black Cat with you Saturday.' Molly spoke hesitantly, wistfully. 'My parents are visiting me this week-end. I got their letter this afternoon.'

She went on brushing her hair as if she had not heard, although her pulse had quickened at Molly's words. If Molly could not go, that would mean that Ann wouldn't go – Ann would never go any place unless Molly went, too. And if Ann did not go, she would have to go alone or not at all. She had yet to go to a night club by herself, and she did not want to now; it was not nice. But she had mailed that letter to Shad – if she did not go, she would miss her chance of meeting him. On the other hand, if she did go she could see him alone without either Ann or Molly to interfere. She was going to go, that was all there was to it! She brushed her hair more rapidly, more vigorously.

'Is Ann still going?' she asked casually, trying to keep her rising excitement out of her voice.

In the mirror she saw her room-mate make a grimace of distaste. 'Ann said she wouldn't go if I wasn't going. I tried to persuade her, but, you know, I don't think she's really interested. Ann's just a tag-along – she hasn't any gumption. I'm sorry, Ellen – I know you wanted to go.'

She saw the smile that hesitated on Molly's face before she replaced it carefully with a more contrite look. Why, she is pleased that she is spoiling my plans! I'll show her! And, without missing a stroke of the brush, she said, 'I'm going anyway. Someone will have to use the reservation.'

'But, Ellen, you can't!' Molly's tone was desperate. 'You can't go there alone. What would people say if they saw you?'

'What would people say if we had all gone and they had seen us?' She turned about and looked at her room-mate, enjoying her discomfort. 'You know as well as I do that no one from the conservatory is supposed to go to the Black Cat. The dean posted a notice on the bulletin board about it. What difference does it make if I go alone?'

Molly stood up and went over to her bed and fell upon it. She began to pound the pillow with her fist. 'Ellen, you can't do it. Nice girls don't go places like that alone. You just want to get him to yourself, that's all!'

She had finished brushing her hair, but she continued to look into the mirror. Molly had sat up again and was looking at her back reproachfully, her mouth compressed, her eyes bright with excitement. 'What if I do want to be alone with him?' she asked her. 'What's wrong with that?'

Molly said nothing. She stood up abruptly and went over to the dresser, pushing past Ellen rudely. She picked up a lipstick and smeared her mouth with it, then patted at her cheeks with rouge. Then she turned around and grabbed her coat out of the closet, went to the door and jerked it open angrily.

'If you're going out, you'd better know it's raining,' Ellen called after her. But the door slammed on her words. She looked back into the mirror and smiled at her own reflection.

As she looked at her own face in the glass, it began to darken, to pulsate and widen. And in the distance on the edge of her hearing, an orchestra sounded, wild, discordant, yet syncopated, the regular beat of a drum, the faint cries of saxophones, the shrilling of trumpets. She leaned forward to see her own face more plainly; but the closer she came to the quickly blackening glass, the fainter and more indistinct her own image became. Then, while she watched, the mirror seemed to dissolve, to lap away as tide recedes from a moonlit beach, revealing a depth, an emptiness, a greatly enlarged interior. Before she was wholly aware of what was happening, this huge area seemed to move forward, to surround her and enclose her – and she found herself seated at a table in the midst of a darkened ballroom, her eyes fixed on a point in space not far from her where a spotlight stroked a silver circle on the floor. All about her couples sat and talked; she heard the tinkle of glasses, and the soft, amorous voices of men, the hushed whisperings and feckless laughter of women; the air was smoke-laden and close and the glass in her hand was cold and wet. Yet she did not feel uncomfortable, or even alienated – her body trembled with eagerness, and the coaxing beat of the music that had ended only a moment before was now replaced with an expectancy, an urgent desire to experience what was about to occur.

A hand clapped, and then another, and another. Soon a mounting roar of applause added to her tenseness as she struck her own palms together, contributing her own sound to the mass propitiation. The silver spotlight wavered and shimmered, then suddenly streaked across the floor to the far end of the bandstand; there it picked out a tall, bowing form and the yellow varnish of a guitar. Someone whistled, and a woman on the other side of the great room cried, 'That's my Jimmy!' The tall figure seemed almost shy and self-effacing. He stood clumsily at the edge of the spotlight, smiling hesitantly at the crowd for another moment before he walked to the centre of the dance-floor with long, loping strides, dragging his guitar behind him. A microphone, glittering in the harsh spotlight, descended on a wire until it hovered in front of him. He looked at it undecidedly and then reached up and caressed it with his hand. 'Hullo folks,' he said into it, and the loudspeaker spoke too, magnifying his soft tenor, throwing it into the corners of the smoky room. 'Hullo folks,' he said again, once more idly caressing the microphone, smiling placatingly at it as if it abashed him, 'ah've come to sing you a song or so. The kind you like, ah reckon.'

And before he had finished speaking, before the softly slurred syllables had ceased echoing, the crowd's roar of welcome had died, and in its place there existed an unnatural quiet, as if some ponderous animal had quit its snuffling and scuffling, had commenced to listen, to be aware, to perceive. This quiet deepened until it was an oppressive silence, as if the tall man at the microphone had thrown a spell on the room. He stood there, smiling to himself, wilfully enjoying his mastery of the crowd, the animal. His eyes glinted in the spotlight, which picked him mercilessly out of the surrounding dark – he knew that soon he must sing, that the wild creature out there demanded it, but that it was also his function to hold it at bay as long as possible. The silence seemed to have been stretched to the breaking point; it seemed that if another instant should pass the tension would be too great, a horrifying roar would burst loose from the animal's thousand throats – it was at this point that Jim Shad chose to sing.

He sang quietly, as softly as he had spoken, and it was as if he sang to her. What he sang did not matter; she did not listen to the words, nor did she follow the melody, sort out its rhythm, its structure, its cadence. Yet his song had more meaning for her than any music had ever had before; it had the effect of an incantation, a direct magic that transformed her. As he sang, she fingered his letter, which had arrived only that morning, his invitation to meet him at the bar after his performance, to go to some quiet place where they could talk. Her throat went dry as he ended one song and began another, a quicker, jauntier one, and her cheeks burned as she remembered that she had not told Molly or Ann about the letter, that she had known they would not have approved of her meeting a man without an escort, that they would have insisted that she did not go out with him alone. But why should she worry about what they thought? – she was old enough to know what she was doing, wasn't she? All she knew was that he had written to her, that he wanted to meet her and talk to her, that he was singing for her now.

As he finished his second song, and the dark, restive audience began to pound the tables and applaud, as the silver spotlight turned and his fingers experimentally plucked a few strange chords on his guitar, she rose and pushed her way through the crooked aisle of chairs back to the bar. She could still see him from there, could still hear his plaintive voice as it related the story of 'The Blue-Tail Fly', but his figure had shrunk, had become impersonal, her heart's frenzied pulsations had subsided, and she found she could breathe more easily. To stand at the bar she had to buy a drink, and it was her third one of the evening – she sipped it slowly, but despite this caution she soon felt pleasantly silly, smiling to herself and giggling whenever she thought of Jimmy and the way he had addressed his songs to her. Until finally she realized that the audience was applauding again, that she no longer heard his voice or his guitar, that now even the applause was dying away. And she knew that the performance was over and shortly he would be with her. She stiffened and held herself as straight as she could, although it occurred to her that there was something very funny, something that if she could just think for a moment so that she might know what it was she would want to laugh at; but she dare not take the time to think now, when Jim was about to appear. So she looked in the mirror behind the bartender, looked at her own face brightly reflected in the vari-coloured light, smiling ever so slightly, holding her head at just the right angle – the angle she had worked out patiently so many times before, the angle she was sure was her best angle, the inclination of her head that made her eyes seem mysterious, that emphasized the beguiling shadow that sometimes hovered over her lips, that made her seem self-possessed and dignified. And while she inspected herself, she saw him approaching, saw his tall form loom out of the surrounding darkness, saw his tanned, tight-lipped face coming closer and closer.

Frightened and shy now that the meeting she had been looking forward to all the week was at hand, she looked away from the mirror, looked down at her drink and the lop-sided cherry that still floated in it, waiting for him to speak. Behind her the orchestra began to blare and, with a scraping of chairs and a muttering of voices, the great animal got to its feet and began to shuffle around the dance floor. She was aware that he stood beside her; she could feel the warmth of his body; if she had wanted she could have brushed against him. But she still did not look up. A tapping sound, hard and metallic, made her jump with surprise – she looked aside and saw his hand, holding a coin, striking it against the bar to get the bartender's attention. Then she heard his voice, heard the sound of it before she heard his words, for an instant thought he was addressing her – as she expected him to – and, conse-quently, looked up at him and smiled before she realized that what he had said had only been directed at the neglectful bartender, 'H'yah, Jack! How's about the usual?'

But he had seen her smile, and it had pleased him; now that she had looked at him, she found she could not look away. He turned his head slightly in deference to her, so that his bright, brown eyes glanced directly into her own, inquiring of her why she had smiled even as his lips pursed and he breathed a long, quiet, admiring whistle. Her cheeks flushed and she felt her own smile freeze, become irretrievable, in embarrassment; for it was obvious to her now that he did not recognize her, that he could not have recognized her, since he had never seen her, that she was only a stranger who had smiled provocatively to him. And yet she could not speak, could not say the words that would clear up the misapprehension that must be forming in his mind, could not even find the strength to lower her head and look away. He took her discomfiture for boldness and his smile broadened into an anticipatory grin. 'Why, hullo, beautiful,' he softly said. 'Wheah have you been all my life?'

The only response she could make was to seize her drink more tightly, to raise the glass tremblingly to her lips and swallow it quickly, cherry and all. He raised his eyebrow slightly and whistled again, this time at the bartender. 'H'yah, Jack. What you keepin' us waiting for? This lady an' myself are prit near dyin' of thirst!'

The bartender bobbed into view and took her glass from her reluctant hand. Without it, she did not know where to look except to look at him. And what was wrong with that? She liked to look at him, didn't she? She had arranged to meet him, hadn't she? She sighed and her smile relaxed, became a little less frightened. In just a moment, she knew she would be able to speak to him, to tell him who she was and why she had smiled. But before the words had formed properly in her mind he had covered her hand gently with his own, a friendly, confidential pressure, and had drawled, 'What's the matter, honey? Has the old cat got yoh tongue?'

His question, although she knew he meant it jocularly, that he had said it only to be pleasant, had not necessarily expected an answer, unsettled her and made it still more difficult for her to speak. Instead, she poked restlessly at

525

her hair, turning away from him as coldly as she dared to stare at the pale reflection of her own blue eyes in the mirror. But, even so, she did not escape his inquiring glance. He, too, turned and looked into the mirror, his elbow leaned against the polished bar, the image of his sunburned face above her own and just beside it, the tiers of amber bottles on either side acting as a frame making it seem that she was staring at a picture of them both, a dull and clouded picture in an amber frame, a picture taken on a dark and rainy day. Then, almost as if he had wished to make the effect complete, he put his arm around her, gently, persuasively. And he was saying, 'Why don't we have our drink an' go for a drive, beautiful? My car's parked just outside an' I hear tell there's a moon –'

While she watched, while she was still too amazed to do anything about his arm that rested so familiarly – as if it had always belonged there – about her shoulders, the mirror shivered and cracked into a million slivers, the night invaded it, the swirling blackness, and she felt herself caught up and held, lifted gently but with a firmness that was reassuring . . . she felt herself carried. Many voices existed on all sides of her, some shrill and demanding, some quieter and more resourceful, but one voice dominated them all, softly but persistently, and then the voices died away and it was quieter and cooler and she closed her eyes and gave herself to whatever it was that was happening.

Slowly the strange sensation grew stronger, gradually it took possession of her, became a part of her that was essential to her being; it was a sensation of freedom, of disassociation – she floated high above all earthly connexions and gloried in her ascension. This cannot be real, she told herself, it must be an illusion. Yet for her, at that moment, it was the only possible reality. She kept her eyes closed, fearing to open them, while she felt herself become lighter and lighter until it seemed she had no weight, no substance, had changed into an essence, an abstraction. Most wonderful of all, she realized, was the happiness she had attained, the sense of contentment, or perfect, immutable equilibrium. She was at peace, at rest, wholly free of the suzerainty of time and space. And then, without thinking about it, she knew what had happened to her, and she also knew that it was what she had always desired, although she had never before had the wit to put it into words: she had become music.

Yes, she had become majestic sound, a rolling, evanescent structure that billowed and cavorted, that made light of time and space because it had grown out of them, was compounded of them, was their inevitable result. She was tone and melody and rhythmic beat, she was harmony and colour. In her the woodwinds blew and the brasses stormed, she inhabited the sweet turbulence of the strings, the intelligence of the keyboard. This was what she had longed for, even if she had not known it; this was her grace, her beatitude . . .

She opened her eyes and saw that she floated high in the air, that the moon was her neighbour and that small clouds raced playfully by her side; below, like an overturned saucer, the earth existed. And she discovered that though the world was far beneath her, she could see anything that happened on its surface, if she cared to look for it. So it was that she found the automobile, the long, low-slung roadster with its bright red body and its chromium exhausts, flying along a country road in the shadow of the clouds, *her* clouds that scudded companionably beside her. And so it was, by looking a little longer at this reckless car, by following it with her eyes and mind, by haunting it with her melody, that she discovered its occupants, the two of them: the lean, saddle-faced man who drove like a demon, eyes hard upon the black streak of road, arm thrown about the small form of the girl, the dreamy-eyed child who nestled against his shoulder, the conservatory student who had fallen in love with a cabaret performer. As she realized that this was another of her selves that she was watching, another, more tangible Ellen, a shudder interrupted the flow of her sound, a discord like a crash of thunder or the scream of a rising gale, a dissonance that was like a premonition of disaster.

Now she began to hear her own sound, to listen to a procession of mournful notes against the funereal crepitation of muffled drums, the solemn shuffle of a dead march. And, as she listened, she looked away from the speeding roadster, away from the huddled, loving figure of the wayward girl, only to glimpse another scene, to take ineluctably the next step on the path to catastrophe. She saw, below her, an ill-lit room. It was as if the roof had been lifted off and she peered down into the interior, as if she were watching a play from the heights of the stage. The time was later—this she half-sensed, half-remembered; weeks had passed, and with them many surreptitious appointments, many careless journeys over country roads. The man and the girl were in this room, the girl sitting in a pool of shaded light thrown by a lamp, resting languorously, her long, bare legs and half-naked torso bathed in its dim effulgence. The man was seated on the brass bedstead, his head tousled and his eyes red and sleepless, a wisp of smoke curling from the cigarette that burned near his lip, a yellowed instrument lying in abandonment across his lap. He, too, was only partially clothed, his brown arms and heavy shoulders bulged muscularly out of his sodden, greying undershirt, glistening with sweat. They stared at each other, the girl and the man, exposing the animosity that belongs only to adversaries who are also intimates, and the girl's bosom heaved under the dully shimmering blue sequins of her *bandeaux*. As she watched from above, her eyes falling down on the foreshortened figures, the gloomy music that was a part of her swelled to a crescendo, a mighty protestation of despair – only to fall away, to cease dramatically, as the man stroked his hand over the guitar's strings and a broken chord rang out with the resonance of steel on stone. At this clarion sound the girl rose ghostily, seemed to hover on her toes above the room's scarred floor. She saw that she was clothed in glimmering blue metalled cloth, cerulean stars on her

528

breasts and thighs. Taut and trembling, caught at a point in the middle of her back, two fragile wings of finest wire and gauze hung in a frenzy of awkward levitation as she pirouetted. Again the man on the bed struck a broken, peremptory chord, but this time he followed it with another and another, each subtly different, each less startling, more anticipatory, until his right hand came in, too, and a melody was formed. The girl began to dance, still on her toes, still taking mincing steps, making fluttering, indecisive motions; and, softly, the man began to sing:

> When I was young I used to wait
> On Massa and give him his plate,
> And pass the bottle when he got dry
> And brush away the blue-tail fly.

Against the humming, somnolent sound of his voice, the twanging chords of the guitar, faint but clear despite the distance in time and space (for the room where this was happening was not only beneath her but in some way in back of her, too, and she felt she must crane her neck to keep it in sight, to keep from losing it, to keep from putting it some place where she might never find it again) – against this sound that rose from the room, replacing the deathly music that had been a part of her, she heard an orchestra, a brassy blare of a band, 'swinging' the melody that Jim was singing – for the man was Jim, she had no doubt of that, and the girl was herself – making a blatant mockery of it. This noise – she could not have called it music – grew louder and louder, drowning out the plaintive insinuations of the guitar, drowning out Jim's melancholy tenor, climbing up into a blasting fanfare with a flourish on the drums and a snort from the trombones. And, as the fanfare rocketed to its climax, she lost her footing among the clouds, the moon was eclipsed and the clouds turned into black spirits that hastened to smother her. Down, down, down, she plunged, oppressed as she felt weight and substance return, drawn to the lodestone earth with dizzying velocity. Falling faster and faster, the blackness commenced to spin about her, to take shape and thickness, to become solid and palpable. Terror struck at her heart when she saw a bright blue dagger of light streak down from above, fly past her like lightning, and end in a lake, an ellipse, a shiny stain of blue fire. Panic mounted in her throat, claiming the scream that had begun there, devouring it, as the shiny stain of blue crept towards her across the blackness, getting closer and closer, seeking her and knowing where she could be found, advancing to engorge her. She went rigid, cold as lunar ice, her ankles tense, her toes arching; she balanced on a point, holding her breath, her arms out, her head back, her eyes on the blue maw. Then, as it grew near, it sprang, drenching her with witch colour and bawd light, stigmatizing her: it, the accusing hammer; she, the accepting, submissive anvil. She stood, on her point, poised for another instant, a blue houri, as she looked up and back, following the bludgeon stroke of blue to its source, a splinter of sapphire fire, acknowledging its mastery – then a chord on Jim's guitar released her, she levelled her head and looked out at what she knew was there, would hear in another heartbeat but would never see: the crowd. And, at the second chord, before Jim's voice came in, she began to dance, hesitantly, delicately, to the plangent sound that entranced her. Like a skirmish, and then a battle, and then Armageddon, the great animal applauded, striking together its thousands of palms, stamping with its thousands of feet, whistling and shrieking its approval. But she continued to dance, inventing steps as Jim repeated chords, until the crowd quieted and they could go on with their act.

Later, she sat alone in their dressing-room, wondering, or pretending to wonder, why Jim had not joined her as he usually did after the last performance. It had been a half-hour since she had bowed to the crowd and run past the bandstand, through the narrow corridor to the dingy room where they dressed. Jim should have followed her a few minutes later – he always sang one more song after she danced 'The Blue-Tail Fly'. But he had not come just as he had not come several nights that week. She had sat in front of the spotted mirror, a kimono thrown over her bare shoulders, buffing her finger-nails and waiting for him. She had smoked cigarette after cigarette, knocking the ashes on to the linoleum floor until there was a ring of grey smudges all around her chair. Still Jim did not come. Finally, she sighed and stood up, letting the kimono slip off her shoulders and fall in a silken wave to the floor. She glanced at her made-up face in the mirror, noting the dark circles that even Max Factor's make-up did not hide, then pawed at the cold cream and splashed it on her cheeks. Of course, she could go out and find him, as she had done the other night; he would be at the bar or at somebody's table. She did not mind that – if he were just at the bar or having a drink at some stranger's table – what she feared was that he would be at Vanessa's table. That was where he had been the other night. She had almost gone up to him, had come within an ace of speaking to him, before she had seen that the woman who was with him was the specialty dancer whose act preceded theirs. Then, as she stood there in the midst of the crowd on the verge of speaking his name, she remembered how on the first night of their engagement she had found him in the shadows of the bandstand watching Vanessa. She had seen the look in his eyes as the tall, auburn-haired woman did her ridiculous dance with the macaw – she danced nude except for a G-string, but she had trained the macaw to cling to her body as she posed and postured, clothing her obscenely with his great green wings and scarlet-and-yellow breast. Yet Vanessa had only one macaw, and it had been trained to cling to that part of her body which she displayed to the crowd; as she turned and pranced and the parrot preened, anyone in the bandstand or lurking near it could make out the secret places of her form in the clarity of the rose-coloured spotlight she favoured. As she had remembered this, she glanced at Jim,

531

sitting across from Vanessa at the table, and she saw the same look in his eyes that had been there when he leaned against the bandstand and watched her pose with the parrot; her face had flushed with certainty, she had not spoken, but had turned and left the night club, had gone to their hotel room and to bed, lying awake half the night until Jim returned – but even then not telling him what she had seen, what she suspected.

She had no claim on him. This she knew, just as she had known earlier that year when she had given in to his advances, had run off from the conservatory without a word to anyone, had let him buy her the blue costume and teach her the dance, that it would not last, that she was only an episode to him, a silly schoolgirl who happened to have enough talent to work into the act. Knowing this, she had gone off with him anyway, partly because when he was near her, when his eyes held hers the way they had that first night at the bar when she had not been able to look away, she felt an excitement, a sense of being alive, of feeling herself and knowing herself to the fullest extent that she never had at any other time – but also partly because of her father, because of the rage he would fly into when he received the telegram from the school, because at night, when she lay beside Jim in the aura of his warmth, she thought of her father's impotent anger, his empty moralizing, and was sure that at last she had triumphed over him.

But, although she had known that some day this would happen, that the time would come when Jim would meet someone else and she would be faced with the choice of leaving him or staying with him and ignoring his infidelity, she had not yet allowed herself to reckon with the predicament. Nor did she now. Instead she rubbed at her cold-creamed face vigorously, threw the dirtied towel aside, pulled open the closet and squirmed into her dress without taking off her costume. She did not care if it did get wrinkled – let him worry about getting her another! Hadn't the whole affair been his idea in the first place?

Hadn't it been he who had thought of the dance, who had insisted on the special costume, who had made her stay up night after night until she could do it with precision and professional polish? Well, if he wanted to throw her out, she didn't care. Let him teach that fat pig and her damn parrot to toe-dance – she was fed-up!

She shrugged herself into her coat and left by the back door to avoid seeing Jim. Outside, it was windy and cold and damp; August was ending in blustery weather. She burrowed her head into the gusty breeze and walked in the direction of the hotel, her skirts fluttering and the fine, misty rain wetting her face like tears. But before she reached the hotel the wind's cold fingers had investigated her legs and found the metalled cloth of her costume, her body had grown stiff and icy, her teeth were chattering. The blinking neon sign of an all-night lunchstand caught her eye, so she pushed open the door and walked into its steamy interior.

She had seated herself at the counter and ordered a cup of coffee before she realized that all the other customers were men of the roughest type. Next to her sat a great hulk with a bulbous nose, a thatch of reddish hair and pro-truding eyebrows; he was blowing on his soup and seemed to be oblivious of her. She looked the other way, and saw a small, shivering man with a face like an axe and watering eyes, one of which was lowering itself in an exaggerated wink. Her hands clutched the marble counter convulsively and she looked neither right nor left; even so she saw in the streaked mirror that all the rest of the men in the lunch room were staring at her. A cup of coffee slid in front of her, stopping abruptly as if it had reached the end of its tether, slopping a chicory-smelling, sticky liquid over the saucer and one of her hands. Its sudden appearance and its novel mode of locomotion startled her; despite her resolve not to look around, she did glance down the counter, and saw the dirty apron and silently heaving belly of the man to whom she had given her order – she even glimpsed his toothy grin.

Picking up the cup, separating it from its saucer and placing a paper napkin in the slop, she decided to take her time, to sip the hot, sugary stuff slowly, not to let the men frighten her. She had dealt with worse than them. In another town, and earlier in the summer, a man had followed her to her dressing-room, had pushed past the open door and stood silently behind her while she changed. Her first knowledge of his presence had been the awareness that someone else was breathing in the room. She had turned around and looked at him, had made no attempt to grab her clothes, had simply confronted his eyes with her own until he turned and fled. Jim had caught him outside the door and had cuffed him, but she had always regretted that this had occurred. She had handled him on her own, and Jim's action had been superfluous.

So she drank her coffee now, slowly and ostentatiously, and pretended not to hear the remarks that were passed. When she had finished, she lighted a cigarette and smoked it long enough to be convincing before she placed a nickel on the wet surface of the counter and walked to the door. But as she reached the street, as the cold wind struck her face and she once again felt the discomfort of the costume beneath her dress, she became less plucky. She had walked only a few steps down the street towards the hotel, when she heard the door bang shut behind her and she sensed that she was being followed. And when she heard a toneless, tuneless whistle, she knew that it was true.

She tried to take longer steps, to move her feet more rapidly, but the costume was too rigid. Perhaps it was better to maintain a steady pace so that whoever it was who was behind her would not know that she was frightened. Which one, she wondered, had made up his mind to accost her? It would not be the counterman, his very girth disqualified him, and he would have to stick with his job. The shifty-eyed one with the rheumy eyes and the sharp, rabbity face? She sincerely hoped not, although, if worst came to worst, he might be better than the lumpish one with the beetling brows and the rotten nose. The footsteps behind her sounded closer, they were all but running.

It was then that her clothes fell from her, dissolving away like spume in the surf. She stopped, ashamed and yet proud. The wind that had been cold now seemed warm and caressing. A great flush spread over her, tinting her flesh with the hue that typifies both embarrassment and the heights of ardour. The gauze wings, which she thought she had removed before putting on her dress, which she must have removed but which now amazingly appeared again just when all decent covering vanished, these wings began to shimmer ecstatically in the warm wind. They gave her a sense of power, a knowledge of freedom, and – instead of running madly on down the street – she turned to face whoever had been following her. It was her father.

Or rather it was not her father, but a faceless thing dressed in her father's clothes, the long-lapelled, black serge suit, the black velvet tie and rolled-brim black homburg, the tightly furled black umbrella. Where her father's sombre countenance should have been was an empty space, a hole in time, a whistling fissure. As the figure advanced towards her, she felt herself drawn towards it, and the sound that she had mistaken for a masher's whistle rose in volume and pitch, became a hellish lament. The wings at her shoulders at the same time gained weight and strength, they ceased quivering and began to beat; but just as she felt that she had the power to rise off the ground, to soar and escape her father, he was upon her. His long, black flags of arms shrouded her in a tenacious grasp – they reached for her beating wings, tore at them, sought to pinion them. She did not succeed in escaping him, but he failed to hold her down to earth: locked in hideous struggle, they both began to rise, and for an instant hung dizzyingly high in the air. Then the shrill sound of doom that issued from the abyss of his face mounted to a scream, a howl, quickly surpassing itself in volume, encompassing her in its violent clamour and, once more, she fell into the pit.

Around, up, on all sides and down, there was only blackness. She existed in a vast, frigid whirlpool of nothingness. Spinning with sickening celerity, she felt that she was disintegrating, that this vertigo that was now her only consciousness was the prelude to oblivion, destruction itself. She could no longer see, since all about her there was nothing but night; she could no longer hear, because the banshee cry stopped her ears. Her sole sensation was that of a horrendous, plunging oscillation; time's flow had frozen, became glacial, space and the objects that had defined it had been swallowed by the vortex. Yet when she gave up, submitted to the frenzy, she saw light.

At first it was just a point, the merest pinprick of radiance, a splinter of brilliance. Still it grew, as she watched in hope and with a wild, hysterical joy, to a mote, and then a ray, and then a beam. It had the lustre of sunshine, the confident yellow warmth of morning. As it expanded, infusing the swirling night with first a glow and finally a blinding illumination, she felt herself breathe again, her pulse begin to beat and time's ice begin to melt, to trickle and ultimately to flow. Four walls settled down about her, and a ceiling – a surface marred with cracks, an enigmatic map of an undiscovered continent. Somewhere a child cried. Footsteps sounded near and yet far – they were in the hall, and she was lying in bed in a hotel room. But – and now she raised herself to another level of wakefulness – something had been happening, a spinning blackness, a sense of shame, her father. As she tried to remember, an image suddenly existed in her mind, an image of her own nudity, of a tall black figure standing near her reaching out for her, of a whirling blackness that fed upon her fear with the voracity of a beast. She sat up in bed, her eyes wide now, awake but still terrified by her nightmare. And as she stared at the door, a metal door varnished brown to look like wood, at the keyhole with its key and its dangling, red, fibre tag, she knew that she was in some place where she had never been before, and yet she knew that a terrible thing was happening again.

It could not be. She could not awaken twice like this, she could not die twice in that pit and yet survive, yet on surviving turn and look and find, twice – that! This time she would not turn, she would not look. She had been tricked, she had been dreaming about that old time (bit by bit it came back to her now), about that night, when she was a girl, that she had fought with Jim, when things had happened that even now she was uncertain had actually happened, that even today, this very moment as she sat up in this strange bed afraid to turn, afraid to look, she did not know whether she had dreamed them then, whether she dreamed them now.

And as she stared at the brown-varnished door that she was certain she had never seen before, even as she made sure in her own mind that *that*, at least, was real, she remembered Dr Danzer's words when, after the first of her 'treatments', she had recalled that confusing night, remembered wholly that terrible awakening. 'I want you to think about what you have told me,' he had said. 'I want you to note its equivocal nature. I want you to decide whether what you remember is a dream, an imagined re-enactment of an early childhood conflict, or whether it did actually occur. But I also want you to know that since you have told me, I have checked with the authorities of the city you mentioned, and they have no record of such a violent death that month, that summer, that year.' And it seemed to her that Dr Danzer was speaking to her, his words echoed so loudly in her ear. 'The guilt you feel is an imagined guilt. The crime you did is an imagined one. It is no less real for all that. To you it is even more reprehensible because you desire it deeply. In your mind, in your imagination, you have committed this crime against this man, have through him struck at your father. He is dead for you, but the guilt you feel is not for this imagined death – but for the real death that occurred that summer while you were away from home with this man, the natural death of your father. You have told me that he died of a heart attack, unattended

537

– that they tried to reach you, but the conservatory did not know where you were, that all the dean could say was that you had not been at school for months and that he had understood that you had gone home. This is the guilt you feel: that you desired your father's death and that your father died because of your neglect. This is what you must face. Once you have faced it, I think you will discover that the other memory is but a distortion of this one, a punishment you have devised for yourself.'

She settled back in bed and shut her eyes again, reassured once more by Dr Danzer. He had told her many times that whenever she became confused, whenever there seemed to be a gap, when she had forgotten something that had happened and wanted to recover the memory of it, that all she had to do was to think back to the beginning of the chain of events, to recall each link and finger it in her mind until she came to the one that was missing. So she knew that this was what she must do now. First, she had to disentangle the truth of that August night from the dream of it – to the extent this was possible. For although she knew that Dr Danzer must be correct, that it only made sense if what she thought had occurred that night had actually never happened except in her imagination, she had never been able to dispel a modicum of doubt. Then there was the dream she had just had, which in many ways corresponded exactly to the reality of that summer and its climax, but which distorted other parts of it unnaturally. It was true that she had visited the Black Cat by herself, that she had met Jim Shad there but had not told him who she was until she had allowed him to make love to her. And it was also true that she had kept on seeing him without letting either Molly or Ann know what she was doing, that she had run away from the conservatory with him because she loved him and because she wished to be free. She knew it was a fact that he had taught her to dance and had used her in his act, had had a special costume made for her that fitted the name of a song he liked to sing. But, of course, in the dream she had just had these events, that had taken months to occur, had slipped into one another in a night, fitting together one inside the other like a Chinese puzzle. Still, it was true that Jim had taken up with Vanessa, that she had grown jealous of her, that one night when Jim failed to return to the dressing-room after the act she had flown into a rage and had decided to walk back to their hotel alone. She also remembered growing cold on the windy street and stopping at a lunchroom for a cup of coffee, and that when she had resumed her walk someone had been following her. But there the dream became fanciful, losing itself in a maze of symbols and a nightmare terror. And it was at just this point that she lost track of reality altogether. She knew that she had begun to run, that whoever it was that was following her – or whatever it was – had come closer and closer . . .

She shuddered and held herself stiff and rigid on the bed. Despite Dr Danzer's good advice, it did not work. She had reached the link but all she remembered was the substitute fancy, the thing that she knew had never happened, could not possibly have happened – had not Dr Danzer gone to the trouble of checking the records? – that could only be a figment of her neurosis. And yet it was the only reality for her. If that had not occurred, what had? But, worse than that, why could she not turn and look around *now*? What was she afraid of finding? Why was she afraid that what had never happened, what Dr Danzer assured could not possibly have happened except in her mind, had happened again?

She would feel better if she knew how she came to be in this strange hotel room that was so uncomfortably like the one in that other city many years ago. But, although she tried, she could not yet remember the events of the recent past, of last night and yesterday. The only way she would discover them, she had long since realized from experience, was to use the doctor's method, to finger the links of the chain of memory – even if one of them were vague and dubious, she could by-pass that one – to follow them up one by one until they led her to the present.

After that night she had been jealous of Jim and had run away from the night club; *after what had probably never happened the next morning* she had been terrified and had left the city, had taken a train to her home half-way across the country, had returned to her father's house to find a funeral wreath on the door. Her father had died of heart failure in the night only a few days before, a neighbour told her. They had tried to reach her, but the conservatory thought she had come home. After this shock she had stayed at home the rest of the waning summer until her father's affairs were settled. The bookstore was sold, the house and all its furniture, even her piano, was sold, and she found that she had money and could travel. That fall she had not returned to the conservatory, but had gone to New York and applied to Madame Tedescu. She had played for Madame, a frail old lady with ash-white hair whose name was known on two continents, and Madame had accepted her for a pupil. Her life for the next ten years had consisted of music: three years with Madame in New York from nine to twelve each morning, from one to six each afternoon, each day in the year with no vacation and only Sundays off; two years in Rome, after she had won a prize, with a spirited Italian master of ancient instruments; and then five more years, with Madame again, all over the face of Europe, concertizing in Paris, Brussels, Vienna, Berlin, Naples, Moscow, London. And, finally, not so many years ago, her first concert in New York's Town Hall, the bouquets of roses and one particular corsage of brown orchids from a tall, blond man who was that season's sensation as a conductor – Basil.

The happy years had been next: their marriage and those idyllic weeks on a New England farm, days like butter with its white froth in the churn, their new house in New York, their friends, Madame Tedescu, the kind words of the critics. And then another summer had come, and with it the difficulty, the blackness that arose out of her harpsichord, even when she played her beloved Bach, and overcame her. That memory had haunted her, the things that went wrong, the little pieces of days that somehow got all mixed up or irretrievably lost, her wanderings. And then her sickness, the days and weeks when there was only blackness, the hospital, the latticed window and the view of the elms . . .

She had that much of it straight, she could think of it, put each link in its rightful place. Except for the early, black, lost weeks, she could remember every incident of her stay at the hospital, recall all the nights when she had fought against the past and emerged victorious. All the days of the last week, the day she left the hospital, the days she went shopping, the interview with Dr Danzer, the luncheon with Nancy and the afternoon at her studio with its terrifying episode -- yes, all this fitted into place, even her meeting Jim Shad, the ride in the taxi, her escape, the woman descending the front steps of her house against the setting sun, the letter in the console table that was inexplicably missing . . . And now she remembered what had happened next. She had gone into the library and found Basil seated at the piano; she had stood looking at him, afraid to speak lest her words betray her thoughts. She had watched him play for many minutes and then had turned about and left the house. As she walked the streets, going towards the midtown section and a small French restaurant where she might have dinner quietly, she had thought of the queer squarish bag she had found in one of her drawers and of the vulgarly scented powder spilled on her dresser. While she sat by herself in the little restaurant, drinking a glass of claret, she had thought of the doctor's warning that her husband might have changed, and she remembered the way Nancy had hinted at the same thing during lunch. And she had grown frightened and sad, and had drunk a few too many glasses of claret.

Later, on an impulse, she had bought a newspaper and

looked in the advertisements for the name of the night club where Jim Shad was singing. She knew that in view of what had happened that afternoon the last thing she should do was to go to where he worked; but she wanted badly to hear him sing again, she wanted to be part of the anonymous crowd, to be there near him and yet in no way connected. She had stopped in another bar and had one more drink, this one a martini, to gather up her courage, and then had hailed a taxi to take her downtown to his night club, a Village cellar.

Once inside the small, low-ceilinged room with bizarrely painted walls that seemed to converge on the minuscule bandstand and even more minute dance-floor, she could not escape. She had not realized that the place would be so intimate – in her mind she still imagined Jim Shad singing in the great barns that were Middle-Western dance-halls – nor that at ten-thirty at night there would be so few people there. The head waiter had shown her to a table near the dance-floor, and only when she insisted had he allowed her to seek a darker corner where she hoped she could not be seen as readily. But no sooner had she seated herself than she realized that out of the dozen people at the bar and at tables around the room were the two she did not want to see her – one of whom she would never have thought would be there – Jim Shad and Vanessa. Even worse, Shad, who sat facing her, had seen her, had apparently watched her discussion with the head waiter over where she should sit, was smiling at her over Vanessa's shoulder, winking at her to let her know that he knew she was there, that he wanted to see her and would be around as soon as he could get rid of Vanessa.

She had wanted to leave, but she had known it was useless. If she had gone, he would follow her. As it was, she was safest in the night club. When he did his act, she would call Basil and get him to come for her. Sooner or later she would have to tell Basil about this – although she feared that if she did it would give Basil the opportunity for which he was probably seeking to ask for a divorce –

tonight was as good a time as any. But in the meantime she had known that she would have to deal with Shad.

She ordered a drink and kept her eyes averted. This stratagem was ineffective: although she did not look at him, she could feel his eyes persistently on her, could not keep the image of his face, his casual smile, from rising up before her, could not divert her thoughts from him. The waiter brought her a drink and a bowl of popcorn and pretzels; she drank the martini slowly, intent on each sip, took pretzel after pretzel, crumbling each one until she had an ant-hill of cracker meal built up on the tablecloth. The cellar filled slowly; she could hear the head waiter speak to each couple as they came down the stairs, and by listening closely to the sound of their feet on the hardwood floor she detected where they had been seated. The piano-player trundled his midget piano to her table, placing it so that it blocked her view of Jim and Vanessa – or the view she might have had if she had looked up; he played several pieces rather badly, but it was a relief to be able to raise her eyes for a time, and when he had finished she gave him money. The orchestra came in – a small combination made up of piano, double-bass, trumpet and drums – and began to play the classics in a modified Dixieland style; they played cleanly, and if her mind had not been on Jimmy she would probably have liked their music. Suddenly she realized that the club was packed with people. They seemed to have come all at once – she glanced at her watch and saw that it was nearly midnight. The orchestra's playing became freer, the solos grew longer and the improvisation more ingenious. She began to watch the trumpet-player, a lean reed of a man who seemed to have the shakes, but he kept to the beat and knew how to develop a melody. A few minutes later she was watching the drummer, and then the big, dark-coloured man who slapped the bull-fiddle. Casually, as if it were accidental, she let her eyes flick over to the table where she had seen Jim and Vanessa. The auburn-haired woman was gone, but Shad saw her look at him,

543

and instantly rose to his feet. Her fingers rolled the stem of her glass back and forth and her lips trembled as she watched him thread his way to her table. Then he was standing over her, a dark shadow on the circle of white of her table-cloth, saying, 'May I?' Of course, she had nodded her head.

Jim had sat down opposite her without another word. He had turned around and signalled to the waiter, who immediately brought him a bourbon. He had thrown this down his throat, squinting as he had used to do as he did it, but making no comment. She said nothing. He took a handful of popcorn and began to roll it kernel after kernel at her tiny, crumbling tower of broken pretzels. By the time he had rolled the last bit of popcorn across the table the mound was demolished.

'I talked to the boss,' he said. He did not drawl.

She did not look at him and gave no sign that he had said anything.

'I don't have to sing tonight.'

She sipped at her drink and looked away from him at the orchestra.

'I thought we might go some place. It's been a long time, Ellen.'

His voice, his presence, moved her, was by turns comforting and stimulating. She did not trust herself to look at him, but it was becoming increasingly difficult to avoid his eyes.

'If you are worried about her, don't be. I've taken care of that.'

To her surprise, she realized that she believed him.

'You are the only one I have ever cared for, the only one who has ever mattered. I would have come to you sooner, but I didn't know how to approach you. You've made yourself somebody, Ellen – you are great. I don't know why I acted the way I did this afternoon. I guess it was the way you looked at me . . . you looked at me as if you were afraid of me.' His voice was quiet, hesitant – she had not heard him stammer before – sincere.

'Let me get your coat,' he was saying. 'I love you and I want to be with you.'

And she had nodded her head.

She opened her eyes again. She sat up in bed, but she kept her eyes fixed on the brown-varnished door. That was the way it had been. She had gone with him. They had walked in Washington Square and sat on a bench and necked like a couple of kids. She had wanted to ask him what had happened that night so long ago, she had wanted to find out if what she remembered was true . . . or if the doctor was right and she had only imagined it. But it had hardly seemed the time.

He had taken her to a small hotel nearby, a place where he knew the night clerk. The only room available was a small one without a bath. She had looked up at the ceiling. She remembered that she had noticed the crack in the plaster when the bellboy had shown them the room, except that it had looked worse in the bald glare of the electric light than it did now in the soft morning sunshine. Jim had bought a bottle, and they had had a couple of drinks – then she had turned out the lights and waited for him while he went down the hall.

That was all she could remember.

Still looking at the door, she threw back the covers and got out of bed. She had nothing on, and there was a dark stain on her hands, her breasts and her thighs. She held her breath and determined to be calm this time, to reason it all out before she did anything, so that she would be sure to remember.

She found Jim's body between the bed and the door. His face was scratched and his throat was mottled. A dark stem of blood had spouted from his mouth and grown a black bud along his chin; when she touched it, it flowered redly. His head, the top of it, had been flattened, and his hair was matted with dried blood. When she looked back to the bed, she saw that there was blood on one of the

545

posts, that there were dark stains on the sheet and the mattress. There was no doubt that he was dead – although she felt for his pulse –and that he had been dead for a long time.

She dressed quickly, opened the door a crack and looked to see if anyone were about before going down the hall to wash her hands. She scrubbed the bowl to make sure that she left no stains, then peered into the hall again and returned to her room. Once back inside, she slowly and cautiously searched the room to be certain that she was not leaving evidence of her presence. She found a bobby-pin, three curling hairs, one with a split-end, and her lipstick. She stood over Jim's body, looking at it, trying to remember. It was no use. She opened the window and stepped out on the fire-escape.

As she was easing the window down from outside, her hands slipping on the dusty glass, someone began to hammer on the door of the room. The sound frightened her more than the sight of Jim's body had; her hands fell away from the window, allowing it to fall to the sill with a loud, slamming sound. She shrank back from the window, colliding with the railing of the fire-escape, losing her balance for an instant, catching a dizzying glimpse of the street many storeys below. It was all she could do to keep from pitching off the iron stairs, and when she had regained her balance she was so weak that she sank down on her hands and knees.

In this position she looked through the window into the room once more – in time to see the door bulge, the flimsy bolt break and the key fly out of the lock, the door swing open. A tall, auburn-haired woman, her face grey with anxiety, lurched into the room. Her hands spread apart as she saw the body; she ran forward and collapsed at Jim's side. Ellen saw that she was Vanessa.

Slowly Ellen crept down the gritty iron stairs of the fire-escape. Not until she was within jumping distance of the alley did she stand erect; then she leaped the last ten feet and landed on the kerb. When she reached the street, she stood on the corner and hailed a taxi.

Vanessa must have followed them when they left the night club; she must have waited outside the hotel all night for them to reappear. When, out of jealousy, she had at last been forced to pound on the door, she must have expected to confront Ellen with Jimmy. She could not have known what she would actually discover.

Ellen sat forward in the cab and, as it turned the corner into Fifth Avenue, looked back at the hotel. She did not think that she had been seen.

5

She did not think that she had been seen. She had stood looking down at the pale stalk of her arm, the white flower of her hand and the glittering crystal of the wine-glass it held, watching the wine-blood pour out on the hearth. A sound, a rubbing of cloth on cloth, made her glance up and into the mirror, where she had met Basil's eyes gravely regarding her own, Basil's head slowly, slightly – so that no one else might see – shaking in disapproval, remonstrating with her. 'Wine is for drinking, Ellen,' he said.

She turned about and faced him, archly bringing the wine-glass back to her lips, pressing its cold edge against them, 'I know,' she said. 'I don't know why I had to do that. Truly, I don't.'

'You did not have to do it, Ellen. No one made you.'

She thought about this for a moment, considering each word of what he said, listening to the sound of each syllable in her mind. 'I know,' she said. 'I didn't have to. I just wanted to. I did it because I wanted to.'

He continued to look at her, without speaking, his eyes clouded with worry.

She smiled at him and held out the glass. 'Fetch me another glassful, please, Basil. I promise I shall drink this one.'

He took the glass from her hand, but he did not smile. He hesitated, seemed about to speak – she saw his lips move. But then he walked away towards the butler.

There was something pathetic about him, she decided as she watched him walk between the chatting couples. Perhaps it was the way he held her glass stiffly in front of him, as if it were a signal or a warning. Or it might be that she was watching him in the mirror, that his reflection diminished him, made him seem smaller, almost childlike. But whatever it was that caused her to pity him – if it were pity she felt and not just heightened sympathy – did not matter; what mattered was that this was the way she felt, this was the way it was, the way it had to be. She shut her eyes as she turned around swiftly, her long, full, black velvet skirts swirling and whispering. She felt for the diamond choker at her throat, the choker that Basil had given her earlier that evening as she sat backstage trembling, waiting for the time to come, waiting to walk out of the wings and into the brilliant space, to stand with her hand on the chill mahogany of her harpsichord, to close her eyes and bow to the great, many-faced beast. Basil had approached her from behind then, too; she had heard his knock on the door, heard her maid greet him, had seen his face swim out of the dim reaches of her mirror into the foreground. She had spoken to him, shutting her eyes then, too, because she had been afraid that she might read on his face evidence of the same fear that she felt; she had only opened them as she felt the hardness, the heaviness at her throat, as if a metalled hand had caressed her reassuringly – but she had opened them to grandeur, to bright fire and glory, to Basil's smile. This time when she opened her eyes, having completed her manoeuvre, having faced about, she saw only the smoke-palled drawing-room, the confusion of bare arms and backs, of dark suits and white shirts and dresses of many colours – and the pinkly enamelled wrinkles of her hostess's face, poor, doddering Mrs Smythe.

A grey, fumbling wraith of a form surmounted by a small, puckered, shiny mask of a face, Mrs Smythe had already clawed at her hand, had caught it and clasped it between her own desiccated bunch of fingerbones. Now she was cooing. 'My darling, you were wonderful. Such tone! Such colour! True, true virtuosity!'

She smiled at Mrs Smythe, feeling the skin of her mouth

stretch, feeling her lips part in the social gesture. Her other hand rooted at the hard stones that guarded her neck, clung there as a sparrow in a storm clings to its nest. To keep the smile up, to display an undaunted face to Mrs Smythe and the room, took all her strength: her shoulders sagged, something within herself emptied, ruthlessly flowed like water down a drain, like wine out of a glass. But just as she was sure that her knees were going to give, that she would in another moment fall forward, sink down, down, a spark of anger flickered in her mind, flickered and finding tinder blazed, grew into flame and warmed her. Damn you, damn you, she thought as she smiled more broadly at her hostess, what right have you to give parties, to know everyone who counts and have favours to bestow? You know nothing of music, of my world of sound, of what it means to set tones down in space and time so that they relate, so that you can build on them other tones, inject into them rhythm, give them weight and meaning, construct with them a reality. You know only people, people you can twist and turn and force to do your bidding; you care only for power. And that is why I am here, why Basil is here, and you know it. Yes, I know and you know that it had to be you who gave a reception in my honour after this, my first 'return' concert, otherwise you might have lost a little of that prestige that is so precious to you. And we both also know that I had to accept your invation, and Basil, too, because old Jeffry Upman always comes to your parties and you tell him what his opinion should be. Jeffry's opinion! Jeffry's fame as a critic! Your opinion and your power! But where, Mrs Smythe, where do you get your opinion? From the music, from the tiny scraps of my sound you heard tonight when you were not chattering with one or another of your friends? Ah, no, not from the music – you have never learned to listen to music. You form your notions in subtle ways, if you can be said to have notions at all. You like those musicians and composers who will do as you suggest, who will add to your fame, who will cluster around you and heed your beck and call. It is like a snow-ball, isn't it, Mrs Smythe? As it rolls downhill it grows larger and larger, and you can grow larger with it, just like all the other little flakes of snow, if you put yourself in its path and allow yourself to adhere. But if you avoid the oncoming snowball, if you resist it, you will be thrust aside to shiver alone, you will be ignored. Damn you, Mrs Smythe.

But, in fact, Mrs Smythe did not resemble a snowball as much as she did a ghost. Except for her face, with its palimpsest youthfulness, she was alarmingly insubstantial. She seemed a shadow in grey lace, a wreathed, two-dimensional shade. Her hands were pink bones, her feet animated shoes. Yet she inspired no compassion, she was not helpless, but a vituperative relic, an awe-inspiring totem, perhaps, that had been placed in your path by an enemy to bewitch you. And as she complimented you, as she smiled her wrinkles at you, she was measuring you, testing your loyalty, calculating your potential fame and its future worth to her.

'What a lovely dress, Mrs Smythe – and what a lovely party! And now you say kind things to me, as well. I'm really overwhelmed!' As she said these polite words, made this fitting response, she noticed with cold amazement that they proceeded in proper sequence, made sense and seemed to meet Mrs Smythe's approval. But you could never tell for certain what Mrs Smythe was thinking. Her eyes, like gems imbedded in a crackled glaze, gave no clues; her gestures were inconsistent with her intentions; those who knew her well averred that the chief source of her power, other than her wealth, lay in her inscrutability.

'I want you to meet a delightful young man,' she was saying, her prehensile hand clutching avidly at Ellen's aching wrist. Bobbing her head solemnly, she began to usher her through the crush, brushing past a painter and his mistress, a bevy of cherubic composers chortling at a boyish witticism, a stern-visaged sculptress who seemed to have been rough-hewn by her own hand out of alabaster, to a tall and gangling fellow, an adenoidal youth with a receding chin and a furtive hand that tried to secrete his faintly moustached mouth as they approached. But he saw that it was too late, that they were upon him, and his hand fell away embarrassedly, grabbed at his pocket and, missing that, fell limply at his side – she saw the crop of uncultivated hairs that littered his lip, too long to be a mistake in shaving, not dense enough to act as an adornment, too red to be ever anything but fatuous. 'Ferdinand,' Mrs Smythe was commanding, 'I know you have been wanting to meet our guest of honour, dear Ellen here. Ellen, this is Ferdinand Jaspers. I'm sure you two will get along famously.'

And Mrs Smythe went on to another solitary victim, standing agape across the room from Ellen and Ferdinand, barely having halted her inexorable progress to introduce them. Ferdinand, she could see, was not used to Mrs Smythe. A flush had started above his collar and would soon threaten his face. His hand flew up to his mouth, jerked there for an instant, then fell reluctantly back again. 'I – I enjoyed your recital, Mrs Purcell,' he said. 'I – I enjoyed it very much.'

'Thank you,' she said, knowing that she should say more, that it would be unkind not to help him by holding up her end of the unnecessary conversation, yet enjoying his uneasiness.

He wet his lips and, as if its action were controlled by a mechanism, his hand skittered up to his head, patted and smoothed his clay-coloured hair. She was amused to see a droplet of perspiration forming on his brow and, while she waited for him to speak again, she chose to speculate as to which side of his nose it would streak down eventually. Then the silence that had held only one youth's shame was broken by a voice that sounded from somewhere in the room, that belonged to some one person in the clutter, a voice she almost, but did not quite, recognize talking about something she did not want mentioned, that she had hoped had been forgotten. '. . . how could you have kept from hearing about it? It was in all the papers. The more sensational ones even printed pictures of them lying there together, dead. A towel was thrown over his body, of course, and she was fully dressed. But, even so, I don't think they should print such things. They said she killed him, you know. Oh, it was based on the time of their deaths – according to the medical examiner he died hours before she did. That was how it was, or so they said. She killed him, for jealousy or for some other reason, and then got to brooding over it. The night clerk said he had rented a room to a man and a woman. No, but then would you expect them to give their *right* names? Yes, she must have felt remorse . . . killed herself. My dear, I was so surprised that you hadn't heard of it . . . a sensation, nothing less than a sensation. Why, I had seen him just a night or two before . . . he was singing in the Village, you know . . .'

Ferdinand cleared his throat and she recovered herself. She realized that all the time she had been listening to the other conversation, afraid to turn around to see who was speaking, she must have been staring at the youth, staring blankly and fixedly; but he might have taken this for a steady inquiry, an indication of another kind of interest. Quickly, she lowered her eyes.

He coughed. 'I – I am a poet,' he said.

Why, oh why, she asked herself, had he told her that? What did his being a poet mean to her? She continued to stare at him, realizing full well that even if he had at first mistaken her glance for coquetry, he could not now – seeing his face tighten, his ridiculous attempt at a moustache quiver as he grew more aware of her hostility, sensed that her look was a weapon.

'I – I mean,' he said, 'that I've had a book published. A little book of verse.' And his hand, like an eager retriever after a bird, swept up to his lip and then swept down again.

But, although she did not avert her eyes, she was not listening to him. She had heard the voice again, the voice that sounded familiar, which she was sure that, if she could

553

only stop to think, she would be able to place. Once more it had risen above the continuous murmuring of the crowd, had broken free of the mass sound, and in its escape had seemed to create an area of quiet, a silence within the general noise, in which it alone existed, which it alone commanded. 'As a matter of fact,' the voice was saying, 'I remember that I'd seen him even more recently than that. Yes, I'd not only heard him sing just a few nights before it happened, but he had been in my studio that very afternoon . . . Oh yes, I knew him well . . . why, he used to drop around all the time . . . Who was she? No one you'd know, my dear. Some dreadful person – a dancer I believe, I read some place that she had been a dancer; yes, I'm altogether sure she was a dancer . . . Why? Why do they ever? She loved him, I suppose. Isn't that always the reason? Her name? Why, I don't think I remember. I read it once . . . it was in all the papers, of course . . . but now I can't remember . . .'

She recognized the voice, knew all at once without question that it could belong to no one but Nancy. And with this knowledge she felt herself compelled to cross the room, to seek out the voice, to confront Nancy and prove to herself once again that she had nothing to fear. Nancy had sounded behind her and at some distance – she must be back towards the fireplace. Thinking this, she turned about blindly and began to push her way through the chatting throng. The youth was aghast, his face lost all colour – she saw this out of the corner of her eye as she brushed past the nearest couple. She felt sorry for him. But she could not bother to return to him, to apologize for leaving him. It was too important for her to find Nancy, to break into her conversation, to hear clearly every word she had to say.

She sensed that her impulsive progress through the densely peopled room was causing comment, she could feel others' eyes on her – but she did not care. Yet she did force herself to walk more slowly, to go out of her way rather than to press herself between a tall man and a robust woman who impeded her passage, to look for Nancy instead of locating her only by the sound of her voice. In fact, she even stood still momentarily, gazing about the great, glittering room, and was rewarded by the sight of the person she sought. Nancy leaned against the fireplace, her granite face contorted by her emphatic speech, her thick-fingered, peasant's hands gesturing broadly. She was relieved to see her, but she did not hesitate any longer. Instead, she pushed forward again, even more impulsively than before, blundering against a sofa, nearly upsetting the butler and his tray.

Nancy saw her approaching. She turned away from her companion, a pallid man with sleek hair and an intense expression, to cry, 'Ellen, darling, you were incomparable. It was really an occasion! But, Ellen – I'm so glad we saw you now – I think you can help us out. Ellen, tell me, do you remember meeting a man, a musician, a singer of folk ballads, very popular, in my studio last summer?'

She nodded to the pallid man, to whom she had not been introduced. Then she looked directly at Nancy's massive face. 'You don't mean Jim Shad?' Her breathing slowed as she waited for Nancy to react, to show any indication that she *knew*.

But Nancy's face did not change. 'That's right. Well, I remember his name, too. But, Ellen, for the life of me I can't remember the name of the woman – she was a dancer, a dreadful person – who killed him. You knew that he was murdered, didn't you? I thought everyone knew, that simply everyone must have read about it – it was such a sensation; she beat his head in, you know! – but Jack here tells me that he didn't know. You knew about it, didn't you, Ellen?'

She smiled, amused by Nancy's chatter. 'It was terrible. I read about it at the time. Did they ever find who did it?' She was proud of her own calmness, her inventiveness.

Nancy's eyes widened and she plainly showed her disbelief. 'But, darling, that's what I'm trying to tell you! This woman, what's-her-name, did it. She bashed his head in, then shot herself – although why she didn't use the gun on him I've never understood. Only I can't remember her name. I thought you might. She was a dancer.' Nancy seemed to have run down.

She looked at her closely, saw her leaning against the mantel, her slouched stance, made sure that her face was blank with curiosity – or was it malice? 'Although why she didn't use the gun on him I've never understood,' she had said. Had she meant that ironically? Was she using this means to let her know that she suspected her? The thought tortured her and made her want to avoid Nancy's eyes. But she knew that she dare not do this, that if Nancy did suspect her such an action would help to confirm her belief. She must brazen it out.

'I remember now. I do think I read something about a dancer. She killed him, didn't she? Did you know her?' She spoke harshly, jerkily.

Jack, who had been smoothing the marble of the mantel with his hand, looked at her in surprise. But Nancy, if she noticed, did not show that she was aware.

'That was it, Ellen. The desk clerk said they registered together under assumed names the night before. Then they found them the next morning. Both of them were dead. She had killed him first, then shot herself. Don't you remember her name?'

She pressed her hand to her throat, felt the diamond choker, was reassured by its unyielding presence. 'I can't say that I do. I'm sorry, but I'm afraid I didn't follow the case. It must have happened just before Basil and I went away. We went to his cabin in the Catskills, don't you remember? I had to get away from everything so that I could practise, and Basil was deep in his scores. We didn't see a newspaper all summer. I'm afraid I missed all the gruesome details.'

Nancy smiled. 'Of course, you wouldn't. I had forgotten that you and Basil were away. Why, you must have left that same week! Oh, well, it doesn't matter. I only wish my memory wouldn't play such queer tricks on me.'

She could see now that she had been mistaken. Nancy had meant nothing by her question, had just been curious, gossipy, as was her nature. But now that her mind had started on that track, now that the special, dry-mouthed fear, the calm panic, had returned, she was forced to remember other details of that morning, that morning that seemed years ago but was only months, that morning that she had returned to the house to find Basil sitting up in his leather chair in the library, sitting stiffly with his head twisted uncomfortably, asleep. She had known at once that he had waited up for her, that he must have been concerned about her absence. She had gone over to him and knelt beside him, had awakened him with a kiss.

His eyes had opened heavily, slowly, his hand had flown to his forehead and rubbed it, before he saw her and accepted the fact that, at last, she was there. He had hunched forward in his chair, feeling in his bones the cramps of an uncomfortable night – he had taken her hand between his own and pressed it tightly. 'Are you all right?' he had asked.

She had been far from being all right. She had been frightened and sick and on the point of killing herself. On the way uptown in the taxi Shad's face had haunted her, and even at that moment she could sense the blood upon her body like a weight or a burning brand. But she had not known how to speak to him of this. She had known that something within her was wrong, badly wrong, that in some way she was both wrong and bad. Yet the pressure of his hands on her own gave her strength, enabled her to lie. 'I'm quite all right,' she had said.

Later, much later, she had decided to tell him nothing about it. She had been clear in her own mind about that. He would learn of it soon enough, she had reasoned, from others – more brusquely perhaps, but less emotionally, than if she had tried to tell him. She had gone to her study, had locked the door, and for the first time since she had returned from the hospital she had addressed herself to her instrument. It had been all that day as if her fingers, her body – yes, even her mind – had not belonged to her; as if, so she remembered it, the hesitant music she made had not been heard by her, as if even her breathing were not her own. She had felt herself to be an instrument, a cruel, polished edge of surgical steel, lying on a sterile cloth, whetted for use. And the music, the sounds her fingers brought into being, had been bright, sharp slivers of tone that had lacerated the silence.

At dusk Basil had knocked at the door and had persuaded her to come to dinner. Later, because he had wanted to and it had not displeased her, they had gone for a walk. He had bought a newspaper at the entrance to the park and they had gone inside, had sat on a bench to read it. If she closed her eyes even today (although she dare not close her eyes now with Nancy looking at her) she would still be able to see that headline, vaguely black in the indirect light of the lamp-post, that had told about Jim Shad's murder and Vanessa's suicide. She had reached for the paper, had torn it from Basil's hands, had read the entire story. At first she could not understand why Vanessa had killed herself, and then she realized that the police did not understand either. It had seemed comic to her that the police should think that Vanessa had killed him; she had wanted to laugh, to sob, to get up and dance like a child in pigtails, but she had known that if she had she could never have explained her action to Basil. As it was, he had wanted to know why she was so interested in the murder. 'This paper features a murder every night,' he had said. But that had been easy enough. She had told him that she had met Jim Shad only yesterday at, of all places, his sister's, Nancy's, studio. She had said that it was the first time that a friend of hers had been murdered and that she was naturally interested.

But a few days after that night, when Basil suggested that they go to the Catskills, she had been relieved at the prospect of leaving the city, of being alone, cut off from everyone, so she could think it through. Of course, Basil was with her most of the time – except for two weeks in

August when he had conducting dates at several summer concerts. Being with Basil had been different, though, had been almost the same as being alone, they had been a part of each other. Her harpsichord and Basil's piano had been transported to the cabin, and they split the days between themselves: in the morning she practised and he did what he liked, in the afternoon Basil read manuscripts and played critical passages while she went up the mountain sides in search of laurel or found a brook in which she could splash and wade. At night they had been together, driving along the twisting mountain lanes or lying back on the dewy grass, their eyes on the stars, their arms about each other.

She had never thought it through. She had made several false starts. One time she had decided that she would go to Dr Danzer, whom she was supposed to have called but had not, and tell him everything. On another occasion she had decided that this would be useless, that Dr Danzer would say what he had said before. He would tell her that this had not happened, that it was an hallucination, a figment of her neurosis that arose out of another, older guilt. But she had believed this for only a little time. Then the other aspect of her self, the sceptical part of her, had scoffed. She knew that whatever had happened that last night with Shad, had happened; it was real. It had not been a dream. Shad was dead, and his death had been recorded in the newspapers. What was more – and the strange thing was that she could formulate the thought, could think of it coldly as a fact, without alarm – it was more than likely, it was probable, that she had killed him.

'I've always said that there was something in the case that never came to light.' Nancy's remark sounded like a trumpet to her ears. Abruptly, her reverie was shattered, and she became electrically aware of Nancy and the danger of her chatting tongue. 'The police said this woman was jealous of him. They found witnesses who had seen them quarrelling, who had heard her accuse him of infidelity only the night before she killed him. But they never mentioned who she was jealous of, never a word leaked out as to who it was he was carrying on with – they made a real mystery of that!' Nancy tossed her head to emphasize her point. Jack, her pallid companion, nodded his perfunctorily – he was plainly bored with the conversation.

She could not decide whether Nancy actually suspected anything or not. But she did seem to keep coming closer and closer to the truth – if she were really clever, this might be a test. 'Oh, I think the police knew!' she exclaimed, trying to make her voice seem exasperated, as if she were tired of talking about an old, sordid crime. 'They undoubtedly questioned the person, found she was innocent and didn't release her name. Would you want to see an innocent woman's reputation ruined?'

Nancy looked at her closely and smiled slightly. 'Why, Ellen,' she said, 'what a horror you must think I am! Of course, I shouldn't want to see this mysterious person's name in print. I'd just like to know who she was, that's all. You see, Jim Shad was my friend. I can't help but be curious, and I should think you would be. Didn't you meet him at my house the very day before he was murdered?'

She opened her mouth to speak, to say something, anything, to keep off the silence and allow herself time to think. But before she could speak, Mrs Smythe, wraith-like, materialized at her side. Her brittle fingers clung to her elbow, her wrinkled face smiled coaxingly. 'Darling Ellen, I am loath to tear you away from these charming people, but dear Jeffry is waiting to see you. He attended your concert, you know, and he is going to do a little piece about it in tomorrow's paper. But, darling, he wants to see you first; he wants to have a little discussion, and he has a deadline to meet. So I'm sure your kind friends will excuse you!'

The birdlike pressure on her arm was surprisingly forceful; she found herself swivelled about by Mrs Smythe and obliquely propelled through the crowd to another part of the room where Jeffry Upman sat, alone and gingerly, upon a gilt chair, tapping at the darker squares of the parquet floor with the ferrule of his tightly-rolled umbrella. He was a thin, palsied, old man whose slight figure was bent into the shape of a question-mark. Whether his bodily posture had anything to do with his aesthetic predilection for the rhetorical question had long been a moot point among the wags of Fifty-seventh Street; however, all his reviews were spotted with indications of interrogation like raisins in bread-pudding. 'Last night in the august halls of Carnegie,' he would write, 'among the accustomed pomps and amid the proper hush, Mr Blizz-Blazz revealed himself to be one of the consummate artists of our time. There was something in his tone that melted, although it at no time lacked the vertebraic rhythm of authority, something that commanded our most subtle emotions and demanded a quality of listener on a level with the quality of Mr Blizz-Blazz's musicianship. Were there some in the audience who noticed, on occasion, a slight divagation from true pitch? Did others seem to feel that, here and there, inflections could be descried that were untraditional, if not debatable? Perhaps, one or more in the audience were aware of certain inconsistencies of tempi, of an unfortunate tremolo, some ill-chosen retardations? If so, these connoisseurs were the exception, as the cataclysmatic applause that greeted the artist after his second number spontaneously attested to the circumstance that unequivocal recognition and enthusiastic approval were Mr Blizz-Blazz's due. Later, the programme promised that this unparalleled artist would return to play concertos by Mendelssohn, Tschaikovsky and Sibelius, as well as smaller pieces by Lalo, Debussy and Thomson; but, unfortunately, the lateness of the hour and the excruciating length of modern programmes prevented our further attendance.'

Jeffry had been a music critic in New York since before the days of Gustav Mahler; he was now not only superannuated, but somnolent, a fact that more than one concert-goer had discovered for himself by glimpsing him drowsing in his seat through the most thunderous of symphonies. Usually he contrived to stay awake through the first number or two, but after that sleep overcame him. To many musicians sleeping critics are not too different from sleeping dogs, and Jeffry's sleepiness might not have become an object of jest if he had not also been inclined to snore. More than one violinist, while playing an unaccompanied suite of Bach's or the quiet movement of a Debussy sonata, had become uncomfortably aware of Jeffry's unintended, but frequently disastrous, obbligato. Curiously, his reputation did not seem to suffer from his habit of catnapping in concert halls; some said this was because of Mrs Smythe's influence, and it did play a part, but it was more probably just another manifestation of our society's respect for anything that is old and accustomed. People were used to seeing Jeffry Upman's signature in the papers, a decade or more ago he had written several books on 'music appreciation' that Mrs Smythe had connived to have distributed by a book club, and to the general public he was as much a fixture, a respectable piece of cultural furniture, as an ageing statesman – most people do not read music criticism anyway.

She knew all these things, and she realized that it was useless to feel bitter towards senility. Even so, as she stood before him and saw his trembling head, his dull, heavy-lidded eyes and his pale, blue-veined, old man's flesh, she felt a desire to laugh at him, to pull him off the gilt chair and onto his feet, to turn him about and display him to the party, to cry out, 'Here you are! Look at him. This is what passes on the music you hear, this is the person whose review you will read tomorrow to find out if what you heard tonight was good or not!' But, of course, she did not do it.

Her presence was a formality, as was his. They both knew it, and showed that they knew it to each other as they fumbled for words. Mrs Smythe broke the silence. 'I was sure, Jeffry, that you would want to speak to dear Ellen. Everyone, *simply everyone*, was amazed at her brilliance tonight.' These were Jeffry's instructions, for which he had been waiting, she knew. And she also realized that Mrs Smythe had forced the encounter, that Jeffry had not been 'eager to see her', but only waiting to discover what his friend's verdict would be.

How Mrs Smythe arrived at her verdict no one knew – least of all Jeffry. But it was not irrevocable, and she would have to play the game out, to be polite to the thin, old figure who questioningly tapped with his umbrella as he peered up at her, whose eyes were already all but shut, who wanted nothing better than to get out of this hot, noisy room, away from all these milling people, so that once more he might fall asleep.

'It was most kind of you to come, Mr Upman,' she said (what else was there to say?), 'I am looking forward to reading your notice.'

Jeffry jiggled a bit on his chair, and the umbrella tapped more loudly. He coughed, drily, once, twice. She remembered that he always prefaced his remarks with this ritual. When he spoke, his voice sounded like a piece of chalk drawn across a blackboard or an out-of-tune piccolo. 'Splendid! Splendid! Splendid!' he squeaked. Then he looked down at his hand and watched it travel to his vest, cautiously observed it as it plucked a gold turnip from his pocket and snapped the lid to reveal two spidery hands converging on an ivory dial. 'Splendid!' he wheezed as he stood up gradually, his knees stiff, his body bent, his feet the dot of the question-mark. 'It's late. I must go.'

'Jeffry, you can't,' Mrs Smyth said firmly and, as he continued to stand, showed that she meant what she said by pushing him down again on to the fragile chair. 'Ellen has promised to play for us, and I know you will want to listen.'

The old man's chin sagged and his lips trembled querulously. But all he said was, 'Splendid! In that case. By all means. Splendid!'

The conversation, if it could be called that, ended as peremptorily as it had been begun by Mrs Smythe's inexorable pressure on her elbow. Meekly, she turned away from Jeffry and allowed herself to be urged by her persistent hostess into the crowd of guests. This time she was directed towards the far end of the great room, towards a raised platform that was decorated with velvet drapes and bedecked with two tall vases of roses and upon which sat the harpsichord Mrs Smythe had foresightedly provided for the occasion. Throughout the evening the drapes had been drawn, the instrument concealed, and even now the butler was still occupied with tying back a flounce, adjusting the position of the rose-filled vases. As they proceeded among the guests, they became gradually the centre of attention. What signal had Mrs Smythe given to invoke this miracle, this sudden, unexpected quieting of talk, this concentrated curiosity? Perhaps none, or perhaps the butler had been instructed to open the drapes when he saw them talking to old Jeffry, or, most likely yet, the entire evening had been planned to conform to a strict time schedule. Whatever her method, the fact remained that Mrs Smythe's receptions always featured these swift, appropriate changes-of-scene, always betrayed the presence of an experienced stage director, no doubt Mrs Smythe herself.

As she thought this, she caught sight of a diminutive person, a slight bowed figure in watered silk – Madame Tedescu. She was standing a little to the left of a group of two men and a vivacious woman that they were to skirt. Forgetting Mrs Smythe, she swerved in the other direction and pushed her way to the smiling old lady whose solitary presence meant so much to her. Madame Tedescu was in her sixties, her face had shrunk with age and weakness required that she lean upon a gold-headed ebony cane. Her hair was white and fell softly upon her shoulders, but her eyes were as bright and her smile as witty as the first day Ellen had come to her studio.

Madame saw her coming. The smile widened and her eyes glistened. She remembered that Madame had many times earnestly told her that she was her favourite pupil, 'the only one to whom I wish to entrust my tradition'. Knowing this, she also knew that Madame would not lie to her, that Madame would tell her sincerely whether she had played well tonight.

Mrs Smythe, surprised at her escape, caught up with her just as she reached her old friend and teacher. As if she sensed that Ellen had a particular reason for breaking away, she managed to place herself between them and to speak first. 'You should be very proud of our Ellen tonight, Madame. Dear Jeffry was telling me only a moment ago that this recital was one of the great events of his lifetime. Of course, you will read his piece tomorrow to find out all he says, but I can tell you now, confidently, that it will be a paean.'

She had thought that she was accustomed to Mrs Smythe's rudeness and her arbitrary statements, but she had also thought that even Mrs Smythe would not be so crass. If she blushed, if she felt her throat go dry, it was not only out of embarrassment, but because she quickly realized that one reason why Mrs Smythe had not wanted her to see her old friend, and why she was now attempting to influence her opinion as she had Jeffry's, might be that even Mrs Smythe, whose taste in music was appalling in its absence, had known that tonight something had been wrong.

'You do not need to tell me about Ellen.' Madame Tedescu spoke slowly and with still a trace of a Viennese accent. 'I was at the concert. I listened.' She nodded her head solemnly, but then she looked at her and smiled. Her eyes were grave and her smile was kind, but by means of a simple change of expression, an admission of melancholy, she conveyed to her that she was concerned. 'I have not seen you in years, Ellen,' she said, but there was no reproach in her voice. 'Could you come to my studio tomorrow? Some time in the morning would be best. We can talk better there.' And, still smiling, she reached out and stroked her shoulder.

The butler had finished with the drapes and the vases –

Mrs Smythe was eager to manoeuvre her prize on to the stage. 'Ellen has consented to play for us, Madame. In just a few minutes.' She shifted her feet restlessly, the grey veils of her frock moving mysteriously, as if to imply a haste she was too polite to mention.

Madame Tedescu stopped smiling, and her expression became wholly serious. 'But you are tired, aren't you, Ellen? You have played enough tonight.' Her tone seemed a little severe.

Mrs Smythe showed her presence of mind. She turned about instantly, her manner sympathetic, but her voice firm. 'I shouldn't want you to play if you are too tired, Ellen darling,' she said. 'I am only too aware of how exhausting your concerts must be! But, darling, Jeffry will be so disappointed!'

Although she did not want to play, although she wanted only to leave this absurd reception, this roomful of outrageous people, to get out of doors and feel the wind on her face, to look up and see the dark sky, to be alone, she understood the threat in her hostess's words, knew that if she did not comply with her wishes and play, Mrs Smythe was capable of speaking to Jeffry again, of changing her verdict and his. And she was afraid, not as much from what Madame had said as from her manner, that she would need Jeffry's little 'paean' tomorrow.

'Of course I'll play,' she said to Mrs Smythe. And to her old friend, pressing her hand, 'You'll see I'm really not too tired. And I promise to visit you in the morning.'

Madame Tedescu was not displeased at her decision, although her nod of acknowledgement was brief and her smile wry. But Mrs Smythe was fairly tugging at her arm, and she knew her reluctance would become obvious if she lingered any longer. So she allowed herself to be led to the platform.

While her hostess raised her voice to announce that she had consented to play, she seated herself at the strange instrument and closed her eyes. In a few moments she would have to place her fingers on the manuals, to arch them and strike notes, to cease thinking about the world of herself and to think only of her world of sound. Or that was the way it should be. It had not been that way, except on a few, scattered occasions, for a very long time. Since the early part of the summer, since the week she left the hospital, she had played some part of every day. Her fingers had played, the notes had sounded as her eyes had read the page or her memory had prompted her. All the old tricks had returned, her virtuosity was if anything greater than it had ever been. But only a few times had it been *right*. Almost invariably all the sounds had been there and in the proper places, the tone had been accurate, the phrasing exactly what she wished it to be. Still it seemed to her that her playing had remained but a procession of sounds, an alternation of tones, a ragbag of phrases. There was no whole; it worked, when it worked at all, in fits and starts, inanely. Yet her technique remained impeccable, her fingers responded to her mind's demands, all the notes were there. If it were her world no longer, if it had ceased to make sense to her – and, truly, it had – where was her fault, what had gone wrong?

Mrs Smythe had concluded her announcement, and now a ripple of applause informed her that they were waiting for her to begin. She opened her eyes and looked at them, at their polished pink faces, their flushed bare arms and backs, their shining white shirt-fronts and flowing dresses, thinking how much they looked like a stiff prosaic collection of porcelain figurines adorning a bric-à-brac shelf. A pattern of sound formed in her head, etched itself precisely, making her feel alive and well: the first measures of Anna Magdalena's aria. If she could only play it once more the way she heard it! For Madame was listening, would be listening with all her intelligence, and if it came out right and good the way it used to come, she would know it and tell her. She looked for Madame among the pink faces, her eyes roving back and forth across the crowded room. She saw Jeffry, and over there was Nancy, still talking to the pallid man. Near them was a striking auburn-haired girl, a beautiful girl in a lustrous black gown, a girl who was familiar. She was talking to a blond man, talking seriously, quietly, as if she loved him. Who was the man? He looked familiar, too; but, then, she could see only part of him – the rear of his head, his shoulder and his hand raised in a gesture that she was certain she knew, that she surely had seen many times before. The girl stood partly in front of him, turned sidewise to face him, obscuring him from her view. Oh, now they were moving! He had put his arm around her; they were walking towards an alcove, a darker corner, where they would not be seen. They were in love – she was pleased that she had seen them, that her eyes had alighted on them just before she struck the first chord; it was a good sign. But who were they? – why did she feel she knew them? She watched them as they worked their way arm-in-arm back to the alcove, watched them enter, and then saw the man's face for the first time as he pulled at the velour drape. He was Basil.

Her hand fell heavily on the manual, and the other followed mechanically. Her eyes settled upon the maze of black-and-white strips, stared fixedly at the two lean, naked rats that scampered back and forth in it in a blind endeavour to run out. She heard laughter, after a few minutes, and excited talk – but she could not take her eyes off the rats and their intricate game in the black-and-white maze. There was a sound, too, a sound of a glass falling, of brittle blood flowing, tinkling, of a thousand glasses breaking, a million drops of blood tinkling. But this sound mingled with the other sound, the laughter and the whispering; it had nothing to do with the poor naked rats and their frightening maze . . .

Then, for no reason at all, the rats stopped running, the maze reassembled itself before her eyes. Someone, somewhere, was clapping, a lonely sound. She looked down at her lap, and saw that the rats had nestled there, had fallen asleep like children after a hard run. The tinkling sound, the noise of a glass breaking, of blood flowing, persisted in her head, but now she recognized it as a melody, a very familiar tune that she had hoped never to hear again, a folk-song that she had just played:

Jimmy crack corn, and I don't care!
My massa's gone away . . .

6

'Jimmy crack corn! Jimmy crack corn!' The words stole
into her consciousness, were placed there as a placard
is placed in a shop window, obtruded from her sleep like a
finger of guilt pointing out her sin – lingered for a long
moment, echoing as the scream she had heard in her dream
still echoed, then lapsed into silence like a stone dropped
into a pool. She lay on the bed, very still, hushed and
quiet, tense. If only she did not remember! – if only, this
one night, she would not have to experience it all again!
By an effort of will she opened her eyes, let her consciousness advance into the shadow world of her room, strove to
see forms instead of the swirling darkness that held her
prisoner on every side. That darkness, that fearsome blackness, was, she knew, a part of her dream; the darkness
of the room was different, as she would see if she could
but keep her eyes open long enough to accustom them to
the small amount of checkered light that filtered through
the window. That darkness belonged to a night long ago,
and to another night even before that – she only dreamed
it now. Say it! Say it aloud! If you can hear yourself
speak it, you will know it is true and you will not have to
live through that night, those nights, again. Speak it!
Say those words! Louder! Louder! '*I am not afraid of the
dark. I only dream the dark. It is not here now, it is only there
then, when I dream. I am not afraid of the dark!*'

Her voice sounded naked, alone and mad. It was not
her voice, but a child's voice, shrill and whining. And she
was afraid, terribly afraid, of the dark. It was here now,
just as it had been there then in her dream. The dark surrounded her, a great, noisome, evil cloak that smothered

her. There was no light anywhere, no alleviation, only shadow devoured by shadow, umbra and penumbra. Worse than that, there was distance and time, a great pit into which she must fall, on whose edge she trembled at this instant. Many times had she fallen into it, many times had she taken that awful plunge, that dizzying descent that was one prolonged, headlong flight down to the depths of the past, to another place, another era. And it had always begun like this, with that sudden wakefulness, those words in her ears, that echo of a scream. Then, gently, the edge of the pit began to crumble. She found herself scrabbling desperately for a handhold in the drifting, shifting, rapidly disintegrating earth. The scream that had been silenced so long was heard again, now a mere thread of sound – it existed in the pit and she was slipping towards it. She fought bravely, trying to crawl back, struggling like a dog in quicksand against the insubstantial ground, the encompasing shadows, the ruthless attraction of the abyss . . .

It was over this time as suddenly, as amazingly as it had been each time before. There was a flash, an explosion – if one could call it either of those things – of absolute dark, a sudden violence of black that was the null itself. In this she ceased to exist, lost all sense of self, of being, of knowing, merged inextricably with this mirror of nothingness... Yet this, too, passed, and she sensed again, saw light again, was seated in the park with the sun on her back, with green, green grass and blue, blue sky, and children.

She was sitting on the bench watching a squirrel eat the nut she had just given him. He was a clever fellow: he held the bulky nut firmly between his claws and nibbled at it industriously with his sharp, rodent teeth; but all the time that he seemed preoccupied with his task, his beady eyes, glittering targets of sight, were upon her, calculating, determining whether to run and hide the nut or to eat it here, whether there would be more to come or if this were all. The sight of him reassured her – he was alive, intelligent, amoral, her kin. This squirrel had his nut, and she had her life, or this present moment of it, at least. They both clung to it, ravened at it, and kept a keen lookout for transforming possibilities into realities. She laughed and the squirrel took alarm, popping his nut into his cheek and running to the nearest tree and up its trunk a foot or more, then freezing on the bark, blending with it, his head cocked, his eyes gleaming, still watching her. She laughed again, experimentally, but this time he did not move. She was quiet, and, after a few minutes of caution, he returned, slowly and circuitously, sat up and looked at her, demanding a relative's due: another nut.

It was the last in her bag, but she gave it to him, crumpling the bag up afterwards and letting it drop at her feet, where the wind caught it and carried it erratically down the slope, then dropped it, let it lie, like a drunken cat playing with a lame mouse. The squirrel eyed the crumpled ball of paper contemptuously, but made no movement in its direction. He knows that there are no nuts in it, she had thought, that if there had been I would not have thrown it away. And he will leave me soon to search for other sources of nuts, other people with other bags. But what about me? Where shall I go now? What shall I do?

She had stood up and began to walk down the path towards the zoo. It was silly to compare herself with a squirrel, silly and melodramatic. She patted the folded newspaper she carried under her arm. She was a person of note, a musician who had given a successful concert only last night. The proof of it was here – she patted the newspaper again – in the words of Jeffry's review, '. . . a genuine experience . . . she reveals a bright, shining world of pristine sound.' The image of old Jeffry came into her mind, flickered before her eyes, obscuring momentarily the sunshine, the trees and the children. She saw the old man as she had seen him the previous night, sitting precariously on the gilt chair, tapping nervously with his umbrella at the polished floor. She heard him squeak, 'Splendid! Splendid!' But anger overcame her, she blinked her eyes and destroyed her sight of the old critic and, to make the destruction complete, she tore the newspaper out from under her arm and threw it in front of her on the path, taking pleasure in walking on it, trampling on it, rejecting Jeffry's lies. For what Jeffry had said, all his blessed euphemisms, his rhetoric and his allusions, had no relation to the truth. She knew what the truth about last night was: she had given a mediocre performance, she had not played as she had wanted to play, as she had been able to play in the past. She was no longer an artist.

Madame Tedescu had told her this frankly, although she had waited for her to ask. She had gone to her studio that morning as she had promised – she had left it only an hour ago. The doorbell of Madame's great, rambling flat near the Hudson River had tinkled enthusiastically when she had pressed it, and before she could press it again and hear once more its tiny clamour, Madame had opened the door itself. The old woman had seemed smaller in her cavernous studio, more like a fragile marionette than a real person. She was dwarfed by her paintings – a huge Léger, a long, narrow Dufy, a massive Rouault – and even by her instruments: the two concert grands, the clavichord, the virginal and the rare harpsichord of intricately carved ebony that was supposed to have been Mozart's. They had sat upon an Empire divan in the farthest room, a high-ceilinged, cathedral-like studio whose many-paned windows overlooked the wharves where liners docked and the travellers sailed for the ports of the world.

At first Madame had asked her the usual questions about her health. They had talked about mutual friends and experiences and had gossiped about the musical world of New York and the Continent, about the strange tricks war had played with the lives of peaceful musicians, the political ones and the victims, the current successes and those to whom music was art, was life itself, whom the larger public habitually ignored. But after a time a natural pause grew into a lengthy silence.

Madame had regarded her, looked at her as she had

573

when she had been her pupil. Her calm, grey eyes had been quietly speculative, her face composed and kind but intent upon its purpose. 'Now tell me about yourself, Ellen,' she had said.

She had looked away at the window, had gazed at the splattered, reflected light of waves until it dazzled her eyes, and when she looked back again at her old friend she saw a blurred face, an indistinct smile. 'I have been working steadily,' she said, and looked down at her fretting hands. 'My technique is sound. My fingers go where I want them to go. When I look at a score, I hear it the way it should sound – as I have always heard it. I am all right.'

Madame nodded her head, but her eyes remained steadfast and did not seem to share in the gesture of agreement. 'I heard you last night. I know you have regained your technique. But that is not what I wanted to know.' She hesitated and seemed to think about what she was going to say next. Then she wet her lips and began again. 'Ellen, there is more to your life than music. There is Basil. There are the other things you do. Tell me about them.'

'Basil is very well. His new concert series is doing nicely. I'm sure you read the notices in the newspapers. Basil's career is assured.'

This time the old woman shook her head briefly, but vigorously. 'I am not asking about Basil's career – or yours. I know all I need to know about both of your careers. I want to know about you – about you and Basil.'

How could she tell her what she did not know herself? She could say that as a husband Basil was kind, considerate, attentive, occasionally distracted and not as concerned with her interests as his own. The letter in the console table, the powder spilled in the drawer, her glimpse of a girl leaving their house burnished by the setting sun – she could mention these facts, too. But what were they? – only impressions, unconfirmed suspicions. She could tell her about their summer in the Catskills, the slow, peaceful days and the long, ecstatic nights. And she could also tell her about the two times during the summer when Basil had been away, the time he was called to the city on business and had been discomfited when she had asked if she might go with him – she had not insisted and he had gone alone, had stayed away several nights – and the two weeks of concert engagements. What about last night? Should she tell Madame the real reason why she had forgotten herself and had played a popular folksong instead of the Bach aria at the reception? What would Madame say if she described to her the beauty of the girl with the auburn hair and told her that she had seen Basil with her, kissing her? But it was nonsensical to think of it – she could not tell her any of these things. Instead, she said deliberately, a little too emphatically, 'Basil has been very kind.'

Madame again shook her head. 'Husbands can be kind, Ellen – and they can be unkind. I do not think it matters. What matters is whether he makes you happy. That is what I want to know.'

At last she could speak, say words that held meaning. 'No,' she said, 'I am not happy with him.'

'What is wrong?' Madame was inexorable. She sat with her hands clasped, her smile patient and just and firm.

'He has not been the same since – since I returned. Oh, he does everything he should. And he worries about me. For a while, last summer, we were happy. We were a part of each other and it was good. But then something happened.'

'Can you tell me about it?'

She shook her head. 'There is nothing I can tell you. Basil seems to withdraw, to be apart from me. It's as if he tolerates me, and does not want me to come near.'

'Have you ever spoken to him about this?'

'No, I haven't. I know that it may be that I imagine it. I imagine too many things, you know. In the past, I have often thought that people were doing things to me when they were not. I have learned not to talk about my fears, to keep them to myself.'

Madame moved to her side and took her hand, pressed

575

it between her own. 'You must talk to him about it, Ellen. I am sure you must. If you don't it will grow in your mind, this fear – it will destroy your life together. If there is something wrong, it will do no harm – it can only do good – to speak openly about it, to discuss it with each other. And if there is nothing wrong, if you are only imagining that he does not love you, you will learn that you are wrong. He will know about your fears and help you to face them. But, if he doesn't know . . . ?'

Madame stood up and walked to the ebony harpsichord. She opened the seat and removed a volume of Bach, opened it to the first page of the score and spread it upon the rack. Her hand brushed against the ebony, rested on it lightly, then fingered the catch to open the cover and reveal the two serried rows of manuals. 'I remember that you were always fond of this aria, Ellen,' she said. She sighed gently. 'That Bach loved it, too, is evident in every one of his variations on it. And a famous king had his court musician play it every night to put him to sleep!' She paused, smiling, to consider the ways of kings. Then she asked, hesitantly, 'Will you play it for me, Ellen?'

If she could ever play it right, she could now. And it seemed certain to her that she would as she sat before the ancient instrument, in the famous old room that she had played in so many times before at so many stages of her life. At this moment there was no compulsion; she felt relaxed, settled and sure, at peace. There was no need to look at the score – she knew each note. She did not have to wait for the audience to quiet, nor did she have to make her stage presence known, to put on the mask of her public self. If she wished, she could sit here forever; it was her place and her time. And, as she realized that this was true, Anna Magdalena's aria began to form in her head. The crystalline notes were all there, the space around them existed as it should, the trills were clean and as neat as a frill of lace, a furbelow, the rhythm was vigorous, the cadences precise. She unclasped her hands, edged forward. Her fingers arched, leant to the attack – the keys moved supple beneath her fingers. She had begun, and it was good.

The movement of the sound, the pace and flow of it, mingled with the movements of her hands, the rise and fall of the melody was the rise and fall of her breathing, the music was alive in her, she lived the song. Her being was as firmly rooted in the chords she played, the counter melody in the bass, as her foot on the pedal. There was no division, no disunity; this world she made herself could not be split up into parts: it was one, mighty whole. She was the essence of time itself, she was the motion that carried the stream of tone along; she found herself at the centre of the hard, exact core of each note and on the soft, reverberant edges as well, where sound married sound and new harmony was born.

The past ended before this began and the future did not commence until this was past. This was now, here and undeniable, an eternal instant. Irrevocable, irrefutable, it had a strength and a reality that defied oblivion. With it she was unique, just as it was unique; without it she ceased to exist, just as it was nothing. This power to evoke music depended upon her reading of black marks on a ruled page, upon the dexterity of her fingers and her body's sense of rhythm, upon her knowledge of the way it was, the quality of its sound. But she depended upon it, too, for without it she did not know herself. Outside its orbit she was a bundle of sensations, a walking fear, an appetite, a lawless creature. But when this sound existed, she understood, her life had meaning, order, morality. This was her end, she was its means.

She played the final cadence reluctantly, lifting her hands off the manuals, releasing the mechanism, but holding them barely above it, allowing them to hover, to reconsider, to continue if they wanted. She could go on to the first variation, and the second, and the third – play on until she had gone through all thirty-two of them, and then she could begin again – if she wished. But she did not wish. Her hands fell into her lap and she looked down at them, smiling at her fears of the night past, confident of herself once more. She would not have turned about and looked at Madame Tedescu and asked, 'Did I play well?' – if she had not felt that she must to be polite.

Madame's face was impassive. She seemed not to want to speak. But she did speak, and she spoke quickly, as a doctor gives orders during a critical point in an operation, briskly, with authority. 'You played competently, Ellen. As you say, you have full command of your technique. Your fingers obey your wishes. And as I listened I sensed that you comprehended the music, as a critic comprehends a painting. But a critic cannot paint, a critic is not a musician. What you played was not Bach, Ellen . . .' She stopped. But her glance went on. Her eyes said, You and I know it was once.

She had felt like arguing. Last night – yes, last night had been bad. She would be one of the first to admit that. But today – no, today she had played well. She had heard Bach in her mind, and she had played Bach as she heard it. She could not doubt it. *It had to be.*

But even as she thought this, even as she insisted to herself that Madame was wrong, she had known that Madame was not wrong. She had failed, as she had many times before, but this failure was final. This time she had not known that she had failed – it had sounded right to her. Only through Madame's honesty, at which she railed, had she known.

Madame came over to where she sat by the harpsichord. She carefully closed the covers on the manuals and turned the key in the lock. 'There are many who do not do as well,' she said. 'And they have fame . . . money . . . recognition.'

This was true. She could not even say that her career was over. Jeffry had given her a good notice, Mrs Smythe had approved, her popularity was assured. She could go on playing competently to filled halls, could become a great success and only a few would know there was a difference. But she would not.

'Madame, I do not understand,' she had said. 'It sounded right to me.' She looked up at her old friend hopefully, waited for her to say something more that would make it possible for her to go on. Tell me to practise twenty-four hours a day and I will do it, she thought. Tell me to memorize all of Couperin, go back and study fingering, play Czerny – anything at all if it leaves me a chance to regain what I have lost – and I will do it.

But Madame had only smiled and had shaken her head, had said nothing more. They had talked of other things, inconsequentials, for another quarter of an hour. And then she had left. She had left and come to the park, had bought nuts and sat on the bench, had fed the squirrel until he ran away, until her nuts were gone, and now she was walking again, walking . . . walking.

She was no longer alone. She was walking in a thick crowd of people, mostly women and children, a noisy crowd made up of calls and cries and childish questions, of balloons above and empty boxes of crackerjack underfoot. She stopped and looked around her, seeing the people for the first time. This was the zoo, and she was in front of the pony track, obstructing the pushing, pulling file of anxious children who were waiting to ride in the pony-cart. A fat, perspiring, red-faced mother – a captive dirigible of flesh held down by two tugging brats – shouted at her, 'Why don't you move on, lady? You're too old to go on this anyway, and you're only blocking traffic!'

Embarrassed, she did move on, past the man with the tank of helium, who sold balloons, past the snorting seals in their barricaded swimming-pool and up the hill that led to the bear-pits. She did not know where she was going, and she did not care, just so it was to a spot where the crowd was less dense. When, at last, she found herself on a rocky promontory that overhung a den of bears, she decided to stop, to remain there for a while and watch the behaviour of the bears as she had that of the squirrel.

There were two of them out in the warm October sun,

579

big, clumsy, brown bears that lumbered like badly articulated toys as they passed their grotto. She saw that each time they came to the blank cliff face, that formed one wall of their enclosure and above which she was standing, they raised their heads, sometimes sitting upon their haunches, and sniffed her. Then, each time, they resumed their pacing, made the complete circuit of their den, before returning to re-enact this ritual.

The brute power of their huge, mountainous bodies interested her as much as their compulsive actions. Each time they padded towards her, the weight of their strides, the hammer-blows of their feet, shook the rock she stood on, made her own body tremble. They stalked back and forth, around and around the grotto, always together, the larger, darker bear slightly in front of the smaller, rangier one. Each bear's movements were perfectly synchronized with his mate's, except for an occasional corner where the lead bear would be taking shorter, pivotal strides while his companion was still lunging straight ahead. They did not seem to tire, nor did they change their course or in any way modify their actions. And every time they stopped beneath her, looked upwards, sniffing, then sat up, she felt a strange pleasure.

The squirrel had been intelligent, canny, aware of causality and wise in the ways of men; the bears were rigidly conditioned, powerful but unintelligent, automatons. Yet they affected her sensibilities in a manner that the squirrel never could – although she could neither name nor express this reaction, she felt it strongly enough to turn her back upon the enclosure and its two restless occupants, to look the other way towards the city and the sentinel apartment buildings that guarded the periphery of the park.

It seemed to her that she was alienated from her life, that since her talk with Madame Tedescu she existed outside of all her previous desires and activities, alone and directionless. Even the bears, who still plodded in their pit although she had turned her back on them, were housed;

in fact, their quarters determined their lives, condemned them to patrol the unscalable walls of their den, to keep casting their eyes upward at the cliff face and the down-curving, pointed bars that would impale them if they leaped. She was not caged, she was free.

Or so it seemed to her. Basil loved her. Basil did not love her. He was being unfaithful to her with the beautiful girl he had kissed the night before, or he was not being unfaithful to her. Either way it did not seem to matter now.

A great mass of dark clouds were forming behind the high towers of the apartment buildings, making their lineaments stand out in stark relief against the leaden opacity of the approaching storm. In a few minutes the clouds would be over the park and it would begin to rain. She knew that she should begin to walk towards the nearest entrance, if she wanted to avoid a drenching. The atmosphere, which had been warm and damp, had grown cold as she watched the clouds; the breeze had quickened, had blown gusty, and all about her bright red and yellow leaves were flying.

She did not move. A strange calmness had overcome her with her realization that she no longer cared. A tension inside her had been released, an enigmatic, ticking mechanism had ceased to operate, and she now floated in the pool of circumstances that had drowned her desires, was held fast in it, like scum on the surface of a pond. Slowly, lackadaisically, she turned around until she faced the bear-pit again. The two brown monsters were coming towards her padding heavily and rhythmically, as if this time they would reach her surely. The larger bear still walked a pace ahead of his mate. still led him, and as she watched, fascinated, she understood just where the resemblance between herself and them lay. But before she could think it through, before the bears could get to the foot of the cliff, the music she had not heard in many months began behind her. A queer, broken humming, an unresonant sound that she could never imitate, a sequence of chords that always seemed about to resolve but never did, this music was the greatest evil she had ever known. Once she had heard it, she could not escape it – she had no control over it – but could only endure it until it lapsed into silence of itself. Yet its evil did not lie in its sound alone, or the terror, the elemental horror, it communicated; the true baseness was *who* accompanied the music. 'I still have time,' she thought, 'to climb that barrier, to throw myself down into the den.' Even as she was thinking this, the discordant humming grew louder and she felt a restraining pressure on her shoulder. She did not have to look to see what it was, she had looked and seen it too many times before; but she did look and saw the hand, the long, white, spatulate fingers, the ring with its deeply-coloured stone that when she gazed into it revealed the night, the swirling blackness, the emptiness of the abyss.

'They are a little like us, aren't they, Ellen?' the sweet voice asked. 'The bears, of course. Look how the old fellow – isn't he tremendous and powerful! – is always in the lead. Now he is sitting up, and in a moment his friend will sit up, too. See, what did I tell you? The second one does exactly what the first one does! Just like you and me, Ellen . . .'

It was Nelle. She did not want to face her. She had hoped she would never see her again. The morning that she had gone up to Dr Danzer's office in the hospital for her last 'treatment' she had said good-bye to Nelle, had told her that she would not recognize her if she came again. And she had thought that Nelle had understood at last. There had been an instant when she lay on the table, while Dr Danzer held her hand and told her that there was no reason to be afraid, that it would all be over in a twinkling, that it was nothing but a shock, an electric shock, that would pass through her frontal lobes, that in some way it would adjust the balance, would make things fit into place again, all things, little and big – there had been this instant, a moment when she first sensed the coldness of the electrodes at her temples, when she had been most terribly afraid despite the warm strength of the doctor's hand, when, ever so faintly, she had heard the humming music, had seen dimly the long, curving fingers, the dark, horrible ring, had known that Nelle was there, too, that she was just lying low, as she always had when Ellen got into trouble, that even after the 'treatment' was over Nelle would not have gone. But this impression had existed for only a moment. Hell had taken its place, white, jumping, searing hell, a blinding, scorching universe of pain. Hours later, when she had recovered consciousness, Nelle was gone. And she had not returned until now.

It would be best to face her, she reasoned – to turn around and look her in the eye and show her that she could not command any more, that she refused to do her bidding. Swiftly, she did turn around, did look Nelle in the face. Nelle had not changed. Nelle still was her twin, her mirror-image. Not that they were the same – they were two different people. Nelle was evil, all evil. Oh, she could be nice, she could cajole – just look at how she was smiling now, how her eyes were dancing, how her long fingers rested lightly, almost gaily on her own. But she would not stay that way. As soon as she was sure that Ellen would go with her, would do as she told her to, her face would change. Those smiling lips would lengthen into a hag's mouth, those sparkling eyes would begin to glitter with the brightness of malice, those long fingers would bend themselves into claws, and that soft brown hair would coarsen, would grow matted and lack-lustre. And Ellen would have to watch her constantly, would not be able to lose sight of her at any time, would have to fight her when she wanted her to go wrong.

Nelle could not stay. She would not let her. Even if she would have liked to have known where she had been all these months, what she had been doing, she did not dare waste time to talk with her. At once, without considering her for even another minute, she must do the two things Dr Danzer had told her to do if Nelle ever came again. She must tell her what the doctor had said to tell her, and then she must go to the doctor at once. It did not matter what time of the day or night it was, or whether she had an appointment or not, she must go immediately to the doctor. If he were not at his office, she was to tell the nurse to get in touch with him, to get her – or whoever answered the bell – to take her to him or to the nearest hospital. She was to say that it was a matter of life and death. But first, before she went to the doctor, she must do the other thing he had said to do: she must say what he had told her to say to Nelle.

Nelle was still smiling. When she smiled, she was beautiful in a way that Ellen had always wanted to be beautiful. The first time Nelle had come to her – the first time that she could remember; Dr Danzer had said that there must have been other, earlier times, although she did not remember them – she had been looking into the old, cracked mirror above the chiffonier in her father's room. She had run away from the store that afternoon to go with some other girls to a show, and when she got home her father had not let her have any dinner, but had sent her up to his room and told her to lock herself in. This had meant that he was going to come up after dinner and make her take her bloomers off, that he would beat her with his trouser belt until she would not be able to sit down or even lie comfortably – hit her again and again with the long, flailing, snake-like strap, his teeth set in a grimace, his eyes afire. She had hated him, she had wanted to kill him, but she had known that all she could do was what he told her to do. So she had gone upstairs and shut herself, hungry and alone, in his big room with the mahogany bedstead, the picture of Blake's 'Jehovah wrestling with Satan and Adam', the tall chiffonier with the cracked mirror. It had been impossible to sleep, and she had soon grown tired of looking out of the window, so she had gone over to the mirror and she had gazed into it and tried to imagine how her face would be if she were beautiful. That had been the first time she had heard the queer, humming music, too, though then it had not frightened her because she had not known what it meant. She had heard the broken chords and she had felt the hand on her shoulder, had seen Nelle's face in the mirror beside her own. She had thought it was her own face, that it was herself who was humming; but as she had continued to look, as she had heard her father's key turning in the lock of the door, she had realized in panic that it was not her own, that it was altogether different, that it was beautiful. Nelle's voice had sounded in her ear, quiet and sweet, persuading her, 'I'm your friend, Ellen. You can call me Nelle, if you like. I'm here to help you. I know how you can keep your father from hurting you – but you must act quickly! Take your lipstick – yes, your lipstick! Yes, I know he doesn't approve of it, that you always wipe it off before he sees you – but hurry, do as I say before he comes in. I'll explain later. That's it. Rub it all over your mouth, make it red, red and beautiful like mine. Ah, that's fine. Now smile. He has come in the door now, he is standing behind you. Smile, smile dreamily and half close your eyes. Now turn around and put your arms around him. That's it! Hold him to you, harder, harder. Now kiss him. No, not there! On his mouth – his mouth! Ah, that's better.

Her father had torn her arms away from himself, had stared at her, and then had struck her face with the back of his hand. 'You little harlot,' he had whispered. He had picked her up and thrown her on the bed, had whipped her worse than he ever had before. And Nelle had stood there and laughed.

Well, this time she would not get away with it. This time she would not listen to her. She would do just as Dr Danzer had told her to do. Although it was difficult to regard her calmly. Her face was so beautiful, so like, and unlike, her own. It was all she could do to say the words.

'Nelle, you do not exist. I imagine you. You have no life of your own. You cannot make me do anything I do not want to do.' But she had said them, and she had said them loudly and clearly.

Nelle had not gone away, as Dr Danzer had predicted she would. If anything, she had smiled more derisively.

'But haven't you always wanted to do what I told you to do, Ellen? And how can you doubt my existence when you, yourself, see me? It's not as if Dr Danzer had seen me. Of course, he doesn't believe I exist – wouldn't I be foolish to show myself to him?'

'I don't believe you!' Ellen said. And, as she spoke, a raindrop splashed her cheek. It had become darker and darker, until it was all but night in midday. In another few minutes the storm would break. The thing to do was to run. If she ran fast enough she would escape the storm and Nelle. But she must not let her know what she was about to do; she must get as much of a start as possible.

Without looking where she was going, she turned about and began to run. A man and a small boy were coming up the path from the pool of seals, and she blundered into them. The man clutched at her, tried to stop her, cried after her angrily. But she was running in full stride now, her legs striking against the confining hem of her dress. The rain had begun to fall – great wet streaks appeared on the path as she veered past the seals and raced towards the balloon-vendor's stand and the pony-track. Was Nelle behind her? If she turned to see, would she be running after her, gaining on her? It was not worth the chance – she must go faster. Already she was nearly out of breath, and she still had quite a long stretch to go before she reached the entrance to the park. It was raining heavily now, and she could feel the wetness spread along her back, feel the water strike her face. Her legs had begun to ache and each breath she took was painful, but she must go faster yet if she was to be sure to lose Nelle. In another moment or two – three or four at the most – she would reach the exit. A blob of yellow caught her eye, a taxi. It was just pulling up at the traffic light. If she could get there before the light changed, get inside and shut the door – she could tell the taxi-driver to drive off without Nelle. But no matter how much she tried, she did not seem to be able to make her legs move faster. It was like trying to run with two weighty pendulums in place of legs. Each step forward she took she seemed to be lifting a great weight by the tip of her toe. But she was almost there. Another stride . . .

She flung open the door of the taxi, jumped inside and slammed it shut. As she looked forward at the cabby, she saw the light change. 'Get away as fast as you can!' she cried. He glanced at her, nodded his head, and shifted gears. The cab catapulted forward, was half-way down the block before the car that had been beside it was moving. 'Keep on going,' she said. 'I'll tell you where in a moment.'

She had succeeded. But she had not yet gained her breath. It was all she could do to sit back on the seat, to hold on to the strap and look out of the window. The blocks went past, Fifty-ninth, Fifty-eighth, Fifty-seventh, Fifty-sixth. The cab had to stop for another light, but by now she should be safe. She opened her bag and began to look for Dr Danzer's address.

'What are you looking for? May I help you?' The sound of Nelle's sweet voice made her hands go limp. She dropped the bag, let it roll on the floor of the taxi. It was as if she had been dealt a vicious blow in the stomach.

Nelle was sitting in the other corner. She was still smiling, but not breathing heavily, nor was her face flushed, and not a hair of her coiffure was disarranged. 'You didn't think that you could outrun me, did you, Ellen? You know that I could always run faster than you. But, tell me, where are we going? To see Basil?'

She said nothing, but stooped to pick up her bag from the floor. As she reached, the driver swerved the taxi to move into another lane of traffic, and the unexpected jolt made her lose her balance. Clinging to the strap, she leaned forward to get her bag again, but it was not where it had been. Nelle had kicked it into the other corner.

'Why don't you answer me, Ellen?' Nelle had her foot on the open bag. 'I won't let you have this until you tell me. Where are we going?'

There was no reason why she should hide the truth.

And there was a good chance that if Nelle discovered that she intended to visit Dr Danzer, Nelle would leave her. At the hospital, when she had been taking her course of shock 'treatments', Nelle had never accompanied her to the doctor. Often she had been waiting for her when she awakened afterwards, but she had not been with her before.

She decided to tell her. 'I am going to see Dr Danzer,' she said. 'He told me to come to him at once if I ever saw you again.'

Nelle's face changed horribly. Her smile was transformed into a sneer, her eyes bulged with anger and her pale skin became suffused with the hot blood of ire. She glared at Ellen hatefully, then bent down and picked up the bag. Snapping it open, she begun to go through it.

Ellen could not let her do this. She threw herself across the seat – on to her enemy – struck out blindly at her face and hands in an attempt to wrest the bag from her. Although she did get her hands on the purse, Nelle proved too strong for her, resisting her as if she were a steel wall, hurting her head, bruising her. In the struggle the bag fell open on the seat and Dr Danzer's card fell out. Both of them clutched at it, succeeded in touching it. But before either could hold on to it, a sudden gust of wind from the open window sucked at it, made it flutter and fly blindly in a small, dizzy circle like a flame-fascinated moth – while both of them stabbed at it with their hands – then forced it to swoop through the window and into the busy street. As soon as this happened, Nelle relaxed, lay back limply under Ellen's weight. The smile returned to her face – her expression became benign. 'You didn't really want to see the doctor, now did you, Ellen?' she cooed.

Tears of frustration and rage filmed her eyes, and she retreated to her corner of the cab, weak with exasperation. The taxi had halted at another light, and she could see the cabby's face in the rear-view mirror, his eyes dull with bewilderment.

'Are you all right, lady?' he asked. And when Ellen

did not, at first, answer, he asked again, 'Are you sure you're all right, lady? You aren't sick or nothing?'

Nelle was signalling to her to answer, to say something sensible.

'I'm quite all right, thank you,' she said. 'Just feeling a little tired.'

'I heard a commotion back there,' the cabby said, turning around and peering at Nelle's corner. 'I heard you talking pretty loud, as if somebody else was there. Have you decided where you're going?'

'I think we'll go home,' Nelle answered sweetly, before Ellen could speak, before she had decided what to say or whether to say anything at all. 'We're a little tired and wet.' And she gave the driver Ellen's home address.

'I don't know why you wanted to see that foolish doctor,' she complained to Ellen. 'He's not your friend, as I am. He would only make you go back to the hospital and take another course of "treatments". I'd rather see Basil. I always liked Basil – I think he's handsome, you know – and I haven't seen him in so long a time!'

Ellen did not answer her. She sat very still in her own corner, holding her aching head, her eyes shut. If she were silent, if she said nothing, Nelle might get bored and go away. But if she did not choose to, Ellen knew from long experience that there was no way she could make her go. She felt sick and weak, frightened, alone . . .

Nelle kept on talking, softly, quietly, but with a deliberate vehemence. 'Dr Danzer has never understood you or me,' she said, 'for all his big words and fancy ideas. He hasn't helped you either. You are just the same as you always were, Ellen – a silly little wretch who is afraid of her own shadow when I'm not there! But I'm always there, Ellen, when you need me, whether you admit it or not, whether you choose to remember me later or not. I was there when you were a girl and your father whipped you – if it hadn't been for me you would never have stood up to him, never been allowed to go out alone or with your friends, never been permitted to go away to the conservatory. And I was there, too, that night when you walked the streets alone and the men mocked you, when you went up to your hotel room to wait for Jim to come back to you, meekly, humbly, ready to forgive him if he only returned! If it hadn't been for me you would have forgiven him, wouldn't you? Yet what thanks do I get? You won't even remember what I did – you let that doctor of yours with his psychiatric mumbo-jumbo persuade you that it never happened, you let him convince you that I did not try to kill Jim that night, that the little you do remember of what happened was only an expression of the guilt you're supposed to feel towards your father!'

Ellen turned away from her and her diabolical words. Gazing out the window at the brownstone fronts, the tenements, the pillars of the Third Avenue 'El', she could almost succeed in not hearing the softly spoken statements, the terrible lies – or truths? – with which Nelle tormented her. But her indifference did not discourage Nelle. She kept on with her spate of accusations, her taunts and her boasting.

'What happened when you told Dr Danzer about me? Tell me, what happened?' she cajoled. But when Ellen refused to answer, she supplied the response herself. 'He told you that I was only a figment of your imagination, didn't he? He said that you had withdrawn from reality – what a catch-phrase that is! – when you found the life you led too unpleasant, too frustrating, and had invented me to be your companion. Do you believe that, Ellen? Do you believe that you invented me? Rather that I invented you, I who am your better part! You can't live without me, Ellen, and you know it.

'What else did that doctor of yours say about me? Oh, yes, the funniest thing of all! Do you remember how we laughed about it at the time, Ellen? When he told you that the best proof you could have that I did not exist – as if you could ever prove that I did not exist, I who am more real than you are yourself – was the fact that my name was your own spelled backwards, do you remember how we laughed, how we rolled on the floor and laughed when he told you that? And do you remember that last concert of yours before you went to the hospital, that concert when you were so frightened and your fingers would not obey you, when I had to play instead of you, when we exchanged roles and you stood beside me and I played? What would you have done without me then, Ellen? Would you have just sat there before your instrument, with the entire concert hall filled with people who had come to hear you play, and have stared at the manuals unable to lift a finger, terrified because you could not hear the music in your head? Yes, that is what you would have done – ah, I know you! – if I had not taken your place, if I had not played for you!'

Ellen let her rave on. Part of what she said was true, but the greater part of it was subtly distorted. At her last concert before she had become ill and Basil had taken her to Dr Danzer, she had forgotten what she was to play, she had not been able to hear the notes sound in her head as she always had before. But she had played – she herself had played and no one else. This much she knew. This much she must hold on to. It had come out wrong, everything had got all jumbled up, her hands had roved the manuals like wild distrait creatures – but she had played, not Nelle. It had been Nelle who had stood behind her, who had mocked and laughed at her, who had tried her best to distract her. And it had been Nelle who had run forward across the stage when she could not play any longer, when the effort to control her wild hands had become too much for her, who had lunged across the footlights at the great, many-faced beast she hated, who had thrown herself screaming upon them, cursing them, reviling them. It had been Nelle, not Ellen.

The taxi parked in front of her house, and Ellen, who had recaptured her purse after the doctor's card had been lost, paid the driver. As she opened the door, Nelle, rudely, squeezed past her and rushed up the steps to the door of her house before she could step to the street. While she fitted her key in the lock, Nelle stood beside her, breathing violently, her lips open passionately, her hands warm and feverish on her shoulder. 'Tell me about Basil, Ellen,' she kept saying. 'Tell me all about him. Is he still as tall, as lean and blond as he was? I can hardly wait to see him!'

She had anticipated a struggle with her when she opened the door, since she had decided that whatever happened she would not let Nelle see Basil first. But as the door opened they both stood motionless in surprise. The hall was filled with the full, sweet tones of a violin. And as they listened, the sound stopped, broke off in the midst of a passage, as it might if someone had pulled back on the hand that held the bow.

Nelle led Ellen into the hall of her own house, led her on tip-toe to the library door. Together, they stood behind it while Nelle pushed it open a crack, far enough to see into the big, book-lined room.

Basil was standing by the piano, his arms around a woman. The violin had been laid aside on the piano bench, forgotten. He held her passionately, and her long auburn hair had come undone, falling in profusion along his shoulders as soft, coppery dusk sometimes falls upon the hills and the sea.

Then Nelle closed the door and turned to Ellen, smiling. 'You see,' she said, 'I am your only friend.'

7

'I am your only friend.' Nelle was present in the darkness, in the foul, seething blackness – Nelle was close to her, bending over her as she lay stiff and tense beneath the bed-clothes, Nelle's sweet whisper echoing in the silence of the room. She had come to expect Nelle's appearance at this point of her compulsive journey into the past, had come to accept it and to make no attempt to fight it off, although she knew that it meant that the greatest terror of all was coming, would be upon her before the night was done. Nelle's hand touched her now, the long fingers grew dimly before her eyes, strips of shadow only slightly lighter than the surrounding, threatening darkness. Against them, slowly, she saw vertical bars – the fingers seemed to rest against the bars, but on the other side of them. Then, as on the other nights, the ring on the longest of the fingers took shape, the horrible stones in its centre flickered and came alive, became a deepness, a soul-sucking vacuum towards which she herself was drawn, upon which her consciousness was focused, into which, inevitably, she must go. She felt herself contracting, growing smaller and smaller, and at the same time moving up towards the bars, the dark aperture of the stone, being pulled into it as thread is pulled into the eye of a needle.

She resisted this magnetism, knowing that she could not resist it long enough. By compressing herself until her bones ached and her skin was taut with the straining of her muscles, she managed to achieve an equilibrium, a delicate poise, on the threshold of the dark entrance within the ring. And it was at this moment that she seemed to stop existing. As she hesitated, by means of an ultimate exertion of will, on the rim of nothingness, the present instant stood still, Nelle's sweet, coaxing voice froze in mid-syllable, her future came rushing towards her, bringing with it a tremendous impact of experience – as if all the events that were to happen had been poured into a funnel and she was at the bottom of the spout – and her past overtook her, swelled up and around her, spread out on all sides.

A nest of bars, a menagerie of vertical and horizontal lines, cage upon cage upon cage, and she herself in the centre of them all – no matter where she cast her gaze, she saw bars, some round and ivoried white, some square and darkly painted and curving downward to end in points, some themselves shadows on the face of a sleeping man (two sets of these, one seen in the silver light of the moon, the other redly in the glare of a neon sign), and a final set – the closest, the most threatening of all – which seemed to press against her temples as if she were peering through them, on the other side of which the vague, dark shapes of the elms could hardly be seen.

Nelle's voice began again, time began again; but the vision of the world of bars did not disappear. Nelle was saying, 'This is you, Ellen. Believe it if you can – for this is what Dr Danzer says – these bars are you. These are the bars of your crib as a child, the bars you saw in the park that were meant to protect you from the den of bears, the bars of shadow cast by two, different blinds at two, different hotel windows on two, different nights upon Jim Shad's face, and the bars on the window of this room, the latticework that casts the checkered pattern on the floor. These bars, so the doctor says, are your fate – you can't escape them, although you can learn to prevail over them by making the best of them, as a caged creature rubs against the bars of its enclosure. Look at them, Ellen; see how they confine you, how they warp and twist your actions, how they influence your thoughts, how they make you.'

A great chill settled upon her – the coldness of the irrevocable – and the fear she had known long enough to grow accustomed to grew in intensity until it regained its pristine force: the terror of a child. She realized that she had been thrown back in time to an unknown period of her childhood, that she was small and bewildered, awakened out of sleep to stare at the darkness, to listen again for the unexplained sound she had heard in her crib. Suddenly the sound came again: a creaking of the stairs, a giggling, her mother's voice protesting, 'But I'll have to look in at the child; she may not be asleep.' Then, a loud noise and a bright streak of light appeared out of which two monstrous forms, two genii as in the fairy-tales, burgeoned and approached her crib. They stood over her, blocking the light, laughing and struggling, bending down to get her. '*Don't you do it!* I tell you she is too young to touch any of that!' More struggling above her. More menacing shadows that grew and wavered and swooped down on her. An hysterical giggle, a high screaming, 'Don't! Don't! Oh, you're terrible!' Again the larger shadow bending over her, coming nearer and nearer, and with it a queer stench. The lights suddenly brighter, blinding her, the hand – her mother's hand with its queer dark stone – upon the bars of her crib, the great fear looming out of her and the great hate – the huge, senseless force of hate that she had never felt before streaming out of her, directed towards the shadow, as her mother cried again, '*If you touch a hair of her head, I'll murder you!*'

The shadows came down upon her, blanketing her, but the terror subsided; she felt herself grow again, move forward in time, move out of the small world of a child into the larger, more complex environment of an adult. The darkness still surrounded her, yet now it was the natural darkness of night. The air was cool on her brow and she lay back peacefully on Basil's arm, her head resting upon his shoulder, as the carriage they were riding in moved slowly through the park. About them the scent of freshly drenched verdure pervaded the atmosphere – the storm had passed and the vaulted firmament above them was

595

brightened with the flashings of a thousand stars. Nelle sat across from them, sulking. For Ellen had not looked at her in many hours, and was now sure that eventually she would become tired of her game and leave them to themselves.

Basil's hand had held her own, Basil's rangy form rested beside hers; she felt almost secure and safe. The long afternoon she had passed shut up in her own room listening to the intermittent sounds of the violin belonged to the past. Throughout the afternoon Nelle had tried again and again to force Ellen to go down to the library and confront the lovers. If she had steadfastly refused to do this, it had not been out of any confidence that her impression was mistaken, or out of dread that her worst suspicions would be verified. Instead, she had sat and looked at a picture on the wall, a print of Picasso's that she particularly liked, had focused all her thoughts upon its form and shape, had studied it as if she were seeing it for the first time. Nelle had kept pacing back and forth across the floor, her smile turned to a scowl, berating her, pretending at times that she could see into the room downstairs, could watch its occupants and describe their love-making to Ellen. She had refused to listen, and had at last reduced Nelle to sullen silence and an even more frenetic pacing.

At the end of the afternoon the violin's sound ceased altogether. The door to the library was heard opening, and the high, musical voice of a woman penetrated to her room. Nelle, gnashing her teeth, flung herself upon Ellen, pulled at her, cursed her, in a final attempt to get her to go out in the hall and interrupt the meeting. But Ellen had shut her eyes and withstood her urgings. When she had looked through the narrow crack of the door and had seen the auburn-haired girl in Basil's arms, the calmness of certainty had descended upon her. She knew then that her husband's infidelity was a fact – from that moment on anything else she might have learned would only have been a detail. Not that it had been possible at all times in the afternoon to suppress her imagination: occasionally the sound of laughter had been heard, of talk and – once – the sound of something falling. But if she had followed Nelle's promptings and had broken in on them, she would only have been adding to her own jealousy.

A little later, after she was certain that Basil's visitor had gone, she went down to the library. Nelle had stayed behind her all the way down the stairs, had walked into the room with her and had seated herself in one of the wingback chairs by the fireplace where she would be best able to see what occurred. Basil had been seated at his desk, but had looked up when he saw Ellen approaching. He had come to her and taken her in his arms and had kissed her complacently on the brow. She had let him do this because she had not felt deeply about it. He was her husband, she was his wife, he was unfaithful to her. The three facts, despite their seeming relevance to each other, had been kept separate and unconnected in her mind. What was happening and how she acted seemed to her to be unimportant, distant matters that were curious to observe and even debatable, but not in actuality a part of her life. Nelle, who sat on the other side of them, sneering at them, was real, her hatred of Basil – which was the greater because of her recent passion – was incontestable, and Ellen felt it as she might feel the warmth of a great fire even at some distance. But Nelle was also not a part of her.

They had gone out to dinner, and had sat and talked afterwards over their coffee. Nelle had accompanied them, had remained near them, watching them. Most of the time Ellen had managed to ignore her unwavering, insolent stare, but she had not been able to forget that it was on her. Nelle's presence had fitted into the back of her mind and nagged her like a worry. It was in the hope that a drive in the park might serve to vanquish Nelle that she had suggested to Basil that they hire a carriage after leaving the restaurant. Nelle had not left them as they

597

entered the park, but she had seemed to grow less oppressive, and Ellen sensed that she would soon give up and go
in the face of their felicity. Nelle depended on violence,
on frustration, on hate.

The carriage slipped smoothly forward along the wide
road, the horse's hooves slopping placidly and the driver's
cocked hat bobbing irregularly as he smoked his pipe.
Nelle had been looking at them intently ever since they
had entered the carriage, but now she looked away. Ellen
sighed and allowed herself to relax even more. Nothing
was right, she realized, but life went on, jogged slowly past
each day in much the same way the carriage moved
gradually past each dark clump of trees. The trick was to
learn to be indifferent.

Then Basil cleared his throat and sat up. He had looked
thin and restless in the reflected light of the street lamps,
and vaguely unhappy.

'Ellen,' he had said, 'there is something I would like to
talk to you about.'

She had looked at him and nodded her head, had waited
for him to continue. But he had hesitated, had fumbled in
his pocket for a cigarette and had taken a long time lighting it before he spoke again. 'It's about your concert,
Ellen. Last night's concert, I mean. I'm not sure you
should give another one.'

She had not expected this. Her face stiffened and,
although she knew it was the last thing she should do, she
had looked across at Nelle. She did not look back at Basil.
Nelle had held her hand up so that the ring with its dark
stone had caught the dim light of the lamps. Its deeps of
darkness had their old effect on her: she felt herself drawn
irresistibly towards its horrible emptiness. Nelle had begun
to smile and to gain substance and distinctness – Ellen felt
as if she were flowing towards her, even though she knew
that she had not moved. She tried to take her eyes off the
ring, but it was impossible.

'Why are you sitting over there now?' Basil asked. 'I
had no intention of insulting you. I said what I did for

598

your own good.' Ellen was startled to see that Basil was looking past her and speaking to Nelle, that Nelle was no longer gazing at her, but at Basil.

'I am not over there. I'm here beside you,' she said. Yet before she had stopped speaking, she had glanced down at where her own body should be, and realized that she could not see herself. Nelle, however, was frighteningly visible.

Basil paid no attention to what she said. He continued to look at Nelle – whose eyes were glinting wildly and whose hair had become disarrayed. 'I went to see Dr Danzer today,' he went on. 'I told him that you had – had difficulties last night. I asked him what was wrong.'

Nelle laughed scornfully. 'You poor fool! I suppose you believed what he told you?' she said.

Basil shook his head worriedly, stubbed out his cigarette and threw it away. 'Don't listen to her, Basil. Please, don't listen to her,' Ellen cried.

But Basil did not seem to hear her. He went over to the other side of the carriage and sat beside Nelle. When he attempted to put his arm around her, she shrank away and clawed at his face.

'Darling, you're ill!' he said. 'You've worked too hard too soon, and now you're on the verge of another breakdown. You must listen to me!' (Nelle was laughing again, showing her teeth.) 'Dr Danzer is quite concerned. He wants to see you, to talk to you. He says it is not at all unusual for a musician, after a course of shock "treatments", to experience difficulty in regaining his previous skills. He thinks that you may well be ill again, that you may need more "treatments".'

Nelle struck his face with her open hand, her nails digging into his cheek's flesh, gouging it, leaving long, deep scratches from which the blood flowed freely. 'Didn't the doctor tell you that might happen when you gave your consent for the "treatments"?' she demanded. 'Didn't he tell you that an artist's skill is lost when that current passes through the brain – that if an adjustment is made

599

later it will be on a lower level?' She stood up in the gently swaying carriage and pointed her long finger at him accusingly. Her face was a mask of hate. Ellen shrank from the sight.

Basil's hand rubbed at his bleeding cheek. 'The doctor told me that,' he said. 'He also told me that your chance to recover was slight without the shock "treatment". I had to make a decision.'

Nelle spat at him, then jumped from the slowly moving carriage. Her hair streaming in wild disorder down her back, she ran swiftly across the road to the path that led to the zoo. Basil jumped out and ran after her, crying, 'Ellen! Ellen! Stop and listen to what I have to say!'

The driver pulled on the reins and halted the carriage. Ellen leaped out, too, and began to run after both of them down the curving path. Basil was a good way ahead of her, and Nelle was almost out of sight; in her desperate hurry to catch up with them, to stop what she felt was about to happen, she deserted the twisting walk and ran down the hill, through brambles and against low branches of trees that she could not see in the night. Nelle, she knew, was running towards the bear-pit.

Ellen got there in time to see Nelle, who had fallen in her headlong flight and whose clothes were torn to ribbons, climbing the bars that overhung the grotto. The creatures below were moving about restlessly; one of them was growling. By the time Nelle had reached the top of the bars, was outlined whitely against the dark iron rods, Basil had begun to climb after her.

'Don't do it, Basil!' Ellen cried. 'Leave her alone – let her do whatever she wants. She is not me! I am here!'

But if Basil had heard, he had given no indication. He had kept on climbing up the bars, holding on with one hand and his twining legs as he reached out for Nelle with the other. She was perched on the outermost limit of the barrier, clinging carelessly to the arching points of the bars. Beneath her the bears, huge, lumbering shadows in the night, padded heavily, sniffing and growling. Then Nelle had started to teeter, to swing back and forth as if she were losing her balance, and Basil redoubled his effort to get to her in time.

Ellen watched helplessly. There had been nothing she could do. Each time she called out to her husband he ignored her – he seemed only to have ears for the blasphemous taunts Nelle threw at him. But as Ellen, her hands clenching and unclenching, had watched the perilous climb, she had remembered a similar experience – a horrifying time – not too long ago. She had remembered awaking in a hotel room with Jim Shad lying beside her. A neon sign blinked on and off outside the window, casting a pattern of red and black bars across his sleeping face. She had left the bed to walk to the window and change the angle of the slats so that the light did not fall on his face, when she felt the familiar pressure on her shoulder, had turned and had looked into Nelle's face. That time she had screamed, and the scream had awakened Jim. He had jumped up and run – not to her, but to Nelle. She had hit him again and again with the heavy base of a lamp, and had beaten him until he had fallen back gasping on the bed. Then she had begun to batter his head against the bedpost, while Ellen watched and screamed her terror.

This time she knew it was useless to cry out. She could not have even if she had wanted to, for Basil had reached the top, the outermost bars, and was working his way laboriously across their points towards Nelle. To scream would have been to startle him, perhaps to cause him to lose his balance and plunge into the pit. Ellen could only stand by and wait.

But Nelle had screamed. Just as Basil had been reaching her, she had begun to shriek – great, full-throated cries. Basil had thrown out his hands in an attempt to save himself, but he had already lost his equilibrium. As he pitched downwards, he caught at the point of a bar with one hand; she saw the flesh torn by the cruel edge. Then his body dropped into the pit with a heavy thud, the cumbersome shadows moved in, and he cried out piteously. Nelle had climbed down as soon as he fell and had run to Ellen, had put her hand over Ellen's mouth and held tightly on to her to keep her from running for help until it was too late and the only sounds that came from the bear-pit were hideously inhuman.

The room was dark, the darkness settled all around her, seething and twisting, claiming her for its own. Even the window was dark now, the moon having passed behind a cloud. She had lived through it for another night and had witnessed it all once again, helpless to intervene. Any time she closed her eyes, day or night, it was likely to begin again; but she did not have to close her eyes to hear those screams. Their piercing ululation filled her ears whether she waked or slept, banishing music forever, creating their own symphony of pain. And another sound was at all times with her: a sweet, lying whisper, advising, cajoling, misleading her. Nelle rarely left her now, seeming almost a part of her, spoke for her, acted for her, often even forced her to think her thoughts. Sometimes it seemed that she was not Ellen, that she was Nelle.